Sicilian Avengers

SICILIAN AVENGERS

A NOVEL: BOOK TWO

LUIGI NATOLI

Translated from the Italian by
STEPHEN RIGGIO

RADIUS BOOK GROUP
NEW YORK

Radius Book Group
A division of Diversion Publishing Corp.
www.radiusbookgroup.com.

For more information, email info@radiusbookgroup.com.

The publisher does not have any control over and does not assume any responsibility for author or third-party websites or their content.

First Radius Book Group Edition: October 2024
Paperback ISBN: 9781635769463
e-ISBN: 9781635769487

Book design by Neuwirth & Associates, Inc.
Cover design by Alan Dingman

Printed in the United States of America
10 9 8 7 6 5 4 3 2 1

Originally published as *I Beati Paoli* in 239 installments in the *Giornale di Sicilia* from May 6, 1909, to January 2, 1910.

This translation is based on the edition published in two volumes by Sellerio Editore in 2016.

Image credit:

"Auto-da-fé in Palermo (April 6, 1724) (François Chiche), M12091.A," Harvard Art Museums collections.

The Romance of Savoy, Victor Amadeus II and His Stuart Bride.

"The Beati Paoli and the Ideology of the 'Popular Novel'" essay provided courtesy of Umberto Eco's Estate.

CONTENTS

PART I

PART II

ABBREVIATIONS

RLD   Natoli, Luigi. *I Beati Paoli*. Introduction and endnotes by Rosario La Duca. S. F. Flaccovio: Palermo, 1971.

AC   Natoli, Luigi. *I Beati Paoli*. Introduction and footnotes by Adriana Chirco. Dario Flaccovio Editore: Palermo, 2015.

SE   Natoli, Luigi. *I Beati Paoli*. Introduction by Maurizio Barbato. Sellerio Editore: Palermo, 2016.

PCG   Chirco, Adriana. *Palermo City Guide*. Dario Flaccovio Editore: Palermo, 1998.

Ustica

SICILY

Palermo
Bagheria
Capo Zafferano
Monreale
Termini Imerese
Cefalù
Partinico
Trapani   Temple of Segesta
Alcamo
Bosco
della Ficuzza
Caccamo
Marsala
Monte Sicani
Mazara
Selinunte
Caltanissetta
Girgenti
Licata

Pantelleria
25 miles
←

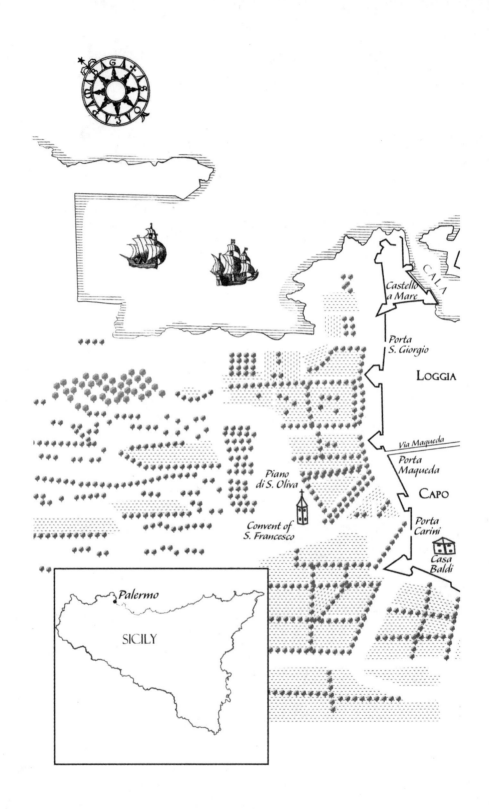

PALERMO

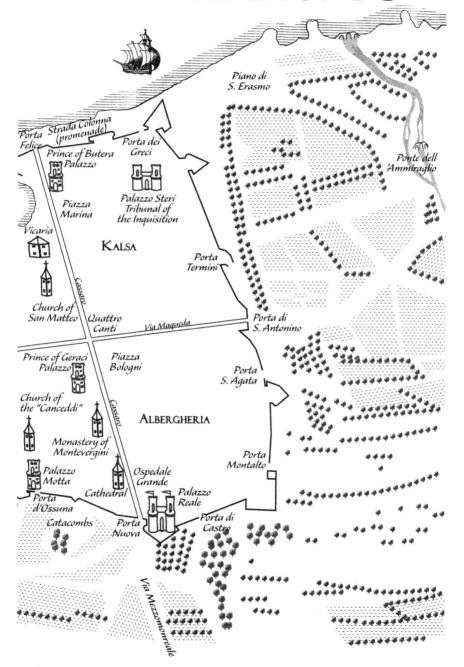

A classic Sicilian litter, transport frequently used for extended journeys outside the city

SICILIAN AVENGERS

AVENGERS

BOOK TWO

Auto-da-fé in Palermo 1724: François Chiche

PART I

CHAPTER 1

On the afternoon of October 24, 1714, a public ceremony took place at Sant'Offizio. The day before, the first procession marking the beginning of the auto-da-fé had come out from the Palazzo Steri. At its head was a procession of cavalieri, followed by the Prince of Cattolica carrying the red banner of Santa Fede, the Compagnia dell'Assunta[1] with lit torches, the poorhouses of lost children and orphans, the friars, the parishes, the Congregazione della Pescagione,[2] whose standard was carried by the Prince of Montevago, and the Cavaliere Filingeri, carrying the white cross; then came the judges of the tribunal of Sant'Offizio, army officers, musicians, and the green cross carried between lit torches by a priest wearing a cope.

The procession went slowly up the Cassaro until it reached the piazza of the Cathedral, where above a large stage about eight palms high, loggias and benches had been built for the celebration of the act of faith. On one side were the loggias of the inquisitors, set higher than all the others; on the other was the one for the Senate; in the center was the bench for the accused; in the remaining space were the altar and the pulpit. Other loggias were designated to accommodate the magistrates of the kingdom.

The procession climbed onto the stage, walked around it until the priest placed the green cross above the altar, then went back the same way.

This was the first function of the auto-da-fé, to which that improvised stage was consecrated and all but devoted to.

On the day of the ceremony, the procession was repeated, but with some differences. The Compagnia dell'Assunta led the procession without torches, and then there were the friars and priests, also without torches, and after them came the *alcade*[3] on horseback; the friars of Pescagione carried weapons instead of torches, and between them walked the accused, who were twenty, behind whom followed

---

1 Composed of experts in canon law, whose task was to disabuse the offenders of their crimes against the faith and to lead them to the light: RLD, 789.
2 Had the task of following and assisting those under investigation during the staging of the Inquisition: RLD, 789.
3 Spanish: mayor.

the captain of Sant'Offizio on horseback, accompanied by cavalieri, and then the counselors, the canon lawyers, the distinguished members of the Tribunal, the delegated standard bearer Teodoro de Lorenzo with the crimson banner of Santa Fede, and, finally, majestic and solemn on their mules, the three inquisitors, one after the other, flanked by nobles and senators and surrounded by the viceroy's halberdiers.

The entire Cassaro was swarming with people, poor and for the most part from the provinces, ignorant and superstitious or frenzied and hysterical, who wanted to see the accused. Another throng packed the piazza of the Cathedral, becoming denser on the Cassaro. In the balconies and windows of the palazzi overlooking the piazza, another crowd sparkled with silk and jewels: it was the nobility, who were used to attending, as the chroniclers of the age expressed it, with "the most exquisite pomp, to celebrate the triumph of faith."

The nearby piazza of the Palazzo Reale and the street behind the Duomo were filled with carriages and portantine.

When the procession arrived at the piazza of the Cathedral and climbed onto the stage, it offered an imposing sight to the eye. From the height of the loggia, which looked like a throne, the three inquisitors of the kingdom held sway over the crowd, and it truly seemed that supreme power and total authority was in their hands. Around them, heads were bowed in fear; the Senate itself, which at times dared to challenge the viceroy's authority, bowed submissively to the solemn and imposing majesty of that gloomy tribunal.

The accused sat on the steps opposite the pulpit; the friars of Pescagione accompanied them there one by one, and they looked around, either astounded or confused, some feeling awkward—all of them with a certain trepidation at the sight of so much apparatus. At first, they had the men sit down, among whom were two or three who wore the frock of a friar, then the women: a Franciscan, a nun, four peasants, and the last one a civilian, dressed in black, extremely pale, who held her head down as if to hide her face. Only when she sat down did she raise her eyes to look over the crowd, as if searching for a familiar face there, and then she lowered them again, full of tears. It was Signora Francesca.

The sermon began. A Dominican friar, with emphatic gestures and voice, after a laudatory apostrophe to the majesty of the tribunal and a praise to the "greater devotion and exemplariness of the nobility present," talked about the Christian faith and divine mercy, which was the inspiration for the holy tribunal and could turn into dismay and terror only through stubborn heretical depravity. And he continued for about an hour in that tone, railing with grand locutions and feigning great emotion against the offenders, whose sins, although not deserving of more serious punishments, were nevertheless very grave offenses to the sanctity of religion and misdeeds in the sight of God.

There were people who were moved at the description of the dreadful sentences and cried; Signora Francesca seemed petrified by her suffering and showed no sign of life. She seemed to be searching for the reason why she was on that stage, and what those vehement words had to do with her.

When the sermon ended, another friar read the proceedings, one by one, calling the offenders who went to listen to the reading below the pulpit, and at the end they confirmed their declarations of submission to the sentence of the holy tribunal. Four of those unfortunate ones accused as heretical blasphemers, who had recanted *de levi*,[4] were condemned to be taken along the street in shame wearing the muzzle[5] and exiled from their towns and neighborhoods, some for one year, some for two or three. A fifth, an Augustinian friar from Caltagirone, a "sorcerer and heretical blasphemer," was sentenced to reclusion in a convent. Two bigamists came after him, one from Girgenti, the other from Patti; they were condemned to the lash along the streets and to the oars for three years. The other friars and deacons were guilty of sorcery and doing business with the devil and of speaking of heretical concepts; Sant'Offizio condemned them to reclusion for five years, some in convents, others to imprisonment in Sant'Offizio. Then came the women. Some old ignorant ones guilty of doing business with the devil and of sorcery were condemned to the lash along public streets and to imprisonment. One, named Barbara, witch, heretic, and sorceress, had the greatest sentence: paraded in shame along the streets, two hundred lashes, and five years in prison.

The reading of these proceedings and sentences continued with a cold and ponderous monotony; those pillories, those public lashings, conjured up sorrowful sights, not infrequent at the time, that left a shameful mark on those who suffered them. The souls accustomed to this felt no pity and their eyes looked on with curiosity; perhaps in secret some lamented the plight of the victims, but they dared not express their own feelings for fear of appearing insufficiently Catholic.

When Signora Francesca's turn came, a certain movement of curiosity was noted in one part of the crowd; named as one being prosecuted for the accusation of being part of the sect, the surname of Ammirata made the wife an interesting subject. Everyone was looking to see if the wives of the Beati Paoli had some mark, some special coat of arms that was like a seal for the mystery that surrounded the sect.

She rose up unsteadily and listened to the proceedings, in which—amid the Latin wordings, a mixture of religious invocations and cruel judicial phrases— it was stated that owing to well-substantiated evidence, the named Francesca Ammirata, native of Palermo, was proven guilty of having blasphemed, of having

---

4 That is, they had publicly recanted their sins: RLD, 789.
5 An iron framework enclosing the head and immobilizing the tongue; a gruesome medieval torture instrument to bring on public humiliation and deter the wearer from speaking.

spoken about heretical concepts, and of doubting God and his Divine Providence; that during the trial, far from acknowledging divine justice and the sacred character of the Holy Inquisition, she had obstinately uttered offensive words and revealed a soul inclined to depravity; and finally that she had given justifiable reasons to believe that she belonged to the sect of the Beati Paoli, which was usurping a property of the Church and making use of rites that were considered detrimental to the holy faith.

However, persuaded by the eloquence of the spiritual fathers appointed to convert her, Signora Francesca Ammirata had renounced her faults, submitting herself to the provident justice of the holy tribunal, which condemned her to public shaming with fifty lashes, to be administered in designated sites with the customary ritual, and to three years of confinement in the prison in Sant'Offizio.

At the reading of the dreadful sentence, Signora Francesca fell to her knees, raised her hands to the sky, and cried out, "I swear in front of God who can see us that I am innocent! I am innocent!"

And from a corner of the piazza, a voice exclaimed, "This is an infamy!"

But this voice, heard only by those close by, didn't spread. It provoked a movement of surprise in that corner; the nearest "forum" members of Sant'Offizio set upon it, scandalized that anyone would dare to offend the majesty of that moment.

The reading having ended, the guilty were consigned to the captain for the carrying out of the sentences, and the procession resumed its journey toward the Palazzo Steri, where it disbanded.

It was about four thirty, and the punishments were beginning. The guilty, placed on top of carts with a miter on their heads, their shoulders bare and their arms tied behind their backs, were flagellated by the executioner and his assistants. The cart stopped in front of the archbishop's residence, in Piazza Bologni, at the Quattro Canti, in front of the Vicaria, and in front of Sant'Offizio, where the condemned were set down. At each stop, the trumpets would blare and the executioner would apply his whip. A crowd of the curious, for the most part young, whose most beastly instincts were aroused by the spectacle, followed the cart. Mud, apple cores, and garbage rained down on the backs and faces of those wretched ones, amid the insults and scornful laughter of the mob, who took particular aim at the old women condemned for sorcery and conjuring up spells.

Evening was falling, and the sad spectacle continued along the Cassaro. The last to walk along that painful ordeal, as the last to have been called onto the stage, was Signora Francesca—upright on the cart, with her head held high, her eyes dry and glossy as if with fever. From time to time her glance would wander over the crowd as if in search of someone. The first blare of the trumpet had been sounded at the corner of the archbishop's palazzo; the first lashes of the whip had fallen on the poor woman's shoulders, and the cart had moved toward Piazza Bologni when, just beyond the corner of the Monastery of Sette Angeli, the executioners who pulled the cart fell to the ground as if struck by lightning. Signora Francesca and the executioner swayed and then fell to the bottom of the cart in a mass. There was a moment of confusion. The members of the forum and the guards of Sant'Offizio immediately hurled themselves on the cart, surrounding it and putting themselves on defense, as if to ensure that they held the condemned woman. In that bustle, a man slipped from between the wheels of the wagon and mingled in the crowd.

The drivers tried to lift up the animals, but they realized that their hocks had been slashed; the surprise of that discovery added to the confusion. A few people tried to approach the cart; some hands reached out, but the points of halberds flashed in the air. Cries of alarm resounded, then the captain rushed to the scene on horseback with a few cavalieri, and the urban guards of the nearby Palazzo Pretorio rushed in. The crowd pushed back vigorously. Signora Francesca was seized, removed from the cart, thrown on the rump of a horse, and surrounded by guards, to be taken away to Palazzo Steri without having been whipped. She didn't look like a condemned woman who was being taken back to prison but like a lady being kidnapped.

The crowd reassembled, approaching the abandoned cart, and the oxen, with their bleeding hooves, bellowed in pain, and from everyone's mouths circulated comments full of surprise and a certain shock.

At the Palazzo Sant'Offizio, they were more than a little amazed by the incident, new in the annals of the Sicilian Inquisition, and unexpected. It was clear that someone had tried to rescue Signora Francesca from the torture of the lash and from public shame and that the perpetrators of that attempt, which seemed like a grave and sacrilegious offense against the majesty of the holy tribunal, could not have been anything but accomplices of her husband, members of the sect—that is, of the Beati Paoli, who thus had given proof of their arrogance.

But that didn't save Signora Francesca from torture, since the sentence had to be carried out in full. The inquisitors postponed it to the following day, limiting the public display to Piazza Marina and encircling the victim with a true army of guards.

The executioner whipped her, but the curious, greedy for tragic spectacles, still noted that from time to time, the executioner looked out among the crowd with a fearful and suspicious eye.

And indeed, among the crowd there were eyes that were following him, menacing and grim.

CHAPTER 2

The nuns and educande of Montevergini, like those of all the other monasteries, had witnessed the processions of the condemned in Sant'Offizio from their covered loggias, and now they were returning to go to supper and to the choir.

The beautiful Violante, still under the shock of that spectacle, was talking about it with her schoolmates; the accused women and especially those guilty of doing business with the devil struck a kind of terror in them that made them shudder. It reminded them of countless frightening stories of diabolical apparitions, descriptions of demons heard in the sermons, in stories told by the old nuns, and in the reading of ascetic books, and they looked around themselves as if at any moment they were likely to see the ground open up and the horns or blazing eyes of monstrous infernal spirits appear.

In leaving the choir after having recited the rosary, in the shadows barely interrupted by the lamps, their fears grew. At night, the corridors seemed frightful, like wide-open and unending gorges, and the sound of their footsteps echoed with the same sense of terror as the voices that had echoed in the dark and deserted church. They huddled together, holding hands. There were, however, the most daring, who would say out loud, "I am a daughter of Mary, and I am not afraid of the enemy." And they would cross themselves. The devil always fled from the sign of the cross.

The monastery stood in part along the front and sides of the church, in part on the other side of the street, in a separate building, connected to the first by a wide covered bridge over the road. The convent school was in this building, together with the novitiate, in two wings separated by a garden.

As in all the monasteries at that time, the girls were separated by age. Violante was among the oldest. She slept in a room with three other schoolmates and a nun. Each one had her little bed enclosed by white curtains; Violante's was next to the window that overlooked the garden, lacking iron bars since it was an interior room and because the building was not cloistered.

The room smelled of fresh whitewash. In fact, during the day some masons had been sent by the procurator of the monastery to do some repairs, which had lasted almost to the Ave Maria. The educande sensed that odor and grimaced.

"Signora Madre," they said to the nun, "may we leave the windows open tonight? . . . This smell is going to our heads."

Although it was October, it was still warm enough to justify that request. Sometimes during very hot nights that stifled one's breath, the dormitory windows would be left open; this time the warmth was also combined with another, more persuasive reason.

But the nun didn't give in: "No, no; the nights are cool now, and I'm afraid that someone could become ill."

Then to the young girls' complaints she offered a glimmer of hope.

"Let's go, let's say our prayers: In the name of the Father, and of the Son, and of the Holy Spirit."

She knelt and began to recite the Latin prayers, which had undergone original and curious transformations, of which neither the good nun nor the educande were aware; the educande also knelt in front of her, repeating those prayers in unison with the same monotonous singsong, followed by invocations, the prayers in verse and in dialect:

> Iu mi curcu 'nta stu lettu
> cu Gesuzzu 'nta lu pettu
> iu dormu e iddu vigghia
> si cc'è cosa m'arrispigghia.
> Cu Gesù mi curcu
> cu Gesù mi staiu
> essenu cu Gesù
> paura nun haiu:
> essenu chi haiu
> st'amici fidili
> mi fazzu la cruci
> e vaju a durmiri.

And then there were some interminable exhortations to the Blessed Virgin, to San Giuseppe, to San Michele Arcangelo, to Santa Rosalia, to San Domenico, to San Francesco.

Some of the educande were dozing and repeating those orations through force of habit; others let the last syllables of each word die out. Finally, louder than the others and like a relief, resounded the word *Amen*. And then the girls got up and kissed the hand of the nun, and everyone vanished behind the curtains of their beds.

For several minutes one heard a whispering of little birds running from one bed to another; then one by one the mouths closed, then the eyes closed; in the silence could be heard the rhythm of their breaths, similar to a light wisp of wind among leafy branches.

The rather large room, with its five beds symmetrically arranged on one side and the other, was immersed in shadow. High on the wall between the two windows overlooking the garden, in front of an image of the Madonna, burned a lamp, a small red flame that barely let one see the pale face of the Madonna on the black canvas.

Violante was sleeping soundly with her head under the covers. She had fallen asleep like that, out of fear of the demons. The other young girls and the nun herself had also had a shiver of fear and instinctively had covered their heads in order to avoid catching sight of the "ugly beast." In spite of the prayers, the image of the crucifix that hung above each bed, the holy water that every girl kept at her bedside, and the relics and medals that hung from every neck, the fear generated by the speeches given and the sight of the flogged sorceresses was still on their minds. But that didn't prevent sleep from taking hold of those pretty bodies.

Slowly a window opened without being heard. A black shadow leaned inside the room and waited a minute, as if spying; then, when it was sure that everyone was silent and asleep, it pushed the window and let itself slip inside.

Another shadow followed it. Both of them were black and one couldn't see the color of their faces; they were barefoot and walked without making a sound.

They approached a bed, gently lifted the blankets, and looked. It didn't seem like what they were searching for, and they passed to the next; it was Violante's. They bent down to look at the young girl and made a gesture, as if to say, "This one!"

Then one of the shadows drew from its breast pocket something like a scarf or a large handkerchief while the other quickly grabbed the girl with all her bedcovers and lifted her up in its arms. Violante, awakened abruptly, made as if to scream, but her scream was muffled immediately, stifled by a gag that covered her mouth. Her eyes, open wide with fear, saw nothing because her head was wrapped in the bedcovers; her hands couldn't move because they were held tightly between two arms that felt like a vise.

The poor young girl was invaded by terror. Devils had certainly come to take her. Her terror was so great that she fainted.

The two shadows moved to the window. One stepped first over the windowsill and went down; its two hands received that little inert body, which vanished in the dark, and behind it the other shadow also vanished.

Although they hadn't made the slightest noise and this scene had unfolded with such extraordinary speed and precision, one of the educande, perhaps due to those vibrations of the senses that escape our attention but that have the same energy as conscious impressions, awoke and pushed aside the curtains of her bed. She saw the black shadow near the window and felt a sense of superstitious terror that made her blood run cold and took away her voice; trembling, with an almost lifeless voice, full of tears and dread, she screamed: "Signora Madre! Signora Madre! Jesus, Joseph, and Mary! Signora Madre!"

The nun awoke, stammering, "What? What is it?"

But the young girl could hardly say a word; it seemed that she had a lump in her throat. She pointed to the window and made the sign of the cross. "The devil . . . the devil," she stammered.

The nun became alarmed. She opened her eyes, looked around, and saw nothing—only a large black square on the wall, but in the confusion of the girl's words, she didn't realize that it was the open window. With some effort, first taking the crucifix down from the wall and then raising it high, just in case, to frighten the spirit of evil, entrusting herself to God, reciting verses, she got down from the bed and, looking fearfully around, approached the girl.

"What is it?" she asked in an almost tearful voice.

"There . . . there . . . the devil . . . I saw him!"

The nun looked around, frightened. "Where? . . . How?"

She didn't dare to go near the window.

The other educande had woken up. They looked terrified, still not understanding what was going on but intuiting that it must be something terrible, and didn't dare to move. Someone stammered, "Jesus! Jesus! What's wrong?"

Now everyone was stock-still out of fear, pale, with eyes open wide, staring at one spot, as if in expectation of terror, and they stayed like that for a while, mumbling prayers.

The nun asked the young girl, "What did you see? Tell me . . ."

But the educanda's teeth were chattering. She was overcome by a nervous shudder and couldn't answer. Her eyes stared at the open window. Who had flung it open? There was no wind. Then she noticed the disorder of Violante's bed, and astonishment was added to her fear. Where was she? They called out to her: "Violante! Violante!"

But Violante couldn't answer; her bed was empty, without its covers. They all looked at one another dumbfounded, with a lump of distress in their throats.

Violante! . . . Violante! . . . Violante!

The educanda who had been the first to wake up stammered, "Demons took her away."

Then a cry of terror and horror arose, and they all burst into tears. The nun picked up a handbell and, ringing it desperately, opened the door and went out into the corridor; the educande followed her. The entire school woke up. The corridors filled with young girls in their nightshirts, their little bare feet, asking one another with voices full of fear, "What is it? What happened?"

They feared earthquakes, fires, a disaster; when the rumor spread that devils had taken Violante away, they burst into tears of terror. They ran to the monastery, awakening the Mother Superior and the nuns.

"The relic . . . let's take the relic."

The Mother Superior took a relic of Santa Rosalia:[1] a barely visible ossicle attached to a piece of crimson cloth and enclosed in a rich gold filigree case. The nuns lit some small torches, formed a procession, and, following the Mother Superior, reciting prayers, they went through the covered bridge into the school and entered the room.

One nun, more courageous than the others, turned toward the window and saw the top part of a ladder; she looked out and exclaimed, "There is a ladder!"

"A ladder! A ladder!"

Everyone rushed over, nuns and educande, struck by that discovery that suddenly unsettled and disoriented the path of their thoughts and rattled their beliefs.

A ladder? But the devil doesn't need ladders because he has the wings of a bat; a ladder is only needed by humans. Therefore, Violante had run away. They all felt reassured; the superstitious terror vanished as if by magic; what demon? The young girl was hallucinating. . . . What dark shadows? Violante had run away!

A new amazement, different from the first, but it, too, distressing, followed the fright of the first. Everyone wanted to see the ladder.

The Mother Superior ordered, "Ring the bells!"

After an instant, in the silence of the night, the bells rang continuously. The peals increased, awakening the neighbors. Balconies and windows opened; fearful faces appeared and were looking suspiciously at one another, asking, "What is it?"

"Where is it?"

"They're ringing the bells of Montevergini."

"Thieves?"

"Fire?"

The nuns of the nearby monasteries of Salvatore and Cancelliere, having awakened from that pealing of bells, not knowing what had happened, also started to ring their bells continuously. The city awakened, surprised and panic-stricken; armed citizens, half-dressed, and guards rushed to the scene; the piazzetta of Montevergini filled with people thronging around the doors of the church and the parlors, amazed at not seeing any trace of fire or any door forced open.

A voice came from the monastery: "From the garden! . . . A ladder in the garden!"

The entire crowd turned toward the vicolo adjacent to the church, where there was a small parlor; others went into Vicolo San Biagio, went up into private homes, in order to try to enter the garden.

A voice suddenly shouted, "This way! It's here!"

"What? What is it?"

They found a narrow lane that extended from Vicolo San Biagio along to the Montevergini building, with a little open door beyond which could be seen

---

1 Patron saint of Palermo.

something that looked like plants. Holding weapons, armed with lanterns, the most spirited pushed ahead, and through a passageway they emerged into the garden of the school. Evidently some people had entered from there. Others followed the ones who had entered first, and the garden was invaded by a crowd that began to rummage everywhere, among the bushes and the trees, in the corners; then they reached the ladder leaning against the wall, which Violante's kidnappers had used.

At the foot of the ladder were the covers from her bed.

The discovery was so glaring that all those people who believed that they would at any moment find themselves in the presence of armed men were unhappy; they started laughing, began to badmouth, to sneer, not without a bit of disrespect toward the monastery.

"A nun ran away!"

"A nun ran away!"

"She ran away with her uncle monk."

"Uncle Monk and Aunt Nun."

"And they woke us up for this?"

"Those swaddled heads!"

"That the devil should take them!"

Some other crude words were flung out; then a whistle; another; the garden transformed into a deafening bird trap; shouts, whistles, mockeries that made the building tremble. The nuns and the educande were afraid. They bolted the doors, fearing they would hear them fall down at any moment under the blows of that multitude, who, having rushed to defend the monastery, had suddenly been transformed into an annoyed and insolent horde.

And it was fortunate that the relatives of the nuns and of the educande, aroused by the pealing of bells, seized by anxiety, rushed there with their servants and neighbors and were able to free the monastery, not without difficulty and with a little violence, from the crowd, which was already beginning to warm up and enjoy the diversion.

CHAPTER 3

The two black shadows lowered themselves cautiously down the ladder, one after the other, carrying the unconscious Violante. When they reached the foot of the ladder, they freed the body from the bedcovers enveloping it, fearing that they were suffocating her.

"Aren't there any cloaks?"

In total silence they crossed the garden and came out of a passage where two men, also in black and unrecognizable, waited by a portantina. One of them covered the girl with a cloak and thrust her inside the portantina, fastening her with a leather strap, as was typically done with cadavers. Out of precaution they tied her hands and gagged her.

The portantina was lifted up; the men surrounded it and quickly set off. Through some dark, narrow, and winding vicoli, they emerged onto Piazza del Cancelliere; a few minutes later, the first bells rang out.

"Come on, be quick . . . those fools will awaken the city."

They crossed the piazza in no time, going up Via del Celso and along Salita Sant'Agata, and taking other vicoli they came out onto Via Incoronata next to the Cathedral. They stopped there for a moment. Violante was gradually coming to, and she opened her eyes, terrified, almost believing that she would see demons, flames, and frightening monsters around her, and she saw herself alone, tied up, inside that large box, which she didn't recognize at first. She felt the rhythmic movement of the steps of the portantini and a different fear took hold of her. Something was obstructing her mouth. She tried to get up and couldn't. She became agitated; she struggled to free herself of all those impediments, trembling through all her limbs.

Where was she? Who was with her? Was this hell? Were demons carrying her? A menacing voice said to her from the door, "Don't you dare move or scream, or we will kill you."

In fact, she saw something flash that could have been the blade of a dagger or the barrel of a pistol. Then she began to cry. Why did they want to kill her? What had she done? Where were they taking her? So they weren't demons, then; perhaps they were sorcerers? Hadn't she heard stories about sorcerers that kidnapped young girls and cut them to pieces and put them in barrels? A more intense terror, like one born from an almost invisible danger, invaded her; her sense of reality, aroused by the voice and the flashing, froze her blood and petrified her. What could she do? How could she resist? How could she free herself? She was tied up in this portantina and there were quite a few men carrying her. Were they sorcerers? Were they "Greeks of the Levant"[1] who with their villainy put so much fear into people? Were they Barbary pirates who stole children and took them as slaves to Muhammad?

She mentally began to recite prayers and to entrust herself to the Madonna, and as she was praying, her heart melted and sobs rose to her mouth, breaking into stifled moans.

The same voice from before tried to calm her down, but in such a threatening tone that it wasn't reassuring.

"Be quiet, we will not hurt you! Be quiet . . . don't be afraid!"

But she was dying of fear!

The portantina resumed its way, passed in front of the Church of the Ospedale dei Sacerdoti and along a vicolo (now closed), emerging into the dark and silent piazza of Palazzo Reale, in whose vast shadow it disappeared.

Where was it going? Now it was entering streets where the steps hitting the pavement didn't resound as before, and where the sound of the bells was fainter. Then suddenly Violante felt a gust of colder air hit her in the face and penetrate between her legs.

Meanwhile the gag was suffocating her; at least they could free her from that torment. She began to groan louder and to struggle inside the portantina. The same voice said harshly, "Can't you understand that we won't do anything to you? Stay calm."

But Violante continued to struggle and to groan even louder and to stamp her feet on the bottom of the portantina.

The voice ordered, "Stop."

Violante then saw the curtain open, and a masked man appeared. Raising a lantern over her, he asked, "What is it? Why don't you want to be quiet? Watch yourself!"

But the face of the young girl must have expressed such suffering, must have appeared so distraught and almost flushed, that the man understood.

"Is the gag bothering you? . . . Well, I will remove it, but I warn you! . . . If you scream I will run through your throat with this."

To those words he added the act of touching the flashing point of the dagger to her throat.

"Do you promise to keep quiet?" the man asked her.

1 Greeks of the Levant, as opposed to the Albanian Greeks living in Sicily at the time, were thought to be sorcerers and descendants of the ancient Thessalian sorceresses.

Violante nodded yes. The man removed the gag and the girl breathed violently, and uncontrollable and convulsive sobs erupted from her chest as if unleashed.

"Don't be afraid, goodness! We're not going to eat you."

The portantina continued on its way. As the curtain opened, by the reflection of the lantern, Violante saw a rustic wall with overhanging branches flash into view. That meant that she was in the countryside. Then she seemed to understand, and a new fear caused her teeth to chatter and her body to tremble. In those days one heard many stories about people kidnapped by bandits who would demand large sums for ransom, and now she had no doubt she was a victim of one of those wicked crimes.

"Oh, signore, help me!"

Why take her, a poor defenseless young girl? Where were they taking her? Perhaps to a cave, a frightening cave where wolves and snakes could penetrate. Oh, better to die! Better to die!

She attempted an appeal for mercy.

"Signore, my good signore," she murmured in a tearful voice.

"What do you want?"

"Have pity on me . . . take me home! . . . I beseech you. I didn't do anything. Why do you want to kill me?"

"Don't talk nonsense."

"If I offended you, I ask your forgiveness; I am begging you on my knees. . . . I will kiss your feet . . . but let me go!"

"Don't talk nonsense!"

"I don't know you; I don't know who you are . . . but I know that you have children . . . if I were your daughter—"

"Don't talk nonsense!" the masked man replied harshly for the third time.

"Oh God! . . . God! Have mercy on me!"

She was crying desperately. The man paid her no attention and let her cry, but suddenly he pushed away the curtain, stuck his face inside the portantina, and said to her through clenched teeth, "Be quiet, for Christ's sake, or I will slit your throat!"

Terrified, she choked back a sob. In that moment of silence she heard the sound of a horse pawing on the pavement, and a sudden hope was born in her heart. She realized that the portantina had stopped and pulled to one side as if to leave the path free or to avoid coming up against someone. The pawing came closer. It wasn't resounding like before, but she sensed she was next to it. The horse neighed and snorted. Then Violante gathered all her strength and screamed: "Help!"

But the man, rushing to the door and thrusting his arm inside, silenced her mouth violently, accompanying the act with a curse.

"Hey!" shouted a strong masculine voice. "What's going on in there?"

The portantina, having come out of the city from Porta di Montalto (now destroyed) along county roads, had arrived at the end of Ponte dell'Ammiraglio at the same moment that, from the opposite side, a man on horseback had reached the top of the bridge and was descending toward the portantina. He had looked with surprise and curiosity in the shadow of the night at that strange retinue, composed of four men and two portantine, at that hour and in that place. It wasn't a supply of provisions, because it wasn't accompanied by torches and large lanterns; it wasn't a doctor or midwife, because there were too many people; it wasn't a person under arrest, because they weren't going toward but moving away from the city, and in the countryside there weren't any prisons. Therefore, it was either a lord who was going to his estate—and in that way and in that hour, it couldn't be anyone other than a crazy person—or there was something suspicious and not quite right about it.

The cry for help, coming from a trembling feminine voice, made him stop and address them in this manner: "Who is in there?" he repeated, spurring on his horse.

But the men blocked his path, and from under their cloaks in which they were wrapped, they took out carbines. One of them threatened him: "Go about your business, or . . . by the Madonna!"

"Oh! Oh! Oh!" replied the voice. "Goodness! My dear bandits, you trouble yourselves too much . . . and at the same time you have the wrong person if you think those contraptions can scare me."

Violante was struggling to free her mouth and scream; the man who had silenced her snapped at her under his breath, "Stay quiet, stay quiet, or I will kill you!"

The portantina rocked back and forth. The horseman was only a few steps from the group. What was he doing? His horse was shuddering all over and trembling nervously. He seemed to want to negotiate.

"My question," continued the horseman, "may be an indiscretion, but it is not meant to be an affront."

"Let's put an end to this! And get out of here!" shouted one of the men.

The man who was preventing Violante from screaming exclaimed, "But hurry up, damnation! . . . Get him out of here!"

He hadn't finished speaking when in a flash the horse darted forward and jumped on the men, who, shocked, and in order to avoid the sudden fury, tried to scatter on one side and the other. They hadn't recovered, nor had they resumed the offensive, when they felt formidable blows descending on them. The horseman, in fact, having brandished the musket he was holding across his saddle by the barrel and wielding it like a club of war, had struck the two closest to him.

Two rifle shots flashed. One bullet knocked off the horseman's hat; the other one flattened itself against the metallic plate of the bandolier in which the horseman was keeping his cartridge box. Everything happened so quickly that the man who was holding Violante had not been aware of it right away. But when he noticed that two of his men were lying on the ground and that the horseman had forcefully thrown himself, with his sword unsheathed, against the other three, he, untying the straps that were restraining the girl, took her in his arms, shouting, "Follow me, Andrea!" and rushed toward the river.

One of the men ran after him.

Violante cried out, "Help! Help!"

The horseman heard the cry, saw the escape, and then, in dogged pursuit of the two that were facing him, battered them with blows, forced them to flee, and turned his horse after the girl's kidnappers, who had gone into the river.

At that point the Oreto isn't so deep that a man cannot wade across it, nor had there been any rainfalls yet to swell it. Those two men, holding the girl firmly raised on their shoulders, cut across the current in order to reach the other shore with a prodigious speed, but the horseman had the advantage of his horse.

"For goodness' sake! You won't get away from me!" shouted the horseman, who was already on top of them.

Then, armed with a dagger, one of the men raised his arm high and, threatening the girl, replied, "Take just one step and I will slit her throat here, like a lamb."

He hadn't finished talking when the horseman, stretching forward over the outstretched neck of the horse, landed a violent blow on the man's fist with his sword, which made the dagger fly out of his hand.

"Damnation!" shrieked the stricken man, looking for something to defend himself with.

His companion suggested to him quickly, "Take the girl. I'll take care of him."

He drew his pistol, while the first one hoisted the young girl on his neck, but Violante, infused with hope and courage by the unexpected help, began to twist about as if to free herself, encumbering her kidnapper and hindering his speed of movement. His pistol, perhaps because it had gotten wet, failed to fire. The man then seized the reins of the horse, forcing it to plunge its head in the water, but the horseman discharged a series of blows on his fingers, some of them deadened by the water, others striking. Swearing, the man had to let go of the reins.

The horseman took advantage of the situation: he seized him by the chest, shook him violently, threw him back; he lost his balance, plunged down, and disappeared under the water.

"Bye, Biondello,"[2] shouted the horseman, spurring his horse close to the man who was fleeing with Violante.

He reached out to grab the girl by her loose and disheveled hair while delivering a blow from his sword at her kidnapper, who let out a cry of desperate pain and dropped his load. The horseman managed to pick up the young girl in time and

---

2   In Boccaccio's *Decameron*, Biondello is beaten to a pulp by Cuccio after having played a trick on him.

pull her up onto his saddle. The horse, as if he had sensed the need to hurry, gave two strong kicks and reached the shore.

"Come on, go!" said the horseman, urging him on.

The horse shook his rump in order to shake away the water, neighed, and thrust himself up along the grassy slope of the shore. Violante's eyes were full of tears and she didn't know what to say. The horseman wasn't looking at her yet; he had turned around to see the two kidnappers, who, having regained their courage, were rushing after him in order to catch up with him. He spurred on and incited the animal, who, having reached the side of the road, began to trot.

"Ah! Now we are free!" said the horseman, and this time he looked at the young girl, surprised to see her looking so beautiful even though she was frightened and tearful. He freed her arms, settled her down better on the saddle in front of him, and added, "We are soaking wet like two chicks in oil! We have to find a place to dry ourselves."

He noticed that the young girl was poorly covered by a cloak and that she was barefoot, and he said, "And then . . . how come you are almost naked?"

And he looked at her face with a curiosity full of interest and with ever-growing amazement.

Violante was looking at him too, but a great joy had come over her face. Then she murmured in an indescribable tone, "Signor Don Blasco!"

The young man gave a start; he looked at the girl and said with intense emotion, "Ah, those eyes! Who are you? How do you know me?"

"I am Violante. . . . Violante della Motta. . . . I have seen you so many times at the monastery!"

"You? . . . Ah! The young nun? The educanda? You! And those men? Ah!"

The truth had suddenly revealed itself, and then, seized by an almost superstitious fear, he thrust his spurs into the horse's flanks and urged him into a gallop.

"Hold on tight to me and don't be afraid," he said to the young girl.

She encircled his neck with both arms, pressing herself against his chest with a confident abandonment of innocence, and she didn't perceive the quiver that ran through the body of the horseman. She murmured with firm conviction, "Oh no, I am not afraid anymore!"

They passed small, poor villages, over which the moon shed a merciful light, arousing the barking of dogs, spreading from house to house, becoming more and more faint. They were alone in the night, along the countryside that was flanked by the mountain that rose gloomily, casting great shadows from its projecting cliffs that looked like dark chasms in the valleys and on the slopes. So tall, so dark, so full of shadows and mystery, the mountain aroused a sacred and religious horror.

They were not speaking. The horse was now moving at a slower pace since they could no longer be afraid of being pursued. Where were they going? He didn't know. Now that they were safe, he was looking for a house, a shelter; the young girl also had to have something to eat and drink. Where was there a house? He saw, by the light of the moon, through the foliage of the trees, one of those rural buildings, between a house and a tower, that are still found on the estates of ancient noble families. There was probably a caretaker there who would not deny them hospitality, and a suitable room could be found for the girl.

He turned the horse and led him down a path, at the end of which, between two rough-hewn pillars, was a wrought-iron gate. Blasco settled Violante in the saddle and dismounted. The gate was locked. He put his hand between the bars, felt for the bolt, and pulled it. Some dogs, barking furiously along the path, ran to the gate. Blasco threatened them, but in order not to expose himself to the teeth of those vigilant guardians, he started banging on the gate with a stone and shouting: "Hello! . . . Hey there!"

A few moments later a voice from the end of the path responded. "Who is it?"

"Call off the dogs. I am a friend."

"What friend?"

"I am a cavaliere! I need a favor . . . please come and open the gate for me."

A lantern moved forward in a zigzag motion along the path; a man armed with a harquebus made himself more visible as he came closer. He stopped at a certain distance, raised the lantern up until it fully illuminated Blasco's face, then placed it on the ground and said, "What do you want?"

"Nothing more than the favor of giving us shelter for a few hours, until tomorrow morning. . . . I will pay you. Are you the caretaker?"

"Yes, signore. Come this way."

He chased away the barking dogs and came closer to the gate to have a better look, still suspicious.

Blasco said to him, "Listen, friend, if you have some doubt, please say so; I will not trouble you, and I will find some good person around here. I knocked here because I saw a respectable-looking villa where the young lady can rest. You can see that we are drenched. . . . And because I assume that you are a Christian."

The caretaker saw the horse, saw the girl, and, having recognized that he was dealing with people of quality, he opened the gate and said, "Your Lordship, come this way, please. This estate belongs to the Prince of Trabia."

"Don Ottavio?" said Blasco. "So much the better, he is my friend."

Blasco took his horse by the reins and pulled it behind him along the path; he helped Violante to dismount and, taking her in his arms, he wrapped her up as best he could and brought her inside into a room, saying to the caretaker, "Now, my friend, we have to take care of this young girl, who has been saved by a miracle of God. As you can see, she is barefoot and soaking wet."

He briefly told him what had happened, not revealing his name or that of the girl. The caretaker listened dumbfounded, but with a slight mischievous suspicion in his heart.

"I am sorry," he said, "that there are no women in the house, but we will make you comfortable. His Excellency's room is upstairs . . . for when he comes to the estate . . . and there is a good bed."

With the lantern, he guided the two young people into a nice room; he took out some linen from a chest made of carved wood, and he prepared the bed, which was made of wrought iron shaped into foliage and painted in red and blue with gilding. It was one of those magnificent beds of rural manufacture that are no longer found, except in museums in Germany and England, and are marveled at for the exquisiteness of the work and the designs.

"Get in bed and rest peacefully," Blasco said to the young girl, who was now shy and bashful. "I'll be in the other room."

But Violante, caught by a sudden terror, clung to his neck, saying, "No, no, don't leave me, Signor Don Blasco; don't leave me . . . I am afraid! I don't want to be alone."

Blasco felt faint and stammered, "But of course, my child; I will not leave you . . . just for the time for you to fall asleep . . . you need it . . . we also have to dry your shirt."

The caretaker seemed embarrassed.

"And where will I get a woman's shirt?"

"It doesn't have to be a woman's . . . there must be a man's shirt here."

Soon after, Violante, bundled up in a shirt made of thick cloth but freshly laundered, was slipping herself under the covers, smiling at this disguise of hers and calling out, "Signor Don Blasco, Signor Don Blasco!"

CHAPTER 4

Blasco spent the rest of the night at the young girl's bedside, holding her hand. She had wanted her savior to stay right there, next to her; she had taken his hands and had curled up in the bed so that her head was almost touching Blasco's shoulder. And she had fallen asleep like that; the weariness and the terrifying emotions of that night had exhausted her. Now, in her sleep, an intense fever stirred her blood and pounded her arteries. Blasco had tried to leave the room several times, but Violante, suddenly awakened, had gripped his hands tightly, murmuring, "No, no . . . I'm afraid!"

It was obvious. During her sleep, the poor girl would give a start on the bed, shake vigorously, and stammer incoherent and incomprehensible words. Blasco was watching over her, looking at her with an affectionate concern, with a tenderness that touched him and almost moved him to tears. Now he recognized who she was, and he recalled that afternoon when, near the same bridge where he had saved her, he had seen her pass by, wearing the black habit of an educanda; her large dark eyes and smiling mouth had remained indelible in his memory. And he hadn't known who she was. Now she was there next to him, with her hands clasped in his, in his care, and he was studying her pure oval face, pale as ivory, suffused with that air of suffering that often gives an ineffable vitality to a beautiful face. The overly large shirt bared her neck to her throat, and he could see the dimple of her throat pulsing rhythmically.

The whims of fate! His fleeting vision lay beside him, and he only had to bend down for it to become his own. Perhaps this thought had crossed his mind; something made him bow his head close to the flaming mouth of the young girl, and he was at the point of brushing her lips with his, but a sudden trepidation—the near guilt that he felt to violate those still unripe and innocent lips, to take advantage of what the innocence and tenderness of her age still made intangible, to forget that respect full of discretion that his circumstances called for with regard to someone who, with the unawareness of her own innocence, was entrusting herself to him—all those things stopped him and made him red with shame. And it became clear to him.

With a sense of dismay he asked himself, "So, would I love this child?"

Violante now appeared to him under a new likeness, and a multitude of new feelings erupted, like a herd of foals who, when their stall suddenly opens, rush galloping and scattering through the countryside.

The duke's villainies, the justice of the cause for which the Beati Paoli were fighting, all faded away from his mind so that nothing was left except this one thought: "Why were they targeting this innocent one?" and an emotion: hatred. He could understand the incessant, bitter, ferocious war against Don Raimondo, but he did not understand why, because they were unable to get their hands on the father, this poor defenseless creature should be sacrificed.

Defenseless? And wasn't he there now? God, providence, fate, hadn't they guided him that night, on that road, and in that hour to free the girl from who knew what horrific revenge?

* * *

For about three months he had wandered through the mountains, hiding, to avoid being arrested. His escape had raised too much of an uproar for it to be forgotten, or for it not to be attended to, and the Marchese of San Tommaso had issued strict orders for Blasco to be arrested. Veritable armies of birri, infantry, cavalry, and rural companies had been dispatched everywhere to hunt down the young cavaliere, who had become, as a result of the incidents, a dangerous figure. Of course, the marchese didn't really think he was dangerous, but he had a veiled jealousy for the young man who was the object of Donna Gabriella's passion and who perhaps still occupied her heart. Donna Gabriella had been satisfied in her heart by Blasco's escape, but she had not dared to lessen the rigors of justice so as not to arouse suspicions, as well as to sustain her role, something that she truly regretted and for which she felt some sort of remorse.

The bodyguards had complained about that severity and had protested about it to their captain, the Marchese of Tournon, but in vain. The Marchese of San Tommaso replied to the captain that the guards had nothing to do with matters of His Majesty's justice. His response irritated the bodyguards; Champ-aux-Arbres, who was the architect of the attempts and of the declarations in favor of Blasco, said, "My word of honor that I am determined not to let this go."

He went to the fondaco where Blasco had taken a room and found that his horse and belongings were still there. The fondacaio complained that he had some expenses and offered the horse to the young gentleman; but he, without answering him, paid the debt and took away the horse and belongings, since that fondaco did not seem to him to be a worthy stable for such a beautiful and vigorous animal.

He said to the fondacaio, "If ever the gentleman comes to take his horse, tell him that I, the Viscount of Champ-aux-Arbres, collected it and that I will bring it to him wherever he would like."

Blasco found out about this two days later, at night, from the fondacaio, to whom he had secretly gone to collect his horse; he considered the words of the viscount as an invitation to fight, as a challenge. He suspected a trap but warded off his suspicion, and without giving an answer to the fondacaio, he thought of making use of a goatherd, one of those men who led his goats to the city in the morning in order to sell their milk. And the following morning Champ-aux-Arbres received a note indicating a rendezvous: *Behind the Castello di Bauso at eight o'clock tomorrow morning.*

Blasco went there a little early. Soon after the assigned hour, he saw a horseman come galloping, pulling behind him another horse: it was his.

It seemed to him that he was seeing a friend again. The horseman was the Viscount of Champ-aux-Arbres. Without dismounting, he handed the reins of the other horse to Blasco, saying to him, "Signore, my companions and I are saddened over what happened to you and we wanted to offer our help to you because, with cavalieri of your standing, matters are not settled with men of the law. There will be plenty of time to slit our throats when we can do it freely. Now I wanted to warn you not to be seen and to get out of harm's way, because you are wanted. I thought I should take care of your horse and bring it to you. Farewell."

Blasco, surprised, amazed, and seized with emotion, stopped him, extended his hand, and replied, "You are a generous heart, and I bind myself to you with gratitude; permit me to embrace you."

The viscount frowned, a little uncertain, and said, "You are certainly not saying this out of fear . . . you are an ancient hero."

And, dismounting, he embraced him affectionately; then he pushed him back. "Come on, saddle up and leave. If you are ever traveling through Savoy, and if no one has killed me yet, come to visit me at the Castello di Champ-aux-Arbres!"

He jumped on the saddle, waved farewell, and raced off like lightning. Blasco waited for him to vanish; his eyes were teary, his heart full of emotion. He stroked his horse and, having found with pleasure that all his belongings were in his saddlebags, that there was ammunition, and that the pistols and rifles were loaded, he mounted and took the path to the mountains. From that day he lived wandering here and there along the fiefdoms, gathering news that forced him to look for hiding places and to move away from the demesnial cities[1] and from the large fiefdoms. The four soldiers of the rural militia had been found, one of whom was still alive and had reported in his own way that they had been murdered by a cavaliere and an abbot who were going to Messina and whom they were accompanying. It wasn't difficult to identify the two alleged criminals, so that new reasons could be put forward to justify searches and persecutions in order to avenge their

---

1   Royal or demesnial (from Latin *dominicus*: belonging to a lord or master) cities were those that were under royal administration and fell outside the jurisdiction of the nobility.

companions, and Blasco felt surrounded by traps and threats. He provided for his safety at night by asking for shelter in a convent, when he came across one, which, as sacred places, were inviolable and enjoyed the right of asylum, or he would sleep in the company of shepherds in a farmhouse, lost amid the vastness of the deserted and uncultivated fiefdoms. In that wandering from one place to another he learned, fifteen or twenty days later, that the king had left, and then he thought that the greatest danger had ended because, with the departure of the Marchese of San Tommaso, his principal enemy, the stimulus was gone, and justice was returning to its customary slow and indolent indifference.

* * *

Amid this wandering and progressing from town to town, he had reached Caccamo. Where could he consider himself safer, if not near the good Father Bonaventura? The Father was gravely ill, and the doctors were giving up any hope of saving him. The convent was distressed over it. Blasco arrived at a good time to lift up his spirits. He sat down at his bedside and wanted to help him, thinking that he could thus repay him in some way for what the friar had done for him as a child. He stayed more than twenty days at the convent in Caccamo and had the consolation of carrying out the pious duty of closing the friar's eyes. Father Bonaventura died on October 18, peacefully, without any complaints.

He kissed and blessed Blasco, who was crying, and said to him, "Remember what I told you."

Blasco attended the funeral rites and the burial; he stayed a few more days at the convent, then left for Palermo, in easy stages, traveling at night in order not to encounter any guards or militia, and choosing the narrow paths. Thus, that night, at the gates of the capital, crossing the Ponte dell'Ammiraglio, he had been able to prevent the kidnapping of Violante and to free her.

The entire story passed very quickly through his mind in a series of images while he looked at the girl that fate placed in his arms; then he gradually gave in to sleep and, leaning his head on the pillow so that his hair mingled with that of Violante and his cheek could feel the warmth of the young girl's face, he fell asleep in a kind of sweet state of drowsiness.

The sunlight coming through the windows hit his eyes and woke him up. As he opened his eyes, he saw over him, anxious and absorbed, the large and shining eyes of Violante. The young girl had awakened first and, still feverish, had sat up in the middle of the bed and was gazing with satisfaction at the sleeping young man, feeling a type of comfort flowing in her heart. Oh! How handsome he was! And how brave he was! But when Blasco opened his eyes, she blushed and felt bashful; she thrust herself back under the covers, hiding and not daring to reappear. Blasco smiled, but he didn't want to disturb her with embarrassing questions.

"Now we will send for Her Excellency the Duchess, so that she will come to get you with a litter. Are you happy?"

Violante nodded yes, but she thought almost immediately and not without regret that in going away with her stepmother, she would no longer see Blasco, whereas she was so happy to see him and feel him nearby.

After some time, she raised her head. Blasco had fallen into an intense melancholy and kept his eyes fixed on the ground without seeing anything. Violante timidly called him with a tremor in her voice: "Signor Blasco. . . . I am thirsty."

He pulled himself together. He went to get a jug and handed it to Violante, who drank eagerly.

"Thank you, Signor Blasco! . . . Oh, I owe you so much. . . . I owe you so much!"

"What are you saying? Perhaps I am the one who . . ."

He didn't dare finish; a flood of redness flushed his face and his heart beat violently. Violante was still waiting for him to finish the sentence, but Blasco shook his head and added, "I am a fool, sorry. But as for you, you owe me nothing at all, my child! Let's take care of you. I think that you have a little fever . . . give me your wrist."

She pulled out an arm, which Blasco felt with intense anxiety, counting the pulsations.

"Yes, yes; there is a little fever, but it's nothing. The fright . . . you were scared, isn't that so?"

"Oh, very . . . I was dying from it. The Lord sent you! What would I have done without you?"

Both of them shuddered at the thought of what could have happened.

"Poor girl!" he murmured. "But don't be afraid now; I will watch over you."

"Oh, I am so happy!" But suddenly, as if remembering something, Violante asked, "Why did they tell me that you were dead?"

"Who told you that?"

"My mother."

"The duchess?"

"Yes."

"When?"

"One morning, in the parlor; I was telling her that I had run into you at the bridge. Do you remember that afternoon, when we were returning from Bagheria? I smiled at you."

"Oh, of course I remember!" Blasco said, sighing. "I didn't know you because I never had seen you before, but I never have forgotten your eyes and your smile."

Violante blushed; she felt a stirring at those words and then a lulling of her heart in a new and exciting sense of joy.

Blasco asked her, "And the duchess told you that I was dead?"

"Yes . . . rather killed . . . and it's not true, because you are here! . . . And it's not at all true that you are bad, because you saved me."

"The duchess told you that I'm a bad man?"

Violante hesitated a moment and ended up saying yes.

"Really. . . . Why did she tell me this, then?"

"But . . . as a joke, perhaps."

"Oh no, she wasn't joking. On the contrary, my mother seemed very angry and she scolded me."

Blasco was looking at her in amazement.

Those revelations were inconceivable to him. He tried to dig deeper, but Violante knew nothing more, and, moreover, due either to fear or emotion or exhaustion, she felt a great weight on her eyes and closed them, gradually dozing off. Blasco then got up, crossed the room on tiptoe, and went to call the caretaker.

CHAPTER 5

Donna Gabriella was about to go to bed when she saw a small piece of paper on the pillow of her wrought-iron bed with a very elegant foliage motif. She picked it up and unfolded it with a certain trepidation and read with amazement these few words:

> *An eye for an eye, a tooth for a tooth; the crimes of the father will fall on his children. Tell this to your husband.*

The meaning of these words seemed incomprehensible, and she was in a pensive and suspicious state of mind when her maidservant rushed into the room, crying out in fear, "Your Excellency! Your Excellency! What a tragedy! What misfortune!"

Donna Gabriella, panic-struck by the sudden interruption, by her appearance and her cry, exclaimed, trembling, "What happened. . . . My God! What is it?"

"They kidnapped the young lady!"

"Violante?"

"Donna Violante! Yes, Your Excellency, they kidnapped her!"

"Violante? How? . . . Who? . . . Who told you?"

"The 'mamma' of the monastery came . . . just now . . . she is still in the other room."

"Have her come to me! . . . At once! . . . I want to know."

She was agitated and didn't know what to think; the news filled her with dismay and devastated her. The matron of the Monastery of Montevergini entered, also quite upset, and amid her sobs she confirmed what the maidservant had said, relating in fits and starts, and in broken sentences, what was being said or imagined in the monastery. The young girl had been taken away by people who had entered the garden. Half of Palermo had rushed there. What a fright! What a fright!

Donna Gabriella didn't know what to say. She would get up, sit down, walk around, murmuring, "My God! What to do? . . . What to do? My God. . . . What misfortune. . . . But who? Who?"

Her eyes fell on the letter, and a shock made the hairs on her head stand up; this letter was the key to the mystery. The Beati Paoli had committed an audacious act in retaliation, and this made the state of things even more terrifying. Where were they? How to attack them? How to free Violante?

"My portantina!" she ordered.

"What does Your Excellency intend to do?" asked the maidservant.

But the duchess repeated more imperiously, "The portantina!"

Twenty minutes later she arrived at the monastery at the moment that the crowd was coming out, buzzing and chattering and letting out wisecracks about the "nun who escaped with the monk."

The Mother Superior, the nuns, and the teachers of the educande welcomed her with tears in their eyes. No one could explain what had happened. The Mother Superior seemed inconsolable; a monastery that enjoyed such a good reputation . . . where nothing of the kind had ever happened! Yes, it was true, there were escapes and kidnappings; there were always girls who would run away, and even some professed nuns. But at Montevergini! . . . Ah! It was a tragedy for the monastery! This was the greatest sorrow.

Donna Gabriella gathered whatever news that she could and, realizing that there was nothing she could do, she left.

"To the Palazzo Reale!" she ordered the servants.

What was she going to do? Arouse the viceroy? Send guards in search of the kidnappers? Call the cavalry to arms? She didn't know; she was appealing to the viceroy, who as head of state was someone who could do anything. But the viceroy was sleeping at this hour; the doors of his palazzo were closed, and the sentinel didn't allow anyone to knock. And then, this was no time for an audience. His Excellency Count Annibale Maffei, Viceroy of Sicily in the name of His Majesty Victor Amadeus, had prescribed the days and the hours for audiences and didn't depart from them. The world could collapse; if there was no provision for it within the rules and regulations, no one could be bothered. All administrative discipline consisted principally of this rigid and pedantic observation of the rules, which was, and still is, the glorious panache of every administration and of every Piedmontese administrator or office head.

Donna Gabriella had to return home, her spirit shaken, upset, agitated, and she spent the whole night unable to sleep, tormented by countless grim visions. The abbreviated and distorted account given to her by her husband about the origins of the persecutions of the Beati Paoli and about the accusations that had been drawn was now coming back to her, reawakening her suspicions and doubts and putting a sort of horror and terror in her blood. It was evident that the abduction was a retaliation. Was Violante perhaps paying the price for that vanished baby, dead, perhaps murdered as soon as it was born? But who could have any interest in this old revenge? Or was she paying, as it seemed to her most probable, for the family of Ammirata, whose nephew was moaning in the dungeons of Castellammare and whose wife had been tortured in that shameful way?

That must be the reason. But why had Ammirata become the avenger of that duchess and that baby who had vanished sixteen years ago? What a mystery! . . . Meanwhile, it was an unrelenting, horrific war that, now that her husband was so far away, she found herself exposed to and dragged into.

The first hours of the day had passed like this when the caretaker sent by Blasco arrived.

"I have important news to give to Her Excellency and to her alone," he said.

The duchess, who was in endless anxiety, ordered that he be brought in at once.

"Well, good man, from where do you come?"

"From Villagrazia, Your Excellency."

"And do you have news to give me?"

"Yes, Your Excellency."

"Then speak."

"Your Excellency must arrange for a carriage, to pick up the young lady."

"Violante!" cried the duchess, jumping to her feet with indescribable joy. "Violante!"

"Yes, Your Excellency."

"But how? Tell me!"

"I know nothing, Your Excellency. I was told to come and inform Your Excellency that the young lady is safe and sound by a miracle of God and of the Holy Mary Mother of God!"

Donna Gabriella felt stung by a myriad of overlapping questions that prodded her, building up and tormenting her in countless ways; she grabbed hold of the bell and rang furiously. "The large litter, with mules," she ordered, "and escorts, at once!"

In a frantic haste she threw a cloak over her shoulders, put on one of those three-pointed ladies' hats surmounted by white plumes, which fashion had just then introduced, and ordered, "Let's go."

A servant in uniform appeared at the door and held out his arm to her, leading with his elbow. Donna Gabriella leaned her hand on that arm and went down the grand marble staircase to the bottom, where she found the litter loaded onto two mules adorned with plumes, and behind it two servants on horseback, armed with harquebuses and pistols.

The news spread throughout the palazzo that the young duchess had been found and that the mistress was going to pick her up, and all the servants crowded around with great interest, up the stairs and along the railings of the courtyard, seeing the duchess off with their good wishes.

The litter left. The caretaker, who had come on horseback, rode next to the door so that he could answer the duchess's questions. The jingling of the harness bells made people turn their heads, and upon seeing the duchess, they greeted her: "At your service, Your Excellency."

The news also spread along the way that the duchess was going to pick up her stepdaughter, and the commoners, greeting her, added, "That Our Lady of Light may be of help to you!"

The retinue emerged from Porta d'Ossuna, went along the city walls, and entered the countryside. Donna Gabriella found the mules to be a little slow, but in truth the poor beasts, urged on by litter bearers, were going at a brisk pace. They certainly couldn't trot, because it would have meant tossing Donna Gabriella about from one side of the litter to the other.

It was already past midday when they arrived in front of the gate.

"It's here," said the caretaker, dismounting and pushing the gate.

Donna Gabriella got down and continued along the path on foot; when she was near the house, she cried out: "Violante! . . . Violante!"

And a voice full of joy answered her: "Signora Madre!"

Donna Gabriella saw her coming bundled up in the cloak, held in place at the sides by a leather strap, and with her arms lost in two loose-fitting deep blue sleeves, but she didn't notice this strange attire, at that moment clutching her stepdaughter with a sincere emotion that also left her speechless.

Following that moment, in which it seemed that those two hearts, free from every fear, were merging, the duchess sat on a stone bench and looked in amazement at her stepdaughter. "Oh, how funny you look!" she exclaimed. "How come you got dressed up like this?"

"If Your Ladyship only knew, Signora Madre!"

"But come now—tell me what happened, why you are here, and why you are dressed in this manner."

Violante sat next to her and ran her hands over her face as if the fear of the danger had resumed.

"Ah, Signora Madre, what terror! What terror! . . . I feel like I'm dying just thinking about it! . . . It was a miracle, really a miracle. . . . Because it was certainly the good Lord who sent him."

"Sent who?"

"My liberator . . . him."

"Him? . . . But who?"

"Oh, didn't I tell you? I am a scatterbrain! And I should have told you before, in order to thank him! The one who freed me from my kidnappers, it was him, Signor Blasco da Castiglione."

"Blasco da Castiglione?! . . . Him!" exclaimed Donna Gabriella, jumping to her feet with an expression in which a thousand opposing and colliding feelings were being stirred up. "Blasco da Castiglione . . . and you?"

A multitude of thoughts and suspicions invaded her mind, clouded her emotions, and disrupted her soul; how ever had that young man been there in order to rescue Violante from danger? Had this sudden and miraculous intervention been planned, by any chance? Where was he?

"So tell me, then," she said to her in a trembling voice. "Tell me!"

Violante told her about her first and frightening adventure with that alertness, that fervor characteristic of adolescence, exaggerating, if it was possible, the perilous course, her impressions, and the beauty of the heroic gesture of the young savior. Donna Gabriella was listening to her, but her mind wasn't paying attention so much to the dangers, the anxieties, the tremors, and her stepdaughter's fear as to the words that were referring to Blasco.

When the young girl finished her account, with her arrival in that house and with her unusual outfit, Donna Gabriella asked her, "And then?"

"And then? . . . I fell asleep."

"And Signor Blasco?"

"Ah! Signor Blasco, poor thing, he watched over me all night. And perhaps for that reason I was able to sleep."

"And then?"

"And then nothing. . . . Your Excellency came."

"And . . . didn't Signor Blasco tell you anything? No words?"

"He gave me courage, certainly."

"I'm not speaking about this . . . I am asking if he told you any of those words that men usually say to women."

"What words, Signora Madre?"

The duchess bit her lip. The young girl's naivete was disconcerting to her. Was it an act? She was silent for a while, tormented by a hidden thought.

Violante then smiled mischievously and said, "Your Excellency told me that Signor Blasco had been killed . . . and instead!"

Donna Gabriella didn't respond; perhaps she didn't even remember having invented that story.

Violante, with the same smile and a tone that wanted to express disbelief and at the same time reproach, added, "And you told me that he was a bad man . . . while he is so good!"

Her praise shook the duchess, who, almost following her thought, abruptly asked her, "And . . . was he always beside you last night?"

"Always!" Violante answered forcefully.

"And he didn't do anything to you?"

"What?"

"He didn't caress you?"

Violante blushed up to her eyes and answered, "No, Signora Madre."

Donna Gabriella looked at her in disbelief and perhaps interpreted that blushing in her own way; pale, with a voice choked up from jealousy and anger, she asked, "And where is your savior now? I must thank him."

"I think he is over there . . . he is uncomfortable, I think . . . he doesn't want to be thanked, he already told me that; but I will call him . . . yes, it is right that you also, Signora Madre, should tell him a few words . . . he deserves it!"

And she got up, went to the foot of the exterior stairs that rose against the wall, and called, "Signor Blasco! . . . Signor Blasco!"

Blasco da Castiglione appeared at the top of the stairs. He was slightly pale and smiling. He bowed to the duchess and went quickly down; Donna Gabriella was looking at him, controlling her emotion but not enough to prevent her face from turning first red, then pale, and her nostrils and mouth from trembling. Standing erect, beautiful, with an attitude that wanted to express gratitude and instead was filled with spite, scorn, rage, and jealousy . . . she forgot to offer her hand to Blasco, who bowed to her again, and she stammered a word of thanks: "I am grateful, signore, for what you have done, and I will write about it to the duke, my husband."

Her words were so icy that Blasco was amazed; nevertheless, he replied, "Your Excellency, if ever I have rendered you some service, it is rather a repayment, which doesn't equal the benefit received. . . . It is I who owe you a great deal, and I thank God that he has given me the opportunity to express my gratitude to you."

They were both silent, awkward—Donna Gabriella due to the torment of her fixation, Blasco due to that cold and almost bitter greeting, the reasons for which he couldn't begin to guess. He was hoping to be greeted cordially and to be able to form a tender friendship with Donna Gabriella based on an unspoken gratitude, and he was feeling led, now that he was in possession of those papers, by that instinctive impulse in his heart that pushed him to defend the weak and to take sides with those who were threatened by a great danger. He felt that the Beati Paoli, having been unable or not having dared to attack Don Raimondo, wanted to carry out their revenge on those two women, who were innocent of every offense, oblivious to the duke's crimes, defenseless; and it seemed to him that it was his firm duty to protect and defend them. But Donna Gabriella's coldness disconcerted him. Was she spiteful because he had abandoned her? Was it hatred? No, it couldn't be hatred, because otherwise she would have let him die in prison. What was it, then?

Blasco didn't have a sharp eye, and moreover he couldn't conceive that the duchess could be jealous of her stepdaughter. Violante was almost a child, and if he had for her a feeling of deep fondness and tenderness, he still couldn't say that he loved her, because the young girl seemed to him still so immature that, in loving her amorously, he would be afraid of defiling her purity and innocence. And thus his emotions were colored with a discretion, with a respect, with a devoutness that almost intoxicated him and infused him with a pure and intense joy. So he had no idea that Donna Gabriella could be jealous.

But she felt something gripping her heart. She loved him; she always loved him with all the forces of her passion, but her pride, self-love, spite, and her response to the revenge were rejecting that passion and concealing it with hatred. She had almost handed the Prince of Iraci the tools for his attack, it was true, but it was precisely because she was consumed with passion. Her desire for revenge was born from that abandonment. The attempted murder and the risk of death had almost erased from her heart every feeling of hatred and had left there a wrathful spite and a raging desire; she had felt, almost unwittingly, moved to protect him from dangers. And this feeling had gotten stronger. In Messina she had understood that if Matteo Lo Vecchio had tried to poison Blasco it had certainly been on behalf of Don Raimondo, and this had led her to say nothing to him of having seen the young man and of having saved him from death. She had felt almost happy to know that he was also free. Perhaps some distant hope was being reborn in her heart; perhaps some dream had hovered within her head at night; perhaps, when her revulsion at her complicity with her husband had tormented her soul, she had focused on the young man as a liberation.

Now a new thought was arising to awaken the flames of her jealousy: her suspicious mind had sunk its gaze into the innermost part of the young girl's heart, and she had seen the image of Blasco carved there. In her imagination she was now seeing scenes and episodes that filled her with pain and swelled her eyes with burning tears. She suspected, rather she was certain, that between Blasco and Violante there had been more than the fraternal and innocent relations that had been revealed by the words of the young girl. The acrimonious desire to investigate, to know, pervaded her blood; she fixed her eyes on Blasco as if to discover on his face the traces of a night of love. And she saw nothing; but she wasn't reassured.

"Come on, get up," she said to Violante, "and let's get your attire in order. We should get you some clothes . . . you certainly can't go back to the city dressed like this."

She called the caretaker.

"In the vicinity there should be some houses of peasants and there must be some women. Here is some money. Get me some clean clothes."

The caretaker left. Donna Gabriella, left alone with Blasco, crossed her arms and, looking at him with blazing eyes, said, "Signore, don't think that I am such a fool as to believe Violante's story."

"What, Your Excellency?"

"I am saying, signore, that your intervention at just the right and miraculous moment gives one all the ease of assuming, rather of believing, that you are in some way involved with Violante's kidnapping."

"Your Excellency!" exclaimed Blasco with his face in flames. "I do not believe that there is anything I have ever done in my life to give you the right to think of such a wickedness."

Donna Gabriella didn't bat an eye.

"It's useless to get worked up; this all points to you. I know that it's not just today that you set your eyes on the Duke of Motta's daughter!"

"Me? . . . Duchess, but what are you saying? But do you really want to think—"

"If it were only just an assumption!" Donna Gabriella cried out desperately, leaving an opening for her jealousy.

That cry was a revelation. Blasco felt his indignation abating and with a gentler voice said, "Your Excellency, on what would you like me to swear? Here." He took out from his breast pocket a silver medal, and in an emotional voice he added, "This silver medal is the only legacy that my mother left me, and to me it is the most sacred inheritance; well, I swear to you on this blessed medal that I didn't know the young duchess before now, that I have absolutely no knowledge of this wicked kidnapping, and that it is only fate or luck that led me to stop a crime!"

Donna Gabriella didn't seem reassured; after all, it wasn't so important to her whether Blasco had had a part in the kidnapping or not, or if he had connections to the Beati Paoli. What was important to her, what was tormenting her, was her conviction that Blasco loved Violante. The vision of the two youngsters clasped in an embrace, joined in a kiss, intoxicated with a joy that she had known and for which she still had a burning thirst, offered itself before her eyes.

"Deny," she said in a broken voice, "deny that you had . . . that you spent the night . . . that you abused your position! . . . Deny even this if you can!"

"But of course I deny it! No sister has ever been safer next to her brother, no child could ever have slept with so much trust in the arms of her mother, as did Donna Violante, last night, in this house, and next to me. Blasco da Castiglione has no family coat of arms, Your Excellency, just as he doesn't have a surname, but he can write on his forehead like the knight Bayard, *Senza macchia e senza paura*."[1]

Donna Gabriella didn't give up but continued with a voice somber with jealously, "Violante is so beautiful!"

"Yes . . . she is beautiful!"

"And so seductive."

"Yes . . . she is seductive."

"Her entire being is an enchantment."

"Yes, it's true . . . she is enchanting."

"Then confess that you love her!" Donna Gabriella shouted, pointing a finger at his chest with a convulsive tremor, anxiously awaiting an answer.

Blasco remained a bit disconcerted by this abrupt and unexpected claim, which suddenly awoke a thousand sweet and tormenting sensations, and he couldn't

---

1 "Beyond reproach and without fear," a reference to Chevalier de Bayard (1473–1524), known as the "knight without fear and beyond reproach."

immediately come up with an answer; then he stammered, "Love her? . . . Me? Donna Violante?"

The duchess savored all the bitterness of her painful triumph.

"Yes, you love her! . . . Swear to me that it isn't true; swear it on that relic!"

"I don't swear," murmured Blasco. "I cannot swear; I don't know; perhaps, yes, I love her, or I could love her. But it is not a love that can feed on hopes, and I am honest enough to know and am able to turn off and stop a feeling in the bottom of my heart that could be, more than a joy, a torture!"

The duchess seemed struck by those words. The pain that filled her heart overwhelmed her; in her nature, which was so fickle-minded that her feelings only lasted as long as their impetus and rapidly alternated, her anger and jealousy were dissolving and giving her access to her pain. She let herself fall on the bench, pale, with her mouth dry, murmuring, "He loves her! He loves her!"

The voice of the caretaker, who was returning with a bundle, aroused her; she regained her composure, took the clothes from the hands of the caretaker, and went upstairs quickly without speaking.

Blasco stayed there like a statue, sad, his heart gripped in a vise, caught in a state of dismay, as if from that brief conversation, and even more from the last words, rose a dark and far-off threat that hovered over not only his head but also over Violante's.

CHAPTER 6

Blasco waited until it was night to return to the city. He unsaddled at Coriolano della Floresta's palazzo, where he was welcomed by the servants with the warmest expressions of joy.

"The master is not here," said the chief steward, "but he will be happy to know that you have arrived. . . . Did Your Excellency have a good journey?"

Blasco was accompanied to his room, and he said to the manservant, "When the master arrives, do me the favor of letting me know."

"Does Your Excellency want supper?"

"No."

He wasn't hungry. All day he had been feeling overwhelmed by the scene that had unfolded between himself and Donna Gabriella, but even more by the image of Violante, who, in the clothes of a peasant girl, a little awkward and ill at ease, had a lovely appearance. He was thinking about that night he had spent next to the young girl—a night that would remain unique and unforgettable in his life—and still feeling the most tender and deeply felt sensations throbbing within his heart, hearing the gentle breath of the young girl and seeing her sleeping there, under his gaze, so beautiful and peaceful, in the disarray and unawareness of her sleep. He was thinking about that night of desires, of dreams, of quivers, of restraint, so chaste, so pure, and meanwhile so intense with emotion, so vibrant with passion, in which he had, one can say, lived a hundred lives and had felt himself lifted into an atmosphere other than where the realities of life kept him.

But who was he? Oh, he well knew that to nourish a hope was madness and that he, poor and without a name, was destined to spend his life without joy; but who could prevent his heart from beating, his mind from dreaming? He threw himself on the bed in order to abandon himself to his fantasies, but sleep gradually won over and he didn't wake until a hand knocked on his door and a voice said, "Are you awake, my friend?"

He jumped to his feet and ran to the door with open arms, shouting, "Oh, Coriolano, my friend."

In fact, it was the Cavaliere della Floresta. Their first words were naturally those that are usually exchanged between two friends who haven't seen each other for some time. Coriolano wanted to know everything that Blasco had done, and

Blasco told him about his travel adventures, the meeting with the abbot, his arrival in Messina, the incident with the king's guards, the arrest, the poisoning attempt, and the duchess's intervention.

"You see?" Coriolano interrupted him. "Don't you see that I was right to advise you to go to Messina?"

"Yes, it's true, and I am indeed grateful to you for that. But I haven't told you everything yet. Now, there are the adventures of my return, especially the last one, that you can't even imagine! . . . Dear friend, I am led to believe that fate is the great mastermind of human events and that the philosophers, who trouble themselves to teach us how to behave in this or that manner in order to achieve this or that result, are true charlatans. Life is about the unexpected. So listen."

And he told him about how he had rescued Violante, who had been kidnapped by masked men, surely emissaries or members of the sect.

Coriolano listened to him showing no signs of surprise, as if it had concerned an everyday occurrence. He got up, saying, "Now rest. I came and bothered you, but I wanted to see you again. Do not leave the house. The viceroy has put all his forces in place to pursue and arrest all those who are justly or unjustly covered by the public warrant. You could be recognized and would not escape. Remember Matteo Lo Vecchio."

"Ah, if that villain should come into my hands!"

"Would you like to give him the honor of being your adversary?"

"Oh, no!"

"Then to kill him?"

"Do you think I'm capable of that?"

"Not at all. . . . I said that in order to show you the emptiness of certain intentions. Let it go and keep yourself out of sight."

"But I have to see Father Serafino."

"You will see him, of course, but with caution, and only when you are sure that no one can find you. I'll see to it."

"I have always told you that you are an invaluable man!"

"Good night."

"Good night."

* * *

In the morning, upon waking up, Blasco saw a letter on the writing table next to the bed; it didn't take long for him to recognize that it was of the same kind as the other one that he had received many months earlier.

"Oh! Oh!" he said. "What might this be about?"

The letter was as follows:

You are a man of courage, but you are wrong to obstruct a work of justice.
Wait at midnight in front of the entrance to the palazzo. A man passing by
will say to you: Do you have any tinder? You will answer: Give me the torch;
and follow that man. Do not be afraid, and have faith.

There was no signature, but there was the well-known seal of the armed hand, in an act of striking a blow. Blasco smiled.

"But yes, of course! From one adventure to the next, and this makes life passably entertaining. Curious these Beati Paoli, who, instead of firing a rifle shot at me or stabbing me, write these little notes that could be mistaken for letters about a lovers' rendezvous!"

He wondered if he should consult with his friend Coriolano but decided against it. To show him this letter would be like letting him in on a secret that didn't pertain to him. He kept quiet about it and waited for the night, with the same anxiety with which children wait for their promised reward. At midnight on the dot he was in front of the outside door, leaning against one of the pillars that flanked it. He had put two short pistols in the pockets of his breeches and a dagger in his waistband, fearing that he would not be able to use his sword if he had to defend himself. However confident he was, he couldn't avoid feeling a certain trepidation for that unknown toward which he was headed, for that mystery that he perhaps would penetrate.

The man passed, glanced at him, gave the password. He answered as had been arranged and followed him. They walked for quite a while. At the turn in Via San Cosmo the man stopped, took a silk handkerchief from his pocket, and said, "Your Lordship forgive me, but you must allow yourself to be blindfolded and promise not to take it off."

"Go ahead, I promise."

When he was blindfolded, the man took his hand and guided him. Blasco understood that in order to disorient him he was being led in circles around one spot, and then he sensed that the street was on a downward slope. Suddenly he was stopped. He heard the creaking of a key and felt a gust of humid, musty air hit his face.

"Come with me."

The door closed behind him. He was now going through a passageway, then he had the impression of going out into the open. The passageway in fact led to a courtyard where a tree spread its branches. Blasco's head brushed against a leafy branch and he imagined he was crossing a small garden. Then he descended again and was stopped once more. He felt a hand quickly disarm him of his sword, accompanying the act with an excuse: "Your Lordship forgive me, it is necessary."

In a gesture of annoyance Blasco frowned under the blindfold, but he thought that he was on the premises of that sinister sect and that finally what was a mystery for others was becoming a reality for him. He wasn't afraid; in addition to his courage, which bordered on rashness, he had confidence in the letters of the Beati Paoli. When they wanted to get rid of someone, they disposed of them at night with a shot from a rifle, not wanting their punishments to have any publicity, in order to set an example.

Blasco heard a soft whisper, after which the same voice said to him, "Enter."

He felt that the air was warmer, and his senses gave him the impression of being in the presence of people bearing down on him.

A voice that made him start said to him, "Sit down, signore."

Two hands gently pushed him onto a chair; the same voice ordered, "Remove the blindfold."

Blasco was forced to close his eyes again, struck by the abrupt change from utter darkness to the bright light of four burning torches fixed into the walls of the room where he found himself, and so was prevented from immediately recognizing where and among whom he was. Reopening his eyes, he saw that he was in a type of rotunda, evidently an ancient crypt excavated in the rock, from which two corridors branched out, fading into the infinite darkness. Here and there were niches hollowed out of the walls. In the center was a type of small stone altar with a Christ on it, between two candles, and the Gospel laid open. Behind the altar on a high bench was a masked man; at his sides were two other men, also masked. Around them, along the walls, other men were sitting, and all were wearing masks on their faces. Blasco looked at his sides and behind him; four men seemed to be watching him and they too were masked. Every man was dressed in a long black robe, similar to a sackcloth for penance, but in its waistband flashed the blade of a long dagger.

A grave and solemn silence hung over everything; Blasco saw eyes shining behind the masks and felt all eyes upon him. He was overcome with amazement and curiosity, and he waited.

The leader said, "Blasco da Castiglione, you are before the tribunal of the Beati Paoli. Your curiosity, which last time we were forced to stop you from satisfying, has now been satisfied; but we, signore, have the right to ask you why you want to get in the way of our work."

Blasco made a gesture as if to speak, but the leader preempted him: "Wait, this is not the time to speak; now you must listen. This tribunal has given you more than enough proof of its goodwill; it has saved you from murder, it has punished an enemy of yours by subjecting him to ridicule. You, without wanting to and without knowing it, have prevented the arrest of two of our faithful companions, but meanwhile you have prevented the tribunal from completing an act of justice."

"Of cowardice!" corrected Blasco.

A threatening whisper ran through the crypt. The leader said in a serious tone, without taking offense, "Of justice! You don't know what you are saying."

"I know that a poor, young, defenseless girl was in the power of armed men who were dragging her away, threatening her with death; and I know that using force and violence against the weak is the greatest cowardice."

"An eye for an eye, a tooth for a tooth! . . . This is written in the holy books, and popular wisdom decrees 'the tree sins and the branch receives.' A woman was killed, and her baby, born a few days before, was saved by a miracle. He is growing up in the shadows, poor and without a name, because his name, his wealth, and his future have been usurped. He lives in the shadows, nor does he know who he is, because if he regained the right to bear his name, if he asked society for his rightful place, the man that killed his mother and usurped his name and his status would take his life. This villain, having been discovered, has one by one killed the witnesses to his crimes; some died of poisoning, some on the gallows, some were murdered. He is persecuting others to their death; the selfless woman who picked up the persecuted child has been thrown into the dungeons of Sant'Offizio, and that child, now a young man, moans in the dungeons of the Castello. The executioner lashed that innocent woman in public shame; he lashed the young man until he bled.

"Now then, in order to prevent this young man from dying in the dungeons— so that he can live and regain his name, his wealth, and his rank—there was only one way to complete this work of justice and compassion: to hold hostage the daughter of that man, to force him, for the love of his own flesh and blood, to stop his fierce, impious persecution and to open the doors of the prison for his victims! Blasco da Castiglione, you have obstructed this act of justice, and you have become an accomplice to a villain! . . . Blasco da Castiglione, Don Raimondo, the Duke of Motta, has accused you of being one of the leaders of this society; he had you arrested in Messina, tried to make you die of poisoning, and you are offering him your support, your courage, so that he can continue his bloodthirsty work. . . . Blasco da Castiglione, you, a loyal and generous heart, have placed the padlocks on the dark and deadly cave where Emanuele Albamonte, the true duke of Motta, groans! You have placed these padlocks on behalf of a thief, a murderer, a disgrace and shame of mankind. Blasco da Castiglione, you are guilty, and the tribunal will begin by judging your actions."

"Do you have anything else to tell me?" asked Blasco.

Everything that the leader had said about Don Raimondo came as no surprise to Blasco, who had read the famous documents taken from Matteo Lo Vecchio; while the leader was speaking, he actually thought to himself, with an inner smile, "If they only knew that I have on me now the evidence they collected!"

What he was unaware of was the torture inflicted on Emanuele and Signora Francesca and that they were still languishing in horrible dungeons. He didn't know Ammirata's wife and had a faint recollection of the young man, but this didn't mean that the knowledge that they were innocent victims of cruel acts failed to arouse his disdain or make him loathe that appearance of complicity for which the leader was reproaching him.

"Do you have anything else to tell me?" he repeated. "Then allow me to say that it is not right to accuse me here of complicity with the Duke of Motta. I am not his accomplice, any more than I was yours when I prevented Girolamo Ammirata from being arrested. You can do what you wish with me, but do not doubt the integrity of my thinking and of my conscience. . . . And now tell me if you have invited me in order to hear your paternal recriminations."

"Blasco da Castiglione," the leader said sternly, "do not joke. No one laughs here."

"I will start—"

"And you will stop!"

Blasco saw some hands move quickly to the handles of their daggers and many eyes turn to the leader, almost as if they were asking him what they should do, but the leader gave no sign and continued: "Blasco da Castiglione, we are demanding that you not get in our way."

After that command, made in a resolute tone of voice, Blasco quickly understood the threat that was hanging over the head of Violante; he saw a new danger, which perhaps she would not have known and from which she would not be able to protect herself, and it seemed to him that his duty at this time was not to abandon the young girl.

He raised his head proudly and said, "And what if I tried to get in your way? What if I tried, with all my might, to oppose your reprisals?"

"We would be forced to stop you, even with violence."

"Kill me, then, because I swear to you on the memory of my mother that you will not be able to put your hands on Violante unless they pass over my dead body."

The leader laughed.

He gave a sign. In an instant Blasco saw twenty arms reach out in one single move; twenty blades were pointed at his chest. He paled slightly but didn't move, nor did he give the slightest indication of fear.

The leader continued: "I would only have to utter one word and you would die right here, riddled with wounds, and no one would know anything; nor would your dead body give us any trouble, because even if we preferred not to bury it in here, we could leave it to be found on some road in the countryside, to the great pleasure of the prosecutors that are searching for you. But your death is of no interest to our cause; what interests us is your absolute neutrality. . . . Do you want to pledge yourself to it?"

Blasco was constantly seeing Violante at the forefront of his thoughts; he answered, "I cannot make a promise that I am unable to keep."

"Blasco da Castiglione, take heed. Even without killing you, I could put you in the position of being unable to do anything; I could leave you in here, where you wouldn't know how to leave, nor would you be able to. Why do you want to force me to take this step?"

"Do it; I prefer to stay here, shut in, rather than be outside and free but condemned to impotence by an oath."

"Is this your final word?"

"Yes."

"Consider that, shut inside here, you will never be able to defend or protect those who are close to your heart."

Blasco didn't answer.

The leader then said, "You will not be able to accuse us of having been intolerant and violent. Brothers, lock him up him for 'reflection.'"

In a flash Blasco saw himself wrapped up in a type of cloak that reduced him to impotence. He was lifted up by strong arms, transported, and put down. He heard a door close even before he could disentangle himself from the cloak. He was in a pitch black place, whose form and purpose he couldn't recognize. He took a few steps along its length and width in order to measure its size; in one direction, as soon as he took two steps, he hit his chest and face against a rough and dampish wall; on the opposite side, his arms groped about a while in the darkness, then they touched a wooden surface, which he identified as the door. But he felt at length and there was no trace of a lock; it must have been locked from the outside, then, with latches and bolts. He searched for the gap in the jamb, pulled his dagger out, and thrust it there, thinking to make it slide along to where the latches were, but the blade couldn't get through. He thought of using it to gradually make a hole in the boards in order to see through. He got to work but soon after felt the point scrape against a metallic surface. The exterior of the door was covered with an iron plate. Therefore, he was in a true prison, from which he couldn't escape. He couldn't take a walk because, not being sure of the terrain and not knowing the surroundings, he couldn't wander around in the dark. Sitting on the ground repelled him. He didn't sense that there were any seats or chairs around him, no matter how much he searched for one by cautiously walking around and around.

He was reduced to helplessness, as the leader had told him. He thought about Violante. Who would watch over the young girl now? She remained at the complete mercy of the sect, of whose intentions there was no doubt. He also thought of the duchess; he thought about that revelation of jealousy that had filled him with amazement and apprehension—the duchess was jealous of Violante, and a woman like her, and in her jealous state, was no less fearsome than the Beati Paoli. The poor girl was therefore exposed to danger from two sides, without a compassionate hand that could rescue her; the duke, her father, the only one who could have defended her, at least on one side, was so far away that he couldn't be counted on. Why ever, then, had he insisted on not pledging his neutrality, when this stubbornness of his was serving no purpose? Would it not have been better to compromise a little, to make a promise with one of those mental constraints, which the morality of the times didn't discourage? Wouldn't an honest and virtuous end justify a failure to fulfill his promise? And was a promise extracted under those conditions, with violence, one that could truly bind him? He reproached himself, hurling insults at himself.

His imagination presented to him in the poorest light the dangers that Violante was exposed to, and he could imagine others. Violante was paying for Emanuele, for this other young innocent life buried in a dungeon, condemned to die, both of them offered up in sacrifice due to the ambition and greed of one man, Don Raimondo.

And he thought about those terrible documents that he had come to possess, trembling at the idea that they could be taken from him by the Beati Paoli, now that he was at their mercy. That man was the father of Violante, and this girl, who was so pure, innocent, and faithful, was unaware of who her father was and at what an infamous and wicked price he had acquired his wealth, of which she was the heiress! What would she say on the day when that terrible secret was revealed to her? And was it not compassionate to hide everything from her?

He was immersed in these thoughts when he heard the creaking of the latches and saw the door open and the bright light of a lantern spreading in the cavern where he was locked up, and which the light suddenly revealed to his eye. The lantern moved and stopped in a wall; Blasco then saw that here and there were some hollowed-out horizontal niches that the shadows rendered darker and more mysterious. From the cone of the shadow in which he had been concealed, one of the masked men in the midst of whom he had found himself a moment before appeared under the light.

For an instant they stood facing each other, watching each other in silence. Blasco had crossed his arms over his chest, still holding the dagger, whose blade gleamed in the light of the lantern. The masked man had let the door close behind him. He was alone and had no weapons in his hands.

He saw the flash of the blade and interpreted it in his own way.

"Do not be afraid; not a hair on your head will be touched. If we had wanted to dispose of you, as I said before, we would have done it."

Blasco recognized the voice of the leader. He threw the dagger away without answering.

The leader resumed: "Have you thought it over? Do you understand that you are in our power? Why don't you give in?"

To be contrary, perhaps out of spite or due to pride, it seemed to him that giving in now would be expressing a sign of fear. Blasco responded, "I have only one word. It is useless to tempt me."

"But you will not leave here until our work has been accomplished."

The young man shuddered but didn't reveal his emotion; he said curtly as one who is annoyed, "Do as you please!"

Another brief silence intervened between them. The leader resumed in a tone of voice that betrayed his inner sadness.

"You are wrong, and you are allowing yourself to be guided more by pride than by reason. Don't you realize that I care about you and that I want to rescue you from the danger to which you have needlessly exposed yourself? Whatever effort you may attempt, whatever your courage, you will never manage to rescue Don Raimondo from our retribution."

"And what do I care about him?" said Blasco.

"Why, then, have you interfered with our work?"

"But it is not on his account; it's about an innocent girl. Why persecute someone who has harmed neither you nor others?"

"It is a means . . ."

"Villainous and repugnant. You have had the Duke of Motta underfoot for such a long time—why haven't you killed him?"

CHAPTER 7

The leader of the Beati Paoli smiled with a sense of compassion and said, "You are a young man, inexperienced in many things, despite having lived intensively amid life's hardships. We do not wish for the death of the Duke of Motta; whether he lives or dies is entirely unimportant to us. We want the title and patrimony to be restored to their rightful owner. The day he falls under the sword of our justice—without us first having snatched from him what he stole with the murder—the entire patrimony would then pass by right, and lawfully, to his daughter, Violante, and would not be restored to Emanuele. Emanuele would be civilly dead; he would be nothing more than an anonymous nephew of Don Girolamo Ammirata, and the theft, the bloodthirsty robbery, would be sanctioned by an injustice that would clothe itself completely in legal guises. No, no. We have respected the life of Don Raimondo only so that he himself, in recognizing Emanuele, can return to him what is rightfully his."

Blasco thought of Violante. Deep down, he could not deny that what this man wanted was nothing but the strictest and most scrupulous justice.

An orphan had been dispossessed and what was rightfully his had to be returned to him. This was right and proper, but Blasco thought that this restitution would in fact entail the dispossession and dishonor of another innocent, of Violante, and in that he saw another injustice. Indeed, what fault did the poor girl have by being born of that man? What offense had she committed to be deprived of a wealth to which she had acquired the right from the moment she was born, and to be forced to atone for the infamy of her father? This idea aroused in him a veiled sense of rebellion, and yet he dared not refuse to acknowledge the justice of the Beati Paoli.

"For the sake of justice, one must not be unjust," said Blasco.

"Toward whom?" the leader replied.

"Toward those who are not guilty."

"What is a man before a violated right? What is a human life before justice that pursues its own unbending course? So much the worse for those who put themselves in its way. It must go forth and crush whoever it meets. An innocent person cries? Their tears compensate for those of other innocents who have cried before them. Justice must not have mercy and must not consider the consequences. Too many tears have been shed: a young, beautiful, rich woman, struck down by a devastating sorrow that took her husband from her while she was bearing his fruit to the world, was then besieged, driven to desperation, and died of terror in a bed that was not her own, where she had been charitably taken in; a faithful and devoted servant was murdered; those people who took in the doubly orphaned child, who hid him and rescued him from death, who performed this admirable act of charity, they now live fleeing like wolves, hiding, forced to defend their lives day by day; others languish in prison, suffer the shame of an undeserved torture; two men, guilty only of having collected the horrific testimony of the murderer, were sent to the gallows like two villains. What are the tears of one innocent victim compared to the blood of eight other victims, innocent as well? Justice must be allowed to take its course. No one will stop it, and you, Blasco da Castiglione, you least of all!"

Blasco heard these words fall one by one, unemotional and relentless, and his inner logic agreed with them, but his heart did not, and it rebelled, and there was something, even in what he agreed with, that encouraged that rebellion.

"Why," Blasco said, "why, if you are so convinced of the justice of your cause, do you keep out of view? Why don't you fight without masks? Do noble causes need to hide in the shadows? Therefore there is something less noble that forces you to conceal yourselves; you don't dare confront the light because you feel faith in your justice wavering!"

"Ah no!" the leader of the Beati Paoli interrupted strongly. "Only faith in *legal* justice wavers; rather, it doesn't waver, it's totally lacking. This is what you should have said. In the shadows? It is necessary. It is our strength and our security. The king's justice is administered by men who see in it not a duty but their wages. They are certainly not interested in deliberating, in recognizing the right of each person, but instead in vouching for the strongest against the weakest. The strong are the feudal lords, the officials of the State, the nobles, and the clergy. Buffered by immunity, abounding with privileges, protected by legal documents, they have a legal system of their own, which is not the legal system of the others, of the weak. The magistrates and the laws defend precisely this personal and privileged right, which is instead an abuse and invites injustice toward the great masses of the weak, who are more numerous. A cavaliere who kills finds in that right and in those magistrates a forbearance and a tolerance that would seem indestructible; a plebe that commits the same crime dies on the gallows, under different terms! . . . A noble can take from his vassal—only because he is a vassal—can take his animals, his weapons, his horse. And his right allows him to do it; this same right sends that vassal to the gallows if he dares to steal a pile of wheat or a newborn lamb from the master. And this is called justice!

"A poor widow owes money; the creditor can deprive her of her home and throw her out in the street, and justice gives him the power to do that. A nobleman, on the other hand, can beat up his creditors and even have them imprisoned, and he can find magistrates who judge this to be in accordance with law. And even this is called justice! Don Raimondo can kill, rob, suppress, and still earn praise and rewards and be put in a position to administer justice. Don Girolamo Ammirata, who defends a weak person, according to justice must instead hide in order not to lose his life, and even this is called justice! . . . The justice of the State is justice according to the laws written to benefit the strongest. . . . But this justice is the most monstrous of injustices!

"Ours is not written in any royal constitution, but it is carved in our hearts. We observe it and force others to observe it. We don't have soldiers, guards, algozini, corporals; we don't pay judges; we don't search the laws for equivocations in order to excuse injustice. We open our ears and hearts to the voices of the weak, to those who don't have the strength to break that dense network of arrogance within which they struggle to no avail, and to those who have a thirst for justice and ask for it in vain and suffer.

"Who acknowledges our authority? No one. Who acknowledges in us the right to exercise justice? No one. Well, we must impose this authority and this right, and we have only one weapon—terror—and a means to deploy it—mystery and shadow. We don't hide out of cowardice but out of necessity. The shadows multiply our army and awaken the faith of those who cry out for our protection. He who would not dare seek the help of a legal magistrate in order to defend himself, his house, the honor of his women—because the appeal would expose him to the ire, to the reprisals, to the revenges of a baron or an abbot—willingly confides, once in the shadow, the pain and violence suffered; a man he doesn't see and doesn't know will listen to his complaint. We determine if he has been wronged. A mysterious warning reaches the oppressor in his own palazzo and the complicit magistrate in his seat; do they heed it? We hope for nothing more. Do they disregard it and carry on with their bullying, and continue with the offense? We punish, and we avenge the offense. No one sees the punishing arm; thus no one can avoid it. . . . This is our justice. It never punishes an innocent person, and it has wiped away many tears."

Blasco listened to him with ever-growing amazement. The man was becoming inflamed as he spoke; it seemed that in front of his eyes was passing a vision of all the injustices that an old social structure, in which arbitrary judgment had taken the place of justice, and an uncertain jurisprudence—stuck between prerogatives, privileges, exemptions, and a variety of magistrates or law courts—was permitting and fomenting.

He continued in an emotional voice, "Why don't you, brave, valiant, loyal, and generous as you are, enter, like me, into the thick of city life and baronial lands? Ah, you would see how many tears, how much bloodshed, how many injustices it is composed of and you would think that not one but a hundred of these tribunals would be necessary in order to stop the abuses of power, the violence, and the villainies of the powerful. I know all about life's sufferings; I have entered the dens of peasants, veritable herds of slaves stooping under the club; I have entered the houses of artisans who live in poverty; I have seen the squalor that conceals itself due to shame and awaits the night in order to search amid the trash for a piece of hard bread, a bone, an apple core; I have seen all the human hardships and a hundred, a thousand, ten thousand mouths sobbing and asking for justice! And so I gathered around me men of goodwill, and I said to them, 'We are in defense of the weak and of the wretched!'

"As long as the world does not change and there are on one side privileged men to whom everything is allowed and to whose benefit laws are created, and on the other men condemned to suffer all the abuses and all the violence, it is necessary to create a force that opposes, stops, and impedes those abuses; it is like a balancing out of powers. And it's not anything new. Do you really believe that the Beati Paoli have just now emerged? Do you know the history? In the times of Emperor Frederick, Adinolfo di Pontecorvo founded the society of Vendicosi; its intentions were no different from ours. The Beati Paoli descend from the Vendicosi. They are centuries old. Sometimes they fall asleep; suddenly, when the situation has become unbearable, they awaken. We will die out and after us there will be others, because the weak will always need someone to protect them, someone to defend them. You yourself, Blasco da Castiglione, with all your courage, with all your valor, you are a weak person."

"Me?"

"You are alone, and therefore you are weak; you are a seed thrown in a field by the whim and arrogance of a baron, without a name and without a future, exposed by your very nature to the persecutions of other oppressors, forced to hide like a bandit. . . . Perhaps you would be dead by now if a hidden surveillance had not protected you, if in you we didn't see someone who could be the strongest pillar of the sect."

"Oh no, never!" shouted Blasco.

"Don't be so hasty," the leader of the Beati Paoli rebutted, "you have unwittingly rendered more than a service to our tribunal; however, sometimes we have been forced to act harshly. Even this time, despite your refusal, you have helped us."

"Me?"

"Yes, you, by accepting our invitation."

"How?"

"But don't you realize that we have gotten you out of our way? Don't you realize that you are leaving the field clear for us?"

He took a watch from the pocket of his waistcoat and, looking at the time, added, "It is already one o'clock in the morning; at this hour the Duchess of Motta and Violante are journeying far from here."

"Ah, damnation!" shouted Blasco, taking out a pistol from his pocket. "Say that you lied!"

"I didn't lie . . . the duchess and her daughter were embarked an hour ago, by my orders."

"Scoundrel!" Blasco cried out and fired.

The shot resounded in the cavern, filling it with smoke. It was answered with a laugh. To his own astonishment, Blasco saw the leader of the Beati Paoli shout out loud toward the door: "It's nothing! Everyone go away!" Then, bending down to the ground, he picked something up and, handing it to the young man, said calmly, "My good young man, choose different bullets next time; these, you see, these get dented. . . . Farewell!"

He made as if to leave, but Blasco blocked his way, saying, "You will not get out of here before I pull off your mask; I want to look you in the face. When I tell you that you are a coward, I want my words to slap your flesh instead of breaking up against that false face."

"Do you really want to know who I am?"

"Yes."

"I could save you the trouble of removing my mask, but it's useless. You know who I am."

"The mask! . . . The mask!"

"Well, yes; it's better this way. Here."

With a quick gesture the black mask came off his face.

"Coriolano!" shouted Blasco. "Coriolano!"

* * *

And his arms dropped alongside his body, his voice grew faint, and he felt his knees weaken.

"You! . . . You! . . . You! . . . ," he repeated in an anguished tone.

"Yes, me. What are you so surprised about? You must have suspected it. Me, who you aimed and fired at!"

Blasco bowed his head not knowing what to say. His heart was torn and troubled by two different and opposing thoughts that could be summed up in two names: Violante and Coriolano.

"What have you done! And what did I do!" he murmured in a tone of indescribable regret. Then, changing his tone and handing Coriolano the other pistol, he added with feverish fervor, "Kill me, I beg you, kill me!"

"Why? What's gotten into you? What you did is, I say, understandable, like what I have done. I bear no grudge toward you, and I would have done the same in your place. Give me your hand."

He took his hand by force.

Then Blasco, overcome with emotion, burst into tears, murmuring, "Oh, Violante! Violante!"

There was such deep pain in that wailing that Coriolano della Floresta was shaken by it.

"What are you afraid of?" he said. "I swear to you on my honor that she is not in any danger—not a hair on her head will be touched, but we need her. Emanuele must be freed and protected from any possible attack. We will not achieve this unless we hold hostage the wife and daughter of Don Raimondo della Motta."

"And if he doesn't give up?" asked Blasco with trepidation.

Coriolano was silent a moment.

"Aren't you going to answer?"

"It would be a very serious matter," replied the Cavaliere della Floresta.

"Ah! So you see that your promise is dependent—"

"No. I have sworn to you on my honor that neither the young girl nor the duchess will suffer the slightest violence, other than limits on their freedom. They will be shut in a castle but treated with all considerations owed to their status."

Blasco seemed tormented by a thought; after a moment of silence he said, "What if I were to guarantee to you not only the liberation of Emanuele but also the recognition of his status and the restitution of his title and his patrimony?"

"You, Blasco?" the Cavaliere della Floresta exclaimed, surprised.

"Yes, me . . . what if I were to guarantee this, would you have any problem entrusting to me the two women of the House of Albamonte?"

"Careful of the pledge that you take on, Blasco!"

"I know what I am saying."

"Do you have this power, then?" asked Coriolano with a penetrating gaze.

"I do."

There was such confidence in the tone of his words that Coriolano looked at him with growing amazement. What could make Blasco so confident? Had he perhaps reconciled with Donna Gabriella and was thinking of using that reconciliation to help him accomplish his goal? It didn't seem to him that it would be enough to give the young man so much confidence, because Don Raimondo had never allowed himself to be swayed by his wife. What was it, then? There was no need to reject Blasco's proposal, but neither did it seem to him that he could accept it entirely.

There was only one way.

"Do you want a truce?" he asked.

"If you want to call it a truce."

"For how long?"

"The time it takes to go to Turin and come back."

"Save yourself this trip because the Duke of Motta is coming here."

"He's coming?"

"In fifteen days, twenty at most. He will find out that his family is in our power."

"And for all this time, that poor young girl?"

"She will not suffer the slightest discomfort, I told you."

Blasco bowed his head, thinking of Violante, and a painful dismay gripped his heart. He murmured with a mixture of regret, sadness, anger, "Ah! Why, why is it you here before me and not an enemy, or even a stranger?"

Coriolano smiled and put his mask back on, saying seriously, "Blasco, inside here only two men have seen my face, you and Don Girolamo Ammirata, and no one else. Those twenty brothers who were in the room, even though they are the heads of the society, they know only this mask; to the other members I am a myth! Neither here nor outside here, not even when we are alone, do you let a single hint slip out!"

"Do you want me to give you my most solemn promise?"

"No, I know you. And now wait for me to send for you, and above all, obey me."

He left, leaving the young man overcome by a thousand thoughts, by a thousand feelings that whirled through his mind and deeply disturbed him.

The tribunal of the Beati Paoli was still assembled; those men had for a moment laid down their masks and were talking among themselves. Some huddled around Don Girolamo Ammirata and were asking for a detailed accounting of the failed attempted abduction of Violante. He had made a narrow escape, but Andrea had been stabbed; if it had been further down he would have been finished off.

"That young man is a demon, I tell you."

Coriolano returned to the crypt at that moment, and soon there was a great silence, and everyone put their masks back on and resumed their places.

The Cavaliere della Floresta said, "We have a new brother, whom every one of you must help and protect if you should find him in danger."

* * *

A moment later Blasco was brought into the room and, caught unaware by Coriolano's invitation, had to swear, according to the wording given, loyalty and silence. Every one of those brothers, in turn, approached him, embraced him, pricked their arm, and with that drop of blood made a small mark shaped like a cross on his forehead. They resumed their places and began with the accounts of the complaints gathered. Misery was howling from the mouths of those men, to whom the masks lent an immobile and a stony impassiveness; the greatest complaints were owing to the collection of the *donativo*[1] decreed by the Parliament, and that usually weighed only on the backs of the commoners. A hundred thousand

---

1   An occasional tax that could be decreed at royal whim to cover any exigency.

scudi were charged for the grinding of wheat; the state-owned cities were charged another almost hundred thousand scudi; forty thousand to the city of Palermo, one hundred thirty thousand to its merchants; twenty thousand to the workers, while the barons were charged only fifty thousand scudi and the clergy less than seven thousand; so that the tribute of the owners of all the land and of all the wealth of the kingdom, nobility and clergy, didn't amount to a third of what the have-nots were forced to pay, and this minor amount they squeezed from the blood of the peasants through their officers, their secretaries, their algozini, with every harassment. An entire history of extortion, seizure, foreclosure, of forced sales, which reduced to poverty the poor people who couldn't pay for themselves, nor for the baron and for the convent of which he was a vassal, passed gloomily time after time through that crypt that seemed segregated from the world. And there were also complaints against bloodsucking moneylenders, judges who caved before friendships or allowed themselves to be corrupted, inhuman and greedy officials who were still trying to extract something from the victims for their own advantage.

Blasco listened and felt a hollow growing in his chest due to the shock; his life appeared to him from a very different perspective, and an entire unexpected world was revealed before his eyes, and the Parliament that had assembled with so much solemn splendor and seemed to be the protector and guarantor of the kingdom and of which everyone was envious now appeared to him as the accomplice of that plundering.

It was almost morning when the tribunal adjourned. The Beati Paoli left one at a time, mysteriously, vanishing into the shadows of a corridor.

When everyone was outside, Coriolano said to Blasco, "Let's go."

But instead of following the same path as the others, he led Blasco through a passageway that led from a small secret door onto a staircase, on whose landing an oil lamp burned in front of a Madonna painted on slate. Blasco noticed that while the first time, upon entering, he had to go down, now, instead of going up, he descended again. The staircase ended in a large vestibule, closed by an exterior door. Coriolano took a key from his pocket, opened the small, low wicket door, went out, let Blasco out, and closed it again.

"You see," he said, smiling, "we are under the protection of the law; this house we came out from belongs to a judge."

It was, in fact, the house of Judge Baldi, on the street that leads from Via San Cosmo to the Capo.

CHAPTER 8

Returning to Palermo with Violante, Donna Gabriella, still emotional and almost feverish, was in the grip of a profound despondency, in which was fomenting a turmoil of anger, spite, wounded pride, jealousy, and hatred. Her hatred bound Violante and Blasco to each other. As much as the young girl's answers had the naivete of innocence, of unawareness, and of being above suspicion, and even though Blasco had pointedly protested against every suspicion and had sworn he had not said a single word nor hinted at any feelings to the young girl, Donna Gabriella could not suppress her innermost suspicion that they were concealing—with a clever fiction—what had happened between them.

She could not believe that a man in love, finding himself in possession of his beloved woman, could impose the greatest sacrifice on himself, that of silence. She was certain that Blasco had expressed his feelings to Violante; he had certainly gotten to the young girl's heart, already predisposed to a fondness for him. However, she would have liked both of them to admit it, to give her a precise and detailed confirmation; she would have liked to savor the bitter joy of tormenting her own jealousy and fueling her own hatred with a detailed account, for her own anguish. By now she was sure that Blasco loved Violante; his outward appearance, the tone of his words, that bewilderment, that immediate blushing and turning pale were telltale signs that didn't allow for even the shadow of a doubt.

The entire way, rocked back and forth by the litter, she did not say a word. But upon arriving at the palazzo, she shut herself in her room with her stepdaughter. Grabbing her violently by the wrists, staring hard at her, she said harshly, "So this is how you preserve the honor of your family, then?"

Violante looked at her in amazement, full of fear; she didn't understand the words, but Donna Gabriella's appearance and the vehemence of the gesture struck her with a terror that disoriented her. What did those words mean? What honor was she talking about? What wrong had she committed?

"Signora Madre," she stammered, "I don't understand!"

The duchess resumed with a convulsive and sarcastic laugh: "You don't understand? At your age, you don't understand! I'll make you understand!"

She was silent for a while, as if to savor the pleasure of the investigations that she wanted to conduct; then with bitterness, she asked her, "When Signor Blasco put you in the saddle, in front of him . . . he put you in front of him, isn't that so?"

"Yes."

"Well, did he embrace you? Did he hold you tight . . . like this?"

She put her arms around her, pressing against her breast, and her hand was trembling.

"No, Signora Madre," Violante replied naively. "He said to me instead, 'Hold on to me' and it was I who held him so as not to fall."

"And . . . did you like holding on to him tightly? You didn't feel any pleasure in pressing yourself against him?"

Violante blushed; her modesty was awakening.

"Tell me . . . speak!"

"I don't know . . . I couldn't say," the young girl stammered. "I was so afraid."

"Don't you think that Signor Blasco is handsome?"

Violante blushed again, then her face turned white and her lips became pale. Her chest seemed to swell. She stammered in an imploring voice, "Why do you ask me these questions that confuse me, that make me want to die?"

Her voice was trembling owing to the suppressed tears, but Donna Gabriella felt she had to be crueler and more ruthless. "Confess," she said in a broken, irascible voice, "confess that you love Signor Blasco."

Violante cried out and covered her face in her hands. Love? What could her stepmother mean? Here that word suddenly awakened strange revelatory instincts in the depths of her consciousness that until then she hadn't understood, or that had gone unnoticed, and they deeply disturbed her. Flushes, one after the other, burned her face; scorching tears rose to her eyes; a great shame, a great dismay, an inexplicable and irrepressible confusion was invading her. That word, *love*, that she had pronounced so many times in her prayers, appeared to her like a new word, full of mysteries, fears, dangers, of things unknown, and yet like something from which she could not escape, like a goal that she had to reach with a man . . . a man! Signor Blasco! The veil within which Blasco da Castiglione had appeared to her was beginning to tear now; the hidden fondness, that tender attraction that seemed to her nothing out of the ordinary, nothing different from what she felt for other people whose sight brought her pleasure; that admiration, that confidence, that abandonment, that joy of seeing him by her side, of knowing that she had been rescued by him, of talking about him; all that was love, then! . . . She loved Blasco! And only now did she tremble at the thought that she had embraced him, that she had held him tightly, that she had slept with her face near his face, with her hands in his hands. She trembled, and a shiver ran through her and at the same time a sadness and languor descended through her blood, and a sob erupted from her chest. She loved Blasco! . . . She was pervaded by fear and shame and yet these emotions caused a desire and a torment to creep into her blood.

Bending over Violante, Donna Gabriella peered at her; her gaze moved down, penetrating the inner recesses of that innocent heart that knew no pretense and was now revealing itself.

"You love him, then?" she insisted.

She angrily tore her stepdaughter's hands away from her face. Violante believed that she had committed a grave sin; the threatening, enraged appearance of her stepmother made what she considered love appear to her like something monstrous.

She threw herself on her knees before Donna Gabriella, sobbing, "Please forgive me! Please forgive me!"

Forgive what? What was she blaming herself for? What had she done? Forgive? . . . Donna Gabriella took those words as a confession; she was blinded by rage and jealousy. She struck her stepdaughter, threw her to the ground, exclaiming through clenched teeth, "You will never see him again . . . you will not have him. . . . No! No! No!"

She went out, locked the door anew, and left the poor girl on the ground, sobbing and terrified.

* * *

The duchess's heart was swollen with a craving to take revenge. She immediately had her carriage hitched and went to the Palazzo Reale to ask for a special audience with the viceroy.

It wasn't actually a day for hearings, so the antechamber was devoid of petitioners; moreover, the antechamber of Viceroy Maffei had nothing in common with that of the Spanish viceroys, to whom the Sicilians were accustomed.

The frugal habits that the king, with his pragmatic sanctions, had tried to impose on the nobility of the kingdom were strictly observed commensurate to how the viceregal court was maintained. Except for the strictly necessary number of footmen, valets, pages, attendants, servants, secretaries, and officials, there wasn't that swarm of cavalieri and parasites that used to crowd the rooms of the Palazzo Reale during the era of the Spanish viceroys and had formed for themselves a sumptuous and truly regal court. The liveries themselves didn't have the ostentation of braiding and embroidery that the eyes of the citizens were accustomed to and that represented the outward sign of royalty that would arouse the pride of the commoners of the capital, who saw in it almost a respect for its importance, a proof of the consideration in which it was held by the king's representative.

The Piedmontese viceroy's antechamber was a modest one, made up of people who get straight to the point and don't care about pomp and vanities. Count Maffei had accepted from Parliament, as the Spanish viceroys had, the donative of a thousand onze for himself and two hundred for his chamberlain, but with this, he had not departed from the habits of his own life, nor had he put the viceregal court on a more magnificent throne.

When the duchess arrived at the Palazzo Reale, Count Maffei was still in his private study with his secretary, putting in order the usual mail to be sent to the king in Turin and trying to orient himself in that labyrinth of laws, customs, constitutions, privileges, pragmatic sanctions, and jurisdictions that constituted the legislation of the kingdom. He had, moreover, the problem of Rome on his hands—the struggle engaged in with the Curia due to the interdict hurled down on two dioceses, those of Catania and Girgenti, which it was threatening to extend to all of Sicily. And yet the duchess's unsettled appearance, and her name, had induced the chamberlain to pass the message to His Excellency. If the secretariat had been closed, if the time allotted to the office had elapsed, Donna Gabriella would have aroused the inflexibility of the chamberlain to no avail.

His Excellency was kind enough to receive the duchess in a nearby room. He was also struck by the sight of Donna Gabriella and feared that some distressing news had arrived from Turin.

"I come to plead for Your Excellency's justice," Donna Gabriella said.

"I am here precisely to carry out the duties of this office, signora; please tell me . . ."

"Your Excellency knows about the educanda who was kidnapped the other night from the Monastery of Montevergini."

"Yes, well?"

"Your Excellency also knows that the young girl is the daughter of the Duke of Motta . . . and is my stepdaughter."

"Yes, I gave the strictest orders to search for her and to punish the culprits."

"There is no need to search for the young girl; she is in my house."

"How—"

"Your Excellency's justice was not as quick as I was."

Count Maffei frowned but couldn't overcome his surprise. "She is in the signora's house? . . . Then they didn't kidnap her?"

"They kidnapped her, Your Excellency, and this morning, having been informed by the poor young girl, I went to get her myself, in the countryside, where they had almost abandoned her . . . and in such a condition!"

"Signora, I am amazed . . . where?"

"In Villagrazia. . . . I know the culprits, rather the culprit."

"And who is he?"

"An opportunist who was formerly accepted into our house by the generosity of the duke, my lord and husband; a certain Blasco da Castiglione, who perhaps wanted to pull off a robbery of the patrimony of the young girl, a coheiress of the duke."

"Blasco da Castiglione? . . . Wait, signora; isn't he the young man who was arrested in Messina and escaped?"

"Precisely."

"But he is wanted by justice!"

"Well, he is making a mockery of it, if he can come to Palermo and carry out, in spite of everything, a feat such as this, of kidnapping a young girl!"

"But the Beati Paoli were accused."

"He must be one of their leaders."

"Can the signora give me any information about the criminal?"

"He wanders about those lands, it seems. The place where I found my step-daughter belongs to the Prince of Trabia."

"Very well. I thank you for this information."

"But we must not rule out, Your Excellency, that he may come to Palermo and that at this very time he is perhaps here."

"Does he have known friends, beyond those of the sect?"

"One that I know of . . . the Cavaliere della Floresta."

"A lord?"

"Yes . . . he is known."

"His protector?"

"Perhaps."

"I will give the appropriate orders."

"Your Excellency, bear in mind that, after this abduction, if the young girl didn't lose her life, she has lost her reputation."

"Signora, leave it to me."

With those words it seemed that the viceroy was dismissing the duchess, but Donna Gabriella added, "Meanwhile, I no longer feel safe in my palazzo. I beseech Your Excellency to find shelter for me in some royal castle, with my stepdaughter, for my peace of mind . . . until my husband, the duke, returns."

The viceroy thought for a minute and answered, "It wouldn't hurt. Would you be satisfied with the Castello di Termini? The family of the viceroy was sheltered there during the disturbances of 1709, if I am not mistaken."

"I would be satisfied with that and I thank Your Excellency for so much kindness. And now, I would like to beseech you to give the appropriate orders, because I will leave immediately."

"Would you like to leave by land? I wouldn't advise it. I have news of a gang of thieves who are wreaking terror on the road to Termini."

"I will depart by sea. I will arrange for a felucca."

"I will have a sergeant accompany you."

"Oh, Your Excellency, I am very grateful to you, and I will write to my husband about your kindness."

This time Donna Gabriella got up, kissed the hand of His Excellency, and returned to her palazzo. As soon as she entered, she called for the chief steward. "At once: go to the Cala, secure a felucca for two to leave for Termini, two or three hours from now at the latest, and arrange trunks for me and for the young duchess."

The order caused a stir in the palazzo, already in turmoil over the extraordinary events of those days. The maidservants got busy filling trunks and sacks with clothes, linens, and jewels, and everything that could be needed for the mistress's wardrobe. Servants came and went to inform the agent, the razionale or *contatore*—as it was then called—and her relatives. Those two hours were a busy time, a running around, a coming and going of portantine and carriages. The servants seemed to have lost their minds. In the street, where for the entire day there had been nothing but chatting and commenting about the kidnapping, the rescue, and the return of the young girl, small groups were forming. The news that the duchess was going to Termini with her stepdaughter was on everyone's lips. Everyone had their own explanation. There were even some who believed that it was a punishment for not having sufficiently watched over the young girl.

When at three o'clock the duchess left the palazzo in a carriage with her stepdaughter beside her, followed by her maidservant and another servant in another carriage, she found the street nearly blocked by the crowd and was barely able to clear the way.

Their closest relatives accompanied them until the Cala, where the felucca was moored, by the Church of the Madonna di Piedigrotta. For the entire time, Donna Gabriella didn't say a word to her stepdaughter. The only words she addressed to her, upon returning from the Palazzo Reale, were these: "Girls like you are shut in castles—get ready to leave."

And she said nothing else to her. Violante was petrified by that announcement and even more by the harshness with which it was said to her. She obeyed, and for the entire journey she stayed in a corner of the carriage as if to escape from everyone's eyes, and with her head lowered so as not to see and not to be seen. She truly believed that she had committed some grave offense and it could be read on her face; but meanwhile, ever since Donna Gabriella's words had pierced the fog of her innocence and had unwittingly enlightened the depths of her heart, Violante thought only about Blasco, and the image of the young man was ingrained in her mind, just as he was when she had looked at him for a long time, with his beautiful face resting on his pillow and suffused with the tender tranquility of sleep.

CHAPTER 9

The afternoon was a splendor of autumn sky and the sea for the entire breadth of the gulf, and up to the edge of the horizon was a great blue plane, its surface gently rippling. Capo Zafferano, suffused with sunlight, appeared to be made of roses and violets, while Monte Pellegrino loomed in a gray shadow.

The felucca had unfurled its sails and seemed to dart over the waves, as light as a large bird. The captain, standing aft, checked the rigging, and behind him the helmsman manned the rudder according to the captain's signals. Donna Gabriella and Violante had sat down on the cushions inside the covered cabin; the two servants had settled themselves under a tent next to them. A big black dog had first approached them, then the cabin, earnestly and quietly sniffing, and had gone to crouch at the feet of the captain. The crew of six men, including the cabin boy, was devoted to handling the sails in order to catch the wind. A small white-and-red pennant hoisted to the top of the mast waved in the wind, producing a continuous and regular fluttering sound. The sergeant who was accompanying the women was taking a stroll.

As the ship put out to sea, the coast unfolded before Donna Gabriella's eyes, and the city was beginning to be seen clearly from the bastions of Gonzaga on the southern side to the bastions of Tuono and Vega, to Porta Felice, all the way to Forte della Garita that marked the mouth of the Cala and to the Castello a Mare that stood on the other side. Beyond the bastions rose the bell towers and cupolas; one could make out the pointed yellow ones of the Cathedral. On one side were the Piano di Sant'Erasmo with the forts of Tonnarazza and Sagramento and then the green of the gardens; in the distance was the ring of the mountains, a wide and magnificent amphitheater, and Monreale lying on a hill, with in front of it the little village of Parco and the ruins of Castellaccio above. Then with the sun gradually falling behind the pointed peak of Monte Cuccio, this entire scene was covered with an ashen shadow, from which emerged some peaks, some rose-colored tips that turned to a luminous copper hue, then faded, retreating to the ashen shadow. A great melancholy enveloped everything. Evening was approaching. Coming from the now distant city, one could hear the soft and gentle sounds of the bells. Other ships passed silently by as they reentered the port.

The felucca had by then reached Capo Zafferano and was now rounding it at its furthest point, beyond which the wider and less calm inlet opens where Termini and Cefalù are located. Monte Catalfano, whose farthest projection forms the cape, is indented at its back with inlets and boulders that look like hiding places. A galley could conceal itself there without being seen, and the Barbary pirates who knew of it often lurked there, eluding the surveillance of the guards that were scattered along the coast in watchtowers, whose ruins can still be found here and there.

The felucca had bypassed that coastal rock formation that marks the farthest point of the cape and was entering, almost coasting, into the great bay of Termini. The captain had lowered some sails according to the new course and had ordered the ship's bow light to be lit, even though the last light of the day was still looming over the sky; and, certain by now of the route, he had sat down on the quarterdeck, where the sailors had lit the fire in an earthenware stove and were cooking a fish soup. Donna Gabriella had asked for a small enameled terracotta oil lamp to be lit and was reciting the rosary; Violante was snuggled in a corner, not moving or saying a word due to her uneasiness with her stepmother and owing to the vague sense of fear that was holding sway over her.

Suddenly a great splash of oars was heard, and a boat darted from behind a large schooner, moving rapidly along the same course as the felucca. It didn't have a ship's light. It looked like one of those high-seas trawlers, long, capable, and swift.

The captain focused his eyes into the half-light and said, "Eight oarsmen and many people on board . . . they must be soldiers, certainly not fishermen. It seems that they are on the same course."

The boat, after having rowed parallel to the felucca's port side, had overtaken it by about forty arm's lengths when, instead of continuing, it stopped, changed tack, and put itself almost on the same course as the felucca as if to close in right up to it.

The captain got up and went to the side of the boat, but suddenly there were flashes from the barrels of rifles, flashes shattering the darkness, bullets whizzing by, piercing and shredding the sail, singeing it in four or five different places.

"Hey there!" shouted the captain, grasping a rifle.

The sergeant took it from his hand and fired, but a second discharge tore the sail in other places, battered the mast, and wounded the sergeant and sailors. The flash of the gunshots revealed the faces of the men.

"We are being attacked by pirates!" shouted the captain.

The smell of scorched air alerted them that the sail was already burning.

"The oars! The oars!" ordered the captain.

But the boat had come on top of them; some men armed with rams and iron hooks boarded the felucca. Twelve men, some dressed in the manner of Barbary pirates, others in a strange fashion but armed with muskets and clubs, jumped onto the felucca, throwing themselves on top of the captain and the sailors, who had been practically nailed to their ship by the fright of that attack.

Those gunshots had frozen the blood in the veins of Donna Gabriella and Violante; they didn't know what it was about, but they feared something sinister. Seizures of ships weren't so infrequent in those times that one shouldn't fear, during a voyage, of having some encounters, and the captain had preferred to sail at night along the coast because darkness afforded a greater margin of safety. Therefore, the terrible danger of falling into the hands of Barbary pirates ran through Donna Gabriella's mind, and her terror was so great that she almost fainted. She knew what fate lay in store for young and beautiful women: the harem. Yes, she knew about young girls sold in the markets of Constantinople, Algeria, and Tunis who then were brought to the sultan or to the bey.

Out of instinct she hid in the bottom of the cabin, crouching to conceal herself, thinking that she could evade the searches of those brigands. But at that point two men appeared at the door of the cabin, shouting, "Not a move or you are dead!"

But they couldn't move; the terror had left them speechless and numbed their limbs. Two men seized them, picked them up, and carried them into their boat. The others, meanwhile, after having beaten and tied up the sailors, the servant, and the maidservant, rummaged through the felucca, taking away the weapons, a tent, the cushions, and the baggage, and with this plunder they returned to their trawler.

The two women cowered there, mute, terrified; in their shared danger they huddled together as if that gave them comfort. The pirates pitched the tent over the aft benches, put the cushions underneath and had the two women lie down on them; then, taking the oars, they went back along the course of the felucca, which they abandoned to the mercy of the wind and the waves with its men tied up and scattered on the quarterdeck.

At that moment the moon was rising behind the ridge of the mountains and spreading its gentle light over everything.

The boat, having passed Capo Zafferano, instead of returning to the city, as Donna Gabriella had foolishly believed it might, raced quickly offshore; the eight oars, in a unified rhythm, cut through the waves, which shattered into a thousand reflections, like white sparks released from a brazier by the stirring of the fire shovel.

At the bottom of the benches, under the tent, the two women held each other tightly, looking at the oarsmen, who were bending with uniform motion over the oars, and staring at the armed men who stood along both sides with rifles at the ready, on the alert and keeping watch over the surrounding sea. Donna Gabriella couldn't see their faces. Some wore black masks; others were concealed under a type of hood. This care to conceal their faces made Donna Gabriella suspicious; did pirates perhaps have a need not to be recognized? And shouldn't they have had a racing ship? This was more like a fisherman's boat than a racing vessel.

Pirates used galleys or three-masted brigantines, and in the wide expanse of the sea there was no sign of any of them. Then who were those kidnappers? Weren't those Oriental clothes with which some had disguised themselves—perhaps a trick? As she was led from one thought to another, amid doubts and suspicions, one suddenly occurred to her that made her shiver and that seemed to her a certainty more than a suspicion: the Beati Paoli! They had failed in their first attempt owing to Blasco's intervention; now they were managing to pull off a more decisive blow by seizing two people instead of one. She was invaded by a mad terror, and a great tremor spread through her entire body. Her teeth began to chatter with a convulsive gnashing that frightened the young girl.

"What's wrong, Signora Madre?" she stammered, starting to feel lost.

Donna Gabriella didn't answer. She was now looking at those men, afraid of seeing them suddenly pounce and try to slaughter her. Her husband's words were coming back to her, the account of all the persecutions that, out of revenge for the sins they accused him of, gave her no respite, and she imagined that if the hatred of the sect was so great, she was certainly destined to be offered as a sacrifice. But what did she have to do with it? Why make her, who had no part in it, pay for the crimes that Don Raimondo was accused of? Violante . . . but Violante was his daughter, and one could understand up to a certain point that the father was punished through his children. She, however, wasn't of his blood; they had tied her to him for reasons of expediency more than of preference, and one could even say that until that time, she had practically separated her life from Don Raimondo's. She regretted being associated with him and having assumed, in defending him, a part of her husband's responsibilities; certainly the Beati Paoli knew what she had done in Messina and were taking revenge for it. This thought filled her chest with sobs because she wasn't strong enough to instill herself with courage and get control of herself; instead, she abandoned herself to fear.

Violante said nothing. Her stepmother's fear was overwhelming her too with a terror all the more indomitable since she didn't know from what new thoughts Donna Gabriella's fear had arisen.

Meanwhile, the boat was racing along. The coast appeared far away, and Monte Gallo, lower and precipitous on the sea, was now visible behind the black and sharp-edged mass of Monte Pellegrino. The valley between the two mountains was bathed by the faint moonlight. Now at the end of the horizon, hazy in the shadow of the sky, the shape of an isolated mountain was appearing, and the boat seemed to be headed in that direction. Donna Gabriella recognized that it was Ustica.

Were they going to that solitary and deserted island, then, a pirate den and hideout? They could be killed and abandoned there, left as prey for rapacious birds, without a living soul finding out about it because at that time the island was uninhabited. She looked at Sicily's distant shore, jagged with mountains, and thought that a few miles away, at the end of a wide beach, on a hill, was Castello di Carini, where no one would have attempted to harm her because it would have been defended by vassals of her family. Why hadn't she thought of taking refuge in that castle? And then the reasons that had pushed her toward Termini flooded through her mind, and she saw in her stepdaughter the source of that jealousy that had blinded her, and the hatred that was made dormant by her fear had reawakened and flared up. She thought with bitter pleasure that her stepdaughter would also be killed, and before killing her those men would certainly make a mockery of that still immature body. Violante would pass from the arms of one to the other, disgraced, degraded by obscene and deviant kisses, before dying—and no one would save her, no one!

* * *

And so the night passed; the moon was already high in the sky, spreading its faint light everywhere. Ustica appeared clearly, with its deep and dark valleys, its jagged boulders just below the surface, its shores fringed with a foam that was turning a silvery white in the moonlight.

The boat finally stopped in a small natural harbor, formed by rocks that sheltered it from the wind. Then one of the men appeared under the tent and said, "Get up, we have arrived."

Donna Gabriella clasped her hands, pleading, "Gentlemen, gentlemen . . . have mercy on me . . . I will give you everything that you want, but don't do anything to me. . . . I didn't do anything. . . . I don't know you! . . . Have mercy!"

The man reassured her: "Don't be afraid; the slightest harm will not come to you and no one will disrespect you . . . but you have to go ashore."

"Are you abandoning me on this island?"

"No, signora. . . . But let's hurry."

Violante followed this conversation, trembling, waiting anxiously for a word that would comfort her. She too now feared that she had fallen back into the power of those men who had kidnapped her the first time, and she stood like a little lamb before the knife that is ready to slit its throat. They had to obey and go ashore. These armed men had placed themselves in front of and behind them as though to prevent any foolish act. They helped them set foot on land and led them up the coast, amid some rocks, where they stopped. Four men sat down, with rifles between their legs, their faces covered with masks, stern and silent; the others returned to the boat. Donna Gabriella saw that the ones wearing pirates' clothes took them off, bundled them up, and hid them astern, and that the others took off their hoods and masks, trusting that the distance made it impossible to see their faces. She also saw, with a heavy heart, that the boat had moved away from the shore and was taking off. Soon after, dawn broke, and a crisp, gentle breeze arose that gave her goose bumps.

One of the men noticed that the two women were feeling cold and handed them some cloaks without saying a word. Toward midday a small two-masted ship with its sails unfurled was seen approaching the coast. Donna Gabriella and Violante looked anxiously, not knowing whether it could be some unexpected help, but instead they were quickly disappointed and trembled at the idea of a new danger.

From the ship, in fact, a type of red pennant was being waved repeatedly at the top of the mast; one of the men who was next to them took out a red handkerchief from his pocket, tied it to the barrel of his rifle like a flag, and, climbing on a rock, waved it three times in repetition in response. It didn't take long to guess that they were signals.

"They are coming to pick us up," one of the masked men said brusquely to Donna Gabriella.

"To go where?"

"We don't know."

"What? You don't know?"

"We don't know," the man repeated in a tone that meant "It's useless to ask, be quiet!"

Soon after, the ship landed a short distance from the coast, and a caïque with an oarsman was lowered into the sea. They had the two women get in, accompanied by one of the masked men, who helped them board the ship; the caïque returned to land to let the others embark, and an hour later the ship veered, caught the wind, and sped along like lightning.

Donna Gabriella and Violante were brought into the commandant's cabin on the quarterdeck, where there was a sort of bed and a small table. They couldn't see anyone but immediately understood that those who were commanding the ship and the masked men all belonged to the same gang. In fact, one man, whom they hadn't seen before then but who had his face masked as well, had looked in on the cabin and, after having a sailor place a chest on the table, had said to Donna Gabriella in a courteous manner, "Your Ladyship must be hungry; there is a bit of cold food in this chest. . . . Your Ladyship should eat and stay calm."

But she wasn't hungry, or perhaps the fear that had taken hold of her had taken away her appetite. She was surprised at those polite manners and the clear signs of respect, due to which it seemed that she wasn't a prisoner but a woman who was traveling for pleasure in a ship of her own.

A sailor with cap in hand had said to her, "If Your Ladyship needs anything, call me by knocking on the wall."

Need? Oh, she had only one urgent need: to know where they were taking her and why she had been captured. She knocked.

The sailor appeared at the door. "Yes, Your Ladyship?"

"Call the captain for me—the commander, the master, in short, whoever commands the ship."

"At once."

An old clean-shaven sea dog, his face tanned and wrinkled, came shortly after, with his hat on his head and his sleeves rolled up.

"Your Ladyship wants me?"

"Excuse me, good man; you are the captain . . ."

"Yes, Your Excellency."

"Well, I beseech you to tell me where we are going."

"I don't know, they chartered my ship. . . . I command the crew, I know that I have to take this course, but I haven't been told the landing point yet."

"But where are we?"

"Near Capo San Vito."

"How come, if you are the captain, you don't know where we are going ashore? . . . Is there anyone else in charge?"

"Yes, Your Excellency."

"You are a good man and I will remember you; I implore you to call the man who is in charge."

"If you need nothing else, I will attend to it immediately."

She waited, anxious to know who this leader was and to find out the reason for her capture. Violante, although she wasn't speaking, was following her, with her mind suspended in an uncertainty full of mysterious terrors. But both of them were disappointed when they saw the man who had invited them to eat enter the cabin.

"I understand that Your Ladyship wishes to speak with me."

Donna Gabriella clasped her hands. "If you are the leader, if you are in charge, signore, I beg you for what you hold most sacred; tell me why you kidnapped me, tell me where you are taking me . . . what you want from me."

"Nothing, Duchess; we don't want anything. We have orders to look after you with all the considerations owing to your social status and to put you ashore at the marina in Girgenti."

"Then you are not in charge?"

"No, signora."

"And who is?"

"God only knows."

"Oh, signore, don't play games with me; do it for the souls of your dear departed ones. . . . Who gave you this order?"

"I told you, our leader."

"But—"

"I thought that Your Ladyship had understood under whose power she was."

She trembled and stammered, "The Beati Paoli."

"At your service," he confirmed, bowing but smiling ironically under his mask.

"The Beati Paoli," murmured Violante, feeling faint and recalling the first abduction. This time she was in their power, without hope of being saved by anyone. Blasco, brave and valiant, emerged from the bottom of her heart to her eyes. So where was he, then? And why hadn't he watched over her?

An oppressive silence fell over the two women, who didn't know what to say, and their terror was so vivid and anguished that the masked man seemed moved by it.

"Your Ladyship take heart that not a hair on your head will be touched, and that you will lack nothing of what a quality lady of your status needs; and I say the same for the young duchess. . . . Have faith. The orders are strict and precise: neither their persons, nor their possessions, nor their honor will have anything to fear. Only that they will be like prisoners and therefore obliged not to attempt any resistance, and not to arouse any suspicion, because in that case we are ordered to kill them immediately."

The tone of his words, at this point, had a cruel harshness that seemed even harsher at the sight of the butt of the pistol tucked under his belt.

"But I am certain," he added in a gentler manner, "that we will not be constrained by this rigor. Besides, why should Your Ladyship scream? We are here only to please you. Your Ladyship wanted to take refuge in Castello di Termini; well, we will instead find shelter for you in another castle, where you will be better served and safer, because you will have nothing to fear."

"But it's an imprisonment! . . . An eternal imprisonment!" Donna Gabriella cried desperately.

"Oh no, signora, it will last only as long as it pleases Your Ladyship and His Excellency, the Duke of Motta, your husband."

* * *

The following day Donna Gabriella and Violante went ashore on a remote point of the southern beach, in a sandy area that rose up to yellowish hills, scattered here and there with mastic shrubs and dwarf palms, green islands in a sea of yellow. The beach was deserted, nor was it marked by any path. Five men went ashore with the women and placed them in the middle of the group. They had false beards and wigs, which rendered them unrecognizable; only one kept his mask on his face, and he was the leader with whom Donna Gabriella had spoken.

They climbed slowly up the hill, on whose summit could be seen scattered on the ground large boulders and sections of huge columns, on which still stood, like a shipwrecked man who stretches out his hand beyond the wave that rises above him, a truncated column. They were the ruins of Selinunte,[1] for the most part still buried under the soil. Near those ruins they met a carter, who was pulling behind him five horses and two mules tied to one another, harnessed and saddled.

Donna Gabriella and Violante were mounted on the mules and placed in the middle of the men who were already in the saddle, and the party, guided by the carter, started off. All around was an unvarying, desolate countryside, without vegetation, that never seemed to end. Far, far away, the backs of the mountains were cerulean blue shapes, behind knolls and hills that were arid or covered with wild plants and mastic shrubs. They encountered some shepherds who leaned on their staffs and played cane whistles, watching over their sheep scattered among the plants and bushes. The trampling made them turn their heads; they acknowledged the two women and took off their caps, imagining that they were two ladies who were going to their lands, accompanied by campieri. It was their only encounter. The lands were deserted; there was not a farm, not a house, not an apple orchard, not a well. The fief, the large landed estate, in all its bleakness.

Above a hill there were watchtowers built since the 1500s along the entire coast, which were mainly used to warn of approaching pirate galleys.

They rode in silence through that vast, solitary place; to the carter, surely the silence seemed depressing, because he began to sing one of those sentimental Sicilian arias that sounded like moans of passion and suffering.

That song descended into Violante's heart like an invitation to cry. In that solitude, in the middle of those people, before the unknown of her distant fate, in an unknown region that could have been to her as much like Sicily as it was like Africa, deprived of a heart that understood her, a breast on which she could seek refuge, alongside that stepmother who was making her feel uneasy, she increasingly turned her thoughts to Blasco, and in envisioning that image, she felt something akin to relief. The song, which expressed the suffering of separation with an expression that responded to the state of her mind with a desire and a passion that she now felt within her, was moving her profoundly.

She felt as though she were listening to her own voice.

Donna Gabriella, on the other hand, was silent, frowning, pale, internally debating between two feelings, one of fear, the other of hope. The fear of a terrible unknown, like the fulfillment of a long-premeditated revenge that was now hanging over her head, since it could not fall on the head of Don Raimondo; the hope that in the end it would be an act of cowardice to take it out on her and that, to judge from the respectful manner of those men and by the sufficient enough excuses from the one who seemed to be their leader, they truly didn't want to use any violence against her.

---

1 Ancient Greek city on the southwestern coast of Sicily. Now an archaeological park with many ruins.

She was thinking only of herself now, not worrying about her stepdaughter; rather, reflecting that this reprisal was directed at Don Raimondo, she found it almost reasonable that Violante should be subjected to it. Besides, the danger that loomed over both of them had not lessened the sting of jealousy in her. She thought with ruthless satisfaction that perhaps Violante would emerge from this adventure ugly and disfigured. Ah, if only that could happen! . . . She would no longer have such a dangerous and hated rival.

They rode almost the entire day, only allowing themselves some rest in the shadow of a solitary tree in order to have a bite to eat. They had reached the line of the mountains and now through deep and wooded gorges, then up steep slopes, or climbing up paths on the brinks of precipices that could make one dizzy, they had continued on, without encountering a city, a village, or a castle. At times, at the foot or at the sides of a mountain, they could more or less see in the distance the confused mass of a city; the two women would think that that was the destination of their journey, but at a new group of hills the city would vanish before their eyes. Finally, on the crest of another cliff, they saw a castle resembling a perched falcon, with its high and crenellated tower and massive walls.

The guide pointed it out to the leader of the group and said, "There."

Donna Gabriella heard and she too looked, wondering how she was going to climb up that cliff, on which there seemed to be no indication of a path.

But the path was there, around the other side, serpentine. The animals, a little tired, climbed up with difficulty; after a half hour they arrived in front of the door, where other armed men seemed to be waiting.

A woman, a polite and humble little old woman, came to meet the women at the foot of the stairway that ran externally along the wall of the courtyard; she looked honest and reassuring, but the manner of the men, although respectful, seemed to say, "Take heed, no one escapes from here."

CHAPTER 10

Matteo Lo Vecchio had returned to Palermo and had gone to see Don Raimondo with the certainty that Blasco was dead and buried. One can therefore imagine his surprise and also his sense of dismay when he learned about the warrant that had been issued for the young man, who had evaded justice for, among other things, the crime of killing four soldiers.

"He killed all four? But he had assured me that the last one had gotten away!"

Then the thought that had tormented him during his brief stay in Messina and that had accompanied him to Palermo took hold of him again; the doubts, the suspicions that had assailed him from the beginning resurfaced stronger than ever. He hastened to ask for a new permit "for the business of justice," and without even being seen by Don Raimondo, he left again for Cefalù. Since the four soldiers who had escorted him belonged to that rural company, that would be the source from which to obtain the most accurate information. This time he didn't resort to any disguise; the black outfit of an algozino, and more than that the order he was equipped with, were the most effective means for an investigation that could be seen as having been ordered by the government.

But the information collected in Cefalù reconfirmed what he had found out in Palermo. The four soldiers were really dead. Two had been picked up still wounded and taken to a nearby town, where one had died as soon as he'd arrived; the other one had lived for another five or six days, then he had died too, but he'd had time to relate his account.

The widows and mothers of the slain were in Cefalù; Matteo Lo Vecchio went to see them. These women, fresh from mourning, unpinned their hair and began to recite the praises of the dead in such dramatic tones as to make it seem that the dead were still at home. He asked if they had found on the soldiers some folded papers, wrapped in a sheet and tied with a ribbon. But no papers at all were found. What papers? Those poor people couldn't even read and had never had anything to do with written or printed things.

Matteo Lo Vecchio was desolated by it; if the papers hadn't been found on any of the soldiers, it was clear that someone had taken them, and this someone could be none other than Blasco da Castiglione.

"The bandit! He had the nerve to give me the saddlebag after having emptied it! Bandit! Of course he gave it to his companions . . . he robbed me! He has ruined me!"

He felt truly robbed, because with those papers in his power he was counting on landing a serious blow against the Duke of Motta, who surely, in order to get hold of them and to destroy those testimonies, would have given half his patrimony. This treasure trove was now slipping away from the birro's hands. The hope of finding them in the possession of any of the soldiers was vanishing; that of being able to take them back from the Beati Paoli, to whom they had certainly been returned, or even from Blasco, was so distant that it seemed impossible to him.

"If that bandit has them, he won't let them go. And then where is he? Where has he gone to find his doom? However audacious, the rascal will not let himself be seen. . . . Let's try," he added soon after in order to get his courage up, "let's try, Matteo, to better sort through our ideas in order to find a way to put ourselves on the right path. Oh, have you perhaps lost your nose, your good nose?"

He returned to Palermo defeated, however much he promised himself he'd be able to find Blasco or at least find out where those papers were, and this goal made him forget about the revenge he wanted to take on the Beati Paoli. Revenge would have to wait.

Entering the city from Porta Sant'Agata, the gate closest to his house, he passed in front of the house of Antonino Bucolaro, whom he had begun to follow and study, in order to take advantage of him.

"I have to squeeze that one," he thought. "It seems to me that he is one of the bigwigs and he must know quite a few things."

Antonino Bucolaro wasn't a graduate *in untroque*, that is, in either canon or civil law, because he had never attended the University of Catania, nor had he taken law courses in the schools of the Jesuits, and yet he regularly attended the courtrooms of the tribunals as a solicitor and pleader of the minor cases of poor people.

He wasn't familiar with the Institutes of Justinian or the Sicilian laws, but he was an expert in technicalities and in subterfuges and was a good friend of quite a few judges, on whom he sometimes exercised an astonishing influence that amazed the most renowned lawyers.

One could be sure to run into him in the morning at the Palazzo Pretorio in front of the magistrates' door, or at the Palazzo Reale, in front of the courtrooms on the ground floor where the tribunals convened, and sometimes at the Palazzo Arcivescovile, which also had its own court in order to judge certain offenses within its competence. In Palermo in those times there were several "tribunals," as they were called, every one of which had claimed rights and privileges granted by the kings. In addition to the royal magistrate, who had authority over the entire kingdom, there was the "tribunal" of Sant'Offizio, which had the power not only to investigate matters of faith and morality but also to judge its "members," namely, those who, as members of the family, by devotion or owing to their offices, had registered for or were dependent on that shadowy tribunal; there was the archbishop's "tribunal," which had its own special jurisdictions also as a feudal lordship, which benefited from *mero e misto impero*,[1] as a sign of which it kept nailed to the door a certain hilt, which is still there and is a source of legends;[2] there was the Corte Pretoriana, which had the right to judge Palermitan citizens; and there was the Tribunal of the Monarchy, which had special jurisdiction over ordinary things and over royal churches and in certain canonical cases.

Often the laws of one contradicted or clashed with the laws of another, giving rise to conflicts, which very often ended up allowing the culprit to evade justice and which the viceregal authority itself didn't manage to settle. Sometimes they resulted in excommunications, interdictions, sieges, and truly comical episodes.

Thus, Antonino Bucolaro was hanging around all these tribunals, where there was always some client to be fleeced, from whom, if nothing else, there were a couple of hens to be had, or a half barrel of Partinico wine, and where human miseries and injustices were revealed in all their nakedness. If not around those courtrooms, one was sure to encounter him in the Perciata tavern at the end of Piazza Ballarò, a tavern frequented by all these advocates of . . . the lower court, like Bucolaro.

Matteo Lo Vecchio was too well known throughout the Albergheria for him to pretend that he needed assistance and legal advice from Antonino Bucolaro, and this time he couldn't resort to his abbot's disguise, which he was sure would attract Antonino Bucolaro's revenge, and perhaps he would then have handed him over to the power of the Beati Paoli. He had to confront him in a different manner. How?

He began to investigate whether Bucolaro had ever had some old account to settle with justice, something that wasn't difficult to do in those times, and meanwhile he directed a rigorous and diligent surveillance on him, to try to catch Bucolaro in the act as a violator of the prohibitions. There was the ban on carrying weapons, there was the king's pragmatic sanction against gambling . . .

But it seemed that Antonino Bucolaro was an exemplary subject of the kingdom. Apart from a sword, he was never seen carrying other weapons; his sword was permitted due to his position, since he wasn't a commoner, a class that was prohibited from carrying even a sword. And as for gambling, he was never seen with cards or dice in his hands in a public place. . . . And yet in the Perciata tavern one could play zecchinetta or primero in a secluded room, which had an exit

---

1 From *mero et mixto imperio*, a medieval Latin phrase that referred to the delegation of all powers—political, administrative, fiscal, military, and judicial—to a feudal lord.

2 According to an ancient tradition, the hilt of the sword with which Matteo Bonello, on the night of San Martino, killed Maio of Bari, Ammiraglio of William I, in 1160. AC, 407–408.

door to the vicolo that now has the name of the celebrated Count Cagliostro[3]—a secret exit, so to speak, which had given the tavern its name.[4]

Antonino Bucolaro sometimes played as well, one game and no more. But more often he would stop to watch the game, almost always acting as a judge in the arguments between the players.

One morning when he had been very busy and was in a good mood, he went to the tavern to drink his glass of wine as usual and made a brief visit to the little room. There were five or six men gathered around a table and they seemed to be wrapped up in the game. Another one was seated, holding a deck of cards in his left hand, thumbing through them with his right. There were three cards on the table that were disappearing under the wagers.

"To you, Don Antonino!" exclaimed the one keeping the bank, looking at him. "Here's a horse . . . aren't you betting? Woman, horse, and king, bet all there is . . . ace . . . five . . . king . . . five . . . deuce . . . seven . . . horse . . . Look! You survived; you would have lost."

Antonino Bucolaro bet on one of the two cards and lost; he bet a second time and lost. He was annoyed, and his irritation got him worked up in the game.

"You," he said, "wouldn't be able to beat me in primero."

"I take you at your word."

They began the game. Antonino Bucolaro won, and his satisfaction was so great that he seemed to have won a resounding victory on a day of battle.

His opponent said to him, "You owe me a return match."

"Not now; it's late and I have to go to the Tribunale del Concistoro to get some information, but, if you wish, tonight or tomorrow."

"Let's do it this evening."

Although a clerk, Antonino Bucolaro's opponent was a spy who was acting as an accomplice of Matteo Lo Vecchio; the birro heard about the new game arranged for that evening and sized things up. He went to find the patrol leader of the Albergheria and alerted him, but in an ambiguous manner full of innuendos, which the excellent corporal perfectly understood.

"You, in short," concluded Matteo Lo Vecchio, "you know what you have to do. Be strict, inflexible, etc., etc."

"But . . . who?" asked the corporal, rubbing his thumb against his index and middle fingers and holding the other two fingers slightly open—an expressive gesture that meant "And the money?"

"Don't worry about it. I'll take care of it."

---

3 Alessandro Cagliostro (1743–1795), the alias of the occultist Giuseppe Balsamo, an Italian adventurer and self-styled magician.

4 The door allowed someone to make a quick escape. In fact, Cagliostro frequented that tavern. From archaic Italian *perciare*: "to make a hole."

"Very well."

At six o'clock, in fact, the patrol stormed into the Perciata tavern and entered the little room to catch the players by surprise; there was a bit of commotion. The corporal shouted, "You are in trouble . . . the royal sanction is clear!"

The players protested; someone offered money, but the corporal was inflexible, counter to common practice. At the shouts and the racket entered—*deus ex machina*—Matteo Lo Vecchio, and with a changed and almost amazed expression on his face, he asked what was going on. He pretended to listen to the patrol head; he looked at Antonino Bucolaro and the clerk, tightening his lips and shaking his head as if to say that it was a serious matter, and pretended to intervene.

"Let's see," he said, "these are respectable people; they are from my neighborhood. This matter can be settled . . . call it a truce and don't mention it again."

"But the offense . . . patrolmen have the right—"

"What right? I will take care of it . . . let it go. For once one can turn a blind eye. Don Antonino isn't a man who doesn't know how to repay a kindness."

The corporal pretended to resist but finally gave in; he promised to overlook everything but gave a warning for the future and left.

The clerk then said, "If it wasn't for you, Don Matteo, that beast would have taken us to the prisons of the court."

"Oh! I didn't do it for you," exclaimed the birro, "that is not the first time, but out of respect for Don Antonino, who deserves even more than this."

"I thank you and will remain indebted to you," said Bucolaro, marveling at the birro's kindness, "and I hope that you will accept a drink from me."

He ordered some wine, which they drank.

"Tell me what I must give to the patrol."

"To them? But nothing, not even a grano!"

"The devil! But they lost out on a fine that they were entitled to."

"It doesn't matter. . . . I will take care of it . . . don't worry. What the heck, there are offenders and there are offenders, and one must have a good nose. If they wish, they can make it up." He lowered his voice and in confidence added, "The lords don't care about royal sanctions," and he made an indecent gesture. "If the patrol leader wants to pay himself for the night, he only needs to lie in wait for whichever baron or count appears first and take a look at their carriage and clothes. He will determine what violation . . . and what tip is required for him to keep his mouth shut. . . . I know how these things are done!"

"Meanwhile, you have gotten us out of trouble," said Don Antonino, still amazed at the "role of friend" played by the birro.

"And he saved us an onza or two!" added the clerk.

"I would have gladly made you pay; you must thank Sant'Antonio."

He was alluding to Bucolaro. They left the tavern and took their leave of one another, but as soon as he took a step, Matteo Lo Vecchio turned and called out: "Don Antonino, excuse me; a word."

The clerk then said, "Take your time. I have some business to attend to and am leaving."

When they were alone, Matteo looked around suspiciously and said in a low voice, "Don Antonino, be careful . . . there is someone who knows where you go on certain nights."

Bucolaro had a blank look on his face.

"I don't understand."

"If it suits you to pretend not to understand, so be it. I tell you, though. . . . In short, I, owing to my position, should not have warned you; they would catch you off guard, you wouldn't be able to run away."

"But what is this about?"

"When I give you two names you will understand: Girolamo Ammirata and Andrea Lo Bianco."

Antonino Bucolaro remained impassive, but there was a flash in his eyes that didn't escape the birro.

"I don't know them," he said coldly.

"So be it, but there is someone who saw you with them in a certain osteria at the crossroads in Brancaccio. . . .[5] In short, I have warned you; do what you believe. I could have been silent, because in the end with my warning I am impeding justice from taking its course . . . but we are from the neighborhood . . . and I have always had a high opinion of you. Realize that I have not told you anything . . . but if you wish, listen to me . . . do not go out at night."

"At night, me? But I sleep at night."

"Yes, yes, as you wish. I, you clearly see, don't ask you what you do and where you go. . . . I say only: *beware*. I would hate to be forced to arrest you. . . . Good night!"

He left him uncertain and shaken. Antonino Bucolaro didn't know if he should believe in the birro's sincerity; he certainly admitted that Matteo Lo Vecchio had to know more than he was letting on, and that silence could very well be useful, having no obligation toward him. And then, even if he had had it, when had a birro ever felt obligations of gratitude or respect toward anyone? Was he perhaps being sly in order to pull some secret out of him? Matteo Lo Vecchio was capable of anything.

"I'll be on my guard," he thought, "yes, but also against you; not for nothing are you the emperor of the birri!"

---

5 Neighborhood in Palermo.

So he thought, but meanwhile suspicion, curiosity, and interest had entered the mind of Antonino Bucolaro, and owing to a natural impulse, he felt from that time on drawn to the birro, a little in order to find out something, a little to keep an eye on him. Matteo Lo Vecchio saw, laughed to himself, and when he was alone he rubbed his hands together and said, "Very well! Very well! Dear Don Antonino, I will put you in a sack!"

* * *

One morning, finally, Matteo hastily said to him, "If you have something to hide or to make disappear, do it immediately . . . the algozini are coming later to search your house. I heard about it just now, and I rushed to warn you."

"Thank you, thank you!" replied an emotional Antonino Bucolaro. "But I have nothing to hide."

Nevertheless he rushed home; after an hour an algozino with a few birri went to search his house and turn everything upside down. He thought, "Matteo Lo Vecchio was right! I absolutely must keep him as a friend because he is a good man after all, whatever they say about him. . . . At least as far as I am concerned."

One night, a few days later, the birro had him stopped by a patrol, lying in wait with a precise strategy. He was sure that Bucolaro had firearms against the ban and that he would be in trouble. So it happened. In an effort to free himself, Antonino Bucolaro tried to bribe the patrol leader—an ordinary and usual occurrence; but this time the patrol leader was firm. Luckily, while crossing Strada Nuova to lead the offender to the prisons of the Pretorio, they encountered Matteo Lo Vecchio.

Antonino Bucolaro, brightened by a sudden hope, called out to him, "Don Matteo!"

The birro, who at first pretended not to see him, turned abruptly, feigning a certain surprise. "Don Antonino? You? . . . What happened?"

He inquired, intervened, spoke in the ear of the patrol leader, had the weapons surrendered, and everything ended with a good glass of wine, drunk fraternally in a tavern in Vicolo dei Mori, where at the sound of Matteo Lo Vecchio's voice the door opened, although it was already closed at that late hour.

When they left the tavern, before parting company, Matteo Lo Vecchio whispered in Antonino Bucolaro's ear: "Be on your guard, I already told you. Strong suspicions are hanging over you and you are being watched and spied on . . . and I cannot always intervene."

This further proof of friendship ended up demolishing any last doubts; a certain friendly relationship began between Matteo Lo Vecchio and Antonino Bucolaro that apparently had no intimacy, owing to the wishes of the birro, who said, "Don Antonino, you know that I like you, but don't let it be seen that we are good friends, because they would be suspicious of you . . . you will understand, my profession . . . and your friends don't look favorably on me."

"But what friends are you talking about?"

"Eh, do you think that I'm a fool? . . . Let it go; rather, watch out for yourself."

Antonino Bucolaro was, in fact, watching out for justice and had become suspicious, but he was not watching out for the Beati Paoli, who had kept an eye on him after seeing him now and then with Matteo Lo Vecchio, and even more after having heard that he had gotten out of some embarrassment due to the birro's intervention. They began to watch him without him being aware of it, and to deal with him with a certain reserve.

Don Girolamo Ammirata, who, as one of the leaders, had received that news, immediately returned to the first envisioned suspect responsible for the disappearance of those renowned documents. Andrea shared that suspicion. Coriolano, who was communicating only with Don Girolamo below the Abbazia del Parco, was struck by it. It was decided to assign to one of the most able brothers, not known as a member of the Beati Paoli by Antonino Bucolaro, the job of watching him to determine whether he had stolen those documents and to whom he had given them.

Thus, from two opposite sides, Antonino Bucolaro was the object of investigations and espionage. Matteo Lo Vecchio set his sights on finding out if the documents had been returned to the possession of the Beati Paoli; they instead wanted to ascertain the path taken by the documents themselves, and whether their companion was a traitor. Antonino Bucolaro, without knowing anything about all this, was gradually falling into a trap.

* * *

One morning Matteo Lo Vecchio, passing by Antonino Bucolaro's house, saw a large crowd of people at his door; he went closer to make inquiries and learned that the algozini were there to seize the belongings of Bucolaro, who had not paid a tax that was levied on his house. Then he went in, taking advantage of this opportunity to render him some other favor, and was able to persuade his colleagues to call off their actions because there could be another way to settle things.

Bucolaro was crestfallen with shame and stood in a corner. Never before had such a thing happened to him! A series of financial disasters had befallen him, which had forced him to miss all his commitments, and even, why deny it, to suffer poverty. Now this invasion of algozini seemed to him like a public declaration of destitution that made him ashamed.

"Come on, cheer up!" Matteo Lo Vecchio said to him. "These things can even happen to a baron of the kingdom!"

And after a moment of silence he murmured, as if talking to himself, "And yet he has riches within his reach. . . . If he wants them!"

Antonino Bucolaro pulled himself together and looked at Matteo Lo Vecchio, who, however, said nothing, and the discussion for the time being ended there.

But those words crept into his mind and began to percolate: how were riches within his reach? And what should he have wanted? He thought about it all day.

The following morning the birro made sure they met; he asked Bucolaro how things were going, sighed with regret, and made a faint allusion to that wealth that could easily be acquired. Antonino Bucolaro was consumed with curiosity and at the same time felt his desire growing.

He said, "Well! If I knew how one becomes rich, I wouldn't be foolish enough to refuse!"

But that time the birro said nothing.

A few days later, Matteo Lo Vecchio went to the Perciata tavern and waited there for Antonino Bucolaro.

"I was thinking about you," he said, "and would like to talk to you."

"No, this doesn't seem to me the right place. . . . I will wait for you in an hour in the Church of the Annunziata near Porta Montalto. We'll be able to talk more freely in the cloister."

When they met under the portico that surrounded the small garden of the Church of the Annunziata, Matteo Lo Vecchio said, "Don Antonino, I know everything."

"What?"

"I know about everything that the Beati Paoli collected against the Duke of Motta."

Antonino Bucolaro gave a start and couldn't control a sudden feeling of amazement and fear. He tried to pretend: "I don't understand what you are talking about."

"It's a waste of time to pretend with me; you know the proverb that says '*fra greci e greci non si vende albagio*';[6] I know that Giuseppico, Peppa la Sarda, Andrea Lo Bianco, and Don Girolamo have given evidence, and I know who Emanuele is, the alleged nephew of Don Girolamo. . . . I also know the role that you have played. . . . And if you want to know more, I can tell you that I also know that the documents collected by the . . . society or tribunal, call it as you wish, were stolen."

Antonino Bucolaro was turning white, red, and yellow; he looked at the birro with ever-growing amazement and didn't know how to respond, because he didn't understand, nor could he explain to himself, how Matteo Lo Vecchio could know about all that.

The birro continued, "As you see, I have so much evidence in hand to be able, now or later, to arrest you and send you to the gallows, like Zi' Rosario and the sacristan of San Matteo. I didn't do it because I had a great fondness for you, and I will not do it. . . . But in exchange for my silence and for my generosity toward you, I ask that you join forces with me."

6 "there can be no agreement between two sly foxes."

Antonino Bucolaro made a gesture of disdain.

"Oh, don't be offended so quickly," continued the birro, "I don't propose that you become a spy and denounce your companions, who for that matter I know. I only offer you the opportunity to become rich; we will become rich . . . on the shoulders of the Duke of Motta. . . . Let me explain. We must get hold of those papers and sell them to the duke, who will pay half his patrimony for them . . . you can imagine!"

Antonino Bucolaro had become grim with disdain and repressed anger.

"Don Matteo," he answered, "if I didn't have any obligation to you, I wouldn't let you out of this convent. . . . You have the audacity to propose to me, to Nino Bucolaro, such a thing?"

"Well! And have I perhaps invited you to come to the captain of justice to denounce your comrades?"

"I have no comrades and I don't know who you are talking about."

The birro made a gesture of contempt.

"Do me the favor of letting go of these pretenses!"

"And if I had any, do you think that I would be capable of a betrayal?"

"Betrayal? Excuse me; where is the betrayal? This is about nothing except pieces of paper. . . . After all, you know what those papers contain, Don Girolamo knows, Andrea Lo Bianco knows, others know and certainly we can't erase it from their minds. Whether they have these papers or not is all the same. What they want to do, no one can stop them, but meanwhile with those pieces of paper we can become rich. Do you understand this word? Rich! To have loads of money, to have servants, carriages . . . to be able to live like the Duke of Motta, to have this lord in our hands . . . what more are you looking for? . . . Anything but fear of the algozini who come to take your belongings and throw you in the middle of the street!"

Antonino Bucolaro was silent; the wealth that flashed before his eyes made him dizzy. Repeating the birro's reasoning, he admitted that he wasn't saying anything strange. In fact, the Beati Paoli would be able to "work" against the duke even without those papers. On the other hand, hadn't they been robbed? Did they still possess them, perhaps?

A great sense of grief gripped his heart; he tried to resist again. "Let's end it with these discussions."

"As you wish. But I wanted to make you understand that I don't want to induce you to commit a betrayal. Imagine that the society no longer has those papers . . . what scruples would you need to make use of them if you should find them? . . . Answer."

Certainly, what scruples could he have? But where were the papers? Who had them? . . . If only he could find them!

"Then do you clearly see that I am right? Come on, Don Antonino, let's talk seriously! Certain scruples are foolish; they are not for a man like you."

"But who has those papers?" Don Antonino asked.

"What, who has them?"

"You know that they were stolen . . . you said so."

"Yes, I know, as you do . . . but didn't you get them back?"

"No, no."

"Then I know who has them; or rather I suppose."

"You?"

"Me, yes. You clearly understand that I know more than your group."

"You know who has them?"

"One of yours has them."

"One of ours?"

"Yes . . . but since you refuse the deal that I propose to you, it's useless to tell you the name."

Antonino Bucolaro was silent; swayed, influenced by the birro, he had answered in such a way that he had implicitly confessed what he had denied earlier, and he realized it now, too late to turn back. He regretted having denied it, he regretted letting himself be caught, he regretted everything, but above all, he regretted not knowing who had those documents.

Matteo Lo Vecchio, who was studying him, sighed and concluded, "Forgive me for disturbing you; pretend that we haven't seen each other. Goodbye, I am going upstairs to visit the Father Guardian, so let's leave separately. . . . *Arrivederci*."

He took a few steps toward the stairway to leave. Antonino Bucolaro roused himself—something quickly went through his mind.

"Don Matteo," he said, "wait a bit, don't leave so soon. For heaven's sake . . . come here, let's talk."

CHAPTER 11

The day following that unexpected reception among the Beati Paoli, Blasco got out of bed with a great and overwhelming sadness. Coriolano's reassuring words had not been able to dispel all his apprehensions; he did not doubt that the two women would be respected, but who could assuage the fear of those two poor women, of Violante? Ah, Violante! Violante! His heart was desperately crying out that name but he was powerless to run to her aid. Where was she? Where had they taken her? As much as he had tried to find out the place where the two women would be taken, he hadn't been able to pull a word out of Coriolano.

"Why do you want to know?" the Cavaliere della Floresta said to him. "You won't be able to do anything; besides, in time, not only will I tell you, but"—and here he smiled—"you will arrive like a liberator, and you will add another page to your novel."

Thus, Blasco had to chase away his pains and desires, but he couldn't stop his mind from thinking. What would he do? How would he spend the days of painful expectation? He couldn't go out, on account of the warrant that was hanging over his head; he would have gotten himself arrested and thrown in some dungeon, and now more than ever it was important for him to be free and to be his own master. Even what had been imposed on him was a kind of imprisonment, but at night he was free and could go out without fear, since justice was not vigilant nor so diligent as to make it dangerous to go out at night, other than having a few spies around. Blasco was counting on this certainty, to be able to take a stroll, until such time as Violante had been freed and placed in conditions where she was no longer exposed to dangers, and once he had sorted out every problem, he would be able to leave the kingdom in order to escape the warrant and to seek his destiny.

The following night, before the tolling of the bells for the dead, Blasco went to the Convent of San Francesco to look for Father Serafino da Montemaggiore. He had a great curiosity to know what the friar would be giving him on behalf of the good Father Bonaventura. Money, perhaps, which he needed and would come at the right moment. Anyway, it would be a new and tender memory for his spirit. He waited in the caretaker's lodge, where Father Serafino came to find him, dragging his feet. He was very old and had snow-white hair and unsteady legs.

Blasco kissed his hand and introduced himself. "I have been to Caccamo, where I closed the eyes of my good Father Bonaventura, and here I am with you. . . . Your Fatherhood has something to return to me, Father Bonaventura told me."

"Yes . . . it's true. And if you hadn't rushed here, who knows if I could have carried out Father Bonaventura's assignment? I am eighty-seven years old, my son, and death is already knocking at my door. . . . Yes, I really have something to tell you! . . . Poor Father Bonaventura! He was my penitent. A holy man, truly a holy man! . . . *Requiescat in pace.* Wait for me a little while, my son, I have to go up to my cell. I wasn't expecting your visit. . . . Poor Father Bonaventura! It was a blow to him . . . he was so attached to the convent! It was a blow! But . . ."

He left the caretaker's lodge repeating those words, in the persistent manner of the elderly. Blasco crossed his hands over his chest and buried himself in his memories. When he was a young boy and evening came upon him in the caretaker's lodge or in the church, lost in the shadows, surrounded by images that gloomily stood out from the paintings, he felt a sort of religious terror, a sense of the infinite. Now, he was seeing almost the same paintings, the same straw-seated chairs, the same lamp, and he thought about his childhood, which seemed to him so distant, so different, like something that had never existed. He hadn't known what sadness was then because he had never questioned the innermost recesses of his own heart; he was bold, daring, loud, ready to fight; he always returned to the convent with some tears on his breeches or on his waistcoat. Father Giovanni used to scold him, and he would laugh it off. Where were his friends from those days? Where was his dog, the good Lampo, who had saved him from the wolf? Where was the tender Elisabetta, who in the escape from Tunis had offered her breast in order to save him from the aggressions of the Saracens? Everyone dead, everyone dead! . . . Memories, names, and nothing else. Nothing else? Oh, no; they still lived in the painful regret that filled his heart.

He heard the dragging footsteps of Father Serafino, who reentered the caretaker's lodge with a small sack in his hand.

"Some money!" thought Blasco bitterly. Perhaps he would have desired something more spiritual and more precious. Father Serafino sat down, placed the small sack on his knees, and took out a slightly crumpled letter, very carefully sealed.

"This is a letter for you," he said, "and inside here are forty onze, which I have orders to give you. Here they are, each one is double. . . . Twenty pieces of gold."

Blasco was looking at the letter more than at the money, with a dark premonition that it contained something that would be of great interest to him. He took and kept everything and, taking leave of the father, he returned home in order to read the letter at his leisure. When he closed himself in his room, by the light of a two-burner oil lamp, he broke the seals with a trembling hand, but as soon as he unfolded the paper, another piece of yellowed and folded paper fell on the table.

He picked it up, read it, and cried out in surprise. The paper said in primitive parochial Latin:

I.M.J.

Fidem facio, die vigesimo mensis novembris a D. MDCLXXXVIII in hac ecclesia metropolitana baptizzatum esse infantum, cui positum nomen Blascus, filius ill.mi magnifici domini Emanuelis Albimontis ducis Mottae, et Cristinae Giurlandae. Padroni m. Agostinus et Maria Magdalena Russus, coniuges.

D. Joseph Cutellius parochus.

I certify that on the twentieth day of November, 1888, in this church in the capital city, an infant was born, to whom the name Blasco was given, the son of my noble Lord Emanuele Albamonte, Duke of Motta, and Cristina Giorlanda. Agostinus and Maria Magdalena Russes, spouses.

D. Jospeh Cutellis, pastor.

Next to the signature was the stamp of the parish, dry-stamped on a small scrap of paper glued with a host onto the paper.

Blasco stayed a while with that paper in his hands, immobile like a statue under the weight of that revelation. An Albamonte! . . . He was an Albamonte! He was the bastard son of Don Emanuele of Motta; and little Emanuele, who was lying in the dungeons of Castellammare, was his half brother, and Violante was his cousin! . . . It seemed to him like something out of the ordinary, a jumble of ideas, of feelings that put him in a state of utter confusion.

"Me!" he exclaimed shortly after. "Me!"

He was speechless. He put the parish document on the table and glanced at the signature on the letters: it was signed "Fra Bonaventura da Licodia." It wasn't long; after the invocation wording, consistent with the three initials *I.M.J.*, that is, *Jesus, Mary, Joseph*, the friar wrote:

My dear son in Jesus Christ, Blasco,

Before leaving this convent, by the will of God, I leave to Father Serafino da Montemaggiore your birth certificate, in order for him to give it to you upon my death, which I expect is near. I do not want to go to the grave with a secret, which I have kept until now out of consideration toward powerful people that you know; but it is not right to bury it with me. I do not know if it can be useful to you; I hope so, and I pray, and I will pray to God to hold his blessed hands over you.

Father Serafino will also give you some money. It is all that I have. I have no relatives; I leave it to you, whom I have cared for like a son, albeit for a short time. Pray to our Lord for me, and always be a good Christian, according to the precepts of Our Holy Mother Church. I bless you in the name of blessed Jesus.

Blasco's eyes filled with tears; a flood of memories, feelings, and affections descended into his soul and seized him with emotion. His mother had died with broken legs, in a house not her own, picked up by the mercy of two friars, on top of the ruins of a city; Father Giovanni, the convent in Catania, his childhood, his escape through the mountains. Oh, Mother! Poor Mother!

Then the portrait he had seen in Don Raimondo's house appeared to him— the portrait of Don Emanuele in front of which he had stopped, struck by its resemblance to him. So, he was the living image of his father, his own origins were imprinted on his face; since the laws didn't recognize his right to bear the name of Albamonte, nature had sealed it on his face with indelible features. And not only did he resemble his father in his features; even his adventurous character, courage, daring, gaiety, and valor came from him. But from his mother, from that poor sweet being, he had taken that good-hearted nature, that vague desire for serene affections, sweet abandonments, that sense of near modesty, and of kindness that lent a special tone and character to his love.

And he thought of Emanuele, who was his brother; he was his younger brother and according to the law, he, Blasco, was, or should have been, the head of the household, because the dishonor of illegitimacy didn't weigh on his birth. But Emanuele was his brother and the wickedness of a villain was torturing him in the dark depths of a prison, and that villain was his uncle: the lean, pale man with a mouth as thin as a line, his face an impenetrable mask. He was wicked, cruel, capable of any crime, and at the same time despicable and contemptible; that man was the brother of that duke who did not begrudge his adversaries and confronted them openly, and he was the father of the sweetest and most gentle being that he had ever known!

"What will I do now?" he wondered. "What will I do, now that I know who I am?"

And what could he and what would it be in his power to do? His life was already mapped out, and it would not be different from what it had been. He would always be Blasco da Castiglione, a man from the shadows, without a home, without relatives, beginning and ending with himself. An ironic smile came across his face; oh, that useless revelation was worth it! What use was it to him? What had the good Father Bonaventura hoped for? He was in that frame of mind when he heard knocking at the door and the voice of Coriolano say, "Are you in bed? May I come in?"

He went to open the door for him.

"I am not in bed," he said with that peculiar tone one's voice has when the spirit is ignited by some passion. "Come in. You cannot imagine what is happening to me. . . . I went to Father Serafino and I came back with a sum of money and a name. Do you understand? I have a name that I don't need and money that didn't come from my father but from the charity of a friar."

Coriolano looked at him in amazement.

"Are you surprised?" Blasco continued with a slight exhilaration. "Well, I will astound you! . . . Do you know who I am? I am an Albamonte; I am the first-born son, so I presume, however illegitimate, of the deceased Don Emanuele Albamonte, Duke of Motta . . . . Well, goodness! . . . Now that I know that, now that I know the name of someone who took a young girl away from the modest protection of her modest home in order to make her his lover, and to make her the mother of his son without a legal name, don't you think that I have added another golden storyline to my life? . . . You who are so righteous, tell me something: Do you think that the bastard of a king is something more or less than the bastard of a mule driver? Do you believe the disgrace that weighs on the birth of one is different from that which weighs on the birth of another; that the anguish of the two mothers before their cradle without a name is different? . . . Ah! I am an Albamonte! Fancy that, if in my situation one could enjoy a greater happiness than this discovery! . . . For now on I will be able to have painted on my carriage, when I have one, the red-and-green quartered shield with green and black alternating bands . . . but with the mark of the bastard!"

Coriolano was silent.

Blasco walked around the room for a while, and his eyes fell on the parish document that he had put down on the table, pointing it out to his friend, resuming: "There is the piece of paper that consecrates my origin, Coriolano; there is my certificate of nobility, which was not enough to save my mother, I do not mean from death, but at least from poverty. The Castello della Motta opened up to let in the kidnapped educanda, welcomed my first cry, but kicked out the mother and her son when it was known that Francesco Giorlanda had died of a broken heart. Look at the odd destiny that unites the two sons of Don Emanuele of Motta, the illegitimate one and the lawful one; both of them were collected by an act of charity from the breasts of their dying mothers, never enjoyed their maternal smiles or care, never knew their paternal home, and grew up unaware of their own origins; both haunted by the same hatred, victims of arbitrary acts; both driven, not knowing each other, onto the same path . . . one fate! Oh! Truly, this is where I identify myself as an Albamonte. This, Coriolano, is the legacy left to us by our father, in equal parts, without a testament.

He sat down, pale and trembling, although his lips were smiling—but it was a bitter and painful smile, and after a minute of silence, he murmured, "It is unfortunate that the duke, my procreator, is dead! . . . But perhaps he was already punished; is not what happened to the Duchess Donna Aloisia and little Emanuele perhaps revenge for what Cristina Giorlanda and her child suffered?"

He again fell into silence. Coriolano was silent as well, as if oppressed by that revelation, and even more by the intimate pain that he read into Blasco's words.

Blasco got up, shook his handsome and proud head with a motion that made the long curls of his hair wave, and he laughed. "Goodness! . . . I believe I got too worked up; it's nothing, my friend! Life doesn't deserve to be taken so seriously. . . . Look here, I remember your wonderful speech of the other evening, that was the glorification of your work! Poetry! My dear friend, poetry. Do you want to rectify abuses, demolish injustices, render justice for everyone? . . . Do you also want to extend your protection over me? . . . Poetry! Poetry! . . . Come on, rectify this injustice that makes me, firstborn son of Don Emanuele Albamonte, Duke of Motta, a stranger in the house to which I belong by blood, an almost shameful being, marked by an infamy committed by another. . . . Life? It's a funny thing. Justice? It's a tragic mask on the face of a fool."

"And then why are you so eager and even audacious when you think that someone wants to commit an act of violence against someone else. . . . Why do you rebel against what you think are abuses and injustices at the expense of the weak?" asked Coriolano gravely. "You have beaten the servants of the Duke of Motta . . . your uncle, because they were about to do in Emanuele; you have jeopardized your freedom by keeping Girolamo Ammirata from being arrested; you have risked your life in order to hand back to Matteo Lo Vecchio the saddlebag stolen by the soldiers; finally, you have rescued—and you knew how to—Violante from our clutches, because you believed that violence would be used against her. . . . You see, then, that your generous heart beats to defend justice, or what seems like justice to you!"

"I am an idiot, Coriolano! . . . I am an idiot who lets himself be carried away by impulses. . . . Ah! Violante, poor innocent young girl! . . . Well, rather consider this, you, Coriolano: your justice doesn't exist without injustices, and Violante is the example of it . . . but what are we talking about? You arouse thoughts and sorrows that I have pushed to the back of my mind, and it is not the time . . . it is the time to laugh, dear friend, to laugh at this mockery that is life. Let's go. Is there anything to fight about? Do you have some job to carry out? Is there the chance to get run through? Here I am. I need to do something, to split someone's head open or to have my own head split open. . . . Laugh! Not for nothing am I the son of Don Emanuele della Motta!"

He took his sword and hat; Coriolano got up and followed him. It was about nine o'clock and the streets were deserted, except for the usual groups of poor wretches who were sleeping behind the doors and on the steps of the churches.

They came out onto Via Toledo[1] and went down toward Porta Felice. From time to time a stately carriage would pass loudly by, preceded by volanti who were shaking their windproof torches. It seemed like the chariot of the god of thunder surrounded by lightning; then, once the last glow and the last echo died out, the street would again fall into silence and darkness.

Blasco and Coriolano weren't speaking; each one seemed to be following the path of his own thoughts.

At that hour patrols were hardly seen, and besides, they didn't stop gentlemen, or if they did stop them, it was enough for them to give their name for the patrol leader to humbly take off his hat. They reached Piazza Marina in the middle of which, in the shadow, the black beams of the mournful gallows were outlined. They saw with horror a human form hanging from a noose, turning on itself in the gust of the wind. In the afternoon a petty thief had been hanged and left on the gallows as an example. He wouldn't be taken down until the following morning.

At the end of the piazza the Palazzo del Sant'Offizio stood, grim and austere; it was the ancient and truly regal residence of the Chiaramonte family, no longer a residence of magnificence and graciousness but a dark cavern of torments and sufferings.

While Blasco and Coriolano were crossing the piazza, the clock, which had marred the face of the beautiful palazzo,[2] sounded the hours, and in the silence and in those sorrowful surroundings, the knells sounded like desperate moans of agony.

"Come, let's go this way," said Coriolano.

They entered the dark vicolo that ran along the palazzo; Coriolano raised his finger, pointing to the top of the building, and said, "Do you see those windows? On that side they are the Filippine. You don't know what they are, do you? They are the most cramped and most horrible prisons in Sant'Offizio and were built at the time of Philip III, in order to lock up those guilty of treachery. Now those on whom the cruelty of the tribunal shows the least mercy are left to languish there . . . and locked up there is a woman who is guilty of having carried out an act of charity. What would you say and what would you do, Blasco, if they had taken Brother Giovanni da Randazzo and Brother Bonaventura da Licodia and had thrown them inside there, to die of privations, miseries, torture, for having saved you from death?"

Blasco looked up in horror and clenched his fists; that hypothesis summoned up all the anger and revenge in his soul.

"Let's go," said Coriolano. "Sometimes, in the depths of the silent night, long, drawn-out moans emerge from those windows, the moans of people who are dying a thousand deaths."

1 The Cassaro was also called Via Toledo—in memory of its extension which took place in 1568 during the viceroyalty of García del Toledo Osorio. RLD, 790.
2 Refers to the dimensions of the clock, which the poet Giovanni Meli, in the poem *La Fata Galante*, compared to that of the eye of the cyclops. RLD 790.

They walked along the vicolo, emerged in front of the Church of San Nicolò della Kalsa, and, since Porta Felice was open, they went out through there. Coriolano turned left, going up along the Cala, the old port defended by La Garita, and the Castello, full of galleys and ships of light tonnage, whose burning lanterns were reflected in long, moving red zigzags in the waters of the harbor. They went along the entire bend of the Cala, to the Church of Santa Maria di Piedigrotta. The Castello projected out, spiked with cannons whose mouths appeared among the battlements. The sea was pounding against the ancient Saracen walls, flowing into the moats that encircled the castle, and passing under the bridge. A few soldiers walked on the ramparts with harquebuses on their shoulders. Coriolano stopped, and here he pointed again, toward the door that had been blocked off by the raised drawbridge.

"And there, in a dungeon, your brother Emanuele is imprisoned! Let's go, Blasco."

He nearly dragged him along Via San Sebastiano.

Blasco said, "Why haven't you tried to help these prisoners escape?"

"Because their cells don't have exterior windows."

"Still," resumed Blasco, "it should be attempted. . . . Perhaps it would be the quickest solution."

"But not the safest. Instead we must hasten the day of justice."

Blasco thought about those two ghastly prisons and felt a shiver of horror and at the same time a feeling of shame. What had he been complaining about? What was his misfortune compared to the greater one of Emanuele, his brother? He, after all, neither had nor could claim rights before society; Emanuele did, and yet they had been taken away from him and denied. He was alone and no one was suffering for him; but Emanuele had an adopted and now absent family, tortured because of him . . . there were three victims. Three? And weren't Violante, and to some extent Donna Gabriella, subject to the same fate that had struck the others?

"Ah, Don Raimondo! . . . Don Raimondo!"

He felt his chest, as if to reassure himself that the famous packet of letters was still there, and he touched it, under his shirt. He thought that perhaps the steps of the Beati Paoli had been stopped after the loss of those papers and that such a loss had forced them to seize Violante and Gabriella; perhaps he could have agreed to hand over those papers in exchange for the freedom and the life of Violante. At that moment it seemed to him like such a good idea that he was truly on the verge of pulling out the papers and giving them to Coriolano, saying, "Take them, here is your evidence; use it to free Emanuele and the wife of Ammirata, and send Violante to me!"

But his hand remained on the front of his shirt, stopped by a doubt: "And what if Violante still remained a prisoner as a pawn, despite the return of these documents?"

And then another thought: "And what if Coriolano delivered these documents to the viceroy?"

Coriolano's voice roused him. As if he had sensed that interior battle, the Cavaliere della Floresta said seriously, "Think, Blasco, that although you are illegitimate, you are also the elder brother of Emanuele and you owe him protection and assistance."

Elder brother! Yes, it was true. But he had only seen the boy on two occasions: the first time he had seen him rise up toward him like a threatening rooster, and the second time he had seen him arrogant and almost annoyed at his intervention. Now thinking back on it, he seemed to discern in that attitude one of those instinctive, indomitable dislikes. As for himself, questioning his own heart, he didn't find any trace of fraternal emotion. The boy aroused his pity and stirred up unselfish impulses neither more nor less than any other boy not bound to him by blood ties. These ties held no meaning for Blasco; for him they were names of feelings, not true feelings, but all that did not diminish this obligation. Their common misfortune rather made it seem to him even more urgent and incumbent.

He remembered having promised Coriolano that he would force Don Raimondo to free the two prisoners. When he had made this promise, Don Raimondo was unrelated to him; now instead he was his uncle, but this discovery, instead of encouraging him, dismayed him. As an uncle, Don Raimondo filled him with an irrepressible feeling of disgust, as would a revolting reptile.

Thus, passing from one idea to another, Blasco walked in silence next to Coriolano. They returned to the Cassaro and were going up it again. Coriolano, as if responding to a thought, said, "Emanuele must not only be set free soon but also reinstated to his rank and patrimony; he must take care of you, he must recognize you and provide for your status."

"Me? Ah, no, Coriolano, you are mistaken. He has no obligation toward me, and I would never accept charity from the House of Albamonte."

"What? Why do you say this?" exclaimed the Cavaliere della Floresta in amazement.

"Everyone has his pride; I have mine. My father made me poor and a 'nobody,' nor did he ever remember having abandoned a poor pregnant woman. Whatever my parish certificate says, I will remain poor and a 'nobody' as I have been for twenty-six years. Emanuele will never know that I am his brother—at least he will not learn about it from me. When I have fulfilled my obligation to help you enact justice, I will leave, I will go far away, and I will belatedly resume my life as a wandering cavaliere until a bullet sends me to another world."

Coriolano looked at him, smiling, and, playfully but with intent, asked him: "And Violante?"

"Violante?" Blasco answered in a voice that betrayed a bitter emotion. "Eh! . . . Once I have peace of mind about her future, what do you want me to do? And what do you think I mean to her? I am just a memory that the kisses of another man will erase from her heart."

And all the way home, they said nothing more.

CHAPTER 12

Donna Gabriella and Violante spent their days in expectation of an unknown event that never arrived. They had asked for the name of the place where they had been taken, but the old woman servant had replied brusquely, sticking her lip out in a distinctive way: "What do I know?" And no one knew. It was clear that a strict order had been given that the two women must not know where they were. However, Donna Gabriella had tried to take notice of the surrounding area, straining to at least recognize that mountaintop and to have a sense of the surrounding countryside.

She was in a castle whose high walls seemed insurmountable and that moreover stood on top of a bluff so high and steep that it made one dizzy to look out from certain windows. Scrublands spread out below, amid which a silver strip twisted and turned. On one side and the other there were hills after hills, and beyond the hills mountain ranges seemed to be painted on a theatrical backdrop, one behind the other in more cerulean and increasingly pale colors.

There was no visible trace of a nearby village, yet when the air was clear and the wind was blowing, the echo of a distant bell reached the castle. Therefore, there had to be some villages in the vicinity, some baronial lands hidden amid the woods.

She had been able to observe that part of the castle was uninhabitable; some rooms had no roofs, the merlons and part of the tops of some towers were crumbling, here and there the curtain walls showed cracks. The part where they were staying was formed by the castle keep, that is, by the main tower, a solid four-sided fortress that towered above the entire edifice and stood at the end of the still well-preserved courtyard.

It wasn't possible to go beyond the courtyard and enter the other wings of the castle. The doors were locked and bolted, some even walled up; evidently, they wanted to prevent Donna Gabriella or anyone else from going beyond the courtyard and the tower. There were stables in the courtyard, but they sheltered only the two mules and three horses. There were no servants other than the neat and well-mannered little old woman, a kind of steward, and two peasants who struggled to fulfill the duties of valets, grooms, and pages. Every night one of them would sleep behind the door to the women's room with a rifle between his legs.

Apart from these limitations, Donna Gabriella and Violante couldn't complain about how they were looked after and served. Their dressing room lacked nothing that a lady would need, revealing the provident and wise hand of a person accustomed to the comforts and refinements of elegant wardrobes. Violante had been amazed to see a whole battery of curling irons to wave, curl, and crimp her hair; there were small scissors, combs, jars of hair cream, majolica jars for hair dyes, powders, and fragrant waters—things she had had no concept of in the monastery.

The wardrobe was stocked with dressing gowns, bathrobes, and embroidered slippers; the two small beds and the table had fine linens; the cutlery and tableware for the table were made of silver. Donna Gabriella could truly believe that she was on one of her holidays among her vassals.

The first shock, that sense of terror that had gripped her as much as Violante, had gradually vanished; they now wondered when their captivity, which was isolating them from the world, would end. The solitude and the silence of the servants had forced Donna Gabriella to look to her stepdaughter for companionship, not that she had any feelings of benevolence or sympathy for her. On the contrary, every time she caught the pensive young girl's eyes roaming the countryside, a thought, a name, would rush into her head, and her eyes would darken and flash in anger. She was sure that Violante was thinking of Blasco. And it was true.

Ever since her stepmother's words had lit up her heart, Violante had lost that sweet foolhardiness that had made the dawn of her youth pass happily by. But this light, penetrating into her still dormant world of feelings and instincts, had awakened them, and they were stirring confusedly, upsetting her with vague desires that at times would drive her to tears.

Blasco's image was before her eyes and she felt a sense of pleasure that she couldn't express, but sometimes sudden flames of desire would rise to her face and she would feel her eyes burning. She now knew that she loved Blasco. She believed that love was all in that incessant thought, in that indefinable mystery, that made her want to see him, to hear him, to be next to him. And this seemed like such an audacious thing to her that she was aroused by it and ashamed of it.

"Oh, yes, it is true," she thought often, "I love him, I love him."

But suddenly a sense of fear would grip her. She would see Donna Gabriella's wrathful stare over her, and she would feel faint.

"Why?" she would think. "Why does she look at me like that? What harm did I do to her?"

One day, a very nervous Donna Gabriella said to her, "Are you thinking about him?"

A lie rose to her lips; she wanted to answer no, but she wasn't accustomed to lying and so she remained silent, except that her crimson face and embarrassed look answered for her. This revelation filled Donna Gabriella's heart with a bitterness full of suppressed anger, and it renewed that resentment and that longing for reprisals and retaliations against her stepdaughter that the distress of the abduction had caused to subside.

And from that day on she began to be more bitter, more tormented in all those moments when it was essential for her to be in contact with Violante, feeling a fierce satisfaction in needling her about Blasco and in denigrating him.

"What are you expecting?" she said once. "What are you expecting? To marry him? It will never happen as long as I am alive, and if I am to die soon, your father will not be so foolish as to consent to it, I swear to you."

It was another idea, an idea that hadn't yet revealed itself, that Donna Gabriella threw into the heart of the young girl and added new anxieties. To get married? To be with Blasco always, alone in another house, without arousing suspicion? This idea overwhelmed her, frightened her and at the same time filled her heart with joy. Before then she had never thought of marriage; now it seemed to her like the most natural path that she should pursue, since she loved Blasco. But it also made her anxious, due to that instinctive fear of a mysterious and terrifying unknown, whose distant vibrations she could barely feel.

Another time Donna Gabriella said to her, "Shame on you! To think of these obscenities at your age!"

What? What obscenities was she talking about? To love a man, to marry, was a shameful thing, then? But why? Many of her schoolmates had left the monastery in order to get married, and she had often heard about the great wedding parties celebrated by the families of her schoolmates—parties that were sources of exultation even for the city and for which sonnets would even be printed. And never from anyone, not even from sister Maria Cristina, who had a formidable hatred for the outside world, had Violante heard such a horrific judgment.

"Such a great marriage with an adventurer, escaped from the gallows! Don't you know, then, that justice is looking for him because he is a criminal? Don't you know that he killed a few guards, and that in Messina he even killed three royal guards? Who knows how many murders and robberies he has committed! . . . Who is he? Where did he come from? . . . No one knows. He is not of our class . . . he's probably some peasants' son, a runaway! The gallows await him. After they have hanged him, they will quarter him and hang him from the Sperone.[1] Then I will take you to see the four pieces of Signor Blasco da Castiglione!"

Violante turned pale and closed her eyes, letting out a cry of horror and pain at the vision of the bloody remains hanging from the gallows of the Sperone—

---

1 Sperone is located along the Romagnolo coast, southeast of Palermo; it takes its name from the use of the *sperone* (a stone pyramid) in the 1700s, where the quartered bodies of the executed were hung on iron hooks. The gruesome spectacle served as a warning and aroused terror. Because the disturbing sight annoyed the nobles who were going on holiday to Bagheria, the stone was demolished in 1788. AC, 425.

a spectacle of cruelty, revulsion, and terror, not infrequent in those days. Then she wondered if what her stepmother was saying was true, but her heart was telling her no, filling her with repugnance for thinking that a man so good, so generous, so loyal, so brave, could be an adventurer, a criminal, worthy of dying on the gallows.

But meanwhile, suspicion, doubt, and fear had entered her soul.

So the poor young girl spent those days pining away, and Donna Gabriella would torment herself, she too becoming pale and sad. The days passed, one after the other, without any news, always the same, amid the same stabs of pain, the same resentments. Sometimes, when her nerves got the better of her, she lashed out at Don Raimondo and at Violante.

"Everything is your father's fault! . . . Your father is a villain, and I am suffering because of him. What do I have to do with the villainies that he committed? Why don't they settle them with him and with you? . . . Oh, how I would like to take revenge! How I would like to take revenge!"

Violante rebelled; she couldn't bear to hear her father, whom she didn't suspect and whom she believed to be irreproachable, insulted.

"Why, Signora Madre, do you also offend my father? What did he do to you? He is still your husband!"

"Be quiet, you have no right to speak. You are of the same breed. A nest of vipers! . . . Your father? . . . I know what he is worth!"

Her invectives against Blasco, against Don Raimondo, against Violante, would grow harsher and more bitter when her captivity, preventing any whim or desire, seemed to her to become more oppressive and unbearable. What made it even more unbearable for her was not knowing exactly when it would end, or what precisely was expected from her. She had questioned the old woman many times but hadn't been able to get an explanation out of her.

She had asked her name, and the woman had answered with reverence, "Nora, to serve you; I am Zia Nora, the mother of Baldassare, the stucco artist."

"Are you here to serve?"

"To serve Your Excellency."

Her answer was ambiguous.

"Who is your master?"

"But, Your Excellency, why do you think I should have a master?"

Donna Gabriella could not get anything else out of her.

Another time she asked her, "Who is expected to come here?"

She at least wanted to know if anyone was expected in the castle, in order to have the keys to the mystery that surrounded not so much her capture as her stay in this unknown, isolated place, cut off from the world. But Zia Nora replied evasively, "The grace of God!"

"Will we be here for a long time?"

"As long as God wishes!"

They were answers that would have made even the calmest person despair. Donna Gabriella felt she could burst; the reserved, impenetrable manner of the old woman, who seemed to have been molded by a secret God, ignited a thousand angers in her and at times gave her the urge to strike her.

About forty days passed like this. Winter was approaching, and cold winds were blowing over that hill; during the evening it was miserable in the rooms. The prospect of spending the winter in that small castle was truly frightening. Donna Gabriella couldn't help but think that this was the season of receptions, of balls where other women were enjoying themselves, surrounded by suitors, enthroned in those little Olympian places that were the halls of grand, elegant palazzi sparkling with mirrors and lights. And then her eyes would fill with tears of sorrow and rage, and in an uncontrollable impulse she would shake her stepdaughter by the hair, screaming, "I wish you were dead, you and your father!"

Her dismay grew when one morning she saw one of the peasants come in with a chest, from which Zia Nora took out some heavy blankets and cloaks. This was a sure sign that her captivity wouldn't end so soon, and she felt such a burning sensation that she struck her temples desperately. Violante, however, didn't seem so desperate; rather, her face lit up with a certain joy.

Entering Violante's room in order to put blankets on her bed, Zia Nora said to her, "I have a message for Your Excellency."

"For me?"

"Hush! . . . It's something that no one must know about."

Violante blushed and looked at her with curious expectation.

"Signor Blasco sends a greeting and says that in a few days . . . but hush!"

Violante could neither thank her nor express any word of hope. Just upon hearing the name of the young man, her heart began to beat so violently that she lost her breath, and her face burned with such a flame that her eyes seemed to dry up. Blasco! Then Blasco knew where she was, and he would come to see her. Perhaps to free her.

Blasco was thinking of her, then. . . . Was it not perhaps because he loved her too? From her heart, from what she was feeling and experiencing, she was sensing and considering what the young man's feelings for her could be, and this thought, while making her face glow, gave her an extraordinary joy she had never before felt, a comfort full of tenderness. It seemed to her that she was no longer alone, that she had a protector, that she was safe. Blasco would take her away from this prison and rescue her from her stepmother's persecutions. She now proudly rejected all of Donna Gabriella's insinuations against the young man; they were false accusations. She would ask Blasco if what the duchess had told her was true. Hadn't she once even made up a story that Blasco had been murdered? And why the spiteful envy? Why the persistence? All these questions crowded into the young girl's mind and persisted there; she addressed them, lingered over them, and tried to penetrate their innermost reasons. Was it hatred? Perhaps. But this hatred, which was directed at her and Blasco equally, they who were not guilty of anything against the duchess—it must have been born from something that still escaped the young girl, inexperienced as she was in the ways of the world, unaware that there could be illicit loves and in fact unacquainted with the great mystery of love.

And yet a type of suspicious fear entered her heart, which painted her stepmother in a poor light. She trembled; her instinct prompted her to conceal her joy. For the first time, Violante was pretending, and this pretense that shielded her joy gave her some satisfaction, as if she had carried out a retaliation or obtained a victory over her stepmother.

But Donna Gabriella had the questioning and astute eye that her jealousy provided; underneath Violante's pretense, she detected that something new had entered the girl's heart.

She began to goad her in order to discover it. "How many days have passed that we have been locked up here thanks to your father?"

"Is it perhaps my father who ordered it?"

"Keep your opinions to yourself; you are not allowed. . . . I know what I am saying. If your father hadn't committed some villainy I wouldn't be here."

She kept returning to this subject that she knew Violante wouldn't like, but the young girl was silent. She had resolved not to respond to any provocation and understood that the duchess had wanted to bring everything up again. Donna Gabriella was expecting an act of rebellion and was astonished at the young girl's silence.

"Aren't you going to answer?" she said.

"I don't know what to say, Signora Madre."

"Eh! Of course you don't know what to say; you are of the same blood. . . . But I don't want to endure this life, do you understand? They can keep you here because you are his daughter, and I don't care; in any case, you will come to a bad end. But they should let me go!"

Violante was silent; an imperceptible smile formed at the corners of her mouth. Keep her! . . . But instead it was she, she herself, who had the certainty of getting out of this prison soon. Donna Gabriella was beginning to find the young girl's silence provocative, and her nerves were starting to quiver, to tense, to cloud her mind. She felt some suppressed passions that urged her to cry, to pull out her hair. She was filled with bitterness. She had a seizure, burst into true sobs that seemed to tear her chest apart. Violante was dismayed and at the same time she was touched. She had never seen the duchess cry, and these desperate sobs aroused her pity.

She clasped her hands, shouting, "Signora Madre! Signora Madre! Whatever can it be?" She moved closer, asking her, "Is it perhaps my fault that you are crying? Did I make you cry? . . . If so, I ask you to forgive me!"

She timidly attempted to take her hand, but on being touched, Donna Gabriella let out a cry as if she had been bitten by a snake.

"Move back . . . move back . . . don't touch me! . . . I don't want to be touched by you! By you! . . . You are hateful to me!"

Violante drew back a step, looking at her in sorrowful astonishment.

"But what have I done to you, in order to be hateful to you?" she asked tenderly, still under the stimulus of her emotions.

"You are asking me?" the duchess exclaimed in a rage. "You are asking me?"

Her voice screeched like rusted metal. Her entire appearance took on an expression of violence and suffering that seemed to reflect a myriad of different and terrifying emotions. In her eyes was a ferocious sarcasm that made Violante shudder.

She said nothing more to her, except, "Get out of here! Leave me alone!"

Violante left in silence and retired to her bedroom; Zia Nora, who seemed to be waiting for her in the corridor, accompanied her to her room, and as she was closing the door, she said to the young girl, "Do not be afraid, Your Excellency . . . do not be afraid. We are here."

Violante looked at her in astonishment. Had the little old woman seen and heard everything? And what did she know, or what had she understood, to reassure her like that?

CHAPTER 13

A ntonino Bucolaro hadn't been able to sleep all night, thinking about those documents, whose contents, moreover, he had never known about until then. He was one of the most active members of the Beati Paoli but had not yet reached the highest ranks, that is, of judges, to whom nothing was secret except the face of the supreme leader, known only to Don Girolamo Ammirata, who was the secretary general and therefore the director of the sect. The other twenty judges, who discussed the complaints and deliberated over them, were chosen after an apprenticeship in which they proved themselves worthy, and when there was a vacancy.

Bucolaro had been initiated by Don Girolamo Ammirata after having befriended him through business connections. He had been in for a few years and had become known for his zeal and hard work; he had first been "executor," then "reporter." Don Girolamo was fond of him, had placed his trust in him, and had chosen him as his confidant. The reporters knew the executors; they were the ones who received the complaints and claims or who verified the information; they directed the initial acts and submitted everything to the secretary and were often called upon to provide verbal explanations to the twenty members of the high tribunal, who nevertheless kept their faces masked.

On quite a number of occasions, Don Girolamo had put Bucolaro to the test and had praised him. He thought he had made a good addition to the sect and often talked about it with Coriolano, with whom he at first would meet in the morning in San Matteo. Now that a warrant had been issued against him, they would see each other at night in a secluded cottage outside Porta d'Ossuna, that same place where Blasco had been taken after he was wounded by the Prince of Iraci's hired killers.

Antonino Bucolaro knew where Ammirata was hiding; he was the only one who knew about it, and he was the means of communication between Ammirata and the executors. Every morning at dawn, he would take his musket, call his dog, and go hunting near the Oreto River, which at the time was teeming with wild ducks. This he did outwardly; in reality, when he was sure that no one was paying attention to him any longer, he would take the paths and head toward San Ciro; in front of a house at the foot of the hills, he would find Don Girolamo and

Andrea waiting for him with muskets between their legs. Antonino would report all the events of the day, receive orders for the secretary, communicate them to the other reporters, and if there was some task to be carried out, he would inform the society of the need to hold special meetings by a simple method: a banditore, followed by a boy who sometimes carried bread, other times macaroni, would walk along the streets announcing that in the pasta shop in the Capo and in the bread bakery near Sant'Agostino very good quality macaroni was being sold at a certain price per *rotolo*[1] or that the price of bread of good weight, as prescribed by law, had been lowered by a terdenari per rotolo. Those two shops were known to the members, who would go there under the pretext of making a purchase and would give a quick and indifferent glance around the shop. If they saw three lamps lit in front of three sacred images—the Virgin crushing the serpent; saints Peter and Paul with their emblems; Saint Michael the Archangel with his scales in one hand and his flaming sword in the other—that was the sign that at midnight that day there would be a meeting in the cave. Other than the members, no one could grasp its meaning at a time when the shops were full of images and lamps. When there were two lamps, one in front of the Immaculate Virgin and the other in front of saints Peter and Paul, the meeting was restricted to the reporters; the executors didn't know what that sign meant. When instead only one lamp was lit in front of Saint Michael the Archangel, the meeting was for the high tribunal, and neither executors nor reporters understood that sign. The bread baker and the pasta seller were two of the twenty judges. The banditore, of course, was unaware that he was an instrument of the Beati Paoli, and he made his announcements in good faith.

Another very simple method was the one resorted to by the executors or reporters if they needed to confer with one of their immediate superiors—so that the executors communicated only with the reporters, the reporters with the judges, and the judges with Don Girolamo Ammirata, who, moreover, knew everyone in his capacity as secretary and director.

Before the sacristan of San Matteo was arrested, that church was the premises for the complaints. A member would throw something in the collection box, located next to the door of the church. The sacristan, after closing the church, would open the box; if he found a terdenari with a hole in the middle and some dents, it meant that a reporter of that neighborhood wanted to confer with one of the judges of his own neighborhood; if there was no hole but only dents, he was an executor who needed to talk with reporters of his own neighborhood. The dents were between one and six; there were six districts, four within Palermo and two rural ones, and each one had a number, corresponding to the number of dents. The Capo, where the cave was located, was indicated by the number one. The sacristan would bring the coins to Zi' Rosario, who then would give them to

---

1 Ancient measure of weight, corresponding to about 800 grams or 28 ounces: AC, 430.

Don Girolamo, who would immediately send those coins, along with others, in a little sack, to one of the judges or reporters of the neighborhood, who, at a certain time of day, would go to sit in one of the agreed-upon osterie.

After the arrest of the sacristan and Zi' Rosario, they would go to the fruit market in Piazza Magione with a basket of lemons, shouting, "*A sciuorta i lumiunaaa!*"[2]

Antonino Bucolaro would go there every day, approach the seller, and exchange the code sign; he would be given the meeting place, set up the meeting, and would then report it to Don Girolamo. As all this was taking place in the open and with means that were part of daily life, it didn't arouse suspicion, and it eluded spies. Although already corrupted from the perspective of enriching himself, Bucolaro hadn't revealed the secret of those means of communication to Matteo Lo Vecchio, who, besides, so as not to arouse suspicion of espionage, had limited himself to orchestrating the blackmail of the Duke of Motta and had not attempted to find out about anything else.

Antonino gave himself a reason that he found to be perfectly logical: "The papers were stolen and, as Matteo Lo Vecchio said, that fellow Blasco— the Duke of Motta's friend who was arrested in Messina and who no one knows the whereabouts of—probably has them. Therefore, the society doesn't have them. Meanwhile, the high tribunal knows the facts and can proceed without a need for those papers. What harm is there if we can take them back from Signor Blasco in order to sell them to the duke? With that act I certainly do not commit myself to protecting the duke from punishment. Quite the opposite. If there is a need to fire a shot at him at night, I will pull the trigger myself. . . . He is a scoundrel, whom it is better to send to hell. And now?"

When he came up with this line of reasoning, he was far from knowing that Blasco had been admitted into the sect before the high tribunal. He didn't know that Blasco was in Palermo as a guest of Coriolano della Floresta, or that Coriolano della Floresta was the secret and supreme leader who drove the sinister ranks of the society to which he had taken the oath of blind obedience and absolute loyalty. To him, Blasco was an enemy that he had to get rid of, if it was true that he possessed those notorious documents. But where was he? Where to find him? To denounce him to the society, which, unleashing its spies, would have certainly tracked him down (so he thought), didn't seem prudent to him, out of fear of losing those papers that were becoming his obsession and that represented for him the dream of infinite riches. Where was he?

Matteo Lo Vecchio, in a second conversation, was surprised by this question. What? He was asking him where Blasco was?

"But he is one of yours!" Matteo Lo Vecchio exclaimed.

---

2 "Lemons by the bagful!"

"Who?"

"Don Blasco, that adventurer!"

"How do you know that?"

"I know it. It astounds me that you don't know it."

"I don't know it . . . because he is not."

"And I'm telling you that he is."

Matteo Lo Vecchio's certainty of this fact surprised Antonino Bucolaro; how could he claim that? What proof did he have? The birro reminded him about the attempted arrest of Don Girolamo and Andrea, which came to nothing, and added, "Who warned them? Who is the spy? Who was in charge of the secret Beati Paoli? Him, precisely him. I saw him with my own eyes."

Antonino Bucolaro was silent; Matteo's argument, for him who knew how the sect was organized, wasn't very convincing, but it was enough to put a germ of doubt into his heart or at least to leave him perplexed.

"What if it were true!" he thought to himself.

He began to cheer up as an evil thought emerged from the depths of his conscience: "What if I attempted to carry out the scheme myself and put a couple of ounces of lead into Matteo Lo Vecchio's stomach?"

It was a deceit on top of a deceit; taking advantage of the birro's information, he would deal directly with the Duke of Motta, eliminating any intermediary, and the reward would be all his. His aroused appetite was turning into a greedy and evil avarice.

If Blasco truly belonged to the sect, Don Girolamo certainly must know it; therefore, he had to begin there. The following morning, he went hunting as usual, then went to meet Ammirata at the agreed-upon place in order to give a report of the day's events.

When he had finished, he asked, as was his custom: "Anything?"

Suspicions about Antonino Bucolaro had already begun to circulate, and for a few days Ammirata, responding to his question, would always answer, "Nothing."

This time, after a brief silence, he added, "And don't come tomorrow."

"Why?" asked Antonino Bucolaro, suddenly suspicious.

"Because I'm leaving . . . some business. Wait until I send for you."

The abduction of Violante from the Monastery of Montevergini had to be carried out that night. At other times, Don Girolamo would have given the job to Antonino Bucolaro to get him everything that was needed: ladders, ropes, men; but this time he didn't think it a good idea to let him in on the secret. The next day, from one of the executors, he learned about the attempt, of the sudden and miraculous intervention of a man who had prevented them from taking the young girl away and how he had not been able to know the fate of the "guard" and Andrea. Antonino Bucolaro then realized that Don Girolamo no longer trusted him, which frightened him. He waited a few days, but Don Girolamo didn't send for him.

"Let's not see each other anymore," he said to Matteo Lo Vecchio. "I'm very afraid that they have spies watching us. . . . Besides, so far I haven't been able to find out anything. No, Don Blasco doesn't belong to the society."

He was losing heart. Matteo Lo Vecchio was alarmed by it, fearing that Antonino Bucolaro would get away from him, something that certainly could do serious harm to him now that his secret was known to someone else. He had to be very cautious, yes, but not let the Beato Paolo get away, as he could be useful to him in other undertakings; for example, flushing the sect out from its lair.

* * *

A few more days passed, and the news spread through the city that a pirate ship had attacked the felucca on which the Duchess of Motta and her stepdaughter were traveling and that the two women had been taken into slavery. A fishing boat in the waters of Solunto had found the felucca at the mercy of the waves, without a man on deck, like a ghost ship. The boatmen, having boarded, had seen in amazement that the sailors had been tied up and thrown to the bottom of the felucca. They had freed them, and then the felucca had brought back the news to Palermo. For the city it was a shock, a commotion, a demand for more news; the viceroy was astonished and saddened, but neither he nor Matteo Lo Vecchio believed that the two women had been kidnapped by pirates. Pirates would not have abandoned the felucca and left the crew, who instead could have some value on the slave market or could be made use of on pirate galleys. It must have been a second and successful kidnapping. For the viceroy it was a slap in the face that sent him into a rage. He dispatched messengers and orders throughout the kingdom, threatening extraordinary hardships to the captains who had not been diligent and zealous, and even sending two galleys to explore the coasts, to gather news and to investigate.

Even Antonino Bucolaro understood that pirates had nothing to do with it and that instead it had been the work of the Beati Paoli, and he had confirmation of it; it mortified him, and he was deeply distressed by it. Were they keeping him out of every decision, then? They should watch themselves: he had only to take one step and he would ruin everyone!

Matteo Lo Vecchio paid him a visit at night at home.

"The viceroy promised a reward of two hundred scudi to anyone who can point out where the two women have been taken."

"And what do you expect me to know?"

"Certainly you would know better than me. Do you think it was pirates—do you? Seriously? Let's not play games. One hundred scudi for you, one hundred for me. That's a lot of money! This deal does not exclude the other, bigger one."

Antonino Bucolaro promised nothing. To find out! How? Every step that he might take would arouse suspicion; he had to leave it to chance.

The following morning he went hunting, but really to see Don Girolamo. He looked for him in vain at the usual place; he pushed ahead up the side of the mountain, even visiting the caves. Neither Don Girolamo nor Andrea could be found there. Had they left? Were they among the women's kidnappers? Were they hiding somewhere else because they were afraid of him?

"Ah, by God! If they put my back to the wall I will sing!"

Meanwhile, as he continued to attend the nocturnal meetings of the Beati Paoli, he couldn't say that he was being treated with mistrust, and he was given some tasks of minor importance, evidently so as not to arouse his suspicion. At one meeting he finally saw Don Girolamo.

"We no longer see each other," he said to him.

"We're together now." And after a minute of silence he took him aside to a corridor in the cave. "Careful, Bucolaro," he whispered to him, "I've always had a good opinion of you; watch yourself."

Antonino gave a start but was able to control himself and responded with sufficient calm: "But what are you talking about? This is the second time, Don Girolamo. If you doubt me, bring me to trial."

"No, I will not bring you to trial; if my suspicion becomes a sure thing, I will kill you with my own hands."

"Go ahead. What do you expect me to tell you? I just want to warn you about one thing: that, by killing me, you will endanger the whole society . . . because you wouldn't know what I know, what I am going to find out, in your interest, indeed, in everyone's interest."

Don Girolamo grimaced in doubt.

"You don't believe me? Well, it's about those papers that were stolen from you and other news that I am gradually gathering for our security. Haven't you understood that I am spying on the spy?"

"What? The papers?" Don Girolamo asked with interest.

"Precisely. The 'friend' knows what they contain; at least if what he says corresponds exactly to their scope."

"What does he say?"

Antonino Bucolaro told him what Matteo Lo Vecchio had briefly related to him. Don Girolamo was astonished, but his face seemed to show no emotion. He responded or commented with a "Hmm!" that meant nothing. But meanwhile he was wondering how the birro knew about the contents of those papers, which were known only to him, the high tribunal, and Andrea; Antonino himself, even knowing that they were the basis of a trial, didn't know what they contained.

"Now if he knows all this, it means that he must know where the papers are . . . And I am trying to wrench it out of his mouth."

Girolamo Ammirata stared at him and asked slowly, "And what are you giving him in exchange for this information?"

"Oh!" Bucolaro answered, smiling. "Nothing that can compromise . . . news of no importance and that drives him away from the truth."

"Careful. The birro is sly. He will catch you."

"Have no fear!"

At that point, the conversation ended. As he left, Antonino Bucolaro passed his hand over his forehead and found it drenched with a cold sweat. He had won a battle, but he couldn't say that it was a decisive win.

Upon leaving, before parting, Don Girolamo said to him, "Be wary and cautious and try to find out where those papers are. I fear that the birro has them; rather, I am certain that he does!"

"Where do you want me to come see you?"

"Nowhere. If I need to, I will come to you."

On his way home, Antonino said to himself, "He believes that Matteo Lo Vecchio has the papers; therefore, the society doesn't possess them. And that Signor Blasco, if he has them, he's not a brother, or if he is, he is a traitor! There's no way out. Don Girolamo doesn't want me to go see him. Therefore, he has moved to a different house and he doesn't trust me."

He was about to open the door to his house when a shadow came out from a dark doorway nearby. Antonino unsheathed his sword, but a familiar voice reassured him: "It's me; stay calm."

"Don Matteo—"

"Exactly. I heard that you had a meeting tonight and I waited for you. Let's go in because the night is damp."

"Do you have anything to tell me?"

"Something very interesting. At nine o'clock I ran into Blasco da Castiglione."

"What?"

"He was coming out of the house of the Cavaliere della Floresta . . . a lord."

"Let's go in, let's go in," Antonino Bucolaro said briskly, pushing the birro inside.

CHAPTER 14

Don Raimondo Albamonte, Duke of Motta, had arrived a few hours earlier after a long and stormy voyage from Genoa to Palermo on a galley of the republic. He had only allowed himself a little rest in order to recover, then had rushed to the Palazzo Reale to find out if the viceroy had any news about the two women.

From Turin to Genoa, from Genoa to Palermo, that heart that was closed to all feeling had been tortured by the most dreadful thoughts and fears; not so much for the fate of Donna Gabriella, whom he had never loved and about whom he had been little concerned, as for his daughter. In his cold and cruel insides, facing the danger of losing his one and only child, through whom he would perpetuate his lineage and the inheritance of his wealth, and before the specter of death looming over that innocent girl, a seemingly unfamiliar feeling of paternal love had been fervently reawakened.

Every obstacle on the journey, the unexpected calm stretches, the sudden storms that either slowed the voyage or deviated the galley from its course, pierced him with a thousand stabs. Would they ever arrive, then? Was Sicily that far from Turin? With every additional hour it seemed to him as if Violante was descending another step of the staircase to her death. Every day at sunset, over that immense sea and sky, he would ask himself, "Will I get there in time? Will I find her alive?"

And his heart wailed with pain. He would go to the captain, the boatswain, or the helmsman, asking anxiously, "How many more days? Will there be a storm? Will we have favorable winds? Why don't you make them row harder? . . . Ah, if I was the galley sergeant! By this time, I would have broken their ribs! Make them row faster . . . put up all the sails!"

He almost would have liked to steer the galley himself. If on the horizon he caught sight of a sail, he would seize the telescope and spy on it with suspicion and trepidation.

"Could it be some pirate ship? Are we in danger? How many cannons do we have on board? We must not allow ourselves to be captured, by God! . . . We have to reach Palermo at any cost, and as fast as possible. I will give you another two hundred scudi!"

Every so often he would reread the mysterious letter that had made him leave so hastily from Turin. It was brief, terse, and marked by the usual symbols. The day when he found it on his writing desk he recognized its handwriting and style and turned pale. "They are pursuing me even here?" he repeated.

The same pallor, the same terror would assail him every time he picked up the letter to read again.

Signore,

You have thrown in jail a poor woman and a boy. A man flees from impious justice armed by you. Your wife and your daughter will answer for them. They are in our power. Make haste to come. It's up to you to get them back.

At first he hadn't wanted to believe this letter. How was it possible that the Beati Paoli had seized Donna Gabriella and Violante? Wasn't Violante shut up in the monastery? He had rushed to the palazzo of the Consulta[1] to see Don Nicolò Pensabene or Francesco d'Aguirre or another of the Sicilians that the king had brought with him to Turin, in order to find out if any had arrived from Palermo; the dismayed expressions of his fellow countrymen were enough to give him confirmation. With the same messenger, in fact, a report had arrived from the viceroy that, according to early rumors, was attributing the abduction of the women to pirates, and he was asking for a flotilla for the safety of the kingdom, since the Sicilian galleys were too few and in poor condition.

"Pirates? Pirates? Do you think they are pirates?" he began to shout in exasperation.

Now he was taking it out on the viceroy, who for a long time—more than a month and a half—had done nothing. If it had been pirates, it would be a different story, but pirates had nothing to do with it.

"This is the work of the Beati Paoli! . . . Here is their letter. Do you understand, Your Excellency? And by God! The Beati Paoli will certainly not have eaten them alive. Where, then, is justice? Where are the rural companies, and what are they doing? . . . I had almost crushed this sect; I had almost destroyed it. . . . Meanwhile, what if my daughter has died?"

This idea was filling his heart, his voice, and his manner with an inexpressible sorrow. An anxiety, a terror, a need to hurry, to act, to think . . .

Of course, the hand of Ammirata was in it; who else, in fact, could have an interest in carrying out that seizure as a means to free Signora Francesca and

---

1 The Consulta was composed of a group of advisers that examined and gave opinions on legal issues or any matters that were referred to them by the king or his ministers.

Emanuele? To free them? Of course! He would have done it himself to save his daughter and take her to safety; and then . . . Ah, then it would be time for his revenge!

The viceroy promised him that he would put the rural companies at his disposal, even those of the baronial lands. But he thought that it would take much more than those forces.

* * *

He returned home depressed, shattered, and had thrown himself on an armchair in his study, as if to organize his ideas and to work out a plan, when a footman announced a visitor.

"Your Excellency, Signor Blasco da Castiglione."

"I am not receiving, I don't want to see anyone," he shouted.

"And Your Most Illustrious Lordship would be wrong," said Blasco coldly, appearing on the threshold with hat in hand and a certain gravity in his demeanor.

Don Raimondo looked at him in amazement, then with a sense of terror. In the doorway, with the door-curtain drawn to one side, immobile, Blasco appeared like a living reproduction of the portrait of Don Emanuele. It seemed to Don Raimondo that his brother had come off the canvas or had come out of the grave to demand an explanation from him for what had happened to Donna Aloisia and little Emanuele.

"What do you want?" he stammered.

With a gesture, Blasco dismissed the servant, closed the door, and, stepping forward up to Don Raimondo's chair, answered plainly, "To talk to you, Your Excellency . . . and uncle!"

Since he had turned in order to move a chair closer, he didn't notice the start that Don Raimondo gave at that last word.

Blasco put down his hat, sat down, and looked at him; he understood by the shock painted on the duke's face the effect of his sudden announcement of their kinship, and said, "Your Lordship is surprised, isn't that so? But it really is true; I have the honor of being descended directly from the illustrious loins of Don Emanuele Albamonte, and of having been born in the Castello della Motta. If I had not come to see you about some grave and very serious matters, this kinship could be something to have a laugh over, but—"

"But I," Don Raimondo interrupted harshly, "have no desire to laugh, nor time to lose, signore; and as to your birth and to your alleged origin—"

"Take it easy!" Blasco rebutted him. "Alleged? I am not alleging anything; what gives me my surname and established paternity is a little parish document, but if I must tell you my opinion, inasmuch as the honor of being a bastard of your brother may lure me, it doesn't lure me to the point of longing for the high honor . . . of aspiring to be the relative of a . . . a man like Your Lordship . . . there is too much . . . difference. But this is not what I came to talk about . . . Your Excellency; I told you that it's about some grave and serious matters."

Don Raimondo thought that Blasco wanted money; in order to cut short the conversation, he got up, saying, "Signore, at this moment I have other and more serious business that I must attend to."

Blasco didn't move; he pointed to Don Raimondo's chair.

"I presume, Your Excellency, that there can be nothing more serious than the fate of Donna Violante and the duchess."

Don Raimondo's appearance and tone changed immediately.

"What? My daughter? Do you know something about my daughter?"

"Yes."

"Is she alive?"

"Alive."

"Oh God!"

His eyes expressed an anguished question, made clear by the torment painted on his face.

He stammered, "Alive . . . she is well, but?"

"As pure as the day she was born and treated with respect, like a saint."

Then that man who had caused so much death and suppressed every sense of mercy, of humanity, felt his knees buckle, fell to the ground clasping his hands and, bursting out in sobs and tears, repeated, "God! . . . God! . . . I thank you!" Then he took Blasco's hands in a surge of joy, gratitude, tenderness, and stammered, "Thank you! . . . Thank you!"

Blasco was touched. He waited until that high-strung seizure stopped before resuming the conversation.

"It's of no use to tell you, and it would take too long to explain how I could have known why and by whom the duchess and Violante were kidnapped; nor will this matter to you; what is important now is to protect—or better—to free the two women."

"Oh, you know well! You are the most valiant man I have known. Do you want one or two companies of soldiers, or one squadron of cavalry? . . . I will give you everything that you wish."

"You are mistaken, Your Lordship, mistaken. First of all, we must find out where they are."

"What? You don't know?"

"No. Secondly, doesn't Your Lordship think that at the arrival of so much force and at the mere thought that the two ladies could be snatched by violent means, that those who are guarding them will hand them over to us already dead? . . . No, no! No display of force."

"And what should be done, then?"

"Come to terms with the kidnappers."

"Who knows who they are?"

"Perhaps I do."

"And these terms?"

"First of all, the wife of Ammirata and his . . . nephew need to be freed, and the warrant issued against Ammirata must be revoked."

"And who can do that?"

"Your Lordship."

"But these are things that depend on justice."

"Indeed, it would seem so, but Your Lordship knows that this justice was arranged precisely by him."

"I can't do anything about Sant'Offizio."

"If this is how things are, then, I have nothing more to do. It means that you will abandon your only daughter to her tragic fate."

"But no, no . . . that's not what I'm saying. Let's see. I don't know what accusations weigh over these people, nor what the trials have been able to establish."

"There are no trials; and that concocted charge against Francesca Ammirata is a lie. . . . But let's not get lost in pointless discussions. Every hour that passes is precious. Your Lordship can do anything. Bear in mind that it is about the life of Donna Violante."

Don Raimondo held his head in his hands; his paternal love was at war with his hate and fear.

Blasco continued coldly and, weighing his words, said, "And careful, Your Lordship, about the revenge of the Beati Paoli—because by now you well know that it concerns them. They will not stop at the imprisonment of the ladies; it will fall mercilessly on you, dragging you in front of His Majesty's justice as someone guilty of incredible villainies."

Don Raimondo turned pale. The muscles of his face twitched; he tried to look indignant and to assume an air of defiance.

"Threats! . . . Ah! The usual infamies, the usual false accusations—"

"Truth!" interrupted Blasco.

"I defy them! . . . Are you one of the Beati Paoli? Well, then, I will start with you; I will have you arrested, I will have you tortured, I will make you suffer most atrocious torments, I will pull all the secrets from your mouth."

"Go ahead, and tomorrow you will receive the heads of Donna Gabriella and Donna Violante in a sack; and the viceroy will receive a formal complaint accusing you of having had an assassin murder a certain Maddalena, the maidservant of Donna Aloisia, your sister-in-law, who had just given birth; of having twice attempted to poison your sister-in-law with powders supplied by the witch Peppa la Sarda; of having done away with Donna Aloisia and little Emanuele, the only and true heir of the title and fiefdoms of the House of Albamonte; of having had Giuseppico, your assassin, killed; of having had Peppa la Sarda poisoned; of having had two poor devils strangled in prison without a formal trial; of having given the job of poisoning me to Matteo Lo Vecchio; and finally, you will be accused of being the fraudulent usurper of the patrimony that is owed to the legitimate heir! . . . There is a surplus of things, Your Excellency, to justify having your head cut off in Piazza Marina ten times, if it were possible!"

Don Raimondo had listened to this tirade, turning white, then pale, and finally ashen; as Blasco spoke, the images of the victims reemerged around him and he felt they were oppressing and suffocating him; with a spasmodic gesture he tried to put an end to the words of the young man, but his fear prevented him from speaking.

When Blasco finished, and with that vision of the torture that he almost saw and felt, he gathered his strength and attempted a defense: "It's not true! . . . It's not true!"

"Be careful, Your Excellency, don't deny it."

"The evidence . . . where is the evidence?"

"They have it. They have everything for a formal trial, with the testimonies of precisely those who were the instruments of the crimes, written depositions, signed by witnesses who are alive and who could come tomorrow to supply other important details. I have read this evidence."

"You? You read it? Where? How? When—"

"By accident, by a mere accident. I was horrified by it . . . and now Your Lordship knows what he has to do."

Don Raimondo was demoralized, defeated, crestfallen; his secret was in the hands of many by now, and that trial would result in his conviction. He thought he had forever silenced the voices of those who could have denounced him, when those voices had actually already spoken in front of witnesses who were still living and whom he didn't know, nor was he able to strike them down; he thought he had nearly destroyed the sect by striking it at its heart, and instead it was rising against him, formidably armed, more powerful and fearsome than before; he thought he could live quietly, an honored man, sought-after, a ruler, and here the vision of a sensational trial, the shame, the scaffold and the hangman's ax, the confiscation of his possessions, the misery and the everlasting dishonor of his child—his Violante—was emerging before his eyes. He was at the mercy of this mysterious and unrelenting sect! He was seized by an anguished fear; he no longer had the strength to put up a challenge, to defend himself, to deny; he thought that his salvation was in the possession of those papers, that destroying them would shatter the source of the accusations and the basis of the testimonies, and he could triumph in a trial, or at least unleash his forces and fight with the likelihood of winning or bending the judges in his favor through schemes and bribes.

"Blasco," he said in a voice hoarse from emotion, addressing the young man in a friendly manner. "Blasco, you are my relative, in short . . . you are my nephew . . . blood of my brother . . . you are an Albamonte . . . I am ready to acknowledge you . . . I will give you an annuity, living quarters in this palazzo . . . I will ensure your future. Do you want a rank of colonel in His Majesty's army? I will obtain it for you . . . I will revoke the warrants against you and Ammirata and release his relatives from prison . . . I will do everything that you require from me, but under one condition."

Blasco looked at him with a questioning eye.

Don Raimondo added, "I want those papers!"

"Impossible, Your Excellency."

"Why is it impossible? Why? What use are they when I have agreed to everything, when I have agreed to free the prisoners? You must do it, Blasco . . . for yourself as well . . . I beseech you. . . . Promise me."

"But I cannot make a promise that I am unable to keep. . . . Those papers are not mine. They belong to Emanuele Albamonte, Duke of Motta, whom you had tried to do away with and who is alive!"

"What? . . . Emanuele? Alive? But I am doomed! Doomed!"

"You can save yourself."

"How do you know this? . . . Then is he the one who gave you the assignment? Is he the one who incited the Beati Paoli? . . . How is he alive? Ah!"

Suddenly a revelation came to him, and his face took on a terrifying expression of astonishment, of hatred, and then of joy.

"Ah! Is it him, him, that boy who is considered the nephew of Ammirata? Is he Emanuele? . . . But then, I have him in my power! . . . Ah! . . . Now then, Blasco, now to us; Emanuele's head will answer for my daughter. In three days either my daughter will be returned to me or Emanuele will die."

Blasco couldn't hold back a gesture of surprise at the boldness of the duke's desperation, that he was clinging to this ploy with all his might, seeking his own salvation with a bold move.

Blasco realized he had miscalculated, but he wasn't dismayed; he got up, took his hat, and said goodbye to the duke. "I ask for your forgiveness, Your Excellency; I have nothing more to do . . . but mind what you said: before me, you are assuming the responsibility for the life and freedom of Emanuele Albamonte . . . leaving here, I will go to His Excellency the Viceroy in order to put my brother under his protection, and as for the life of Violante . . . she will know that her father doesn't value it enough to forego his hatreds and his crimes for her. Farewell, signore."

He started for the door; Don Raimondo leapt up and grabbed him by the arm. "Where are you going? Wait!" he said to him in a somber voice. "Forgive me; what do you want? My distress and anger made me go too far. You are right. Yes, you are right. I am a fool. We will reach an agreement. . . . Who must I reconcile with? With you?"

"No! I wanted, of my own accord, to put myself in the middle, so as to avoid a scandal that would have overwhelmed you and your daughter . . . and your daughter is innocent! That's all. I thought that you are a father, and that the life of an angel who believes you to be the best of fathers must be important to you. . . . I thought that you could find a way, so that silence spreads over the past and Emanuele is acknowledged and has in you a father, not an enemy; you yourself, a man of laws, would have found a way. . . . I didn't pursue my own personal gain, Your Excellency; I will be happy when I have ensured the futures of my brother and of Donna Violante and shattered forever the reasons that incite the sect against you. . . . When everything is finally settled, I swear to you that you will have those papers, so that no trace remains of a dark and bloodstained past! . . . Now with you, in your hands, is the fulfillment of this desire of mine, which aims for the peace and happiness of everyone. Do you want to fulfill it? I am here for you. You don't want to? I will go to the viceroy and allow destiny to take its course."

"The viceroy will have you arrested."

"I don't care. Then you think that my life matters to me? If it mattered to me, I wouldn't risk it. . . . My arrest will not save you, or your daughter."

Don Raimondo was trembling, grinding his teeth, delirious as if he had a fever; he felt unable to free himself from the iron hand that had taken him by the hair and that there wasn't even the chance to prevaricate, or to look for excuses. Blasco spoke with such a firm tone that there was no doubt about his resolve. He gave in.

"What do you want me to do?"

"I told you. You must start with the liberation of Emanuele, Signora Francesca, and Don Girolamo Ammirata."

"I will try to obtain it."

"You must not say *try*, but *I will obtain it*."

"I will obtain it."

"On the same day when they have been returned to their homes, Your Lordship will embrace the duchess and Donna Violante."

"Who will guarantee it to me?"

"I will."

"Then can you do something about the Beati Paoli?" asked Don Raimondo with a flash in his eyes and his nostrils flaring like a dog sniffing for hidden prey.

"Right now, yes . . . and solely to save you. . . . Oh, don't think it's because I hold you in great esteem—on the contrary; and neither because I bear, by chance, a name that on the other hand I will not use, but rather for your daughter, for that poor and innocent creature that I freed the first time, by force, whom I want to be free even now, whom I want to save; because it is not only her life that must be guaranteed, but her name, Your Excellency, her name and her wealth! . . . She must have no idea that her father is a villain and that the wealth in which he lives is usurped; she must not see her father walk up a scaffold, among the Bianchi,[2] and place his head under the ax! . . . She must not curse her own life and the one who gave it to her!"

Don Raimondo shivered.

"Shut up! Enough! . . . There is no need to discuss this further; I will go to the viceroy at once . . . provided he agrees. Do you want to come with me?"

"No, I trust you. Besides, it's in your interest."

A few minutes later, Don Raimondo went down the stairs of his palazzo to enter the carriage he had already called for, while Blasco got into a portantina that was as modest as that of a doctor.

As they took leave of each other, Blasco said to him, "It is not necessary to send me a response. I will know myself if Emanuele and Signora Francesca have been released from their prisons."

* * *

The time for audiences with the viceroy had passed, but for a high magistrate who was coming from Turin and for a serious matter that was keeping the government busy, such as the mysterious seizure of two ladies and the failure of justice, there were none of the usual prohibitions. Don Raimondo went into the private work study of the viceroy, Count Maffei, who asked him solicitously, "Well, is there any news?"

"Yes, Your Excellency."

"Is it known where the ladies are?"

"No, it is not known, but I have confirmation that they were taken by the Beati Paoli. . . . Death hangs over them if we don't give in."

"Give in? Must we give in? About what?" the count said, frowning.

"Listen, Your Excellency, I could act and put together my own mission because I still have authorization to do so from His Majesty, who gave me full powers to act against both the sect and bandits, but out of respect for Your Excellency, I will not use it without the consent and agreement of Your Excellency."

Without going into details or mentioning Blasco's name, he demonstrated to him the need to settle the case against Emanuele, a case that, as it had revealed nothing against the young man, could only end with an order for his release, unless, in order to speed things up, and so that His Excellency's generosity could be given a greater honor, he should decide to pardon the young man himself and order his release.

---

2   The Compagnia del SS. Crocifisso was composed of aristocrats who had the task of assisting and bringing comfort to those condemned to die; called "Bianchi" for the hooded white tunics they wore.

Count Maffei was astonished. If there wasn't anything against the young man, if he had been arrested, imprisoned, and tortured under mere suspicion—and even worse, as a retaliation—then why had he been kept in prison for so long? What kind of justice was that? And what honor would come to His Majesty from such arbitrary proceedings? Things had to be put right. He sent a secretary down to the rooms of the Tribunal in order to read the proceedings, but the proceedings didn't contain anything except the transcript—as it would now be called—of the torture inflicted on the young man.

"But what kind of proceedings are these!" shouted the outraged count.

He promptly ordered that Emanuele be set free.

Don Raimondo asked that the order be given to him. "If you allow me, I will go myself to give this comfort to that boy."

Leaving the Palazzo Reale, Don Raimondo thought, "This has gone smoothly, but with Sant'Offizio it will be more difficult. Besides, for now we'll negotiate, then we'll think about it. They will have to deal with me!"

A wicked smile passed over his thin lips. The Grand Inquisitor who presided over Sant'Offizio was Monsignor Don Giovanni Ferrer, an eager, fanatic, arrogant Spaniard who regretted never having officiated an entire auto-da-fé, that is, with its beautiful pyre lit to the glory of God. Snatching a victim away from his clutches would be a difficult undertaking. Perhaps there was only one way: to tempt his greed, under the pretext of donating a sum to Sant'Offizio. And Don Raimondo had had to reluctantly cling to that approach.

The tolling for the dead sounded in the night sky when Signora Francesca, astonished and somewhat dazed, was in the Duke of Motta's carriage on her way to the Castello a Mare to receive and embrace, amid tears, the young Emanuele, who was no less stunned by his sudden release from prison and at seeing his second mother in that carriage. But when he noticed Don Raimondo, who was standing in a corner, almost in the shadows, and recognized him, a sudden flame rose to his face and his eyes blazed amid his amazement and hatred.

"Ah! . . . Him! Him!"

The young lion gnashed his teeth, smelling revenge, but Don Raimondo's cold and calm mask had opened into a benevolent smile. "Is it really so strange that, after having been, owing to my duty, your judge, I am now, out of conscience and Christian charity, your liberator? Give me your hand, then, and have confidence in my protection."

The duke held out his hand; Signora Francesca, whose heart was still pounding with emotion, implored Emanuele with a glance. The young man slowly gave his hand, but upon contact with the duke's cold and clammy one, he shivered with disgust. Was it the hand of a corpse or the body of a reptile? In that instant, his eyes met with those of Don Raimondo. His hatred lit up his eyes with hostility.

CHAPTER 15

Don Raimondo had returned to his palazzo, fuming with hatred, thirsty for revenge, gnawing inside from anger at his own impotence. He had come to an agreement with Blasco under the threat of those revelations that would have destroyed him, but that had just ignited in his soul a furnace of hate against that bastard. He even forgot about Violante, his Violante, in the surge of rage to which he abandoned himself when he was alone in his study. Where were those papers? Did the bastard possess them? He had to get them back, and then, a stab from a dagger or a rifle shot, at night, would be more effective than having him arrested by virtue of the warrant that was hanging over him. . . . Once he was arrested, the Beati Paoli would emerge to tear him away from him with other threats, and revenge would escape him.

He was mulling over plans and alternate plans when a servant came to announce the arrival of Matteo Lo Vecchio.

"Let him in!" he shouted. "Let him in!"

The birro entered, bowing. Don Raimondo assailed him: "Well, so bandits can rise from the dead and walk with impunity throughout Palermo, now that I am no longer vicario generale!"

"Eh! That's not what should surprise Your Illustrious Lordship, but that the doors of Sant'Offizio are opening!" the birro replied with some insolence; and, changing his tone, he added, "Besides, Your Illustrious Lordship teaches me that sometimes it is wise to let a bandit walk free and to make him almost gain confidence that no one will bother him. . . . What does the cat do? He lets the mouse run; when he sees it move away—Pow!—a leap and a blow with a paw. . . . I know who Your Lordship is referring to . . . I am following him and keeping my eye on him for other reasons. . . . It would be necessary to tell Your Lordship a long story, but it doesn't matter. I will only tell you that Don Blasco—"

"Who, according to you, was dead and buried."

"Exactly. What fault is it of mine if the mice died instead of him? The scoundrel knows more than we do; he made a narrow escape, but he will not get away."

"You are a fool."

"If it pleases Your Lordship, I will be one, but what if I tell you that just by playing the fool I discovered something that precisely concerns Your Illustrious Lordship?"

Dom Raimondo gave a start. There was something sarcastic and piercing about the tone of those words. What did the birro mean?

"Concerning me? What could concern me?"

"Certain pieces of paper that are in the hands of Blasco da Castiglione."

Don Raimondo turned pale; there was no doubt as to what those papers were; the allusion was clear, and yet he feigned surprise and asked, "What papers?"

"Papers that are enough to hand a man over to the venerable Compagnia dei Bianchi."

Don Raimondo felt his blood run cold, but he held back his emotions, and on his impenetrable mask there was only a slight contraction of his jaw.

"And why do those papers matter to me?" he said.

"They are of more importance than Your Lordship believes . . . because they make reference to Your Illustrious Lordship. . . . Not that I even believe what they contain, far from it! They are nothing but skulduggery and false accusations, and whoever wrote them should be given a beating. . . . But meanwhile, this could appear to be a serious matter."

The Duke of Motta felt his throat tighten as if gripped by an iron hand.

Who had made the birro aware of the existence of those documents? And what did he know about them? Had he read them? Was he another one sharing in that secret, which he presumed had been buried with the last victims? He tried to laugh and probed further.

"Ah! Ah! What you are saying has all the appearance of a serious matter . . . and it would be frightening . . . it could be said that you are acquainted with the contents of those papers!"

"Yes, Your Excellency."

"You are familiar with it? You? How?"

"I had them in my hands."

"You had them in your hands . . . and you didn't hold on to them?"

His voice seemed swollen with anger. So Matteo Lo Vecchio had held those terrifying and damning papers; he knew what they contained; he was also another soul, another voice who could suddenly rise against him; he was another enemy force who had to be stopped and done away with.

"How could you let them be snatched from you?" Don Raimondo asked, pretending not to believe Matteo Lo Vecchio.

"Does Your Lordship perhaps doubt me?" the birro answered. "Do you think I'm making this up? The thief, the one who took them from me, is Blasco . . ."

"Blasco?"

"Precisely him. Blasco da Castiglione stole them from me. I had stolen them, I know with what danger to my own life . . . and I was planning on giving them to Your Illustrious Lordship, in order to demonstrate my devotion and attachment to you, but that scoundrel took them from me. . . . How did he discover them?

I haven't figured that out yet. Meanwhile, it's certain that he has them. . . . Now, Your Illustrious Lordship understands why, even though I can arrest Don Blasco, I allowed him to go free."

"You should have arrested him and searched his house."

"If he had his own house."

"Does he perhaps sleep out in the open?"

"He is a guest of the Cavaliere Don Coriolano della Floresta."

Don Raimondo's eyes widened. And Don Coriolano was giving hospitality to a man of that sort? Was he giving shelter to criminals, then? By God! Perhaps the example of the Prince of Mezzojuso, who had been arrested and thrown in the Castello a Mare precisely for aiding and abetting bandits, was not enough? Here was a man to report to the viceroy . . . perhaps he was an accomplice, perhaps he was also familiar with the contents of those terrible documents; he too was an enemy to defend himself from.

He wanted to find out if Matteo Lo Vecchio really knew the contents of those papers, and also to find out and verify what Blasco had said. He questioned the birro, who explained to him in detail what he had read in the trial prepared by the Beati Paoli, but interspersing his account with objections and with declarations of esteem toward such an illustrious gentleman as the Duke of Motta.

"It must be all a hoax by people who want to blackmail Your Illustrious Lordship."

"Yes, precisely!" said Don Raimondo, whose heart was still in turmoil, grasping at that hypothesis.

By now there was nothing left for him to find out; even the birro knew everything and was a very dangerous person, whom either he would have to irrevocably tie himself to or he would have to crush. Meanwhile, it was necessary to have those documents that had become his nightmare.

"I would be curious," he said, "to see those papers!"

"That is what I plan to have in my hands, if Your Illustrious Lordship will help me."

"Of course! . . . Are you sure you can succeed?"

"I have a way."

"Meaning what?"

"I was able to win over one of the Beati Paoli, a friend of Don Girolamo Ammirata."

"Ah!"

"And I am following with him, step by step, what the sect does. . . . However, it would be good to search Don Blasco's room . . . and in order to accomplish that, the servants should be bribed. . . . I am sure you understand."

Don Raimondo understood; he took a sack of money from a cabinet and threw it into the birro's eager hands. "Here is some money."

"Thank you; I will get to work at once."

"Do not arouse any suspicion. . . . Try to get hold of those papers, although they don't scare me and are nothing but nonsense; I will pay you a fortune for them."

Mentally, Don Raimondo added, "Except that I will make you disappear from the face of the earth an hour after you have handed those papers over to me."

* * *

He dismissed the birro, and when he was alone he abandoned himself to the desperation that until then he had repressed in the depths of his soul.

"Everyone! Everyone!" he shouted furiously, beating his head with his fists. "Then does everyone know? Everyone?! My secret is no longer! From every side and from every shadow, witnesses and informers are rising up. And I am in their power; I am at the mercy of the vilest individuals! . . . So I have sown death along my way, then, I have caused tears and bloodshed all around me in order to bury my secret in the shadows, and from the earth, from the air and from every side, thousands of voices are shouting it and divulging it! Can I never hope to have silence and oblivion surround me, then?"

And in his swollen heart ran the thought of a colossal revenge, with which he could crush with one blow all those known and unknown enemies that were surrounding him, laying traps for him, tormenting him. To crush them! The ability to make one single head out of all those heads and to cut it off with the swing of a gigantic ax!

"Ah, are you the bastard son of Don Emanuele, Duke of Motta, and are you the legitimate son? Go join your dear paternal shadow! And are you the Beati Paoli? Go to enjoy the reward of your beatitude!"

With his nostrils flared, he yearned for a merciless revenge, the crueler and more frightening as the terror that made him tremble grew more intense.

A superstitious and uncontrollable terror left him feeling subjected and dejected. To take revenge? Ah, yes, it was his dream, but meanwhile, "they" were stronger, and they had him in their power, and they could, if he transgressed an inch, throw him into the arms of the executioner. They were stronger and their strength derived from mystery, from the unknown. How many were there? Beyond those he knew, how many were there that were unknown to him and therefore even more terrifying?

This thought made his revenge appear distant and uncertain to him. Perhaps after the initial victims there would emerge other and newer avengers; perhaps, indeed, his desire for revenge and his attempts to obtain it could lead to and give rise to newer and greater reprisals against him.

Amid these anxieties he had nearly forgotten about his daughter; that paternal impulse that, when he wasn't yet aware of the tremendous threat that was hanging over him, had driven him from Turin to Palermo and had made him fall at the feet of Blasco da Castiglione seemed to have faded after he learned that Violante was suffering, but undefiled, and that she would be returned to him. No longer fearing for her, he could think about himself. His daughter would come within one or two days, but under those circumstances it was almost preferable to send her away, somewhere else, to safety, in order to keep himself free and to prevent her from knowing about the crimes that tainted her father's conscience. Owing either to a feeling of sensitivity or to vanity, he wanted to remain in Violante's eyes the honest and virtuous man that his daughter believed him to be.

In this way his mind passed from one series of thoughts to another no less tormenting one, and between one and the other he passed the night staying awake and tormenting himself.

* * *

Meanwhile Matteo Lo Vecchio, leaving the Palazzo Albamonte, was starting off in search of Antonino. He thought that it was time to act, out of fear that, taking advantage of the favorable circumstances, such as the arrival of Don Raimondo in Palermo, Blasco would keep for himself the full profit of the sale of those papers. Therefore, it was necessary to get those papers back—something that, truly, Matteo Lo Vecchio could do himself, considering that in the investigations to determine who was holding those documents, Antonino Bucolaro had been of very little help to him. But there had been many new developments, and other unforeseeable events could occur, so it was prudent to keep a firm hold on Bucolaro and to compromise him in such a way as to force him into espionage and betrayal.

Crossing Piazza San Cosmo, he looked at Girolamo Ammirata's house, whose balconies were closed. But from certain cracks a trace of light was shining through, a clear sign that despite the late hour, someone was awake there.

"Of course there is a gathering there, and Don Girolamo and Andrea must be inside. What a coup! . . . If only a patrol would pass by! . . . But at this hour the patrols are sleeping peacefully. And what if I went to the San Giacomo quarter? It's not that far . . . yes, it's true, it's not far, but while I go to call someone, they have all the time they need to vanish . . . there are so many spies! . . . And then, perhaps it's better for now to let it go!"

His thoughts went in a new direction. That afternoon the birro had seen Don Raimondo leave the Palazzo Reale in his carriage, and he was astonished.

"What?" he had said to himself. "The duke in Palermo? Since when? Certainly he must have come back due to the disappearance of the two women. . . . Eh! It will take more than the viceroy!"

He had started running behind the carriage and had been able to catch up with it and sit on the rear footboard, like a street urchin, thus being transported and following the duke closely without being seen. He had followed him that way—not without a certain amazement—until Sant'Offizio, where it hadn't taken him long to find out what Don Raimondo had gone there to do; it seemed to him so wonderful and unexpected that he made the sign of the cross with his left hand. After having waited a good while, he had seen Don Raimondo and Signora Francesca come out of the main door of the palazzo and get into his carriage.

"Well! Well! . . . Well! But is this really what I am seeing or am I hallucinating? . . . What does this mean? . . . I could have imagined anything, except this! There must be some big devilry behind this. Watch out, Matteo!"

But his surprise had turned into astonishment when he had seen the carriage go to the Castello a Mare to collect Emanuele. It had seemed to him like the world had turned upside down and that men were walking with their heads where their feet should be. Everything he had seen had seemed to him to belong to the realm of the impossible and the incredible, and he was unable to grasp the reasons that had compelled the duke to take that step.

"Certainly," he thought, "there must have been big developments! The man is clever, and if he is doing this, it must be for his own personal gain."

Now, passing in front of that house, he made the same observation: "It must have been for his own personal gain!" And a vague premonition made him fear for his plans.

"Nino Bucolaro must know something. For heaven's sake, they would certainly have invited him! . . . A family gathering like this!"

He had reached Ballarò when he thought he heard footsteps ahead of him, but the darkness of the street didn't allow him to see the people who were walking. He quickened his pace without making noise, and he thought he caught sight of two shadows, one of which was recognizable, or nearly so, by its gait.

"Is that him? Is it not him? . . . And who could the other one be?"

The two shadows, after crossing Piazza Ballarò, turned toward the Albergheria and stopped at the corner of the street. Had they heard him? Had they seen him? Perhaps, and it wasn't wise either to stop or to turn back, because he would have aroused suspicion. It would be better for him to keep walking like someone who is going about his business; and he passed in front of the two motionless shadows wrapped in cloaks.

Matteo recognized one as Bucolaro. He had not been mistaken. But the other one? Who was the other one? He continued on toward his house, and after about twenty steps he stopped and turned, concealed by the shadows. He thought he saw him and then realized that the two shadows, after leaving the street corner, had vanished.

He went back, walking on tiptoe, and arrived just in time to hear a door close in a narrow street behind the Church of the Carmine Maggiore, and he no longer had any doubt. It was Antonino. But would the other one leave soon?

He waited about an hour, but the door didn't open; then he gave a commonplace whistle and waited, but the small balcony remained closed; he waited some more, but in vain. He went home. At dawn he was awakened by a whistle similar to his own; he got up, and in his nightcap and underclothes he appeared at the windows. Antonino Bucolaro was below, under the balcony, wrapped in a cloak with his nose in the air. Matteo gave him the sign to come up, then pulled the cord to the latch.

"What the devil got into your head to call me when I'm with someone?" Bucolaro said angrily.

"I needed to see you."

"Me too."

"Who were you with last night?"

"Didn't you recognize him? Andrea Lo Bianco."

"Oh, the devil! . . . If I had recognized him I would have stretched out the net for him."

"A waste of time . . . my dear friend. . . . Don Girolamo and Andrea can walk right under your nose . . . they have safe-conduct, to be followed by a pardon . . . and you can hope in vain."

"And this miracle is naturally connected to the release of Emanuele and Signora Francesca."

"Precisely."

"Things are coming to a head, Don Antonino; it's time to strike."

"I think that scoundrel Don Blasco did it."

"What?"

"This morning he met with the duke . . . and then all this happened."

"Ah! The rascal!"

"The duke must have burned those papers by now."

"No; he has instructed me to retrieve them."

"A pretense!"

"Well, no! Do you expect me not to notice a pretense? That scoundrel must not have handed them over yet. . . . By this evening, we must take them from him. I will take care of him; you should attend to his friend, the Cavaliere della Floresta."

"That is not possible."

"Why?"

"Because Don Blasco left."

"He left?"

"Last night, he went to pick up the duchess and the duke's daughter and to bring them safe and sound to the Duke of Motta."

Matteo Lo Vecchio had a flash of genius that lit up his face with a savage joy.

"An idea just came to me."

"Let's hear it."

The birro bent down and began to speak in a low voice. At first Antonino Bucolaro displayed amazement, then admiration, but reluctance; finally, persuaded by Matteo Lo Vecchio's reasoning, he concluded, "Very well. I'll do as you say."

"In two hours, I will go to the duke; you get that information for me. We'll see each other at midday."

"Where?"

"At your house."

"But are you off your head? Do you want to ruin me?"

"Don't worry. No one will recognize me."

In fact, at noon, Antonino Bucolaro saw coming to meet him, at the door of his house, an abbot from the provinces, and he let out a cry of surprise: "Ah! The abbot from the Castello a Mare! . . . Signora Francesca's confessor. . . . Now let me make you comfortable."

But at the sound of Matteo Lo Vecchio's laugh he was astonished. "You! . . . So, even then . . . when did you come?"

"Yes, yes, we'll talk about it later, but let's go in, otherwise you will have me recognized. I am a poor abbot of the kingdom, come to see you about some business, a batch of wine to find a market for. . . . Do I make myself clear? So let's go in, then."

CHAPTER 16

Violante had sat down at the window of her room, which overlooked the valley. She was gazing at the mountain ridges, which gradually faded into the distance amid the vapors of humidity rising from the earth. Large cirrus clouds billowed over the peaks of the rugged and bare mountains. Below, wide expanses of land stretched out that appeared to be abandoned, scattered with wild plants, small and sparse or in thickets, without a tree, without a house or a hut. Here and there was a solitary tower; in other places a stone enclosure to gather the flocks at night; between the hills, or at the foot of a mountain range, were some dark patches: a wood; and some whitish spots: a village or a city.

Violante could also see a stretch of the path that led to the fortress, on top of which stood its prison. That path, emerging between several boulders that concealed it, turned soon after toward the side of the cliff. Ever since Zia Nora had spoken those encouraging words to her and mentioned Blasco, Violante would position herself at the window to spy on that stretch of path from which Blasco would surely come. Along there, in fact, every so often she would see the mule that brought provisions to the castle going uphill, and she had inferred that it was the access road and that Blasco would come from there.

She preferred to spend the days in that sweet expectation, which, as it kept her far away from her stepmother, it spared her from those violent and hateful rows that would open wounds in her heart. And she would limit any contact to the short time spent at meals, when she couldn't avoid being next to Donna Gabriella; nevertheless, either because in her solitude she was becoming sadder or because seeing her stepdaughter shun her stirred up all the bad feelings that had been lurking in her heart, Donna Gabriella sometimes went into the girl's room and always found an excuse to torment her.

One evening while preparing her room for the night, Zia Nora said to Violante, "He is coming tomorrow."

The young girl's heart began to beat violently; there was no need to ask and yet, embarrassed and blushing, she said, "Who?"

"Signor Don Blasco."

Blasco! . . . Finally, he would come; there was only one more night, but how long it would seem to her. And at what time would he come? At dawn, her own desire would promise her; in the evening her dread would dishearten her. The hours passed like that amid two internal voices contending with each other, but there was always that one great certainty that had the name "tomorrow."

"He's coming tomorrow," the young girl thought. "Why hadn't he come before?"

She turned that question over in her mind, but it remained unanswered; that Blasco in her mind's eye did not speak, but he was looking. How would he come? At that new question, a sense of fear stirred her heart. The men who were keeping guard over her, who didn't permit them to leave, who didn't allow anyone to approach the castle—those men, while showing themselves to be helpful and respectful, like vassals, had something hard, inflexible, and threatening about them; would they allow her and her stepmother to be taken away without putting up any resistance? And what if they killed him? This idea filled her with so much dismay that she truly thought she could see Blasco killed; and then she felt capable of sacrificing herself to ensure the safety of the young man.

"He doesn't have to come, I don't have to see him, I can remain here forever, provided that he comes to no harm."

But another voice encouraged her. What was she afraid of? Who was as brave and courageous as him? He would knock down and overcome every obstacle and no one would be able to hold out against his power. Her faith in the invincibility of her liberator, of which she had had much evidence, rose in her, somewhat lessening her anxieties and fears of the danger.

She didn't close her eyes all night, and in the morning she got up from bed with a feverish impatience.

To Zia Nora, who came to tidy up her room, she asked anxiously: "What time will Signor Blasco come?"

"I don't know. This I don't know."

Violante thought for a moment, then asked again, "Does the duchess know that Signor Blasco is coming?"

"Oh, no; there was no need to tell her. And then, they didn't order me to tell her as well."

"You were to tell only me?"

"That is so."

"Who ordered you?"

Zia Nora shrugged, as if to say, "What a question!"

And she added nothing more. Violante remained at the window, staring at the path.

Even Donna Gabriella was nervous and impatient. Zia Nora had told her of the imminent arrival of someone, but she had told her, on the surface to comfort her, but in reality to prepare her: "Let's hope that you don't remain here longer than this week, and that you spend holy Christmas in your palazzo."

"What do you know about it?" the duchess asked strongly.

"I know nothing . . . but I heard some talk."

"And what talk did you hear . . . what talk? . . . Tell me. . . . I want you to."

"Oh, Your Excellency, talk . . . what do I know? They were saying, 'We still have a little more of this exile and then we'll return to Palermo.' That's what they said."

"Who said it?"

"Eh! The men."

Donna Gabriella gathered from these few and incomplete answers that some new development was imminent, and she waited impatiently. This long imprisonment had exasperated her. But a new thought made her even more restless and nervous: "What if the men had been talking only about themselves? What if relief was coming only for them, with a change of guards?"

Therefore, she was also waiting not for a liberator but for the day her guards would depart, in order to find something out about her fate. That morning, sitting behind the window, having nothing else to do, she looked down that stretch of path that she could see.

Thus, at the same time, Violante and Gabriella saw two riders emerging between the boulders, climbing up the short visible stretch of path and disappearing again behind the high boulders. Both of them followed the two riders anxiously, not recognizing them because they were wrapped in cloaks; but Violante already knew who one of them was. Both of them, seeing the riders, had a joyous thought.

Violante thought, "It's him."

Donna Gabriella thought, "This is not a changing of the guard; they are coming to get us, then!"

And at the same time, for that need of the spirit to expand and communicate its joy, they left their rooms, met each other on the threshold of the common door with the same words on their mouths, words that expressed hope, relief, happiness, an accumulation of feelings: "People are coming!"

Donna Gabriella asked immediately, "How do you know?"

"I saw them from the window."

The duchess thought, "Then she too was at the window; did she also know?"

And they waited. In that solitude, the arrival of those two riders represented for Donna Gabriella an event of great emotion because in their arrival there was something unknown; for Violante the emotion was different because she knew that one of those riders was Blasco.

"Who could they be?" said Donna Gabriella.

Violante was on the verge of answering "I know" but was silent. After what had occurred between her and her stepmother, she was always afraid of betraying herself and of inciting one of Donna Gabriella's furious rages against her. She was silent and waited.

Zia Nora went into the duchess's room smiling, with her hands at her sides, saying, "Your Excellency, get ready to leave, and the young lady too . . . they have come to get you. Be of good cheer . . . the men are also leaving."

Donna Gabriella thought that if the men were leaving with them it could mean that they were changing their place of imprisonment, and this thought darkened her spirit and brought forth a wave of suspicions to her heart.

In her harsh and imperious tone, she ordered her stepdaughter, "Get your clothes ready."

She too, helped by Zia Nora, began to collect all that belonged to her. Suddenly she asked the old woman, "Have those gentlemen that I saw from the window arrived?"

"Yes, Your Excellency. But only one is a gentleman; the other one is a *campiere*."

"For whom?"

"Who knows! . . . Perhaps for the gentleman."

"Where is this gentleman?"

"In the dining room."

"Go tell him that I wish to speak with him and for him to get ready to receive me."

Zia Nora gestured with her head, which could have meant "Listen to that tone of voice!" and left.

A minute later Donna Gabriella went into the dining room with a defiant manner, while Violante called Zia Nora and quickly asked her in a low voice, "Well, Zia Nora, has he come?"

"Yes, my lady . . . he is in the dining room . . . with the duchess."

Without knowing why, Violante felt a pang in her heart. Upon hearing that her stepmother was with Blasco, she must have wanted to run to hear what they were talking about, if the rules of good manners had allowed her.

"What are they talking about?" she asked.

"Who knows?"

Donna Gabriella, on entering, had not seen the man who was in the dining room, who was looking out the window with his back to her; nor did it seem that he had heard the noise she made upon entering.

It was necessary for her to call out: "Signore."

But as soon as Blasco, shaken by that voice, turned, Donna Gabriella let out a cry of amazement. "You? . . . You, Blasco?"

Blasco approached her in order to kiss her hand, like a good cavaliere, but he didn't seem surprised, since he was evidently expecting this encounter; only he was unable to conceal a slight blush.

"It's me, Your Excellency, very happy to serve you."

Donna Gabriella's dark eyes shot arrows at him and she murmured with bitter irony, "Is it really to me that you are rendering a service? . . . Have you faced the troubles of a long journey for me? . . . This confuses me and makes me proud, signore, because I was not accustomed to your sacrifices."

Blasco looked at her with fraternal affection and his voice seemed filled with a compassionate and profound tenderness. "Do you perhaps think that your life, that your person, are not important to me? I certainly did not come for you alone, I would fail in my duties of loyalty if I said this, but believe me that if it had only been about you, I would still have come, to free you from an imprisonment."

"It's mysterious to me; not to you, apparently, since you know where they have banished us, and without putting yourself in danger, you are able to open the doors for us."

The irony that gave the tone to those words was so vivid that Blasco asked, "What do you mean by that?"

"In short," Donna Gabriella said bitterly, "take off the mask, signore! . . . And have the honesty or the openness to tell me for what purpose have you had us seized."

"Me? Do you think I was the one who had you seized?"

"Oh, it's useless to pretend, but keep in mind that as long as I am alive, you will never attain your objective!"

"Your Excellency, I believe that you are mistaken. . . . What objective are you talking about? I know of only one. To ensure your freedom. In this castle, which I did not even know existed until three days ago, there are five men, devoted to the point of sacrificing themselves, who from today depend on me . . . only on me. Well, Your Excellency, I will place these men at your command and leave at once, relinquishing the pleasure of accompanying you and serving you."

And when he reached the window that overlooked the courtyard, he shouted, "Cristiano!"

A moment later a man in a short doublet and tall boots, with a pistol in his waistband, appeared at the door.

"Cristiano," Blasco said, "what order have you received?"

"To blindly obey Your Lordship in all respects."

"Very well. Then listen to me. From now on you will only receive orders from Her Excellency. You will take orders from no one but her."

"If Her Excellency orders me and my men to throw ourselves off this fortress, we will not think twice about it."

"Thank you, Cristiano; go and wait."

With his own hand Cristiano performed the act of kissing the hands of Blasco and the duchess; as soon as he closed the door, Blasco said to Donna Gabriella, "And now my presence is no longer required. I am leaving you."

He bowed respectfully and started to leave. Donna Gabriella, who up to that point had remained mute, immobile, and sullen, shook her head and shouted, "Where are you going? Stay here!"

"Why?"

"Because I don't believe in this farce. . . . You or that Cristiano, it's all the same; I am still your prisoner and I well know that I am leaving here in order to enter some other prison . . . only tell me, if you please, what you expect."

"Me? What do you think I expect? What I desire, and the reason why I came, I have told you. Must I repeat it for you? You don't believe me. And I can't force you to believe me . . . but you are wrong; excuse my frankness. . . . If I could tell you how and for what reasons you and Violante had been seized and how I could have found out, after so much time, where you were confined, and how I obtained your freedom, you would surely believe me; but I would be revealing secrets that are not my own. The duke, your husband, to whom I promised to bring you back, will be able to, if he thinks best, tell you something . . ."

"My husband? Then has he returned?"

"Four days ago."

"And is he in Palermo?"

"Where he is waiting for you and his daughter."

"Then he knew what had happened to me?"

"He had been informed."

"By you?"

"No, others preempted my desire to tell him."

"What interest did these 'others' have in informing Don Raimondo?"

"I don't know, nor could I say. . . . Besides, what does it matter to you? During your imprisonment, I am sure that no one touched a hair on your head, nor was any disrespect shown toward you; now you are regaining your freedom and you will be taken with the utmost respect to the place where the duke, your husband, will receive you. No trace of this episode will remain, except for its memory, like a dream. . . . I would have liked to hand you over to the duke myself, as I had promised him, but you will be kind enough to excuse my absence. Do you have any orders for me?"

"I have begged you to stay," Donna Gabriella said in a somber voice, "and since my husband expects to receive us from your hands, you will accompany us."

"As you wish."

Donna Gabriella stayed a minute in silence, then with a smile full of bitterness added, "Certainly you will not mind the company, since . . . you will not escort only me."

Blasco felt a sudden flush on his face but didn't respond. Donna Gabriella noticed that and turned pale; her lips lost their color and twitched with anger.

She couldn't restrain herself and, seizing him by the arm, assailing him with a fiery look, in a voice that seemed made of sobs, she resumed, "Why did you tell me that you loved me? Why did you conquer my soul? Why did you ignite a passion in my heart that devours me, that destroys me? Why did you make me feel the rapture of your kisses? Why does one night, one passionate night, whose memory burns in my blood, disturb my mind? One unforgettable night, why did you make me drink from the cup of joy, make me believe I possessed you completely, body and soul, forever, until death, after death? Why did you abandon me? What did I do to you? What did I do to you, Blasco? Hadn't I given myself to you entirely, completely, my magnificent conqueror? And you threw me away with an excuse . . . you filled my heart with all the torments, with all the agonies, with all the rages, with all the desperations; you drenched me with rancor and bitterness; you made me, and still make me, burn with hatred. . . . Only with hatred; and now I live for this hatred and this hatred envelops both of you . . . you and her! And listen to me well: if you want to be with her, you will have to kill me first!"

Blasco had listened to this impetuous torrent of words with sadness, pity, astonishment, trying to stop it with a gesture, interrupting her with one word: "Duchess . . . Duchess."

She let out an anguished laugh. "Duchess! . . . This is my name now, but when your mouth sought mine and your hands were trembling with caresses, you called me Gabriella! . . . Now this name has been erased from your soul under the mark of another name . . . but I will dig up that name with my own hands, and you will see it blaze and burn at night, implacable, tenacious, like my hatred, like my revenge."

"Gabriella. . . . In the name of God!"

"God? Why do you invoke God? What are you hoping for? He will not save you!"

"Gabriella!"

But the duchess, overcome by her outburst, burst into tears and collapsed onto a chair. Blasco was seized with emotion; the conjuring up of the past, the still untamed passion of this woman, her pain, filled his heart with pity and tenderness.

He took Donna Gabriella's hand, calling her name tenderly and imploring her, "Gabriella, then have mercy on yourself and on me."

He bent over her and she could almost feel his words brushing against her hair. At that moment the door opened and Violante appeared, saying, "Signora Madre."

But on seeing Blasco in that pose, she let out a piercing scream, as if wounded, and she staggered.

"Violante!" Blasco shouted in an indescribable tone of voice. "Ah! Her!" Donna Gabriella shouted, jumping to her feet, blind from pain, jealousy, and hatred. And grabbing a small fruit knife with a slightly pointed curved blade from the table that was still set, she rushed at Violante, roaring, "Ah! . . . You will die!"

Blasco saw and assessed the situation and in a flash threw himself between Donna Gabriella and Violante, who was falling to her knees. The knife struck, moved downward, and tore Blasco's waistcoat, grazing his skin.

Blasco forcefully grabbed the duchess's wrist, disarmed her, and threw the knife away from them, reprimanding her: "Damn woman! What are you doing?"

Donna Gabriella's eyes opened wide, saw Blasco in front of her, on whose waistcoat was clearly visible a large red stain. The horror was painted on her face; she took a step back, stammering, "You . . . blood . . . me!"

Blasco let her go, and then Donna Gabriella passed a hand over her eyes and forehead with an instinctive gesture; then, as if mad, she let out a shriek and ran to the window.

"Signora Madre!" a frightened Violante screamed, slumping to the ground.

But Blasco had already made a move, had grabbed Donna Gabriella by the waist and placed her on a chair, quivering and frightened.

"Gabriella! Gabriella!"

The duchess let out another shriek and fell into convulsions, while Violante, aghast, screamed, "Signor Blasco! Signor Blasco! . . . What is it, then?"

CHAPTER 17

The journey to Palermo was sad and silent. Blasco had two litters ready for them down at the foot of the cliff; Donna Gabriella went in one and Violante and Zia Nora in the other. The armed men, on horseback, in two groups, preceded and followed the two litters, with Blasco riding next to Donna Gabriella's and Cristiano next to the other.

After that crisis that had almost caused the duchess to become a murderer and a victim of suicide, she had withdrawn into a dark and distraught silence. Blasco had attempted some words of comfort to lift her spirits and to bring her back to her senses, but she didn't respond to him; only once did she stare hard at him with a dark and intense gaze, and another time she raised her eyes up to the cliff on which towered the castle, partly in ruins, whose name and location she still did not know. It was the ancient Castello della Pietra, whose ruins were still visible at the top of the fortress, from which nearby Alessandria had taken its name, built in 1570 by Blasco Barresi, lord of the castle.

The path ran along the sides of tall mountains, here and there covered with thick woods; it left Santo Stefano di Quisquina on the right and plunged into the slopes of Monte Carcaci. They spent the night in Pizzi, where they departed at dawn for Mezzojuso. The travelers looked like a group of lords who were returning from their fiefdoms. The harness bells on the mules attached to the litters jingled, and it seemed as if other groups were traveling through unknown and mysterious roads. In the shadow of its high ridges, Rocca Busambra[1] enveloped the travelers, who crossed the State of Godano, where the Bosco della Ficuzza[2] created a large gloomy and frightful thicket. The following night they stayed in Marineo; everyone slept except Blasco and Donna Gabriella. They had been guests in the marchese's castle, but Blasco had separated the women and, doubly fearing that Donna Gabriella would either make an attempt on her own life or let herself be carried away by her jealousy of Violante, he had settled down in the room in front of Donna Gabriella's. But she had almost become an automaton, letting herself be led everywhere without a will of her own, and for the entire night did not make herself heard.

1 The highest peak in the Monte Sicani chain.
2 Today the Bosco della Ficuzza is a vast nature preserve near Palermo.

When the following morning Zia Nora knocked on the door to ask her if she needed anything, she was surprised to see her fully dressed, like the day before, sitting next to the window with her forehead leaning on the palm of her hand, just as she had left her the night before.

They departed toward daybreak. The journey proceeded toward Misilmeri in silence. By then they were approaching the city, where they would arrive a few hours later, since Misilmeri isn't more than nine miles from the capital. The road crossed a ravine, called Portella, that was a den of bandits and thieves, where passersby and carters were almost always attacked and robbed.

The group had traveled over regions and districts heavily infested with thieves but had taken the precaution of taking paths that were not frequently used and staying away from the road taken by travelers and canceddi, along which the thieves of the countryside would lie in wait in order to profitably carry out their attacks. They had then, up to that point, completed their journey without any incident that could have frightened or jeopardized the personal integrity of the women. But here they had no other road to choose; even if they had wanted to take some shortcut, they would have had to first cross that road. Fearing some encounter, Blasco sent Cristiano and one of his men ahead in order to explore the road. He and another man placed themselves in front of the two litters, and he positioned the other two escorts behind.

They were six determined men who would not retreat in the face of a battalion.

Cristiano and his companion spurred their horses to a brisk pace, but they hadn't gone a third of a mile when they ran into a rural company, with its captain and algozino. The algozino was Matteo Lo Vecchio.

They stopped Cristiano, greeting him in the manner of peasants: "Jesus and Mary!"

The captain asked, "Are you campieri?"

"Yes, signore."

"Whose?"

"Of the illustrious Cavaliere della Floresta."

"Fine. Have you noticed any suspicious people along the way?"

"No one, Captain."

Meanwhile, the militia had surrounded the two campieri, cutting off their retreat to the litters with a double file. At a nod, they leveled their rifles at the campieri.

"On the ground!" the captain ordered.

Cristiano turned pale and bit his finger, letting out a loud curse; then, as if with a sudden resolution, he let himself drop from his horse and, drawing his pistol from his waistband, he went to fire at the captain, but a few soldiers spurred their horses on top of him and knocked him down. In no time, Cristiano and his companion, despite defending themselves with punches and kicks, were tied, beaten, thrown on top of their horses like two bundles, and taken away by a few soldiers.

"And this is one thing," said Matteo Lo Vecchio. "Now comes the best part. Go ahead, I will come at a distance; but be careful because the beast is wild."

The captain gestured as if to say that he was dealing with him. He was one of those bravacci who, although not lowborn, threw themselves into the underworld, becoming thieves, blackmailers, bullies, murderers, and then ending up in the service of justice; the rural companies were in fact recruited from among the cream of the crop of the banditry of the countrysides.

They often aided and abetted the gangs of brigands, especially if they were left to fend for themselves; they would become ruthlessly impudent if they had a promise of rewards from some barons involved in the undertaking.

The company moved away in step, while Matteo Lo Vecchio, after dismounting from his horse, sat on a rock. They went along in a tranquil and unassuming manner so as not to arouse suspicion; turning the corner that the road formed on the slope of the hill, they found themselves opposite the party.

Blasco was startled but didn't show it and continued to advance calmly. The path wasn't wide enough to allow the litters and the squadron to pass through at the same time. The captain greeted Blasco respectfully and gave the order to his men to stop and to allow them to pass. The soldiers divided themselves into two flanks, drawing up on either side, leaving the party in the middle. They held their rifles across their saddles, on their thighs, and Blasco, having looked at the soldier closest to him, noticed that the rifle was cocked. A suspicion suddenly occurred to him; the suspicion turned into certainty when he saw the path blocked by two men who positioned themselves in the center and the others raise their rifles to take aim at him and the three campieri.

"Stop!" shouted the captain. "No one move, unless they want to die!"

Blasco turned pale—not for himself but for the women, who at that shout had peeked out of their litters, frightened, not knowing whom they had run into.

Blasco said to the captain, "Signore, perhaps you misunderstand."

"I'll give you something to misunderstand!" the captain replied arrogantly and, turning to his men, added, "If anyone moves, make him dance like a bear."

Blasco felt his nerves stiffen, and his jaw clenched from rage.

"The first one who dares to lay a finger on me will be killed like a dog! . . . What do you want?"

"Nothing other than to arrest you, to tie you up. And bring you to the Castello a Mare."

"Me?"

"By order of the king."

"Precisely me?"

"Precisely you, the renowned Blasco da Castiglione."

There was a minute of silence; Blasco, trembling, looked at the three campieri who were standing immobile, impassive, and at the militia with their rifles leveled; he looked at the litters; opposing thoughts contended with each other in his mind. Certainly, if there hadn't been any women in the middle who could have been hit in a shoot-out, he wouldn't have debated much about which decision to make, but on the other hand to let himself be taken in that way . . .

He lived an instant so intense and dizzying that it seemed to him like ten years; a cold sweat dampened his brow. He assessed his position with a strategic glance. He was surrounded on three sides by about ten men, and the litters were on the remaining side. He couldn't open a passage for himself at the sides because the path was sunken, nor from behind, because the litters, his campieri, and other militia were there. If anything, he could try from the front, where the passage was blocked by the captain and a soldier. To force that passage? It was certainly tempting, since the soldiers facing one another would run the risk of killing one another if he evaded their aim with a lightning-fast move. But in this case, how could he leave the women at the mercy of this gang? All these thoughts followed one another almost at the same time, at the same speed that at night, with a flash of lightning, the monstrous specters of the clouds flicker in the dark sky.

"Excuse me, Captain," he said with an amenability that was concealing a slight trace of irony, "in order to arrest me and bring me to the Castello a Mare, you must certainly have an order."

"I have it, and it would be all the same even if I didn't."

"Bravo! One can see that you are a man in the true sense of the word. And it almost gives me pleasure to be arrested by you. However, you will do me the favor, at least, of telling me if even these ladies I am accompanying, and these campieri who don't belong to me, must be arrested."

The captain puffed his cheeks a little. "The ladies," he said, "no. . . . As to the campieri . . . we'll see."

"So have the kindness, then, to accompany the most illustrious duchess and the young duchess della Motta to their palazzo, since I was supposed to carry out this assignment on behalf of the duke. . . . That means that the ladies will excuse me to the duke, and the duke then will then think to . . . reward you for what you are doing."

These words made the captain a bit embarrassed. To arrest Blasco was fine; Matteo Lo Vecchio had the order and had promised him, in addition to the bounty, a large reward on behalf of a lord. But the two ladies, who belonged, no less, to one of the kingdom's highest-ranking figures . . . he not only had to set them free, but he had to treat them with every respect, and to have them accompanied to the duke's palazzo.

"That's right," he said and, turning to his men, added, "Have you heard? Then take heed."

Blasco smiled to himself and resumed: "And now, Captain, if you don't mind, first let the ladies pass, so that it doesn't look like they are traveling with an arrested man."

The captain found this suggestion reasonable and, nodding to two of his men to stay close to Blasco, said, "Put him in between you, and if he tries to run away, kill him."

And while one of the men was taking Blasco's horse by the reins, the captain ordered those who were blocking the road to clear the path so that the litter bearers could go ahead.

But Donna Gabriella, who, pale and silent, had witnessed that scene from the window of the litter, called out to the litter bearers, "Stop!"

The captain was taken aback by that counterorder, but Donna Gabriella, opening the door of the litter and showing herself in all her dark beauty, said to him, "My litter only takes orders from me . . . and as for the gentleman, I warn you that I will not return to my palazzo unless I am presented to the Duke of Motta, my husband, by Blasco da Castiglione. Mind what you do."

The captain would have wanted to respond with his insolent arrogance, but as the matter had to do with the Duke of Motta, he let himself be advised by prudence and apologized: "Your Excellency . . . they are the orders."

"Who did you get them from? From the viceroy? . . . From my husband?"

From her litter, Violante, with her hands clasped, her face suffused with fear, watched in silence; her heart beat violently in her chest, and her inner voice invoked divine help with fervent prayers. At that moment, in which she saw her stepmother defending Blasco, she forgot what she had suffered from her and in her heart was blessing her.

But while the captain, embarrassed because he did not want to displease the duchess, from whom he could hope to reap some benefit, could not make up his mind, and because his men, owing to their curiosity, were letting themselves be distracted to watch, an extraordinary event occurred.

With his spurs, Blasco had badgered his horse, who, restrained and held by the bit, trembled under him with all its muscles wriggling. Taking advantage of that moment of inattention, and finding a path open before him, as he was bending over the noble animal's neck, he gave a formidable punch to the arm of the soldier who was holding the bit and dug his spurs into the horse's flanks.

The soldier relaxed his hand; the horse, now free, impatient, and excited, jumped, went through the passage at a gallop with a terrifying howl.

In response, there were shouts of fear, astonishment, and anger, immediately followed by a frightening round of rifle shots; the litter was enveloped in a cloud of dust.

"Go after him! . . . Come on! Get him!" shouted the captain, foaming at the mouth. "Take him at any cost!"

The gunshots had been fired at the moment in which Blasco was vanishing behind the curve of the path, and not one hit him directly; only one bullet, bouncing off a stone, crushed against his leg. In the commotion of that instant, in rushing for that bold and unexpected escape, the militia forgot about the camp-ieri, who, taking advantage of the confusion, fled to the opposite side, toward Misilmeri, but not without firing three shots at the militia, increasing the confu-sion among them due to the fear of a counterattack at their backs.

The gunshots had made Matteo Lo Vecchio jump to his feet; he, suspecting some devilry—and from Blasco he expected all sorts of tricks—and armed with a rifle, looked for the path and recognized Blasco. He acted intuitively; he flung himself to the side, pointed his rifle, and as he saw him pass, shot him almost at point-blank range.

Blasco's roar revealed that he had made contact; in fact, he thought he saw him wobble, but instead he had shot the poor horse in the shoulder, and after taking two steps, it fell to the ground.

With a cry of triumph, the birro ran, but Blasco was already on his feet holding his harquebus; as soon as Matteo Lo Vecchio was within reach, he shouted, "Ah, you dog! Are you here?" And raising his weapon, he sent him flying with a blow to his head from the butt of the rifle.

The birro fell without even saying "Ah!" A trampling of horses made Blasco turn, and he saw five or six soldiers coming upon him at a gallop. His horse blocked the path; if he knocked down another man, it would almost put a barricade between himself and the soldiers. He took aim at the one galloping in front and fired; horse and rider reared up and fell heavily to the ground. Blasco then rushed up the side of the hill, bristling with stones and hedges, where he had a certain advantage as, on foot, he could escape by twisting and turning and evading the aim of others; it was difficult, however, for the horses, who were forced to jump over obstacles at every step. . . . Several gunshots pursued him. The soldiers spurred their horses up through the hill, but Blasco had the advantage of time and the agility of his instinct for self-preservation. At Blasco's escape, Donna Gabriella had cried with joy and had anxiously jumped down from the litter; Violante had followed her. At the sound of gunshots they were both seized by fear; the young girl had thrown herself to the ground, screaming, "Oh God! Oh God!" Nor could she find any other words.

Donna Gabriella, on the other hand, began to shout: "Captain! . . . Captain! . . . Tell them not to shoot!"

But the captain, who saw his prey escaping, paid her no mind. In a flash his men dispersed.

A few, dismayed by the surprise of the three gunshots from the fleeing camp-ieri, had gone down the path toward the valley; the others had joined the captain to follow Blasco. The narrowness of the path prevented them from all running together, and the two horses and the fallen soldier had formed a barrier that forced them to lose some time.

Donna Gabriela and Violante quickly found themselves alone with Zia Nora, the litter bearers, and the mules, who, in the middle of such a sudden racket, after having pricked up their ears, stood with their snouts hanging down, perhaps dreaming of a sack of oats and bran. The duchess looked around, and her eyes fastened on Violante, whose appearance expressed a multitude of emotions; they had a dark and menacing glimmer but soon fell back into their gloom.

She said to her stepdaughter in an imperious tone of voice, "Get into the litter."

Violante obeyed without saying a word.

Donna Gabriella also climbed into her litter, but she didn't give orders to the litter bearers to start off because from the other side of the hill, where the rural militia had disappeared, rifle shots echoed, and fear held her back. Soon after, they saw two soldiers return, bringing a lifeless and immobile Matteo Lo Vecchio, stretched out on the back of a horse with his head and face horribly covered in blood.

That sight, with that blood, filled the two women with horror, and they drew back, closing their eyes. Donna Gabriella was afraid of encountering other wounded, other dead men, of seeing more blood, of having to cross through a field of battle; her fear grew, and she ordered the litter bearers, "Let's turn back! . . . Let's go back to Misilmeri!"

But Violante thought of Blasco. What if he was wounded, dying, in the middle of the road, at the mercy of those brigands?

"Signora Madre," she said timidly, sticking her head out of the litter, "do you want to abandon Signor Blasco? And what if some misfortune has befallen him?"

Donna Gabriella turned pale and resumed her somber expression, lit up by an ironic and jealous flash of her eyes.

"Would you like to run and save him?"

One of the litter bearers intervened. "If Your Excellency is pressed to go to Palermo, we could take a different route instead of turning back."

"What route?" the duchess asked.

"A shortcut. It's a difficult path, but it's safe from encounters."

Donna Gabriella thought it over a moment, then said, "Let's go."

The mules, shaking their harness bells, spurred on by their litter bearers, went back on the road traveled for a while, then turned down a small path between the boulders and the thickets marked by the peasants who crossed the mountains. The path twisted and turned on the rather steep slope, and the climb was long. Around four o'clock, Donna Gabriella and Violante were back at the Palazzo della Motta.

Zia Nora had gotten out at Porta Termini and had vanished, on foot, into one of those vicoli.

CHAPTER 18

Pursued like a wolf, running zigzag through the bushes and boulders, loading his rifle in his escape and shooting at his closest pursuers, Blasco reached the top of the hill. Behind him, the rural militia were running out of breath; at first they had all thrown themselves into the pursuit, as a column, but the captain, at Blasco's first accurate shots, spread his men out in a chain. He sent off some along the road, some on the opposite side in order to outflank and cut off the young man's escape. But to be able to truly confine him in a circle and seize him, he would have needed triple the amount of forces that he had under his command. One of the soldiers had fallen; two had picked up Matteo Lo Vecchio in order to take him to Misilmeri; he had sent four others earlier to accompany Cristiano and the campiere. Therefore, of his twenty-four men, seven were missing. He could only complete his movement with seventeen men, which made it difficult to successfully take Blasco alive; he gave orders to his men to advance while firing, so as to make the one pursued believe that he was hemmed in and threatened from all sides.

The frequency of the shots made it seem from a distance that a true and real fight had been engaged, and from two opposite points, two different groups, hearing the more or less distant echo, assumed it, even changing some elements of their assumptions.

Cristiano, the campiere, and the four soldiers thought that the bulk of the squad had come to grips with the other campieri; the three escaped campieri instead imagined that Blasco had found a house or shelter where he sustained the fire.

"Do we leave him alone?" said one of them.

"Let's go!" answered the other.

Guided by the shots, they spurred their horses. They encountered the two litters, gathered some information, and then after making their decision, they spurred their horses and rushed at a gallop along the path where the prisoners had set out. They quickly caught sight of them. The soldiers had stopped, straining their ears to orient themselves, and in this position were suddenly struck by three gunshots and shouts: "Leave them alone! Leave them alone!"

Surprised by those bullets that whistled over their heads, the militia was seized by anxiety and fled, abandoning Cristiano and the campiere, tied to their horses; their escape was a counterblow to the main body of the squadron that was giving chase to Blasco, up through the hill. The sound of those gunshots and the fright of the militia, which the captain could see fleeing from above, made him think there was a counterattack, which he thought it wise to oppose and, after gathering his nearest men, he prepared himself. The campieri, after untying the two prisoners, had begun firing toward the hill at the soldiers; this naturally produced a diversion and slowed down the chase. The campieri, shooting and retreating, attracted the attention of the soldiers to themselves, toward the path; then they fled, allowing themselves to be chased.

While everyone was moving away from that place, Blasco, having gone past those hills and those knolls, descended toward the city. He was lacerated, slightly wounded in the shoulder, bruised, panting, running wild; his appearance would have attracted people's attention and would have exposed him to new dangers. He asked for shelter at that tavern where he had first seen Violante pass by, dressed as an educanda; an expressive glance was enough for the tavern keeper to understand. There he waited the night, hidden in a loft, and saw, but without being seen, the militia returning from the fruitless exploit, stopping to drink and talk about it, amid cursing and swearing; and he heard that Matteo Lo Vecchio had died.

When he was sure he could come out, Blasco disguised himself with a cloak and a round felt hat and left. Coriolano saw him appear in that getup shortly after the Ave Maria and was astonished.

"Well," he asked, concerned. "What happened?"

"Dear friend," Blasco answered cheerfully, "I think I have received a gift from my father, and I don't know if I should be grateful or not; he gave me neither a patrimony nor a regiment but a certificate of immortality."

He told him this jokingly, but under the joking manner there was a bitterness about what had happened from his arrival at Castello della Pietra up until his arrival at the tavern. Coriolano went from one amazement to another. He would interrupt his friend's account with some interjections; at the end he seemed to withdraw a little into himself.

"What I am anxious to know now," said Blasco, "is if the ladies have arrived home without another incident."

"They have arrived," Coriolano replied, "safe and sound. But excuse me, it's not them that we must be worried about."

"About whom, then?"

"About us."

"What do you mean?"

"Well, it doesn't take much to understand what will follow. A new and more ruthless warrant against you and the power given to anyone to kill you, willingly, at no cost to them, or rather earning a large bounty for it, and a variety of troubles directed at me, as a consequence of my campieri; but this is the least—I will manage to get myself out of trouble."

"Instead what pains me most is precisely the nuisance that I am creating for you. As for myself, I don't think about it. Didn't I tell you that I am immortal? And then I have already made my decision."

"And that would be?"

"I am leaving."

"Why are you leaving?"

"And what do you think I should do now? I had only taken on a twofold commitment: the release of Emanuele and his benefactors, as well as that of the ladies of the House of Albamonte. Now there is nothing left for me to do."

"You think so?"

"How can one think otherwise?"

"Then you would abandon Violante to the jealous hatred of Donna Gabriella?"

"And who else should she be jealous of if I am not there?"

"But precisely because you are going away, the duchess, losing all hope of winning you back, would take it out on the young girl."

"What you say is, in fact, true, but—"

"But you must keep Violante safe from any attack."

"There is her father . . ."

"A father is not a lover . . . or a husband."

"Oh! . . . Perhaps you want me to marry Donna Violante Albamonte?"

"Why not?" Coriolano said calmly.

Blasco let out a loud laugh, which deep down had the anguish of a sob.

"Ah, of course! A fine marriage: the daughter of the Duke of Motta, an Albamonte who becomes the wife of one such Blasco da Castiglione!"

"Well, no! It would be instead Violante Albamonte, daughter of the Cavaliere della Motta, who would become the legitimate wife of her cousin, Don Blasco Albamonte."

"Dear friend, in four days I hope to leave for Spain; I will go to serve the old kings served by the Albamonte. Get me some English or French vessel in order to ensure my safety; it will be the last favor that I ask of you. . . . And let's talk about something else . . . have you seen my brother Emanuele?"

"I have seen him. Don Girolamo brought him to me."

"Does he still not know of his origin?"

"I believe that he knows nothing, nor does it seem to me appropriate and advantageous to reveal it to him now. . . . It's better to wait until his twenty-first year. When he will be of legal age and able to administer his patrimony, I have already told you, then it will be the time to convey it to him. Meanwhile, go clean up, my friend. I will expect you at dinner, and at midnight you will leave with me."

"Is there perhaps a meeting?"

"Yes."

"And you will attend?"

"Yes."

"Is there some important business?"

"Extremely important . . . and that may concern you."

"You are making me curious."

"Go and get dressed, dear Blasco."

Blasco went to his room, undressed, tended to his wound as best he could, and flung himself on the bed, a bit tired and still shaken by such diverse and intense emotions. That idea thrown out by Coriolano as a solution filled him with an agonizing and intense sadness, which made him feel all the brutality of his situation. But youth and nature overpowered his pain, and he fell into a deep sleep.

Coriolano was alone and pensive in his large dining room, sitting on a nail-studded leather chair; he had a leather bag next to him, from which he would from time to time draw out some sheets of paper that he would read carefully, jotting down a few words on them with a pencil.

Three knocks resounded on a wall at equal intervals. He drew near a small mirror enclosed in a tortoiseshell frame inlaid with ivory rosettes and pressed his finger on one of them. A perfectly concealed door opened in the wall and Don Girolamo Ammirata appeared.

"Come in," Coriolano said to him.

And he went to lock the door of the antechamber.

Don Girolamo, at a nod from the Cavaliere della Floresta, sat down.

"Well?" he asked.

"Everything is ready."

"Have you informed our notary?"

"Yes, signore."

"The witnesses?"

"They are ready."

"Very well. Is there anything else?"

"I have evidence that Nino Bucolaro betrayed us . . . he sent Matteo Lo Vecchio and Captain Mangialocchi's rural company against the campieri and Signor Blasco."

"Are you sure it was him?"

"Quite sure. I had put the *Orbo*[1] on the heels of the birro. The Orbo saw the birro go to Antonino Bucolaro's house at night."

"And then?"

---

1   *Orbo* translates as a "blind person." Presumably used here to refer to a person that Coriolano has sent to spy on the birro, without being seen.

"Then, the following day, Antonino came to see me at home, in order to talk to me."

"And what did he tell you?"

"He began to speak about a hundred things; then he confirmed that Blasco is in possession of our documents and that he is a traitor, because instead of working according to our orders and statutes, he acts on his own behalf. I pretended to believe him. I ordered the Orbo to keep an eye on him as well. On the same night as Blasco's departure, the Orbo saw Antonino Bucolaro and Matteo Lo Vecchio in disguise go to Zi' Alessio's tavern, below Santa Cristina la Vecchia, where soon after a carriage stopped, without a coat of arms or servants. Antonino Bucolaro and Matteo Lo Vecchio came out and went into the carriage, which then pulled away at a good pace for Via Papireto. Near Le Mura[2] those two got out. The Orbo, who had crouched down on the rear footboard, let them go and followed the carriage to the Palazzo della Motta."

"Well?"

"The duke was in the carriage. The following day Matteo Lo Vecchio was seen with Captain Mangialocchi, and this morning they took the road for Villabate, clearly going toward Misilmeri, from where Signor Blasco was supposed to come."

Coriolano was listening in silence, knitting his eyebrows; it was the only sign of emotion that his face would reveal. When Don Girolamo fell silent he said, "Was Nino Bucolaro informed about tonight?"

"Yes, signore."

"Very well. We have to get the rifles and get ready in the event of a surprise."

"I understand."

"You may leave."

Girolamo Ammirata went out from the same passageway from where he had entered; the wall returned to its place. Coriolano went to turn the key in the lock; no one entering would ever have imagined that a minute earlier another person had been there.

Blasco woke up soon after and, remembering that he was expected, dressed in a hurry and went down to the dining room, where Coriolano, stretched out on a large chair, was sleeping or pretending to sleep next to the brazier that was burning in a brass basin.

At the noise he made upon entering, Coriolano opened his eyes without moving.

"Well! It's you! I was no longer expecting you. Have a seat."

"I fell asleep. I was so tired . . . and I also had some small wounds to tend to."

"What? You are wounded and hadn't told me?"

"Oh, it wasn't worth the trouble; a singe on the shoulder and a bruise."

2   The ancient wall of the city.

"Thank goodness; then they aren't enough to take away your appetite."

"On the contrary, I'm starving."

"I am happy to hear that."

He rang and ordered dinner to be served: vegetable soup, roast chicken, cheese and dried fruit, and a couple of bottles of old wine from Castelvetrano.

"This is good wine," said Blasco.

"Do you like it? . . . When you have your own house, I will send you a few barrels."

"Well, I will never have one!"

"Why? That depends on you."

"On me? Ah! Ah! I understand! Becoming Don Blasco Albamonte and marrying . . . and so forth and so on. Excuse me, Coriolano, have you become a matchmaker?"

"For you, yes. . . . Let's talk seriously, Blasco."

"You really want me to take these things seriously?"

"Why not? Only that you leave it to me, putting yourself entirely in my hands."

"You arouse my curiosity and compel me to entrust myself to your patronage."

"Be truthful, Blasco, but forgive me if I question you about details that you certainly and naturally like to harbor at the bottom of your soul. Do you promise to answer me in all sincerity?"

"I promise, although your preamble is such as to put me on guard."

"Do you love Donna Violante?"

Blasco blushed and tried to evade answering.

"What a question!"

"Answer yes or no, goodness! You aren't an educanda."

"Well, yes, I love her. What do you want? It's a strange love, made of tenderness, that is also paternal, and at the same time has all the commitments of an undying devotion."

"I am not asking for a justification of your love, which I know is loyal, pure, and chivalrous. . . . Just tell me sincerely if you would like to marry her. Don't question the probability, answer yes or no."

"Yes, yes, yes!"

"Finally! One would say that you have made your first confession. Now I am telling you that it's up to you and to me to get you to marry Violante."

"To you and me?"

"Yes. It's very simple. . . . You, Blasco, will begin by handing over to me a packet of papers stolen from Don Girolamo Ammirata by Matteo Lo Vecchio and taken by you from a saddlebag that came into your hands in well-known circumstances. A packet that contains documents that do not concern you, that you should have given back—forgive me—to those to whom they belonged and that any day now

I was expecting to see you return to me. . . . I will take care of persuading those responsible about the advantages of the wedding that I will propose to them."

Blasco had heard those words marveling, blushing, biting his lips. Although the tone with which Coriolano had pronounced them had its usual calm composure, there was in them and in Coriolano's manner a strong and resolute will, whose weight Blasco could sense. In truth, he found himself in a difficult position: as a guest, protected and aided by Coriolano, to whom he was bound by countless obligations, he could not assume a hostile attitude toward him; as a holder of something that in the end was not his, he couldn't lay claim to any right to keep it; as a member of the society and bound to them by an oath of obedience, he couldn't refuse to obey its leader. And yet a hidden and indefinable instinct prompted a great suspicion and a greater reluctance to hand over those papers, as if, in that act of his, he imagined or sensed a grave danger for Violante.

Nor was the mirage of marriage to the young girl appealing to him, for even if it was his burning dream to have and to hold her all to himself for his entire life, united in love and with indissoluble bonds, he considered it nothing but a dream, unattainable and crazy.

"So," he answered, "if I had destroyed the papers, which you think are in my possession, then this beautiful dream of a marriage would vanish?"

"You haven't destroyed them," Coriolano said coldly.

"That doesn't mean that I can't destroy them," Blasco replied with the same coldness.

Then something unexpected happened. Coriolano got up; his face, usually so pleasantly courteous in its immutable tranquility, altered frightfully. His eyes blazed with an insufferable rage, his jaws clenched, grinding like a wild beast; his entire being was shaking in anger. Blasco couldn't contain his amazement but didn't waver, even though the resolve in Coriolano's gaze caused a continuous stirring and disturbance in his blood.

"Blasco da Castiglione," said the Cavaliere della Floresta in an unrecognizable voice, "look!"

From a corner, behind the window shutters, he took one of those fairly sturdy iron bars that were put up diagonally for security and, grasping it at both ends, added, "In my hands you wouldn't be stronger than this iron bar."

His hands tightened, his sleeves seemed to burst from the swelling of his arm muscles, the bar bent like a twig, and Coriolano threw it to the ground with a clang.

"I could take you by the waist and snap you in two with less difficulty than this iron," he resumed, staring at Blasco, who seemed turned to stone owing to his astonishment and due to an indefinite sense of malaise that numbed him. "I could snap you like this, Blasco da Castiglione, but you are my guest, and I have had for you, from the first day, a more-than-fraternal fondness, but you . . . you will hand over those papers."

"Never! Never!" stammered Blasco, stepping back and murmuring, "Don't look at me like that!"

As he was stepping back, Coriolano was drawing closer, always looking at him with an imperious gaze. Blasco stumbled over a chair and fell; the fall removed him from the peculiar spell of that gaze and restored his spirit. But Coriolano was on top of him, grabbed him by the arms, lifted him up, and, softening his voice, said to him, "Why? Why do you want to force me to use violence? Even if you were my brother, my father, I wouldn't spare you. Above me, higher than me, there is an idea of justice, of which I am the instrument, and to which I have entirely devoted myself; if justice ordered me to bring down my hand on my father, on my own son, I would do it without hesitating. Don't force me to use violence. Obey. You have taken an oath . . . do you want to break it? Do you want to be considered a traitor? Do you want me to denounce you myself?"

"Yes, I'd rather die, but those papers, in which are written all the infamies that will inexorably fall on the name of an innocent young girl, I will never hand those papers over to you . . . I would rather destroy them!"

"Don't do it, Blasco."

But Blasco was getting carried away; he had lost the exact awareness of what he was saying and doing. Humiliated by the superiority of this mysterious man who seemed inordinately large to him, he was embarrassed and he rebelled. In his words, in his attitude, there was also his wounded pride, there was the rebellion of his spirit against what seemed to him like a bullying, an abuse. With his trembling and convulsive hand, he opened his shirtfront, took out the sack that contained the papers, tore it, tore the cloth and, after removing the papers, folded as they were, he threw them on the brazier.

"Fool!" Coriolano shouted in horror, rushing toward the brazier.

But Blasco drew a pistol from his pocket and blocked his way. "Not a step, Coriolano."

The Cavaliere della Floresta, however, with the agility of a cat, grabbed his wrist and, twisting and tightening it as in a vise, forced him to loosen his fingers and let the pistol fall to the ground. Then he pushed him back and bent over the brazier, where the corners of the papers were already turning black and crumpling up, smoking.

"No! Coriolano, no!" yelled Blasco, trying to stop him.

But Coriolano had already taken hold of them and, pressing them against his clothes, extinguished the incipient flame that was glowing at the edges of the papers. A minute more and they would have been consumed.

Blasco felt himself blinded by anger, shame, and passion; his eyes full of burning tears, his voice choked, his spirit devastated by a hundred different thoughts and emotions, he drew back and said, "Signore, what you have done is an act of cowardice; before you were the leader of a villainous sect, you were a gentleman. If the sword that you gird is not a sign of dishonor for you, out with it, by God! Either you or me, one of us will leave this room alive."

Coriolano shrugged with a smile. He had resumed his reserved and smiling expression.

"Child!" he shouted.

But at that same moment, three knocks resounded on the wall; an odd smile flashed on Coriolano's face. He went to press the button concealed in the tortoise-shell frame, shouting, "*Appannate la lanterna!*"[3]

The wall opened; a man appeared in the shadows, in the act of adjusting the mask on his face.

"Is it time?" Coriolano asked him.

The other one nodded.

"*Caiffasso grande?*"[4]

"*Nel paniere.*"[5]

"Very well. Blasco da Castiglione, do you see this secret door? There, if you wish, I could make a legion come, seen by no one, without leaving a trace. But a solemn duty calls me; take your hat and come. What will happen tonight closely concerns you."

He pointed with an imperious gesture to the space open in the wall and said to the masked man, "Go ahead and light the lantern."

The masked man obeyed. Blasco collected his hat without saying a word, but before going into the dark passage he said to Coriolano, in a haughty tone of voice, "I hope, signore, that we will resolve our game as soon as possible."

"Have no doubt; sooner than you think."

They entered the space that the man's lantern was illuminating in front of them, and the wall closed again silently.

---

3 "Cover your face!"
4 "The high magistrate?"
5 "He fell into a trap."

CHAPTER 19

The same evening that Signora Francesca and Emanuele set foot in their house again was a celebration for the entire neighborhood. The neighbor women went up in large numbers; some kissed the signora's hand, others asked her how she was, and all assured her that they had felt a great sorrow at her arrest and even more on account of that unjust sentence. Oh! If they had been asked for information, the good woman would not have suffered so much. And you should see what happened since they arrested her! The birri had overrun the neighborhood, it was a true battle, indeed! Even through the stairs of the house!

Signora Francesca looked around. In fact, traces of that invasion could be seen in the disorder that reigned over the house. She begged a neighbor to go upstairs to the painter Bongiovanni to announce her arrival to him. Pellegra ran down, shouting with joy, and in her rush she embraced Emanuele, thinking that she was hugging Signora Francesca. Emanuele took advantage of this misunderstanding by kissing the girl on the mouth; she freed herself with a cry, if not of joy, certainly not of displeasure.

The painter came down slowly, repeating to himself a speech he had prepared, and entered, saying, "Welcome! Welcome! . . . But you know that it's a serious matter . . . serious! The Vicaria, you know; it's nothing to joke about! The Vicaria; he told me that if I meddle in certain things. . . . So, Signora Francesca, I'm glad . . . but far away. You understand, I don't like the Vicaria. . . . I don't like it!"

He was smiling, looking at everyone as if to win their approval. His dementia had worsened and was making him appear ridiculous. Pellegra would allow him to speak, at times reproaching him and stopping him, when she could, from saying and doing something foolish. But now no one was paying attention to him. . . . Signora Francesca and Pellegra had gone around, like good housewives, tidying up the house, dusting and sweeping, and Emanuele was helping them a little, and he was teasing Don Vincenzo a bit, who was taking up his lament again: "Ah! The Vicaria, it's a serious thing! You came from there, my son, and you could talk about it . . . do you think I could endure such a punishment? I would die from it, I would die. . . . And Pellegra? My poor daughter! . . . Ah, my unfortunate daughter! My unfortunate daughter!"

He would start whimpering as if he was actually about to be arrested and sent to prison. Then Emanuele, who was enjoying this scene, would calm him down.

"But no, there's nothing to worry about, everything is over, you know; just imagine, the duke himself came to pick me up in his carriage."

"The duke? Himself? In his carriage?" Don Vincenzo repeated with his mouth agape. "But then we are all friends? Oh goodness! Why didn't you tell me before? . . . We must drink, we must drink and have a good time! Pellegra, my daughter, go fetch two bottles . . . two of that aged one! . . . That one that Father Messana da Partinico sent me . . . just wait until you taste that wine! Long live happiness! . . . Oh, oh! . . . But that matter of the Vicaria, that matter! That one, then, no! . . . No prison!"

Meanwhile Don Girolamo and Andrea arrived, and then there was a celebration for the entire house. The painter started to dance and shout. "The wine, Pellegra, go get the wine. I want to get drunk, by the beard of Michelangelo!"

"But of course we must celebrate our arrival!" said Don Girolamo, in a good mood. On the spur of the moment they put together a supper with some hot fried foods bought from the vendor in the piazza of the Capo market, and they stayed late into the night, laughing at the painter's foolishness. Pellegra and Emanuele had sat down next to each other. The young man had left the Castello much changed; he had taken on the role of a man who knows the world, and under the table he gripped the young girl's hand with squeezes that made her blush. To make fun of the painter, Don Girolamo suggested playing a game of tressette—himself, Andrea, and Don Vincenzo, who agreed to the idea by clapping his hands.

Thus they gathered around one side of the table while Signora Francesca was clearing away the dishes, and on the other side Pellegra and Emanuele stayed as if isolated in a half-light that blurred their profiles. No one was paying attention to them; the players were studying their cards, Signora Francesca was doing the dishes and tidying up. So they could consider themselves alone. Emanuele was looking at Pellegra, flaring his nostrils like a colt setting out to the pasture among mares; new desires pulsed in his blood and encouraged his transgressions, which unnerved the young girl, causing heat to rise to her face.

"You know," he was whispering to her, "I love you, but not like before, I love you more than ever. . . . If we could speak to each other alone, I'd give you so many kisses, so many, so many on your lips."

Pellegra blushed, turning pale; the idea of those kisses, which she almost seemed to feel on her lips, was upsetting her.

"Quiet," she stammered, confused, "quiet, don't say these things."

But he persisted: "Oh, I guess you don't love me!"

"Me? . . . I don't love you? . . . If you only knew how many tears I have shed for you, and what I have done!"

"So then why don't you want me to?"

"Want what?"

"For me to kiss you."

"Because . . . it's not right."

"So then what is this love? When one is in love he wants to be with his beloved, to hold her tight, to kiss her. . . . I have all these desires and it's killing me!"

"Oh, Emanuele!"

"No, no; don't say my name. . . . Anyway, I am convinced that you don't love me."

Signora Francesca came near them and the youngsters stopped talking, but as soon as she went away, they resumed.

"My father," Pellegra said, "wants to take me to our relatives in Rome. He says that I am now grown, and he doesn't want me to be alone anymore."

"And you are leaving?"

"How can I not? How can I refuse?"

"Do you see that you don't love me?"

"My God! Then what do you want me to do to make you believe that I love you?"

Signora Francesca came near them again, and they were silent. Emanuele became annoyed. When his adoptive mother moved away, he said, "Do you see? One can't even utter a word!"

"What fault is it of mine?"

"None, I know, but meanwhile we can't talk, and I need to talk to you . . . to tell you so many things."

"My God, what should we do?"

"Soon. When your father is asleep."

"Oh, but what are you saying?"

"So then don't think about me anymore!"

Emanuele got up and went toward the players, leaving Pellegra pale and nearly in tears. The young girl loved Emanuele with all the devotion and submission of a first love; that attitude struck a strange blow to her heart and knocked away the defenses that her instinct for modesty raised against the young man's expectations. Now she was looking at him, hoping that he would turn his eyes to her, in order to silently implore him to come next to her; but he kept looking at the players, which exacerbated the young girl's sorrow.

Finally, he looked at her distractedly; she begged him, implored him with her misty eyes and a nod of her head. With an air of condescension, he came near her again and sat down.

"Well?" he asked.

"I will do as you wish."

"Then tonight—"

"Well, no, not tonight. How can I if the door is locked and my father keeps the key?"

Even Emanuele could see this large obstacle rise up against him. Don Girolamo or Signora Francesca were in the habit of locking the door, so it was no use to insist.

"Instead," said Pellegra, "tomorrow morning, early, I will go up to the belvedere . . . you can come to your balcony."

"Leave it to me. Oh, how I love you!"

The following morning, they were alone under the still-cloudy sky, while the rest of the house was still sleeping. The belvedere of the Bongiovanni house rose above the roofs by barely two arm's lengths and a terrace overlooked one side, lower than the level of the roofs by at least three arm's lengths, and therefore it remained enclosed by the walls of three houses and that of the belvedere. In order to climb up to the belvedere it was necessary to have a ladder, or rather to have the ability to climb, taking advantage of the holes and projections in the rough unplastered wall. Pellegra really didn't mean for Emanuele to climb up; they could easily talk to each other from his spot below, but the young man had other ideas in his head.

During his stay at the Castello a Mare he had learned quite a few things, including how to climb. He examined the wall and smiled; in a minute she saw him climb up and jump onto the belvedere, and before she had time to recover from the surprise, she felt herself almost tense up and lose her breath in Emanuele's strong arms, then she felt his mouth on hers.

She felt an indescribable sense of bewilderment, confusion, and fear.

"Oh no, Emanuele, no! Let me go! Not like this!"

She burst into tears, and those tears dismayed the young man. "Why? Why are you crying? What did I do to you? Good God, is this how you love me, then?"

He tried to calm her down, caressing her, speaking tender words to her, which was at odds with the violent nature of his manners, and he persuaded her to sit on the ground, pressing against her to talk. They told each other the most trivial, most futile, and at times foolish things. They talked about getting married and of never leaving each other again. Gradually, Pellegra, enchanted by that dream to come and by the words of Emanuele, and perhaps also by the contact, by the warmth, and by feeling his hair tickle her face, felt drawn to surrender her mouth to his and they kissed for a long time, intensely, in that first blossoming of sexuality, which to them seemed like a deeply felt passion.

The voice of the painter calling Pellegra aroused them from that tender moment of discompose. They promised to see each other again the following day at the same time. And they met again. Emanuele returned home in a state of intoxication; at midday, at the table, he said once again to Don Girolamo, "I am in love with Pellegra, and I want no other wife than her."

"Your mouth still stinks of milk," Don Girolamo responded.

"Me? But, after all, I'm a man. I'm no longer a boy!"

"Oh, listen! But are you aware that you have really taken on airs? But be quiet! You shouldn't talk about these things at your age. Besides, you are not free to marry whoever you please. There are many things to take into consideration. . . . And put it in your head, once and for always, that Pellegra will never be, can never be your wife."

"Why?" Emanuele asked, both astonished and annoyed.

"You will know why when it is the right time."

"And why not now?"

Don Girolamo stared in amazement at this cocky young man who suddenly was raising his cockscomb and ruffling his feathers.

"But do you know," he said to him, "that ever since you left the Castello a Mare you have been a little impertinent, like never before? What is this new development? It annoys me!"

"But—"

"But now be quiet; you have no right to speak."

Emanuele reddened and his eyes flashed in anger. He looked at Don Girolamo and hurled words at him that wounded him deeply in his heart: "After all," he said, "you are not my father, you are my uncle; but I have never found out how and why you are my uncle, nor who gave you authority over me."

Don Girolamo turned pale; Signora Francesca, with her face altered by a painful sense of disbelief, let out a cry and clasped her hands. Was that really Emanuele who was speaking in that haughty and ungrateful manner? He, the little one she had picked up and raised with her own milk? Whom she had loved like a son? He stood there surly and ill-tempered, perhaps dismayed by his own audacity and regretting having let himself get carried away but resolved not to give an inch and not to take back what he had said.

"It's true!" Don Girolamo murmured with a swollen heart. "You are right; I am not your father and I never explained to you how our kinship came about. . . . You are right. Kinship? But who can say to what extent we are related? Perhaps we are not in the slightest. . . . Authority? I have no legal authority over you because the Gran Corte Civile didn't entrust you to my guardianship; but one night, a cold winter night, I picked you up from the middle of the street, and you had been born a few days earlier. . . . I collected you and your dying mother and brought you to my house; and that woman there, Francesca, she had been my wife for a few years, and we had a baby. Your mother died; she was unable to give you a drop of her milk and so my wife shared her breast between you and our baby. And after six months you were strong and healthy but our baby died; perhaps it died because you were stronger and more demanding and took everything for yourself. And so then you became the only child. . . . I have no legal authority, certainly, and you are right, but I have some other responsibilities over you that perhaps you still don't understand. . . . Go! Go! Those words of yours reveal who you are. . . . I know what I am saying. In any case, pay attention to what I tell you: I will stop you from marrying the daughter of a painter, just as I would stop you from marrying any young girl of our class. I will stop you. . . . And that's enough now, and keep quiet. Until you are twenty-one, and while you are staying here in this house, I'm in charge."

Emanuele had listened to this speech at first sulkily, then with an astonishment that had turned into confusion, and finally with a veiled contempt toward himself and everyone else, which at the last words turned into a sense of rebellion. But he didn't say a word. This unexpected, unimaginable revelation had silenced him. So then he was a lost child, a foundling, an orphan of who knew who, something like an anonymous person! That was why they had put him in the Collegio dei Turchini! . . . And then that surname they had given him and that story of his mother who died in childbirth? Why had they lied? And why all that secrecy that he sensed in Don Girolamo's words? Was there a mystery surrounding his birth, then? And what was the mystery? And was what Don Girolamo was saying now the truth or was it another lie? One thing was certain, that between him and the razionale Ammirata there was no bond of kinship. Well, then, he could do as he pleased.

He went to bed that evening with his mind full of all these thoughts that gave his life a new direction. Signora Francesca must certainly know whose son he was; she could, indeed, she had to tell him. She loved him so much that she would not deny him that secret. His dilemma was clear: either to find out who he was and how he came to be in the Ammirata household, or to go away forever. His adoptive mother would have to choose.

All this didn't prevent Emanuele from seeing Pellegra the following morning on the belvedere. But he was silent about what he had learned and about the obstacles that stood in his way, and he continued to intoxicate her with kisses and caresses. But Don Girolamo went to see the painter and said to him outright that their friendship would last only on condition that he kept a close eye on his daughter. And he spoke in such a harsh and threatening manner that it frightened Don Vincenzo.

"Have no doubt, have no doubt . . . I will do as you wish. Of course I will do it. We are good friends, goodness! . . . And we must remain good friends! . . . You will see what I am going to do. . . . Pellegra! Ah, yes? But I will take care of her! . . . I'll send her to Rome, to Rome, to Rome."

Fear was turning Don Vincenzo into a beast; he screamed at, threatened his daughter and even wanted to beat her.

"Now you've done it! Surely now you've done it! And you want to plunge me into this mess? Me? With Don Girolamo? . . . That man will shoot me in the back, do you understand? . . . In the back, and kill me! Do you want to get me killed? But I am going to kill you first!"

Don Girolamo had ordered him to keep an eye on Pellegra, and Don Vincenzo didn't allow her to take a step without hurrying after her; and at night he locked her in her room, so the following morning she wasn't able to go up to the belvedere. But neither did Emanuele have the opportunity to go there, because Don Girolamo forced him to go with him to the Ospedale Civico.

The young man was defiant.

"But what do you want me to do at the hospital?"

"Nothing; you will be with me."

Don Girolamo was inflexible, and Emanuele had to obey. When he returned home, the young man was seized by a fit of such violent rage that he tore his clothes. Signora Francesca was so scared by that sight that she knelt at his feet and, hugging him, she begged him, crying, "Emanuele! Emanuele! . . . For heaven's sake!"

Emanuele seemed agitated and paid no attention to her; with his face in flames and his eyes full of tears, he beat his temples and ground his teeth. When he was able to speak, he said to his adoptive mother, "Why? Why?"

He was naturally alluding to those prohibitions that seemed to him like violent abuses.

"You tell me, why? If you don't tell me I'll throw myself off the balcony!"

Signora Francesca tried to calm him down, but Emanuele didn't intend to give in; more than once he attempted to rush to the balcony. Finally the poor woman, who felt her insides being ripped apart, said to him, "I will tell you; calm down and obey, and I will tell you."

"Well?"

Signora Francesca seemed uncertain, but Emanuele threatened.

"Well, your uncle is right. . . . You cannot marry a common girl, because . . . because she is not of your rank!"

"Then what am I! Am I a prince?"

"Almost. . . . Until now it had to be concealed, but the day is not far off when you will be acknowledged . . . and you will have your titles, a grand palazzo, servants, fiefdoms . . . and then you will marry a lady. . . . That is all."

Emanuele looked at her in amazement. Was he the son and heir of a great lord rich with fiefdoms? Then how had he ever been picked up on the street? Why had his mother died after having been sheltered in the house of that modest worker? What mystery was hanging over his birth? But perhaps that was just a tale?

"It's not true," he said. "Tell these tall tales to others, not to me."

"It's not true?" moaned Signora Francesca. "I wish. . . . Oh, why do you think that your uncle was pursued and I was thrown in prison? Precisely because Don Girolamo has tried and is trying to restore your status and to restore the wealth that

belongs to you and that was usurped from you! Therefore, be good and obedient
. . . we are doing it for your sake. When you are no longer poor Emanuele, ward
of Don Girolamo Ammirata, and you are a count, marchese, duke—whatever it
may be—you will marry a lady of your rank! You cannot marry another woman
because it would be a disgrace, and the viceroy wouldn't allow you to. . . . He
would banish you to a royal castle, in Trapani or Termini, and she would be shuttered in a monastery. That's how it is. Everyone in their own class. . . . This is the
sacrosanct truth before God, who sees us and listens to us!"

Emanuele remained dumbfounded by this revelation, whose truth he now no
longer doubted; he raised one last resistance, so as not to immediately give in,
and out of curiosity more than anything else: "I will believe you when you tell
me the name that I bear."

"Ah, no! I said too much . . . and if Don Girolamo found out . . . God, what
grief it would be for me! Do you want to expose me to such grief? For now, you
cannot and must not know . . . for now you must not be anything other than the
nephew of Ammirata. . . . Woe to you if it were known! . . . You don't realize . . .
and I cannot tell you more; I can only tell you that you escaped death by a miracle. For now, do not persist. . . . Then, perhaps soon, you will know everything."

Emanuele remained pensive. His thoughts took a different direction, and some
new aspirations of nobility and power sprang up from the bottom of his consciousness. Noble, rich, he would be able to do what he wanted and whatever pleased
him; no one could stop him.

Pellegra? He liked her, loved her, he would love her forever. As for marrying her
. . . he would even marry her secretly. What did he care? The viceroy, the castle,
the monastery. . . . Nonsense! He would be noble and rich! . . . He felt seized by
a longing for his own domain. In reality, given that he was a lord, he was the only
one to have the full right to be in charge and impose his will. Gratitude? Oh yes.
He would put up his benefactors in his palazzo, would give them a sum of money,
and thus settle his debt to them. These and other similar thoughts began to teem
in his head. He promised Signora Francesca that he would be calm and no longer
talk of marriage; but he made this promise with the attitude of a little overlord
who knows to concede rather than obey.

"But meanwhile," he thought, "why can't I continue to see Pellegra?"

The blood of his lineage was beginning to reveal itself, and lust glowed on the
face of that still-callow young man who had left the Vicaria debased and experienced in the mysteries of life.

CHAPTER 20

Donna Gabriella, after arriving at the palazzo, had just exchanged greetings with her husband and answered a few of his questions, and then she had gone to withdraw to her rooms. The intense emotions of that journey had deeply disturbed her soul, already depressed and upset by what had happened at the Castello della Pietra, and she felt the urgent need to be alone and to abandon herself to her thoughts.

Violante, on the other hand, stayed with her father.

Don Raimondo, relinquishing the gravity and sternness that he usually assumed in front of his daughter, had let himself be overcome by paternal affection, and after having impulsively hugged his daughter, he had sat her tenderly on his knees like a child and was asking her a thousand questions. He wanted to hear the account of her imprisonment in minute detail, and in his legitimate curiosity was lurking a terrible suspicion.

The paternal caresses, to which Violante was not accustomed and which gently surprised her, the questions that he was pressing her with, and the affectionate concern with which he encouraged her had dissolved every reluctance and every uneasiness, and the girl felt almost happy to be able to tell her father about the extraordinary adventure that had happened to her and that still seemed inexplicable to her.

Indeed, there was more than one extraordinary adventure. And so she began by telling him about her abduction from the monastery and the miraculous intervention of her liberator. Unwittingly, she was constantly mentioning "Signor Blasco," her voice taking on some gentle and affectionate intonations that were equivalent to adjectives, but she didn't notice that whenever she mentioned "Signor Blasco" a flash of hatred would appear in her father's eyes.

"Oh," she would say, "if not for Signor Blasco, I would have died, Signor Padre!"

She was silent only about the scene with her stepmother, either out of discretion or fear or from that instinctive reserve that warned her to be silent about an event that could amount to a revelation or to a confession.

"Now go rest," said Don Raimondo at the end. "You must be very tired; no one will touch a hair on your head, and besides, in a few days, as soon as the first large English vessel leaves, I will bring you with me to Turin."

"Leave?" moaned Violante, dismayed at the idea of not seeing Blasco ever again. "Why? Why?"

"Because I must return to court, and I will certainly not leave you exposed to more dangers."

The tone of these words was quite harsh, and Violante, seeing once again the stern and cold mask return to her father's face, lowered her head and said nothing more. She kissed his hand and retired to her room. She truly felt a great need to be alone. Alone? Oh, no; there was an image and a name that were always in front of her eyes and in her heart, and she wanted to shut herself in her room in order to abandon herself to her thoughts.

But what a multitude of thoughts and emotions! Where was Blasco? She had seen him boldly escape and get away from that militia and then had lost sight of him, but she had no doubt that he was safe. Her great faith in the invincibility of that hero of hers rendered her confident and calm about his fate. To her mind he was one of those princes or one of those marvelous characters from fairy tales who overcome every obstacle, knock down giants and monsters, who are invulnerable and protected by some benevolent fairy. Certainly he had to have a secret power to be able to get out of so many dangers unharmed and victorious.

But where was he? What was he doing? When she abandoned herself to this investigation, a dark and threatening figure appeared in the back of her mind: her stepmother. She now saw her armed with a knife as if ready to brandish it, not against her, but resolutely against Blasco. She was gripped by a cold sense of dread; her illusion was so vivid that it took away her perception of reality, and it seemed to her that the door to her room was opening and Donna Gabriella was slowly entering and coming toward her. The silence immobilized her.

* * *

Donna Gabriella had, in fact, opened the door and had come in and was approaching Violante. When she was close to her, seeing the girl immobile and with eyes wide open, she shook her arm, saying, "Well, are you not getting up?"

Violante let out a cry and jumped up, passing her hand over her eyes.

"God, what a fright!"

"Why are you afraid?" the duchess asked her in a harsh tone of voice. "Why are you afraid? Have you done something wrong?"

"Oh, Signora Madre! . . . Me?"

She tried to regain her courage. Donna Gabriella was standing in front of her, giving her an inquisitive look that searched the depths of her soul. After a moment of silence, she said, "Did your father ask you anything?"

"What should he have asked me?"

"Stop playing the fool. He certainly wanted to know what happened to us."

"Yes, Signora Madre."

"Everything?"

Her expression of this word was significant enough to leave some doubt in Violante's heart, who, with a sweetly sorrowful smile, answered, "Everything, no . . . about some things I was silent."

"About what?"

"What could cause my father great pain."

Donna Gabriella stood silently for a moment, gazing around the room without seeing; then she said, "Watch yourself! Say just one word about that episode and I will kill you! And no one will save you. I will kill you at night, in your sleep, so that no one could run to your aid."

She ground her teeth with a savage ferocity, clenching her fists, pleased with the fear that she saw spreading over the young girl's face.

"And before killing you, I will tell your father that you are the mistress of Blasco da Castiglione."

"Signora Madre!"

Clasping her hands, with her face in flames, she begged her to stop.

"Are you afraid that I will talk, then?" the duchess continued mercilessly.

"But what have I done, Signora Madre, to deserve your anger? What have I done?"

"Quiet! I forbid you to speak. . . . Be quiet! What have you done? To me, nothing. It is your father to whom you have brought dishonor; it is the family that you have shamed. . . . Oh, it is useless to deny it. I know everything."

"What, Signora Madre, what?"

"Oh! The innocent one!"

"I swear to you, Signora Madre, that I have done nothing wrong."

"Quiet! . . . Be quiet! . . . You are of your father's blood and you cannot slip up."

She felt the need to abuse, to lash out in order to give vent to her embittered, unfulfilled, cold, and rapacious spirit. She well knew that Violante was innocent, but what did it matter? It was enough for her to know that Violante loved Blasco and that Blasco loved Violante, and that she, she a woman full of her every desire, every impulse, every passion, had been abandoned and scorned. All that was more than enough to light a volcano of hatred in her heart against the young girl. This idea pounded at her fiercely; in that instant she had a clear vision of that love, and all her nerves shook.

She approached Violante, seized her wrists, and, shaking her roughly, screamed, "You must not love him! Do you understand? . . . You must not love him! . . . I do not want it; I do not want it!"

Her voice had the pang of a sob.

A helpless Violante begged her again, "Signora Madre, have mercy!"

Then suddenly a voice resounded from the back of the room. "Gabriella, what are you doing?"

It was Don Raimondo; he rushed forward and hugged the girl, whom Donna Gabriella had released.

"What?" she answered, standing haughtily like a woman whose dignity was wounded, and, pointing to Violante, she said, "I defend your interests and your dignity, which she defames."

"Who? Violante? . . . Her?" And, changing his tone of voice, he added, "But you, you are mad!"

"Ah, I am mad? But ask her yourself if she isn't the mistress of Blasco da Castiglione."

Don Raimondo jumped back as if struck by lightning.

"Her? . . . Her?" And moving again toward Violante he raised her head, shouting in amazement in which his disbelief, pain, and hatred were resonating together: "You? You . . . and is this true?"

Violante looked at her father in the eyes and said boldly, "No, it is not true."

"She is lying, lying, the impudent girl!"

"Be quiet!" yelled Don Raimondo.

"I am not lying."

"Deny, then, if you can, that you love Blasco da Castiglione. There is the crucifix, swear!"

"I love him, yes," exclaimed the young girl, standing tall in her diminutive self with the dignity of a mature woman. "I love him, but I am not his mistress."

"She has slept in the arms of that man!" Donna Gabriella retorted, embittered.

Don Raimondo bent over his daughter. "So, is it true?"

"Yes, it's true, he slept next to me, only at the bedside, but I have never felt so safe, not even in the arms of my mother."

Don Raimondo was looking first at his wife, then at his daughter, tossed between the accusation and the defense; one moment believing, then not. It was repugnant to him to think that his daughter was guilty, but meanwhile it was also true that Violante loved the hated bastard and one night had found herself at his mercy. In her first account, Violante, out of modesty, had kept silent about that idyllic moment, which the duchess was now hatefully revealing, altering and making it worse.

"Is she innocent? Is it possible?" Don Raimondo asked himself. An excruciating doubt took hold of his heart. With clenched fists, almost threatening, he shouted to his daughter, "Then defend yourself! Exonerate yourself if you can!"

"Exonerate herself? But she confessed!" Donna Gabriella shouted.

Then Don Raimondo turned to his wife, and his face was blazing with hatred and pain.

"Be quiet!" he yelled. "I well know what drives you to accuse my daughter; I know you well enough, Donna Gabriella, and you are not the one who should be protecting my dignity. Get out! I will see to my daughter."

Donna Gabriella became livid; blinded by her own anger.

"I will leave, yes, and not only from this room but also from your house. I have stayed here too long and no longer want to be an accomplice to your villainies."

"Wretch!" shouted Don Raimondo, appalled, and in an impulse of anger and fear he unsheathed his sword and was about to fling himself at her, but Violante leapt up and clung to his neck, crying, "No, Father, no!"

Donna Gabriella didn't seem daunted; she drew back slowly and after reaching the door she turned and hurled these last words: "You don't surprise me. These walls are accustomed to blood; in fact, it is here that you murdered Maddalena!"

"Ah, you will not live!" shouted an exasperated Don Raimondo, and he rushed forward, but Donna Gabriella had gone out and had bolted the door behind her, and Violante had already caught hold of his arm.

At that point a servant knocked on the other door that led to the corridor. "Who is it?" shouted Don Raimondo, promptly sheathing his sword.

"Your Excellency, the most illustrious captain of justice is here."

"I'm coming." He looked at his daughter uncertainly and said, "Put on your cloak and follow me."

As he was leaving, Don Raimondo commanded the servant: "Have my private carriage harnessed at once."

Then he went into his study where the captain of justice was waiting for him, leaving Violante in the antechamber with the old maidservant. "Wait here for me."

* * *

The discussion between the duke and the captain was brief. Don Raimondo escorted him to the grand staircase and parted by saying, "Then I will wait for you here."

Entering the drawing room, the servant told him that the carriage was ready.

"Come," he said somberly to Violante.

At the foot of the staircase, a small man, blind in one eye, took off his hat and, extending his hand, he asked in a whining voice, "Charity, Your Excellency, for the love of God!"

Don Raimondo turned rudely and was about to have him chased away when the blind man quickly added, "Don Antonino sent me."

Don Raimondo gave a start, then approached the blind man.

"Who, Don Antonino?"

"Bucolaro . . . about that matter."

The duke looked around suspiciously and put a silver coin in the blind man's hand and asked, "Well?"

"At midnight at Zi' Alessio's."

"Take it, good man," Don Raimondo said loudly, nodding, "and God be with you."

The blind man left, and Don Raimondo, after climbing into the carriage where Violante was waiting for him, directed, "To Santa Caterina."

CHAPTER 21

The nuns of the magnificent and noble Monastery of Santa Caterina were coming out of the choir, where they had recited the evening service, when Don Raimondo's carriage arrived, much to the astonishment of the nun in charge of the revolving wheel and the office—that is, the "Mamma." Although his two older sisters were in the convent, the Duke of Motta wasn't in the habit of visiting them often; except during important religious holidays or times when nuns took the veil, he was never seen in the monastery's parlor. His arrival, and even more the unusual hour, naturally must have aroused the astonishment of the nuns.

He asked the nun, who had rushed behind the grates at the sound of the doorbell, to invite the Mother Abbess to be so kind as to come, together with Sister Clementina and Sister Maria Rosaria—his sisters—to the parlor.

"Whatever could this be about?" exclaimed the three frightened nuns as they rushed there.

Don Raimondo wasted no words; after having praised the monastery and the wisdom of the Mother Abbess who governed it and having mentioned the danger faced by his daughter, now free due to a true miracle of the Blessed Virgin, he begged the nuns to keep her in the monastery from that evening on.

"She returned a few hours ago, but I do not want to keep her at home or take her back to the convent school in Montevergini; I want her to devote herself to God and take her vows, and I cannot find a better monastery than this."

Violante wasn't saying a word; pale, with downcast face, she silently let her tears flow. Her father's last words had made her heart ache, but she could do nothing except cry and be silent. An act of rebellion against these coercions, against these forces against her will and her personal freedom, in those times was not even to be imagined, and young girls knew from a tender age that they were destined for the monastery.

She entered the cloister that night, perhaps like the guilty ancient vestal virgins would enter the tomb. Her father didn't kiss her, did not say a loving word to her; harsh, cold, and impassable, he accompanied her to the door of the cloister, pushed her through the open doorway, and returned to his carriage without expressing any sign of emotion.

His mind was preoccupied with thoughts of a much more serious nature. Donna Gabriella's allusions and her rebellion had revealed a new enemy to him, formidable not only because he himself, although denying the truth, had confessed which crimes his mysterious enemies were accusing him of, but also because he understood by what emotion she had been driven: the emotion that more than any other takes away a woman's perception of reality and command of her conscience—jealousy. What were the interests of the family and the dignity of the name for her, before the worm that was gnawing at her heart? And, thinking back to its origin, he felt his hatred for Blasco growing.

An obligation toward him for having rescued and brought him back his daughter? He didn't feel any. Their freedom was nothing but the price of an agreement; he had bought his women in exchange for his enemies. But besides, he thought, by this time Blasco must be in a secure place; he was rather surprised that Matteo Lo Vecchio or Captain Mangialocchi hadn't shown up. Perhaps they had remained in Misilmeri or, for who knows what reason, they were waiting in order to travel at night. He had no doubt that Blasco had successfully been ambushed. Indeed, as soon as she had arrived, Donna Gabriella had told him about the encounter, and, in fact, she had strongly complained that that peasant, the captain of the rural company, hadn't submitted to her commands, since she presumed that Don Raimondo would never have tolerated any abuse to a person sent by him. Violante had added that she had been very afraid because they were firing several shots. Therefore, Blasco had fallen into the hands of the militia and, dead or alive, they would have taken him to Palermo. Perhaps dead or gravely wounded, he thought; but meanwhile by this time Matteo Lo Vecchio should have arrived.

Blasco dead or captured, the famous papers in his possession, and the sect surprised, caught in its lair, as he had already orchestrated . . . what could he be afraid of? He had put everything in place in order to play that last and most decisive game, and he felt a blind faith in his heart that he would come out victorious, since nothing more remained unknown to him about that secret society, about its objectives, and about the causes of its ruthless, relentless, never-ending war against him.

Meanwhile Antonino Bucolaro wanted to speak with him at midnight in front of Zi' Alessio's tavern, below Santa Cristina la Vecchia. Why? Was there some new development? Hadn't all the agreements been made? He returned to his palazzo; his faithful manservant told him that the duchess had gone out a quarter of an hour earlier in her portantina and had had herself taken to the Palazzo La Grua, ordering the servants to bring to her, at the latest the following morning, her wardrobe and all that belonged to her.

"Very well!" he replied curtly. He was expecting them to say that someone had come to look for him but to no avail.

"What the hell is Matteo Lo Vecchio up to?" he said to himself, worried; and with that unspeakable delay was associated the thought of the meeting requested of him by Antonino Bucolaro. Was there some connection? Had that demon of a bastard perhaps escaped the ambush and upset everything? That suspicion made him shudder. He waited impatiently for midnight, counting the hours by the clock of Monte di Pietà.

When it seemed like the right time, he left, on foot and armed, and he had two faithful servants accompany him, armed as well. They only had to walk along the last stretch of Via Sant'Agostino and turn downhill toward the Church of the Angelo Custode, all the way down to the Papireto.

Except for the houses that still today face Via Papireto, there were no others at that time along the descent between the Church of the Angelo Custode and the Duomo, and the deserted area still retained traces of the ancient swamp that had been drained. The little hill, now reduced to the foundation on which stands the Ospedale Grande dei Sacerdoti, rose in its wild state above the ancient basin and was scattered with short thin reeds. A few streets emerged from the interior of the city, almost perpendicular to the plain. At the end of one of them, behind the historic Capella dell'Incoronazione, was the Church of Santa Cristina la Vecchia, a small Norman building that still retains the arches and ogives of the original architecture. At that time a small garden stretched alongside the church, bordered by a vicolo that descended toward a street, and at whose corner stood Zi' Alessio's tavern—a tavern so famous that the street was named after it. The night was dreadfully dark, without a star in the sky, only a dense canopy of black and impenetrable clouds. There were no lamps, the streets were dark, and one couldn't see a single step ahead.

Don Raimondo was descending along the steep Via dell'Angelo Custode, poorly cobbled and slippery due to the nighttime humidity and on account of the soft mud that the rains and the citizens' trash would spread there. One of the servants went ahead with a lantern in order to light the way so that the master wouldn't trip amid the filth that the housewives would throw out from their balconies and windows at nightfall, since almost all the houses at that time lacked toilets.

The vastness of the uncultivated and squalid plain, whose boundaries the night seemed to obliterate, rendered the darkness even more frightening.

Reaching the entrance of the street to Zi' Alessio's tavern, Don Raimondo ordered the servants to stop.

"Wait for me here and put out the lantern."

He entered the street alone and walked along it at a hurried pace until he reached Zi' Alessio's tavern. He turned to see if his servants could see him, but the shadows were so dense that he couldn't even see the beginning of the street.

* * *

The door of the tavern was closed. He went up to it and tapped gently; no one answered. He knocked a little harder but, at the moment he was straining to listen, he felt himself overwhelmed by a sort of whirlwind, a frenzy, something indescribable and inconceivable that covered his eyes and mouth, enveloped his arms and legs, lifted him off the ground, and thrust him into the void. He had no time to be surprised, to move, to scream. He couldn't even understand what unknown and mysterious force had overwhelmed him.

He struggled, trying to free himself, and only then did he realize that he was enveloped in a type of thick net, as if wrapped with a thousand straps. He felt no contact from any hands; he was neither in an upright nor a horizontal position. He couldn't even understand how he was curled up. He was sure he was being carried somewhere. Where? How? By whom? He wanted to scream but couldn't since his mouth was gagged. Who had gagged him? Had he fallen into an ambush, then? That half-blind man who had come to invite him on behalf of Antonino Bucolaro was an emissary, perhaps one of the attackers; perhaps Antonino Bucolaro himself had drawn him into this trap. He felt lost.

He didn't hear any sound of steps around him. The people who were carrying him had perhaps taken off their shoes so as not to be heard. However, he could sense that they were going along slightly inclined streets and that they turned two or three times. From Zi' Alessio's tavern to Piazza San Cosmo, the route wasn't long; he, who from the beginning had understood into whose hands he had fallen, was calculating how long it should take to reach the Beati Paoli's cave. He wanted to get there soon in order to get himself out of this situation. And then he had one thought on his mind: he was counting the steps and the time; within an hour and a half, perhaps everything would be clear. One just needed to have the ability and cunning to get to that point.

After fifteen minutes, perceiving the difficulty and irregularity of the steps, he felt that they had entered a passageway. They had arrived. He waited to be freed from the net, and soon after, in fact, he felt they were removing the wrappings that were confining him, the blindfold and the gag.

His eyes had to close again, struck by the bright light of a few lanterns that illuminated that place, already known to him. It was the underground rotunda where he had been led one night, with its stone counter, side passageways, cupola, and niches. About twenty men stood there, armed, dressed in black sackcloth, their faces concealed by masks. Two others sat at the counter. In the middle of the room, near a table, there was a small desk furnished with everything needed for writing. Don Raimondo wasn't surprised by that paraphernalia, which was already familiar to him and which he was already expecting; he was unable, however, to control the sense of fear that ran through his blood at the sight of those unknown, immobile, and menacing men in their silent poses.

After the brief moment that was necessary for everyone to take their places and get ready, the leader made a gesture from the counter where he was and began, in a slightly ironic tone: "Duke of Motta, the means chosen to have you come here tonight among us are certainly not the most fitting and adequate for your person and your esteem; please forgive us, but we were sure that if we had invited you by courteous means, you would not have thought to cede to our wishes. *Necessitas non habet legem*;[1] and for us it is an inevitable necessity to have you here tonight."

Don Raimondo didn't respond. He had immediately resumed his cold and impenetrable mask and was pressing his thin lips together in order to prevent any nervous twitches that could betray him.

"Duke of Motta," resumed the leader, abandoning his ironic affability and assuming a harsh and imperious tone of voice. "Duke of Motta, you have had the clear proof that we can do anything, and that we keep our promises. We must now complete the work already begun."

He took from the counter some papers, whose edges were singed, and continued: "These papers, Don Raimondo Albamonte, contain the case that our tribunal has initiated against you."

Don Raimondo couldn't control a chilling sensation in his blood. How? Then those documents that he had hoped were already in Matteo Lo Vecchio's possession were in the hands of this terrifying tribunal. Had he been deceived?

"You are familiar with the contents of these documents, at least in their totality, because someone has let you know about them, and there is no need to tell you, a man of the law, what consequences they would produce for you if they were to be presented to the king's justice. . . . Your head, signore, is no longer safely on your shoulders."

The duke felt the cold blade of the ax on his neck.

"But we are generous. We will not hand these papers over to His Majesty unless you force us to do so. Tomorrow a vessel will leave for Genoa. You will agree with us that it will be easy for us to have it leave with either a cavaliere, a man of the law, or a prosecuting magistrate, and for him to go to Turin and introduce Emanuele Albamonte and present these documents to the king. . . . This man could, moreover, accuse you of having had Giuseppico murdered by Matteo Lo Vecchio; of having poisoned Peppa la Sarda in prison; of having had strangled in prison—without a regular trial—two alleged criminals; of having attempted to have Signor Blasco da Castiglione poisoned by Matteo Lo Vecchio in the prison in Messina; of having tried to have him murdered this morning on the road in Misilmeri, by Captain Mangialocchi's company."

"It isn't true!" stammered Don Raimondo.

---

1 "Necessity has no law."

"Don't deny it!" the leader rebuked him. "Don't deny what we have evidence of . . . lying makes your situation worse. . . . Don Raimondo Albamonte, are you prepared to acknowledge your crimes before us?"

The duke attempted an audacious retort: "I do not acknowledge your right to pass judgment," he said with some effort.

The leader looked at a clock that was on the counter.

"I grant you five minutes to reflect on your situation. Beware. You are in our hands and will never get out of here, except when it is time to hand you over to justice. Think about it."

A great silence followed, in which he heard only the ticktock of the clock; no one was moving, but Don Raimondo could feel everyone's eyes on him, flashing through the holes in their masks. He wasn't weighing his situation; he seemed to be counting the minutes, listening intently, almost waiting for a sign, a noise. But time passed by silently without any sign.

"Well," the leader resumed, "five minutes have passed. Don Raimondo, what is your answer?"

The duke pulled himself together, felt a shiver, sensed some hope fading away. He resorted to the only ploy he could think of: to waste time.

"What do you want me to do?"

"Nothing more or less than your duty: to acknowledge Emanuele Albamonte, your nephew, Duke of Motta."

"Me? Acknowledge a boy when I don't know who he is? Who can prove that he is my nephew?"

"Don Raimondo, don't try to evade us with your prevarications; there are twenty men here who can prove it, but remember one more fact, that sixteen years or so ago, you, pretending to be crushed by the disappearance of your nephew, issued public proclamations promising great rewards to whoever found him, and provided, based upon the statements of Sister Mary, the midwife, some definite clues: the baby had a small heart-shaped brown mark on his left shoulder blade. The proclamations from that time still exist; here is one, stamped with your coat of arms. And there is the revealing mark . . . what greater proof do you need than this?"

Don Raimondo felt doomed.

The step that the leader was asking him to take with such simplicity entailed the confession of his crimes and was equivalent to a voluntary offer of his head to the executioner or to a suicide. He saw in a rapid vision all the horrors of the suffering, the shame, the gallows.

His instinct for self-preservation made him cry out: "No! . . . No! . . . They are all lies."

"Don Raimondo Albamonte, beware. We are not here to waste time but to enact justice. Do you want to make a formal declaration signed by you and by witnesses that acknowledges Emanuele as your nephew and reinstates his status and his rank?"

"No!"

"Well, then, tomorrow Don Girolamo Ammirata will take your proclamation and Emanuele's birth certificate to the viceroy and will introduce your nephew to him; meanwhile in turn, someone will be leaving for Turin. You will wait here . . ."

And, turning to two of the silent and immobile men, he added, "Open the pit."

The men bent down and, after hooking a rope around a large iron ring, lifted a slab. A black and putrid square space appeared before the eyes of Don Raimondo, who stepped back in fear.

"Lower him!" ordered the leader.

The two Beati Paoli lifted him up, despite the fact that he planted his feet on the ground and tried to resist.

"Just a moment! . . . Just a moment!" he screamed desperately.

"Lower him!"

The men carrying out the order dragged his feet into the void; he almost lost his mind. The emptiness under his feet gave him the impression of an infinite void that would open up beneath him and swallow him up; it seemed to him that death had snatched him by the hair in order to toss him into that black, bottomless abyss. The terror, the fear for his life, and the desperation stifled every other expression except a desire to live.

"I consent!" he shrieked in a choked voice. "I consent!"

The leader motioned and the two men pulled Don Raimondo back up and put him back on his feet. During that brief scene, one of the masked men had given a sign of impatience and disdain that was barely suppressed but visible from his trembling hands.

"If . . . if I consent," Don Raimondo asked, "will you then give me those documents?"

"We will see. Now is not the time to impose conditions. Besides, have no fear, the declaration that you will write and sign and that will be ratified by a notary and by witnesses will not implicate you at all; on the contrary, it will bring you praise for your magnanimity, and you will be able to add one more hypocrisy to the others that make up your masquerade. Bring in the duke's notary."

A Beato Paolo left and returned almost at once, leading by the hand a pale and trembling man whom Don Raimondo recognized with shock and anger as his own family's notary.

"Don Raimondo," ordered the leader, "write."

The duke sat at the desk, took a pen, and wrote as the leader dictated:

In the name of the Blessed God and of the Holy Virgin, I, the undersigned Don Raimondo Albamonte, as Duke of Motta, with a joyful heart hereby declare to acknowledge, due to undisputable evidence and known details, the young boy Emanuele, an orphan picked up and raised by Don Girolamo Ammirata, as my dear beloved and precious nephew Emanuele Albamonte, legitimate son of the late Duke Emanuele, my brother, and of the late Donna Aloisia Ventimiglia; and I declare and acknowledge that to him alone, as legitimate heir, by virtue of royal pragmatic sanctions and of our constitutions, belongs the title and the investiture of the Duchy of Motta and of the other lands and fiefdoms pertaining to the House of Albamonte; and in formally renouncing the possession of said fiefdoms and lands with their attached titles, now wrongfully held by me, in favor of my nephew Emanuele, I acknowledge him as the head and lord of the family. And I thank Divine Providence for having granted me the singular grace of having found this dear lamented nephew of mine again, and for being able to restore his patrimony to him. With that, other than to provide for the health of my soul, I also intend to restore the blessed souls of my brother, the late Don Emanuele, and of the late Donna Aloisia. This declaration, written and signed by my hand, today, the day of the glorious virgin Santa Lucia, whose care has enlightened me, I entrust to my notary, Don Antonino Di Bello, so that he may keep it with his documents and take care of the execution of all the legal documents that may follow.

In Palermo 13 December 1714
Don Raimondo Albamonte
Of the Duchies of Motta

"And now you, Master Notary," the leader ordered.

In his turn the notary sat at the desk, and at the bottom of Don Raimondo's declaration he appended the necessary judicial wording. Four of the masked men signed the document, to which the notary affixed his seal and added his signature.

"Bring that document to me," commanded the leader, and having read it, he gave a sign of approval and placed it on the counter, saying, "Very well. Now let's proceed to the next matter, Don Raimondo."

The duke raised his head in fear.

He was a truly unrecognizable and terrifying sight; the head of Medusa would not have provoked a different effect.

"What else is there?" he moaned with barely a voice.

"A very simple matter," said the leader in a cheerful tone of voice. "You have some obligations toward a relative of yours: Blasco da Castiglione. If we limit ourselves to asking you for a declaration instead of handing you over to the executioner, it is solely out of consideration for this loyal and generous young man, to whom you have not shown your appreciation and neither have you acknowledged him. Don Raimondo Albamonte, I ask you for the hand of your daughter for Blasco da Castiglione."

Then the body of that trembling and terrified man shuddered violently; he stood up and with blazing eyes exclaimed, "No! . . . Not this. My daughter is mine! Mine!"

From the circle of black and masked men one came forward and, extending his hand with a solemn gesture, said, "Blasco da Castiglione renounces."

All eyes turned to that man with a sudden feeling of astonishment; the same Don Raimondo was unable to control a certain emotion.

That one continued, "Blasco da Castiglione renounces and says to this tribunal: that justice be done and that the ward's name and fortune be restored, but do not deprive an innocent girl in order to clothe another! He says to you, righteously, he says to you, Don Raimondo Albamonte: give your daughter to Emanuele so that the ducal crown may remain on her innocent head!"

A murmur of approval ran across the lips under the masks. Don Raimondo seemed illuminated by a ray of light; in a flash he saw all the advantages he could derive from such a proposal, in which generosity and self-sacrifice overpowered his cold reasoning and obscured his perception of the future. He clasped his hands in a gesture of assent and gratitude, but at that moment the shot of a pistol resounded outside, and a voice shouted, "Lock up! Lock up!"

CHAPTER 22

That evening Antonino Bucolaro had crossed the Rubicon; compromised by Matteo Lo Vecchio in the eyes of the Duke of Motta, and incited by him, he had placed himself completely in the service of justice and had informed the captain of the city. A little before dawn a half dozen soldiers were lying in wait in the house of Judge Baldi; others, in groups of twos and threes, were lying in wait in the church of the Canceddi; the greatest number were hiding in the nearby Convent of San Cosmo; and another half dozen, in disguise, occupied an empty house in the courtyard of Ecce Homo[1] next to Vicolo degli Orfani. And they remained there all day, without seeing a living soul, awaiting the night, when another half company of soldiers would arrive in battle formation.

A rare and almost new occurrence in the conventions of justice, these operations of lying in wait were carried out without arousing any suspicion, with maximum caution so that the two entrances to Vicolo degli Orfani and the two entrances to the underground of the Beati Paoli were watched over by a truly invisible army.

Midnight had passed more than an hour earlier when these soldiers began to emerge from their hiding places and to draw up, assembling in their assigned places, and in the meantime a half company was arriving silently from Via Papireto.

Cautiously they formed a closed circle. Two large squads advanced from both ends of Vicolo degli Orfani; another occupied the courtyard of Casa Baldi; some reserves were spread out in Piazza San Cosmo, in the Capo, and in front of Casa Baldi.

The two lookouts of the Beati Paoli, stationed at the entrances to Vicolo degli Orfani, were thus caught by surprise. One fell into the hands of the soldiers; the other managed to reach the door to the underground, firing a pistol shot and shouting a warning.

That shot reverberated through the vaults of the underground, creating a moment of confusion and almost of disarray, but Don Raimondo wasn't able to contain his joy and cried out, "Finally!"

But that cry came as a shock.

---

1   This courtyard on Via Sant'Agostino is so called due to the existence of a small church by the same name. RLD, 791.

"*Scaffarate il bambino!*"[2] shouted the leader.

A few of the Beati Paoli flung themselves on Don Raimondo, knocked him down, tied his arms and feet in an instant and with such skill that before the duke had a chance to recover from the surprise he was already tied up like a salami.

Meanwhile, at the door at the end of the vestibule and at the door to Vicolo degli Orfani, powerful blows were heard, perhaps from axes or poles, that resounded deeply through the underground. And at the same time other blows resounded from the end of the corridor that led to the courtyard of Casa Baldi.

The leader ordered, "*Coprite il rosso e lasciate un occhio.*"[3]

They extinguished all torches, leaving only one. The blows were increasing. Don Raimondo waited, anxiously hoping and keeping an eye on the movements of the men who were holding him. Every blow on the two doors made his heart jump; he thought, "Now they are knocking them down; now they are coming in, and they will get them all."

The creaking of the wood and the squeaking of the hinges filled him with joy, as though they were steps toward his being freed.

"*Ammanicatevi i soffianti; e voi scarcerate la fumosa e rotolatela nei tubi.*"[4]

A few of the Beati Paoli bent down and took out rifles from under the benches; others grabbed some bundles of firewood from niches dug into the walls and piled them up at the end of the corridors, next to the doors where the blows were heard.

The leader ordered, "Follow me."

He started off toward a corner of the room, and after he thrust both hands into a niche, he pushed back a boulder with both his hands. A large space capable of allowing a person to pass through opened up, at the same moment when one of the doors fell under the blows of the axes.

"*Vampa,*"[5] the leader ordered.

Two men ran to set the bundles of wood on fire; immediately, large clouds of smoke and tongues of flame rose up that put a barrier of fire between the door and the corridor. Some gunshots echoed, and the bullets got crushed, chipping the walls; the corridors and the room began to fill with a dense and suffocating smoke.

Meanwhile one man, who had gone unnoticed, began to groan loudly; the leader turned energetically and noticed the notary, who had been seized with terror upon hearing the shots and, throwing himself on his knees, was begging them to save him. At a nod from the leader, a man with a torch passed through the opening; another followed him, and they pushed the notary through.

"Stop crying, good Lord! And go in," they said.

---

2 "Take the prisoner and tie him up!"
3 "Put out all the lights except one."
4 "Get the rifles ready and lay the wood in front of the doors."
5 "Light them."

One by one the Beati Paoli plunged into the opening and vanished, while from the door that had been knocked down there were more and more frequent gunshots on the wood in order to scatter the flames, and some shouts ordered: "Surrender!"

Don Raimondo, having been rendered immobile by the rope, consumed by rage and at the same time anxious, looking and waiting, took heart again at those shots and tried to draw attention to himself. "Help! Help!"

"Silence him!" ordered the leader.

A crashing of the other door was heard; more shouts, more shots resounded. Don Raimondo's heart jumped for joy and he exclaimed, "You are trapped!"

"Not yet," the leader said calmly, throwing aside his sack and drawing two pistols from his belt. He gave a sign to his men. "Stuff this salami!" he ordered.

Don Raimondo suddenly felt himself lifted up in the air, thrown feet first into the opening, pushed and pulled before he could resist, protest, call for help.

Only two men were left in front of the niche, the leader and one other, he too without the sack and armed. Through the holes of their masks they looked at each other in silence for a moment; then the leader said, "Go in."

"After you!"

"Go in, there's no time to lose."

Amid the clouds of smoke that had already filled the underground, the flames were dying out and were sparse and diminished. From the end of the corridors could be heard the steps of soldiers, who were coming in firing their rifles.

"I'm staying."

"Do you want me to make you go through by force, Blasco?" said the leader.

"Don't touch me, Coriolano, don't touch me!"

A voice shouted from the end of the corridor: "Surrender!"

Coriolano stepped forward and fired his two pistols, then with a quick gesture pushed Blasco toward the opening, murmuring, "You surely don't want to let yourself be caught!"

He also passed through and pushed the boulder back into place. It was a narrow, low, humid corridor; a narrow passage that seemed to stretch into infinity, in whose darkness the lantern shed no light but instead seemed like a tiny red speck.

The Beati Paoli were waiting, in file—the notary among them, trembling, Don Raimondo, pale, mute, terrified.

Coriolano ordered, "Forward."

All those men, preceded by the lantern, began to walk silently through that corridor, enveloped in the shadows and in mystery; the last to come was Blasco, with his head bent down, his chest swollen with rage, spite, and regret, troubled by a hundred thoughts and a hundred different emotions. They had been going forward for some time, following the corridor, when it suddenly seemed wider; there was, in fact, a crossroads.

"Stop!" shouted Coriolano.

He called for the small lantern and had one of the wings of the crossroads lit up. There was a stairway carved into the volcanic rock. He summoned two companions. "Have the notary go up, and accompany him. You will quickly see where this stairway leads. . . . Go, signore; your services will be generously rewarded."

The notary followed the Beati Paoli up the steep and hard-to-climb narrow stairway, which entered into the vault and then faded from view. The group resumed their journey. The corridor was now wider, lined with niches; it was some branch of the ancient catacombs, of which the cave of the Beati Paoli was only a segment.

After about forty steps or so, a circular room with encrusted walls opened up; there were puddles of water on the ground, a sign of the seepage raining down from above.

Coriolano ordered everyone to stop. Don Raimondo was watching. He still didn't know what his fate would be, but he had lost all hope; fear was now rendering him a coward. He had put his hopes on the surprise attack by justice, and when he had heard the doors give way he had thought that no one would be able to escape; instead here they were all safe, and he was at their complete mercy. What kind of soldiers were those, who were afraid of a little fire and a couple of pistol shots? So was this how the State was being served, then? The death that awaited him made him furious at the captain of justice, at the soldiers, and at the viceroy himself; he blamed everyone in his heart for his impending doom.

"Cowards! Cowards! To abandon me like this!" These thoughts reverberated in his head, but he couldn't say a word; his lips were shut tight, he had a lump in his throat. When the Beati Paoli, at a sign, put him down on his feet, his legs gave way and he fell in the mud like a rag, with his teeth chattering.

The terror was making him even more miserable.

They formed a circle around him; the lantern held high by one of the Beati Paoli—it was Andrea—cast a scant and reddish light that at times illuminated a chin here and there, fading away on the black masks. Amid the dark clothes and in the gloomy space, those chins, glimpsed in the tenuous reddish glow, seemed cut off and rendered the scene grotesquely surreal.

In the profound silence, in which could be heard the gnashing of Don Raimondo's teeth, Coriolano said slowly and somberly, "Don Raimondo Albamonte, you have arranged an ambush in order to catch us! You—who we so far have saved from disgrace, and for whom a few moments ago, generously, we wanted to retain your rank and your name—you were expecting to hand our heads over to justice! Raimondo Albamonte, you have lost every right to forgiveness and to mercy!"

"Pity! Have pity on me!" stammered the wretched man.

"Do you know where we are? Here above, above our heads, rises the Palazzo della Motta; we have brought you back to your house because it is not right that the likes of you die elsewhere. You will die here, and the palazzo for which you have so much greed and that you filled with blood and sorrow will weigh heavily on your head, a large and immovable lid to the tomb that is receiving you alive!"

Don Raimondo still didn't understand what type of death was intended for him; he had understood nothing and was watching, terrified, in the manner of someone trying to catch a word, a sign, a gesture. But under the masks, the faces were impenetrable and in his ear those words resounded confusedly: *death, palazzo, greed, blood, sorrow, tomb.*

Coriolano gave a key to Don Girolamo Ammirata, who was standing next to him, and said, "*Scoffate; piantate l'occhio*;[6] the good men of the tribunal guessed right."

Most of the men moved and went forward, led by Coriolano.

Coriolano cautioned them, "*Sfumate*,[7] at once."

Andrea with the lantern, two Beati Paoli, Coriolano, and Blasco stayed in the rotunda, and in the middle of them, with his arms tied, collapsed on the ground, immobile from the terror, was Don Raimondo.

Coriolano said brusquely to Blasco, "Why are you staying? Go, you go!"

"I will not leave, except with you. . . . You know that."

"It is not your place to be here."

"Tell me what you intend to do with this man."

"What justice commands!"

"I warn you! I will not allow any violence toward him!"

Coriolano clenched his jaw, trying to control himself, and the other three Beati Paoli murmured disapprovingly. Blasco repeated what he had said.

"Do you want to strike a man tied in that way, incapable of defending himself, shattered with terror? Oh no, I cannot consent to an assassination!"

Don Raimondo felt heartened by a thread of hope; he looked with astonishment at the man who was suddenly rising up to defend him. It was the same voice in the room of the tribunal that had—in the name of Blasco—renounced the hand of Violante. Who was he, then? Was he perhaps the bastard whom he had, unjustly, tried to kill? He was trembling, panting, watching with wide-open eyes, weighed down by a thousand emotions that stirred up a tumult in his lost soul. Coriolano had crossed his hands on his chest in a gesture full of anger.

"Then you want to stop the course of justice?"

"I want to stop an act of cowardice!"

"Careful! . . . We will strike even you, if necessary!"

6 "Disperse; put out the lantern."
7 "Disperse."

"Just try! But I will not allow you to kill this man, whose fear renders him as worthless as a rag that's been thrown in the garbage!" He stepped back and, after tearing off his mask and throwing it on the ground, shouted, "Like this, openly, and without a mask!"

"Blasco!" stammered Don Raimondo.

There was a moment of silence; Andrea, who had placed the lantern in a small niche, removed his sackcloth and took out a long dagger from his belt; the other two Beati Paoli followed suit; their blades, with that gesture, flashed gruesomely.

Coriolano motioned everyone to stop and turned to Blasco; the effort to control himself was heard in his voice: "Do not squander your generosity, signore; it's not worth it. . . . You will not save him, and his life certainly doesn't matter as much as that of his victims. Justice will take its course, even passing over you. Save your life for nobler causes, Blasco da Castiglione . . . and carry out your own work!"

The two Beati Paoli advanced toward Don Raimondo, but Blasco threw himself between them and the victim and, leveling his pistols, he shouted, "One step and I will kill you!"

Then Coriolano erupted into a beast-like roar and in his turn put himself between the Beati Paoli and Blasco, shouting, "Ah, by God! Now this is too much!"

He rushed at Blasco. A shot boomed; a voice said amid the smoke, "It's nothing." There was the sound of a brief but furious scuffle. In the faint glow of the lantern, as the smoke cleared, one could see two entangled bodies and hands that were searching and fiercely striking. Those two men, once so friendly, now seemed to have turned into two furies. Coriolano had deflected the pistol shot, but not enough to keep the bullet from grazing his shoulder, and he had managed to grab hold of Blasco's wrist in order to disarm him; the young man, recognizing the muscular strength of his adversary, had jumped on top of him and seized him by the neck, coiling his legs around him in order to wrestle him to the ground. They flailed about violently, gasping, grunting, with rough, almost wheezing roars.

"Do what you have to do!" roared Coriolano while trying to imprison Blasco between his arms and prevent his every movement.

"No! . . . No!" Blasco shouted desperately.

But at that moment, a cry, a groan, and a thud were heard.

Andrea said, "It's done."

Then Coriolano made an effort and with all his strength shook Blasco and, bending him in half, called his companions. "Help me to take him away."

They held him tightly; one threw a rope around his arms and prevented him from resisting, and like that they lifted him up and carried him away.

Passing by, Blasco, whose eyes were full of tears of rage, saw in the faint light on the ground, bent over like an abandoned bundle, the body of Don Raimondo. He saw, or thought he saw, a quiver shake that body, and he was startled. With indignation mounted on his face, he gathered all his strength in one last curse and spat it out energetically into the face of the one nearest to him: "Cowards! Cowards! Cowards!"

They didn't respond to him. By the light of the lantern, they started off for that mysterious underground, leaving that wheezing body on the ground. After about two hundred steps they climbed up a stairway. Blasco was no longer resisting, abandoning himself to his misery; he sensed that they were opening a door and a gust of cool air blew across his face.

"Let me go!" he said. "Let me go! . . . I no longer have anything in common with you!"

They paid him no mind. He looked around and in the dark night it seemed to him that he was in the countryside. Where was he, then? Finally, he felt that they were laying him on the ground.

"Leave him there," ordered the voice of Coriolano, "and *vento*."[8]

Blasco looked around. He was alone.

8 "clear out."

CHAPTER 23

B lasco remained on the ground, with his elbows on his knees, head buried in his hands, silent, eyes burning with tears of rage and misery, in the throes of a profound depression. His efforts hadn't saved the man that he, moreover, despised, and they had cut him off from the sect and from Coriolano; between him and the cavaliere an abyss had been dug, even acknowledging that Coriolano had shown great tolerance toward him and had spared him. He was isolated and lost in the world; the night enveloped his being and his spirit.

It began to drizzle; some cold drops fell on his neck and descended down his back, left uncovered by the way he was sitting. That sense of cold shook him; he raised his head and looked around. The first light of dawn was breaking the darkness, spreading a dim light full of sadness, rendering visible its tears falling from the trees. Blasco was in a shallow vegetable garden, nestled between a hillock and the walls of the city. After a moment of concentration, he recognized it as one of those vegetable gardens that extend beyond Porta d'Ossuna, on the ancient bed of the marshland of the Papireto. He stood up and realized that he had no hat or weapons and that his clothes were in disarray; to head out and go back to the city in these clothes would effectively bring attention to himself and perhaps lead him straight into the hands of justice. He knew that he was still under a warrant and he could no longer count on anyone's help; it wasn't in his plans to fall into the hands of the guards. Therefore, he would have to hurry, find himself a refuge and a means to retrieve his things from Coriolano's palazzo, and attend to his future.

He started off slowly, making his way out of the garden, looking around to see where they had brought him from, while he rearranged his thoughts. The first idea that came to him was one he had already entertained at other times: to find a vessel and to leave, to go to France or Spain, to throw himself into the adventures of wars, and to resume his wandering life living in the present, until a stab or a bullet took him from the world. But as soon as this idea emerged, a pressing concern suddenly occurred to him: "And Violante?"

And behind the name of the young girl, the image of Don Raimondo appeared to him: a tangle of clothes, piled on the ground, in the mournful and gruesome stillness of death. He felt a disdain, a mortification, an anger with himself, blaming himself for having been unable to sufficiently defend that wretched man whose own cowardice combined with the inflexible inhumanity of his judges made him appear to be worthy of compassion. Now it even seemed immoral to him to abandon that bloody corpse there, isolated from filial tears and compassion. His death was obliterating his crimes and rendering him sacred.

Oh! If only he could at least deliver that body to Violante, since he had been unable to keep her father alive for her!

This idea troubled him, tormented him.

The Palazzo Albamonte wasn't far away, and when he arrived it was still dark. Nevertheless, he found the door open and the servants in great distress. After having waited for over an hour on the street corner, the two portantini, at not seeing their master return, began to feel some apprehension, which increased as the night wore on. They ventured out, looking at the doors of houses, listening intently, but the houses were immersed in the profound silence of sleep, and no door gave the indication that there were any people awake. They walked up to Santa Cristina, along Vicoletto dei Pellegrini, and made their way down to the Cathedral; everywhere there was the same solitude, the same silence.

"What does this mean?"

They couldn't find any explanation; if Don Raimondo had had romantic liaisons they would have had a laugh, but he, on that front, had never given a reason for the slightest suspicion and led a strictly chaste life. Therefore, some misfortune must have occurred.

"Might he have returned home?"

They lingered a while longer, like good faithful servants carrying out orders. A pistol shot, which the night made still louder, made them jump; they feared something sinister and began to search, calling out: "Your Excellency! Your Excellency!" They pushed ahead like that toward Piazza San Cosmo, where they saw some lanterns and armed men; they approached anxiously, but as soon as they were seen they were arrested and tied up.

Their livery saved them; by the light of the lantern the official recognized the shield from the green bands. They said that they had left their master at the corner of the street below Santa Cristina and that they hadn't seen him again; they had waited two hours, had searched for him, fearing something sinister, but they couldn't account for his disappearance. They wanted to go to the palazzo; who knows, might he have returned another way? The official detained them a short while, then decided to let them go, accompanied by a birro. Fearful, they set out for the palazzo.

At the Torre di Montalbano, no one had seen the duke; the arrival of the two servants, their bewilderment, and the pistol or gunshots that had broken the silence of the night put the servants into a fluster; they scattered through the most isolated vicoli, on the suspicion that the brigands had murdered him in order to rob him. And for the rest of the night they roamed through the neighborhood, stopping in front of the site where the underground fight between the guards and the Beati Paoli had taken place without imagining that exactly down there, in the darkness and mystery, the fate of the man they were looking for was being decided, and while they were searching all over, Don Raimondo was in the throes of death below their feet.

From Via San Cosmo and from Vicolo degli Orfani the guards were emerging, black with smoke, filthy, quick-tempered due to the futility of their searches, railing at the servants and at the curious onlookers on all sides who were flocking there. They had ransacked the rotunda, the two corridors and the niches, not sure where those men in black had vanished. They had seen them in the dim reflection of the flames, through the smoke, wandering like ghosts and fading away in the distance, one by one, enveloped in the smoke. It was a frightening sight that in those primitive and superstitious souls had evoked visions of hell.

They had found nothing; the underground was not very long, and it didn't take much time to search it. They turned Casa Baldi upside down and opened up the poor houses of the adjacent ground floors. In vain. Were they demons? Were they spirits? Were they under a spell? So many stories were told of spirits that vanished at the touch of a finger, or that could never be grasped. This belief began to enter into everyone's hearts, and that underground, which was perhaps an opening to hell, seemed so full of mysteries and fears that in order to get out of there they came to a decision that any search would be useless.

So they abandoned the search, leaving guards at the two entrances, the one on the vicoli and the one to Casa Baldi, and reassembling again on Piazza San Cosmo to await orders from the captain of the city.

The servants returned to the Palazzo Albamonte discouraged, terror-struck, not knowing what to think; the day that was beginning, gloomy and rainy, found them downtrodden by that painful silence, full of dismay, that one is almost afraid to break with voices that are too loud. They looked at one another and whispered, in that grand palazzo whose masters were all gone, as if a great scourge hung over the family in order to scatter it and wipe it out.

* * *

This was how Blasco found them, presenting himself as he was, in disarray, pale, and bewildered. His appearance in that state aroused apprehension and fear. They crowded around him; he was unaware of the scene that had taken place between Don Raimondo and Donna Gabriella. He said, "Wake up the duchess; tell her that I need to see her at once."

"What about the master? . . . The duke? . . . His Excellency?" they asked him anxiously.

"Inform the duchess!" Blasco insisted.

"But the duchess left last night!"

"She left?" Blasco exclaimed. "Left? For where?"

"For the house of her relatives, of the Prince of Carini."

"And . . . Donna Violante?"

"She is in the monastery. . . . But the master?"

Blasco clasped his head in his hands. He said, "Bring me a hat and a sword! And two men of goodwill should come with me."

Quite a few volunteered. Blasco chose two and set out for Vicolo degli Orfani, but he found the door guarded. He turned down Via San Cosmo, and the door to Casa Baldi was guarded. It wasn't possible to enter; what to do? He went back, almost defeated, with his head downcast. The servants followed him in silence, without knowing what all this coming and going was about. Along the way, Blasco recalled a few words he had heard down in the underground. Don Raimondo had been assassinated under his own house. . . . Here was a way. From which side and how to go down? And what part of the house was directly over the underground?

He again recalled that the ground where that swift and gloomy scene had unfolded was slippery with mud and that water had trickled down through the labyrinth of the volcanic rock and was dripping from the vault. Therefore, corresponding basins or fountains, and in any case, structures subject to the infiltration of water, had to be above. He entered the courtyard, at the end of which, placed against a wall, was a basin into which water flowed continuously from a bronze pipe. The basin was full, and from its edges, water dripped onto the ground. The well and the ground were covered with a murky green layer that had thin fronds of maidenhair ferns growing in it.

"Perhaps there," thought Blasco and, turning to the servants, he said, "Close the gate, and don't let anyone enter; get some shovels and pickaxes."

A minute later he and the servants were digging furiously around the basin, pulling up the cobblestones and slabs, removing mounds upon mounds of earth. They worked for an hour. The day had risen and was illuminating their feverish faces. The pickaxes hacked away at the volcanic rock; one blow resounded deeply, reverberating with an indefinite sense in everyone's heart. Blasco felt his scalp tingling. There, below, was the void.

Blasco began to test the ground, as if to determine where it was resonating the most; between the corner of the courtyard and the basin the blows gave off a more resonant sound, so then he furiously began to dig up the volcanic rock in order to create an opening. One of his blows sank down, there was some soil; with a second blow some stones broke away and caved in.

Blasco shouted for joy and feverishly resumed his work, helped by the servants. Due to the collapse of stones, a large hole suddenly opened up under their eyes, and the soil fell down with the dull thud of a basket of debris that is turned upside down. It was perhaps a skylight that provided light into the underground during very ancient times, walled up since then and now concealed by an accumulation of debris and earth and buried under the cobblestones.

"A rope and a lantern!" shouted Blasco.

The servants were stunned by what they were seeing; they were rushing and obeying every direction. They ran into the stables and returned with everything that had been asked for. Blasco bent down on the ground and lowered the lit lantern into the hole in order to have a closer look. In fact, a vast cavity had opened below, and the darkness prevented the bottom and sides from being visible. Was it a well? A cistern? Was it the underground? He didn't doubt it; he took a long pole, resting it across the opening, tied one end of the rope in the middle, and let the other end fall into the opening. The bottom wasn't deep enough to cause concern.

He said, "Pay attention to what I tell you to do."

And, taking the lantern, he descended into the hole, holding on to the rope. He touched the ground and measured the height: it wasn't more than four meters. Then he lit up all around him and a great joy gladdened his heart; he recognized the underground and precisely the rotunda where the dark and ruthless scene had unfolded. Don Raimondo had to be there, or not far away. He turned the lantern toward the ground and saw him, still curled up, immobile, as he had left him. He bent over him, raised his arms, turned his head, tried to lay him on his back. His body didn't have the stiffness of a corpse, and it had some give; and although five hours had already passed since he was in that underground, it didn't have the icy cold characteristic of death.

He placed his ear to his heart and exclaimed, getting up, "God! He's still alive!"

Then he tried to lift him and carry him under the opening and, grasping him under the armpits, he tried to stand him up straight so that he could hoist him up; with that movement Don Raimondo's head reclined to one side and revealed two deep wounds that ran from the front to the back of his neck and another long one creeping along his skull.

Blasco made an effort and, hoisting him on his arms, moved him under the skylight, shouting, "Another rope and a sheet."

They threw them down to him. He laid Don Raimondo's body down on the sheet and tied the four corners together tightly so that it formed a sack; he passed the rope that they had thrown down to him through there, and, placing the other end around his waist, he climbed the rope that was hanging from the pole, leapt into the courtyard, took hold of the pole, and, holding the end of the rope that was secured around his waist, he said to the servants, "Come on, slowly, we have to pull . . . He's there!"

They shuddered. There? Their master was there? Who had brought him there? How had he found him? Alive? Dead? Four of them began to pull cautiously, until the gloomy-looking bundle that had already been spattered with mud and blood had reached the rim of the opening, too narrow to allow the bulky mass to pass through.

Then Blasco said, "Hold on."

He and another servant knelt down, one on each side of the skylight, and bent down over the bundle; they thrust their hands into the hole, where they caught sight of Don Raimondo's hair and pulled him up by the armpits, delicately lifting him out. A moment later the body was lying on a bed, undressed and washed.

"He's still alive," said Blasco. "Send for a surgeon."

In fact, perhaps due to the sensation of the coolness and the abrupt movements, his chest seemed to stir gently.

"Now that I have given him to you, I have nothing more to do here. Go and tell the duchess and Donna Violante; farewell."

* * *

He picked up his hat, took a cloak from the antechamber, wrapped it around himself, turning the collar up above his eyes, and left, but instead of heading for the interior of the city, he followed the city walls, went out through Porta d'Ossuna, and returned to the countryside. Where to go? Where to rest after so much excitement and so much exhaustion? Now he felt heartbroken and longed for solitude. He had a great sorrow, which gripped his soul in an icy vise; he at least wanted to have the ability to give it free rein. Having pulled Don Raimondo up from the bottom of the underground and returned him to his daughter so that the duke would at least have, through his own act of mercy, the utmost tribute, it seemed to Blasco that he had accomplished all that he could.

He had been unlucky; he had been defeated; his hopes and his dream had vanished in the face of something stronger. Now he had nothing more to do. Nothing?

The vision of Violante—rejected as an outsider from the house where she was born, covered in shame by the revelation of her father's crimes, which seemed to him inevitable—passed in front of him in his imagination. After all, wasn't the young girl an Albamonte? And didn't he have the right and the duty to defend her, to protect her now that she was left an orphan? He thought that perhaps it would be a consolation for the young girl to send her a word, a sign, and this thought touched his heart. She too, at that time, was crying and feeling alone and lost in the world; she too, who at that moment was crying over her father's body, perhaps was turning her thoughts to him and looking to be consoled.

Pondering those thoughts across the vegetable gardens and paths, he had reached the Convent of the Capuchins, and it seemed to him that he had been guided by the hand of God. He entered the little portico, whose walls were covered with numerous little votive paintings and with arms and legs made of red-stained wax, and he sat on the low wall between the pillars, waiting perhaps for a friar. He was gradually overcome by sleep; he stretched his legs out on the wall and fell asleep. A friar, having spotted him upon closing the door of the church, approached and shook him gently, then a little harder. "Signore! . . . Signore!"

Blasco opened his eyes.

"If you need anything," said the friar, "you can go into the caretaker's lodge."

"Well! Actually, what I would need now is just a bed, good Father."

"There is no lack of them in the guest quarters. If Your Lordship"—taking a good look at him, he had realized he was dealing with a gentleman—"needs . . . I don't know if I'm explaining myself . . . sometimes one knows . . . this is a sacred place and there is the right to asylum."

"Yes, very well, but it's not necessary. It's only that I'm a little tired right now, that's all."

"Your Lordship may stay in the guest quarters. Does Your Lordship come from far away?"

"Yes."

"On foot?"

"To make an offering to the Madonna," Blasco said a little rudely, as he was becoming annoyed at the friar's inquisitiveness.

"Ah! To make an offering? . . . To Our Lady of the Assumption! I imagine that you have brought the torch, is that true?"

"One shall be purchased."

They arrived in front of a room; the friar opened the door.

"Your Lordship, please; I will inform the Father Guardian."

Blasco went in and threw himself on a large chair. He could stay in the convent undisturbed, at least until justice, finding him there, would order the Father Guardian to evict him; besides, he wasn't planning to stay there for long, just a few days to rest, to sort things out, to collect his things and find a vessel on which to sail off.

"The mendicant friar," he thought, "will do me this favor."

The favor was to first go to the Palazzo della Motta and then to the Palazzo della Floresta; another place was coming to mind, but he dared not consider it.

"What does she really need from me? The Branciforti are her relatives, after all, on her mother's side, and they are a large and powerful family with fiefdoms and friendships; they will not leave Violante to the mercy of fate, and they will take care of her . . . they will protect her . . . surely they will protect her!"

The Father Guardian was reviewing the accounts and did not think it necessary to inconvenience himself just to greet the guest. He ordered that they give him something to eat and a place to sleep, as was customary, and to inquire if he was a lord; perhaps in that case some other courtesies would be offered to him. So Blasco had the good luck of being left in peace in those moments when his mind was troubled by worries and by different and contrasting affections; he was able to sleep deeply for a few hours.

The friar woke him.

"If Your Lordship has any orders to give me, I am going to the city."

But of course he had some assignments for him! He had given it a great deal of thought; there were his belongings to retrieve and news about Violante to ask for. In a hurry he wrote a brief and point-blank letter in which he asked Coriolano to have his clothes and everything belonging to him delivered to the cave in Denisinni at a certain hour. Not a word more, not a greeting, not even a mention of where he was sheltered.

"Since you are so kind, do me a great favor and take this letter to the Cavaliere della Floresta."

"Ah, the cavaliere? I know him; he is a good benefactor of the convent."

"All the better, but . . . I would like you to leave him this letter without even mentioning that I sent it. He must not even know that I am here. . . . Can I trust you?"

"Rest assured, Your Lordship."

"And there is another little errand . . . go to the Palazzo della Motta."

"I know it. In the Capo."

"Very well. You will be so kind as to ask for news of the duke and if the duke's daughter, Donna Violante, is already at the palazzo."

"Your Lordship will be obeyed. Is there anything else?"

"Nothing, thank you."

The friar left, and Blasco followed him in his mind along the way, calculating the time that it would take to get to the city, complete his errands, attend to his other business, and return. He didn't want to leave his cell for the entire afternoon, waiting and letting his mind roam from one thought to another and no longer finding in his life a goal, a dream, or a hope that would illuminate his future. Was everything finished, then?

"Bah!" he said, shrugging his shoulders with a nonchalance that concealed his private bitterness. "Ah! What got into my head in the end? But fancy that, that I was wiser when everyone thought I was off my head. It's madness! Madness! . . . Get yourself together, Blasco. Weren't you living well before you met the Cavaliere della Floresta, the Duchess of Motta, Donna Violante, and this entire world full of mysteries, of artifices, of cowardice, of crimes, of villainies, of hypocrisy? What got into your head to make you come to this city that seems to be the nest of all evils? Are you perhaps something more now that you know you are the illegitimate son, yes, but the firstborn son of the Duke of Motta? Firstborn? And who knows if suddenly another one won't show up, given that my father sowed children throughout the land and sea? Let it go. Life is a very sad thing and we shouldn't add to the reasons for its sadness. Don't take it so seriously, Blasco, my man, and you will be better off!"

But all this philosophizing of his collapsed when toward the Ave Maria the friar returned. He had left the letter at the Palazzo della Floresta—but this mattered to Blasco only up to a certain point—and he had gone to the Palazzo della Motta . . . and what misfortune! The duke was between life and death; they had tried to assassinate him at night, three stab wounds! . . . Terrifying . . . an extraordinary thing! The palazzo was full of people: the entire court, all the nobility, the captain of justice, even the viceroy, even the viceroy! . . . Throughout Palermo nothing else was being talked about.

What was most astonishing was the site where they had miraculously found him. Everyone wanted to see that opening, well or cave, whatever it was. And the gate had to be closed because the courtyard was filled with a mob. The duchess and the young duchess were there, yes, signore, and also the relatives. An extraordinary thing, incredible . . . who had taken him down there? And how did they know about it?

Blasco allowed him to speak. What he wanted to know was if Violante was in the palazzo; the reason for this interest wasn't clearly defined in his mind. Perhaps there were quite a few reasons; perhaps some intentions not yet well defined, some vague hopes, some intermittent intuitions, were wandering and wavering in his heart.

When the friar had completed his litany, Blasco said to him, "Now do me a favor."

"Tell me."

"I would like a trustworthy man."

"I know one . . . the carter, here . . ."

"Can he be trusted?"

"Like Your Lordship himself."

"Call for him, please."

The friar carried out the request; Blasco gave some instructions to the carter, who had that characteristic demeanor of a man who knows how to be useful and to be called upon, and two hours later he received his bag, his weapons, and his clothes. Then he took off his muddy clothes, spoiled and ragged from the events of the night, dressed in a more suitable manner, girded his sword, wrapped himself in his cloak, and went out.

CHAPTER 24

The news of the attempted assassination of Don Raimondo had filled the city with an enormous sense of disbelief due to the circumstances that surrounded it. The mystery of that pit, that no one knew from where or how it had been entered, proved to be inexplicable, and to that disbelief was added a vague sense of dismay.

The first ones to rush there were Donna Gabriella and Violante. Donna Gabriella didn't feel, to tell the truth, a profound sorrow; she didn't cry, she didn't despair; she felt a kind of disconcertment but had no doubt about where the attack had come from. The sight of her inert husband, pale, still clotted with blood, corpse-like, inspired in her a certain compassion mixed with a sense of terror. She seemed to see the armed hand that had struck her husband rise up again and hang menacingly over the heads of the entire family.

But Violante let out loud cries, burst into tears, and had to be led away from her father's bedside. Her cries annoyed the duchess, as if they had aroused reprimands or regrets in her heart.

"Be quiet!" she shouted to her. "Be quiet. This is not the time to cry, your cries are upsetting."

Two doctors had been summoned and they were both studying the wounds, shaking their heads.

By dint of aromatic waters and other stimulants, they had been able to shake the lethargy that was overpowering Don Raimondo, who had regained consciousness and had begun to stare with a great fear in his still-confused eyes; then he had closed them again and was now moaning softly while the two doctors, after having applied certain balms to his wounds, were dressing and bandaging them.

Meanwhile, lords and government officials flocked to the palazzo; the captain of justice, who should have brought him news of the capture of the Beati Paoli and who instead hadn't dared to confess his own defeat to him, had made haste now that he had learned what had happened, and he raced to gather the first details. And soon after, the captain of the halberdiers of the viceroy had arrived, who had been surprised, and not only on account of the victim but also by the audacity of the assassins.

The Branciforti, the La Grua, the Ventimiglia—all great dynasties allied by marriage with the Albamonte had been touched by it; the palazzo filled up with people.

Everyone wanted to hear some news from Donna Gabriella, a trace, a clue in order to have the key to the mystery that would lead to the discovery of the assassins. But she was uncertain, fearing the consequences of those revelations that she could have made. At this moment she wasn't thinking about revenge or reprisals. After all, the wounded, dying man was her husband, and it was her duty to defend him and to defend the name that she had acquired from him.

Several times the name of the Beati Paoli had risen to her lips, but how would she explain her reference to the sect?

She didn't reveal anything and claimed that she had no suspicions, but her silence rang hollow. From even the initial investigations, three very important clues emerged in which the magistrate found the common thread: first, the name of Blasco da Castiglione, who "knew"; second, the fact that he had initially led the servants to the two entrances of that underground, now known to be the Beati Paoli's meeting place. Therefore, the attack had been carried out by the sect, and Blasco da Castiglione must have been present and must have been familiar with the locations; third, the Beati Paoli's cave had to extend below Palazzo Albamonte and have an opening from where its mysterious members had vanished.

He had to have Blasco da Castiglione in his hands, but here was where the difficulty began, because, being under a warrant, he was certainly keeping himself out of view. Added to this was another fact that complicated matters, indicating a link between him and the events of that night.

Captain Mangialocchi, upon returning to Palermo at night, as he was embarrassed by the fiasco, had reported that Blasco, having escaped arrest, had killed Matteo Lo Vecchio and a soldier. Blasco then, fleeing from justice, had entered Palermo and was at that gathering where the Duke of Motta, who had ordered his arrest, had almost been killed. Had this then been Blasco's revenge? But then why would he have saved him? This was the enigma that justice was unable to solve.

The viceroy instructed Don Francesco Cavallaro, a judge from the Gran Corte, to direct the trial, and the first thing was the confirmation of the warrant issued against Blasco da Castiglione, with a large reward for anyone who handed him over alive or who revealed his hiding place.

Captains, algozini, guards, and rural militia were put in motion; every part of the Beati Paoli's cave was ransacked, but without the secret passageway being discovered; and to account for every eventuality, it was ordered that on the same day, in order to prevent the gathering of curious onlookers, the two entrances were to be solidly walled up.

* * *

Blasco knew nothing of all this. But under the cover of night, he descended from the Convent of the Capuchins toward the city and was able to pass through Porta d'Ossuna undisturbed by the gabelloti, who would pass the time playing cards and drinking and would never concern themselves with gentlemen; and, while walking along Via Sant'Agostino, he gathered here and there bits of news concerning himself from the discussions of the small groups of people lingering in the vicinity of the Palazzo Albamonte.

He stopped in the piazzetta near the Mercé, looking at the palazzo, behind whose windows he could see large shadows of people wandering about. He didn't think it wise to enter. Why, for that matter, would he go in? By what right? And to what end? In truth, he found it scarcely believable that he had gone to that palazzo, which he no longer had anything to do with. But in the shadows the figure of Violante would appear before his eyes, and his heart, dejected from so many emotions, would be moved to tenderness. He waited a long time; he saw portantine and a few carriages leave the palazzo and recognized to whom each one belonged by the colors of their liveries.

A much simpler portantina, carried by porters of the piazza, indicated to him that it was a doctor; he approached, poked his head inside, and asked, "Your Lordship, forgive me, can you give me some news about His Excellency?"

"Ah, it's serious, serious! Let's hope for the best!"

So death had not yet come, and the doctor hadn't despaired. He waited some more. Night enveloped everything, but for this occasion, on either side of the gate of the palazzo, two windproof torches had been affixed in order to illuminate that stretch of the street; by that light, Blasco was able to observe who was entering and leaving without himself being seen. The shadows behind the windows had gradually become fewer in number and would now rarely appear; even the portantine and carriages had thinned out; then no more were seen leaving. Perhaps only a few of the closest relatives and some friends had remained in the palazzo in order to keep the women company.

A servant came out carrying a bottle, perhaps to go to the nearby *aromatico*, as the pharmacists were then called. Blasco recognized him and called to him.

"Oh! Your Lordship?" exclaimed the servant, frightened.

"It's me, yes; I came to get information. The doctor gave me some news . . . Are there people upstairs?"

"The Marchese of Regalmici is there, the duchess's brother."

"Ah, good! Do me the favor, dear man, of asking the duchess if she would be so kind as to accept my visit."

"Right away, but . . ."

"But what?"

"Is Your Lordship aware of the warrant?"

"What warrant?"

"I don't know . . . I wouldn't want to say . . ."

"Please tell me, without fear."

"Be that as it may, in short, I mean no harm; well, there is a warrant against Your Lordship and a large bounty on your head . . . watch out for yourself; if anyone should see you . . ."

"Thank you. Don't worry; you certainly will not betray me . . ."

"Me . . . ?"

The servant went back up the stairs of the palazzo and returned soon after.

"The duchess is waiting for you . . ."

"What did she say when she received the message?"

"She turned pale and at first I thought she wanted to say no."

"Is anyone with her?"

"At this moment she is alone."

"Very well, thank you."

He parted from the servant and slipped through the entrance; in his haste he saw that a portantina, preceded by two volanti holding windproof torches, was coming from the piazza in the Capo toward the palazzo. Entering the drawing room where Donna Gabriella received visitors, he was unable to control an intense emotion. Donna Gabriella was there, standing next to a chair, quite beautiful amid the different and opposing emotions that passed over her face, like clouds pushed by the wind against the blue of the sky. For an instant her beautiful face was altered by her pain, anger, hatred, jealousy, and desire; however, it promptly resumed a gravity suitable to the occasion. But she didn't offer her hand to Blasco, remaining on her feet in a pose full of dignity and sorrow, which for a moment embarrassed the young man.

Before he could think of a word to say, Donna Gabriella said to him, "I know that the discovery of this wicked crime is owed to you and I am grateful, although you still haven't explained to me how you found out that the duke had almost been assassinated."

Blasco, struck by the cold tone and the veiled sting of those last words, felt reassured, since nothing could relieve him of embarrassment as much as having to assume a pugnacious manner.

He replied with the same cold tone. "I had come only to find out about your husband's condition and to express my sorrow, not to receive thanks, nor to give explanations that, forgive me, at least in this moment are out of place; I had also come to determine if the duke was being attended to by his family . . . who I knew were scattered about."

Donna Gabriella bit her lower lip in a spiteful manner.

"You can see, signore," she said, "that I am where I belong."

She stressed that "I" in a meaningful way as if to say, "And it's pointless for you to inquire about other people." There was an indifferent and barely restrained hostility between them; harsh reproaches rose to their lips and the storm seemed to be building up in their chests and was close to bursting, when a servant announced, "The Cavaliere della Floresta wishes to kiss the hand of Your Excellency."

Blasco made a gesture of great astonishment, but Donna Gabriella gave a nod of approval and soon after Coriolano entered with his calm and cool manner, his refined and gracious smile, and his perfect manners, with his long-tasseled cane in the same hand as his hat. He approached the duchess, kissed her hand gallantly, and with a friendly and familiar nod greeted Blasco, who looked at him bewildered, full of indignation and anger.

"Believe me, Your Excellency," the Cavaliere della Floresta said softly in a remorseful tone of voice, "that I was terribly surprised by the misfortune that befell the duke . . . it is an unprecedented thing that has struck the entire city."

Donna Gabriella sat down and pointed to a chair for Coriolano. Blasco remained standing, with a hand on his hip; pale, menacing, he could barely contain his anger and clenched his jaw so that the words rushing to his lips would not come out, and in order to contain the storm that surged in his chest.

Coriolano was inquiring about the wounded man's condition.

"Three wounds!" he exclaimed, visibly horrified. "But it's a dreadful thing! . . . What doctor did you call?"

"Don Francesco Pignocco, the chief physician of the kingdom."

"You did well; and does he give you any hope?"

"Very little."

"My God! . . . To think that they could have killed him! And that without the miraculous intervention of Signor Blasco da Castiglione, the poor duke would be dead by now."

Blasco clenched his fists till his nails dug into his flesh; beneath the apparent emotion, he grasped a slight tinge of irony in those last words, which completely escaped Donna Gabriella.

She murmured with bitter conviction, "Indeed, that is so."

"And are there any well-grounded suspicions?" Coriolano asked.

"Justice seems to be on the trail."

"Yes? I am pleased to hear it."

Saying these words, the Cavaliere della Floresta cast a scrutinizing glance at Blasco, who, perhaps surmising Coriolano's thoughts, frowned in an expression of anger and contempt. There was a moment of silence, during which Donna Gabriella had the opportunity to notice that Blasco and Coriolano, who she knew were close friends, looked at each other with great indifference and reserve. This discovery gave her a certain pleasure, not because it corresponded to her own interests, but out of malice. Devoid of this friendship, Blasco would be left alone, without any protection in that dangerous predicament, with his life and freedom at stake. A wicked idea suddenly occurred to her: that of covertly sending for the captain of justice and handing the young man over to him. But she didn't act on it. Her instinct for revenge was followed by a sense of repugnance for such a cowardly act, and also—why deny it?—by that vague, intimate desire to repossess that young man again, not because she loved him, but out of spite and jealousy.

Coriolano picked up his hat again, said a few more polite words with the same courteous and impeccable manner, kissed Donna Gabriella's hand, and started to leave; but, in saying goodbye to Blasco with a nod of his head, he said to him, "They told me that you are leaving, signore. Is it true?"

It was worded like a question, but with an ulterior motive, which Blasco understood perfectly: it was almost an order to leave.

Blasco replied, "Not yet, signore, I still have some obligations to fulfill, here—"

"Ah! . . . it's only right. You cannot abandon your good work as savior. I hope with all my heart that your efforts are rewarded with the most joyful success, but . . . be careful, because justice is on your heels."

"I am not afraid."

Coriolano left. Blasco then approached Donna Gabriella and said quickly, "Allow me to return. . . . I will tell you the reason, but I warn you that the duke's life is at stake."

The duchess gave a sign of fear.

"Don't be afraid of anything . . . I will return soon."

He left before Donna Gabriella had the time to say anything; he crossed the antechamber and asked the servants if the Cavaliere della Floresta had already left.

"No, Your Excellency; he went to see the duke in his room."

"Ah!"

Blasco didn't just enter but leapt into the room where the duke had been put: a large, plain, and almost austere room, in the middle of which they had placed a bed. Don Raimondo lay motionless, with his head bandaged, his eyes wide open, staring at the ceiling, pale. He looked more like a wax statue than a living being. At that moment at his bedside were the Marchese of Regalmici and the razionale of the house, and two footmen stood in front of the door, awaiting orders. Coriolano approached the bed, looking coldly at that body over which the scythe of death seemed to hang; his face didn't betray the slightest emotion.

Blasco, his voice sounding like a roar, said, "Signore." He then murmured beside him, "Signore, don't you think it is time to leave the wounded man in peace?"

Coriolano made as if he hadn't grasped the meaning of that observation and replied with apparent calm. "Indeed. . . . There are too many of us here."

His words also had a hidden meaning that Blasco seemed to understand.

"I will go with you," he said.

They left, but upon reaching the gate, Blasco, no longer able to control himself, said under his breath, "Signore, your conduct is despicable!"

"Do you think so?" Coriolano replied coldly.

"And if I have a sorrow, a regret, a shame in my life, it is to have known you and to have shaken your hand!"

"Which would mean?"

"That the piazzetta there is deserted, the night is dark, and two people of good-will can fight each other there."

"A duel? . . . With you? . . . Here? . . . But if you want to fight me at least allow me, according to good custom, to choose the place and time. For now, I am busy. . . . Goodbye, Signor Blasco."

"You will not leave, by God!"

"Listen to me, Blasco da Castiglione; I still want to give you some proof of my tolerance and of my friendship, whatever you say. . . . You do not know what you are doing; I warn you, however"—and here he lowered his voice—"that you are a condemned man, and you know why . . . and if you are here, you owe it to the luck that comes to your aid and to the concern that I have for you. You want to fight me? I will give you that satisfaction and will wait for you tomorrow at four o'clock at Via Colonna Rotta, in the vegetable garden where you found yourself at dawn. But be on guard because from the Palazzo Albamonte you are closer than you realize to the ax in Piazza Marina; and put it in your head that neither the duel nor any other thing that you can do will bring to a halt the path of justice! . . . See you tomorrow, Blasco da Castiglione; see you tomorrow."

Blasco was about to reply, but Coriolano, pointing to the corner of the Capo, where a swaying lantern could be seen approaching, said, "Look: there is the patrol! Leave, unless you want to be caught like a mouse."

And, taking advantage of Blasco instinctively withdrawing into the shadows, he got into his portantina and left quickly.

Blasco shouted to him, "See you tomorrow, I will be there for sure!" and he went back into the palazzo in enough time to avoid being seen by the patrol, who, at a cadenced pace and pounding their pikes on the cobblestones, kept on toward the Piazza dei Noviziato.

Blasco went up to the drawing room, where Donna Gabriella had remained, still surprised and curious.

"Your Excellency," he said to her, "let me spend the night here in order to watch over your husband."

"Why? Aren't we enough? Aren't the servants enough?"

"Perhaps not. Allow me to keep watch. . . . I will not be a bother to you. . . . It could be, rather, that I may render some service to you."

"You frighten me. What has happened now?"

"Nothing, but isn't my desire to complete the work already begun legitimate?"

Donna Gabriella didn't seem satisfied with his response; certainly there was a hidden meaning to Blasco's desire and persistence, which aroused in her a sense of terror. Then a suspicion suddenly came to her: Violante. She was her fixation, her torment. A wave of jealousy, on top of her fear of the unknown, passed over her face, filled her mouth with bitterness and her eyes with a spiteful envy.

"Then," she said, "I will keep watch with you."

"Why do you want to wear yourself out?"

"Why do you want to be left alone?"

Her reply revealed to Blasco what suspicions were going through the duchess's heart. He smiled sorrowfully and with a voice tinged by sadness said, "Why do you want to torment yourself? Do you think, then, that I am capable of taking advantage of a misfortune in order to satisfy a desire, assuming that I had one? Instead, I thought that I had given you proof of my lack of interest and of being able to even renounce the joys of life, in the face of a great obligation. . . . Go and rest and be more fair. . . . When you learn—and perhaps the day will not be far away—about the terrible secret of last night and why your husband is lying on that bed, and why I saved him, and what I have proposed, oh! then, Donna Gabriella, you will give me my due and recognize that here, under this chest, there is an honest and disinterested heart, and above all a lover of justice . . . even against himself, indeed against himself more than against others."

He fell silent for a moment and covered his face with his hands, as if not to allow his pain to show through, or in order to collect his thoughts; then he raised his handsome head and, shaking his thick head of hair, resumed with a bitter smile.

"Do you know who I am? Do you know if anything compels me here, beyond a sense of human kindness? Perhaps the Duke of Motta has kept it from you; but why leave you in the dark? . . . What is the good of keeping a secret, when others know the truth? . . . It amazes me that you have never looked at the portrait of Don Emanuele, the dead duke. . . . Call it to mind . . . and look at me, Donna Gabriella!"

The duchess looked at him and then, for the first time, she seemed to grasp the signs of his resemblance to the great portrait; her astonishment caused her eyes and mouth to open and she murmured, "How? . . . Perhaps you? . . ."

"Are you surprised? Indeed, no one would ever have suspected that this nameless Blasco—owing to a whim of the noble Duke Don Emanuele—had Albamonte blood in his veins. I myself never even suspected it until a few months ago. . . . A bastard, yes! That is what I am, but, since my birth certificate is not silent about the name of my father and gives me the right—if I so want—to bear the name of Albamonte, you will acknowledge my obligation to watch over and to defend this house."

Donna Gabriella still hadn't recovered from the shock; she continued to murmur, "You? . . . Indeed, it is true. . . . The same face . . . the same likeness! . . . Oh God!"

"Yes, my father wanted, in fact, to give me a token of his love, of his foresight, leaving to me his features as a legacy, so that by carrying them around, they would reveal to the world the disgrace brought upon a poor young girl and the shame of my birth! . . . And you fear . . . you ascribe ambitious aims to me! What ambitions do you expect me to have? What dreams might I entertain? . . . Love, wealth, power? They belong to the young man, the legitimate son of Don Emanuele, his heir, the heir to his title and his fortune!"

"What?" Donna Gabriella cried out, jumping to her feet with even greater shock. "What are you saying? . . . The little Emanuele . . . the missing child? . . . He is alive? Where? How?"

"He is alive! It's a long story. Why do you care to know? It is full of blood and sorrow; he lived and perhaps still lives in the mystery and oblivion of his status, but tomorrow, led by those who raised him, he will enter here, with his name, with his title of Duke of Motta."

The duchess, pale and trembling with fear, looked at Blasco, struck by this unexpected revelation whose gaps she had quickly filled with the half-confessions given to her by her husband, who appeared in her memory under a sinister light. The missing young man was still living, and the man in the next room, lying immobile and blindfolded, was a usurper and had achieved that usurpation by means of a criminal act. . . . Therefore, he wasn't a victim of hatred but a criminal struck down by divine, infallible, and inexorable justice.

So, from the darkness now emerged the young boy, robbed of what was his, deprived of his mother, stripped of his name; the seed of Don Emanuele was coming to call out the crime committed by his uncle! . . . Here an entire tale of wickedness emerged from the depths of oblivion and crushes the one who had been, up until the day before, the arbiter of the city! How many victims did she see rising up from the dark corners of that palazzo, holding unforgiving hands over the bed of that man?

She was afraid. Certainly not for herself, who had nothing to do with Don Raimondo's past, but of all that threatening and terrible unknown that weighed on the house and of which she could see there, in the next room, one of the first frightening manifestations. And that bastard? What did he want? Did the legitimate brother come first or was he placing himself against him?

So it would seem; but why, instead of protecting him, was he moving closer to and assuming the position of defending the man he should have instead abhorred? Concern for Don Raimondo? Oh, no, certainly not! . . . For her? She was an outsider, and her life and her dowry could not suffer harm. Violante, then? . . . Yes! She could see it, she could feel it in Blasco's own silence and in his constant effort not to mention her.

So her jealousy was taking hold of her again, then; her impressionable heart passed from one emotion to another, with an equal fit of passion. What did the existence of the young legitimate son of the Duke of Motta matter? What would it matter if the new lord came to take over his palazzo and drive away the usurpers? Could all that perhaps prevent Blasco from loving Violante, from seeking to possess her? And didn't those events perhaps help this ambition? Wouldn't Violante, alone, orphaned, exposed to threats, in danger, even out of necessity, throw herself into the arms of her cousin, who appeared to her as her natural defender?

She felt a knot in her throat. She looked at Blasco and with a stifled voice said, "You, however, are not here for him . . . for Don Raimondo, nor for your brother . . . admit it."

"No, I am not here for them."

"Nor for me."

Blasco didn't answer immediately; his loyalty had suggested a word to him that propriety and discretion prevented him from saying. With a turn of phrase, he softened his response: "If I knew you were exposed to any danger, I wouldn't hesitate to offer you my arm and my life."

"It is, then . . . for Violante!"

"Yes, why should I deny it? Don Raimondo atones for the death of Donna Aloisia; I tried to save him not for himself but for his daughter. Violante will be alone . . . and perhaps disgraced by the memory of her father. It is necessary that she not be aware of who she had for a father, that she not be crushed by the house where she was born, that she remain the Duchess of Motta."

Donna Gabriella looked at him in astonishment.

"What do you mean?"

Blasco continued, "You are wrong, Donna Gabriella; you should join me to prevent the atoning of her father's guilt from extending to the young girl."

The duchess shrugged nonchalantly. What did it matter to her? These words didn't ease her torment.

"You love her!" she murmured sullenly, her voice quivering with hatred and pain. "You love her! . . . That is the truth! . . . You want to make her the Duchess of Motta! And what does this mean? Will it perhaps prevent you from making her your mistress?"

"Oh! Donna Gabriella!"

Their eyes met and each one read in the other the many memories of the past.

Blasco resumed in a lower and more sorrowful voice: "I will leave in three or four days . . . and forever! . . . Therefore, your suspicion is unwarranted."

"You are leaving?"

"What do you want me to do?"

Donna Gabriella glanced quickly into Don Raimondo's room, and perhaps a wicked thought crossed her mind. A brief silence enveloped them; then, as if answering herself, she murmured, "Only I will be alone and abandoned."

Behind these words was a feeling of such suffering that Blasco was seized with emotion, but he didn't respond. He bowed his head, sighing, perhaps with a regret for the past and a discomfort with the present. After a moment he stood up and went toward Don Raimondo's room; the servants were sleeping on the chairs, the razionale had thrown himself on a sofa and he too was sleeping, snoring lightly. The wounded man's eyes were half-open, and his appearance was so frightening that Blasco feared a calamity and rushed over to the bed to examine him. As he stood, with his mind reassured, his eyes rested on the window, and he seemed to see a shadow through the glass, which quickly faded away. He ran and opened it; the window overlooked the courtyard. In the darkness he seemed to see that shadow sinking into the ground. He stepped back, closed the window again, and barred all the doors and windows.

Donna Gabriella saw him return with his face pale and his forehead damp with sweat.

"What is it?" she asked, frightened.

"Nothing!"

"The duke?"

"He is resting. Go to sleep, I beg you. I will keep watch."

But Donna Gabriella asked him gently, "Don't you even want me to stay next to you at this time? Have I become so hateful to you?"

Blasco was not able to refuse; he sat by a little table in the middle of the room, from where he could see Don Raimondo's bed through the open door, and Donna Gabriella sat next to him in an armchair, looking at him silently. The she murmured softly and meekly, as if talking to herself, "If you leave, I will follow you."

CHAPTER 25

A volante had rushed to the Monastery of Santa Caterina to bring the momen-tous news to Don Raimondo's two sisters and ask them to send the young girl, Violante, to visit her father, so that she might arrive in time to see him alive. She had spent a sorrowful night, shaken by visions of ghosts, and after the morning prayers had thrown herself on her bed, more to conceal her pain than to sleep, when a lay sister came to call her on behalf of her aunts and the abbess.

"What will it be this time?" she asked herself.

But when she went down into the small parlor she found her aunts and the abbess talking quietly, and they seemed to have been surprised by unexpected as well as painful news. As soon as she entered, the two aunts embraced her and the abbess stroked her hair.

"My child," she said, "they want you at your house, your father is not well."

"What has happened to him?" a frightened Violante asked.

"A minor sickness. Unexpected. I will have Father Mongitore, who is down in the confessional, accompany you. A volante from your house is also here."

She could never have imagined finding her father in the condition in which she saw him, and believing him to be dead, she threw herself at his feet, sobbing. Only the presence of Donna Gabriella, who, having entered at that moment, reprimanded her for those excessive outbursts of sorrow, could force her to stifle her crying and to get control of herself. It was again her stepmother who after nightfall ordered her to go to sleep, and she obeyed, either because in that moment of suffering and frailty she was putting up with everyone's authority or because, after what had happened the night before, the sight and the voice of that woman made her blood run cold.

Now, having gotten up and thinking that she could resume her place next to her father's bed, she walked on tiptoe so as not to make noise. In order to go from her bedroom to where—due to that circumstance—Don Raimondo's bed had been placed, she had no choice but to cross the sitting room, where Blasco and Donna Gabriella had spent the night.

On top of the little table, one of the burners of a brass oil lamp was still glowing, and the other was extinguished; the light, weakened due to the dwindling amount of fuel, barely illuminated a small circular area, within which the outlines of things were merging or could be guessed at due to some brighter highlights. Violante saw next to the little table a human form whose back was turned to her, and, hesitating, she stopped, but the stillness of that figure and its slow and deep breath made her sense that sleep was weighing on that form, not yet well defined to her eye. She crossed the room with a light step like an ethereal being, turning to look, and she recognized the face of Blasco. The young man had fallen asleep with his head thrown back on the low back of an armchair; his mouth was slightly open, and a profound sadness was spread over his face. Violante stopped for a moment, clasping her hands, but her eyes descended along the young man's body, immersed in the half-light where something overly massive had caught her eye.

She stifled a cry of sorrow and disbelief and, feeling faint, leaned heavily on the little table.

Next to Blasco but much lower down, she had seen Donna Gabriella, with her head resting on her arms, folded on one of the armrests of the chair, with her hair almost touching Blasco's chest, in a pose full of tender intimacy. She was sleeping. Perhaps sleep had come upon her in that pose of devotion and abandonment.

Violante felt a cold blade pierce through her heart; a sense of horror, an undefinable sorrow, a surge of tears filled her chest, and yet she was unable to take her eyes off that sight. She pulled herself together to go enter the room, and perhaps she didn't have enough control to soften the sound of her steps or to avoid bumping into things. Donna Gabriella woke up and saw, without recognizing her, the shadow of the young girl, and she leapt up, confused, and drew near her. Then, added to her confusion, she had a surge of spite, anger, and jealousy.

"You!" she screamed. "You! Are you coming to spy?"

Her scream woke Blasco, who, fearing something sinister, leapt up as well, grasping the sword that he had within reach on the little table, but he found himself in front of the two women and stayed there like a statue, not understanding what had happened and what new reason would put them, at that hour, against each other.

He had been so overcome by sleep that he hadn't at all been aware that Donna Gabriella had moved close to him during the night and had nearly fallen asleep on his chest. He was now stunned to see her threatening and menacing the young girl.

Clenching her teeth, the duchess repeated, "Are you coming to spy?"

Fighting back tears, Violante raised her head and with a pride beyond her years said, "No, signora, I am coming to look after my father."

And once she was in the room she went to resume her place at the foot of the bed, without turning, without bowing her head, without betraying the slightest emotion.

But Donna Gabriella, the torment of her jealousy removing any sense of caution, followed her and said, "Your presence is not needed when I am here."

"You, signora?" said Violante, staring into her eyes.

"Return to your room."

"I hope you will recognize my right to be here!"

The servants and the razionale, roused by those words, had gotten up, embarrassed by having allowed themselves to be overcome with sleep and having been discovered, and they stammered a few words of apology; but Violante dismissed them: "Go and rest, you are too tired; I will stay here. Go!"

The servants and the razionale looked at the duchess, undecided, as if to ask if they should obey, but Violante added imperiously, "Well? It seems to me that I have released you from your watch. Now leave."

Although initially stunned by this unexpected behavior, Donna Gabriella nevertheless recognized that her authority was being damaged and diminished in front of the servants.

She said haughtily, "Are you forgetting that I am here?"

"No, signora," answered Violante, "I am not forgetting anything, but I am relieving you of the trouble of looking after my father, and I believe that if he could express his wish, he would not want anyone at his bedside other than me."

And turning again to the servants and the razionale, who were standing aside, immobile and a little embarrassed, she added, "Go; even the duchess finds it more suitable for you to get some rest."

They bowed and left; the razionale thought it best to again offer his help: "If you need anything, Your Excellency . . . I am in the secretariat . . . feel free to call for me."

When they had gone out, Violante drew a chair near to the foot of her father's bed and sat there without saying a word. Donna Gabriella felt consumed with spite, with hatred, and by the need to put that young girl under her feet. Remembering how she had slandered Violante in front of Don Raimondo, she felt a thin-skinned humiliation for having been discovered in a manner that gave her stepdaughter the full right to slap her with the harshest words of revenge. She wanted to crush her at any cost, to throw back her own defeat against her, to torment that twice-broken heart.

"You certainly don't expect," she said, "that I will leave you by yourself."

"What is Your Ladyship afraid of?" the young girl answered, turning halfway around in the high-backed chair. "Besides, won't you be in the other room . . . with Signor Blasco? You will be more comfortable there than in front of this bed."

Donna Gabriella bit her lip, and Blasco, who didn't understand the reasons behind the painful irony of these last words, murmured softly, but with a tone of great regret, akin to a slight reprimand: "Violante!"

"Nothing, signora. . . . But I can think with satisfaction that . . . now you can no longer accuse me of being the mistress of Signor—"

"Wretched girl!" screamed Donna Gabriella, interrupting her and making a move to grab the young girl.

But Blasco didn't give her the chance; he held her back, reprimanding her: "But what are you doing?"

Violante had stood up and gestured toward the wounded man, and at that moment all three of them saw him open his eyes and look at them with an expression of sorrow that he was unable to communicate with his voice. That look stopped and froze Donna Gabriella, penetrated into the blood of Blasco, and struck them both into a state of silence full of thoughts, dismay, and mercy according to each one's conscience.

Violante approached the bed and asked him gently, "Do you want anything, Signor Padre?"

Don Raimondo turned his eyes toward her and looked at her for a long time; his lips quivered imperceptibly but nothing escaped except a moan. With her eyes full of tears, the young girl stood gazing at him; then, following the direction of her father's gaze, she saw that it rested on the duchess and Blasco. She thought she understood what it meant.

"Signore," she said, turning to Blasco, "I beg you, leave him in peace."

The word was addressed to the young man, but evidently her plea was also directed toward the duchess. Donna Gabriella shrugged her shoulders in contempt.

"Come with me, signore," she said imperiously, extending her hand so as to rest it on the wrist that Blasco had yet to offer her.

Blasco felt nailed to the spot; a multitude of thoughts, suspicions, and questions raced through his head. There was in Violante's hard, haughty, and rigid attitude—as there was in Donna Gabriella's disquietude—a mystery that he couldn't manage to decipher. He had wanted to question the young girl, to have some explanations, in order to prove his innocence and to defend himself, but the duchess was waiting for him, annoyed at the delay. "Signore, I have asked you to come with me."

"Forgive me," Blasco said, "but everything that is happening here is so strange, and I feel so embarrassed, without knowing anything, that I think it's a legitimate desire that I have to ask for some explanation."

Violante coldly, and not without bitterness, answered him, "The duchess can explain everything better than I can. . . . Be so kind as to go with her."

She was forcefully directing him to leave; why? Of what crime was he guilty in her eyes? He looked at the duchess, who was waiting for him in a pose that fully reflected ladylike dignity, and with a glow of malicious satisfaction on her face. Violante had turned her back to them and had resumed her position in front of her father, who with astonishment in his eyes gradually followed the movements of one and then the other as they were talking, as if he hadn't heard the words clearly or understood what they meant.

Donna Gabriella grew irritated with Blasco's vacillation; annoyed, she said, "I'm waiting for you!"

Then slowly, with his head down and his heart in turmoil, he held out his arm to her; the duchess rested her hand on it, and he went with her into the sitting room where they had spent the night.

Donna Gabriella was uncertain for a little while, then she resumed her place next to the little table and pointed to a chair at the back of the room for Blasco to sit in, from where he could neither see nor be seen. "Sit down."

She gave orders imperiously, as if she had caught others at fault, out of a need to carry out a revenge, to hide, to retaliate, and out of a desire to overpower, to vindicate herself on someone.

Blasco, however, didn't sit down; he felt a disdain, a covert sense of rebellion against this woman who had no respect even for that bed where her husband was dying, in order to abandon herself to her blind instincts; he didn't want to obey that imperious, irrational gesture and said, "I have nothing more to do here. I hope that Don Raimondo recovers. In order to fulfill my obligation, I need not remain in this house, where, moreover, with the coming and going of people, I would not be safe. It is not yet daylight; the streets are still dark, and I can get out of harm's way."

"You're leaving? Are you going away? How? Why?" the duchess asked hastily.

"Because I must."

"I will not allow you to leave."

"You will not stand in my way!" Blasco replied firmly, dominating her with his will.

Then she felt her heart shatter, and her eyes filled with tears.

"Why do you want to leave me?" she moaned.

"I must go. I have other things to do. I cannot leave my work unfinished . . . perhaps I will return tonight . . . if it will be possible . . . in any case, you will hear from me, have no doubt; and have faith in me that I will watch over this house."

"What do I care about this house!" Donna Gabriella exclaimed, full of pain and spite.

But Blasco didn't react to her interruption; he took his cloak, his sword and hat, and said goodbye to her. "Farewell! Be more fair and more understanding; and remember that at this moment you have a great obligation to fulfill because for now you alone represent the House of Albamonte."

He kissed her hand with an indifferent sense of propriety and left. Donna Gabriella couldn't hold him back, she couldn't even utter a word; the nervous tension of her impulses had naturally given way to a weakness of will and an exhaustion of strength, which found no other outlet except in her tears.

Blasco went out wrapped in his cloak, with the collar turned up above his nose, and took Via Porta Carini in order to get out of the city as fast as possible. It was already daylight; the shutters of some windows were half-open, some sleepy faces were appearing behind the glass panes, the shops were opening their doors.

The gabelloti had already opened the city gate, behind which were waiting carters with teams of mules loaded with barrels or sacks, and carts pulled by oxen. Blasco hid among them and, following the line of the bastions to the left, he soon reached the vegetable gardens, and following a path he returned to the Convent of the Capuchins, where he would wait for the appointed time of his duel with Coriolano.

* * *

Responding evasively to the friar who accompanied him, he went into his cell and threw himself on the bed in order to think and to rearrange his thoughts. He had to protect Violante from every threat and from any violence by the duchess and at the same time to attend to her future. There was only one way: to reveal everything to the Ventimiglia and Branciforti families, to the relatives of Emanuele and of Violante, the two orphans, and to put them under their protection. He wrote two short letters, signing them "Blasco Albamonte," and, calling the young friar, who was about to go begging for alms, he asked him to deliver them to their address.

"Goodness! . . . They are the most high-ranking lords," said the friar. "Are they friends of Your Illustrious Lordship?"

"Yes."

The friar put the letters in his knapsack and left. Blasco had requested to meet with both lords owing to matters that were very serious and that were of concern to their families; he asked them to excuse his boldness if he did not go himself to their palazzi, as he should have, but he was unable to because he was constrained by a greater power. He gave each an appointment at a different time, in the woods of the Convent of the Capuchins.

The two lords arrived at the convent at the established hour, with their carriages, and both were more than a little astonished in recognizing that Blasco Albamonte, who had invited them and whom they believed they didn't know, was that young man Blasco da Castiglione, whom they considered to be an adventurer of unknown origin. Blasco had to prove his birth two times, to his annoyance, which filled the two lords with wonder; having learned that in the end the young man had noble blood in his veins, they seemed to reconcile with him, and they looked upon him with greater benevolence. But their astonishment reached its height when they learned that the heir of Don Emanuele, Duke of Motta, the legitimate duke, the son of Donna Aloisia, was alive, saved by a miracle, and that it was necessary to remove him from the guardianship of his saviors and to restore his rank, especially since there was a document in which Don Raimondo acknowledged his nephew, and that document was in the possession of the notary Di Bello. Now that Don Raimondo was between life and death, it seemed necessary to him that the maternal relatives of the young man take steps to integrate him into his status; but meanwhile, out of consideration for the house, and to obviate any inconvenience and not scatter the patrimony, he was proposing the marriage of Emanuele and Violante. As natural guardians of the youngsters it was up to the relatives—given the gravity of Don Raimondo's state of health—to agree about their future status. All this news, all these proposals didn't astonish the Marchese of Geraci, Emanuele's grandfather, in whom the idea that the son of his poor Aloisia was still alive produced a sweet and tender emotion, and it didn't even astonish the Prince of Butera, to whom the solution proposed by Blasco seemed the most logical and suitable. For the moment, they didn't come to a decision; they had to have in their hands the document issued by the notary and to gather all the elements. In any case, it would be necessary to wait for Don Raimondo's state of health to resolve itself in one way or the other.

In his revelations, Blasco had kept silent about things that could endanger Don Raimondo and about what part the Beati Paoli had played in all those events; he only mentioned one thing in the ear of the Prince of Butera: to protect Violante, his niece, who was threatened by grave dangers in her father's house.

While the two lords, who had ended up being together, were leaving, the Prince of Branciforti said to Blasco, "But you, my son, with this warrant that hangs over your head, what devilry have you committed?"

"None, Your Excellency. I wanted to do good, but I wasn't able to, and I had to defend myself. That is a summary of what I have done. If I have a warrant issued against me, I owe it to Don Raimondo, whom I saved. But it doesn't matter. Your Excellency will obtain a passage for me. The warrant is issued for Blasco da Castiglione, and I am instead Don Blasco Albamonte, of the Dukes of Motta. Blasco da Castiglione is dead, by the hand of justice."

"What the devil! Here's an idea that I like. Leave it to me."

Blasco accompanied them to their carriages; when they left, he felt as if a weight was taken off his chest and he took a breath, but a tear came to his eyes and he felt a painful sob rising up.

CHAPTER 26

After they had placed Blasco on the ground in the vegetable gardens that stretched out onto the ancient bed of the marshland of the Papireto, Coriolano, Don Girolamo, and Andrea went off, crossing through the plants, and, walking far and wide, they emerged onto a tree-lined road outside Porta Nuova. They walked along the city walls up to Porta Termini and lingered until dawn waiting for the gate to open, and, in order to enter unnoticed, they mixed in with the carters who were arriving from Messina. Coriolano hadn't taken off his mask; when it was time to enter the city, he quietly exchanged a few words with Don Girolamo, who made a slight nod and said to Andrea, "Go by Nino Bucolaro's house, give him the sign, and wait for me with him in front of San Michele Arcangelo."

As soon as Andrea left, Coriolano took off his mask.

In Fieravecchia[1] he parted with Don Girolamo and went home; when Don Girolamo went to San Michele Arcangelo, he found only Andrea there.

"Well?" he asked him.

"I gave the sign three times and even knocked, but there was no answer; indeed, no one showed up at all."

Don Girolamo looked grim.

"The scoundrel," he said, "he must not be home. Where might he have gone?"

Slowly they started off for San Cosmo, unaware and not imagining that the area was, so to speak, in a state of siege, but when they walked down from Sant'Agata alla Guilla, at the windows and in the doorways they saw people looking with curiosity in the direction of the piazza, and after seeing guards and soldiers at the entrance to the street by the church, they stopped and became worried.

"What on earth!" said Don Girolamo. "This is serious business. Let's go to Piazza del Monte."

They slipped away under the Sant'Isidoro arch, and from Piazza del Monte, along Via dei Lettighieri—now known as Via delle Sedie Volanti—they went back toward San Cosmo, but even on that side there was a squad of soldiers, behind which some onlookers were gathering.

---

1 A fifteenth-century marketplace.

Don Girolamo and Andrea mingled among them and took a look in the piazza, where some windproof torches were still burning, their flames growing faint at the first light of day. They saw that Vicolo degli Orfani, the church of the Canceddi, and the entrances to Via San Cosmo and to Porta Carini were guarded by soldiers; it seemed that the entire garrison had rushed there. Officials and algozini came and went from one point to another; the captain of the city was in the middle of the piazza, very angry and taking it out on whoever he came across.

Don Girolamo picked up the impressions, the comments, and the gossip of the crowd.

"They tracked down the Beati Paoli!"

"No way, they haven't found a damn thing!"

"I'm telling you!"

"You don't know anything."

"They went into the cave!"

"Really?"

"Where is the cave?"

"But can you imagine! It was right under their nose!"

"In Vicolo degli Orfani."

"But no; under the house of Judge Baldi."

"It's here in the vicolo!"

"He says that there are two entrances!"

"Who would ever have imagined it?"

"Jesus! Jesus! . . . And they found them?"

"Did you hear the gunshots?"

"It was a battle!"

"Poor souls!"

"You can't imagine the fright. I was sleeping when suddenly I heard a bang! bang! I woke up and wanted to go outside, but my wife told me, but no, Peppe, don't go anywhere; it's probably thieves . . . bullets don't have eyes, you know!"

"And are there any dead?"

"Who knows!"

"Someone had to be a spy, surely!"

"Well! Not even God was able to avoid traitors!"

"If it's verified, they will be celebrated."

"You can expect it."

"But can't one get through?"

"Corporal, signore, excuse me, can we get by?"

"Fine story, the captain's order! And what if I lived on that side?"

"But what kind of an order is that!"

Meanwhile some gardeners with donkeys turned up, loaded with *zimmile*[2] full of cauliflower and lettuce, as well as some carters with their train of mules; the church bells were ringing for mass; around the piazza people were coming out of their houses to go about their daily business; the cordons of soldiers had, without anyone having given the order, broken up, and the piazza filled with people who were coming and going.

The comments began to rain down and were certainly not favorable to the captain of the city, who that year was Duke Don Luigi Gaetani.

"That's a fine impression they've made on us!"

"But did they think they were dealing with children?"

"The Beati Paoli are like spirits; they are seen, they are heard, and they are never caught!"

The Beati Paoli were well liked by that populace, inclined to admire everything that had a hint of the supernatural or that was a sign of rebellion against the authorities, of which it knew nothing except their cruelty and acts of violence. In its eyes, the sect exercised a type of vindictive justice in favor of the weak, and for that reason it was its natural and legitimate defender. Therefore, the widespread satisfaction in learning that the forces of law and order had failed miserably was quite understandable; even if they had found the stable, the oxen had already taken off, and there was great pleasure in taunting the incompetence of the leaders and of the captain.

"What a sorry state of affairs!"

The exclamation, repeated amid sneers and ironic laughter, and the futility of every search suggested to the captain that he should order the withdrawal of the soldiers. He left some guards at the two entrances of the cave and then abandoned that inglorious field of his failure.

* * *

Don Girolamo and Andrea went up to the house, where Signora Francesca was in a state of great anxiety. Waiting up for her husband, she hadn't gone to bed, had heard the gunshots, and had run frightened to the small balcony. From there, by the light of windproof torches, she had seen that bustling of soldiers and, trembling, she had begun to pray, appealing to the saints, not moving away from the balcony and fearing to see her husband—either killed or arrested—emerge at any moment from the vicolo amid the soldiers. And she had spent the entire night in this state of painful anxiety, jumping at every sound, watching every group, trying to guess what would happen.

---

2   Word of Arabic origin: a type of saddlebag made of dwarf palm, which is loaded onto the backs of beasts of burden, usually to carry vegetables or fruit.

She experienced an initial sense of relief at seeing the guards and soldiers walk away amid the laughter and mockery of the crowd, but when she saw her husband, she was overcome with tears of joy.

"What was that about? What happened?"

"Nothing, minor things. Emanuele?"

"I think he's sleeping . . . I didn't notice. You were on my mind. What a fright! . . . But how did it go?"

"Who knows? Someone must have tipped off justice."

"Did something terrible happen?"

"Nothing."

"Praise be to God!"

Signora Francesca was unaware of what had happened that night at the tribunal of the Beati Paoli. Although she knew the role that her husband played and she knew some secrets, especially regarding Emanuele, Don Girolamo never revealed to her the business that occupied the tribunal during its meetings, nor had he ever told her the identity of his companions. She only knew that Antonino Bucolaro and Andrea belonged to the sect. However, the presence of Andrea—unusual at that hour—and his outward appearance as well as that of her husband were enough to make her understand that it must have been some very important business; but as she was not in the habit of meddling and was submissive to her husband, she dared not ask anything, and like a good housewife she had begun to tidy up the house.

"One can now say that my work is done," said Andrea. "I have achieved what I swore to myself I would do, and now I will be able to kiss the hand of my young master, and even if I were to be struck by a bolt of lightning or be sent to the gallows, I would die content."

"We are not afraid of dying on the gallows."

"We had a narrow escape . . . and, excuse me, now that we have that document, what else is there to do?"

"Goodness . . . it will be taken to the viceroy or to the Gran Corte Civile. . . . I don't know; it is what the leader will decide. He knows everything."

"I have nothing except one burning desire—to see the young master in his palazzo and to drive away the interlopers."

Don Girolamo shook his head.

"Who knows? Don't forget that there is the bastard—"

"Ah! If he wasn't of the blood of my good master, I would have rid the earth of him by now! What do you want? What do you expect? Did you see how he defended that scoundrel? It takes courage—"

"*Baccaglio!*"[3]

---

3 "Silence!"

"You are right."

Don Girolamo got up and went to Emanuele's room, but as soon as he entered, his astounded voice was heard saying, "Francesca, where is Emanuele?"

"What do you mean, where is he?" an astonished Signora Francesca answered. "He's in his room sleeping."

"He's not there."

"What? What?"

And the good woman ran, interrupting her work, and she too saw that his bed was empty and the covers in disarray.

Don Girolamo frowned, looked around, and noticed that the glass doors to the small balcony, although they seemed closed, weren't bolted shut; he opened them and looked out. That small balcony opened onto a small interior terrace that was formed by the bottom of an air shaft, over which the windows of the upper floor opened, and there was a ladder that was used to climb into a loft above the kitchen. Don Girolamo saw that the ladder was propped under a window of the terrace and that its upper rungs weren't so far from the window that a young man of Emanuele's height couldn't reach the windowsill with his chest. He immediately intuited everything.

"Now," he shouted, "I'm going to get him, and word of honor, I will teach him a lesson."

He went back indoors and took a key, opened a small door, and climbed up a narrow wooden stairway, amid the amazement of his wife and Andrea. Soon after, a trampling noise was heard that came down at an almost precipitous pace, and Emanuele appeared, red with anger and annoyance, followed by Don Girolamo, who was shouting, "I forbade you, by God. . . . I forbade you! . . . It's disgraceful. . . . I will shut you in a convent!"

The sight of Andrea, instead of embarrassing the young man, incited him.

"Who? . . . Who will you shut up? . . . But end it for once!"

"Ah, ill-mannered boy!"

"Watch out!" Emanuele shouted at him in an angry and arrogant tone of voice. "Watch out!"

"You are threatening me?" exclaimed Don Girolamo with both astonishment and rage. "Do you dare this too?"

"No, I am not threatening you, but sooner or later you must stay in your place!"

"Are you talking like this? Are you talking like this to me? . . . I will put you in your place!"

He took a rod from the wall and went to flog Emanuele, but Andrea came between them with a resolute determination to protect Emanuele, exclaiming, "This, no . . . I will not allow you to!"

"You? . . . Get out of my way, by God! . . . Who do you think you are? Get out of my way!"

"Get out of the way!" Emanuele added with a self-important arrogance. "I don't need your help! . . . Let him come, if he has the heart."

Don Girolamo was enraged. "Body of God! As long as you live under my roof you are still my adoptive son and I will beat you!"

He raised his hand, but Andrea tried to grab his arm. "Don Girolamo, don't beat him."

"Ah! For Christ's sake! So do you want me to take my anger out on you? . . . But get out, leave! . . . I am the master here! Get out or I will regret what I have done!"

Signora Francesca intervened, trying to calm her husband.

"You are right, Don Girolamo, but forgive him; he doesn't know what he is saying, and you will see that he will be sorry."

"Me? Far from it!" Emanuele interrupted with a sneer. "I have nothing to be sorry for!"

"Do you hear him . . . but may my reputation be lost, if . . ."

He pushed Andrea aside and unleashed a blow that Andrea was quick to block with his elbow, while at the same time grabbing the rod in order to stop Don Girolamo from beating the young man. Signora Francesca, with a scream, had flung herself in the middle. Emanuele, however, retained a defiant manner. Don Girolamo was almost beside himself with rage; now he was taking it out on Andrea.

"Get out!" he shouted. "Get out! . . . Out of here!"

"Don Girolamo!" implored his wife.

"I will leave, yes," Andrea responded, "but not alone . . . by God! Are you mad?"

"Yes, I will do crazy things! . . . That little ingrate, that viper, who I supported with all my heart!"

"If you supported me, do not fear; I will pay your expenses, as soon as you put me in possession of my patrimony!"

Don Girolamo was staggered by those arrogant words of Emanuele's. His anger was overwhelmed by the unexpected; there was an entire revelation in that arrogant and cruel response.

"What? Patrimony? What did he say?"

Signora Francesca seemed at a loss. Andrea, coming to his own conclusions, exclaimed, "What, then he knows!"

"Yes," said Emanuele with a tone of triumph. "I know that I grew up in this house, humbly; I also know that I am a lord and another status awaits me. And I know that I am owed respect . . . and if someone must give orders, it is me!"

"Ah! Finally!" Andrea shouted with joy. "Finally, I can relieve myself of the weight of this secret! Oh, Your Excellency, my master!"

He threw himself on his knees before Emanuele and, taking his hand, he kissed it with respect, amid the young man's feelings of pleasure and amazement and the bewilderment of Don Girolamo, who repeated, "How does he know? . . . Who told him?"

Signora Francesca was trembling. Emanuele, who after all knew nothing more than what Signora Francesca had told him, was dying to know what Andrea and Don Girolamo were imagining that he already knew. That Andrea, who was kissing his hand, paying him honor, calling him master, and who appeared overcome with great emotion, now appeared to his eyes as the solver of the great enigma that he could in any case decipher. But meanwhile the amazed reaction of Don Girolamo, and the words and gestures of Andrea, confirmed to him that he had to be the descendant and the heir of a great family and increased that haughtiness, that arrogance, and that vanity that were rendering him almost loathsome.

Don Girolamo pulled himself together.

"Ah! Pay me!" he said bitterly. "Your Lordship wants to pay me for what I spent? . . . But if you handed your entire patrimony over to me, as well as all your titles, it would never be enough to pay me for what I did for you, what risks, what dangers that I encountered and how many times I endangered my life. . . . But not even your life would be enough to repay me! . . . Get out! Your blood doesn't lie; I realize that. And you are right, you alone have the right to give orders. . . . We are, it is true, the ones who saved you and who struggled to prevent you from being dispossessed, but, in any case, we are poor people and it is up to us to obey . . . it is right. Tomorrow I will accompany you to the relatives of your mother; I have nothing more to do for you. And when you leave, I will close that door, so that you will never again be tempted to enter. . . . Your money? Ugh! If I had wanted to have sacks full of it, I would have handed you over . . . to someone I know, who would have paid a fortune for you."

"Don Girolamo!" Signora Francesca implored again.

"Don Girolamo," added Andrea, with a tone between a plea and resentment, "these words do not seem worthy of you."

"At least allow me to speak! . . . His money! Would he have it if I had not saved him from death? If I hadn't hidden him and confronted the dangers that I encountered? But keep it for yourself! . . . Who wants it? It would burn me. . . . Today here, tomorrow somewhere else, and if I meet you I will act like I don't know you. . . . But, as long as you are here you will obey me. If your relatives want you to marry the daughter of a street cleaner, I don't care. If they are happy, everyone's happy, but that I will have a hand in getting you entangled with just anyone, don't even think about it! . . . And I will tell everything to your relatives; I don't want to have misgivings. . . . Meanwhile you will stay here, in this room. . . . You will see that your relatives will take away these silly notions from you. In a convent! There, or a few months in a castle, and you will know how that feels!"

He was silent. He had a bitter taste in his mouth and his chest swelled from both sorrow and anger. The others were silent as well, overcome by the righteousness of that outburst; but Emanuele stood there glowering, spiteful, arrogant, as if he had made a great effort to tolerate those words.

After a moment he said coldly, "Why don't you take me at once to my relatives? In the end, I've been here much too long; you should have done it before."

"Do you hear him?" Don Girolamo said. "Do you also hear him, you who nursed him, Francesca? You, who didn't want to give him up when I wanted to take him to the Prince of Geraci."

"Ah!" shouted Emanuele with a surge of delight. "Then am I the son of the Prince of Geraci?"

"You . . . But what? Then you don't know whose son you are?"

"He doesn't know?" an amazed Andrea said. "But then . . ."

"But your words?"

"No, I don't know everything, but now will you tell me. . . . In the end, I must know. You, tell me," added the young man, turning imperiously to Andrea.

"Yes, Your Excellency."

"No, Andrea, not yet," Don Girolamo said bitterly.

"Why? I don't think there's a reason to keep it from him. And then he is my master and I cannot disobey him. . . . Your Excellency is the son of the forever blessed memory of my late master Don Emanuele Albamonte, Duke of Motta."

"Albamonte!" exclaimed Emanuele, with an astonishment in which there was some regret at not being a prince. "Then I am an Albamonte!"

He remembered Don Raimondo, his footmen, the torture inflicted on him in the Castello a Mare, and his nostrils flared with hatred and of a desire for revenge.

How had that man become duke? How had he usurped his name, status, wealth? . . . If he, Emanuele, was duke as the rightful heir, then Don Raimondo would have to leave the palazzo, surrender the patrimony to him, and return to the shadows as a private citizen! . . . This was clear; and he would enjoy the splendid revenge of having that man driven away by the same servants who had served him before! This thought filled him with so much joy that he no longer regretted that he was a duke instead of a prince.

"Ah! Therefore I am the Duke of Motta!"

His eyes flashed with joy and he looked around with arrogant disdain, marveling at having been able to live in this poor home, among inferior people who had addressed him informally. Around him there was silence, and it seemed that a great distance had immediately inserted itself between Emanuele and those three people who had risked their lives for him. The difference in rank had broken every bond and had raised a great barrier between them. Everyone was regaining an awareness of their own status and feeling that the old relationships had ended right then and there, with that name and that title.

Emanuele said coldly to Don Girolamo, "I hope that you have informed my relatives of my existence."

Don Girolamo indicated that he had not.

He was a little uncomfortable, not knowing what forms of address he should use toward his former adoptive son, and he was resorting to gestures that did not require formal etiquette.

Emanuele resumed: "I believe that now it is necessary to make it known."

He had taken on, not without ostentation, the manners of a great lord and was giving orders as if that little family had had the obligation to raise him, to look after him, and now to obey him. But Don Girolamo's discomfort couldn't last long; he got up his courage and replied rudely, "I will do it when it is the right time. Meanwhile, Your Illustrious Lordship will be content to continue to be the person you have been; and your Signor Andrea, since he has nothing to do here, will do me the favor of leaving and never coming to this house again, unless I tell him to."

Emanuele turned red from spite and shame; Andrea was humiliated.

"Are you banishing me, Don Girolamo?"

"Take it as you wish!"

"But I want to be served by my servants!" shouted Emanuele, exacting his revenge.

"And what have we been and who are we, if not your humble servants?" Don Girolamo said ironically. "There is no need to have others in this house."

Andrea took his hat, turned it over in his hands like one who can't make a decision, then, mumbling his words a little, took his leave. "Enough . . . I will do as you wish. . . . This is your house and I cannot speak. . . . Goodbye. So then we will see each other again . . . and Your Excellency may rest assured that as I served until the end, faithfully, the blessed memory of the duke, your father, I will also serve you. I kiss your hand."

"Have patience, I beg you," said Don Girolamo, "and as for Emanuele, have no fear, I had him as a son!"

Emanuele couldn't hold Andrea back; he followed him with his eyes and when he saw him vanish he felt part of his boldness fading. He looked at Don Girolamo, almost waiting for him to speak, but the razionale threw the rod on the little table and said, "This is no longer necessary, but meanwhile go into my room. You will sleep there . . . and don't say a word. . . . For now, I am the master. Be off."

The young man felt his face flush; he would have wanted to react, but Don Girolamo's manner was such that it convinced him to be cautious. Without giving up his air of a master and acting more like a man who does someone a favor than like an obedient boy, he went into the room. Don Girolamo locked him in there and thrust the key in his pocket. Then, dressed as he was, he went to throw himself on the young man's bed and fell asleep.

CHAPTER 27

Toward noon, Don Girolamo went to visit Coriolano; no one could see him enter by the usual secret passageway. He found the Cavaliere della Floresta troubled by a veiled anger that revealed itself in the contractions of his jaws.

"Well!" he muttered under his breath, as soon as Don Girolamo came in. "*Caifasso è sbottonato.*"

"What?" the razionale exclaimed, amazed.

"And he's still *allumato.*"

"How is that possible! . . . He had three *salassi*!"[1]

"He slipped through your fingers! . . . What an embarrassment!"

There was a moment of silence. Don Girolamo asked, "But how did he get out? By himself?"

"They pulled him out."

"What? . . . They went down there? They found the passageway?"

"No. They entered by digging up the courtyard of the Palazzo della Motta."

"And how did they know about it? Who could have told?"

Coriolano shrugged; Don Girolamo understood, and with a thinly veiled reproachful look, he remarked, "I know! It was surely that damn bastard! . . . I had told Your Lordship that he would bring us bad luck, that he would create obstacles for us! . . . Your Lordship never wants to listen to me. And now we have to start from the beginning. . . . Why don't you let me go? A rifle shot, at night, not even God can get him out of this!"

"Do not make a move without my orders! He too is a victim of injustice."

Don Girolamo mumbled something unintelligible and remained silent for a moment, worried by this news, which seemed to shatter his plans. Coriolano wasn't saying anything; with his hands in the pockets of his waistcoat he looked up, like someone who is searching for something or concentrating on a thought.

After a while Don Girolamo asked, "And now what do we do with the *Caifasso*?"

"Nothing. We must watch and weigh matters. Now, more than ever, we need to *astutare la lanterna*. If he is able to *cantare*,[2] he can obstruct us. I realize that

---

1 *Caifasso è sbottonato*: the magistrate got out; *allumato*: alive; *salassi*: wounds.

2 *Astutare la lanterna*: kill him: *cantare*: talk.

in the end we have all the weapons, but some of us could pay the price. . . . I will pay him a visit. Meanwhile, go to Di Bello the notary, pretend you are keeping him company in his study, and watch over him."

"Oh, we can be sure about this. The poor man is so afraid that he won't even dare to be seen."

"More reason to watch over him and anticipate him. Fear is a bad adviser. Meanwhile, keep the Orbo in Nino Bucolaro's ribs."

"I already have him on it."

"I have news about Matteo Lo Vecchio."

"Yes? Is he really dead?"

"That scoundrel is still alive; he is at the prince's castle, being looked after with every possible consideration, and it seems that he is recovering."

"Fine, we'll bash in his teeth so that he doesn't bite."

"We'll talk about it later. For now, let's leave him alone; he could be useful. And he is a witness. Do you have anything to tell me?"

Don Girolamo then told him what had happened between him and Emanuele, and about how the young man already knew about his status. Coriolano listened to him without saying a word, knitting his eyebrows.

"The world belongs to the ungrateful," he then said. "Emanuele has the vices of his father and the soul of his uncle, without any of their virtues. But this has to do with him; it will certainly not change what we do. It means that we will see if there's a need to hurry."

He dismissed him with a wave of his hand; Don Girolamo asked him, "Do we need to *pizzicare la vecchia al refettorio*?"

"Not now."

"Your Lordship will tell me when I have to *sonar la campana*. . .[3] But in any case, where?"

"Outside Porta d'Ossuna."

"Very well."

When Don Girolamo left, Coriolano called for his carriage and went to visit the Duchess of Motta, where he met Blasco and where that brief quarrel and challenge took place, which, although Coriolano was able to conceal every emotion underneath his cold mask, had opened a great wound in his heart.

By now every bond was broken between him and Blasco. He had relied on the young man and had almost wanted to prepare him for his succession in that dark realm in which his guidance was blindly obeyed. A young man, alone, without a future, rejected by society, a rebel by habit and instinct, brave, handsome, and enterprising, he had all the qualities necessary to lead an army except one: caution.

---

3 *pizzicare la vecchia al refettorio*: convene the council of the sect; *sonar la campana*: send out the invitations.

He had hoped to make him acquire it by pulling him into the sect, getting him accustomed to that masked struggle, to the duplicities of the executioner, and he had been sure he would succeed and turn Blasco into the most feared enemy of the legal authorities.

And instead, that young man was evading him; in truth he was resolutely confronting him, in order to fight him, he was holding back his punishing arm; he was taking away the condemned from him; he was revealing, perhaps unwittingly, the secret of the sect; he was becoming an enemy, and moreover a dangerous one, against whom the avenging daggers of the Beati Paoli were being sharpened. He was an enemy, which the supreme interests of the sect itself would ask him, and perhaps force him, to eliminate for their collective safety.

Cold reasoning did not justify Blasco's conduct to him, nor did it conceal or mitigate the disastrous consequences resulting from it; nevertheless, a remnant of his earlier fondness made it hard and painful for him to clearly put forward any judgment; and if it wasn't suggesting excuses or compassion to him, it gave him a sensation of suffering that was bothering him. His inflexible and merciless heart perhaps felt the need for some tenderness, and, since he was indifferent to women, while looking for it in friendship he had become attached to Blasco, whose qualities had struck him from the very first day.

But then that beloved young man, over whom he had extended the protection of the sect, without his being aware of it, and whose standing he had tried to reestablish, drew his sword in front of him with the harsh and severe manner of an executioner.

"What a pity!" his aching heart would murmur.

"He must die!" his inflexible logic and vested interest would decree. "He failed in his oath, he betrayed; he must die, as traitors have died and will die! It is the law!"

That night he convened the tribunal.

Don Girolamo personally went to invite the members, including Andrea.

"Outside, and wherever we may meet," said Don Girolamo, "we don't even know each other, and I no longer want to hear anything about you, but as far as the society is concerned, it is another matter. Besides, it is proper that the tribunal should decide between the two of us, and whoever has transgressed will pay."

"As you wish," Andrea replied.

* * *

The Beati Paoli were convening in the catacombs of Porta d'Ossuna, which, until that terrible night, only Coriolano and Don Girolamo had known existed. The catacombs of Porta d'Ossuna, discovered and explored more than half a century later and now visible, were not isolated. By way of underground tunnels that the passage of time had covered up and wiped out, they were connected to the other group of catacombs that extended underneath the high ground of the Capo and of which the cave located in Vicolo degli Orfani was only one end, perhaps the point of entrance, and was almost detached from the main body due to the buildings that had risen above it, whose foundations had cut off or obstructed the passages. Coriolano, exploring those undergrounds, had discovered that the cave of the Beati Paoli could be connected to the catacombs of the Capo and, digging in a niche, he had found the passageway, which he had then concealed so that it would remain secret even to the members themselves.

With Don Girolamo, he had then explored those underground areas, pushing forward, and he had found a narrow stairway excavated in the volcanic rock at the top of which was a trapdoor, which the passage of time and mud had almost glued to the jambs. At first with caution, then reassured by not having heard anything, they had struck harder; the silence had encouraged them to be more daring. Coriolano had used his strength to leverage his shoulders against the trapdoor, shaking it loose, and lift it with the creaking of rotted wood. They found themselves in a room that looked like a cellar, an abandoned, partly destroyed storeroom full of cobwebs and grime. It was the ruins of a house that overlooked the church of the Noviziato, of the Jesuit fathers, recently consecrated to the sect, and it may have still been standing at the time, a remnant of the demolitions that had been done in order to build the church. The discovery had pleased Coriolano, as it represented a sort of secret exit for any event. Going back down, and having resumed their journey through the narrow labyrinths, similar to sewers, they quickly reached another group of catacombs. A hole in the vault, blocked by stones and earth, indicated an opening to them. It was sufficient. They then returned there, cleared that opening, and found themselves out in the open, amid the vegetable gardens along the side of the ancient, large Papireto marsh.

Here, then, Coriolano convened the tribunal. They had created an entrance there from an opening that looked like a fissure in the volcanic rock, which rose almost vertically over the marsh bed and concealed the entrance so well that no one was aware of it.

The meeting was serious. Coriolano explained the situation in which the sect found itself. A warrant had been issued that same morning that promised large rewards to whoever would discover, reveal, and identify to justice the members of that "pernicious sect"; other warrants had followed. Their meeting place had been walled up; spies, guards, tribunals, and Sant'Offizio were all in motion. Justice knew some names; some insignificant arrests had been made, and from them it was perhaps possible, through torture and bribery, to go back and track down the leaders. The arrests of Blasco da Castiglione, Don Girolamo, and Andrea had been ordered.

That evening they had been able to keep themselves out of view, but it was necessary to find a way for them to get out of the kingdom, to take refuge in Tuscany or Rome, or perhaps even better, to send them to Spain, where they would be safer. As for the society, it was prudent, until the fury had died down, to be silent, to disappear, almost to make people believe that it had dissolved and dispersed; it was necessary to eliminate all traces. Whoever needed to send a piece of news to the leader could do so by putting a lit candle with a cross marked at the bottom in front of the statue of Ecce Homo dei Biscottari at ten o'clock in the morning, and waiting at midnight in front of the opening to that underground.

Someone asked to speak. It was Don Girolamo.

"It has resumed for me," he said, "the wandering life. But this time I will leave, I will go with my family outside the kingdom, in order to live a more peaceful life. Now I have nothing left to do here . . . but before we leave one another, I ask that two men who until yesterday we considered to be our comrades, and who have been protected by the society, be declared traitors and left to the vengeance of the society. I formally denounce them. They are Blasco da Castiglione, whose behavior and rebellion everyone has witnessed, and Antonino Bucolaro, who, betraying the brothers, has become Matteo Lo Vecchio's spy. And of this I state that I have hard evidence."

A murmur of approval and menace greeted those words. Everyone's eyes, through their masks, turned to the leader, but Coriolano remained immobile, silent, like a divine being, without giving any sign of approval or disapproval.

One of the Beati Paoli took the floor: "If Antonino Bucolaro has betrayed, and the Beato Paolo brother who accuses him provides evidence of this, let him be judged and punished; but as far as Blasco da Castiglione, I beg my brothers not to rush to judgment. It is true, he tried to oppose our justice and he disobeyed the laws of our sacred society, but was he a spy? Did he betray our secret? Perhaps he acted out of the goodness of his heart, out of mercy, without considering the step that he was taking. But I rule out the claim that there is treason, and it doesn't seem to me, dear brothers, that he should be punished like Bucolaro."

Another brother interjected, "Our statutes, that we have sworn on the Holy Crucifix to respect and enforce, are clear and precise, and there are no excuses. Whoever disobeys deserves to die. He disobeyed and rebelled at gunpoint. . . . Furthermore, he pulled Don Raimondo out of the underground and violated our secret."

Andrea said, "Let's hear the words of the Wise One."

The "Wise One" was the leader, Coriolano. He said, "The law must be imposed!"

The executors of the law had to be named, and Coriolano resumed, "I will carry out justice."

The meeting broke up; the Beati Paoli left, one by one, vanishing into the darkness of the night. Don Girolamo and Coriolano were the last to leave.

Coriolano asked him, "So what do you intend to do?"

"I will entrust Emanuele to his relatives. Now that I can no longer watch over him, and I can't even make a brief visit to my house, it is the only option that remains. To leave him with my wife, now that he knows whose son he is and has been putting on airs, it would be the same as having that poor woman die of a broken heart. . . . I will hand him over, or better yet, I will have him handed over to his relatives, then Francesca and I will leave for Spain."

"Very well. I will provide you with the means. Regarding Antonino Bucolaro, I will think about it. . . . We will see each other before you leave."

* * *

They parted company. Coriolano returned home absorbed in thought. He had taken upon himself the serious task of rescuing Blasco from the perils of the Beati Paoli, but now he was feeling all of its weight and responsibility. To punish—the law required it, and inevitably it would have to be imposed; he had passed judgment and taken on the responsibility himself and he couldn't escape it. Meanwhile, at four o'clock of the following day he had to fight Blasco, in front of the Beati Paoli's new meeting place. So then: to fight and to kill in a duel was an expedient way to do away with any odiousness of the vengeance or justice of the sect. Blasco would have the opportunity to defend himself; Coriolano, if anything, would kill or gravely wound him (which he didn't doubt) in an entirely fair match. That thought calmed him and allowed him to sleep almost until noon.

He waited for the agreed-upon hour, attending to things as usual and providing for the safety of his fellow members; then, when it seemed to him time, he thrust a pair of small pistols into the pockets of his waistcoat, took his sword—the best one, flexible and light—wrapped himself in his cloak, and left in a portantina.

He passed in front of the Palazzo della Motta and made inquiries about the duke's health, with that politeness that was customary for him. He rejoiced upon hearing that the duke had shown signs of consciousness, wished him a speedy recovery, and asked that they tell the duchess that he would return.

He came out of Porta d'Ossuna and, having made the portantina stop, he dismissed it, saying that he would return on foot. When he was sure that his servants could no longer see him, he made a wide detour, and through an opening in the hedge he entered the vegetable gardens. He walked for a while, then noticed Blasco sitting on a rock with his arms crossed, waiting. At the sound of his steps the young man raised his head, recognized Coriolano, and got up, greeting him coldly, but not without a certain emotion that he wasn't able to control.

Coriolano took a watch from his breast pocket and looked at it.

"It's exactly four o'clock, signore; I hope I haven't made you wait."

"No, signore," answered Blasco. "I too have just arrived."

"Since the matter that we have to settle is by its nature reserved for the circumstances that determine it, I didn't think to inconvenience a friend to be my witness; I notice that you have made the same decision."

"Indeed," said Blasco.

"So, whenever you wish, I am at your command."

"Me too," repeated Blasco, taking off his hat, frock, and waistcoat, remaining in shirtsleeves.

Coriolano did the same. When, having chosen the terrain, they stood facing each other with their swords in hand, Coriolano said, "I warn you, signore, that I will do everything I can to kill you. You have been condemned as a rebel and a violator of the oath you swore. I have wanted to spare you a death unworthy of you, that is, by a single stab or a rifle shot in the back, so I reserved for myself the responsibility of carrying out justice. This way, you will not die ignobly but as a cavaliere; you cannot say that you are being assassinated but rather that you are being killed fairly, having been given all the means to defend yourself. It is the last consideration that I wanted to extend to you, due to the respect that I have had for you."

"Do your duty, signore," said Blasco gloomily, "and know that I am grateful to you for this deference. However, I must faithfully inform you that I have revealed the existence of Emanuele to the Prince of Butera and to the Marchese of Geraci."

"You did well; I will tell you, in fact, that you have anticipated my plan. On guard, then."

They crossed their swords, which clashed against each other with a noise that made one shiver; Coriolano tried to guess Blasco's strategy but immediately realized that he had none and that he was offering only a weak and passive resistance. Knowing him, he was surprised by it and lowered his sword.

"Signore," he said, "I did not come here to play."

"I well know that," replied Blasco, "nor do I intend to play."

"It seems to me that you want neither to attack nor to defend yourself!"

"What do you care? I certainly am not asking you to do the same. . . . Do your duty."

"But put up a fight, by God!"

"I will do what I want."

"Then must I force you to put up a serious fight?"

"No. Why would you want to force me? You have a duty to kill me; I am making it easy for you. Do you really believe that life is so desirable and precious that one should defend it even when one knows that it is better to throw it away? . . . Come on, on guard!"

"But I want an all-out fight; you yourself asked for this confrontation, and I welcomed it as a respectable means for both of us to get out of a situation that is awkward and ambiguous for you and for me."

"And so what? Until a few days ago we were two brothers—well, almost. . . . Fate has wanted to pit us one against the other. Now you are an executioner, I am the guilty one. I acknowledge that I have done wrong to your society, and I am not looking for excuses, because I am not in the habit of apologizing; in fact, I confirm to you that if I had to do it all over, I would do everything the same again. I am sorry for you. I know whether I suffered in breaking our friendship and seeming like an ingrate to you. But remember a lesson that you gave me. . . . You said that you had before you a noble idea of justice, and that if in order to carry it out you had to ride roughshod over your brother you would not hesitate. I had a noble idea of mercy toward someone who had been vanquished and I didn't hesitate to break a bond of friendship. . . . I wronged you, I repeat, and I disobeyed the society. Punish me; to die by a stab from a sword or by a shot from a rifle is one and the same to me. I have completed my time on earth, and I have nothing more to do in the world. If you want to do me the favor of sending me to the Eternal Father, I will have a final thought of gratitude for you, and I will consider this an act of fraternal friendship. You recognize that, for me, to receive this favor from your hands, rather than from an unknown person, is more gratifying. . . . I would even say kinder. So let's go, what more are you looking for? Do you have an assignment, a duty to fulfill? Carry it out without quibbling."

Coriolano listened to him, and his knitted eyebrows and clenched jaw revealed a dull, barely controlled rage. He was angry with Blasco and with himself—with Blasco because with that behavior and with those words he was preventing him from getting worked up and finding a reason to kill him in fierce combat; at himself because he couldn't find any words to counter Blasco's and he blamed himself for being weak.

"Very well," he said, "I will do as you wish; put yourself on guard."

They again crossed swords. But a shout suddenly brought them to a halt: "Gentlemen! Gentlemen!"

They turned to look; on the top of the embankment that overlooked the vegetable gardens and concealed the catacombs behind it stood a short and haggard man nervously waving his hands, looking frightened.

"Gentlemen! Gentlemen! Stop . . . a rural company is coming this way . . . they will arrest you."

Blasco looked with amazement at that little man, whom he recognized as Michele Barabino, the tailor who had saved him once before from the police; he saw that, having found a suitable point, he was descending precipitously, repeating, "There is a rural company that is poking around . . . immediately, get dressed! . . . Oh! Your Lordship?" he cried out, recognizing Blasco. "Immediately, hide! Hide!"

Coriolano said somberly, "Let's get dressed, signore, and pretend that we are here just observing."

They dressed quickly, sheathing their swords, and began to look around, while Don Michele, next to Blasco, asked him in a low voice, "Your Lordship, forgive me, but what was that about? . . . A good gentleman like Your Lordship . . . and the Cavaliere della Floresta? You were such good friends. . . . How much it pains me! If I could be of some service. . . . Do you hear?"

He was silent and listened closely; indeed, one could hear a trampling of horses. Coriolano turned; among the trees that surrounded the embankment, he thought he saw some men passing through on horseback that the foliage didn't allow him to distinguish clearly.

"It was the good God who sent me," the tailor said. "I went to the Capuchins for a bit of soup . . ."—he had, in fact, a little terracotta pot under his arm—". . . I go there after lunchtime because so many people are there at noon . . . and I'm ashamed, I'm not used to doing that. . . . Enough. I always come back this way. I heard talking and I had a look. . . . I saw the soldier searching inside the houses. . . . Your Lordship must hide . . . are you aware of the warrant?"

"This man is right," Coriolano said to Blasco. "You know where you can hide, without anyone seeing you."

"Thank you, allow me not to take advantage of it . . . if you think it best, you go there . . . we will have time to see each other again; I will let you know where we can meet. . . . Leave."

The tailor had gone up to watch the company of soldiers and was returning very frightened.

"Be quick, be quick, they are coming this way."

Coriolano wrapped himself in his cloak and started off toward the ridge of the embankment because he had no need to run away or to hide; he could go ahead and run into the rural company, confident of being revered rather than harassed. As soon as he reached the top of the embankment, he saw the company, which was coming through the trees. It was led by Captain Mangialocchi.

"Good evening, Your Excellency," greeted the captain, who came forward with a musket across his thighs. "Have you seen anyone, Your Lordship, around these parts?"

"Of what sort?" Coriolano asked, in a slightly mischievous tone.

"A dangerous sort."

"Oh! . . . I saw a couple, Captain, but they weren't dangerous. . . . I would advise you not to disturb them, unless you want to incur the wrath of Venus, goddess of lovers. . . . There is no one else. Good evening, and good service."

"I kiss Your Lordship's hand."

The captain paused and looked around, then glanced at the silent and deserted vegetable garden. He seemed reassured and said, "There's nothing, let's go. It's pointless to go down there."

Whistling, he turned his horse and the company moved slowly away, heading toward the gardens of San Francesco di Paola.

Below, under a sort of cave that had been excavated, or perhaps eroded in distant times by the waves of the sea, the tailor was holding on to Blasco—who would have liked to get out of there—begging him, "Your Lordship, don't move. Holy Mother! . . . They are here, above us. . . . Can't you hear them talking? If we move, if we take a step, they will see us and bang! bang! With two shots we will die like rabbits. By San Bonomo! I know that to Your Lordship the soul is enough . . . but here you would die like a mouse! Leave it to me . . . allow me to lead the way. . . . Wait. . . . I think they are leaving. . . . Yes . . . now I will see."

He stayed another minute, listening intently, as if to pick up the slightest sound, then very slowly he came out of their hiding place, climbed up without making noise, and looked.

"They are gone! They are gone! . . . Your Lordship, come out. Oh, goodness gracious! How scared I was!"

Both of them went out into the garden again.

"Where does Your Lordship intend to go?" the tailor asked Blasco.

"To the Convent of the Capuchins."

"Is Your Lordship sure of finding the road clear, to be able to go back? The entire countryside is overrun with guards, birri, and rural militia . . . it will take cunning. . . . We'll do this: I will go ahead, and I will be the scout, like a dog. If there is anything I will start singing, for example . . . the tale of Saltaliviti. Let's go."

They climbed up the embankment and set out along a path. Michele Barabino went in front, with his pot under his arm, and from time to time he would dip three fingers in it and pull them out holding some cooked greens, which he would eat eagerly, wiping his lips with the back of his hand. Blasco followed him with his head full of thoughts. At a certain point Michele Barabino began to sing.

Blasco stopped and looked around; he saw Michele Barabino, who, still singing, was turning to the right amid the vegetables, and so he too went back, making a detour so as to cross the tailor's path. And then he joined him.

"The birri were there," said Michele Barabino. "We'll have to go a different way . . . but I fear that the convent is surrounded. . . . Who did Your Lordship tell that you would be in the convent?"

"No one."

"No one at all? . . . And did you send any message, any letter?"

"Yes . . . to the Prince of Butera and to the Marchese of Geraci."

"With whom?"

"With Fra Rosario."

"I don't need to know anything more. He is a gossiper. Without meaning to do you any harm, he must have let a few words slip. . . . There are so many spies . . .

and, with this blessed problem with Rome, the convents are being spied on! . . . We mustn't even think about going to the Convent of the Capuchins."

Blasco was thinking, saying nothing, looking at that little, ragged, and meager man with his little pot under his arm who was scurrying along quickly without a care in the world. Evening was falling, and the sky behind Monte Cuccio had clouds that were made fiery by the last rays of the sun and were gradually turning gray.

Suddenly Michele Barabino stopped as if struck by a thought and said, "Do we want to outsmart justice? I will bring you the frock of a Greek priest, a fake beard, and a pair of glasses, and Your Lordship will enter Palermo and will walk through the streets as if you came from Piana dei Greci or from Contessa,[4] without anyone recognizing you. I guarantee it. . . . What do you say? Yes? . . . Very well. Let's see, where will you wait for me. . . . Down below, again, in the ravine where we were. . . . At seven o'clock at night I will return, and before the bells of the Castellana[5] we will be in the city, at my house. . . . It's not a big deal, my house: a hole, a lair, and then . . . but a life for a life! . . . San Bonomo! . . . This is a good one. Let's go, there is no time to lose; Your Lordship will not want to spend the night walking around."

More than leading, he dragged Blasco back down; he left him in the garden and took off toward the city with the short and hurried steps of a busy man. Blasco was thinking about the peculiarity of fate, which for the third time had sent that man to save him.

An hour or more had passed when the good Michele Barabino returned with a bundle. He quickly had Blasco put the garments and robe of the Albanian *papas* over his clothes, encircled his hips with the purple sash, disguised his face with a beard, and, looking at him, cried out, "Goodness . . . I would like to see who could recognize you!"

He put on Blasco's cloak, under which he hid the sword and hat, and said cheerfully, "Papas, let's go."

---

4 Piana degli Albanese, a town fifteen miles south of Palermo; Contessa Entellina, in the province of Palermo, one of the oldest Albanian settlements in the city.

5 The bells signaled a curfew.

CHAPTER 28

They were gathered in Don Raimondo's room, silent and dismayed: the Prince of Butera and the Marchese of Geraci. Violante, next to her father's bed, looked distraught; Donna Gabriella, almost off to one side, next to the Marchese of Regalmici, her brother, seemed stunned rather than saddened. Emanuele next to his grandfather, the Marchese of Geraci, stood stiffly in his rich and elegant clothing, with one hand resting on the hilt of his dress sword, looking every so often at the rich lace of his sleeves. Sometimes he would look at Don Raimondo, and in those moments he thought it suitable to assume a contrite manner, as would be expected under the circumstances.

For five days he had been in his ancestor's palazzo, whose magnificence had filled him with wonder and made him think that he had entered paradise, but two or three days had been enough for him to become familiar with the surroundings and assume those manners of a demigod that were seeming indispensable to him in his new status.

The following day the Marchese of Geraci went to the study of the notary Di Bello in order to read the statement that Blasco had spoken to him about. The notary, however, was ill with fever. The terror of that night, and even more so the fear of being arrested as an accomplice of the Beati Paoli, had made his blood run cold; only the news that Don Raimondo, whom he feared the most, had been found gravely injured and was thought to be as good as dead had somehow, selfishly, comforted him.

The announcement that the Marchese of Geraci had come to ask him about that document had nearly killed the poor notary, who had imagined the Corte Capitaniale coming after him; it had taken some persuading to assuage his terror, which proved to be inexplicable to the marchese. The latter, having read the precious document—and having had a copy released to him, being the grandfather of the young man whose guardianship he would claim—had rushed to the Ammirata house in great haste in order to embrace the son of his poor Aloisia. Signora Francesca, who had already received from her husband the pertinent instructions, told the marchese how her husband had found and taken in Donna Aloisia and her baby, and how she had died, without having been able to say anything. When the news of the murder of Maddalena had spread through the city, and it was learned that unknown assassins had kidnapped the duchess and her son, they had remained silent for fear of being considered the authors or accomplices of the crime; they remained silent even after that, when they had strong suspicions that the life of the child, brought up by them as a son, would be threatened. Now, however, the mystery was revealed, and Duke Don Raimondo had acknowledged his nephew, and the good woman, though with sorrow, was surrendering the handsome, strong, and healthy boy to his relatives.

The Marchese of Geraci, seized with emotion by that story and by the sight of Emanuele, in whose face he thought he recognized some traces of his daughter, said to Signora Francesca, "You, dear signora, you will not be separated from the young man that you have raised as a son; there will be a small apartment for you in the Palazzo Geraci."

But Signora Francesca turned him down. The marchese offered her a handsome sum to reward her for her labors, but she refused even more vigorously. "If we had wanted to take advantage, we could have enriched ourselves and we never would have suffered; nor would Don Girolamo have been pursued and persecuted again."

"At least accept my protection," said the marchese.

He took Emanuele away in his carriage. The young man hugged Signora Francesca, showing no sign of emotion, rather annoyed by her tears and by the intensity of her embraces, and he couldn't wait to get into that grand gilded carriage, whose presence in front of the razionale's small, modest house had aroused the curiosity of the neighbors. The news that Emanuele was the son, grandson, or another relative of great lords had suddenly spread, and everyone was running to see him leave, with the satisfaction we feel for the good fortune that rains down on people we love. But Emanuele looked with so much contempt at those poor people that he dampened all their feelings of fondness for him.

He didn't even look up to a balcony on the second floor, where a young girl with tearful eyes saw him get into the carriage and leave without saying goodbye, without any sign of affection.

The Marchese of Geraci had already announced to Donna Gabriella that he had found his grandson, "the true and legitimate Duke of Motta," and that for now he wasn't taking any legal action to recognize his rights or to obtain the investiture of the feudal baronies, out of regard for Don Raimondo's state of health. He would, however, take his grandson to visit his uncle as soon as he was able to receive him. Don Raimondo was recovering, at least so assured Don Francesco Pignocco, who was looking after him. The great doctor, who was also the head of the Academy of Physicians, had held a consultation in order to assess the wounded man's condition, and the opinion of the doctors had been unanimous in its judgment that the duke would be healed of his wounds, none of which seemed to have harmed vital organs. Only the injury to his head was a cause for concern. Although it hadn't penetrated the skull, it was nevertheless keeping Don Raimondo in a daze. He would look around dumbfounded, without speaking, or he would stammer some incomprehensible words under his breath; at times it seemed like a sudden burst of understanding would come to his eyes and that he would recognize people, but then a sense a terror and an intense sorrow would be painted on his face. More often, however, he would fall into a state of apathy or stupor, with no awareness of the outside world, with no sign of an inner life.

That day the Marchese of Geraci, thinking that it was by then the right time, took Emanuele to the palazzo where he was born, and of which he was the true and absolute lord. When he entered, Don Raimondo, with his back resting on a mountain of pillows that kept him more upright, was in one of his conscious moments and had stammered some louder and more intelligible words. He seemed to recognize the Marchese of Geraci, whose sight disturbed him.

The marchese approached the bed and, introducing his grandson, said to him, "Don Raimondo, do you know who this is? This is Emanuele, our grandson Emanuele, the son of Donna Aloisia."

The duke's eyes opened wide with fear; he looked at the young man. An intense tremor ran across his face and spread through his limbs, his pale, thin lips twitched nervously, his pupils dilated with an expression of terror that was transmitted even to the bystanders; then suddenly he let out a ghastly and terrifying scream that shattered the silence and reverberated in everyone's hearts with an indefinable shudder. And keeping his eyes fixed on the young man, soon after he let out another scream, more frightening than the first, and, extending his trembling hands before him in an act of defense, with an effort that seemed to muster all his terrors and all his horrors, he screamed, "No! . . . No!"

A frightened Violante came forward, asking, "Signor Padre . . . Signor Padre . . . what's wrong?"

Donna Gabriella shivered. Only she could guess what was passing through her husband's mind, and her heart began to beat violently, fearing that in that state of mind he would let some words slip out.

The Marchese of Geraci, who didn't quite understand, said, "Don Raimondo . . . what is it? . . . Don't you know him? . . . He wants to kiss your hand."

But the duke, his pupils dilated, was perhaps looking at a vision that ran through his newly awakened memory, filling him with terror. A cold sweat glistened on his forehead and his hands were groping about in the air. His mouth moved and he cried out in a choked voice that seemed like a sob: "No! . . . Enough. . . . Enough! . . . Mercy!"

"Signor Padre!" implored Violante.

"Don't touch me!" Don Raimondo was still crying out, his tongue loosened. "Don't touch me!"

Everyone looked at one another in anguish.

The Prince of Butera said, "What are you feeling? . . . Don Raimondo, what are you feeling?"

He was no longer looking at anyone; he was looking at the back of the room, his face expressing terror mingled with disgust.

"They are coming!" he stammered in a lifeless voice. "They are coming. There!"

"Who?"

"The Beati Paoli! . . . They are over there! There! The daggers! . . . Ah!"

Again, that cry that made everyone's blood run cold tore at their hearts. Everyone felt a sense of cold and emptiness inside. That name of the Beati Paoli and that momentous terror revealed the tragedy of which he was a victim. Violante, looking around as if imploring for help, tried to take his hand to reassure him, but as soon as he felt her touch, Don Raimondo gave a start and let out another feral scream.

"Giuseppico! . . . Giuseppico! Don't let her get away!"

That name was a mystery to everyone. Donna Gabriella, suspecting something, remarked, "I fear that the sight of this young man has made the duke very emotional."

"Yes, that must be it," said the Marchese of Geraci.

He started to move away from the bed; perhaps his movement mixed in Don Raimondo's mind with other images, and it exacerbated his terror. He sat up on the bed, putting his feet on the floor as if to stand up, and, holding out his gnarled hands as if to grab something, he shouted, "Seize her. . . . Can't you see that she is coming down from the balcony? . . . Kill her. . . . Where is she? Where did she go? . . . No, no! Don't kill me! . . . The other one? . . . Yes . . . Emanuele! Where is Emanuele?"

"Here he is, Don Raimondo . . . but stay calm."

They thought that he was looking for his nephew, but the eyes of the duke didn't see the young man that they had pushed in front of him, and his ears heard nothing.

"Where is Emanuele?" he shouted, foaming at the mouth. Then, after a minute of silence, he screeched in a gloomy and piercing laugh: "Ah! Ah! Ah! Did you want to catch me? . . . Captain! . . . Captain! . . . Captain! Here they are! . . . Captain! . . . Captain!"

His voice was beginning to tremble from the terror and the weeping, "Captain!"

He called out again with a desperate cry of anguish that crushed everyone's spirits, emptied their veins of blood, sapped their energy. There was another moment of silence and, letting out another scream, more intense, more agonizing, more hair-raising, he suddenly fell back onto his pillows, gasping for breath with a mouth full of drool and wide-open eyes.

Violante, crying out from fear and sorrow, threw herself on the bed, calling out to her father; Donna Gabriella and the others were immobile, speechless, as if overcome by something horrible and monstrous that was beyond their comprehension.

At that moment Don Francesco Pignocco arrived, and as soon as he glanced at the wounded man, he couldn't hold back a gesture of distressing surprise.

"What is it? Why such confusion?"

He took the sick man's pulse, closely examining his face with ever-growing wonder; Violante was sobbing. The Prince of Geraci briefly explained what Don Raimondo had done, as well as the incoherence of his words, his terror, his outburst.

"His pulse is truly chaotic," said the doctor.

He tried to lift Don Raimondo, who was keeping his face buried in the pillows, gasping for air like a wounded beast, but as soon as the duke lifted his face and looked at the doctor, his eyes lit up with a bestial fury and, seizing him by his arms, trying furiously to bite him, he roared, "Ah! It's you! . . . I've got you! . . . Murderer! . . . You shouldn't have written!"

The poor frightened doctor struggled free, leaving a torn scrap of his sleeve in the hands of Don Raimondo, who sank his teeth into it, tearing it in a triumphant fury.

"Here is what I do with it! . . . Here! Here!"

A still frightened Don Francesco looked at him in amazement, murmuring, "These are outbursts of madness! . . . Yes, of madness!"

During that interchange, the bandages on his head and those on his shoulders had come loose, the gauzes had fallen off, the sores had reopened; a trickle of blood ran down his ear, stained his chest. Mechanically, Don Raimondo brought his hands to his neck and to his chest, withdrawing them covered with blood. He looked at them in horror; the features of his face were distorted. From horror, he transitioned to fear, then to anguish, and finally to prayer.

"Blood, blood! . . . My hands are drenched with blood! . . . Take this blood away from me; take these dead people away! . . . Mercy! . . . Mercy! . . . They are tormenting me. They are ripping apart my heart. . . . Ah! So much blood! I'm drowning! I'm drowning! I'm drowning!"

His voice died out amid the sobs that violently shook his chest, and nothing was more agonizing than seeing that man stained with blood, with hands outstretched as if to push away something terrible, moaning amid the sobs that were rending his chest, with his tired, terrified eyes.

Don Francesco drew near him again to redo the bandages, but Don Raimondo shrieked and started to scream again. "Don't touch me! . . . Don't touch me! Everything is bleeding! . . . Blood is everywhere! . . . A river! And there has to be more. They have daggers and they kill. . . . They kill! . . . They kill! . . . Where is Blasco? . . . He is here too! . . . There, they killed him! . . . Blood! . . . There is blood! Always blood! Always blood!"

Don Francesco, the Prince of Geraci, and the Prince of Butera were trying to comfort him with kind words; they were trying to persuade him that there was nothing, that he was among his own, that he should keep calm.

"Don Raimondo, look at your daughter! Look at Violante, poor girl!"

The duke was silent for a minute, turning around with an astonished gaze and fixing it on Violante, who was in front of him, weeping.

"Violante," he sobbed. "Violante! . . . Where is Violante?"

"She is here; don't you see her?"

"Where is Violante?" he continued, pressing on and gradually flying into a rage. "I want Violante! . . . I want my daughter! . . . Give me back my daughter! . . . Violante!"

"Father, my father!" implored the young girl.

"Violante," Don Raimondo howled desperately, rising again in the middle of the bed, with his eyes staring into space, not recognizing anyone, not hearing any words, fixated on an inner vision or thought. He burst into tears.

Then the doctor said, "I won't risk redoing the bandages unless there are some strong men who can hold him tight."

Donna Gabriella rang and ordered four portantini to come and, reassured by their presence, Don Francesco began his work. The wounded man was still crying, now softly, and allowed him to work with deference, unconsciously following the work of the doctor with a slight bend of his head or his arm. They cleansed the wounds, replaced the gauzes, and bandaged him again, more securely; then, pushing him gently, they forced him to lay back on the pillows.

"It would be better," said Don Francesco to Donna Gabriella, "to tie him to the bed with bands in order to stop him from moving. We have lost almost everything that had been gained."

"Do what your profession advises you," the duchess replied.

Violante, on whom this measure made a painful impression, dared to stutter, "But he is calm now."

"Now, yes, but the outbursts will return. . . . They could be even more violent."

He took the wounded man's pulse.

"He has a fever!" he said, vexed. "A high fever."

Meanwhile a servant brought some long bands that were soon passed and interlaced with each other around Don Raimondo's body and fastened to the sides of the bed in order to keep him from moving. Don Francesco prescribed sedative potions and then left.

"Let's go, son," the Prince of Geraci said to Emanuele, who was silent, struck by everything that he had seen, but not so much as to get him to drop his patronizing attitude or stop looking every now and then at the furniture and decorations of the room, thinking that it belonged to him. He kissed the hand of that very young and beautiful aunt of his, dressed so elegantly, and he followed his grandfather, asking him why they still hadn't given him possession of that house, or why they at least hadn't allowed him to live there.

The Prince of Butera said to Violante, "You should go rest, my child; you can't stay here day and night . . . it has already been five nights that you haven't closed an eye; you will get sick."

"Oh, Your Excellency, forgive me, but I will not abandon my father."

"What you say is fine; and you will not abandon him, but rest is also necessary so that you can look after him."

"Wait! Excuse me . . . he is saying something."

Don Raimondo, in fact, was moving his lips as if he were trying to speak. He lay on his back, immobile, with wide-open eyes. His beard, which had grown during these days, thin and interrupted by gaps, put black spots on his cheeks and lip, making his appearance more frightening, and the bluish circles into which his eyes sank enlarged them immensely. The prince and Violante had bent down to listen, thinking he might have been asking for something.

"What are you saying?"

But he wasn't responding, continuing to stammer; then, gradually, his words became more intelligible.

"All of them. . . . Kill all of them! . . . We have to kill all of them. . . . Even Blasco! Yes, even Blasco. My nephew? What does it matter . . . a bastard. . . . Even Emanuele! . . . All mine! Everything is mine! . . . No, don't touch me. . . . I'm burning! I'm burning! . . . A spasm. . . . Hold my head, they are taking it away from me. . . . They are taking it away from me!"

His entire body trembled within the bands, shaking the bed, which was making a dull metallic sound; a great agony altered his face, and it seemed that all his energies had coalesced into that last cry of desperation in order to stop him from losing his mind.

"Hold my head! Don't let them take it away from me! . . . Don't let them take it away from me!"

All day and all night, at intervals, suddenly waking from slumber, he would let out wild and bestial cries and words—incoherent, but they were the fragmented expressions of images that followed one another in his brain.

This torment lasted two days; for two days Don Raimondo, burning with fever, with gangrenous sores, writhing about between outbursts of madness, tormented by his visions of blood, filled the house with alarm and horror. One thought above all dominated his spirit, and often, twisting and turning under the safety bands, he would cry out in desperate fear: "The Beati Paoli! Save me! . . . The Beati Paoli!"

The third day, after a long slumber in which it seemed that his vital signs were gradually diminishing, he awoke, without giving any sign of agitation. His manner instead expressed an ineffable and taciturn sorrow, like someone who feels death approaching. Perhaps wanting to make a gesture with his hand, he realized that he couldn't move, and he sensed that he was strapped and tied down.

He looked around, saw Violante, and asked in a faint voice, "Why have you tied me down? Have them untie me! . . . What thirst!"

There was such an intense plea in those words and so much submissiveness in his manner that after silently questioning one another with their eyes, the servants untied him and Violante gave him something to drink.

At that time there were only his daughter, Donna Gabriella, and two servants around his bed, but at that moment the Prince of Geraci and Emanuele arrived. Don Raimondo saw them enter; he saw the young man and had the impression that his face wasn't new to him, but the richness of his clothing and seeing him in the company of the Prince of Geraci prevented him from recognizing him at first. But when the prince approached the bed to ask him how he was feeling and he had the young man move closer, calling him by name, Don Raimondo, with an extraordinary quickness and lucid mind, understood, having connected what had happened with the events that had followed one after the other. He became paler and a sense of terror distorted his face.

He stammered, "Emanuele! . . . Emanuele! Oh God! It's . . ."

"Yes, it is him," said the prince. "He wants to kiss your hand."

"No . . . no." He trembled with an expression of supreme loathing. "No, have mercy on me. . . . What a horror. . . . What a horror!"

He closed his eyes for an instant, then reopened them in fear. He looked around, and with intense terror, chattering his teeth, he yelled, "A priest! Have mercy on me. . . . A priest, I'm dying!"

A servant rushed out.

Don Raimondo looked at his nephew, and with terror in his eyes, he groaned, "Why? Why have you brought him here? . . . Take him away from me! . . . I don't want to see him! . . . I can't. Ah, what burning inside here! What burning!"

He dug his nails into his chest in a desperate gesture; under the covers his body could be seen twitching and jerking, and his face underwent rapid and agonizing strains.

"A priest," he stammered, terrified, "a priest!"

Almost at the same time, the servant returned, pushing forward an Albanian papas, who seemed reluctant.

"I found this man," he said. "I dragged him here; after all, even Greek priests are priests like the others."

But the papas was hesitant. "No, no . . . I'm not a confessor, I can't. . . . Go get someone else."

His voice roused Donna Gabriella and Violante and made Don Raimondo open his eyes; all three looked at the papas, who had stayed in front of the bed, struck by the wretched appearance of the duke, who upon seeing him began to tremble and repeat, "What burning. . . . What burning! . . . Help me! . . . Father, help me!"

The papas moved closer to him, an intense sense of mercy painted on his face. He bent over Don Raimondo, looked at him, and murmured slowly, so as not to be heard by others, "May God forgive you for all the wicked deeds that you have committed, as I forgive you for those that you have done unto me!"

Don Raimondo looked at him in amazement and fear and he stammered, "Confession! . . . Confession!"

"I cannot hear your confession; now a priest will come."

He got up and moved away from the bed, while Don Raimondo scratched at the blankets with his frenetic fingers. Donna Gabriella and Violante looked at the papas; of course, they recognized those eyes, that nose, that voice, but in his bearing and in his movement they saw nothing inherently sacred that conveyed the practice of the priesthood. The papas was made uncomfortable by those questioning glances and, perhaps in order to evade them, he gave a slight bow and started to leave.

"Are you leaving?" the Prince of Geraci asked him. "It doesn't seem very Christian to me to abandon a man in these conditions; if you are not a confessor, you can provide some comfort, though . . ."

The papas stopped, hesitated for a moment, then with a gesture he took off the long thick beard that was disguising him.

"Don Blasco!" exclaimed the prince.

"Blasco!" Donna Gabriella repeated, amazed.

Violante turned pale and turned her back to him; Emanuele looked at him arrogantly, asking himself who this Blasco could be who was disguising himself as a Greek priest and arousing so much astonishment, but noting that perhaps he had seen that face somewhere else.

Blasco responded sadly, "Myself, yes. . . . You will understand why I had to resort to this disguise: in order to find out about the duke's state of health."

Don Raimondo, at the sound of the name uttered by the prince, had looked at the young man and was overcome by a new, stronger tremor.

"All of them," he rasped under his breath, "they are all coming out!" And once again he let out a desperate cry: "I am burning up! . . . Send for a priest! . . . Why . . . are you making me die a damned soul? . . . Why? . . . Don't you see how many crimes! . . . I see everyone coming out of the grave. . . . I see them coming for me. . . . I feel they are clutching me, dragging me. . . . A priest! . . . A priest!"

Those were his last words. A convulsive wheeze stifled his voice. When the chaplain of Sant'Ippolito arrived a few minutes later, he found him with his eyes half-closed, with his chest laboring from that wheezing that, with every draw of breath, had the painful sound of a sob; he took him by the hand and the man let out a scream, without giving another sign. He called him but there was no response; that wheezing and those sobs filled the room.

Thus it went on all day, all night. At first, as soon as he was touched, he would scream, then even these screams died away, but one could see that he was shaken and torn by terrible spasms. The wheezing had grown louder. Sometimes it seemed like a gurgling, other times like the rolling of a heavy object; then it began to weaken again and to become longer and with greater intervals, until the convulsive movements ceased.

At dawn, he died.

Victor Amadeus, King of Sicily and Sardinia

PART II

CHAPTER 1

On the morning of July 1, 1718, the citizens were deeply moved and shaken by a momentous piece of news, whose first inklings had been heard during the night. The *fani*, or flames on the watchtowers, in fact, had transmitted the warning that a great fleet was sailing along the seas of Sicily, and soon after, a messenger sent by the Prince of Carini had brought a letter to Viceroy Count Maffei, with which, in haste, the prince himself informed him that the fleet was crossing the Gulf of Castellammare.

In the morning the fleet had appeared within sight of the city; its ships were so numerous that it filled the horizon. There was no doubt that it was the Spanish Armada, which was known to be massed in Sardinia and was four hundred and thirty-two ships strong, between combat vessels and landing ships, with twenty-two thousand men and fifty thousand horses, pieces of artillery, provisions, and everything that was needed for an invasion, under the command of the Marchese of Lede, an experienced captain.

No one knew, however, whether the Armada was coming to Sicily as friend or foe; most of the citizens would have welcomed it, just to get rid of Savoyard rule. While aiming to improve conditions in the kingdom and to restore the full and complete autonomy and precedence of secular authority over the ecclesiastical, with regard to temporality (as in the good old days of the ancient monarchy), Savoy perhaps hadn't been able to adapt its tactics to accomplish this goal; it had believed it could—through violent means—suddenly change prejudices, prerogatives, and deep-rooted material self-interests, and, moreover, it had stripped Sicilians of offices and ranks to appoint Piedmontese citizens.

Due to both the long and bitter discord with Rome, which troubled people's consciences, and the rigid, excessive taxation by government agents, Sicily went through such a period of financial difficulties as to arouse a deep discontent; so much so that someone by the name of Victorius Amadeus was given the anagram *Cor eius est avidum*,[1] and in a popular song, the name of the House of Savoy represented the devastation and desolation:

---

1 "His heart is greedy."

Pari ca cci passò Casa Savoia[2]

The work of the clergy had not been unconnected to the fomenting of dissent; with few exceptions during the struggle between the State and the Church, the clergy had openly taken sides with the pope against the secular rights of the monarchy, which at other times had been steadfastly defended by the clergy itself. But perhaps it wasn't that the Sicilian clergy was so loyal to the pope (in a hierarchical and spiritual sense) as much as that they were opposed to the Savoy king, whose government was not inclined to be generous toward the convents and churches with regard to prerogatives, privileges, exemptions, bequests, etc., unlike the previous Spanish government.

All these things, and the financial difficulties that a change of monarchy would inevitably bring about, had made that Spanish government desirable, as its work in Sicily had been carried out according to a very simple formula: to make money, to enrich the clergy and the nobility, to hang as many people as possible, and not to care about anything else. For at the time, those who were in charge were free to do as they wished, and the commoners had holidays, pageants, acts of faith, processions, and carnival-like revelry, and bandits could infest the countryside and tyrannize the city; how could one not feel nostalgic about Spanish rule?

For this reason, the announcement, and then the news of the sighting of the Armada and the knowledge that it was sailing under the Spanish flag, spreading throughout the city, had seized it with emotion and had attracted a crowd of the curious to the Marina, among them those who harbored some fears, not on account of the foreign invasion but due to the potential dangers of a conflict that would have the city as its battlefield. Nevertheless, it was more than a little surprising that the viceroy wasn't the least bit alarmed, and that the Piedmontese soldiers were mingling among the crowd to see the Spanish ships sail past.

To those lords who had gone, as usual, to pay their respects to His Excellency, the viceroy had given reassuring words.

"Have no fear, gentlemen; Our Lord the King, whom God watches over, had already warned me by messenger about the passage of this fleet, which is going to Naples. Indeed, I have orders to offer them refreshments and anything else that they may need."

But toward the Ave Maria more news arrived, which gave the city cause for concern. Prince Lanza had rushed back from his vacation in the village of Aspra, announcing that militias in full battle dress were setting ashore from the ships, and that the abbot, his brother, had approached a superior officer to ask him what it meant and had gotten the reply that His Majesty Philip V was taking back the kingdom because King Victor had not upheld the treaties. Almost at the same

2 "Looks like the House of Savoy passed through."

time, a campiere of the Prince of Cattolica took the same news to his lord, and the prince rushed to inform the praetor, the Count of San Marco, who, without delay, ran to the Palazzo Reale to see the viceroy.

Poor Count Maffei was astounded. What? A landing? An invasion? Just like that, by surprise, treacherously, without a declaration of war, against time-honored traditions? There was nothing to do except to get ready, in a hurry, to fortify the city.

"I don't have sufficient forces to repel the attack; the city must arm itself."

"But, Your Excellency, a defense cannot be improvised against an army that has a strong artillery!"

"So then there is only one alternative left. Your Illustrious Lordship must negotiate an honorable surrender; meanwhile, I will set in order the defense of the kingdom."

"Very well; but I would like Your Excellency to put this in writing for me."

The same evening the praetor rode through the city, giving orders to the consuls of the workers' guilds for them to go in full battle order to occupy the bastions, and the city was full of the sound of drums beating the call to assemble, thus spreading a sense of anxiety and consternation about the great events.

The following morning the bastions were occupied and equipped by the workers' guilds; the artilleries were at the ready, but more out of a need to stage a scene than to put up a true resistance. A reconnaissance during nighttime had been ordered by the viceroy, but the troops had not carried it out until morning and, returning on the run, in disarray, they said a defense would have been pointless because the Spanish were so numerous. The oddest and most varied rumors were circulating; those who praised the past, all those who had formerly enjoyed the benefits of the Spanish government, those who until then hadn't dared to reveal their hostile feelings toward the Savoy government, now, encouraged by hope, were loosening their tongues; someone compared the Marchese of Lede to Gideon.

"As soon as the trumpets sound, the walls of Jericho will fall down."

"And Don Gaspare Narbona? Where is he, where is Don Gaspare Narbona?"

"That one? But he left for the battlefield. He knew everything, that old sly one!"

Don Gaspare Narbona was the solicitor of King Philip V for the county of Modica; because, in accordance with the agreements of the Treaty of Utrecht, Philip V, in ceding Sicily to Victor Amadeus, retained for himself that ancient and vast county and was keeping his garrison and a solicitor there. The previous year a great quarrel had arisen over a tax matter. Narbona was claiming that the county was exempt from any obligation toward the Kingdom of Sicily; the avvocato fiscale, Don Ignazio Perlongo, instead maintained that since the county was a fiefdom of the kingdom, King Philip, Count of Modica, was in fact a vassal of the crown of Sicily and owed to her all the obligations of vassalage. He therefore wanted to send a Savoyard garrison there, but the people of Modica revolted; thus the wrath of the viceroy against Narbona.

It was thus understandable that the solicitor of the King of Spain would now issue a rebuke and take his revenge. The entire day passed in a state of great anxiety. The viceroy summoned the nobility to the palazzo in order to justify himself, showing them the king's letter and proposing a defense, which everyone rejected because by then it was too late. Someone even bolder murmured that to him it seemed like a farce.

"It's all a pretense, a farce, to come upon us so suddenly; do you seriously believe that King Victor and King Philip disagree? This one says, 'I'll pretend to come as a friend and I'll disembark my troops; you'll pretend to know nothing and to be deceived; four cannon shots, and then we'll reach an agreement!' And we have been duped! . . . Defense? What defense?"

The viceroy's proclamation, issued that same day, didn't make a better impression: "Given the imminent necessity of defending the kingdom, all barons and feudal lords subject to military service, and in accordance with their obligation, should be provided with men, weapons, and horses within twelve days exactly," and it ordered them to assemble in Piazza Armerina armed with "two pistols, a sword, and a carbine or a hunting rifle," threatening the indignation of His Majesty toward whoever disobeyed. No one paid it any heed because even before that proclamation was issued, couriers from the Spanish camp had been sent everywhere to announce that from that moment on only King Philip was to be obeyed; and also because no one felt like fighting the Spanish, given that their leaders had come to a concerted agreement in the Senate to negotiate the surrender of the capital and had formulated the terms of surrender to be submitted to the Marchese of Lede.

For this reason the anxiety of the city was losing that little bit of consternation, born out of uncertainty and curiosity more than anything else, arousing that unusual commotion, that chatter, that asking for and giving of news, since the commoners, who did not benefit at all from the dynastic changes, were now only interested in the double spectacle of the departure of the Savoyard troops and the viceroy, and the entry of Spanish troops.

The Marina was full of people who were going there to see whether the Armada was entering the gulf and approaching the city: commoners with their wives and children, ladies in carriages, in portantine, lords on horseback; modest clothing and silk outfits, doublets of the commoners and the liveries of the footmen and volanti; friar's habits and short abbot's robes. Carts for transporting goods and magnificent carriages pulled by mighty Friesian horses would join up, mingle, and separate again.

Three young lords, the oldest of whom might have been twenty-two, were making their horses trot in a high-spirited manner that, now backing up, now rearing up against the crowd of people walking, was creating a commotion among the women, who with high-pitched shrieks would disperse and run away. The scene seemed to greatly amuse the three horsemen, who, instead of riding in the wide street, thrust their horses among the people, under the pretext of looking at the ships that were moored in the Marina and making maneuvers toward Capo Zafferano.

"Well," one of them asked, stroking the neck of his chestnut mare, "well, Emanuele, when are we celebrating this wedding?"

The youngest, Emanuele Albamonte, Duke of Motta, replied with an air of displeasure, "As far as I'm concerned, the later the better."

"Your grandfather doesn't agree."

"Not so much mine as her grandfather."

"They say that she is beautiful," said the third one.

Emanuele shrugged his shoulders.

"I saw her a few times, two or three, I think, when her father died. . . . Yes, perhaps she is beautiful and charming, but I don't like her at all."

"She has a large dowry."

"I know. She is a Branciforti and that will do."

"Now we'll have to see how things turn out with the war."

"So, you see," said Emanuele, "my grandfather discarded the viceroy's proclamation regarding military service, but if I had been of age, as for me, I would have enlisted my feudal militias. Because I would have liked to go to war. They tell me that my father was the same way."

"Would you have served under King Victor?"

"He like any other; it's war itself that I like!"

"Everyone knows that. You are the best jouster in the arena."

"But that is a mock war. I would much more like to do it for real. Who knows? If all that is said is true, there will be plenty of opportunities! . . . Ah, to be twenty-one years old, to be free and one's own master, to be able to manage one's own income without being forced to ask one's guardian for a tarì. . . . There's still a long way to go: six months and fourteen days!"

"Goodness! Do you have an accountant who gives you a day-by-day countdown?"

"I do it myself; with each passing day I subtract one from the count, but I think there are still too many left: one hundred ninety-seven days!"

Chatting thus, they spurred their horses here and there, laughing at the fear of the crowd and making fun—with the insolent manner of rich young men from powerful families—of those who grumbled. Emanuele had grown tall and strong and seemed older than his age. His grandfather had given him an education suitable to his status, including riding, fencing, and dancing; there was no need for literary culture, either because Don Girolamo had provided that or because Emanuele didn't have a strong predilection for reading. The only knowledge that Emanuele desired was to learn about his patrimony.

The acts of acknowledgment and his right to inheritance were asserted immediately after Don Raimondo's death, and the guardianship and administration of his vast patrimony had been entrusted to the Prince of Geraci, not only because he was his grandfather but owing to his prestige. However, the dotal property of the first wife, mother of Violante, and of Donna Gabriella had been recognized, and in order to avoid quarrels, as much with the Branciforti as with the La Grua, they had come to amicable agreements.

With an excessively gallant gesture, the prince had proposed that Donna Gabriella could, if she was so inclined, continue to live in the Palazzo della Motta, but she refused to live as a guest in the house where she had once been lady and mistress, and for the time being she withdrew to her brother's house. But shortly after, having acquired a villa behind the Convent of San Domenico, she went there to conceal her widowhood and her torments from view. Her dowry and an annual allowance given to her by her family were sufficient to allow her to live with the prosperity that her status required.

Violante, placed under the guardianship of the Prince of Branciforti, returned to the monastery. The two nobles had thought it quite natural that the two cousins, both orphans, whose wealth until then had been accumulating in the hands of Don Raimondo, would marry and thus keep it intact.

The two young people had nothing at all to do with the discussions about or the final decision regarding the marriage, nor was it necessary, because, even though it should have been of interest to them more than to anyone else, the conventions and customs of the time didn't allow them to get involved, nor would their inclinations be consulted before taking the big step. Marriages for love were infrequent and not typical among nobility; marriage would be concluded owing to the interests and advantages of the relatives and, according to custom, the youngsters would not see each other, nor would there be any contact between them. The future bride was usually in a monastery, where she would complete her education and from where she would leave a few days before the marriage, thus moving abruptly from a cloistered life to one amid the tempests of the world.

By common agreement, the two nobles had decided that the wedding would take place when Emanuele came of age and that Violante would wait in the monastery until that day. Violante's dowry was made up of not only her maternal inheritance but also that of the personal patrimony of Don Raimondo: the fruit of his labor, his savings, and some profitable speculations, such as usury, that he had discreetly exercised through loans and mortgages to lords. And it was a substantial dowry, worthy of a true princess, that would have made Emanuele one of the richest lords of the city.

At first Emanuele had not had any objection to these plans; although his cousin had not wielded any charm over him and hadn't even aroused any affection, the idea of a marriage to a lady of nobility and wealth equal to his still seemed like the most natural thing in the world to him. But gradually the relish for his new life, the gallant exploits to which he had devoted so much time, with the lust of a young satyr, and even more, a feeling of rebellion, arrogance, and authoritarianism had made this marriage—orchestrated without his will and imposed on him—seem to him like something burdensome and unpleasant, to which he felt decidedly averse.

He felt no affection for that cousin, whose cold and distant manner had irritated him. There was something insurmountable between them, a kind of tall barrier and a deep and very wide abyss, which made them feel distant and unrelated.

In the spring of that year he had wanted to visit his estates. The nobles and the giurati of the great estates, the secretaries of the villages, the captains, had gone to meet him, receiving him under triumphal arches of greenery to the sound of gunshots and firecrackers; in the parishes, the parish priests and the curates had blessed him with the Holy Sacrament, after a short speech in which they wished— rather were sure—that he would have the same zeal for religion as his elders. In the great room of the castle he had received homage from the officials of the fiefdoms and the kissing of his hand never seemed to end; the vassals improvised bullfights and fireworks, and some local well-read men made up encomiastic Latin verses in which Emanuele was compared to Hercules or some other ancient hero, or playing on the etymology of his name, he was, of course, called the one sent by God, as if he were another Messiah.

All these celebrations—which gave him a measure of his power and made him aware that there were a multitude of people who depended on him, who were obliged to work for him, who owed him the veneration worthy of a god, who the magistrates chosen by him could have made hang—had intoxicated him. Why on earth, if he was so powerful and master of being able to do and undo, if he had a will to impose, why must he obey his grandfather and accept that marriage that he didn't want, that he didn't desire? He had no longer thought about Pellegra, except as a gracious and pleasing adventure that had left no trace of passion in his heart. Just that, in comparing her to Violante, who was so cold and reserved, he found her to be charming and desirable.

The poor girl had waited in vain for her prince, although the sudden fortune that had transformed him before her eyes from the nephew of the razionale from Monte di Pietà into the heir of the Duke of Motta had given her a painful pang in her heart and had severed in her any hope for the future.

From her balcony she had seen the young man leave in his grandfather's carriage and had hoped for a glance, a greeting, a nod—but in vain. He had gone without remembering that there was a suffering heart up there, and she had felt her heart going away forever with that carriage.

Nevertheless, she waited for him. Was she hoping? In truth, she wasn't, but she couldn't resign herself to being abandoned and she didn't want to believe that Emanuele had completely forgotten about her. But he never showed up again.

Sometimes, going out with her father, already half-senile and dragging himself along on unsteady feet, she would see Emanuele in a carriage or on horseback or with his tutor or with other young men; her heart would pound, would race, but in vain. He would pass by without even looking at her.

After two years, Pellegra left for Rome, taken there by her mother's relatives, since by then Don Vincenzo had become completely senile, and it was best to entrust him to the care of one of his distant relatives, with a monthly compensation. In Rome, Pellegra had begun her studies, becoming passionate about poetry, and had begun to pour out her soul, composing sonnets in which she pretended to be Laura, replying to Petrarch—sonnets that a prelate who was a relative had liked and that later earned the young girl admission to the Arcadia[3] and the hand of a Roman lawyer; once completed, the sonnets would be published and praised as a miracle of poetry.

After her departure, Emanuele thought about her from time to time, but only as a means of comparison with Violante and nothing more. His heart, or rather, his vanity, had other aspirations, and he was meeting too many beautiful ladies in the new society into which he had entered. That aunt, for example, so young, so beautiful, was alone. . . . Oh, why had she ever wanted to leave the Palazzo della Motta?

They almost never saw each other, except on formal occasions, such as on New Year's Day, Christmas, and Easter, and in general on all the occasions where it was mandatory to go and kiss the hand of one's older relatives or superiors in order to wish them happy holidays. They were brief visits that didn't go beyond the limits of the strictest good manners, at the behest of Donna Gabriella, who had shut herself into a truly eccentric self-restraint and solitude, and who perhaps found unpleasant and aimless that tall and strong young man in whose face was a certain something reminiscent of Blasco. There was a family resemblance, the imprint of the lineage, but what a difference between him and Blasco! She couldn't help but recognize that the bastard was worth much more than the legitimate son and that, when comparing the two, the latter would lose as much as the former had gained.

Perhaps this comparison prevented her from availing herself of cordial and pleasant greetings to Emanuele that would encourage intimacy and familiarity. Thus the young man would refrain from going to his aunt's house, even though he found her to be beautiful and charming and, moreover, unguarded territory.

Emanuele was in this state of mind on the eve of his coming of age, and the nuisance and annoyance of that marriage, which threatened to imprison his youth, would be renewed whenever he would ride with his friends, the tone of whose words seemed to him to contain a tinge of irony.

---

3 Accademia dell'Arcadia, an Italian literary academy founded in Rome in 1690.

CHAPTER 2

On July 3, the surrender of the city, formulated in six articles, was concluded between the Marchese of Lede and the ambassadors of the Senate, Don Francesco Gravina, Prince of Palagonia, and Don Girolamo Gravina, Prince of Montevago. And on that same day Viceroy Count Maffei, with the vicereine and family members, the clerks of the court, and the counselors, left the city, departing through Porta Nuova, where cavalry and infantrymen were waiting for him and with whom he started off for Piana dei Greci. Out of courtesy, none of the lords accompanied him past a certain point; no one bade him a polite farewell; hearts had turned to the new sun that was reappearing after an absence of five years.

The workers' guilds, by order of the praetor, took possession of the Palazzo Reale, where nothing of the archive was found, since Count Maffei had burned all the writings, as well as the copies of Mongitore's *The Parliaments of Sicily.*

The piazza of the Palazzo Reale, empty of soldiers after the departure of the court, seemed like a deserted town. The San Giacomo quarter was empty; all the Piedmontese families of workers and soldiers had left that morning with their belongings. It was a sad exodus, devoid of mourning.

Only in the Castello a Mare did a garrison remain of four hundred soldiers, with the order not to harass the city but to defend the royal flag and not to give in, except when a defense was impossible. Six soldiers tried to escape, but two were caught and put to death.

The Spanish Army entered Palermo on the morning of July 4, with a swarm of families, amid the cheers of the citizens, who greeted those who, as it was emphatically said, had come to liberate them "from the tyranny of the Savoyard Pharaoh"; they didn't know that with those cheers they were preparing the homeland for the most pernicious servitude. The fleet, following the movement of the troops, entered the gulf lined up in battle order and then commenced a violent bombardment between the garrison of the Castello and the ships, which attracted the population to the Marina and onto the bastions so they could admire the sight of that contest that reverberated in the city, arousing trepidation and fear.

Meanwhile the Spanish troops, in order to subjugate the Castello, were setting up camp at Sant'Oliva and, in order to defend themselves from possible attacks and cut off all communication from the Castello, they were extending their line down to the Convent of Baida. And from those places they gradually pushed forward, continually shortening the line until they established their batteries in the vegetable gardens outside Porta San Giorgio, where populous neighborhoods are now located.

* * *

On that same evening of July 4, a young soldier from the Spanish dragoons, probably with a permit from his captain, entered the city from Porta Carini, set off toward the Capo, and, turning at the Mercé, stopped for a minute to gaze at the Palazzo della Motta.

The balconies were closed, the front door shut; there was something sinister and gloomy about the house's appearance, almost like the external sign of a grim and dark history. From there, descending slowly, he passed by San Cosmo and stopped again to look at the front door of Casa Baldi; then going around the piazza, he went back up Vicolo degli Orfani and stopped again in front of a little walled-up door. He shook his head and resumed his way. It seemed that his memories, which had been reawakened, had left their imprint on his face.

From Via Sant'Agata alla Guilla, then along Sette Angeli, he emerged onto the Cassaro, which seemed to be in a state of celebration. Here and there one could see some portraits of King Philip V and some priests who were talking animatedly, as if reassured, like people who were witnessing a moment when all their hardships would come to an end. It was hoped, in fact, that with the return of the old regime, the interdict and the persecutions of which they considered themselves victims would cease. A crowd of people, lords and ladies in carriages, commoners on foot, were rushing to the Marina in order to be present at the sight of the cannonade between the Castello and the Spanish ships. Some older people were saying that it was a match that compared with the famous naval battle fought in the gulf between Holland and Spain on one side and France on the other, more than forty years before. That had truly been a terrible and grandiose spectacle. The entire gulf was full of ships shrouded in clouds of smoke, shattered every minute by cannon shots; vessels as large as mountains that were ablaze would become immense craters or would explode with a boom that made the city shake. And what carnage, what death, what destruction! What was that battle all about? Something similar to fireworks! Nevertheless, it was still a sight to admire. One could follow the trajectory of the cannonballs and have fun guessing where they would fall. The bombs from both the vessels and the Castello would often fall into the water, raising columns of foam and smoke, which amused the spectators even more.

The dragoon walked down the Cassaro, admired by all those who saw him, and they were pointing to him as if he was one of the liberators, but he noticed that many eyes looked at him with an insistent gaze, with that singular expression that means "I think I know you." Reaching the Quattro Canti, he stopped, glancing at the four streets that extended out from there and that seemed so beautiful to him. But while he was standing in that pose of silent admiration, he was suddenly startled, and his face turned a bright red.

A voice next to him, one that he knew well, shouted, "Stop!"

From a carriage, pulled by two horses who at that command had stopped with a great patter of iron on the pavement, appeared a face that looked in astonishment at the dragoon. For an instant they both looked at each other, recognizing each other, without speaking, immobile, but not without emotion; and it seemed like they were torn apart by different feelings and even more by a kind of repugnance or reserve, which perhaps prevented them from being cordial.

The lord dismounted from the carriage and, approaching the dragoon, said sternly, "Then am I not deceived in recognizing Signor Blasco Albamonte?"

"It is I indeed," Blasco replied coldly and indifferently.

"Well, since fate brings us together after four years, if you wish to resume that duel that we put on hold in the vegetable gardens, I am at your disposal."

Those were Coriolano's words, but his lips were on the verge of a slight smile and his eyes flashed a look that revealed very different wishes than those alluded to by his words.

The dragoon, that is, Blasco, didn't answer immediately but, suddenly shaking his head with his radiant face and extending his hands, said, "Blasco da Castiglione had some accounts to settle with you, but Blasco Albamonte, dragoon in His Catholic Majesty's army, extends his hand fraternally like before, without rancor and without resentment, Coriolano."

"Ah! Bravo! I recognize you. Now let me embrace you, my old friend."

And, overcoming every reluctance, they threw themselves into each other's arms, hugging affectionately and kissing each other's cheeks.

"Where are you going?" Coriolano della Floresta asked him.

"I'm wandering about. . . . I have no destination."

"Then come into my carriage so we can talk more freely."

"Gladly."

They climbed into the carriage and started off along the Cassaro. Coriolano looked at Blasco with both satisfaction and amazement.

"But look here! I would never have imagined running into you. . . . Why do I find you in these clothes?"

"Homesickness, my dear friend. I felt a great need to come to Palermo, and the only way to come here without fear of a nasty surprise was in this uniform."

"Then you were sure that you would be able to take Sicily back?"

"Quite sure. . . . Although I am nothing but a simple soldier, I had some friends at court, from whom I ascertained all that was most secret. So I am able to affirm with complete confidence that I alone in the army knew the purpose of the expedition from its beginning—what the Marchese of Lede himself didn't know until he was on the high seas, when he opened the envelope that had been given to him."

"Goodness! Then you have such well-informed contacts in politics?"

"Oh, no. . . . But I was, and I am, a good friend of His Eminence Cardinal Alberoni, the king's prime minister."

"Ah, bravo! . . . Now I understand everything. . . . And where are you staying?"

"My regiment is in the summer house of the Prince of Sperlinga, where the headquarters are located."

"I hope that you will come to my house; you will find that your room is still there."

"Thank you, but are you forgetting that I am no longer Blasco da Castiglione but a dragoon who can't move away from the camp? And then," he added, smiling, "don't you remember the second article of the terms of surrender, which also forbids soldiers to lodge in the houses of civilians, or any other private citizens?"

"Let's go, come on; it certainly doesn't forbid two good friends. . . . We are friends, aren't we?"

"As before."

"Excellent! Then as I was saying, it doesn't forbid two good friends from dining together. . . . At least do me this favor. We have so much to talk about, because I assume that you know what happened during the four years of your absence."

"Hardly! . . . If you only knew where I've been."

"I can imagine. You must have gone to look in the windows of the Monastery of Santa Caterina!"

"The Monastery of Santa Caterina?"

"Yes, but only the windows, because she is betrothed to your brother, as you had wished."

Blasco turned pale but immediately resumed his good mood.

"Oh, no, you are mistaken. The Monastery of Santa Caterina? . . . I hadn't thought about it and I didn't even know that she was there. . . . Instead, I wanted to revisit other places. . . . And I went to Vicolo degli Orfani."

"Ah. . . . It is walled up."

"I saw that; so, you are like the Jews, dispersed!"

"No. Premises are not lacking, and our objectives are the same. . . . But let's talk about something else. Have you seen any of your acquaintances?"

"No one. I only arrived in the city a few hours ago."

"Well! Look!"

Coming toward them were two young horsemen mounted on magnificent horses, followed by footmen. Coriolano pointed to one of them.

"There is your brother."

Blasco couldn't hold back a cry of wonder.

"That one? How tall he has grown! I wouldn't have recognized him. . . . And he's also a handsome young man."

"Yes, that's what everyone says. . . . I believe that he goes to the arena in Villafranca to practice. He is a strong rider and a good jouster."

"Really? . . . I'm glad."

"Are you going to see him?"

Blasco darkened a little and replied curtly, "No."

"You are right; perhaps there's a little too much pride in your 'no,' but you are right. . . . And you don't plan on seeing any of your old acquaintances?"

"No one. Why should I see them again? My dear friend, now I am nothing but a poor soldier of the dragoons who lives from his pay, when they give it to him, or from whatever he finds, and he goes to war happily, waiting for a cannonball to knock off the head that was never quite right to begin with! . . . Let's go. . . . I assumed my birth name and surname only for expediency, and so that to everyone's eyes Blasco da Castiglione might be dead, banished, pursued like Saltaliviti or some other criminal of that sort. But when I am alone with myself, then I feel that I am that same Blasco who entered Palermo riding a nag that would make Don Quixote feel ashamed, picking a quarrel with the Prince of Iraci. . . . Ah, how I would like to go back and wipe out those two years from my life! . . . By the way, what about the young Prince of Iraci?"

"I believe he is in Rome, in King Victor's embassy; you can be sure he will be back."

"Poor devil! . . . And the duchess, Donna Gabriella?"

"She bears her widowhood with great dignity."

"A repentant Magdalene?"

"Perhaps."

"And your friends? . . . Don Girolamo?"

"Don Girolamo is living in Naples under another name; his wife died of grief. The poor woman loved her foster son deeply and grieved so much from the separation and from having left Palermo that she fell ill. Her foster son, Emanuele, never saw her again, and never even sent her a note."

"Oh! Is that possible?"

"Unfortunately, it is. . . . Andrea is in service to Emanuele; he took him with him, not out of gratitude or any other feeling but to make a lordly gesture."

As they were talking, they had arrived at the Palazzo della Floresta, where they dismounted. The roar of the frequent and menacing cannon shots from the direction of the sea could still be heard. The two sides didn't seem to be disposed to giving in, although the Savoyard garrison was meager and recognized that it would have been more of a pro forma defense than that of a true resistance with any hope for success, nor could they rely on relief, since Count Maffei, with his few thousands of soldiers, was retreating above Caltanissetta, allowing those thirty thousand or so Spaniards to swallow up the small Savoyard garrison.

During their meal, Blasco and Coriolano listened to that cannonade and talked. Blasco gave him information about the strength of the army, the generalissimo, the officials, the regiment of foreigners (for the most part Italian); the artillery had set up their trenches among the vegetable gardens all the way down to Porta San Giorgio. After the official entrance of the Marchese of Lede, in his capacity as Viceroy of the Kingdom of Sicily on the side of Philip V, there would be a decisive action to overwhelm the Castello.

This news, which seemed to interest Coriolano, was alternated with other news about the life that Blasco had led during those four years. He had lived for a little while in Genoa, from where he had left for Barcelona. Then he had gone to Madrid and stayed there until the day when Cardinal Alberoni had decided to reconquer the Kingdom of Sicily, claiming that Victor Amadeus had not complied with the obligations imposed on him by the transfer of the kingdom, given to him under the Treaty of Utrecht. Blasco had lived as a master-of-arms and, by teaching the young son of a lady, a friend of Cardinal Alberoni, he had become so familiar to her that to leave and follow the Spanish Army he had had to resort to cunning.

Coriolano della Floresta was also sharing news about the events of city life, providing curious and interesting details, as well as about his daily life.

An hour later Blasco took his leave; he was perhaps a little late and was expecting to be punished. He resumed his way to the camp, this time going up toward Porta Maqueda in order to take the shortest route. On the road that, later ennobled by the Marchese of Regalmici, gave rise to the Quattro Canti of the countryside[1] and later took its name from Ruggero Settimo, he came across those two cavalieri, one of whom Coriolano had pointed out to him as Emanuele.

He looked at him carefully, not without some sadness, and, with his spirit oppressed by all these new thoughts that the encounter and the conversation with Coriolano had aroused in him, he returned to camp.

---

1   At the time of the events in the novel, the location was in the open countryside and was known as the *quattro canti di campagna*, in order to distinguish it from the Quattro Canti in the city.

CHAPTER 3

After eight days of resistance, the Savoy garrison agreed to an unconditional surrender. The city was then under the full power of the Marchese of Lede, who had by this time made his solemn entrance as viceroy in the Senate's carriage, amid the salvos of muskets and artillery, and had already reorganized the government. The Savoy had been concentrated in the fortified cities, such as Termini, Messina, Castel Mola, and Siracusa, where Count Maffei had ended up after many adventures.

As they took place at about that time, there was nothing unusual about the feasts of Santa Rosalia, which were considerably smaller due to a furious rainstorm that hampered the procession, and also as a result of the interdict. The conflict between the Papal Court and the Monarchy of Sicily had, in fact, become so acute during those four years that most of the clergy, who would side with the pope against any law, were banished. Perhaps there was never a more appropriate motto than "a small spark arouses a great fire" with regard to the Bishop of Lipari's refusal to pay the maestri di piazza for that handful of chickpeas that had given rise to a war of reprisals and persecutions that lasted about eight years. Despite the fact that two grani worth of chickpeas had been returned to the bishop—not due to his right but for the sake of peace—he, as we related previously, had demanded that the civil authority give him a formal apology and acknowledge a nonexistent right; and since the civil authority hadn't complied, and since the bishop, owing to his restlessness, had been admonished by the viceroy—who had the power to do so due to the rights inherent in the crown of Sicily—it gave birth to an open rebellion. The Papal Court, seizing upon a pretext to intervene in Sicily, supported the bishop and sent instructions that were disseminated by several bishops without the necessary permission of secular authority, and hence measures were taken first against the Bishop of Catania, then against the Bishop of Girgenti: an interdict and excommunications, which extended to all of Sicily.

With few exceptions, the clergy, very different from that of the past, perhaps due to its hate for the new regime, sided with the pope; the pope issued excommunications and papal briefs and bulls that would abolish the secular privileges of the monarchy, and so the State took up arms to defend itself. The king instituted a council that included men distinguished for their learning and their uncompromising character, and the council imposed on the clergy a choice of either submission to civil authority or exile. To acquire the crown of martyrdom with a relatively light punishment, or in any case a bloodless one, seemed like a fine and easy choice; most of them, in order not to incur canonical punishments, preferred exile. The instrument of that council was principally Matteo Lo Vecchio.

* * *

The birro, after recovering from the blow given to him by Blasco on the road to Misilmeri, had returned to Palermo in February 1715 and no longer found anyone that he once had dealings with. Don Raimondo was dead, Blasco had left, Don Girolamo also had left, and Andrea had moved on to be in the service of the Motta family heir, and consequently in the shadow of a doubly powerful family. Antonino Bucolaro had vanished, and no one knew where he was; the Beati Paoli seemed to have scattered, nor was anything more being heard about them; there was only Coriolano della Floresta, leading his life, irreproachable and beyond suspicion.

Thus, Matteo Lo Vecchio saw all hope of enriching himself being snatched away, and the secret that had come into his possession had turned out to be completely useless. Emanuele had been acknowledged, Don Raimondo was dead, and Donna Gabriella mattered little. It could be of interest only to one person that Don Raimondo's reputation should not fall into disgrace, and that was Violante; but she was in a monastery, still a young girl, and therefore unable to arrange for money to buy the birro's silence, and furthermore, she was Emanuele's fiancée.

Angered by these setbacks, the birro threw himself headlong into the conflict between the State and the Church. No one was more capable than him of drawing out the priests who, so as not to incur excommunication, would refuse to attend religious service; he had compiled lists of all the priests, of all the friars, and was inquiring whether they were going to choir and whether they were participating in religious processions. Since the processions took place quite frequently, it was easy to determine who the absentees were; then he would descend on their houses like a hawk and threaten them with arrest. If they wanted to live quietly and without being harassed, they would give him enough money to satisfy him, and then he would leave; if they refused, he would declare them exiles, arrest them, lead them through the most crowded streets, and force them to stay on a tartan or outside the gates of the city. Often those who had bought peace of mind were arrested the following day and would sustain a double loss.

Matteo Lo Vecchio's pockets were always full of orders of eviction, arrest, and imprisonment, and he used them widely, finding that the laments and grievances of his victims would lift his spirits. And meanwhile he was making money and enjoying himself.

The arrival of the Spanish Armada, the surrender of Palermo, and the installation of a new government had cut short his prosperous career. The council had been dissolved by the new viceroy and the persecutions had ended; Matteo Lo Vecchio returned to his position as algozino, losing not only the font of his illegal earnings but also that degree of power that he had attained through the terror of his violent acts.

Thus he hated the return of Spanish rule, of which he considered himself a victim, but he dared not oppose it, nor appear to be a partisan of the Savoy king. He devoted himself to his position apathetically and through force of habit, waiting for luck to come his way by chance, so that he could seize it and find a new source of earnings in the new order of things.

Meanwhile, out of habit and in order not to lose sight of those people who were of interest to him, he would spy on the lives of Emanuele, Donna Gabriella, Andrea, and Coriolano della Floresta.

On the day of the entrance of Viceroy Jean François de Bette, Marchese of Lede, Matteo Lo Vecchio had had a great deal to do and was staying, due to reasons related to his work, near Porta Nuova when the procession entered, at whose head a squad of dragoons rode on horseback with their swords unsheathed, which naturally brought out the initial curiosity of the crowd of people. Matteo Lo Vecchio saw and recognized, to his great astonishment, amid the dragoons at the end of the first line, Blasco, who passed by, almost bumping into him with the tip of his foot.

"Well, well! . . . Look who's back! . . . Ah, have you returned, my friend? Now we'll settle our accounts. I want to return the gift you gave me. . . . Goodness, these are debts that must be paid!"

He made inquiries about what kind of soldiers they were and found out that they were the first squadron of the Numancia Dragoons.

"There are six squadrons from Numancia, six from Lusitania, three from Batavia, three from Tarragona—"

"Enough, thank you!" Matteo interrupted, frightened by the detailed enumeration of the squadrons that his informant was giving him. "Apparently Your Lordship knows how the army is composed."

"Eh! Eh! I know: thirty-five infantry battalions, including eight of guards, one of artillery, twenty-four squadrons of cavalry, twenty-four of dragoons, a company of four hundred gunners and bombardiers, one of miners, one of workers' guilds, and fifty engineers."

"Good heavens! . . . How do you know all this?"

"Eh! Eh! . . . How do I know? I am the scrivener for the master razionale of the army."

"Ah! . . . And . . . and does Your Lordship know the soldiers? Do you know all of them?"

"All of them? I can't know them all. There are thirty thousand! The leaders, yes, I know them well."

"But the foreigners, for example . . . those of other nationalities . . . there can't be many."

"Oh, there are. . . . Even Sicilians. Most Illustrious Field Marshall, Don Domenico Lucchesi, isn't he from Palermo?"

"Yes, it's true . . . but what about soldiers?"

"There must be about fifty, for sure."

"Even in the dragoons? I thought I recognized one."

"In the dragoons as well. The first one on the right, who passed by just now, he is from Palermo; his name is Blasco Albamonte."

"Albamonte?" Matteo Lo Vecchio said, amazed. "Albamonte? But I know him by another name."

"What do you mean?" the scrivener asked.

"Exactly what I said."

"What name?"

"Oh! You well know."

"But then is he an extradited criminal?"

"Eh! Eh!"

"Excuse me; you say 'eh! eh!' with a certain air."

"What air?" Matteo Lo Vecchio asked with a naive expression but grasping immediately the advantage that he could draw from the turn in the discussion.

"An air of someone who knows many things and wants to conceal them."

"Me? . . . But I don't know anything, dear signore . . . signore . . ."

"Alonso Apuente, at your service; and you?"

"Matteo Lo Vecchio, corporal of the algozini, at your command," the birro replied with a mischievous smile.

"Splendid! . . . Then that's why you know so many things. Dear man, when it has to do with service to His Majesty, may God watch over him, there is no need for silence. . . . He could be some bandit wanted by justice."

"No, it's not that, but . . . in short, Signor Alonso, they are not things that I can share with you."

"You can speak of them; rather you must tell them to His Excellency."

"Yes, yes, it's something that will be seen to later; you keep an eye on him or have him followed, one never knows . . . he must have some files, he certainly must have some files. . . . I will also spy on him, have no doubt. You find out about everything that he does, and if necessary, we'll go to His Excellency; you will obtain a special audience for me. . . . And have no fear, for I will be able to show my gratitude to you. . . . Good heavens, when one can earn money honestly, in the service of the king, may God watch over and protect him, it is blessed money. Isn't that true, Signor Alonso?"

"Quite true. Tell me where you live so I can know where to find you."

"In the Albergheria. Ask for me and they will tell you right away."

"Then goodbye, Signor Matteo."

"Arrivederci, Signor Alonso."

When the master razionale's scrivener left, Matteo Lo Vecchio rubbed his hands together out of satisfaction and started off behind the procession to enjoy the ceremony, for the sake of appearances, but really in order to see Blasco again. He knew that the viceroy had to go to the Cathedral to take possession, and to swear observance to the constitutions of the kingdom and to the conventions and privileges of the city, as expected by the constitutions themselves and by tradition; so he made haste in order not to remain behind the crowd that was swelling and building up in the large square of the Cathedral, behind the line of infantry that was keeping the passage clear for the Senate's carriage, which carried the viceroy and his retinue. He arrived at the moment that the viceroy was in the act of taking the oath; the soldiers were firing salvos and artillery was being fired from the bastions of the Palazzo Reale, and from all the bastions of the city walls and from the squadron's ships, the salvos would in turn reply, filling the air with a terrifying noise.

Matteo Lo Vecchio stationed himself at the corner of the Cassaro so that he could overlook the street of the archbishopric and the main door of the Duomo; out of necessity, Blasco had to come opposite him and pass by him, and he would see him at his convenience. The procession, in fact, moved with its squadron of dragoons at the head. Blasco was in the first row. He was, or seemed to be, very distracted, and his eyes, even if they noticed Matteo Lo Vecchio, didn't recognize him or weren't entirely aware of him.

The birro wanted to enjoy the moment.

"Ah," he said to himself. "So, His Lordship changes his name and is wearing the deep blue uniform of His Majesty's dragoons, and he has the nerve to come to Palermo as if nothing had happened, without thinking that he would find this little nail here, ready to meet him; but splendid! Mountains don't meet, but men do. . . . Now I'll fix you. First of all, we must take away that name that doesn't belong to you, and this we'll take care of at once! We'll take care of the rest later. . . . Have no doubt; Matteo Lo Vecchio is here, and he has enough in store for everyone. Praise be to God! Finally, here is a hunt to enjoy! . . . Should I kill you? Never again! To kill a soldier of His Catholic Majesty, that the devil may take him, is the same thing as letting oneself be shot in these times of war."

With those thoughts, after the wave of people that were following and cheering the viceroy to the Palazzo Reale for the official reception had passed, Matteo Lo

Vecchio went down the Cassaro until he reached Piazza Bologni, where the palazzo of the Prince of Geraci was located.

The prince, the young prince, and the prince's grandson, that is, Don Emanuele Albamonte, had gone to kiss the hands of His Excellency, and they wouldn't be delayed long because the Ave Maria took only a few minutes.

"Then I will wait for them to arrive. . . . I wish to speak with the most illustrious prince . . . it's about something that concerns him."

He leaned against a pillar and waited. The Ave Maria sounded; he took off his hat, made the sign of the cross, and devoutly recited the Angelic Salutation, as did the passersby. Soon after, a magnificent carriage, preceded by volanti and grooms and followed by two Moorish slaves, went through the main entrance. Matteo gave a heartfelt greeting, and, allowing time for the lords to go up and make themselves comfortable, asked for permission to honor the prince and to speak to him about something very important.

"To me?" the prince said. "Why me? What does this excommunicant want? Or doesn't he know that to have anything to do with him will incur canonical penalties? I refuse to see him."

The Prince of Geraci's rejection was motivated by the fact that, due to his active role in the persecutions of the clergy, Matteo Lo Vecchio had been hit by the excommunication *vitanda*, which forbade all the faithful to have any dealings with the excommunicant or else they would incur the same spiritual punishments.

Matteo Lo Vecchio was inwardly annoyed by the rejection, but he maintained a meek and humble outward appearance and said, "As His Most Illustrious Lordship commands . . . however, tell him that I was coming to render him a great service, for the protection and honor of his relatives, and especially of his grandson Don Emanuele."

He left very angry, not renouncing, however, his plan to stir the Prince of Geraci against Blasco—owing to Blasco's usurpation of the surname Albamonte—and to bear out his charges with the authority of a person as illustrious as the Palermitan patrician. The prince wouldn't receive him out of fear of excommunication? Fine. He would approach the young Duke of Motta and tell him himself—along the street, while strolling, at the arena in Villafranca, or anywhere—and the young duke himself would take care of arousing his grandfather's grievances and anger, as well as the objections of the viceroy. With this idea in mind, he went home for the day.

* * *

Blasco was quite far from expecting that some plot was being hatched against him, and he was surprised when on the following day he found himself stopped three times, first with one excuse, then with another, by Signor Alonso Apuente, the scrivener of the army's master razionale, who was always hanging around him—and even more so when the captain of his squadron asked him if he had relatives in Palermo.

"Relatives? . . . No. . . . They are all with God!"

"Friends, at least, or acquaintances . . ."

"Perhaps I do . . . one can have some anywhere . . . I must have some in Palermo."

"Then make sure that someone who knows you comes to the camp."

"Why?"

"There is no need to tell you. You are a soldier. Obey."

Blasco said nothing more. He gave a military salute and ducked into his tent, where some fellow soldiers asked him what had happened.

"Nothing. . . . They wanted to promote me to sergeant."

"And?"

"I refused, of course."

"Oh! Oh!"

"If I had accepted, I would no longer be able to play the usual game of *calabre-sella* with you. That's for sure."

They understood that he didn't want to talk, so they started playing cards on top of a drum. But every so often, Blasco would think back to those questions. Why on earth did the captain want an acquaintance of his? This was a new development. Did he need to be introduced, or had he perhaps been recognized as an extradited criminal? Surely there was something behind his words. He would have to be on his guard. He could give them as many acquaintances as they wanted, and all of them people of virtue. He listed them in his mind: the Prince of Butera, the Prince of Geraci, Coriolano, Donna Gabriella . . . a hundred more lords. But did he really have to inconvenience someone without knowing what it was about, and whether the reason was acceptable for his own dignity?

The following day the captain sent for him and asked if he had informed any friends.

"Listen, Captain, signore," Blasco answered respectfully but firmly, "I am as fine a gentleman as any other cavaliere who serves in the ranks of His Majesty's army, and if I had the necessary amount of money, instead of joining as a simple dragoon, I would have bought a company or squadron, and I would be your equal. Now, precisely with regard to this, I tell you, with all due respect, that I will not trouble any of my acquaintances or friends unless I know what is requested of them that concerns me."

The captain frowned at him.

"Do you know," he said, "that your answer would force me to put you under arrest for insubordination?"

"I could only suffer the punishment in silence, Captain, but you will not dissuade me from my decision."

"Very well; go back to your tent and for today you won't leave the camp. Go."

Blasco returned to his tent, where his curious comrades renewed their questioning.

"Well, did they still want to promote you to sergeant?"

"Tut tut! Sergeant? Captain, dear friends, nothing less than captain!"

"And you refused again?"

"Of course. I would have to treat my fellow comrades as inferiors. Don't you think so?"

Toward evening, since there weren't any rooms that could serve as a prison, Blasco was put in shackles in the same tent and guarded by a sentry armed with a musket; it surprised the squadron a bit since Blasco was well liked for his geniality, his courage, and for the two or three blows he had dealt with his sword in the first days of his enlistment, in order to make himself known to his comrades. His sudden arrest was inexplicable; they presumed that Blasco had committed a serious offense against the captain, but in times of war, depriving himself of a good soldier like Blasco—come on!—it was much too harsh.

Blasco took the matter philosophically. Since he wasn't prohibited from drinking, from gambling, or from reading and writing, he had a jug of wine, a deck of cards, and some writing materials brought to him; he drank, had a little fun drawing lots with cards (as he had learned from a gypsy), and then wrote a note to Coriolano della Floresta, informing him that he was sorry if he didn't show up, since due to orders from above he had been seized by a very singular case of the gout that prevented him from walking.

The sentry was a poor Catalan, a drunkard and an obliging one, who had looked with a loving eye at the jug and felt his heart ache to see it empty.

In order to strike up a conversation, he asked Blasco, "Are you writing to your beloved, *señor*?"

"Yes."

"Is she *hermosa*?"

"Very beautiful."

"*Bueno!* . . . I guess you were drinking to her health."

"That's true, and goodness! I forgot to invite you. . . . One really mustn't drink alone."

"Yes, exactly so. . . . No harm done, I can join, you know."

"There's an idea. Bravo! Then come drink, there is still some."

"Gladly."

Blasco offered him the jug, which was more than half-full.

"May I drink it all?" the Catalan asked.

"But of course! What the hell!"

The soldier drank, gurgling the wine in his throat until the last drop; then, after putting down the jug and sighing with satisfaction, he wiped his mouth with the back of his hand and thanked him.

"Good! Good wine!" he said, smacking his lips.

Blasco let him enjoy the moment a bit and said, "How long will you be on guard?"

"Another hour."

"That's fine; do me a favor."

"Two, *señor*."

"Take this letter to this address."

"A letter for your beloved?"

"But what beloved? He's a man."

"Your relative?"

"No."

"Then your friend?"

"No."

"What the devil! Neither relative nor friend; then who on earth is it for?"

"Someone that I don't know, but who is my creditor."

"Do you want me to beat him up?"

"On the contrary, my friend. He's a person deserving of every respect."

"Then that's different. Give the letter here. . . . Where is this gentleman?"

"This is difficult to describe; you are not familiar with Palermo."

"Well! And was I a stranger to Sicily before the Savoy seized the kingdom? I know the city."

"Then it will be easy. Everyone will point out the Palazzo della Floresta to you, in Strada Nuova, toward San Antonino."

"I know, have no doubt. Should I wait for a reply?"

"I don't know. He may give you one. Ask him."

After less than an hour, the Catalan dismounted from his horse; with a nod of his head and a smile, he reassured Blasco that he had completed the task, and Blasco, in order to while away the time, went back to pulling lots from the deck of cards.

* * *

He was very far from imagining that on that same day, Emanuele had come to the headquarters to pay his respects to the Marchese of Lede and to complain that someone had usurped the name Albamonte, which belonged solely to him. Whoever was masquerading under that name perhaps had his reasons, but certainly not that of claiming an illustrious name of the aristocracy that his father had borne nobly in service of Their Majesties Philip IV and Charles II.

The Marchese of Lede recognized the legitimate grievance of the young man, promised that he would investigate, and dismissed Emanuele, who left puffing his cheeks, walking past the soldiers with his fist on his hip and with the air of an angry sovereign; he inquired in the offices if among the Sicilians who served in the army there was someone by the name of Albamonte.

Signor Alonso Apuente, then, believed he had to demonstrate his zeal and asked for permission to personally bring him the news for which His Excellency had asked. And he went there and told the Marchese of Lede what he had heard from the mouth of Matteo Lo Vecchio. It wasn't much, but it was enough to arouse suspicion; hence the order of arrest.

"Find this Matteo Lo Vecchio," the viceroy ordered him, "and bring him to me. I want to interrogate him."

Blasco, after having mused for quite a while about that arrest, believing that being put in shackles was too severe a punishment for such a frivolous act of disobedience, ended up falling deeply asleep, with his usual indifference in the face of dangers, which had something heroic about it. He forgot about the irons, and only when, in his sleep, it occurred to him to change position would he realize that his legs were imprisoned. But he would fall back asleep right away, following the images that he gladly conjured up in the silence and solitude.

Ever since Coriolano had given him all the news about the people who had been in his life the most, he would think about Violante secluded in the monastery or about Emanuele, and however much he himself had proposed and advocated for that marriage, he would feel his heart ache just at the idea of it happening, and he would think bitterly about his situation. Quick thoughts and bitterness that he immediately pushed back.

"Are you turning into a fool, then?" he would ask himself, trying to think about anything else and to fall asleep.

The following morning, the Catalan showed up at the entrance to his tent with a contrite look that at any other time would have made Blasco laugh.

"Well?" he asked.

"Excuse me, señor . . . but I don't remember well if you gave me a letter last night or not."

"What? If I gave it to you? But of course!"

"Really?"

"I'm positive, goodness!"

The Catalan grimaced and shook his head.

"If you say so, it must be true. . . . But now where the devil did I put that letter?"

"You didn't take it?"

"Since I'm not sure I had it, it means that I didn't deliver anything. . . . It doesn't take much to understand!"

"Ah, rascal! Thank your saint that I can't throw these irons on your head."

"Don't be upset, señor. I certainly didn't do it on purpose. . . . But the innkeeper had a horrible wine."

"What innkeeper?"

"I'm sorry! I went for a drink because I had a parched throat. Fancy that, the more I would drink and the more . . . . I was parched. . . . If I had the letter, I certainly must have misplaced it. . . . Couldn't you write another?"

"Get out; I no longer need you. When they free me from these irons, I'm going to cut off your ears! Get out!"

The Catalan left grumbling, while Blasco, giving in to his irritation, blamed it all on his unlucky stars. "I'll have to find someone who is less of a drunkard," he thought.

But soon after midday, instead of finding a good friend, he saw a sergeant enter the tent, who took off his shackles without saying a word.

"Ah, finally!" Blasco exclaimed, drawing up his legs, which were numb from inactivity, and getting up on his feet again. "I assure you that that position is not very comfortable!"

"Sorry," the sergeant said, taking out of his pocket a chain with two rings, "but, instead of your legs, I have been ordered to tie up your hands."

"My hands?"

"Exactly. Look."

He pointed to the entrance of the tent, and only then did Blasco notice a group of soldiers armed with halberds, who were waiting outside.

"Then am I under arrest?"

"It seems so. It is by order of His Excellency. So what have you done?"

"Me? If I only knew!"

"Come on! Who are you trying to fool?"

"When I tell you that I don't know, you have to believe me, by God!"

"If you wish, I will believe you . . . but you must have done something because a soldier isn't arrested for nothing, by thunder!"

With those words he had firmly tied Blasco's wrists and, holding one end of the chain, added, "Come on, that's a good man! And don't resist."

But Blasco was so stunned by this arrest, which had turned from being shackled into a full-blown imprisonment, that he gave no thought to putting up a resistance. Perhaps if he had found himself alone with the sergeant and the four men on some secluded road, he wouldn't have thought twice and wouldn't have had handcuffs put on him; but in the middle of the camp, escape would have been impossible, and to attempt it would be sheer lunacy. He had to obey, even if only to have the key to the mystery.

He saw that they were taking him to the summer house of the Prince of Sperlinga, where the general command was located.

"The viceroy," he thought, "perhaps he will interrogate me."

But he was mistaken; instead they locked him in a room on the ground floor, whose window was fortified with iron bars and looked out over the little village.

"So, I'm in prison!" he said to himself. "But at least I know why! Just as well, however, because if nothing else I could go for a walk."

And, in fact, he began to walk back and forth over the length and width of the room, which wasn't very big, singing softly to himself and looking out the window when he turned toward that side as he walked. On one of these occasions, he saw some figures on the other side of the iron bars of the window, and he stopped; but soon his face expressed the greatest wonder, rather an amazement, an astonishment, as if at the sight of something not only unexpected but also incredible. It was the captain of the squadron, Signor Alonso Apuente, and Matteo Lo Vecchio, whom he had thought was dead.

"Him!" he exclaimed. "Him!"

The captain asked the birro, "Well, then, do you remember that soldier?"

"Yes, Your Excellency; he is definitely Blasco da Castiglione, on whose head there is a bounty for being a member of the sect of the Beati Paoli, and for committing several crimes."

"Ah, dog!" shouted Blasco, to whom those words revealed everything, but soon after, he burst out laughing, which took the captain and Matteo Lo Vecchio aback. "Ah! Ah! Ah! . . . Blasco da Castiglione? Member, etc., etc."

"Silence!" the captain commanded. "And think about your circumstances. What do you have to say to the contrary?"

"Nothing, Captain, except this: I am Don Blasco Albamonte, of the duchies of Motta, and that man is a bandit for whom the gallows itself would be a great honor."

"We'll see whose legs will sway in the wind, my good man," the birro said, emboldened by the iron bars and by the presence of the captain.

But the captain pushed him back, threatening him harshly: "Be silent, scoundrel; after all, as of now he is a soldier of His Majesty. Be off!"

They went away, leaving Blasco feeling stunned, angry, and spiteful. He clarified everything for himself: the birro had run across him and had reported him, and he would have to expect a judgment with all its consequences unless some powerful help arrived. Certainly there was nothing about dying by the hand of the executioner that was appealing or thrilling to him.

He spent that day hoping to be questioned so that he could defend himself, and above all to clear up the misunderstanding; but, except for the sentry, whom he would hear walking behind the door, and the soldier who brought him dinner, he saw no one else. He had to get out of this mess. More than once the idea came to him to seize that soldier, gag him, tie him up, take the keys, open the door, throw himself on the sentry, disarm him, and flee to the countryside; but since it was a time of war, this seemed to him something that would bring him dishonor, and he rejected the temptation.

"Let's wait some more," he said to himself.

It seemed that they had forgotten about him, and the viceroy—occupied as he was with the siege of the Castello that was still dragging on and by the news that arrived from Caltanissetta and Girgenti—was probably no longer thinking about Blasco. It was enough to have imprisoned him, and he would think about the rest later. In fact, the one who was always thinking about it was Alonso Apuente, who was interested in getting the bounty for himself.

He was intentionally going to visit the captain in order to find out if the prisoner had been interrogated, as well as to arouse suspicions and fears. He had heard so many stories about that sect called the Beati Paoli that he wouldn't at all be surprised if one fine day they found the room empty. It was better to speed up the trial; what need was there to wait? The testimony of the algozino, who was an official of justice, should suffice; and then wasn't there the warrant?

But the captain paid him no heed; rather, one fine day he told him outright that he had annoyed him and for him to get involved with something else; for which reason the worthy Signor Alonso decided to take the place of the magistrate and start to gather the elements of the case on his own behalf, with the hope of formulating a precise and detailed charge. And he returned to Blasco's prison, by the window, with the demeanor of someone who is taken by a keen interest and regret.

"Good day, signore; well, what are you doing?"

It was a silly question, but he couldn't come up with anything better to strike up a conversation.

At that moment Blasco was walking; he turned at once and recognized the razionale's scrivener and said, "You can see, I'm walking."

"Poor young man! . . . You can't imagine how sorry I am to see you here!"

Blasco shrugged and thought that Signor Alonso must have known something, because he had come with Matteo Lo Vecchio; without responding to the commiseration, he asked in an evasive manner at what stage the siege was.

"Batteries are stationing themselves at Porta San Giorgio, in order to strike the Castello at close range, but this shouldn't matter to you. Do you know what you've done?"

"What?" asked Blasco. "Do you know? I don't."

"Come on; to lie about one's name is not a whim. And then, have you heard? The Beati Paoli, the warrant, a bounty . . . there is enough to get you shot! . . . You should find a way to save yourself, Holy Virgin of the Pillar!"[1]

"And who says I am lying about my name?"

"Well! Haven't you heard? That algozino . . . he knows your real name. And didn't the young Duke of Motta come to complain that there are no other people that bear the name Albamonte except him?"

"Ah! The young duke?"

---

1 A name given to the Blessed Virgin Mary.

"Precisely! . . . Then you are well aware that everything is stacked against you."

Blasco didn't respond; his heart was aching. So his own brother had come to disavow him, perhaps without knowing it, and perhaps not knowing what his complaint would mean. The disappointment was so bitter that he stayed silent for a moment, pensive and sad—something that Signor Alonso, who thought of himself as having great insight, interpreted as the bewilderment of someone who finds himself caught in the wrong. He was satisfied, and resumed: "They will torture you to find out what crimes you have committed . . . a horrible thing! You could spare yourself by confessing of your own accord. . . . Excuse me if I dare to give you advice, but it's on account of the concern that you inspire in me."

"Thank you. If necessary, I will take advantage of it, but . . ."

"But?"

"You are a good friend, isn't that so?"

"You must not doubt it."

"Good, then you should tell me, more or less, what I am being accused of . . . so I can know how to behave, not for any other reason."

"Well . . . actually . . . I wouldn't know the precise accusations. You have heard them; the algozino maintains that you resisted justice and you tried to kill him."

"Ah! Very well. Thank you, friend."

"Is it true?"

"What?"

"What the algozino said."

"You want to hear that from me?"

"Goodness! Who would you expect to know it?"

"I don't even know."

"Come on!"

"It's like I told you."

Signor Alonso understood that there was no point in continuing.

"If you need anything," he said, "speak freely."

"Nothing. Thank you . . . I mean, yes, for example, if there was a tavern nearby, I would like to dine as I am used to and to my own taste."

"You can do it. . . . There are at least a half dozen in the camp that have built huts . . . you would have seen them."

"It's true. Then, with the captain's permission, do me the favor of having an innkeeper come here, the first one who appears the cleanest."

"I will take care of it. May God watch over you, signore dragoon."

"God be with you, signore scrivener."

* * *

A few hours later a Spanish soldier entered with a young man, whose apron, twisted around his hips, immediately revealed his profession.

The soldier said in Spanish, "You asked for an innkeeper? Here he is."

Blasco looked curiously at the young man and gave a barely perceptible sign with his eyes, while touching his forehead.

He thought that the young man had reacted to it, and then he asked him, "What neighborhood are you from?"

"The Capo."

"Ah! And *chi c'è 'nto puortu?*"

The young man gave an astonished look and replied, "*Calia.* Where was Your Lordship born?"

Blasco replied, "In the *Cuncuma.* Then how about this: a good plate of macaroni . . . and go to the *Guardiano* . . . a slice of beef . . . you will tell him that one of the *colleganza attapanciato* . . . some cheese, some peaches, and some good wine . . . but hurry, and some bread with a *muzzica surda.*"[2]

"Your Lordship will be served, as you deserve."

When the young man went away, Blasco, left alone, began to jump, rubbing his hands together; the sound attracted the attention of the sentry, who was behind the door, and not knowing what it was, he called the sergeant, who opened the door and, amazed that Blasco was so cheerful, said, "What was that? What are you up to?"

"Nothing, Sergeant; I'm trying a dance, a new rural dance, an amazing and most gracious one. Judge for yourself."

"You are quite mad!"

When the young man returned soon after midday with a basket, from which an appetizing aroma emanated, a glance was enough for Blasco to understand, and he waited for the soldier and the young lad to leave in order to take out, before anything else, the loaf of bread and to break it. A small triangular file was ingeniously hidden inside, which he hid behind the straw mattress. Satisfied and happy, he ate with the greatest appetite, waiting for the completion of the errand entrusted to the young lad.

"We'll see how it turns out; but in any case, dear viceroy, Blasco will not let himself be hanged by you, or by anyone else."

---

2   *Chi c'è nto puortu?*: who do you belong to?; *Calia*: the group; *Cuncuma*: Garden next to the cave of the Beati Paoli; *Guardiano*: Leader; *colleganza*: members; *attapanciato*: has been seized; *muzzica surda*: file inside.

CHAPTER 4

Coriolano della Floresta hadn't seen Blasco for several days. At first he had assumed that he was being detained by the urgent needs of the war, but the prolonged silence made him suspect that something sinister must have happened to him, so he had begun to investigate. But during those days, he hadn't been able to enter the camp due to the strict rules that had been imposed.

Upon visiting the hospitals, he had felt confident about only one thing: that Blasco wasn't wounded. Then he had also been able to find out that the first squadron of the Numancia Dragoons hadn't left from the camp.

There was only one sure way: to find out from Marshal Lucchesi, who was living in the palazzo of his relatives at Lo Spasimo.[1] But as he was getting ready to go ask him, he received the news that one of the group had been seized. He didn't doubt that it concerned Blasco and went immediately to visit the field marshal.

His first words, as soon as the name Blasco was mentioned, amazed Coriolano.

"He's lying about his name? In what way is he lying about it?"

The marshal told him that he had heard about Matteo Lo Vecchio's accusations and depositions and about Emanuele's complaint.

Coriolano listened, smiling, then he said, "I can assure Your Illustrious Lordship that the dragoon, my old friend, is indeed Don Blasco Albamonte, and that he is the illegitimate son of the late Duke Don Emanuele."

"What? What is Your Lordship saying?"

"The truth. I can bring you two other reliable witnesses to confirm what I am saying, the Prince of Butera and the Prince of Geraci."

"So then that dragoon is a true gentleman?"

"Indeed."

"Oh, leave it to me. . . . If nothing else, until we see how that other business of the warrant turns out, he must be put in a more suitable prison. After all, he hasn't done anything against military honor or Our Lord His Majesty Philip V. . . . It's about some old accusations and edicts of the former government that don't concern us."

---

1 The bastion of Lo Spasimo enclosed the southeastern area of the city.

"Very well. Your Lordship has laid out the matter as it truly is. And then, you may assure His Excellency that in the entire army he will not find another soldier, or officer, who is the equal of Don Blasco Albamonte. . . . If they test him in a risky undertaking, they will find out."

"I'm happy with what you are telling me, and I thank you for your visit."

That evening, while Blasco—whistling in order to cover up any noise—was getting ready to cut the iron bars, the door opened and the sergeant called him: "Come on, dragoon, we are changing quarters. . . . You must have friends in high places. Let's go!"

"Where to?"

"To the city."

"What?"

"Yes, signore. The dragoon is going to stay in the military quarters in San Giacomo."

Blasco thought he was joking, but when he saw in front of the door a portantina surrounded by guards armed with muskets, he feared that the joke was a bitter, sarcastic remark.

"Who knows where they're taking me?" he said uneasily and looked around to see if there was a chance to attempt an attack, but he brightened up when he caught sight of the young lad from the tavern, who was giving him meaningful signals with his eyes as if to say, "Go ahead and don't worry, it is our doing."

The portantina, in fact, after traveling along the outer roads, entered the city through Porta Nuova and set out for the nearby Spanish military quarters, named after San Giacomo, where the officers' rooms and a capable garrison of troops were located. Next to the church was a building on whose ground floor were prisons for soldiers and in the upstairs rooms those for officers, where a prisoner would not be denied certain comforts that would mitigate the harshness of their confinement. Blasco was escorted there.

"Thank goodness," he thought, "it's more comfortable here and it will be possible to see some friendly faces."

He spent the night peacefully, expecting some news and putting trust in his good luck.

* * *

Meanwhile Coriolano had gone to see the Prince of Butera and the Prince of Geraci and explained Blasco's case to both; the Prince of Geraci expressed surprise at the step taken by Emanuele without his knowledge and asked for an explanation. The young man confirmed what he had done.

"Does Your Lordship believe it is consistent with my good name to allow an adventurer sought by justice—who knows for what knavery—to usurp the Albamonte name?"

"And what if he isn't usurping anything? What if he has the right to bear that name?"

"Are there others with the Albamonte name?"

"There is your brother, my boy; illegitimate, I know, but still your brother and older than you; and he is precisely Don Blasco, who, however, doesn't use his name in order to ask you—in memory of his father—for the crumbs that fall from your table."

Emanuele looked at his grandfather in amazement; he would never have imagined that this brother existed, but he felt no remorse or regret that he had gone to complain about him.

"In the end," he dared, "he is not legitimate and cannot be recognized as a true Albamonte, and he has committed some crimes."

"Be quiet, you don't know what you are talking about; you are an ingrate. You should learn a few things from your brother."

The old lord went to the viceroy, making use of his social standing as Grandee of Spain in order to have the right not only to enter without being kept waiting but also to keep his hat on before the king, and he testified on behalf of Blasco.

The viceroy, who had already received the first news from Marshal Lucchesi, was shocked. He objected, "But there is the complaint of that birro, Lo Vecchio, if I am not mistaken, and there is the warrant."

"The warrant," the prince remarked subtly, "was issued against Blasco da Castiglione, not the present Don Blasco Albamonte, who has the honor of serving in His Majesty's army. And as for the birro Matteo Lo Vecchio, it is my duty to inform Your Excellency that he is affected by the excommunication vitanda."

"What!" the Marchese of Lede exclaimed. "He is an excommunicant vitando? And I received him?"

"Do you see, Your Excellency? He cannot testify, he cannot take an oath, he cannot be admitted into the Christian community. He is a downright villain!"

The viceroy, who had the superstitious conscience of a Spanish zealot, seemed greatly shaken by this news, which to his own soul was worth more than the assurances in favor of Blasco.

"Thank you, signore, thank you; I will give the appropriate orders. I already had him change prisons. I will set him free and I will follow the marshal's advice. I will send him to take part in the assault on the Castello di Termini. If he truly is a valiant man and carries out some brave deeds, he will earn a pardon for all his offenses; if he should fall, there will be no need to investigate his past. Fate will have done justice. What does Your Excellency say?"

"I can only admire and offer praise for your wisdom."

* * *

Thus Blasco's imprisonment ended, and as soon as he was out, he rushed to embrace and thank Coriolano. On the same day that he emerged from prison, the Castello—violently shelled by the Spanish and weakly defended—raised the white flag and had to surrender unconditionally; it was July 15, the first day of the Feast of Santa Rosalia, and Blasco's pardon coincided with two events that could have appeared to be opportunities.

The following day, during the cavalcade that the lords conducted in the Cassaro, in honor of the "Santa," with the attendance of the viceroy, Matteo Lo Vecchio couldn't believe his eyes when with the utmost amazement he came across Blasco in the company of Coriolano.

"What? He's free? Out? What does this mean?"

But his amazement grew when, having rushed to look for Alonso Apuente, he was not received, and he heard that His Excellency, having learned that he was an excommunicant vitando, had given orders for him not to be received by anyone. Kicking himself out of vexation, the birro went back like a beaten dog, swearing in his heart that he would make him pay dearly in some other way.

"This is entirely the work of the Cavaliere della Floresta!" he thought. "I must begin with him. Ah! Is this how it is? We'll see about that, cavaliere, we'll see!"

He felt confident about the support of the council elected by King Victor, due to the controversy with Rome (of which he had been the most ruthless and fierce enforcer), but on that same day the viceroy issued a decree that abolished the council, thus hinting at a new direction in ecclesiastical policy. This was a blow to Matteo Lo Vecchio. By now everyone was turning their eyes toward the new sun and it seemed that they were trying to leave behind the services rendered to the Savoy monarch, so as to be absolved from excommunication and to regain favor and positions in the restored Spanish dominion, and the birro felt that he was alone, without support, without protection. The only thing to do was to throw himself resolutely under the new flags—something that wasn't at all repugnant to him, since in his capacity as birro, he, like all of the birri of all times and places, would adapt himself perfectly well to any regime and to any politics, and he would rage against the members of the council with the same ferocity with which he had previously raged against the disobedient priests.

The viceroy departed on July 16, with the army, toward Messina, in order to storm that stronghold, giving his instructions for the assault on Castello di Termini, assigning to it, among others, the first squadron of the Numancia Dragoons and entrusting the command to the lieutenant general, the Count of Montemar.

The departure of these troops would not take place for another eight days, so Blasco took the opportunity to relive a little of the life of that city where he had experienced so many and such different emotions.

The city, vacant of any commotions of war, had resumed its normal appearance; in the evening the promenade of the Marina would fill with carriages and portantine, and the musicians on the beautiful stage that had been erected there in 1681 were playing pieces of the most popular works.

The promenade retained the sumptuous decorations that had been made under the government of the Viceroy Count of Santo Stefano, by the Prince of Valguarnera, praetor, in 1687. On both sides of the stage or "theater" for the musicians, in a baroque style not lacking a measure of grace, there were two fountains, one of which had been erected there by the Viceroy Marcantonio Colonna, who in the figure of the Siren had wanted to portray his beautiful mistress Eufrosina Corbera, Baroness of Misilindino; the other had been moved there from Fieravecchia. The curtain that stretched between Porta Felice and the bastion of the Tuono, which stood near Porta dei Greci, had been painted, and a portico of marble columns had been added, and under every arch was a statue rendered in chiaroscuro, representing a virtue or a deity, whose name could be read at its base. And there were thirty-nine, beginning with Prodigalità and ending with the three theological virtues.

At the top of the curtain, a balustrade of stone had been erected, interspersed with plinths that served as a base for statues, and there were twenty statues of whitewashed limestone, representing the twenty kings of Sicily from William II to Philip IV, excluding Roger II and William I. And between one king and the next was a small pyramid between two spheres, surmounted by a smaller sphere at the top. Between the Marcantonio Colonna fountain and Porta Felice, the statue of Charles II had been erected, and perhaps one of Victor Amadeus would have also been put up if his reign had been longer and more prosperous.

Surely this expanse, between the beautiful monumental gate and the bastion, thus decorated and adorned, must have given an impression of magnificence from the side facing the sea, and those who had conceived it certainly hadn't thought that the devastating fury of men, combined with that of time, would, without reason, replace the painted representations with a massive rusticated stucco wall and allow all those statues to be eroded and, after moving the Marcantonio Colonna fountain somewhere else, sell it for rubble. . . . They hadn't thought that its monumental and sumptuous presence would be removed from the promenade, which rendered it truly unique.

During the summer, it was the most enjoyable meeting place for people of every class, who went there, as they do today, to enjoy the cool air and the music; and in those days, almost to make up for the forced withdrawal during the bombardment of the Castello, it was more crowded than usual.

Blasco had gone there and, stopping in front of the iron fence that encircled the statue of Charles II, looked at the magnificent equipage that, moving on from Porta Felice to the Marina, passed in front of him. From the liveries of the volanti and footmen, and from the colors of their shields, he would know to whom they belonged; sometimes they were his acquaintances and he would greet them courteously, smiling at their amazement as they recognized him under the dark blue garments of the dragoons. Some lords on horseback, followed by footmen, would pass by; Blasco would recite their names one by one. Among them were old acquaintances whom he had met in the grand soirees or at a gaming table when he would accompany Donna Gabriella; and that time, which now seemed to him so far away, would come back to him, with that sense of melancholy that is also one of life's sweet pleasures.

And he thought about his status. What was he? A poor soldier, without a future, without hope, who was barely worth a glance. It was true that, due to the habits he had acquired, his uniform wasn't as ragged and dirty as those of the other soldiers, and that in his air and in his manners there was something that set him apart and revealed his origins; but nevertheless he was still a soldier, nothing more than a soldier without a name, that those lords didn't even care to glance at.

He had no regrets about this, nor did he feel any envy, but he was unable to prevent a certain bitterness from rising up inside him, and he felt a type of dissatisfaction with himself. Oh! He had been so much happier before, when, unaware of his origins and not yet having tasted the life of that rich and gallant society, he had lived a very jovial life, like a bird searching for food in the fields, and he hadn't even known what tears were! Now he had tried to return to what he was before, but in vain—a new layer of memories, of sorrows, of desires, of joys had superimposed itself on that old, so impervious one, that these couldn't break it and thus restore or revive his spirit.

The images that were most associated with the sight before him came to his mind.

Donna Gabriella!

Oh, the carriage rides, alone by themselves! And that nighttime journey along the outer roads, when she had thrown herself into his arms, palpitating with passion and trembling with desire! . . . But behind her, the pensive and solemn face of Violante would appear to him. He had never forgotten her, even when he tried hard not to think about her, and he couldn't remember her without a feeling of regret. Sometimes he would ask himself what demon had inspired him with that appalling idea to propose and push for the marriage of Violante and Emanuele, instead of following the advice and opinion of Coriolano della Floresta; perhaps by now he wouldn't have been a blue dragoon, alone, leaning on one of the spears of the iron fence; he would have been happy.

He recalled that he had parted company with the young girl without exchanging a word, without seeing her again, without even saying goodbye. She must already be eighteen years old, and certainly she had become a woman and even more beautiful. . . . Ah, yes, she must be more beautiful! A secret desire to see her again tormented his soul, but the rules he had imposed on himself forbade him from taking a step in order to please his own heart.

While his soul was aching from those images, his eyes would follow the coming and going of the carriages and portantine; he might see someone: Coriolano, for example. Instead, he saw the young Prince of Iraci pass by, heavier, almost chubby, inside his carriage, with a young lady next to him, for whom he was flaunting his self-importance. Then he saw—appearing even smaller and more haggard looking—dressed in a threadbare jacket with a small stick in his hand, Michele Barabino, and he didn't dare call out to him, owing to the pity that the poor and crestfallen man aroused, and since he was unable to offer him any help. And almost at the same time he saw Emanuele, his brother. He was advancing on horseback, with a fist on his hip, head held high, with a haughty manner, dressed in a very elegant silk fabric, with rich lace on his sleeves, buttons made of gems, and diamonds on the buckles of his shoes. The footman who was following him on horseback wore the livery of the House of Albamonte, green with gold braid, on which was repeated the quartered shield, green and black in two opposing quarters, with alternating green and black bands in the other two.

Whether indignation, pain, or regret swelled Blasco's heart at the sight of him, he couldn't be certain; it was an undefined feeling, in which, however, affection played no part. He didn't love that strapping boy, to whom he wasn't bound by any familiarity during their lives, no tender memory, no obligation. He had defended him, had protected him, had even laid out for him that happiness that he assumed was unattainable and insurmountable—the marriage to Violante—but he had done it more for an ideal of respect toward the name, perhaps more out of a sort of unconscious vanity than of love. Emanuele appeared unpleasant to him; he didn't hate him, but he felt a certain repulsion toward him.

He followed him for a while with his eyes, then lost sight of him, mixed up amid the crowd, which, seen from that spot, looked dense and tumultuous.

The sky had turned gray and Capo Zafferano looked as though it was covered in ash. The water of the sea had taken on the color of steel-gray silk, with iridescent reflections. There was no longer a ray of sunshine in the sky. Nighttime was falling. Suddenly, the bells for the Ave Maria rang, and from a hundred different and opposite points the tolling spread and interwove, so that the entire city seemed to be bending down under the peals of those bells. And then that whole crowd on foot and on horseback, all those carriages stopped, heads were uncovered and bowed down, and the whispers of thousands of voices that recited the salutation flowed through the air; then there was an exchange of greetings: "Good night, holy night, bless me," and life, after that brief interruption, resumed its restless and tumultuous movement.

Already the musicians, who had fulfilled their obligations since the concert took place during sunset hours, were on their way home with their instruments under their arms, and the crowd of bourgeois and commoners, having nothing more to hear, followed them, flowing like a stream through the narrow opening of Porta Felice; they were dispersed, pushed back, and often broken up by the voices of the volanti who were walking in front of the carriages, and by the carriages themselves, the clanging of whose huge iron-reinforced wheels seemed to say, "Make way for the lords."

Blasco didn't move. The shadow enveloped him, rendering the contours of his face vague and indefinite; by the light of the torches of the volanti that were being lit and that he saw tossing about over the heads of the crowd, he recognized the lords he had seen pass by. He saw the young Prince of Iraci again, he saw his brother again, he saw everyone again; Michele Barabino passed almost in front of him, with his short stride and his demeanor of resigned poverty. And finally the grand and beautiful road was almost deserted, with its twenty kings gleaming white above the curtain against the dark sky, its murmuring fountains, and the empty little music "theater." Then he also started off, but not to reenter the city; he set out for the sea, stopped in front of the parapet wall, and gazed at the waters, above which the moon, which appeared red behind Capo Zafferano, cast a fiery, shifting, and undulating ray of light.

And as he looked on, without knowing why, Blasco asked himself, "Why did I come back?"

CHAPTER 5

Blasco went very slowly up Via Toledo again in order to return to the San Giacomo quarter, and he had just gone past Piazza Bologni when a group of people and some shouts near the Palazzo Geraci caught his attention. He moved closer and saw two footmen mistreating a poor soul, pushing him along with violent shoves. The poor little man was shouting, "It's not charity . . . leave me alone . . . it's not charity." People were stopping to look, not knowing what it was about. The sight of servants mistreating a poor wretch was nothing new or extraordinary in those times; it was almost a sign of the power of the lords, so no one sided with that poor man, small but bold, who instead of running away somehow passively resisted the shoving and punching of those liveried bullies.

"Be off! Get out of here! The duke doesn't tolerate beggars!"

"I'm telling you, keep your hands to yourself."

"Hey there . . . look how he resists!"

Blasco moved closer, and the indignation that had come over him at that sight turned to anger when he recognized that the man who was being mistreated was Michele Barabino. He made his way through and, stopping the two servants with his arm, he ordered them, "Leave this man alone."

At the same time Michele Barabino and the servants looked at him in surprise; the old tailor looked astonished, rubbed his eyes, and cried out, "Signor Don Blasco! . . . Signor Don Blasco!"

And taking the young man's hand, he kissed it with great enthusiasm, but the two servants haughtily looked Blasco up and down and said, "Do you know who you are talking to? Go about your business! . . . And as for you, ugly beggar . . ."

But Blasco, grasping the arm of the servant closest to him and shaking him forcefully, said to him through clenched teeth, "I am not in the habit of saying something twice. Leave him alone, and go away, scoundrel!"

At those shouts, other servants, some armed with clubs, came out of the palazzo; the two footmen had turned furiously toward Blasco, shouting, "We are from the house of the Duke of Motta and we are going to rid you of your fondness for meddling in matters concerning Palermitan lords."

"Oh, really?" Blasco said. "Splendid! It won't be my first time teaching manners to the servants of the Palazzo della Motta!"

And after quickly snatching Michele Barabino's little cane from his hands, before the four or five servants were able to take up the offensive, in a dizzying whirlwind he unleashed a sibilant torrent of blows on top of them. The cane was made of a good hazelwood, hard and knotty, which in Blasco's hands was turning into a club.

The servants, scattered by the force of the assault, ashamed of being beaten by one man in front of a crowd, especially since they were so many, rallied around with their clubs raised; someone had run inside and come back out with a dagger, but Blasco, with his legs wide apart, left hand at his hip in order to hold firm his sword—which could have encumbered him by going between his legs—moved from one to the other, keeping them in check, striking them on their heads, on their arms, with a lightning speed from which his adversaries couldn't escape.

The crowd was applauding and laughing. Siding with the poor man who had been mistreated by the ill-mannered arrogance of the servants, they had immediately followed the intervention of the dragoon with approval; and now, assured of his valor and swept away with admiration, they encouraged him with their applause, which, though embittering the servants, also discouraged them. The shouts and the racket drew people to their balconies; from the balcony of his palazzo, Emanuele, who at that moment was in the company of two young lords, the young Prince of Iraci and the Count of Gisia, looked out to see what was happening; the darkness didn't allow him to see anyone clearly, but he thought he recognized some of his servants by their voices. He immediately went inside and called to find out what had happened, but upon learning that they really were his servants and that the entire domestic staff was outraged at this soldier, he flew into a rage.

"Ah, by God! An affront like this to my house?"

And he rushed down, followed by the two lords and by other servants carrying torches. He shouted at the servants, "Sluggards, cowards! . . . Be off! . . . Be off! We'll deal with you later!"

Confused and disheartened, the servants withdrew; Blasco lowered the formidable weapon, handing it back to Michele Barabino, who was rubbing his hands together and repeating to those close by, "What did I tell you, eh? What did I tell you?"

Emanuele approached Blasco with his head held high and his eyes blazing with anger.

"Who gave you the right to beat my servants, the servants of Casa Albamonte?" he shouted.

Blasco, who had been unable to control a certain emotion upon seeing Emanuele come in front of him, raised his head at hearing him speak in that arrogant tone and looked into the eyes of his brother.

"Usually," he replied calmly, "I don't ask for anyone's permission to teach bullies about Christian charity toward the poor and the weak."

"Do you know who I am?" Emanuele erupted, furious at Blasco's composure.

"I do, you are the Duke of Motta."

"Well, then, you know that I don't tolerate disrespect from anyone."

"Bravo! That's what I like to hear."

"And thank your saint that you are not a gentleman of my rank, because I would teach you how one should respect me. . . . But I will have you beaten by your superiors."

"Here . . . you are mistaken, my boy!"

At that designation of "boy," not only Emanuele but also the two lords who had come forward flew into a rage and assaulted Blasco, who hadn't paid attention to them.

"You are ill mannered and insolent!"

But the Prince of Iraci, recognizing him by the light of the torches, shouted in surprise, not without a tone of hatred, "Blasco da Castiglione!"

"Ah! Finally, here is a lord who knows me!" Blasco said, recognizing the young prince, and then, with a ludicrous gesture, he took off his braided hat and bowed, adding, "Good night, prince, are you well?"

Emanuele had been left speechless; he looked at the dragoon with contempt and a poorly concealed anger, repeating, "Blasco! . . . Blasco!"

"Did you hear? The gentleman knows me; we had the pleasure of seeing each other on other occasions, before I was a dragoon serving His Majesty; and you too have seen me. . . . What can you do, it seems that fate obliges me to always thrash the servants of Casa Albamonte . . . and in this area . . ."

Emanuele turned red, recalling that precisely in Piazza Bologni, six years before, Blasco had rescued him from Don Raimondo's footmen, just as he was now rescuing some other poor soul from his servants. The memory, taking him back to a past that in his present state he would have preferred to forget, annoyed him. He chose to pretend to be unaware of the blood ties that existed between him and Blasco, and, pushing back the bitterness of his memories, he said, "Whatever you say, signore, I cannot tolerate an affront to my house . . . unless you prefer to apologize."

"Forgive me, I didn't hear you well; what did you say?" asked Blasco with a naive look on his face.

"That you apologize!" Emanuele repeated angrily.

"You are right," Blasco replied, and, turning, he looked for Michele Barabino, took him by the hand, pulled him into the middle, and resumed, "Good man, the Duke of Motta asks me to apologize in his name for what his servants did to you."

A howl, a formidable laugh, an applause that shook the houses greeted Blasco's words, to which a trembling Michele Barabino kissed his hand, saying, "What is Your Lordship saying? What are you saying?"

Emanuele and his two friends felt the utter ridiculousness of their situation; all three became furious and advanced menacingly against Blasco, shouting, "Signore!"

The Count of Gisia, quicker than the others, unsheathed his sword, fuming, "It's time to end this!"

But Blasco, who had no reason to have any respect for this newcomer, raised his voice as well: "Hey there, young master! Are you perhaps looking for a whipping?"

"This I will not tolerate!" shouted the count, attacking Blasco, who, without wasting time, had jumped back and once again plucked the cane out of Michele Barabino's hands, putting himself on guard, saying, "Here I am, boy!"

The Count of Gisia took a step back and lowered his sword, reddening with rage amid the laughter of the crowd. "A cane?" he roared. "A cane? . . . Someone the likes of me gives you the honor of dueling with him and you brandish a cane? . . . You insult me like this? . . . You dishonor me like this?"

"My God!" Blasco said with comic regret. "I didn't think I was displeasing you, my lord. . . . I was using the weapon that seemed most suitable to me . . . for you! I usually don't draw my sword except to deal with more serious matters."

The Prince of Iraci and Emanuele intervened, pulling back the Count of Gisia, who was wailing with rage and thrashing about, and trying to calm him down.

"Let it go, he's not worth the trouble!" the prince said to him. "He's a trouble-maker, I know him. Shrug it off. Move back . . . we'll have the servants do him in . . . he deserves nothing more."

Emanuele was reassuring him too.

"Come, come upstairs. . . . A loss can happen . . . there will be an opportunity and the time to teach him good manners."

But the count was still flailing about.

"His name. . . . I want to know his name!" he fumed, foaming at the mouth.

"My name, signore? I believe the Duke of Motta knows it, but if it pleases you to hear it directly from me, I am at your service: I am Blasco Albamonte, dragoon of the First Numancia Regiment."

"Albamonte!" the Prince of Iraci exclaimed in disbelief.

"Precisely; I realize that this displeases Signor Emanuele, but it's not my fault that when I was born in Castello della Motta I was given this name. . . . Now that you know who I am and where I am, I bid you farewell, gentlemen!"

The Count of Gisia and the Prince of Iraci turned to Emanuele, who was biting his lips, while Blasco quietly went away, followed by the crowd, which was commenting on what happened and nearly carrying the young man in triumph.

"Then he is your relative?" the prince asked.

Emanuele made a contemptuous motion with his shoulders and replied, "Tut, tut! He's a bastard."

"Of your uncle Don Raimondo?"

"No . . . of my father, apparently."

"Then he is your brother?" they exclaimed with even greater amazement.

"So he says. . . . But who can confirm it?"

Talking like this, they had gone back into the palazzo, where the servants were still standing, armed with daggers and pistols, waiting for an order from their master to attack Blasco; but the three young lords didn't even glance at them, blind as they were from rage, from humiliation, from the unsettling revelation.

Blasco, meanwhile, had crossed through the crowd, pulling Michele Barabino after him, and since a few of them had stuck close to him, he turned and gracefully bade them farewell.

"Dear friends, now do me the courtesy of leaving me alone with this good old man. I am not the Blessed Sacrament for you to follow me like this. . . . I thank you, but . . ."

That "but," however polite, could mean so many persuasive things that the people dispersed to both sides and Blasco found his path unobstructed. But he hadn't even taken six steps when he sensed someone behind him, and at the same time he heard a well-known voice say to him, "Goodness! You never change."

"Hey! Is that you, Coriolano?"

"I saw everything. Splendid. I had lost track of you, I had lost my Blasco of bygone times, and now I've finally found him!"

"Do you think so?" Blasco said with a sense of bitterness; he was about to say something else, but, realizing that Michele Barabino was standing next to him, he changed the subject and asked him, "What were you doing at the Palazzo Geraci?"

"Oh, Your Excellency, what poor people like me do . . . I ask for a little charity . . . that's all!"

Blasco rummaged in his pockets, found some bronze coins, and put them in the ex-tailor's hands, saying in a low voice, "This is all I have; for this evening it should be enough for you, but tomorrow come to the military quarter . . . now go."

In an expression of profound thanks, the poor old man kissed Blasco's hand and went away, exclaiming with emotion, "What heart! What heart! If only everyone was like him!"

Blasco and Coriolano walked for a while in silence, one next to the other. Coriolano was the first to break the silence. "Where are you going?"

"To the military quarters, as you can see."

"Is it mandatory to sleep there?"

"Mandatory, as you are well aware, no; rather, it's a little uncomfortable, because all the lodgings have been taken up by the families of the soldiers and workers."

"So come with me, then, for heaven's sake! I don't understand why you have to refuse my hospitality, or rather, why you cannot resume living in your former home. . . . Come, we'll dine together."

"But I invited Michele Barabino to the military quarters tomorrow morning."

"Oh, we'll let him know to come to my house."

"What do you mean we'll let him know?"

"Don't worry. . . . I'll take care of it. . . . Let's go."

He linked arms with him, and they retraced their prior route, going back toward the Quattro Canti, passing again in front of the Palazzo Geraci.

A carriage that was coming out of Piazza Bologni, pulled by two Friesian horses and preceded by two volanti, forced them to stop. They looked inside, and Blasco couldn't hold back a cry of surprise. A lady was inside whom he had recognized as Donna Gabriella, but she seemed not to notice the two friends.

"Perhaps she is coming from the Palazzo Villafranca," Coriolano said.

Blasco didn't respond; he had become saddened by the wave of visions awakened in his memory in rapid succession, which had constituted a monstrous whole. Again, they had fallen into silence. Coriolano broke it once again.

"Well," he said. "What do you think? Come on! I don't want to see you with this long face; after supper we'll go to a 'soiree.'"

"Oh, do you think so? Wearing such a poor uniform as this?"

"Of course not. You almost have the same build as me. Choose an outfit from my wardrobe. It's settled. We'll go visit one of your acquaintances: the Prince of Butera. He took an interest in you and it's a good idea to thank him. . . . You will probably meet other people you know, and we'll laugh at the expression on their faces."

* * *

After supper, in fact, they went to the palazzo of the Prince of Butera, who some years before had left his former home, behind Santa Cita, in order to live in his other one, formerly belonging to the Branciforti dukes, above the city walls at Porta Felice. There was a beautiful terrace on which he was planning to build a theater, but then, having designated the rooms adjoining it for other uses, he transformed it until it later became part of the Hotel Trinacria. The terrace was adjacent to one of the reception halls, and the prince had transformed it into a type of hanging garden with trees planted in enormous pots, trimmed according to the fashion, amid whose foliage a great number of lamps and lanterns would spread a beautiful light. A fountain gurgled at its center. The prince would entertain on clear summer nights and, unless they liked to gamble, everyone preferred to stay on the terrace to enjoy the cool sea air. The rank of "first peer of the kingdom," the customary elegance and magnificence of Casa Branciforti, made his "soirees" very well attended; a virtuoso would often participate, fresh out of the Conservatorio dei Dispersi, or the Buon Pastore, to great acclaim.

The Prince of Butera gave Blasco a friendly welcome, saying that he was happy that his troubles were over. Blasco thanked him, exchanged a few more words, and mingled among the guests with Coriolano, who, when introducing him to his acquaintances with the name of Blasco Albamonte, aroused their curiosity. At that time, to be an illegitimate child of a great lord, especially if acknowledged and with the full right to bear his name, was not a mark of dishonor or shame. It wasn't uncommon in cases of feudal succession that an illegitimate child, in the absence of legitimate heirs, was invested with the fiefdoms and the rights of the house; nor were marriages of nobles to high-born illegitimate children disdained. The most probing asked in Coriolano's ear whether Blasco's mother was a lady, since that naturally would have greatly attenuated the original stain, the young man thus possessing all the virtues of an aristocrat. But Coriolano was evasive: she wasn't a great lady, but she wasn't a commoner; the family were provincial smallholders, landowners, not yet barons, but more or less. Such a response was sufficient to attenuate their qualms and make those lords less mistrustful of Blasco.

So, after four years of absence, he reentered that society from which he had withdrawn, and perhaps it wasn't displeasing to him. The scene that had taken place two or three hours earlier stayed with him a little, in imperceptible stirrings, which gave him a certain desire to see those two young lords again, and perhaps his brother, who might come to the "soiree."

He exchanged a few words with old acquaintances who deigned to ask him where he had been, in which corps he was serving, marveling that he hadn't at least asked for command of half a squadron. "The vicissitudes of life!" he answered jokingly; but while he was chatting near one of the large glass doors that led to the terrace, under the curved leaves of a palm tree, there were the Prince of Iraci and the Count of Gisia coming out of the hall. At the sight of Blasco, they stopped, stunned, unable to conceal their contempt and surprise. Blasco looked at them with supreme indifference, as if he had never met them, and the two young lords passed in front of him haughtily, casting a glance of arrogant defiance and hatred in his direction.

A moment later Donna Gabriella came into the hall too, on her way to the terrace, lightly resting the tips of her fingers on the hand that Emanuele gallantly held out to her. Three or four lords hurried toward her, lavishing her with bows and kissing the hand that she regally held out to them. She was dressed in black silk, which made her pale beauty stand out and rendered her enchanting. Those four years had given her face a certain serene austerity and her body a greater fullness, but not enough to subtract from that harmony and elegance that were particular to her and almost formed the essence, the scent of her femininity. Blasco was amazed, moved as if by a sudden and unexpected apparition, and he couldn't take his eyes off her, though he didn't dare to approach and revere her as others were doing.

Donna Gabriella hadn't noticed him and moved on with her brisk and graceful step, responding to the greetings; but when she came close to the glass door and caught sight of Blasco, she couldn't hold back a cry of surprise. She turned pale and was about to faint. Two or three young men dashed over to hold her up, asking her how she felt; someone took a bottle of smelling salts from the pocket of his waistcoat and held it out to the lady. These attentions were enough to enable Donna Gabriella to get control of herself, or rather, to get her strength back and conceal her emotion.

"It's nothing, thank you!" she said.

But her eyes returned to Blasco and naturally were followed by the curious onlookers, who in fact remembered that Blasco had been that cavaliere from some time ago (and many were saying also the lover) of the duchess.

He felt that his situation at that moment was extremely awkward and that he had to get out of it as soon as possible, in an honorable and courteous way; thus, moving from his spot, he approached Donna Gabriella and, bowing with devotion, said—not, however, without a slight tremor in his hand—"Will the duchess grant me the favor of honoring her?"

Donna Gabriella, without speaking, offered him her hand; she could barely stammer, "It's you! . . . Here!"

She was unable to add anything else and, in order not to give in to the impulse of the thoughts and feelings that stirred inside her, she moved on, to greet the princess who was mistress of the house.

The incident was noticed, notwithstanding the coolness of the words and the brevity of the conversation; her emotional state was noted, followed by mischievous if not malicious comments.

But the most amazed of all was Emanuele, who, completely unaware of any relationship there might have been between Blasco and the duchess, couldn't figure out how they knew each other, or why she had become so emotional. He didn't even address Blasco with a nod of his head.

The two brothers looked at each other coldly, not without prompting the astonishment of those who had already heard about the blood ties between the two young men.

Someone whispered to Coriolano, "Tell me something: doesn't the young Duke of Motta know his illegitimate brother?"

Coriolano apologized for not knowing anything.

"Perhaps they know each other, but I am unaware of whether they know they are brothers. Perhaps not."

He was lying in order to remove Blasco from that humiliating situation that Emanuele's behavior could create for him, and his lie seemed to please everyone, since the reality of those two brothers, who didn't know each other and yet had found themselves together, had for them the tantalizing flavor of a novel or comedy. It was, after all, quite a coincidence!

Emanuele had accompanied the duchess and, after having greeted the other ladies, had returned to the entrance hall with his two friends, the Count of Gisia and the young Prince of Iraci. The expressions on their faces were so agitated that all three seemed to want to tell one another something urgent and extraordinary.

Going back into the hall, in fact, and withdrawing to a corner, the Count of Gisia said, fuming, "It's a provocation! Absolutely a provocation!"

"Be quiet! Let's not cause a scandal here," the Prince of Iraci remarked. "Let's speak softly, so that he can't tell that we're talking about him. I know him well."

"You know him?" Emanuele asked. "For a very long time?"

"Unfortunately, yes. . . . I met him four or five years ago, when, excuse me, he was nothing but an adventurer."

"And he's known the Duchess of Motta since then?"

"Eh! Then you don't know? . . . Indeed, they say he was something more than a friend of Donna Gabriella!"

"What are you saying!" a pale and spiteful Emanuele exclaimed.

"What everyone knows, my friend."

"But we're getting lost in things that don't concern us," the Count of Gisia remarked. "This is certainly not anything we should be worried about."

"Worry? No . . . ," the Prince of Iraci corrected. "At most, it can only hold our attention for a moment."

"Possibly—I'm not arguing about words. . . . What I maintain is that that gentleman came here to provoke us . . . and we must not let ourselves be overwhelmed like this. Forgive me, duke, if he is your brother, but what I said is true."

"Oh, don't worry about this relationship, which, word of honor, I don't care at all about! If my father had some passing fancies in his youth, it doesn't mean that I have any obligations to the consequences of his whims. Isn't that true?"

He smiled at this witty remark, looking at his two friends as if to welcome their approval, but they were content to nod their heads and said, "We must challenge him."

"Since he is a gentleman, although illegitimate, we can well duel with him."

"Let's formulate a written challenge," Emanuele said haughtily. "Though I have told you that I don't meddle in his business, you will understand that for reasons of propriety, I refrain from taking part in the drawing up of the challenge . . . so I will walk away for a moment."

He was lying; what was pressing him inside was to find out if Blasco had been the lover of that Duchess of Motta, of that beautiful, desired Donna Gabriella, who had an almost disdainful coolness toward him.

The lady now appeared to him in a different light, and it seemed to him that, in possession of that particular secret, he could take advantage of it. His was not a jealousy arising out of love, but a baser and more vulgar emotion: that of his vanity as a handsome, noble, and rich young man being shown less consideration than a bastard. This feeling of his intensified when he saw Donna Gabriella approach Blasco and speak to him.

She, in fact, having gotten over the first impression and resumed control of herself, was dying to know what Blasco had come to Palermo for, after so many years away, unaware that he was serving in the Spanish Army. Not wanting to give the appearance of calling out to him, but on the other hand unable to resist the urge that tormented her, under the pretext of saying something, a greeting, a gracious word, she moved closer to the various groups of ladies that were scattered here and there about the terrace. This way she would be forced to find herself near Blasco, and the proximity would take care of the rest. She was too skilled in the arts of a beautiful woman and in the pretense of not paying attention to what she had set her sights on in order to get there more assuredly for there to be any doubt about the success of her move. Thus she found herself a couple of steps away from Blasco, as if led there by chance, and when, inadvertently turning, her eyes met those of the young man, she again pretended to be taken by surprise and was so charming that Blasco had no choice but to smile and to say to her, "So, is the duchess amazed by my presence?"

"My God! Yes; I would never have imagined seeing you here again after all this time."

He drew closer to her.

Donna Gabriella, taking advantage of the fact that no one could hear, said quickly, "Rescue me, I beg you, from that boring and tiresome young duke . . . your brother. When I leave, escort me to my carriage."

Blasco had no time to voice any objection or ask a question before Donna Gabriella had already moved past him. He thus found himself committed and unable to exempt himself from what he well understood was an invitation. He went to find Coriolano, who was getting ready to leave, and told him what had happened.

"I assure you that I regret having you leave alone, but what can I do? I'll catch up with you at home."

"Go ahead, but be careful. Are you familiar with the legend of Circe?"

"I will be Ulysses, have no fear."

They were about to take their leave when two young lords approached Blasco and, greeting him with ceremonious gravity, said, "If Your Lordship would like to grant us a minute for an audience, we have something to tell you on behalf of the Count of Gisia."

"To me? Forgive Their Lordships, but I don't believe that I have the pleasure of knowing the Count of Gisia, except that he is a slightly intense young man."

"We cannot, owing to our social class, allow any judgment on behalf of our friend, who honored us with his assignment."

"Ah! He honored you with an assignment. Splendid; I am delighted with Their Lordships . . . please tell me—"

"This does not seem to us like the most suitable place."

"Of course . . . then, here: I am asking my friend Coriolano della Floresta to take my place or, if it pleases Their Lordships more, I will instruct him to accept the assignment with which they are entrusted."

And, bowing, he left them there, while Coriolano, smiling his usual smile, said, "I am at the disposal of Their Lordships."

CHAPTER 6

Donna Gabriella left soon after, and to Emanuele, who had approached and offered to escort her, she answered, "Thank you, duke, but I had already asked Don Blasco"—and here she changed her tone, lowering her voice—"your brother."

Emanuele turned red and looked with sullen and jealous fury at Blasco, who, drawing near, had offered her his arm, smiling subtly at Emanuele's gaze.

"If you prefer the company of the duke," he said to Donna Gabriella, "have no concerns about me."

"Thank you, signore," Emanuele replied haughtily.

"Signore?" Donna Gabriella remarked, surprised, looking at the two brothers. "What? You address each other as 'signore'?"

"As a matter of fact, I wouldn't know how else to address him," Emanuele said in a tone that betrayed his contempt.

Blasco, who had turned pale, shrugged his shoulders and limited himself to telling the duchess, "Whenever you wish, Donna Gabriella."

She rested her hand on Blasco's arm and crossed the hall, while Emanuele followed her with burning eyes, biting his lip.

Going down the stairs, Donna Gabriella remarked, "But do you know that your brother Emanuele really surprised me?"

"Why, signora? He has no reason to love me, just as I really don't know why we should think of ourselves as brothers rather than as two strangers."

The footman opened the wide door and lowered the footboard, and Donna Gabriella climbed quickly into the carriage, visibly content, saying not without a certain degree of silliness, "That boy is truly crazy."

Blasco didn't respond but kissed Donna Gabriella's hand and closed the door of the carriage, wishing her a good night.

She said to him, "Won't you come visit me? Are you still angry with me? Now you certainly have no reason to be. . . . And I have suffered so much . . . so much. We can talk about so many things."

"Thank you for your invitation, but I am leaving in a few days."

"You're leaving? Again? Why?"

"Oh, didn't I tell you that I am a dragoon in the First Numancia Regiment? . . . I am going to the siege of Termini."

"Oh, God! To war? . . . But then so much the better." She lowered her voice and said quickly, "Go and wait for me at the corner of the church of the Catena. I will have my carriage go slowly. I have many things to tell you. . . . Go."

Blasco's mood darkened somewhat, but to refuse would have been a true incivility; he bowed and hurried out of the palazzo while Donna Gabriella's volanti were lighting their torches outside the gate. The carriage indeed started off slowly and turned into Via Alloro, making the pavement resound under the iron-shod hooves of the two horses and the rolling of the wheels. Near the Church of Santa Maria della Catena—a precious jewel of fifteenth-century Sicilian art—it caught up with Blasco and stopped. The street was deserted, the houses shut, and the darkness was barely broken by the flames of the two volanti; except for the servants, no one could have seen Blasco climb into the carriage at the duchess's call. Appearances were thus preserved; this was important to Donna Gabriella due to her status as a widow. The servants were, as their masters generally believe, discreet people, and besides, the duchess wasn't even dreaming of anything that would go beyond the door of her palazzo. The route to get there wasn't short, and she could speak freely and at length.

Blasco then climbed into the carriage and sat next to her, and for a moment they remained silent. Donna Gabriella had sat back in a corner in the shadow, but by the faint light that the torches of the volanti let into the carriage, one could see her eyes shining. If the noise of the wheels on the surface of the Cassaro hadn't nearly deafened Blasco, he might have heard the tumultuous throbbing of that feminine heart beside him. But he could see those eyes shining, and he sensed everything that that silence was expressing.

She seemed to be waiting for a word, but he also, for his part, was waiting for Donna Gabriella to tell him some of the things she had to say.

After a while she sighed and murmured, "How much time has passed!" And a minute later: "We parted in anger . . . and I was always afraid you would hate me. . . . Tell me, first of all, if I am mistaken."

"Yes, you are mistaken," Blasco replied. "Perhaps I even committed some wrongs against you, and I allowed myself to get carried away by resentments . . . but so much time has passed! You said so yourself . . . so I am not angry with you . . . nor do I hate you. I am giving you proof of that, it seems to me."

"Thank you, it's true. . . . But let's not talk about wrongs. . . . I committed many more of them. . . . I have always thought about it, do you know? But . . . I was so blinded by the pain . . . by jealousy! Let's not talk about it anymore. . . . If you only knew how I have lived during these four years! A widow, yes, in a strict widowhood that almost everyone interpreted as unwavering fidelity and respect for the memory of Don Raimondo . . . but really it was and is the widowhood of my dreams, of my hopes."

Her voice trembled with emotion and her tearful eyes shone even more in the shadows. Blasco was silent, he was thinking about Circe.

Donna Gabriella had a burning question on the tip of her tongue, but she didn't dare ask it; she let a moment of silence pass and said with apparent indifference, "And . . . have you seen . . . your cousin?"

Blasco gave a start; the name of the young girl rose to his lips, but it didn't turn into a sound. Then he answered in a broken voice, "No, I haven't seen her."

"Do you wish to see her?" Donna Gabriella persisted, and with that question her heart was trembling.

"No," Blasco replied again.

"You are right. . . . Do you know that she is engaged?"

"Yes; for that matter, it was my wish."

"Did you know that the wedding will take place at the end of next January?"

"No," Blasco said, barely controlling his emotion, "I didn't know."

Donna Gabriella studied him; at the core of that statement she sensed a tremor of pain and passion, which awakened in her heart dormant but not yet extinguished torments, jealousies, and hatreds. She fell silent again, creasing the sumptuous laces of her sleeves with a brief and nervous gesture. Did she no longer have any charms, then? Did her beauty, which had triumphed so often, no longer have any power?

She moved a little closer and asked in a gently suggestive voice, "Are you suffering?"

"No, why should I suffer? And about what? You were willing to assume something that had never happened, you created a novel of pure fiction and believed it to be an actual account, thus tainting an innocent young girl's puberty; you poisoned three lives, you pushed away those who would have been your best and most faithful friends. . . . Oh! When I think about all that you have done, Donna Gabriella, I feel overwhelmed by such an intense and profound pain that I should almost hate you."

"And do you hate me?"

"No, I don't hate you, because I wasn't born to hate; my father must truly have conceived me in a moment of great kindness and love in order to give me a heart like this! . . . I don't hate you, but certainly, Donna Gabriella, you have broken something inside here, and it can't be mended!"

She fell to her knees on the carpet in front of the seat, murmuring with an unbound expression of sorrow, "Forgive me! . . . Forgive me!" And, taking his hands, she kissed them hesitantly.

Blasco drew them back, confused, upset, saying, "What are you doing? No, no . . . get up. I beg you. . . . I want you to get up."

Since she wouldn't move, he, sitting as he was, took her by the waist and forced her to get up and sit down, but Donna Gabriella was so emotional and out of her mind that she pressed herself against his chest, and he felt her tremble and shake from the force of that emotion.

Blasco was confused. "Donna Gabriella," he murmured, "I beg you . . . do it also out of respect for yourself."

She shook her head in denial, her eyes full of tears that flowed down between one sob and the next, dropping onto Blasco's hands. Those impassioned teardrops seemed to penetrate his blood, multiplying until they became a wave, rising from his veins to his heart and drowning it in an undefinable emotion. Pity, tenderness, sweet memories, youth, and above all that vague and ineffable desire to mingle one's own heart with that of another made him grow weak; the wax that Ulysses had believed plugged up his ears was melting, and he felt all the stirrings of that love again.

She continued to shake her head, with her eyes shining amid the tears like two stars seen through the rain, and she found some passionate words: "It has been five years since I first met you, five years that my heart has been closed and has never again opened to another emotion, as though you had taken away the key; it has been strictly closed . . . and in these four years of widowhood none of those who tried to seduce me received even a single smile, because my heart was full of sorrow, the sorrow of having lost you, perhaps forever. A sorrow without hope. . . . I felt your hatred over me, like a curse, and I wanted to know where you were in order to escape from this place full of anguished memories, to come to see you, to throw myself in your arms and tell you, 'Here, now I am free, and I still love you. Take me!' And to pull out a word from you, a tender word that my soul is thirsting for! . . . And now I have you here, Blasco, here next to me, I can feel you. I have your hands in mine, I have your mouth here, next to mine, like this . . ."

She had pressed herself against his chest as she spoke, her voice low but vibrant with passion, like a caress, and as her words flowed in that dizzying state of desire, she moved her face toward Blasco's face, with her eyes locked on his eyes, until in a mad impulse her quivering lips sought out his lips.

He felt as though his temples were bursting.

"Donna Gabriella! . . . Donna Gabriella!" he pleaded without retreating, abandoning himself to triumphant youth, almost happy to have been vanquished.

Meanwhile, the carriage, after passing the Quattro Canti and having gone along Strada Nuova, was turning into Via Bandiera. At Donna Gabriella's request, it had taken a long detour, precisely so she could have Blasco in her company as long as possible; now, approaching the house, she was worried that Blasco would leave her.

And in the anxiety of this fear and in the full intoxication that flowed through her blood, she resumed, more tenderly, suggestively, almost with a virginal modesty, "In these four years I have saved myself for you, without expecting you, owing to a vow I made. Because I haven't yet met a man who is like you and who is worthy to stand beside you. . . . I have wanted to devote my life, my youth, my solitude to you, whom I could never hope to see again, to you, the one and only true love of my life. . . . Now I look at you, I feel you, I have felt your kisses and it seems like a dream to me. . . . A dream? . . . Don't wake me up, I beg you . . . allow me to dream . . . here on your mouth!"

She pulled him to her; their huddled bodies seemed like one. And blessed are the cobblestones that made the wheels clang so loud in the narrow street that they drowned out the sound of their kisses.

The slowing of the horses released Donna Gabriella from this embrace. She whispered quickly, "I will wait for you. . . . But don't come now. No one must see you come in. Come back in a half hour, this way, from this vicolo."

She pointed it out to him; it was a vicolo enclosed between her palazzo and that of the Prince of Pantelleria. And she added, "Now pretend to leave."

The carriage had arrived and entered the vestibule; one of the footmen opened the door. Blasco jumped to the ground, took Donna Gabriella's hand, and accompanied her to the foot of the stairs, where he kissed gallantly—but not without desire—the beautiful hand that the lady held out to him, wished her goodnight, and went away, immediately vanishing around the corner of the street that went down to Piazza San Giacomo La Marina. But as soon as he heard the entrance door being bolted, he went back and thrust himself into the vicolo, and he was so full of that adventure, which was brightening up the night and adorning it with roses for him, that he didn't notice some shadows at the corner of Via dei Crocifissari that seemed to be spying on him. Instead, he heard a balcony door open after a while and a voice calling out softly, "Blasco!"

And almost at the same time something swaying passed in front of his eyes and hit him in the legs; it was a rope. He caught hold of it, tested it, felt that it was securely fastened, and then quickly jumped up and clung to it.

Not for nothing had he spent a few years at sea; he climbed the rope in a flash, jumped over the railing of the balcony, and found the nearly naked arms of Donna Gabriella waiting for him, trembling.

CHAPTER 7

With rage and jealousy, Emanuele had seen Donna Gabriella leave with Blasco; and, giving in to an impulse, after taking leave of his friends with an excuse, he had left the palazzo, but instead of getting into his carriage, he took with him his faithful servant, a sort of squire and bravaccio, dismissing the carriage and the others.

He saw Blasco moving away in a hurry and Donna Gabriella's carriage moving slowly, and he followed it at a certain distance, not really having any prearranged plan, but mulling over thoughts of revenge and reprisal.

Nothing seemed more mortifying to him than to have been rejected in favor of Blasco; perhaps he would not have felt so much contempt if Donna Gabriella had chosen some other cavaliere. To provoke him, challenge him, fight, or send him to kingdom come were things that he could have done without anyone intervening, but Blasco, after all, was his brother; however much he felt no respect for him, he nevertheless feared the judgment of the world. And besides, he was well aware of the fact that Blasco would never have picked a quarrel with him. And meanwhile, there he was once again: lucky, popular, desired, summoned by that beautiful woman who for two years had stirred his instincts of a young colt. Now, seeing the carriage move slowly, he wondered what it meant. But the answer was not long in coming when he saw it stop near the church of the Catena and a man climb in, whom he recognized from his build as Blasco.

Then he clenched his fists in anger. Since the horses had quickened their pace a little, he wouldn't be able to keep up with them, and assuming they were going to San Domenico, he thought he would shorten the distance by going through the side streets. He turned into Via Porto Salvo, which would lead him once more into the piazzetta where the entrance to Donna Gabriella's house was located, and he felt relieved when he saw Blasco go into Via dei Crocifissari.

"She," he thought, "must have dismissed him, so she's alone. Good."

But he hadn't finished consoling himself with this thought when he realized that Blasco was still there, standing in the shadows of the street, like someone who is waiting for or wants to chance upon something. Then, afraid of being identified, he crouched on the steps where some poor people were snoring. He saw Blasco go back and enter the vicolo, and so he went cautiously down the steps, without making a sound, peering into the shadows. He heard a balcony door open and a white shape appear. It was her!

"What is she doing?" he wondered, with his heart in the clutches of rage and jealousy.

A faint light came from the room and was shining on Donna Gabriella's back. He could see what she was doing and in fact he saw her go back in and stretch out her hands, and in the light that struck the balcony's iron railing, he saw Blasco appear and saw him climb over it and go inside.

He blurted out a curse, raising his fists toward that balcony. In an outburst of fury, the thought had come to him to bang on the door, even to smash it, to storm into that house and lay bare the shame of that woman, but the image of Blasco rose before his eyes and stopped him. A wicked idea suddenly came to him. Trembling, with a bitter taste in his mouth, he bent down to his servant's ear and quickly whispered a few words to him.

"Did you understand well? Go, hurry."

The servant didn't need him to repeat it. Emanuele withdrew into Via dei Crocifissari, walking in a glowering and threatening manner and savoring his revenge. How slowly the time was passing! It seemed so long to him, almost endless, and he trembled with impatience, stomping his feet and cursing the servant.

From time to time he would look up at the balcony of the villa and some tormenting visions would fill his head and swell his heart with a storm of hatred, and the more time that passed, the greater his torment grew. After less than an hour he heard a trampling of feet approaching, and soon after he saw a group of people coming from the end of the piazzetta, preceded by a lantern.

"Finally," he said.

It was a pack of beggars, hoodlums that had perhaps been scraped together from the benches of the nearby market, armed with stones, who were laughing boorishly. Leading them was the servant, who, pointing to Donna Gabriella's house, said, "It's there. We are clear; shout, knock the stones together, say anything you want. I don't have to repeat their names for you."

"Leave it to me," said one of those ruffians, who appeared to be the ringleader.

They entered the vicolo, lined up under Donna Gabriella's balcony, and began to make a dreadful racket, knocking one stone against the other and imitating the sound of trumpets with their voices. Then they suddenly fell silent, and one of them, in a resonant voice, began to sing.

And right after, the dreadful racket of the stones started again, which resounded in the vicolo and transformed it into a living hell. Then there was silence, and the voice resumed.

And again the stones clattered, and howls and laughter and whistles and curses filled the air. A few plebian jokes echoed: "Hey there! Hey there! . . . And what do you want, to win the race? . . . Take this, duchess! Take this, dragoon! Brr!"

And tremendous laughter accompanied those shouts.

A few windows opened, and some drowsy and curious faces looked out of them and asked, "What is it? Did some old fool get married?"

Then they would follow to where the shouts were directed; they would see, they would guess, be amazed, take pleasure in the sight, and laugh. Little by little everyone in the vicolo was awakening; those ruffians became more boisterous as the number of spectators grew, and their allusions became clearer, bolder, more audacious. The entire neighborhood was waking up to witness that shameful and craven denigration.

Emanuele was happy; he was looking at the windows, looking at that strange rowdy crowd, and from time to time he would send his servant to incite them more and more, and to those incitements, in order to spur them on, he would add handfuls of bronze coins. A few carriages that were coming from a soiree would stop; some faces would peer out, watch and marvel. Some portantine would also stop.

Some cavalieri would emerge, notice Emanuele, and wonder what was going on.

"Who knows!" Emanuele would reply, playing dumb. "I don't know. It seems like they are upset with the duchess."

"Donna Gabriella?"

"So it seems. . . . It's disgraceful, don't you think?"

"Disgraceful, indeed! . . . But why?"

"Who knows anything about it?"

But however disgraceful, the ruckus was entertaining, and after that observation, everyone would go on their way; Emanuele would pretend to leave, but then he would go back to enjoy the show. But then, suddenly, while the mob in the vicolo was knocking those stones together and laughing scornfully, the door opened and a man wielding an unsheathed sword flung himself at them, raining down a veritable tempest of blows with the flat part of his blade; it was so sudden, unexpected, and furious that all those people, turning their laughter into cries of terror, fled and dispersed without even bothering to see where the blows were coming from.

Blasco chased them, striking them on all sides. "Rascals! . . . Cowards!"

Two of those formidable blows struck Emanuele's servant, who, not so much out of sheer fear but from the worry of being recognized, drew back, creeping along the wall. Blasco noticed him, but as he was striking him, he recognized that the man was not dressed in rags like that rabble was, and in the dark he could make out that he was wearing livery. He jumped on top of him and grabbed him by the neck. The servant tried to free himself, thrust his hand in his pocket, and drew it out armed with a dagger, but Blasco was quick to grasp his wrist and twist it so violently that the servant let out a howl of pain and prostrated himself on the ground, pleading, "Ah! . . . You are breaking my bone, signore!"

Emanuele was livid. He would have liked to come to the aid of his servant, since abandoning him to Blasco's revenge seemed to him like a cowardly act, but he didn't want to be recognized; nevertheless, spiteful envy, jealousy, shame, an entire wave of emotions surged in him and, overcoming any reluctance, he moved closer, as if drawn by those cries, and with an expression of surprise, he asked, "What is it? What happened to you? Where are you?"

He found himself in front of his servant, who was moaning on the ground with his wrist in the grip of Blasco, who was perhaps about to teach him a lesson. But upon recognizing the voice of Emanuele, he stopped.

"Emanuele!" he shouted, looking at his brother.

Emanuele, who was choosing to pretend that he didn't know anything and didn't recognize him, was disconcerted. He stammered, "You?" But, resuming his arrogant tone, he added, "Leave my servant alone! . . . I haven't given you permission to beat my servants."

"Ah! Is he one of your servants? Goodness, Your Excellency, I never would have imagined that you recruited servants from among the riffraff of the market! He is your servant? Well, since you don't teach them good manners, I will do it. Take this, lout, and go get yourself hanged somewhere else!"

And to those words he added such a violent kick in the back that the unfortunate soul tumbled five steps away, unable to get up again.

Emanuele was beside himself with rage; he unsheathed his sword, shouting, "Ah! This is too much!"

He rushed at Blasco, who, with a lightning-fast movement and a skillful blow, disarmed him, making his sword drop away. Taking him by the arms before he had time to recover from the surprise, lifting him up high like a plaything, and shaking him with every word, he said to him in a voice tinged with anger, "Thank your saint that you were born of the same father, because I would have slit your throat like a rabid dog, but I am not Cain, or even Abel; meanwhile, since I now understand the utter cowardice of your doings, and because I am ashamed on your behalf, you are going to ask for forgiveness—on your knees—for having dishonored the name of your father."

And, still holding him up high by the arms, shaking him violently, he carried him away, went through the entrance, climbed the stairs, crossed the halls amid the astonished servants, and after entering the bedroom where Donna Gabriella was crying with pain, shame, and anger, he threw Emanuele down at her feet, saying, "Donna Gabriella, the Duke of Motta, my brother, begs me to implore you to forgive him."

She raised her frightened and astonished eyes, looked at Blasco, looked at Emanuele, and covered her face in her hands. On the ground, Emanuele was livid, like a corpse, showing no sign of life.

Meanwhile, the curious and still astonished servants had crowded the doorway, and someone, noticing the duchess's clothing and the disarray of the bed, was smiling maliciously. But Blasco, holding his hand out to Donna Gabriella, looked everyone in the face and said with a noble sense of pride, "Listen to me well, all of you; the duchess has given the honor of granting me her hand. From this night forward I am your lord. . . . Take away the young duke and show him every consideration; and close the doors."

Two footmen rushed in and lifted Emanuele; they carried him away, closing the door to the room, with a whispering full of astonishment, while Donna Gabriella, with her radiant and still tearful face, clasping her hands, stammered, "What did you say?"

"What I had to. . . . Could I possibly have left your reputation to the gossip of others? Can I leave you defenseless?"

She flew into one of those wild outbursts of gratitude, love, and passion; she threw herself at Blasco's feet, took his hand, and kissed it as if in a state of delirium while murmuring, "Thank you! . . . Thank you!"

But suddenly her face darkened; she realized that Blasco wasn't responding to that delirium and that he seemed to be struck by a grave and sad thought, and so her enthusiasm cooled. An icy wave coursed through her body; at first she rose timidly, stepping back toward a chair, but then a thought came to her and her eyes flashed with a sullen gleam.

"Why," she asked, with an indescribable anguish in her voice, "Why do you deceive me?"

These words startled Blasco; he looked at her and, seeing her so upset, moved closer and said, "Who is deceiving you? . . . Do you mean me?"

"Yes . . . you . . . you said something in front of the servants . . . that is not possible. It was a lie, in order to save me . . . you said it yourself . . . but it is a deception."

"Oh, no, don't think that, Gabriella."

"Yes, yes, it is a deception. . . . I feel it. You cannot and must not marry me. . . . I know why. . . . It's a horrible thing. . . . Why? Why?"

She wrung her hands in sorrow.

"Gabriella! Gabriella!" Blasco said with boundless compassion. "You are wrong . . . it's not what you think."

But she shook her head, abandoning herself to the delirium of pain and jealousy that was seizing her.

"I am not mistaken. I know myself. . . . I am not as I should be in order to come to you, to be able to believe that you are all mine, to believe that your words, so solemn, are dictated by love and not by generosity."

Her voice became bitter and tremulous.

"No, I don't want your generosity! . . . What does it matter to me? It is your heart that I want . . . it is your heart that I don't have . . . it is elsewhere!"

"No, Gabriella!"

"It is elsewhere, I tell you! . . . I feel it. She is pure, and still a young girl, and I have a past. . . . I am a woman who everyone accuses of being frivolous . . . and it's true. . . . I have been frivolous, and you know it! . . . You take me, you intoxicate me with your kisses, but your heart . . . your life are not with me! No! No!"

Blasco felt enormous compassion for that poor woman whose passion was perhaps rendering her almost too unfair toward herself; he took her hands, drew her close to him, murmuring tender words in her ear. "Oh, Gabriella, why do you torment yourself? But who am I, a poor bastard without a future, without a fortune, to aspire to your hand? . . . Perhaps I have presumed too much, perhaps I have dared too much; in that moment I could think of nothing else to explain my presence here . . . this is the truth. . . . A minute ago I was thinking about that scoundrel Emanuele. . . . I was thinking about very sad things, Gabriella . . . that were wrenching my soul. Why do you want to tear your heart up with ghosts that are now gone and scattered? . . . Do not poison this night. Don't you see that they threaten our joy? . . . You wanted me with you, you opened your arms to me, why do you now close them? . . . Don't you still want me, then?"

Donna Gabriella looked at him deeply and with intense passion, then suddenly she opened her arms and with a sob said, "Come!"

Their lips sought each other's again, but it seemed that something chilly, something immovable, had come between them.

CHAPTER 8

In the morning, after breakfast, Blasco went to see Coriolano; he was so pale and solemn that it stopped his friend from voicing the joke that instinctively rose to his lips.

"What is going on with you? You look like you've been to a funeral!"

"My friend, I challenge you to find a man that fate treats as treacherously as me!"

"Then you fell into the snares of the law?"

"That's not what I'm complaining about. I'm still grateful to Donna Gabriella, and I feel I still have toward her that esteem and devotion that I have always had for her!"

"Here is one thing that doesn't surprise me but that already says a lot, mind you, as long as you don't lose for the duchess the same respect that you have had for all the beautiful ladies. So, is it serious this time?"

"Yes, I rather confess that I had been mistaken in my judgment of the duchess. Her love for me today is the same as it was five years ago, deep and unchanged. . . . She has touched me."

"She has conquered you!"

"Perhaps. What does it matter? Mine is one of those defeats that displease no one."

"Do you love her? Tell me the truth."

"I don't know. In some moments, yes, I think I love her deeply, with tenderness; at other times, no, or rather, I feel something that weighs on me like a type of dismay. . . . But this is not what makes me look like I've been to a funeral, as you say, nor do I blame fate for this."

"Well, then, what is happening to you?"

Blasco told him about everything that had taken place during the night, including the violent scene with Emanuele. The tone of his voice reflected the bitterness that was filling his heart.

"Do you understand, my friend? . . . And he's my brother and I can't just lift him off his feet and smash his head against the wall! Otherwise, I wouldn't owe him anything, and perhaps doing away with him would be no different from purging society of a reptile that, in the end, would become poisonous. . . . It would also be the liberation of a poor creature that I myself—I who had and still have a true affection for her—destined to be with him! And meanwhile, he is an Albamonte, and he is the head of the household, its recognized head!"

Coriolano, who had listened to this story with great amazement, didn't know what to say; a slight flaring of his nostrils and knitting of his brow were the only clues to his disgust and his anger.

After a while he asked, "What do you want me to do?"

"Nothing."

"Emanuele doesn't seem to me to be the type to give up; he will think about taking revenge."

"I know, I'm expecting it."

"And not only against you."

"I know; this worries me even more, because, as you are aware, I am forced to leave."

"If this is the case, it goes without saying that you don't have to worry: Donna Gabriella will be guarded and protected."

"Thank you, Coriolano; you are taking a weight off my mind. . . . Oh, you can't believe how I suffered during the night and how that incident made my blood run cold."

"I believe it, but what can you do about it? By now you are accustomed to twists of fate, and you should expect all kinds of them. You are a bit of a philosopher, my friend. And rather than dwelling on what has already happened, think about what must still happen. I say *must*, because it seems that you are forgetting that you still have a matter to settle with the Count of Gisia."

"Well! That is true!"

"Behind whom, as you can imagine, there is an old acquaintance of yours: the Prince of Iraci."

"I thought so. Well, did you come to an agreement?"

"Fully."

"So, we will duel?"

"After the war ends."

"What? After the war?"

"But of course, goodness! Do you expect me to go through the trouble of taking a soldier like you away from His Catholic Majesty? It would be a mistake, and the count's seconds, who are very loyal subjects, agree with me that it is right and proper to postpone the duel."

"But why have you done this?"

"Why? Well . . . to have a little fun behind the backs of those lords. When I see such comical examples of oppressors and bullies, I feel a certain satisfaction in making fun of them. Let it go; anyway, after what you have done, they will not think that you lack any spirit. We'll let them lie, and when it's time, we'll wake them up and give them a good spanking, and that will be it. Meanwhile, you have one less thing to worry about. Do you mind?"

"Whatever you do, I have no complaints. Perhaps I would have liked to settle things quickly. . . . And then, imagine that a bullet sends me to kingdom come; I would leave with an unpaid debt to that amiable count."

"But in that case, which I do not wish for and that I do not foresee, I will take care of paying off those lords; don't worry about it. Will you dine with me today?"

"No, thank you. I can't."

"I understand. A wedding feast!"

"Perhaps it is not just a joke, Coriolano."

"What? What are you saying?"

"I am saying what I haven't yet told you. That after what happened last night, I felt almost driven by a mountain of emotions toward a solemn promise. Only that, for my own dignity, I will not give her the wedding ring unless I have at least one company of soldiers under my command."

"Goodness! Goodness! So the matter is more serious than I thought. . . . But if you have thought, as a good gentleman, to take this step, I will not blame you, and I instead congratulate you. Go, then, I wouldn't want to incur the wrath of the duchess."

* * *

After putting his uniform back on and leaving Coriolano, he went to his quarters and, since he had to walk along the Cassaro, he passed in front of the Prince of Geraci's palazzo, at whose entrance two or three servants were talking excitedly. He noticed that there was an unusual movement about, as if due to something extraordinary, and he couldn't prevent his curiosity from getting the better of him. But he thought that if he addressed the servants, it would appear as if he wanted to provoke them.

At that point, a leather-covered portantina came out of the palazzo, carried by porters from the piazza, that looked like it must belong to a doctor.

He drew closer and politely asked the old doctor if someone in the palazzo was sick.

"The young prince. . . . An attack of bile."

"Is it serious?"

"Eh!"

That "eh" had such a clear meaning that Blasco thanked the doctor and left, with his expression a little darkened.

"It was his own doing," he thought. "Why should I make an effort at this point?"

He kept this news from Donna Gabriella and he probably would have said nothing about it anyway, since the duchess that day was so gloriously beautiful and enchanting that he, upon entering, couldn't help but exclaim with heartfelt emotion, "How beautiful you are!"

Oh, yes; even she had realized it while standing in front of the dressing table. Her face had a soft pearl-colored pallor, with very slight pinkish and pale blue touches, and her eyes, in the blue that surrounded them, had a moist languor, full of flashes, of desires, of promises. And in her whole presentation there was something like a certain enchanting abandonment, full of a serene and profound joy. And that morning she had armed herself with all her seductions, choosing a mauve silk dress full of lace and veils, which, pinned to the wide neckline, concealed as if in a white and light cloud the top of her white bosom, on which some more indiscreet veins marked lines that were barely visible. She had not put any jewelry around her neck; she had left it bare, displaying the beauty of her fleshly contours. In total there was such a harmony of colors and shapes and in her somewhat slow movement a grace full of desires, and in her eyes and in her smile such invincible charms, that Blasco felt their sway down to the intimate depths of his soul, and after that exclamation he couldn't restrain himself from kissing Donna Gabriella's hand with intense passion.

"Do I please you?" she asked him in an ingratiating and quivering voice full of happiness.

His kisses answered for him.

"Oh, you don't know," Donna Gabriella said while they were dining, facing each other, smiling at each other and at times holding hands, "you don't know how your love transforms me. I feel good, willing to have compassion for everyone, even for those who have hurt me; I almost feel a desire to embrace everyone, to bestow on each person a part of the joy that fills me. . . . So, is it happiness that disposes our souls to kindness? . . . And remembering the past . . . an unpleasant past, it seems to me almost impossible that at times I could have been bad. . . . How happy I am! . . . And it was you who performed this miracle . . . you . . . my one, my only great love! . . . Don't you believe that you are my one and only love?"

"Yes, yes, I believe it," Blasco answered, intoxicated.

He forgot everything in front of that breathtaking figure of a woman who seemed created by love: Violante, Emanuele, the war, everything. He found himself on the threshold of a life where the hands of rapture were interweaving joys into the fabric of his dreams, a life still new to him, even though he had reached the age of thirty. And, in a moment of supreme joy, he said, "My entire life, Gabriella, is not enough to reward you for these moments."

But a few hours later drums were heard on the streets, beating the general call to assemble. Blasco got up.

"Whatever is this?" Donna Gabriella asked, turning pale.

"Don't you hear it? The call to assemble. We have to part."

"So soon. . . . Why?"

"Unfortunately, this evening my squadron is leaving for Termini."

"You're leaving? . . . You. . . . But no, it can't be! I don't want you to go! . . . You must stay with me."

"I can't. . . . I am a soldier!"

"But I'll go to the captain myself, to the colonel. . . . I will speak to the general myself. . . . Who is it? Lucchesi? Montemar? . . . I will say that you are sick. I don't want you to leave, do you understand? . . . I found you, I got you back, and you want me to lose you again? Now?"

"Of course not, Gabriella, you aren't losing me. . . . After all, I'm not going far; it doesn't take more than four hours to return from Termini, and I will come back. . . . I will come. But I must leave. Listen to me, I made a solemn promise to you. . . . I must keep it. . . . But I also have my pride. . . . I have no title, I have no name. . . . I am an unknown soldier! Allow me to earn my captain's sash."

"What do I care? What do I care about all that? I love you! . . . And aren't you an Albamonte? What do I care about the rest? No, no. . . . Don't leave, I beg you! I beseech you. . . . I will die from it!"

Sobbing, she fastened her arms around his neck. Blasco was suffering but resisted.

He asked her, "If I were a coward, would you think me worthy of you?"

She looked at him, bewildered, not knowing how to respond.

"You see?" he said. "And yet you want to have me look like a coward to everyone, and to be shamed and accused of being a deserter."

"But what if I lose you! What if I lose you!" she said, sobbing.

"Don't be afraid. . . . You well know that bullets have yet to learn the way to strike me. . . . And then, surrounded by the protection of your love, I feel invulnerable."

Donna Gabriella tried a little longer to hold Blasco back, but he, freeing himself gently from the tender trap that encircled him, after kissing her for a long time and giving her courage, left.

Before they parted, the duchess asked him, "At least let me say goodbye from afar when you leave. I will wait for you along the road . . . at the Ponte dell'Ammiraglio, in my carriage."

As soon as Blasco had left, she dropped onto a chair, sobbing violently, and this outburst of sorrow only abated toward evening, when, as the hour of departure was approaching, she called for her carriage and went to wait for the passage of the dragoons on their way to Termini. She saw Blasco and, stretching her hand outside the curtains, waved goodbye to him. Instead, he went to the carriage and kissed that hand.

"Whatever you may need during my absence," he said, "you can count on my only and faithful friend."

"The Cavaliere della Floresta?"

"Yes, Coriolano."

The squadron moved forward in a disorderly fashion, followed by carts and curious onlookers; beneath the iron-shod hooves and the wheels of the carts, the bridge resounded thunderously. Donna Gabriella was looking with curiosity and even with a certain sense of regret at that hodgepodge of people, who no longer had anything in common with the cavalry of past centuries that she had heard stories about. They wore tattered uniforms, adapted as well as possible; they had sunburnt faces, rapacious and brigandish; any appearance of a gentleman was rare, except among the officers.

Her heart ached seeing Blasco in the middle of those people, and she thought it would be necessary to pull him out. . . . Who in fact was more worthy than him to command that squadron? Wasn't he an Albamonte? Oh! He should have been the one to assume the ducal crown, which instead adorned the head of Emanuele!

She followed the squadron with her eyes until, due to its distance and the darkness, she lost sight of it, other than from the dust that it raised; only then was she again lost in thought and aching, ruminating about some thoughts that had come to her.

The Ave Maria sounded, and she gave the order to go home; she issued strict orders to her servants that she would receive no one, not even her friends, neither that day nor the following days, except for the people she explicitly would name herself. She shut herself in her bedroom, which still seemed full of sweet words and the scent of her love.

She spent those days in an even stricter solitude, even forbidding herself from going to the Marina to take in a bit of fresh air; she would only go out in order to attend early mass in the nearby Church of San Domenico. Her solitude was brightened by the letters that came to her from the camp in Termini, in which Blasco would inform her about what was happening; she would read them several times, moved and cheered by the tender words in which Blasco poured out his heart, and it truly seemed to her that she was being reborn and starting a new life.

CHAPTER 9

After three or four days, Emanuele, no longer seriously ill and on the road to recovery, left the house in a carriage with its curtains drawn, in a sullen and grim frame of mind and with a heart full of a desire for revenge. No one could get him to say what had happened to him; he wasn't wounded, had no bruises, and there was no trace of violence except for his clothes in disarray. His servant, after getting up again, not seeing him and believing that he was gone, had rushed to the palazzo, but, upon finding out that his master hadn't been home, he had gone back with some other servants and they had found him unconscious in front of the steps of San Domenico, among a few of those vagabonds, who, having woken up, were busy stripping him of whatever he had. They arrived just in time to stop who knows what other devilry, and they carried Emanuele to the palazzo, which was turned upside down over that return that was anything but ordinary or imaginable.

Doctors came rushing, herbalists were awakened, all kinds of remedies were used. Emanuele came to, but he was assailed by violent convulsions that lasted almost the entire night.

The Prince of Geraci, his grandfather, was distressed by it; when questioned, the servant made his excuses by saying that he knew nothing. His master had sent him away, and when he didn't see him return he had become worried and had gone to look for him.

"Perhaps," he said, "he was attacked by thieves."

But his explanation didn't convince the prince, especially since there was something fishy and contrived about Emanuele's silence; it was as if an emotion, a desire, compelled him to keep a secret. Except that some rumors began to spread: two trickles of gossip. One circulated with a great deal of malice and many embellishments about the indecent ruckus that had taken place that night under Donna Gabriella's window, and it is understandable that, lending itself to the most audacious slander, the little story spread rapidly through the salons, provoking laughter and salacious comments, especially among those who, in vain, had tried to conquer that unguarded fortress. No one knew the identity of the victorious adventurer who triumphed over the ban that the beautiful lady had imposed on herself, or of the envious, cruel, and disappointed lover who had arranged for that racket.

The other trickle of gossip, emerging, as can be easily understood, from the mouths of Donna Gabriella's servants, spread the news about what had befallen the young Duke of Motta, who had been forced, on his knees, to beg for the duchess's forgiveness; and due to that metamorphosis that transforms true facts into legend, what had been a promise had become a fact, and it was said that Donna Gabriella had secretly gotten married to a cavaliere whose name was Don Blasco Albamonte. The change, or in this case, the addition, was beneficial to the lady, removing every reason for blame and replacing it with a noble and inexplicable wonder.

The two trickles of gossip merged; the two little tales complemented each other and explained each other in turn. Emanuele found that he was at once the target of condemnation and of mockery, which filled him with shame and anger. The extent of it reached its peak when his grandfather, the old prince, saddened by the news, reproached Emanuele and threatened to shut him in a convent and keep him there until the time of his marriage.

"No one of our family—no one—has ever committed such a villainous act, and your father, Don Emanuele, was a true and perfect gentleman. . . . Shame on you! I am not only saying that such vile acts should not be carried out against a lady, but not even against a poor little girl of the lower classes! . . . And if it is true, and I want to hope that it really is, that Don Blasco took you upstairs and forced you to ask for forgiveness, he did very well indeed, by God! And when he returns from the war I will go visit him and pay him a compliment. . . . Yes, yes, me, the Prince of Geraci. . . . That bastard is much more of a gentleman than you, and he did well to teach you a lesson. Well deserved, by God! Well deserved!"

The scolding embittered Emanuele's soul, increasing his hatred and his desire for revenge. Ah, he would have to exact such a spectacular revenge on that bastard and on that lady that the affront would be immediately forgotten. For several days he avoided meeting his friends; he would go out in his carriage or on horseback, but he would travel outside the city gates, taking one of the roads that led to the villages or hamlets that were already appearing on the outskirts of the city. At home, he would spend long hours with his fencing master, who was renowned in Palermo for certain of his special modes of attack.

One evening toward the end of August, while traveling in a portantina outside Porta Nuova, just past the Palazzo della Ginestra, he found himself greeted respectfully by a man who didn't seem entirely unknown to him.

It was Matteo Lo Vecchio.

He barely responded to the greeting and moved on, but the birro, undaunted, approached him at the window, saying, "Your Illustrious Lordship, forgive me if I dare to approach . . . but it is to serve Your Lordship. They don't want to let me enter the palazzo . . . and yet, if I had been able to offer you my servitude, what happened to Your Illustrious Lordship would not have happened. . . . Perhaps Your Lordship no longer remembers me."

Emanuele frowned and was about to chase him away, but the last words jogged his memory and, looking at the birro with an annoyed scowl, he said, "What do you want?"

"Do you remember, Your Illustrious Lordship, that I, due to the obligation that I feel toward your noble house, and due to the servitude I had toward the illustrious Signor Don Raimondo—a good memory—hastened to reveal to you that someone, a soldier in the dragoons—"

"Yes, yes! I remember well. What do you want now?"

"I would have many things to tell you. . . . I could give Your Lordship information about him and . . . about her. . . . And then. . . . Does Your Illustrious Lordship know that I am a corporal in the algozini? Haven't you ever heard of Matteo Lo Vecchio?"

"Ah! . . . It's you? . . . But you are excommunicated!"

"No, Your Excellency. I have been absolved by the vicario generale. You may ask him. This morning, for example, I went to confession. . . . You see, there is no danger in receiving me."

Emanuele's cheeks had reddened and after a moment of silence, he asked, "So you were saying?"

"That I am completely at Your Lordship's service. . . . But these are not things to be said on the street."

"Very well, come this evening at seven o'clock. I will give the order to let you enter."

"At seven o'clock I will be at your service. I kiss your hands."

Matteo Lo Vecchio went back the same way he had come and reentered the city. Ever since he had learned that Blasco was free, he had been consumed by the impotent rage of avenging himself; he could have fired a shot from a carbine at him at night, but he didn't want to take the risk, fearing that he might miss and thus expose himself to a certain danger, since he had a kind of superstitious belief that Blasco was invulnerable. Meanwhile, he was following him, tailing him, and spying on him in order to study his habits and his schedule and determine his chances of striking him with certainty and with impunity.

Thus he had watched the scene unfold between Blasco and Emanuele's friends; he had then followed him to Coriolano's house, had followed him to the Palazzo Butera. Then he had learned about what had taken place between him and Emanuele on account of Donna Gabriella, and it pleased him, having intuited in this the *ubi consistam*,[1] the point of support for the leverage that he would use to get rid of his hated enemy.

"So, Emanuele is in love," he thought. "What could turn a man into a beast more than love?"

---

1 From Archimedes: "Give me a fulcrum and I will raise the world."

He had to proceed on this basis. Now Blasco had left for war and Donna Gabriella was alone; he would have to take advantage of that situation. He formulated his own diabolical plan, one that would give Emanuele a victory to dig the abyss into which Blasco would disappear forever. However, it would be necessary to lure Donna Gabriella into an ambush.

* * *

In those days news would arrive frequently about the siege of the Castello di Termini, which was continuing without any certain outcome due to the valiant resistance of the Savoy garrison that benefited greatly from the impregnability of the fortress.

The garrison, amid the commotion in the city, had withdrawn and barricaded itself in the Castello, compelling the citizens to supply it with whatever it needed; and having welcomed with cannon fire the first dragoon companies that had attempted to occupy the city, it had forced them to steer clear and make camp a mile and a half from the walls, in a place then called Impalistrato. But after the other militias arrived and the artillery and mortars were unloaded, the camp was set up at the Convent of the Capuchins and they began to position the batteries: the mortars at the slaughterhouse, the cannons at Porta Felice. From the Castello, the Savoy were impeding the construction with calibrated fire, and a covered road had to be urgently built in order to protect the batteries. Blasco was assigned with a squad of dragoons to harass the Savoy so that time could be gained for the road to be built.

Since these men, defended by the site itself, could, without danger to themselves, harass the Spaniards who were below, Blasco thought to divert their attention by attacking and threatening them from another position. After going around the southern hills and entering the upper part of the city along the walls between Porta Girgenti and Porta Palermo, he plunged himself among the houses and came out into Piazza del Duomo, from where he scattered his men and with heavy rifle fire began to cause chaos among the troops stationed on the bastions.

That sudden attack terrified the citizens, already frightened by the frequent explosions of grenades and bombs; a widespread stampede followed, which allowed Blasco to carry out an even more audacious action.

He pushed forward into the open, on horseback and alone, holding a rifle, following the line in a spectacular act of provocation, which filled the Savoy themselves with astonishment.

A fiery repetition of shots took aim at him from all sides; he seemed to be laughing at the attack. Taking off his hat, he saluted the whistling of the bullets, shouting, "Savoyards! . . . Come out of your cage, by God!"

His fellow soldiers called out to him, "Get out of the line of fire! . . . Come under cover!"

Then two, three, five dragoons, ashamed of leaving him alone, spurred their horses next to him and they all started galloping under the hail of gunfire, shooting and shouting in a pointless heroic madness. Two fell. Blasco was hit by two bullets. One grazed his head above the ear, taking off a lock of hair; the other broke the buckle of his baldric, to which his cartridge box was attached, and wounded him above the breastbone, but not seriously.

"It's nothing!" he shouted. "Savoyards, your bullets are made of ricotta!"

But the other dragoons took the reins of his horse and forced him to find cover.

On August 29 the batteries began to operate; it was a dense combat of bombs and grenades on both sides, all the more admirable since the Savoy numbered no more than three hundred, while the besieging forces were more than ten times greater.

Blasco, who, although wounded, hadn't wanted to abandon the siege operations, was now calling for and carrying out the riskiest undertakings; amid the smoldering rubble of the Castello and the trench he had set out to attain either his captain's sash or his death. He was waiting for the breach to open in order to go first on the assault and was feverishly following the collapse of the Castello's curtain wall, under the terrifying rounds of the Spanish mortars.

* * *

This news reached Palermo. Matteo Lo Vecchio, who had been spying on Donna Gabriella's house for a few days, had noticed a carter who would come every two days, and he had gathered that he must be some messenger sent by Blasco. He took note of him and kept on the lookout for him; calculating the day when the carter was due to return, he waited for him at the corner of Via Materassai and, as soon as he saw him, made him stop. "Excuse me . . . you are coming from Termini, isn't that so?"

"From Termini, yes, signore."

"Were you sent by Don Blasco Albamonte, a Numancia dragoon?"

"Exactly . . . how does you Your Lordship know that?"

"Excellent! I am waiting here especially for you! . . . You are bringing a letter to my mistress, the duchess—"

"Ah . . . !"

"I am the house steward. . . . The duchess—one can say that I saw her being born, because I was in the service of her father—called upon me an hour ago and said, 'Cosimo, do me a favor'—so she says, 'a favor' due to her kindness!—'I have to visit my brother, the marchese, and I cannot wait. A letter from Don Blasco should arrive today; wait for the carter and have him give you the letter. I will take care of sending him a reply today.' And here I am. I have already seen you come three times . . ."

The carter didn't suspect anything; Matteo Lo Vecchio had such an honest face, and then he knew everything so well that it wasn't possible not to believe him.

He didn't hesitate to hand the letter over to him. Matteo Lo Vecchio wrapped it in a handkerchief and put it in his pocket.

"Come for a drink," he said, leading him toward Piazza San Giacomo La Marina, where some taverns were located. An hour later the carter, half-drunk, was straddling his mule again, on his way to the fondaco, where Matteo Lo Vecchio had promised to bring him the reply.

As soon as he was alone, the birro drew the letter out of his pocket and was on the verge of breaking the seal when he thought better of it, placed it back in his pocket, and hurried toward the Palazzo Geraci.

Emanuele let him enter immediately.

"What is it?"

"I already have my plan! . . . Would Your Illustrious Lordship like to have one of the letters that Don Blasco sends to the duchess?"

"A letter?" he said. "How . . . where did you . . . ?"

"I got it due to the kindness of the carter who is the go-between. At this moment Your Excellency has before him the humble house steward of the duchess, and the confidant of her secrets."

Trembling, Emanuele took the letter that the birro was holding out to him, but at the sight of the intact seal, he stopped, hesitant to break it.

"Your Lordship, open it; what the heck! This letter must be read . . . it serves my plan."

"What plan?"

Matteo Lo Vecchio seemed annoyed. "In short," he said, "does Your Lordship want the duchess in his power? If you so desire, leave it to me, and tomorrow the duchess will be in your arms."

His face turned bright red again, and his nostrils flared in a catlike manner.

"Give it to me. I have no qualms, and then no one can say that Your Lordship broke the seals."

He took the letter, opened it, and handed it to Emanuele, saying, "Your Lordship, read."

As soon as he gave it a look, the young man's face darkened, and he became ferocious; the letter began with the vocatives used at that time: "*Dear breath of my heart,*" and the signature said precisely, "*Your slave who sighs for you —Blasco.*"

He scanned it quickly with a veiled rage, as if he had been a betrayed husband or lover, and with a spiteful envy and ravenous desire; when he had finished reading it, he asked in a broken voice, "Well, what do you intend to do now?"

"Can't you guess? Signor Blasco was slightly wounded; he doesn't say so in the letter, but I learned it from the carter. Now then, what harm is there if we assume that he is gravely injured?"

"And then?"

"And then? . . . The wound is serious, he is alone. . . . Of course he will express his wish to have the duchess by his side, who, frightened upon hearing the news, will not think twice about packing her trunks and departing with her litter for Termini. . . . The roads aren't safe, especially in Portella, above San Nicola . . . and . . ."

Emanuele's eyes gleamed; more than the words, the insinuations and the expressions of the birro's eyes and lips completely revealed the highly imaginative plan.

"Goodness!" he exclaimed with joy. "You are a talented rascal! . . . Then let's write this letter. . . . But who will deliver it?"

"That's my job. . . . Can they recognize your handwriting?"

"No."

"So then Your Lordship should write; imagine yourself as a fellow soldier or chaplain of the squadrons. . . . Write those words. . . . If Your Lordship permits me, I will dictate the letter to you."

Emanuele had become infatuated with this dirty trick, in which he could only see his revenge and his vengeance; he took a sheet of paper and, under the direction of the birro, who was keeping an eye on Blasco's letter, he wrote:

Dear breath of my heart,

Don't be frightened, my darling, if this letter is written by another hand; I had an accident of war, a wound that prevents me from using my hand. Don't be frightened, my love, it's not very serious; although it forces me to stay in bed. . . . Your last letter, so full of tenderness, enchanted me, and it took away the pains from my wound. I imagine the effect that your white hands would have on me if they were lovingly placed over it! . . . As for what you write to me, do not doubt me: I yearn for the end of this campaign so I can spend the rest of my life at your knees, entirely for you. I thank you for the handkerchief and sash, which I tied at my hips like a talisman.

I kiss your hands with all my love, and I am
your slave who sighs for you.

From Termini, on this August 1, 1718.
Blasco

"Well done!" the birro exclaimed, praising himself. "Now we must fold it and seal it. Let's look at the seal. To be fair, Your Lordship has better eyesight than me."

Emanuele looked and said, "It's not a coat of arms. I think it's the impression of the butt of a pistol . . . or of a metal button."

Matteo also looked at it carefully, then he took out a short pistol from a pocket of his breeches and compared the metal button that adorned the stock with the wax imprint.

"It seems to me that it's a button; it's not the same as this but it's similar and can pass for it. So let's fold the letter and seal it."

When everything was done, the birro kept the letter and said to Emanuele, "Your Lordship, get a half dozen determined men ready for tomorrow. . . . I will return this evening . . . with the duchess's reply."

He went away, leaving Emanuele dumbfounded by what he had seen, heard, and done, and above all by that man who was so clever, so ingenious, so villainous, prolific with tricks and energetic, whose interest he didn't yet know what to attribute to.

A half hour later Donna Gabriella received the letter, which filled her with fear. She wanted to see the villager who had brought it and was surprised that it wasn't the usual carter. What could this new development mean? The villager immediately explained to her that his comrade Cosimo had felt sick, perhaps a case of sunstroke, and he had had to dismount at the fondaco in order to lie down; he had called for him, who was from the same village, and had asked him to take the letter and collect the reply, which he, Cosimo, would take to the gentleman.

His answer was so obvious that it couldn't arouse any suspicion. Donna Gabriella sat down at her writing desk and with a hand that trembled, like her shaken heart, she wrote two or three lines, folded the paper, sealed it, and handed it to the villager, giving him a nice two-tarì coin, saying, "Take this letter at once to your comrade Cosimo and tell him to leave immediately; I will give him a good reward tomorrow, as soon as I know that he has promptly carried out my order."

She was overcome by a great anxiety, suspecting that the wound was much more serious than what Blasco was trying hard to make her believe. She would have wanted to leave at once, rush to the camp, take the dear wounded man with her, safeguard him with her care, with her love, and she was getting carried away in her imagined mission as a gentle nurse, picturing in her mind a series of tender and moving scenes. Ah! How long that night would be! She ordered that her travel litter be ready at dawn and had her brother provide her with two armed servants on horseback that could go with her to Bagheria—so she said, in order to divert her relatives—where she was planning to stay for fifteen days in her little villa.

Dawn was still far off, and Donna Gabriella was impatiently counting the hours. She wondered where comrade Cosimo might have gotten to by that time, or whether he had arrived, and what effect her brief and feverish letter might be having. What was Blasco doing? Who was looking after him? How serious were his wounds? Oh God! And the day seemed to go on forever! How long those summer days were! She was delirious the entire night, passing from one vision to another, making and unmaking plans, and during moments when she would be overcome by sleep, she would close her eyes and dream of Blasco, sometimes dying, other times on horseback at the head of a squadron, dressed as a general, and sometimes embraced by her. And she was seized by palpitations and frightful and tormenting visions.

Finally, daybreak brightened the sky. She heard a loud shaking of harness bells under her windows, a sign that her litter was waiting and that the mules were growing restless. She dressed quickly, wrapped herself in a black silk mantilla that covered her entire body, and went downstairs. The litter bearers and two servants on horseback were waiting, as she had wished. With assistance, she climbed inside the litter, and at her signal it moved ahead with a great loud jingling of harness bells, which resounded in the silent piazzetta.

It was a beautiful day, and the first rays of the sun were shining in the clear blue sky. The litter crossed Via Materassai, Via della Loggia, and Via Cintorinai and set off for Porta Termini, and amid the awakening of the city, they encountered only a few citizens, carts, and teams of mules.

The journey proceeded without incident until Bagheria; there they made a brief stop in front of an osteria, where the litter bearers had a simple country breakfast, while Donna Gabriella—to whom that stop seemed too long—stomped her feet on the bottom of the litter, urging them to get moving.

They resumed their journey. Now the road, or rather the rural path, climbed over the hills in a deserted countryside, where patches of prickly pears and fruit trees alternated, among boulders that seemed to have fallen from the top of the mountains. The stark solitude instilled a sense of dread.

Suddenly the litter bearers stopped.

Donna Gabriella stuck her head out to ask why they weren't moving but then became alarmed when she saw at the sides of the narrow path, with rifles leveled, some men whose faces were covered by handkerchiefs.

Evidently she had fallen into an ambush of thieves. She thought she was doomed, not for fear of being robbed but of something much worse happening to her.

The two servants who were accompanying her, overwhelmed in number, had had to give up their weapons so as not to be pointlessly killed. She was therefore at the full mercy of the bandits, who, without abandoning their threatening stance, had forced the litter bearers and the servants to throw their weapons to the ground and to get down on their knees in one group.

Then a masked man emerged from a thick bush, approached the litter, opened the door, and said in a voice that betrayed his emotion, "Do not be afraid, signora, since not a hair on your head will be touched. We only ask that you follow us."

Donna Gabriella clasped her hands in an act of prayer; her presence of mind was fading at the thought of not being able to complete her journey.

"Take whatever you want, I promise to send you whatever you ask for, but, I beg you, let me go!"

The masked man let out a roaring laugh. "Ha! Ha! Ha! Then you think we are highway robbers? Thanks for the honor! It's not your money we want; it's only your company. . . . Be quiet and obey; anyway, you cannot put up any resistance."

He closed the door again and, posting himself close by with a pistol in his fist, he ordered the litter bearers to pick up the reins of the mules who were standing still, waiting, with their heads down; and, pointing to the servants, he said to his men, "Tie up those two and take them you know where; at the slightest sign of resistance or escape, slit their throats and don't be afraid of anything."

The servants, bound tightly by these criminals, were pushed forward along the path by the butts of the carbines, while the trembling litter bearers picked up the reins and, following the orders of the masked man, turned left, where the countryside sloped down to the sea.

Donna Gabriella pleaded in vain, alternating her pleas with threats. She mentioned her relatives, who would never tolerate such an offense, but the masked man laughed. Between one prayer and the next she observed him closely; that well-built person, that bearing, that gesture, the same tone of voice, although artfully disguised, all seemed familiar. He aroused confused and vague memories from the back of her mind.

Certainly, despite the rural clothes, the masked man didn't look like a commoner, and he didn't seem to be one of those bandits who were roaming the countryside. There was something refined about his hands, and his linen was finely made. But these observations only increased Donna Gabriella's terror; the man was probably some gentleman persecuted by justice who wanted to provide himself with a day of amorous adventures.

How could she defend herself from him?

She looked with bewilderment at the road the litter was traveling over, and she thought of Blasco. A painful pang tore at her heart at the thought that he was perhaps languishing far away from her, in the desire to feel her close to him, while she moved farther away, the prey of another, one who would have resorted to any means to possess her and take her away from Blasco forever.

The sight of the sea, whose spray she felt on her face, startled her and made her blood run cold. Could they be putting her on a ship? She remembered when she had been kidnapped by the Beati Paoli; at that time she had been treated with respect, and perhaps never had her body been so inviolable as among those people. But that time she wasn't the target, Don Raimondo was; she and Violante were nothing but sacred hostages. But now? Now she felt the savage impulses of the man next to her, who had been waiting at the passage in order to attack her and capture her. This was something different; there was something more discreet, more sacred that was being threatened and that she could already see was in imminent danger.

Blasco's love had aroused in her a profound feeling of fidelity: a new modesty, tender and strong at the same time; a conjugal chastity that had almost renewed her soul and her life. Now all this seemed already close to crumbling down, to being shattered, under the brutal violation of the boundaries that love had erected between her and other men.

Behind this violation emerged the specter of the death of every beloved thing, of her reason for living! The abandonment, the loathsome solitude, the endless despair!

How could she defend herself?

The sea was just a few steps away; a small boat gently rocked on the surface, hidden in a small natural cove sheltered by rocks. No ships were in sight. A small castle with a big round tower rose above the rocks; was that where they were taking her, then?

It was the Castello di San Nicola, built in the sixteenth century by Tomaso Crispo, now owned by a certain Gastone, a friend of Emanuele and his companion in their bullying and gallant adventures. Was the baronet of San Nicola her kidnapper, then? He too had been one of her admirers; he too had desired her and had tried to seduce her. But that man didn't have the same build; no.

The litter entered the castle; the two litter bearers were locked in a room on the ground floor that had one window, fortified with iron bars. Donna Gabriella was pulled almost by force from the litter and carried upstairs.

The castle appeared to be abandoned; she called for help, but not a window opened, nor did a face appear in a doorway. The stairs that she went up, carried by two rogues, were deserted.

She was put down on a sofa in a room dominated by a wrought-iron bed on top of a raised platform between red damask curtains. The masked man stayed with her, and at a nod from him, the servants disappeared.

"Now," he said to her, "you are in my power!"

But the imminent danger infused Donna Gabriella with a courage that until then she had lacked, restoring the spirit that she had lost; she quickly assessed her own strength and the possibility of resisting that strong young man, and she sensed that she would not be able to resist for very long and would have to give up. She would have to resort to cunning, and with it obtain those results that would not be possible through her own strength. Trembling inside, she armed herself with all her seductions. Feigning emotions, in the state of mind in which she found herself, wasn't difficult for her; the same tremor that fear was spreading through her body and voice added a more graceful charm to the bewildered expression that her face had assumed.

With an indignation that was, after all, quite real, she said, "Signore, I could understand all the audacity, but not that of committing an act of violence worthy of horsemen on the main road! . . . Your conduct is most despicable, and a well-born lady can only feel disgust at the touch of your hands."

Emanuele was a little taken aback at this reaction, which he hadn't been expecting. However accustomed he was to gallant undertakings, he had never found himself in that unique situation and with a lady like Donna Gabriella; the same emotion that had overcome him as he nearly found himself master of the situation had also disarmed him a little.

He stammered, "Signora, do you think that if I didn't love you with all the passion that a fervent heart is capable of, I would have dared to kidnap you? . . . Forgive a heart that beats for you!"

"Forgive you?" she said. "You want me to forgive you? Who are you? I don't know you, and I cannot forgive a despicable act, or at the least an unseemly one, by a person who I do not know is worthy of it—I don't mean of my forgiveness, but of my even speaking to."

Emanuele had a moment of indecision; he felt stung, and besides, he wanted nothing more than to be recognized.

Donna Gabriella noticed his indecision and pressed on: "A gentleman, even if he pushed his audacity to the point of violence, as you have done, would not hesitate for a moment to make himself known . . . and to honestly and openly assume responsibility for his actions."

Then Emanuele took off his mask with a quick gesture and, falling to his knees before the duchess, who was surprised by this astonishing reveal and trembled with disdain, said to her, "Here I am! Forgive me!"

But this time Donna Gabriella's disdain wasn't feigned.

"You!" she exclaimed. "You!"

Amid the various conjectures that had occurred to her, only this one, which really was so obvious, hadn't presented itself to her: that her kidnapper could be Emanuele. She knew him to be overbearing and prone to violence; she had been pestered by him, annoyed by him; she had suffered public abuse by him. And yet the idea that it was him had never occurred to her, perhaps because, believing him to be ashamed of what he had done, she had never supposed him capable of imagining such a romantic kidnapping, or of coming before her again.

But her indignation was greater than her shock. So it was Emanuele who was invading his brother's territory. He, more than anyone, should have had a duty to respect him, as something inviolable and sacred—he, the author of that vile and disgraceful ruckus under her windows.

"You!" she repeated, unable to control herself. "You!"

All her plans of cunning, of duplicity, dissolved in front of this reality, which recalled to her, in a burst of hatred, that abusive, defamatory episode that had caused her to shed so many tears of pain and anger. She stopped thinking about her weakness and disregarded the fact that she was at the mercy of a young man who was capable of the most vulgar and indecent violence. She exclaimed, "And you dare to appear before me!"

Standing, with her eyes blazing with all the storms of anger and hatred, with her finger outstretched, as if she had wanted to strike the insolent young man dead with that gesture, with a new energy coursing through her entire body, and almost deluding herself into thinking she was stronger than she really was, she screamed, "Get out! Get out! . . . I'm ashamed to find myself in front of a despicable soul like you. . . . I am disgusted by you! . . . Get out!"

Emanuele had become pale, then red, as if flushed by those words that were smacking him full in the face. His violent and quarrelsome nature was reawakened, and his face took on a beastly expression. With swollen veins, blazing eyes, and clenched fists, it seemed that he was about to explode.

"Me?" he roared. "Me? Ah! You are ashamed, you! . . . You! . . . Then are you forgetting that you are in my power, and that only I am in charge here? . . . Ah, duchess! Did you believe that someone of my status, an Albamonte, would tolerate your contempt? . . . I will have you, not out of love, not because I am so crazy about you—as you may have believed—but to teach you and your lover how to treat my peers! It is my revenge, duchess, and I will not give you up."

"Coward!" Donna Gabriella shouted in his face. "Coward! You want to take revenge on a weak and defenseless woman, surrounded by your hired thugs; but if Blasco were here . . ."

"I would be twice as happy to see you both at my feet . . . and it would give me the utmost joy to possess you right under his own eyes . . . it is the only revenge that could immediately right the wrong."

"Coward! Coward! Coward!"

Donna Gabriella could find no other words, but her anger, her insults, and her combative attitude fomented Emanuele's passions; the animal in him trembled with all the violence of his cravings.

He sneered, "Coward! . . . I may well be, I don't care . . . . But I will subdue your arrogance."

He rushed to seize her, but Donna Gabriella, nimbler, darted under him and put a large chair between her and Emanuele as if to take cover, and with her eyes full of burning tears, she threatened, "Mind what you do. . . . Mind you! . . . Any violence on your part will cost you bitterly."

But Emanuele was no longer listening; his judgment was overwhelmed by the impulses of a lustful wild beast. With a leap he seized her, clenching her wrists in the grip of his hand in order to stop her from reacting and force her to bend backward. She flailed desperately, trying to bite the hands that were gripping her, to raise her knee against that body that was pressing against her; her hatred and her loathing multiplied her strengths, but in the struggle the man had lost all sense of respect and humanity, and she gradually felt the superiority of those muscles, which seemed to grow increasingly more powerful.

There was a moment when she was afraid.

She felt that her resistance was fading.

In that instant she felt all her pains and all her desperation, and her heart roared, her eyes filled with burning tears, and her breath seemed like a wheeze or a sob.

One more minute and she would have suffered the shame . . . another moment.

A shot rang out in the courtyard; at the same time the windowpanes shattered and fell.

Emanuele stopped, got up, and looked around in short-tempered astonishment. Another shot rang out; more panes shattered.

"Damnation!" he shouted, rushing toward the window.

Donna Gabriella leapt to her feet, her face lit up by a great hope, and, pressing her chest as if to suppress the beatings of her heart, she murmured in an indescribable tone, "God! God!"

Almost at the same time, some violent blows landed on the door. Emanuele, fuming, went to it, holding his sword.

"Who is it?"

He was answered by more furious bangs, under which the door gave way and burst open; three masked men appeared on the threshold with rifles leveled, with pistols and daggers on their waistbands. The one who appeared to be the leader stood behind them and, not without sarcasm, said, "It seems that the duke is having a good time, and that we are disturbing him. . . . I am sorry, but I am sure that the duchess does not find the duke's choice of amusements to her liking. Therefore, we have the duty to ask you in a friendly manner to set the lady free."

Donna Gabriella clasped her hands in a surge of joy, shouting, "Thank you! Thank you! . . . Oh! I am saved!"

"Who are you? What do you want?" Emanuele bellowed, livid with rage at his powerlessness to respond under the threat of the black and terrifying rifles. "How dare you to break into my house?"

"Take it easy, signore. I will bet that when Signor Gastone, who after all has no brigandish habits, finds out what you were using his castle for, he will have something to say about the expression 'my house.' As far as daring, the duke should know that we can enter anywhere we want . . . it is our duty and at the same time our right."

And, turning to Donna Gabriella, the masked man added, "If the duchess so wishes, her litter is waiting at the door."

"You will not get out of here alive! Neither I nor anyone else!"

He tried to run her through with his sword, but then, agile as a leopard, the masked man leapt on top of him, grabbed his arm even before Emanuele had time to put up any resistance, and said, "You are an ill-mannered and nasty little boy!"

Emanuele struggled to free himself from the grip of his arm, which was rigid and strong as steel.

The man dragged him over among the three armed men.

"Persuade yourself," he said, smiling under the mask, "my dear duke, that women who belong to others deserve respect."

In an instant, Emanuele, though struggling like a wild beast caught in a trap, found himself caught in a tangle of ropes, as if in a net, powerless to move his arms or legs, lifted up, and carried down into the courtyard, where, astonished and exploding with rage, he saw his men bound by their hands and feet to the flint rings that were used to tie the horses to. And in front of them were other masked and armed men.

He erupted in a violent burst of anger at his men; unable to otherwise vent the furious rage that roared inside him, he spat at them, shouting, "Cowards!"

But the men who were carrying him didn't give him a chance to say another word. After slipping one end of the ropes through one of the large rings that were once used to secure the chains of the drawbridge, they pulled him up, leaving him hanging by the arms alongside the jamb of the entrance door, laughing at him and cackling in his face. Emanuele was howling, groaning, cursing, foaming at the mouth, livid and shaken by savage impulses. His face no longer had anything human about it.

He saw Donna Gabriella's litter coming out of the castle, at whose door the leader of those masked men was walking. Passing in front of Emanuele, he raised his head, looked at him with a teasing smile, and, tipping his hat in a farcical manner, said to him, "Goodbye, and have a good stay, Don Emanuele!"

Emanuele saw the litter move away and vanish amid the boulders that lined the path, followed by the armed men. In the silent castle his men, tied to the rings, were swollen with anger and yellow with fear, and he swayed alongside the doorjamb like a man hanging from the gallows.

The Prince of Geraci saw him return in the evening on a type of stretcher, carried by villagers. His arms were dislocated.

At the same time a servant delivered a mysterious letter. The prince opened it and read:

Most Illustrious Prince,

Only out of consideration to your person are we limiting ourselves to giving a little warning to your grandson. Persuade him that the time for violence and bullying is over.

There was no signature, but a little seal, whose imprint bore a cross cut through diagonally by two rough swords.

The prince read, looked with astonishment, and murmured with an air of dismay, "The Beati Paoli!"

CHAPTER 10

On the afternoon of August 8, Blasco returned from Termini.

The Castello had surrendered unconditionally, powerless to resist, and now the three hundred defenders, unarmed, surrounded by dragoons and Spanish infantry, were returning as prisoners to the same city that they had entered in triumph four years earlier.

Blasco rushed at once to Donna Gabriella's house.

The beautiful woman still hadn't recovered from the intense excitement of the abduction and was lying in bed. This was more than a little surprising to Blasco, who was unaware of what had happened.

"Why didn't you let me know? How are you feeling? If I had known you were ill, I would have flown here, to your side."

She couldn't respond; she hugged Blasco tightly, feeling a tremor run through her entire body as if the fear of danger were being renewed. She couldn't speak; the joy of seeing her Blasco, combined with her renewed fear, filled her heart with dismay.

Blasco was surprised by that silence, by that silent and sorrowful embrace.

"What's wrong? Why aren't you saying anything?"

Then she said, "I have been so sick, and I was afraid of losing you . . . of losing you forever!"

"You could think that?"

"Yes."

A tremor ran through her body at her recollection of the images that for six days had tormented her, and in a fit of passion her arms held tight the man she loved, as if she wanted to cling to him so as not to be parted from him ever again.

"You are a child," Blasco said, caressing her; then, joking, he resumed, "And why did you think you were losing me? Was it I who was leaving you?"

That question relieved Donna Gabriella of any embarrassment; she answered immediately, "Yes, yes . . . you were leaving me, to run after another woman more beautiful than me."

This was her way of escaping an investigation that she wanted to avoid, and she didn't imagine that she was opening a door in Blasco's heart that had been locked by a desire to forget. A shadow passed through his mind and fell over his face like a cloud, and in that shadow he saw a dense grate, and behind it the stern and sad face of Violante: Violante alone and lost in the vast monastery, without love, without protection, pushed to sacrifice by the selfish wishes of others, like an innocent lamb; Violante, whom he himself had almost handed over to the knife of the sacrificers, due to an aberration of his conscience, a qualm, or an illusion that he was making things better and doing some good; Violante, whom he had loved, like a tender vision of pure and serene joy, like a dream, as something indescribable, superhuman—a rapture, an enchantment of his entire life.

Why was Donna Gabriella unlocking the door to that shrine carved inside his heart, in which he had preserved the image of Violante? Why? Perhaps feeling the weight of that memory, she raised her face and looked at Blasco.

"Have I displeased you?" she asked him affectionately.

"No," he replied, "no, but what a notion!"

And they were silent for a moment. Did Donna Gabriella sense that she had made a mistake? That she had summoned up some ghost that she had thought was forgotten? She got on her knees in the bed, with her elegant nightshirt in disarray, and, hugging Blasco's neck with her bare arms, trembling from doubt and passion and with a quiver of jealousy in her words, she begged him in a whisper, with her mouth close to his, "Tell me that you love only me, and that you will always love me. . . . Tell me!"

"Yes, yes, I love only you!" Blasco replied, clinging to that answer as if to a safety rope in order to escape from the waves of that painful vision.

* * *

Donna Gabriella had never written to him or mentioned anything about her perilous incident; upon leaving the Castello di San Nicola, the masked man had said to her, "Signora, I beg you not to write anything to Signor Blasco and to keep silent even when he comes to see you."

She had looked at him in amazement, and the masked man, smiling, had added, "We are his best friends, and we have the pleasure and the good fortune to protect you and to defend you. . . . You have seen proof of this. . . . Perhaps we should have arrived sooner, but it wasn't our fault; on the other hand, we did arrive in time."

"Oh, signore, whoever you and your companions are, believe that I am very grateful to you. However, I beg you to escort me to Termini."

"Why must you go to Termini?"

"But don't you know that Blasco is seriously wounded and is dying?"

"Blasco wounded? Dying? Of course not! . . . Who told you this?"

"He wrote to me."

"That's not possible."

"I have his letter here. . . . Look!"

After taking it out from her bodice, she had given it to the masked man to read; as soon as he glanced at it, he understood everything and exclaimed, "But don't you realize that this letter is a fake, and that it was written to draw you into a trap?"

"What are you saying?"

"But it's obvious, good God! . . . Blasco isn't wounded. I received letters from him yesterday."

"Ah!"

Donna Gabriella's face lit up with an intense joy and, looking at her savior, she exclaimed, "I recognize you. You're—"

"Quiet! . . . It doesn't matter who I am; you only need to know that you have a faithful friend beside you, who will not fail to carry out the most scrupulous watch over you. However, I beseech you to say nothing to Blasco; it's better that he not know anything. As for the other one, you have witnessed the lesson that we gave him."

Donna Gabriella had one last doubt. "I believe you, but if Blasco has written to you, why didn't he write to me?"

"This is a mystery that will need to be worked out."

"That letter that I showed you even replies to something that I had written to him about . . . and uses the same phrases that Blasco uses."

"Look no further. It had to be traced from Blasco's letter, which, of course, was intercepted by Emanuele. . . . Leave it to me."

He had then told her about the way he had been able to run to her aid, naturally keeping silent about what he didn't want revealed. A servant whom he had sent, as he would usually do, to inquire around the neighborhood whether the night had passed peacefully, had told him that the duchess was about to leave for Termini; and so he and a few servants had mounted their horses in order to reach her, fearing the roads were infested with thieves. Close to the San Nicola gorge or to Calatorre, he had encountered the two bound servants, accompanied by several bandits; he had recognized them, freed them, and from them had learned everything. So then he had come rushing to her aid.

It wasn't necessary to explain the reason for his urging, that is, for keeping Blasco in the dark about everything.

"The hatred between the two brothers would intensify, and I don't want that," Coriolano had concluded. "Emanuele must instead acknowledge and grant a proper and suitable status to his older brother, more worthy than he of wearing the ducal crown."

"Oh, yes, it's true! Blasco deserves a kingdom!"

Coriolano, smiling at this exaggeration, which could be excused, coming as it was from a woman in love, had then obliged her to return to Palermo and she had complied, also because she was not feeling well. And she hadn't written anything and had also kept silent about not feeling well.

During those days of her illness, the Prince of Geraci had gone to visit her, but Donna Gabriella had given strict orders that she would not receive anyone, unless it was the Cavaliere della Floresta's trusted manservant. To her relatives, who were astonished to see her return so soon, she had said that she had suddenly felt ill, and the fever that had seized her justified the excuse; as for the men who had accompanied her, with a sum of money and with a pledge, they had agreed not to say a word. This was something not difficult to obtain from men from whom torture itself would not be able to extract a confession.

So nothing had leaked out from Donna Gabriella's side and neither could anything have leaked out from Emanuele's side. The bravacci that he had recruited had scattered, afraid of falling into the hands of justice or of the duke's revenge. Moreover, they had every interest in not implicating themselves in the assault and abduction by recounting that stunt, which had turned out badly for them.

Emanuele hadn't said a word. Either because the serious illness that he had come down with had endangered his life, or due to his own will, he had stubbornly refused to reveal what had happened to him or to make even a vague allusion to it.

Light could only be shed by that mysterious letter from the Beati Paoli, which had filled the Prince of Geraci with dread. But that light was quite faint!

He had gone to see the Prince of Carini, vicario generale for the Val di Mazara, in order to have him read the letter and to denounce the great crime that the sect had committed against his grandson.

"As Your Illustrious Lordship can see, the sect is far from extinguished, as had been believed. And now it dares not only to kill our children but to spread these rebellious principles against our authority and our class."

The Prince of Carini was astonished. Of course it would be necessary to investigate and to take measures, but some facts would have to be heard directly from Emanuele. He had no idea that it would have been sufficient to ask Donna Gabriella, his niece, in order to get the keys to that mystery and to thank the Beati Paoli instead of punishing them.

But Emanuele said nothing.

"I have no need of justice!" he said. "A Duke of Motta can assert it himself."

Surely, the prince, his grandfather, was thinking, there had to be a woman behind all this.

He knew Emanuele to be quite licentious, and it didn't take a great deal of intelligence to construct a little drama about an offended husband's possible revenge. In order to stop Emanuele, fixated as he was on the notion of avenging himself, from running the risk of a greater danger, the prince could envision only one means: to make him leave for a while, and upon his return have him marry Violante, although it might be even better to hasten the marriage. He talked about it with the Prince of Butera, who approved; the two grandfathers, convinced that they were doing the best thing, settled on the date of December 8, the Feast of the

Immaculate Conception. As soon as he recovered, Emanuele would bring the engagement ring to Violante in the Monastery of Santa Caterina, and then he would leave.

"Send him to Naples or Rome," the Prince of Butera suggested. "We'll entrust him to His Majesty's ambassador. You are a Grandee of Spain."

But Emanuele's recovery was slow.

* * *

During this time news had arrived from Messina about a revolt of the people against the Prince of Lardaria, and of the events of the siege of the citadel and of Forte Salvatore, still in the power of the Savoy. As he needed to speed up operations in order to take Milazzo by storm, the Viceroy, the Marchese of Lede, asked for the squadron that had been at the seizure of Termini, and Blasco was ordered to depart.

"Oh, I won't let you leave by yourself," Donna Gabriella told him firmly. "I will come too."

"No, dear," objected Blasco. "I would be afraid for you."

"And I don't want to stay here, alone and far away. Does the gentleman understand? . . . No, no. . . . I would be afraid. If you only knew how afraid I was! . . . Take me with you. You'll see, I won't bother you, I won't be any trouble. . . . And you'll have a friend close to you, who will take care of you. . . . Near you I will feel more courageous."

He had to give in.

The squadron left by land. The sea wasn't safe after the battle in Messina, where the Spanish ships, attacked by those of the English, had received the worst of it.

England had suddenly entered the battle against Spain, which, provoked by the restless Cardinal Alberoni, was putting the peace of Europe at risk. The Quadruple Alliance had joined forces against Spain precisely for this reason; and while the English fleet, twenty-eight ships strong under the command of Admiral Bing, was sailing from Naples in the direction of Sicily, Austrian regiments were entering the citadel in aid of the Savoy.

The English fleet had arrived in the Mare del Faro without displaying hostile intentions, but after an exchange of questions and answers, it had declared that it was under orders to guarantee the neutrality of the peninsula and to maintain the treaties of the Peace of Utrecht, which amounted to a declaration of hostility. And so the Spanish Armada went into action. It was thirty-seven ships strong, nine more than the English, but the Spanish had at their disposal 7,142 men and 1,038 cannons; the English had 9,063 men and 1,440 cannons. The numbers were to their advantage, as was their greater skill. The Spanish Armada was commanded by Admiral Castagnedo, incompetent and irresolute, who let himself be attacked and defeated, then made excuses for himself by accusing the English of being *assassinos, fuera de toda regla de milicia nacional.*[1] The Spanish ships that had escaped took shelter in Palermo, and the sea remained at the mercy of their enemies. Venturing into it galleys loaded with militia was the same as allowing them to be captured by the English. Hence the order to have the Spanish troops leave by land, which was longer but safer.

The carters who had to travel that road, and whoever else had to go to one of the towns between Palermo and Messina, took advantage of the favorable circumstances to travel safely, so a type of caravan extraneous to the militia followed the squadron of infantry. Therefore, Donna Gabriella's litter wasn't alone, and she had no need to be accompanied by servants. Indeed, since no one knew where she was going, she hired a public litter and didn't take anyone but her trustworthy maidservant with her.

At home she let it be known and let it be said that she was going to spend autumn at one of her estates, near the Castello di Brucato.

So when Emanuele was well enough to leave the house and yearning inside for revenge, he sought out Matteo Lo Vecchio, found out that Donna Gabriella had left, and burned with anger.

"She left? For where? How?"

"Eh! Naturally her lover would not have left her here alone. She left with Signor Blasco for Messina, where it will not be so easy for either Your Lordship or others to reach her."

"Oh! We'll see about that!"

But he didn't know what his grandfather and guardian had decided for him.

---

1   "murderers, beyond all regulations of national militia."

CHAPTER 11

On the first Sunday of October, the Feast of our Lady of the Rosary, Via Butera was full of elegant carriages, portantine, and servants in sumptuous braided livery that formed groups in front of the entrances, talking or gossiping about their masters.

For every carriage that arrived, preceded by volanti, the groups would separate into two wings to allow it to pass, amid winks, whispered comments, and deep bows. The most well informed on the day's top story would give interpretations and bits of news about the betrothed.

"A marriage of convenience."

"They say that when they went to collect the bride from the monastery, the poor girl was pale as death."

"He's not a good husband."

"Why not? He's a handsome young man."

"Rich."

"He's fit to be hanged."

"Have you heard what happened to him?"

"Ah! Yes. . . . Given a thrashing."

"What! They as good as hanged him."

"The Beati Paoli."

"He got laid."

"Who knows with who."

"Some poor girl."

"He takes whichever one he sees."

"He will end up murdered."

"Poor bride."

"Is she beautiful?"

"A Madonna!"

"A tasty morsel, by God!"

"She's not for us . . ."

"Look! If she wants to trade him in, I'm ready."

Petty quarrels and salacious allusions commenced amid laughter and were immediately stifled upon the arrival of a new carriage.

The drawing rooms of the palazzo filled up with ladies. The Prince of Butera, both due to the natural generosity of his house and since it concerned an orphaned granddaughter, didn't want people to think that he would do anything less for her than what he would do for his own daughter. He had wanted to give the promise of marriage the greatest solemnity, worthy of his rank as well as that of the groom's family.

But all the extravagance and pomp of the invitations and the hospitality contrasted dreadfully with the look on Violante's face.

The poor girl, in her bedroom, among her married aunts, was waiting for her turn to come out and be presented to society; and she had the same expression as one of the condemned who, in the chapel, among the priests who assist them, waits trembling and at the same time anxiously for the fatal moment when the door opens that leads to the gallows.

She had left the monastery that same morning in order to receive the ring; she already knew from the day before that she had to get ready for the sacrifice.

Her grandfather had gone to tell her.

At his first words Violante had taken on a deathly pallor and had almost fainted.

"Why so soon?" she asked.

"Oh, it's not too soon; on the contrary," said the prince. "At your age you should already be married. We put off giving you a status, but now it is time, my child; you can't stay shut up in here."

"But I am comfortable here, I don't wish for anything, and I've grown fond of these good mothers. . . . Why does Your Lordship want to have me marry?"

"Goodness! But you almost have an obligation to do it. You have a considerable inheritance that you cannot, and must not, let pass into the hands of others, apart from those of your children."

"Oh, signore, I beg you . . . put it off for another year, give me time . . . this is a serious matter."

"Childishness! What is the meaning of these entreaties? It has been agreed to. I'm sure it's what your father would have wanted."

"But what if I had a calling for the monastery?"

"It will pass."

"And if I didn't have a calling for marriage?"

"It will come to you."

"Your Excellency, it will not come. . . . I swear to you that it is something that frightens me . . . please leave me here in the monastery with my aunts."

"Oh, let's put an end to this! Since when does a girl meddle in these matters? We will pick you up tomorrow morning, and tomorrow evening we'll bring you back here, where you will stay until the day of the wedding. And let's not talk about it anymore."

The prince left her there, pale and deathlike, while repeating indifferently, "Childishness! Childishness!"

Violante followed him with her eyes through the grate, then suddenly she burst into tears and went back up to look for her aunts in order to plead for their help. She threw herself into their arms, sobbing and begging, "Mother Rosalia, Signora Concezione, save me! Save me!"

The two nuns were frightened, asking her anxiously and with concern, "What was it? What has happened to you?"

"I am lost, if you don't save me, my kind aunts! . . . Do it in memory of my father."

"But tell us, speak up! Blessed Virgin of the Rosary! What happened?"

With her words broken by sobs, pale and helpless, she told them about the conversation with her grandfather.

"I don't want to marry him! . . . I don't want to!" she then exclaimed forcefully, shaking her head.

The two nuns fretted over her.

"My child, you must obey . . . if the Lord wants you to enter the world, you must do as he wishes. Your grandfather is thinking of your own interests."

"Ah! So even you are abandoning me?"

"Of course not, we're not abandoning you, child, you must be reasonable. Entrust yourself to God and to the Blessed Virgin and you will find some comfort."

"Oh God! God! God! . . . Why do you want to have me die?"

The nuns tried to console her; they were concerned, but what could they do? They had no authority and certainly couldn't prevent that marriage arranged by her grandfather.

"I want to be a nun!" Violante said, sobbing. "I don't want to leave the monastery. . . . I want to be a nun!"

As for them, of course they would have been happy to have their young niece with them; they would have been happy to see her become a nun in order to extol that calling with all the glory that it deserved, but how to go against the will of the Prince of Butera? Once he got something into his head, there was no way to convince him otherwise. To console her, they promised that they would plead her case and write a note to the prince, but he replied with much courtesy that there was no need to take such childish behavior seriously.

Violante spent the night in the deepest despair; her entire past came back to her, and the images she had tried to forget appeared again before her eyes.

Oh, how many things she was seeing, and how the dreams of her youth, which had already seemed so distant, now seemed close and vivid to her, as if to increase the torments in her soul. What slight hope then would remain in her heart, if that marriage filled her with fear and sorrow, like the threat of a premature and violent death?

Emanuele? But she detested him. She had met him only briefly and had felt an insurmountable repugnance toward him. Although she had sworn to herself and forced herself to forget Blasco, that same Blasco who one night had slept with his head resting at her bedside, that same Blasco who had shown so much gentle tenderness toward her and in whose arms she had almost surprised her stepmother, his image now leapt before her again like that of an intensely desired and irreparably lost love!

Where was he? What had happened to him? She had heard nothing more about him. For four years she had jealously harbored the secret of her early youth and had not dared or wanted to ask for any news about Blasco. On the day when the Viceroy, Marchese of Lede, made his solemn entrance into Palermo, she, from the suspended loggia that overlooked Via Toledo, where she watched the dragoons as they rode by, was suddenly startled because one of them resembled Blasco, but she was very far from imagining that the handsome cavaliere could be one of those foreign soldiers and had thought it was just one of those unusual but not uncommon resemblances.

Where was he? What had happened to him? Was he alive?

Ah! She didn't know, and perhaps it was better for her not to know, that that dragoon was indeed Blasco, and that while she was despairing in the darkness of her cell on account of that marriage that was digging a deep grave for her last fading glimmer of hope, Blasco was in the arms of another woman, her stepmother!

Thus Violante spent the night, amid these agonies, pulled in spite of herself toward her former dream, virtually holding out her arms to the one who had appeared to her as a liberator.

She realized that she was alone—alone in the world!

The following morning her grandfathers came to pick her up in their carriage and take her to the palazzo. She was frightfully pale.

The prince joked a little about that dreadful pallor and about that fear, but under the veil of the joke was something imperious and irrevocable, which took away every bit of hope and courage from the young girl.

She allowed herself to be dressed, without any desire or spirit for it, detached and mechanical as if she were a doll.

The maidservants and the Butera aunts couldn't get a word out of her and thought it was due to the emotion of that ceremony. In fact, she was beset with emotion, but it was from her suffering, and she stared into space, seemingly lost in the depths of her dark and tragic fate.

When, led by her grandmother, she entered the salon, which was crowded with invited guests, her pallor had some bluish highlights that gave her such a corpse-like appearance that a murmur of astonishment and pity hovered on the mouths of those who saw her.

Violante made superhuman efforts not to faint and to maintain a calm and dignified demeanor.

She was immediately assailed with compliments and best wishes, every one of which was an acute blow to her heart. Only the sight of Emanuele revived her, due to a sudden flash of hope to which she would cling for the slightest reason.

Emanuele, who was moving forward alongside his grandfathers, was also dreadfully pale, and his face had an expression of unflinching reluctance.

She detected from his manner that in his heart the same feelings of aversion and almost of repugnance that she felt were rising to the surface. So even Emanuele was being subjected to the will of others! Even Emanuele was approaching this marriage without desire, without joy, as if it were a sacrifice.

He didn't love her. Violante felt the same way, and her heart had a thrill of joy. If Emanuele didn't love her, if he instead hated her, he would be her best ally. A crazy idea whirled through her mind: to ask the young man—whom they had chosen as her lifelong companion—if it wouldn't be better for both of them to refuse this marriage with an act of single-minded will.

But Emanuele was drawing near.

When he was in front of her, the Prince of Geraci, taking him by the hand and introducing him to the Prince of Butera, asked the prince for the honor of granting the hand of his granddaughter and ward, Donna Violante Albamonte, to his nephew and ward, Don Emanuele Albamonte, Duke of Motta.

And, having received a response full of superciliousness and studied courtesy, he asked Emanuele to ask Donna Violante to be kind enough to accept a pledge to exchange vows—the engagement ring—as dictated by tradition.

Violante had to hold out the ring finger of her right hand for the ring to be slipped on. Her forehead had become damp and her hands icy cold. Her pride prevented her from abandoning herself to her sorrow before those hundreds of eyes that were looking at her.

But she didn't say a word, she didn't reply, either to the gracious words of her future relatives or to the good wishes that came to her from every side.

An army of servants in formal dark green livery, embroidered with gold, with an extravagance and an astonishing sumptuousness, served refreshments, while in an adjacent drawing room the notary of the family, with the two grandfathers and with the witnesses, drew up the marriage agreements. Emanuele stood grim and silent amid those compliments.

"You are a lucky man, you have beauty and wealth!"

"I hadn't yet met Violante, she is truly beautiful. I offer you my congratulations."

"You are an enviable couple."

"Bravo! Bravo!"

All these comments, largely dictated by social convention, annoyed Emanuele. At times he would look at Violante in order to discover all this beauty they were singing the praises of, and he would admit that she truly was beautiful but that he was not attracted to her at all. In any case, it was not so much for the bride they intended for him that he had such a profound aversion as for the idea of marriage, which seemed to him like a kind of imprisonment.

He was still so young! And he wanted to enjoy his life. His father hadn't taken a wife until his forties; why did they want him to tie his youth to an unwanted yoke, not enlivened by any ideal, by any dream? He too, like Violante, when he was still an adolescent, hadn't thought much about this marriage. There was still time! And in such a long time so many unpredictable things could happen. . . . But time had passed so quickly that it didn't seem real, and what seemed far away to him was already imminent. Indeed, he was there on the threshold and there was nothing to do except cross that threshold.

Only one thing comforted him: his departure for Rome, which, in addition to exempting him from the formal visits that he should make to his betrothed in the monastery (behind the grating of the parlor), could have some unexpected consequences.

Forced by his grandfather, he had approached Donna Violante to speak to her, but the young girl had remained immobile, pale, with her eyes fixed on the ground like a funerary statue; this attitude upset Emanuele and, as usual, it excited and aroused in him that rude lack of polish that was the foundation of his upbringing in a modest and humble bourgeois environment.

"It seems," he said to her, seizing the opportune moment, "that you are not very keen on this marriage."

Violante didn't answer, nor did she seem to have heard him.

Her silence intensified Emanuele's contempt and angered him.

"Anyway," he added, "I am not keen on it either!"

And then he turned his back to her, pleased at having said these insulting words to her, like a slap, which instead opened up Violante's heart to a sudden hope. From the depths of her heart, she murmured a "thank you" that was the expression of all the feelings that tormented her.

Those who saw her cheeks turn pink imagined, smiling, that the girl had blushed due to her modesty at the words that her future betrothed had spoken, and no one imagined that it was instead due to her joy at knowing that she wasn't loved or desired by that loathsome man.

She returned to the monastery the following morning, with her heart torn between the faint hope that Emanuele himself would break that bond of matrimony, the pain of having tied it, and the comfort that for some time she would not see her fiancé, who, as it had been decided, would be leaving for Rome.

In fact, Emanuele left that evening, with two Tuscan galleys that would put ashore in Civitavecchia, from where he would travel by land to Rome. He would be accompanied by three servants and was bringing four horses with him and had been provided with letters and introductions—other than for the Spanish ambassador, also for His Eminence the Vicar and for Father Don Antonino Inguaggiato, one of the many priests exiled under the Savoy government, who, like the majority of exiled priests, was living in Rome.

Father Inguaggiato was to be Emanuele's confessor during his stay in Rome.

CHAPTER 12

The Citadel in Messina had surrendered to the Spanish on September 29, and the event gave rise to great joy throughout the kingdom; however, the Savoy still retained control of several fortified locations of some importance, such as Syracuse and Milazzo, and it was immediately necessary to conquer this last city in order to clear the entire route between the two major centers of the island.

The Viceroy, the Marchese of Lede, then concentrated all his available forces against Milazzo, around which a blockade had already been set up since July, though it was unable, due to the meagerness of its forces, to prevent the city from supplying itself with new defenders.

At the beginning of October, the Spanish Army moved on Milazzo in successive stages and at various intervals; additional German reinforcements arrived at the garrison by sea, so it seemed that the fate of the kingdom would be decided in Milazzo.

The Spanish began to construct batteries that certainly would have damaged the fort if they had been able to operate. The commanders of the Savoy and German troops realized this, and they decided to attack the Spanish and destroy their batteries.

The garrison in Milazzo could no longer be said to be Savoy since they were only a small fraction. Of eleven infantry regiments, ten were German. Under the pretext of helping King Victor Amadeus and to preserve the agreements of the Treaty of Utrecht, Emperor Charles VI, who was already ruler of Naples, aimed to enlarge his dominion by setting his sights on and by seizing Sicily.

At dawn on October 14, the eleven Austrian-Savoy regiments of infantry and six squadrons of cavalry, under the command of General Caraffa, left Milazzo to attack from the left the Spanish trenches, which were defended by fewer than four thousand men.

The inferiority of the Spanish forces was striking. They had to abandon their trenches, even though they retreated in an orderly fashion and never ceasing to fight; then a quick movement spread through their ranks, and as if a bursting stream had broken its banks, pushing and pulling along everything in its fury, the Spanish saw themselves pushed to go on the offensive again.

The Viceroy, the Marchese of Lede, entered the battle with seven battalions of infantry and two regiments of cavalry.

The Marchese of Lede had left on October 13 from Messina and had made camp in San Pietro. Hearing the cannonade of four Neapolitan galleys that were supporting the movement of the German troops, and sensing the action, he moved quickly and managed to invigorate the Spanish, halt their retreat, and resume the offensive. The battle grew into a fierce and terrifying struggle.

A squadron of Alemanni cavalry, supporting the Piedmontese Susa regiment, was mercilessly slaughtering the Spanish from the right. The Marchese of Lede then ordered that two Numancia squadrons drive back the German cavalry and attempt to outflank the infantry.

The two squadrons launched the assault with swords held high, in close ranks, strong and formidable.

Blasco was in the front line, at the end. With his nostrils flared, and hunched over his horse's neck, he chose the spot to attack.

Facing him, the Alemanni cavalry was approaching at a gallop. The clash was terrifying. Blasco found himself carried under his own impetus beyond the line of the enemy horsemen, and he was soon surrounded by three or four German horsemen. He brought one of them down with a pistol shot, another with a stab of his sword. Two dragoons rushed to his aid. At that point, the battle became spirited and deadly. Men and horses seemed to be possessed by a ferocious spirit of destruction; blows of swords alternated with gunshots; amid the smoke that enveloped everything there was a flash of blades, a blaze of flames, a procession of horses and riders, and cries and wails. The German squadron, defeated and decimated, withdrew; however, the Piedmontese infantry used its artillery fire to temporarily halt and unnerve the dragoons.

Blasco said to himself, "Here I will either earn my captain's sash or I will die."

He rushed forward. A bullet wounded his horse; he was quick to jump off the saddle while the animal was dropping to the ground. As another dismounted horse passed by his side, he grabbed the bit and with a leap mounted it and continued on. The entire squadron, after that first moment of hesitation, had thrown itself on top of the infantry.

Blasco had pushed himself toward the flag, around which a group of defenders, infantry and horsemen, had formed, and the battle became more violent and ferocious than ever. Battered, wounded, ragged, and bloody, he waved his sword with a fury that trounced the enemy and cleared his way.

The infantry was yielding; only a group of horsemen and officers resisted. Blasco saw a Savoy officer surrounded by a few dragoons, desperately and valorously trying to defend himself. He was wounded in several places; a little more and he would have been killed.

"Castellammonte!" he shouted in amazement, flinging himself among the dragoons.

The man was, in fact, the old royal guard, now captain of a company of infantry.

The Cavaliere di Castellammonte raised his head attentively and looked at Blasco, who had gone to stand in front of him. Then, recognizing him, he handed Blasco his sword and surrendered.

"Take him to the encampment and treat him with all due respect; he is a brave and loyal cavaliere."

He pressed ahead still more. His goal was the flag.

After four hours of struggle, the Germans and the Piedmontese were routed, driven back until they were below the walls, taking refuge in Milazzo; the Spanish retook their trenches. Blasco was taken to San Pietro on an improvised stretcher, but in his hand was the flag snatched from the Piedmontese standard bearer.

His body had been run through by two stabs, and there was a bullet in his right calf.

Bandaged as well as possible, he was taken with other wounded men to Barcellona Pozzo di Gotto, where Donna Gabriella, having been given the news, rushed to his aid.

Whether due to the season or to the nature of the wounds themselves, his healing was slow and his convalescence long. At the same time, Blasco received his commission as lieutenant of the Numancia Dragoons and an indefinite sick leave so that he could make a full recovery.

He took advantage of the situation by returning to Palermo at the beginning of February of the following year, while his squadron remained below Milazzo, which, supplied with forces and provisions, was still enduring despite having been under siege for more than five months.

During the most acute stage of his wounds, fearing that he would die, he had revealed to Donna Gabriella his desire to keep the promise made to her, but she objected.

"No, not now," she said, "I don't want our marriage to be blessed during a time of sadness. We'll wait until you have recovered."

"And if I were to die?"

"Oh, you will not die! No! I feel it, I am sure of it."

* * *

For this reason, when they set ashore from the felucca that had taken them to Palermo from Messina, Donna Gabriella went ashore first and went home alone in her carriage; Blasco was met half an hour later by Coriolano, who was waiting for him in his carriage. When he arrived at the Palazzo della Floresta, though tired, he felt an overpowering need to tell his friend about all his adventures. He felt a tender affection for Donna Gabriella and a deep gratitude that was very close to love, but he didn't feel that undefinable something between a dream and an abandonment of self and of all things, that sort of sublimation of spirit, that mysterious melancholy and that tenderness of rapture of one's entire being that are the essence and the poetry of love.

Coriolano listened to him not without satisfaction. A confirmed bachelor, he didn't understand certain mysteries of the human heart. When Blasco finished, he said, smiling, "You can't believe how pleased I am to know you are happy! I must be grateful to the duchess as well, to whom I beg you to offer my compliments. And I am all the more happy, as I am sure you will learn some news of the day without being seized with emotion."

"What news?"

"News that you should be expecting."

"That is?"

"Of Emanuele's wedding."

"Then has it happened?" Blasco exclaimed, suddenly turning pale.

"Oh, no, but it will take place soon, on the last Sunday of Carnevale, which falls on the nineteenth of this month."

Blasco said nothing; a cloud of melancholy had lowered itself over his eyes.

"They should have wed earlier, during the Feast of the Madonna, but Emanuele returned from Rome with an illness . . . that prevented him from getting married. . . . I don't even know if he is in any condition to do it now, without endangering . . ."

"What illness?" Blasco asked, merely to say something but without any interest. Coriolano told him.

"In Rome, nothing could be easier; it's the most corrupt city in Italy. I believe that Emanuele didn't restrain himself. Allegedly, he led a wretched life in Rome. Courtesans, gambling, duels . . . twice he was locked up in Castel Sant'Angelo. . . . The Prince of Geraci had to open his purse many times and finally had to recall his grandson to Palermo. He arrived in such a state of health that it wasn't necessary to resort to restrictions, which, moreover, would not be very effective since Emanuele has already come of age."

"Really?"

"The prince has consigned the accounts over to him and put him, as one would say, in possession of his fortune."

"So then he is now the head of the House of Albamonte!" Blasco said, not without a touch of bitterness.

"Indeed!"

A moment of silence passed, then Blasco asked, with a touch of emotion, "And is Violante happy about this marriage?"

"If I said yes, I would be lying."

"Poor young girl," Blasco murmured.

"You are right!"

And yet another curtain of silence fell between the two friends, and once again Blasco was the one to break it.

"Oh, Coriolano. . . . I think that when I defended Violante, even against Emanuele, I wasn't wrong. . . . Your harsh justice has protected a scoundrel and created a victim."

"Who could have foreseen that that young orphan, unwanted, deprived, pursued, and threatened with death, would have been undeserving of all our protection? And yet on the other hand, does justice measure a right using the scale of dignity? Justice doesn't recognize people but actions, and where there is a violation of a right, it intervenes in order to protect and to defend. . . . It can make mistakes and even protect a man like Emanuele; this does not mean that the one protected today cannot fall under its harshness tomorrow."

"But meanwhile the victim remains—"

"She is a fatality. But you can be sure that I am watching over her."

And he added soon after, smiling, "You won't be jealous, then, if I substitute myself for you in this surveillance."

"Jealous? Why?" Blasco said bitterly. "It's all over now. Fate has marked everyone's path; I will go my own way. I have no complaints because I would be an ingrate to a woman who, with a life of devotion and passion, has almost redeemed herself in my eyes, and to whom I am now bound, more than by a promise, by gratitude and affection. Certainly this wasn't my dream. . . . But I, a poor bastard, tossed to his fate, couldn't and shouldn't have any dreams! . . . Now, you must well understand for what delicate reasons I must abstain from putting forward any action in favor of Violante; indeed, I must be grateful for what you will do for her."

"Don't worry! . . . I give you my word."

For that entire day, Blasco was sad and pensive. The image of Violante, dragged to that wedding, in the arms of that vicious lout, depraved in body and soul, stayed with him and tormented him.

* * *

Donna Gabriella noticed that sadness and didn't dare to investigate. She too felt surrounded by something like a shadow, and there was something weighing on her that she didn't want to speak about.

She had heard the news about Violante's imminent wedding, which, given her status as Don Raimondo Albamonte's widow, she almost had the obligation to attend. That news had upset her, recalling to her the image of Violante, whom she had not forgotten. In the four years of her widowhood, she had gone to visit her stepdaughter only during solemn holidays, more to be seen than out of affection. Since she had reconciled with Blasco, since she had begun her new life of love, she had never seen her again, either for the mid-August holiday, or for the Feast of the Immaculate Conception, or at Christmas or on New Year's Day. The distance had served to excuse her absence, but now she had returned to Palermo and surely couldn't get out of fulfilling her duty. Her absence might attract attention and be interpreted in a sinister manner.

In truth, in her heart, she was satisfied that Violante was getting married, and even more so that she would be marrying Emanuele. In this, her satisfaction had a degree of malice, because she knew that the two young ones didn't love each other, that Emanuele was already a half-defeated man, and that that marriage was, for both of them, an unbearable yoke. Thus she was exacting revenge without inciting it, indeed without pursuing it.

Nevertheless, despite this selfish and malevolent satisfaction, she was troubled, and Blasco's unhappy silence was increasing her distress and filling her heart with a certain anxiety. That night at supper not a word was spoken; Blasco's arms didn't reach for her with the same excitement as at other times, and she felt her eyes fill with tears.

"Why are you sad?" she asked.

"No, I'm not sad," Blasco replied, "perhaps I'm tired."

Donna Gabriella didn't press him. She sat on his knees, wrapped her arms around his neck with that gesture of abandonment and tenderness that rendered her enchanting, and she put her head on his shoulder, sobbing, "You don't love me!"

Those days passed quickly, and the last Sunday of Carnevale was coming soon. Donna Gabriella had received an engraved note, in a decorative frame, that said:

> *On the most welcome occasion of the marriage that will be concluded between the Duke of Motta and Signorina Donna Violante Albamonte e Branciforti on Sunday, February 10, the kindness of your presence is requested in order to heighten ever more the magnificence of the occasion, in declaration of their allegiance to you.*

The receipt of that engraved invitation gave her the opening to respond as she was planning to all along. She replied at once, expressing her pleasure at the gracious invitation but saying regretfully that her state of health wouldn't permit her to express "in person" her "dutiful affections" and that, "confirming the honor of the most esteemed requests," she was "again very devoted and obliged."

When she sent this letter she felt lighter, as if a great weight had been lifted from her chest, because in truth, her presence at the wedding would also have embarrassed others, since it was no longer a mystery to anyone what had taken place between her and Emanuele.

She said nothing to Blasco; she had searched the depths of his soul, had discovered a poorly repressed anxiety, and her lover's heart had guessed the reasons for it. She would watch him suspiciously, keeping her own pain to herself, but at times her eyes would blaze with the old flames and a thought of hatred and revenge would cloud her mind.

They spent those days in a state of anxiety, hiding their feelings from each other and avoiding asking each other about the reason for their melancholy and telltale silence, as though they were afraid of hearing the revelation of what they already knew.

Sunday came.

Donna Gabriella was feverish.

"When she is married, he will no longer be able to think about her," she would tell herself. "He must forget about her. And then he will be mine, all mine!" But while she was thinking this, a sorrowful inner voice would respond, "No, no, no! He will never be all yours, never!"

And at this dark and secret voice that only she could hear, her heart would freeze, and sobs would start to rise to her throat.

* * *

She had her carriage harnessed, as if she were going for a ride or to enjoy the show of the masks and costumes that were spreading enjoyment all along the Cassaro that day, but in reality she was going out to find out some news about the wedding.

The Cassaro was full of people who were waiting for the floats. Comical masked characters slipped into the crowd, provoking laughter and causing a sensation; they would run and jump on people's shoulders. A cadenced roll of drums made heads turn to one side. A man dressed in the Spanish fashion of the sixteenth century, with a feathered velvet hat on his head, a cape over his shoulders, and a wooden sword in his hand, would climb quickly up a ladder, making a thousand ridiculous faces, and hurl himself down among the mad laughter of the crowd. It was the *Mastro di Campo*, one of the oldest and most cherished characters of the commoners, who had forgotten its historical origin. The Mastro di Campo was a remnant of a ludicrous portrayal of the loves of old Bernardo Cabrera, Count of Modica and Grand Justiciary of the Kingdom, and subject of the very well-known episode of his climb up the castle wall to kidnap the beautiful and young Queen Bianca.

More drums and fifes poured into the Cassaro from another street, and the besieged crowd opened up to make way for an army of a new sort, infantry from who knows what period, dressed in cuirasses and helmets made of silver paper, armed with staffs, commanded by generals. They split into two groups, beating and chasing each other, making a frenzied racket.

Farther on was a "dance of slaves," characters whose faces were smeared with lampblack and oil who, while dancing, would run into people in order to kiss them and leave a black mark somewhere on their face; then there was a running around in order to avoid those embraces, begetting comic scenes that gave rise to rowdy and unrestrained merrymaking.

But even livelier was the merriment aroused by the *mamme Lucie*, men disguised as courtesans, who danced with swaying hips or lewd movements, hugging one moment this one, the next that one, and provoking mockery, gestures, and licentious comments that brought about vulgar laughter among the large crowd.

And everywhere was a rhythmic roll of drums, a shrillness of fifes, a clacking of castanets, a furious racket, in the midst of which oranges, apple cores, and eggs full of powder or chalk flew from both sides. Sometimes a cane would be raised, shouts would be heard, people would scurry in fear, a hundred voices would blend into one, then a head red with blood—a wounded man—would be taken away and the space would close up again, and the gush of mad and carefree joy would erase it from memory; the merrymaking removed, swept away, and dispersed that bloody scene.

From time to time Donna Gabriella's carriage was forced to stop due to the great mass of people. Some of the masked people would take advantage of it, appearing at the door of the carriage with that freedom that a piece of papier-mâché or silk on one's face confers, and a few rattled off the characteristic sayings of Carnevale.

Donna Gabriella would keep to the back of the carriage while her volanti tried to chase away the nuisances, who after leaving their mistress alone would keep close to the volanti and every now and then burst air-filled bladders at their backs.

The carriage could barely move along the Cassaro until it reached the Ospedale di San Bartolomeo near Porta Felice; it stopped there, near the Church of San Nicolò, and Donna Gabriella, sticking her head out the door a little, looked down Via Butera, attempting to see something.

She saw the street full of carriages and portantine, and a flush of satisfaction rose to her face.

"Ah," she said to herself. "They are obviously getting married now! . . . Thank goodness."

At that moment she would have liked to be in a corner of the palazzo to see the newlyweds, and in her desire there was a certain wicked pleasure of revenge, since she imagined that no wedding had ever been so sad and funereal as the one that would unite those two lives.

She gave the order to go back along the Cassaro, when she saw a wagon that looked like a ship, with a mast in the middle, its sail lowered and a dozen sailors, sumptuously dressed in Turkish style, on its deck, from where they were throwing handfuls of confetti over the crowd and tossing onto the balconies the finer sweets, wrapped in golden paper. A rabble of street urchins fought over the fallen confetti, hitting each other desperately amid everyone's laughter and cackles.

Donna Gabriella hid in the back of her carriage so as not to be seen, but she noticed with amazement that the mock ship, instead of turning into the Cassaro, turned instead to the right, onto Via Butera.

"So, where is it going?" she wondered.

The ship stopped below the balconies of the Palazzo Butera; some musicians who were out of view in the bottom of the ship struck up a melody to the sound of violins and guitars, which drew people to the balcony. But while the musicians sang and played, the Turks were jumping down from the ship with their scimitars unsheathed and climbing up the grand staircase, which was covered with luxurious carpets.

Donna Gabriella was pleasantly surprised, but when she saw ladies and gentlemen in masks step down from the carriages and portantine, she understood that the prince, following the whims of his lively and novel imagination, was giving a masquerade party. A thought then occurred to her that made her smile, and she ordered the coachman to return home at once, avoiding the crowds in order to make better time.

* * *

Three-quarters of an hour later, at the foot of the grand staircase, a lady stepped down from an elegant portantina; she was dressed in a pale blue domino,[1] with a large white ribbon on her shoulder, and her face was covered by a black half mask, leaving uncovered her lovely rosy lips.

She went up very quickly, in a hurry, but when she reached the great hall she stopped, a little timid and undecided. The prince went to greet her, holding his hand out to her. The gloved hands and the small and delicate feet of the domino had revealed to him a lady of class, but the understandable curiosity of the master of the house made him look at the domino closely, trying to determine who she was.

"Your Lordship," the domino said, "allow me to keep my identity secret, even with you."

"Nor would I, beautiful masked lady, dare to reveal it. On the other hand, one senses that you must be one of the most charming ladies of our city, and that is enough."

She thanked him with a gesture and plunged into the crowd of guests that filled the halls, in one of which there was dancing.

Violante was there, in her white wedding dress, with a long veil pinned to her head by a delicate garland of jewels. Her face was even whiter than her veil

---

1 A robe-like costume, worn by both men and women, concealing the identity of the wearer, producing an element of intrigue and mystery, thus enabling them to move freely and converse with whomever they pleased.

and dress, and only her black eyes, sunken in their bluish shadows, could put a dark blemish on so much whiteness, and they gave her a somewhat ghostlike appearance.

Next to her was Emanuele, he too dressed in white satin embroidered with gold and gems, standing stiffly in a contrived and affected pose; his face, however, was red, as if his collar, squeezing his throat, was choking him. An irritation could be detected in his bearing, a hateful contempt, a desire to resort to arrogance and retaliation, to take revenge for something, to vent—and there was no sparkle of joy, no flashes of sensuality. By that time the newlyweds had finished dancing and withdrawn to the back of the hall. They had danced because they were expected to begin the dances, but they did so without desire, without enthusiasm, without any pleasure; rather, neither of them could wait to withdraw. It seemed that the intonations of the violins created a sensation of indescribable irritation on their nerves.

The masked characters abandoned themselves to an exuberant merriment, like an effervescent wine, making jokes about ladies and their suitors, dancing, jumping, laughing, dispensing sweets along with witticisms. They took aim at the newlyweds and especially at Emanuele, in whose ear they would whisper funny things or double entendres or offer advice that was a little off-color.

Emanuele had defended himself, but so as not to appear ridiculous with his haughtiness, he had gradually allowed himself to be carried away, and he would respond with quips of his own, he too teasing, also for his own relief. Then, after asking permission from Violante—who after all wished for nothing more—he too mingled amid the hubbub of the party, not so much to enjoy himself but to escape that unpleasant and embarrassing situation, beside a bride who still hadn't shown that she was aware of him.

The domino approached Violante; she looked her up and down, and shaking her head she said in a falsetto voice, "Poor child! . . . I pity you!"

Violante gave a start. Then there was someone who guessed or could read the feelings inside her heart. This domino was the first one who, instead of whispering a compliment or one of the usual good wishes, was sympathizing with her. The domino drew closer to her and, lowering her voice even more, whispered to her, almost in her ear, "You have two people to thank for this marriage: your father, may God forgive him, and Don Blasco da Castiglione."

This name aroused a sudden and fleeting blush on Violante's cheeks, and she came to her senses; she looked hard at the domino, as if trying to recognize her face from the flashing eyes behind the mask. What did she know about it? How could she say such a thing? How did she know Blasco?

Not only her curiosity but a need within her heart enlivened her face. The figure seemed to have been imbued with a breath of life, and Violante's heart, which seemed to be closed, suddenly opened up to a multitude of feelings. She would have liked to ask but didn't dare. Who was this blue domino? . . . Why had she said those words to her? The domino was looking at her. It couldn't be said what wicked sentiment had driven her to speak because her appearance was so impenetrable, and it would take a much keener sense of observation to discover, in the curve of that mouth, a smile of ruthless satisfaction.

"Are you surprised?" she whispered to her in an insinuating voice in which some quivering could be sensed. "But it is just as I tell you: if not for the crimes of your father, and if not for the generosity of Signor Blasco, who arranged this marriage, you would be happy."

These words were even more mysterious than those first spoken, but they also tightened Violante's heart in an icy grip. The domino, certain of having filled her heart with dismay, walked away.

But Violante tried to detain her.

"Wait . . . listen to me."

But the domino shook her head and thrust herself into the crowd of guests, leaving Violante astonished, shaken, anxious. Had Blasco arranged this marriage? Why had he thrown her into the arms of Emanuele? What interest did he have, then? She knew that Blasco was an Albamonte. A thought crossed her mind: was the marriage perhaps a service rendered by the bastard to his legitimate brother, for some compensation? Then was the man she had loved in all the dreams of her early youth such a despicable human being? And Emanuele? He disgusted her; the man had never appeared as repulsive to her as at that moment.

The domino had looked for Emanuele and come up to him while some of his friends were teasing him.

"Leave him be, gentlemen. The duke is very worried at this moment."

"Really? Worried about what? Kind masked lady, we want to know why he is worried."

"Oh no, not this, gentlemen! This is a secret that I cannot reveal."

Emanuele, making an effort to smile, asked, "Can't I even know?"

"You? . . . You want to know from me? But the secret is yours. Ha! Ha! Ha!"

She walked away laughing. Emanuele, who didn't understand a thing, was disconcerted, but his dismay was interpreted as an implicit confession that he indeed had a secret, and then they surrounded him, provoked him, teased him. They wanted to know his secret.

He rudely freed himself in order to catch up with the domino and stopped her at the same time that she, seeing Coriolano della Floresta pass by, said to him, "Offer me your arm, signore, and protect me from the Duke of Motta."

Emanuele hinted at a smile and said, "Kind masked lady, I am not someone who attacks beautiful and gracious ladies—"

"Eh!" the domino interrupted intentionally. "Are you sure that one cannot prove you wrong?"

Emanuele bit his lip.

"Who are you?" he asked. "You are making me die of curiosity."

But the domino evaded the question. "My God, how can you leave your charming young bride alone? Don't you see? Your remoteness pains her so much that she looks like a ghost. . . . Go and console her. . . . I don't want to steal her groom."

"Oh, don't be afraid of—"

"She could be jealous."

"Don't give it a thought."

"Then isn't she jealous of you?"

"Of course not!"

"No? But doesn't she love you? Ah, poor duke! . . . How I pity you! . . . Be careful: she is the daughter of Don Raimondo. . . . Ask Girolamo Ammirata who killed your mother."

"Who are you?" Emanuele insisted, unable to control his anger, his annoyance, and a sense of fear.

But the domino pushed the Cavaliere della Floresta forward and walked away once more in order to return to Violante. The Cavaliere della Floresta had heard her last words and couldn't control a sense of surprise. He looked at the mouth and hands of the blue domino and a suspicion crossed his mind. He bowed and said in a barely audible voice, "Be careful, duchess, you could be recognized."

It was the domino's turn to be taken aback with an air of alarm.

"Quiet!"

She had reached Violante.

"Farewell, young bride, you will never see me again, but I want to leave you with a warning." And, moving closer to her ear, she whispered, "Above all, beware of friends . . . and remember that your father was murdered."

Rather than simply leaving, she fled, leaving Violante in a state of anguished shock, with the vision of her father on the bed in the throes of death.

Emanuele was following her with his eyes; as soon as her saw her go out, he called a servant. "Ten scudi for you if you follow that domino and can tell me who she is."

Half an hour later, the servant returned. Emanuele, who was waiting for him impatiently, went to meet him.

"Well?"

"Excellency, she is the duchess, the Dowager Duchess of Motta."

"Donna Gabriella! Her!" Emanuele exclaimed in a voice in which hatred, rage, shame, and the spirit of revenge coalesced like whirlwinds in a hurricane.

CHAPTER 13

The parties for Emanuele's wedding lasted two days. On the second day they took place in the palazzo of the Prince of Geraci, who didn't want to be outdone by his illustrious relative. The people had their own festivities. Following the traditions of their houses, the two lords wanted the commoners to participate in their more or less heartfelt joy, and there were in Piazza Bologni, as there already were on the Mura delle Cattive, makeshift fountains pouring wine and greased poles with plenty of little baskets filled with all that a poor devil would need to live it up in the last days of Carnevale. Handfuls of coins were thrown from the balcony onto the crowd, who fought over them with their fists, amid the great laughter of the generous noble lords, and in honor of the newlyweds.

Those newlyweds, however, didn't appear to be moved by all that, nor by the sumptuous banquets, nor by the formal balls, nor by the fistfights among the commoners.

Violante dreaded the time, now approaching, when all these parties would end. Emanuele was still under the shock of Donna Gabriella's audacity and her words. The appearance of that woman had awakened all his desires of possession, vengeance, revenge, hatred.

Two hours after midnight on Monday, the newlyweds were escorted to the Palazzo della Motta, which after a long time was seeing its rooms opened again to its masters, and they were left there with the most ardent good wishes. Violante was going back into that grand and vast palazzo where she had once been mistress by hereditary right and was now nothing but the wife of the master; she was going back into that palazzo so full of painful memories, where her father had died. Nothing of the former layout of the rooms and furniture had been updated. The large double bedroom, with its alcove framed by friezes and stuccos, with the large wrought-iron bed with a motif of blue, pink, and gold enameled leaves; the curtains of crimson damask; the large silver filigree reliquary inside the tortoisehell and gold case; the inlaid chest with handles of gilded bronze; the locked writing desk; the small damask sofa; the oval mirror in its frame of gilt scrolls; the slightly darkened painting of the Madonna—everything was there as she had seen it in her childhood, as it had been handed down for two or three generations, intact, like a family tradition, and from every object arose the memories of her life.

She was born there, in that room; her mother, of whom she had no real memory but only a small portrait miniature, had died there.

All at once her entire life offered itself up to her memory like one of those large canvases by the old masters, in which around the main figure all the events of their life, from their birth to their death, are recorded in little paintings. Her innocent and happy childhood in the Monastery of Montevergini; her stepmother, the abduction, the sudden and miraculous intervention of Blasco; the castle where she and Donna Gabriella had been kidnapped; the death of her father, assassinated. . . . And every scene of this story placed Blasco in front of her and with him her stepmother. . . . She saw again the knife in Donna Gabriella's hand and then saw again Donna Gabriella herself resting in languid abandonment on Blasco's chest. . . . A sharp and acute pain was renewed in her heart, which in those four years seemed to have become accustomed to the idea that everything was dead and forgotten; the wound that she believed was closed opened again, bleeding, in that room and in front of that bed, where she seemed to see their two faces, Donna Gabriella's and Blasco's, dozing on the same pillow, as she had found herself one morning, the sweetest of her mornings in the room at the villa.

Now she too would enter that bedroom but with another man, and the hands that were pushing her were Blasco's! . . . Blasco whom she had loved, Blasco who had betrayed her. Had he sold her? Sold her to Emanuele, perhaps for the right to call himself an Albamonte? Perhaps to gain a status? The words of the pale blue domino still echoed in her ears: the crimes of her father and Blasco's wish had thrown her into the arms of Emanuele. What crimes? What was her father guilty of? Some vague bits of information, heard here and there on people's lips, were accumulating or blending in her mind. She recalled everything that had been said upon Emanuele's appearance onto the scene of aristocratic society—this legitimate scion having suddenly emerged from the shadows on the same day that her father was assassinated. The words *usurpation, crime, Beati Paoli,* on which she hadn't dwelled and whose meaning she hadn't understood, came back to her, making her blood run cold. It seemed to her that Emanuele and Blasco both had some connection to those terrifying events that had suddenly made her an orphan and had cast her away from that palazzo, where she was now the wife of one of those two due to the complicity of the other.

Her heart was crushed by all her sorrows and her desperations. This marriage now seemed to her more odious than ever, and all her rebellions, held back by a resigned suffering, now burst forth from her with a violence that emboldened her.

Emanuele was there, on the threshold of the bedroom, where she had stopped, caught off guard by all these thoughts; he was behind her, so close that they were almost touching each other. He had never seemed so repugnant and so loathsome to her as at that moment.

She looked at him with a sullen expression.

He too seemed overwhelmed by a thought. The idea of this marriage, of having to spend his life with this young girl who didn't arouse even a quiver of sensuality, frightened him. Crossing this threshold, embracing this woman, because it was imposed on him and because at least for that first time it was necessary, seemed to him like something that was beyond his own strength. He couldn't overcome his intense aversion.

This house, to which he was returning as lord and where he had never lived, still retained the memory of Donna Gabriella, and he felt a type of raging desire for that woman that he had not been able to nor had known how to possess.

He also looked at Violante, unable to restrain the feelings that stirred in his chest and gave him an expression of reluctance, of rancor.

They couldn't bring themselves to utter a word to each other, but they had a silent understanding of what wasn't being said.

Emanuele was the first to break the silence: "It's not necessary, I think, to tell you that I didn't wish for this marriage, let alone ask for it, and that it is only the wishes of our relatives that imposed it on us."

"I know, signore," Violante replied, satisfied with the tone that the discussion was taking, and to whom those words "the wishes of our relatives" recalled those of the blue domino: "Blasco's wish."

"I am glad; this relieves me of having to offer any explanations. . . . There is no emotional bond between us. I am sorry to have to say it, but I don't feel for you what is called love, and I would like to inform you from the beginning that our relations will be those strictly necessary so that the Albamonte lineage does not become extinct."

Violante didn't understand. She was completely unaware of what such relations could entail, and she looked at Emanuele with a certain astonishment. "I don't know what you are talking about, but it is only right that I tell you honestly that I don't love you either, and that I will never love you."

Emanuele turned red, his self-respect stung. He wanted to retain only for himself the right to refuse and to reject the young girl, and her declaration provoked him.

"I don't care," he said. "I'm not looking for and do not ask for your love, nor will I ever ask for it. Rather, except for those relations, we will live like two strangers. I intend to enjoy all my freedom, without you having the right to accuse or to complain about me."

"It's only that I have but one regret, signore: that of being tied to you forever. . . . And as for living like two strangers, it is what I ardently desire. I rather ask you to let me prepare the room I had as a young girl. I am giving this one over to you because it arouses too many painful memories for me."

Emanuele nodded.

"It makes no difference to me. This one or the other is the same thing, although it seems to me more convenient that you stay here, but we'll talk about this later.

Now that we are clear, and since I don't think you want to spend the night and talk here, on the threshold of this room, I beg you to get undressed and go to bed."

Violante blushed with shame; a shred of reality was revealing itself to her. Trembling, she said, "But I'm not sleepy, signore: I will be fine sitting down."

"It's not a question of being sleepy," Emanuele said with a vulgar smile.

He stayed a minute, waiting for a response that wasn't coming, and he repeated, "We can't spend the night like this, sitting down talking."

The young girl sensed the danger. Flushes of shame mingled with those of scorn and repugnance.

"I don't understand why I can't—"

"But you will understand later, for heaven's sake! . . . Besides, they are not things that are talked about. . . . Come on, go to bed."

Violante became sullen but made a decision. "Well, then, leave, signore."

Emanuele smiled, shrugged roughly, and said, "This is silly. But even so, I will indulge you."

He went out, adding, "Be quick. You don't want to leave me outside."

But Violante bolted the door.

Fearing the attacks and surprises of the Beati Paoli, Don Raimondo had fortified the doors and windows of the rooms with iron bars, which made them secure. Violante barred the door, mentally thanking God for that defense, and she felt safe. At first Emanuele heard the squeaking of the key and the bolt and he laughed at it; then he heard the sound of the iron bar and became suspicious.

"What are you doing?" he asked from behind the door.

Violante didn't answer. He waited a little, then knocked and said through the door, "Donna Violante . . . well, then, why aren't you opening the door yet?"

But no answer came. Violante had curled up in a corner, pressing her hands against her heart, which was pounding due to the emotion. The door was solid, the windows also barred; in order for someone to get in, the shutters would have to be smashed with axes, and that would throw the palazzo into turmoil.

Emanuele waited another moment and shook the door, trying to open it, but in vain; in an angry voice he called out, "Donna Violante! Donna Violante! Come on, open the door, by God!"

Then she answered.

"Leave me alone. I will not open it. There is no point in shouting and having the servants hear you. Don't create a scandal."

He clenched his fists, cursing, and was on the verge of giving a couple of kicks that would have knocked down the door, but he realized that he would expose himself to ridicule; the servants would rush there, realize what it was about, and roll about laughing, and the little story would be known all over the city, adding to those of his misadventures with Donna Gabriella.

There was only one way out: to leave. To go from rejected husband to giving the appearance of a husband who is doing the rejecting, which, in saving him, could also harm Violante. But his stubbornness, his vanity, and his anger, which were taking the place of any reasonable inner emotion, kept him there, behind that door, undecided. He insisted a little more, then he made a decision, the least noisy one possible, so as not to expose himself to the comments of the servants. Slowly, he crossed two or three rooms, went into Don Raimondo's old study, which retained the austere silence of learning amid the high shelves of books, and sank into a large armchair in front of the table, like someone who has a great idea ready to put down in writing.

* * *

The three-burner oil lamp that he had placed on the table cast a reddish light into the middle of the room, while the rest of the study remained in a dim half-light. On the ceiling, on a large stucco panel, was painted the Albamonte coat of arms; opposite the writing desk, hanging on the wall between the bookshelves, was a large portrait of Don Raimondo in the robes of presiding judge of the Gran Corte Criminale, with one hand resting on top of a book, perhaps the statutes of the kingdom, the other on his hip, in a pose of authority. In the half-light his features weren't clearly visible, but from the thin contour of his mouth and from the corner of his jaw one could divine that undefinable feline and evil nature that made one's blood run cold upon seeing him.

He recognized him. He was the man who had had him thrown shamefully into the prisons of the Castello a Mare and whose daughter, by a twist of fate, he had now married. Emanuele had never forgotten that disgraceful whipping punishment, and every time that a resurgence of memories reminded him of it, he felt the blood rushing to his head. Now the image of that man stood before him and was joined with that of his daughter, from whom he was receiving a treatment that seemed to him no less insulting than that torture, and he wrapped the father and daughter in the same feeling of hatred.

And now, comparing the cold and unhappy features of Violante with those of Don Raimondo, he seemed to discern in both of them something in common: the same sharp-edged and menacing expression. So, had the young girl inherited this from her father? Was she perhaps capable of driving a dagger into his back while pretending to embrace him?

"Tomorrow," he thought, "I will have that portrait taken down; I will have it thrown in the attic. Why did they leave it there? Why didn't they tell me about it?"

But he was lying. Two days before, invited to see if everything was in good order in the palazzo where he was going to live, he had seen the portrait and had made no remark about it. Perhaps he had glanced at it absent-mindedly, preoccupied as he was with his imminent and not eagerly awaited wedding.

"I'll let the mice chew it up."

It was the only revenge he could take on that man. But his bride? What would his bride do? In truth, he was astonished not to feel at the bottom of his heart anything but an exuberance of hatred for her person, but no true deep resentment for her action. She didn't want him? But in this they were equals. He didn't want her either. What offended him was the obstacle created by the young girl on whom he wanted to, indeed *had* to, take revenge, for so many reasons, and his revenge had to be full, open, complete.

Meanwhile he had to make sure that nothing leaked to the eyes of the servants about what had happened that wedding night, or at least to make everyone believe the opposite of what had occurred. He immersed himself in the search for the how and ended up falling asleep in the large armchair, under the immobile gaze of the portrait, which seemed to be watching over him.

The bells of the goats that were coming to bring their milk to the city early in the morning awoke him with a start. He was afraid of being discovered by the servants and having them guess that he had spent the night outside the bridal chamber. He returned to the antechamber, pretending to have just come out of his bedroom, and he pulled the bell cord.

His manservant rushed in, astonished to see his master wearing his evening clothes instead of his dressing gown, but even more astonished at being told to arrange for the portantina.

"Is Your Excellency going out? At this hour?"

"Quiet!" Emanuele whispered with a meaningful smile. "The duchess is sleeping; we must not wake her. . . . Get the regular portantina ready."

A quarter of an hour later he was leaving his palazzo and being taken to Signora Nina Manfredini, the celebrated prima donna who during Carnevale had sung at the Teatro di Santa Lucia, which, although it could not rival Santa Cecilia, the main opera house, nevertheless put on fine performances.

Emanuele, a frequent visitor to the theater, had conducted a steady and successful courtship of the prima donna Manfredini and up to the eve of his wedding had spent some pleasant hours with her. Jokingly, she had said to him, "How much I would pay to see Your Illustrious Lordship in his groom's suit!"

Emanuele had let slip a promise: "Why wouldn't you see me?"

He had suddenly remembered his promise and had seen salvation in it. They would judge him reckless, but he would avoid the ridicule and perhaps an excuse could be found for his escapade.

That season Signora Manfredini's beauty and voice had sent the young men of Palermo into ecstasy, and quite a few had fought over her favors. But Emanuele had the advantage of having met her in Rome, and for that reason he had been chosen as her natural protector.

His success had so pleased Emanuele's vanity that he had showered the beautiful singer with gifts, to the great satisfaction of her husband, who at first hadn't seemed happy with the choice made by his wife. The relationship had to be severed upon Emanuele's marriage, which coincided with the final performance of Scarlatti's *Inganni Felici*, in which Signora Manfredini excelled and which was also the final performance of the theatrical season that went on in those days—at least in Palermo—for Carnevale only.

On the last evening that Emanuele had seen Signora Manfredini, the beautiful woman had shed abundant tears of sorrow, which would have moved a stone and had thoroughly excited the young man's vanity, and it was amid those tears and that emotion that she let out that exclamation, and Emanuele let slip that promise to which he had clung.

Signora Nina was sleeping when she awoke to knocks beating on her door. She was no less surprised, as sleepy as she was, at seeing Emanuele appear before her, who, smiling and gallantly extending his hand, said to her, "Here I am for you in my groom's suit."

She seemed to be touched by this attention, which had the power to silence the good signora's husband, who in truth had woken up reluctantly to do the requisite honors to his wife's patron.

The astonishment of the servants, when it was found out that the Duke of Motta had spent the night in the singer's house, locking his wife in her room, had no bounds. The maidservants almost wept for their mistress's bad luck. But their astonishment grew when, still not having been called for, they realized that Violante had locked herself in from the inside and was refusing to open the door.

Meanwhile close relatives were beginning to arrive to wish the bride and groom a good morning and to give them their best wishes for male offspring. Only then, when she heard the voices of her grandparents, did Violante unlock the door. Her first words, without waiting for her grandparents to ask for an explanation for that new development, were, "Take me back to the monastery, I beg you!"

The prince laughed, interpreting the young girl's dismay and plea in his own way.

"Come on! What is this childish behavior? Of course it had to be like this . . . but it's all over now."

The princess hugged her, she too smiling, whispering some words in her ear, but at the astonished look of the young girl, who had understood nothing and didn't know how to answer, she hesitated.

"But where is your husband?" she asked.

"My husband? Oh, but I haven't seen him. He didn't sleep here. I don't want him to."

"Oh."

Then they noticed that the bed was untouched.

"What does this mean?"

CHAPTER 14

Marriage annulment proceedings were initiated by the Prince of Butera, in accord with Emanuele della Motta, and in the meantime Violante went to live at her grandfather's house. Those events had so shaken her health that she had become ill over them, and so the doctors didn't think it advisable to let her return to the monastery, as she wanted. Emanuele couldn't have hoped for more.

Now master of himself, he could do as he pleased. The annulment of the marriage gave him back his full and complete freedom, and he was using it and abusing it. He had again drawn close to Matteo Lo Vecchio, whose perspicacity, investigations, and discoveries he was familiar with, in order to learn in detail what role Blasco had played in the Beati Paoli and how Don Raimondo's death had come about.

The birro told him what he knew; he naturally added something of his own and lent a degree of certainty to what was an inference or a hypothesis.

"Your Excellency," he concluded, not without malice, "you must be grateful to the Beati Paoli and to your bastard brother, because without them who knows what would have happened! I am sure that you would merely be the son of that beggar Girolamo Ammirata."

Instead of opening his heart to a benevolent sentiment, those words stung Emanuele, who said harshly, "I would still be a duke."

"Your Excellency, permit me to have my doubts. The sect had prepared a serious case against Don Raimondo and it is because of that case that he, fearing the ax, had signed that document of acknowledgment that served as the basis for putting Your Excellency in possession of your inheritance and to obtain the investiture."

"So did that case contain terrible things?"

"Simply the testimonies of quite a few people who knew about or had carried out the crimes ordered by Don Raimondo so that he could usurp the Albamonte inheritance and the ducal crown."

"What? What?"

"The plain truth."

"What about me, then?"

"Your Excellency, as you know, was picked up on the street, but perhaps you don't know that your mother, in order to escape from two attempts to poison her and in order to save Your Excellency, who was born a few days before, lowered herself from the balcony. She wandered through the night, lost her way, and was picked up by Girolamo Ammirata. If he had arrived a little later, she would have fallen back into the hands of Don Raimondo, who would have had both of you put to death."

Emanuele shuddered, then said, "And idiot that I am, I had to give back or let the daughter benefit from what the father had stolen from me! . . . But can there be anything worse? Why didn't you tell me all these things before?"

"Your Excellency no longer gave me the privilege of requesting me . . ."

"And this evidence?"

"Signor Don Blasco had it."

"Him?"

"Now I couldn't say if he still has it. . . . But either him or someone from the gang."

"Matteo Lo Vecchio, I would give an eye to have it."

"An eye is too much for Your Excellency and it is nothing to me. We should find out for sure who is in possession of those papers and try to obtain them rightfully, or by stealing them."

"How does one go about finding out?"

"We will try. . . . If Girolamo Ammirata were here, we might be able to find out."

"Where is Don Girolamo?"

"In Naples. He doesn't dare come here. Perhaps he would be useful to us. . . . Owing to the affection that he felt for Your Excellency, I believe he would do anything you would ask him to do. Your Excellency should ask for him to be pardoned; they would not deny him, and it would be justified due to your former relationship."

The birro didn't use enough tact this time, or perhaps he didn't imagine that Emanuele would be making an effort to forget the past and that he wouldn't feel any gratitude toward the razionale of the Ospedale Civico.

Emanuele, in fact, had reddened at those words and felt a sense of repugnance, but his personal interest was stronger, and he answered evasively with an "I will try" and dismissed the birro after giving him a purse of money and urging him to investigate on his own.

Matteo Lo Vecchio was on his way home with his usual stride, racking his brains; no one could dissuade him from believing that Blasco had returned those famous papers to the sect, and most likely they had to be in the hands of either Don Girolamo or Coriolano della Floresta, since he had no doubt that the cavaliere had some role in the sect itself. He had no certain proof of it, so he had not been able to report him, but he was thoroughly convinced. His friendship with Blasco provided him with the most reasonable grounds.

How to get to Coriolano and Blasco? He was too well known, had been too public about this matter to act directly, and if he had proposed the name Don Girolamo, it was because it seemed to him the most direct and speedy means. But as he walked along, another face came to him: Andrea. How come he hadn't thought of him before?

Andrea was still in Emanuele's service, something not at all uncommon, since in those times a servant was certain to die in the same house where he had served since boyhood, but he was not satisfied with his situation.

He was hoping that for services rendered, and for having been the late duke's trusted servant, Emanuele would make him his majordomo, his house steward—in short, provide him with the means to attain a certain level of comfort. But Emanuele, by keeping him in his house, had thought he was doing something great, and Andrea had been treated like any other servant, without any distinction. That had made him unhappy, a bit sullen, and a lover of idleness.

He was getting fat and would always find excuses to leave the palazzo and wander aimlessly through the streets, not even disdaining to stop in some taverns to drink with the porters of the piazza or with some artisans.

In the first days of his service, invigorated due to his past experience and the dangers he had encountered, he had thought this authority would carry weight over the other servants, but, convinced that he was not being supported by his master, that he was surrounded by hatred and that he was isolating himself, he put his foolish ambitions aside and made that more comfortable decision, one with fewer problems. But all that idealized love, that sense of unlimited devotion and readiness to sacrifice, which he had sworn to his dying master and with which he had thrown himself into its pursuit, had vanished from his soul.

Sometimes it would reawaken when Emanuele got into some misadventure. Then he would get angry: "Why are you pushing me aside? Why don't you have me accompany you? . . . I'm not one of those who run away! . . . I have fought against the Turks."

His contempt reached its peak when Emanuele left for Rome and didn't choose him to be part of his retinue.

"Now it's over!" he said bitterly to himself. "It's really over. If I could find another house, I would leave . . . but where can I go when I am devoted to this one?"

In one of the taverns where he hung out, he had met and gotten to know Michele Barabino, who was still poor but no longer a beggar. Now he was beginning to make some clothes for the poor, since he didn't have enough to reopen his shop and seek a better clientele. On one occasion when he saw Blasco pass by, he started to talk enthusiastically about him to Andrea.

"What a man! What a man!"

"I know him," Andrea said brusquely.

"Ah! You know him! I'm glad. What a man! What a heart! If you knew what he has done for me!"

He began to tell him about all the episodes in which Blasco had been the subject or the instigator at one time, and his words resonated with that intense and profound admiration that fills devoted souls.

"Believe me, he deserves to be the Duke of Motta, not that clown Don Emanuele! . . . Yes, him! He's better-looking, taller, generous, valiant. What more do you want?"

From that day on the good old man was so pleased that Andrea knew Don Blasco that he always found a way to talk about him, telling the same stories, with the same enthusiasm.

"Yes, listen: I sold him his first suit!"

Andrea also began to think that Blasco would have been more worthy to come into the inheritance and the title than Emanuele. Blasco was just like his father: the same valor, the same generous and chivalrous nature, the same lack of interest in refined manners, the same daring. Emanuele, instead, was wicked; there was something lacking in him.

He had even thought so earlier, when he had desperately thrown himself against Don Raimondo in order to reinstate Emanuele into his inheritance, he had felt a jealous mistrust and an almost natural aversion to Blasco. He would even have killed him, and in the meantime, on account of both the tailor's stories and what he himself knew, he had ended up wondering whether it had been worth slaughtering Don Raimondo in order to make Emanuele the person he had become.

Matteo Lo Vecchio tracked down Andrea in a tavern in the Capo, having a drink with Michele Barabino, but he didn't approach him. He too went in and asked for a glass of wine, but without taking a seat, standing in front of the counter and pretending not to have seen Andrea.

With a knowing glance Andrea pointed him out to his companion.

"There is the patriarch of the birri," he said under his breath.

"*Libera nos domo!*" said Michele Barabino, who took pride in sprinkling his conversation with Latin phrases.

Matteo Lo Vecchio took three swigs, savoring the wine, turning indifferently to look around the tavern. Just then he pretended to notice Andrea and made a gesture with his head as if to say, "Alas! There is that fine individual."

He paid and went out.

A few days later he returned a second time, repeating the same meaningful gestures, which made Andrea suspicious.

"What the devil does that son of a bitch want?" he said to himself.

And when the birro had gone, he let loose a curse and a threat.

"Blood of . . . it will end up that I *scucio il sacco della* . . ."[1]

And he said a repulsive word.

The third time they saw each other, in fact, Andrea looked at him with an air of resentment and of challenge. "Well, then, do you have something to say to me?"

Matteo Lo Vecchio shrugged his shoulders, as if to say, "What an idiot!"

Then he said loudly, "Me? Nothing. If I had wanted to tell you something, my friend, you wouldn't be here drinking now."

"What do you mean?"

"Nothing, my friend. You are so intelligent! . . . Be well."

He went out, but Andrea got up and ran after him, while Michele Barabino tried to hold him back.

"Let it go. . . . You know who he is. You'll bring yourself to ruin."

But Andrea paid no attention to him. He stopped the birro, repeating his question: "I want to know what you have to tell me."

Matteo Lo Vecchio made a sarcastic face. "If you really want to know, I could have the captain of justice tell you, or better yet, the auditore fiscale. . . . You don't have to look at me with those eyes and put your hands in your pockets, my friend, because you should understand that, if I had wanted, you wouldn't be here talking to me now. . . . You would have already made the acquaintance of the gallows."

Andrea turned pale and in a humbler tone of voice remarked, "I believe that you are mistaken."

"Oh, no, my goodness! . . . It would be a fine thing if I didn't know you, Andrea Lo Bianco. I would have some accounts to settle with you, personal accounts, mind you, and apart from the power of the Gran Corte Criminale, but you should have noticed that I smiled when I looked at you. . . . That is the clearest proof that I have no hostile intentions against you. . . . Far from it! And then. . . . You should have seen me at the palazzo, since the most illustrious duke, your beloved master, has given me the honor of calling for me many times."

Andrea had had plenty of time to calm down and to mentally make this reflection: "He is right. If he had wanted to report me, he would have done it, and if he had bad intentions now, he wouldn't be having this conversation with me."

Nevertheless, to affirm his position, he objected again. "I don't know what you are talking about. I have no account to settle with you, and I haven't seen you at the palazzo."

"Ah, liar!" Matteo Lo Vecchio said, laughing, giving him a pat on the shoulder. "But let's let it go. Come drink with me; not here. That chatterbox the tailor is here. . . . I know him."

He dragged him toward Piazza San Cosmo, to a tavern from where one could see Girolamo Ammirata's former house and Vicolo degli Orfani, and, feigning

---

1 "knife him in the stomach."

to choose a random spot, he pushed him to sit at a table in front of the door, so that he could see out.

Pouring a drink, the birro winked at the house and said, "Do you remember, eh? . . . Poor Don Girolamo. He's a widower, I think. Isn't that true?"

Andrea nodded, upset by the reference and at the same time by the people who seemed so far away to him.

"Actually," the birro continued, "I never would have imagined that the duke wouldn't take his savior with him, or that he wouldn't at least provide him with a fortune."

Andrea gave a start. How did he know?

Matteo Lo Vecchio went on with apparent warmth: "Because in the end he not only owes his status to him, but Don Girolamo risked losing his neck. . . . He was a hair's breadth away. I should know. And you too, Andrea. Don Raimondo knew everything. These are things that can now be talked about. It's all in the past. But then! . . . Do you remember that vicolo? One night when I nearly arrested you, the bastard, Don Blasco, saved you. . . . You must remember. . . . I had you in my hands and Don Raimondo knew about everything . . . even the case against him. The case that you had put together with all the witnesses. Peppa, Giuseppico . . ."

Without meaning to, Andrea was feeling uncomfortable and no longer knew how to respond.

Matteo Lo Vecchio continued: "I was forced to search for you and to persecute you, but, my word of honor, I didn't know that Don Raimondo was the villain that he was. I thought he was a victim. But when I read the evidence . . ."

Andrea leapt from his chair, white as a sheet.

"You read it? How did you read it?"

"I had it in my hands."

"Ah! . . . You? . . . That's why it was never found again! . . . Then you have it?"

"Me? No. . . . I don't have it."

"Did Don Raimondo have it, then?"

"But of course not! He would have paid a million for it. . . . But I suppose Don Girolamo has it."

"No, he doesn't have it, he doesn't have it anymore!" Andrea groaned.

He was afraid. From that case, it had been clear that he had participated in the sect of the Beati Paoli, and although he had withdrawn four years ago, he also had reason to fear that justice could lay its hands on him for the assassination of Don Raimondo and for other crimes yet unknown. A thought suddenly occurred to him: that Matteo Lo Vecchio had skillfully drawn him into a trap in order to extract the confession that he had inadvertently let slip. He looked at the birro and read in his face an amazement and a regret so sincere that he was somewhat reassured.

"So who has that evidence, then?" the birro asked.

"I don't know anything about it, but we will have to find it, at any cost!" Andrea said.

Matteo Lo Vecchio remained a little pensive, then said, "I have my suspicions, but I can't investigate them."

"Meaning what?" Andrea asked strongly.

"I would bet that Don Blasco has it."

"Him? How would he have it?"

"Because I know from a reliable source that he had it in his hands. Now, either he gave it back to Don Girolamo, or he has it with him, unless he destroyed it . . . which would be desirable. . . . If you really wanted to know, you could verify it."

"Me?"

"Well, I certainly can't. First of all because it doesn't concern me and secondly because I would be suspected. But as for you, that's another matter. . . . It will be said that it is in your master's interest. But we have to be sure, very sure, that it hasn't been returned to Don Girolamo . . . and Don Girolamo is in Naples."

At this time the discussion went no further. Andrea returned to the palazzo with a troubled mind, feeling that he was in the birro's power; nor did the friendly manner that Matteo Lo Vecchio had assumed or the fact that he hadn't been harassed until then serve to reassure him. It was obvious that that conversation had been sought, and that the birro needed to get some information, and that perhaps he had gotten it out of him. Andrea went over the conversation in his head, trying to recall if he had let any compromising words slip out.

From that day he no longer had any peace. In spite of himself, he would follow in Matteo Lo Vecchio's tracks, or rather, he would let himself be encountered, thinking that he could thus keep an eye on him and more easily surveil him. The birro didn't cast off that kindly and almost protective manner and no longer spoke about the past. He would inquire about the proceedings for the annulment of the marriage, which was fascinating the city.

"It takes money, my friend; one must go to Rome with a pouch like this, as the 'bronze king' in Piazza Bologni says. The monsignors have big hands and pockets like saddlebags."

But Matteo Lo Vecchio's silence and his caution to avoid any discussion about the famous papers made Andrea increasingly suspicious and stirred up this thought in his mind: "The birro is plotting some big mischief."

And he was in a way obsessed with it and became bitter, irritable, and suspicious, taking offense at every little annoyance and believing that he was being watched and spied on. His suspicions grew when, a month later, he ran into Don Girolamo Ammirata.

"You?"

"Me, indeed! . . . I arrived this morning."

"Pardoned?"

"Pardoned!"

"Oh, how wonderful. . . . I mean, I don't know if I would take comfort in it, my friend, or if it would have been preferable to have stayed in Naples!"

"Listen! Why are you saying that?"

"Do you know who had you pardoned?"

"But of course I know. And I come precisely to thank Eman . . . the duke, for his kindness to have remembered me."

"Are you sure it was the duke?"

"Who the heck do you expect to have gone through this trouble?"

"Who? Matteo Lo Vecchio."

"Eh!"

"It's like I'm telling you. We are in his hands. The scoundrel knows all about that case that was made against Don Raimondo. . . . And it contains our names and surnames. . . . He has had us reunite here so he can hand all of us over to justice. Listen to me; we have to find refuge."

Don Girolamo was at first disconcerted by this news, but, reflecting on it, he didn't think it held up. They knew that he belonged to the sect, and he had had to flee for precisely that reason. And if they pardoned him now, it meant that they were exonerating him for that crime for which he had gone away. And then there was a way to verify it, and that was to approach Emanuele.

He wasn't home, and Don Girolamo sat in the servant's hall waiting for him, talking to Andrea and inquiring about a thousand silly things. Andrea spoke to him about Emanuele's marriage, about the scandalous events, about the annulment, but to each of these bits of news Don Girolamo would say, "I know."

"How do you know?" Andrea asked, vexed.

"That's a good one! How do I know. . . . What world are you from?"

"Even from Naples, then?"

"But of course! . . . I understand that you are surprised, because now 'you are a Turk.' But . . ."

The noise of a carriage in the vestibule, the immediate bustle of servants, and the deferential manner in which they lined up signaled that the duke was arriving.

Andrea rushed to stand in line with the others, saying, "The master is here."

Don Girolamo got up and looked, not without an intense emotion. Although he had parted from Emanuele with a saddened heart and had never received a word, not even a goodbye, he couldn't erase from his heart that for more than sixteen years he had treated him like a son, and for all that time he had been the apple of poor Signora Francesca's eye. And all the memories of the past, sweet and sad at the same time, gushed from the depths of his soul. His heart was pounding, and his eyes were tearing up.

He saw two valets leading with torches in hand, as if they were accompanying the Eucharist, and behind them came Emanuele, in very sumptuous and elegant attire, proud, with his back straight and head erect, not lowering his gaze, his stride stiff, followed by two other valets, one of whom was carrying his cloak with great care on his outstretched arms and the other one holding a red silk umbrella.

He crossed the hall between the servants, who were divided into two rows, bowing not in a submissive manner but one more of adoration; he passed in front of Don Girolamo, barely deigning to glance at him, and went into the rooms, whose doors closed behind him.

Don Girolamo felt his heart tighten. One glance, and nothing more! Hadn't he recognized him? Or had pride and vanity dried up every feeling in Emanuele's heart? He waited until he was allowed to be in the duke's presence, but after a wait of three-quarters of an hour, a valet came to tell him that His Excellency, while appreciating Don Girolamo's consideration, could not receive him right then because he had to change his clothes before going to a soiree.

Don Girolamo went down the stairs with his head lowered, embittered by a scornful sorrow, and he went to the Palazzo della Floresta.

He told everything to Coriolano and concluded with a sigh of profound regret. "And this is who we have carried out justice for!"

CHAPTER 15

Violante's marriage had caused Blasco to be withdrawn, and on the day of the wedding, under a pretext, he had avoided Coriolano's company and that of Donna Gabriella as well by going away to the countryside and not returning until Ash Wednesday, when the news was spreading throughout the city that Emanuele, like the young rake that he was, had spent the night at the home of the prima donna of Santa Lucia.

He was outraged by it, but at the same time he couldn't conceal his own joy, and he wanted Coriolano to give him the details that were common knowledge. His joy increased when he learned that Violante had denied the groom access to her bedroom.

"What can you do?" concluded Coriolano, smiling. "Emanuele was hungry, didn't find his dinner at home, and went out to dine; it's excusable, and I think he acted with spirit."

"Well done! Well done!" Blasco exclaimed, certainly not thinking about Emanuele's appetite. "Do you know that that young girl has character? I would never have imagined it! . . . I am so happy!"

"Excuse me, what are you happy about? About her character, if this is what you would like to call it, or about the bars that barricaded the door?"

Blasco blushed slightly. Coriolano, who was looking at him with his calm and gentle but at the same time investigative eye, said, "It's a short-lived consolation. These are sieges that always end with a surrender. If this state were to continue, it would end up showering the participants with ridicule, and the ridicule would also fall on the authors of this marriage. Therefore, it's natural for the bars to fall down and for the doors to open."

"Do you think so?" Blasco said, turning pale.

"For heaven's sake! . . . But excuse me," added Coriolano, "why are you so pale?"

"Me? . . . No, I'm not."

"Yes, you are! . . . Tell me the truth, are you still in love with Donna Violante?"

Blasco shook his head; he didn't dare say no. Coriolano's words stirred up too many memories and too many dormant emotions for him to declare something that wasn't true. But he didn't want to admit it. He was by then no longer free himself; he had tied his destiny to Donna Gabriella's, and it would seem like a disgrace to him, a dishonorable, cowardly act, to break the promise that, in one critical, extraordinary moment, he had made. If up until that day Donna Gabriella hadn't legally become his wife, it had only been because she hadn't wanted to.

"I want to be loved by you freely, without any constraint, without any obligation other than from the heart. . . . I fear, my friend, that the day on which I become your wife I will earn the right to go out on your arm without meeting anyone's disapproval, but I will lose your love, and I want your love."

These words had tied him to Donna Gabriella even more strongly than the blessing of a priest would have done.

But meanwhile he felt that there was something in his heart that he couldn't give; there was something preventing him from it. Even he could see it clearly now—he had bolted the innermost chambers of his heart before Donna Gabriella because in those chambers he had locked the image of Violante with his dreams, with his hopes, with the sorrows of a solitary love.

Coriolano shook his head and murmured, "Alas! How much you have changed! Where is my Blasco whom I met one day on Strada Colonna, he face-to-face with the Prince of Iraci?"

Blasco also smiled at this recollection, but it was a sad smile. It really wasn't him anymore; a muddy river had descended to flood the green fields of his happy-go-lucky manner.

"I am growing old, my friend."

"At the age of thirty? Come on! Don't even think it. . . . I know what kind of old age you mean. But let's talk about something else."

A few days later, news circulated through the soirees that the annulment proceedings for Emanuele's marriage had begun, and Coriolano conveyed it to Blasco.

"What!" he exclaimed, lit up with joy. "What? An annulment?"

"Of course. It's the best solution. They will lose two hundred onze, and both will regain their freedom."

"Oh, what are you telling me!"

Blasco was unable to conceal the profound emotion he felt upon hearing that news; his face had resumed, as if by magic, its old joviality. Violante would regain her freedom, Violante, still a young girl, untouched, pure!

"Do you know," he said, "that it is an extraordinary thing?"

He could find no other words except such silly ones, but what did he care? It wasn't that he wanted to say anything; he just wanted to conceal everything he would have liked to say instead behind a sentence. Of course, he dared not nourish or express any hope, but the mere idea that Emanuele would never possess the young girl and would never have any rights over her was enough to make him happy.

Donna Gabriella, upon noticing that he was more outgoing, more cheerful, almost restless that day, like she hadn't seen him in a few days, was at first surprised, then she took umbrage over it and suspected the truth. So then it was her turn to become gloomy and withdrawn. It was clear that if the news of Violante's separation filled him with joy, then he still loved her. What until then had been vague and uncertain suspicions now turned into reality and filled her heart with jealousy. She wondered whether the behavior of the newlyweds on their wedding night hadn't been the effect of the poison that she had sprinkled into their souls, and, exaggerating the significance of her words, she now blamed herself for having provoked, due to her burning desire to carry out those little reprisals, that process that would render Violante free, desirable, and dangerous once more.

She saw the bright star of her happiness fading away. Was there something destined, then, something inevitable that would take away her *entire* hold on her beloved man? Or, sooner or later, would he not free himself from her arms in order to follow the illusion of his yearning heart? Then what could be done to prevent it? If only one could reverse that annulment and reconcile the spouses!

* * *

That year spring was balmy and cloudless; in March the weather seemed like May. The promenade on the Cassaro was busy, as was the one outside Porta Nuova, but in the afternoon there were some carriages that would push forward as far as the Marina, just as there were some solitary souls who, leaving the hubbub of the main street of the city, preferred the tranquility of that vast piazza by the sea, whose spaciousness would extinguish the noise made by the few carriages. Even on the rampart that ran along the curtain wall between Porta Felice and the Palazzo Butera, with its terraces on the Mura delle Cattive (so called because they provided a secluded promenade for widows), one could see some figures draped in black or a few portantine with plumes, curtains, and black fringes.

One afternoon Donna Gabriella, sad and troubled, had herself taken to the Mura delle Cattive. She was still wearing widow's weeds, but some of the signs of mourning had already disappeared from her portantina. In the middle of the rampart she had the portantina stop and got off to enjoy the beautiful sight of the sea, which spread out before her eyes along the entire width of the gulf. To her right, the bastion of the Tuono stretched out like a buttress, with its heavy iron artillery; behind her, twenty steps away, rose the long palazzata of the Palazzo Butera, with its terraces.

Donna Gabriella glanced up at it and was startled; leaning against the parapet of the terrace she saw Violante, wrapped in a mantilla; she too was looking at the sea and at Capo Zafferano, and at the tiny little clouds that looked like bouquets of roses and gigantic violets spread across the sky, which took on a slight amethyst hue.

She watched the absorbed young girl for a while and it seemed she had attracted her attention because Violante looked down at her and reacted with astonishment; so then she waved at her, her face hinting at a smile.

She had made an effort to smile, with her heart filled with bitterness, seeing Violante even more beautiful than before, and in a pose that had, in its melancholy profile, a mysterious charm. Violante seemed to marvel at that unexpected greeting, and yet, following the customs of her upbringing, she acknowledged her with a ceremonious and reserved curtsy.

For an instant they looked at each other. Donna Gabriella's mind was weighed down by thoughts and schemes that followed one another and competed with one another. She was torn; a sudden daring was immediately opposed by an unconquerable despondency. Her eyes burned with jealousy, her love tormented her, her desires and hatred pulled her back, her self-interest pushed her forward. Violante, for her part, looked at her as if expecting an explanation for that greeting. They hadn't seen each other for a long time. Donna Gabriella had not taken part in the wedding celebrations, and she had neither mourned nor rejoiced at the young girl's restored freedom; she hadn't even reached out with a greeting, with a nod. Why on earth was she greeting her now? Had she come to the Mura delle Cattive to see her? When she realized that Donna Gabriella wasn't going to say anything, Violante, in order to avoid a situation that would require any sacrifice on her part, gave her another curtsy and went back into the house.

The duchess felt a surge of contempt for both herself and the young girl.

What she wanted and what her plan was still weren't absolutely clear in her mind, but it seemed to her that Violante's gesture took away from her the chance of a successful outcome.

She didn't dare return the next day, yet she wanted to see her again, in the vague hope that from a conversation with Violante she would manage to gain something to help her win Blasco back again. After two or three days she returned to the Mura delle Cattive, but she didn't see Violante again. She instead saw Matteo Lo Vecchio, who greeted her with a deep bow. The sight of the birro sickened her; she remembered that he had tried to poison Blasco in the Castello in Messina, and a sudden impulse urged her to have him arrested, even though five years had passed.

The birro reached the far end of the rampart and came back, passing again in front of the portantina and bowing once more, casting an oblique glance at the duchess with a malicious smile. He had noticed the impatient looks that Donna Gabriella directed toward the terrace of Palazzo Butera.

* * *

That evening Emanuele heard about it.

"What on earth was she doing under Butera's terrace?" the young man asked himself.

That she would go to see Violante had never even crossed his mind; he assumed that it was about something else, and a veiled jealous rage stirred up his blood. Mentally, he smothered the duchess with insults and curses; he had never forgiven her for the humiliations he had suffered, without even having had the satisfaction of kissing her, and he had always entertained the idea of a sensational revenge on her, one that would make Donna Gabriella the talk of the town. He drowned her with insults and obscenities, believing that some new whims had led her to that terrace. This pleased him only because it would bring shame upon Blasco. "By God! It's the doing of that devil of a bastard! I can taste it! We'll put him under the protection of San Pasquale! Ah, if I could have some proof, if I could find some information!"

"Matteo Lo Vecchio, I want to know what the duchess is doing on the Mura delle Cattive."

"Your Excellency will find out."

A few days later the birro came to tell him.

"The duchess is courting someone."

"Ah! I knew it."

"Only it's not a man."

"What?"

"She is courting her stepdaughter."

"Donna Violante?"

"Precisely."

"You are joking."

"Me? I have never made so much sense. . . . I saw the duchess talking to Violante . . . the duchess from the Mura delle Cattive and her stepdaughter from the terrace of the Palazzo Butera."

Emanuele wasn't convinced; perhaps they had seen each other that time by chance, but Donna Gabriella would certainly not have bothered to go there on account of the beautiful eyes of Violante, of whom she had never been fond. Matteo Lo Vecchio had misperceived it. He would have to go back there.

The birro bowed. "If Your Excellency orders me to, I will obey, but I assure you that the duchess doesn't go there for any other reason."

After another two or three days he reported the same thing. The duchess would ask her stepdaughter if she was reentering the monastery, or if she was going to visit her aunts; she wanted to see her up close and to talk to her about a thousand things.

Emanuele was astonished. So they were on good terms? Then he remembered the blue domino and her venomous words: a duplicity in order to prevent him from entering the bridal chamber, in order to provoke that scandal of the annulment. It had been Donna Gabriella's revenge. It seemed so clear to him, so logical, that he had no doubt.

"Ah! So madam duchess isn't satisfied? Madam duchess, after exposing me to ridicule, takes my wife away from me? Ah! Then is she the author of everything that has happened to me? Very well, duchess, very well! We'll see if I'm clever enough to teach you a lesson that will last the rest of your life . . . even with all the protection of the Beati Paoli!"

Matteo Lo Vecchio pricked up his ears: the protection of the Beati Paoli? Was there something he didn't know? But fancy that, even the duchess might be a member! Watch out, Matteo!

Emanuele walked up and down, fuming; suddenly he stopped in front of the birro. "And you? What are you doing? I arranged for Girolamo Ammirata to come back at your request, I gave you carte blanche, but those papers. . . . And now they would be useful to me on account of that slut Donna Violante! I could tell her to her face: 'Your father was a criminal, and I will tell it to the four winds; I will slander his memory and I will avenge my mother and myself!' That's what I want to say to her! . . . What have you done? Where are the papers? I want to humiliate, to shame those two women, I want to see them at my feet . . . to have them, and to throw them to the dogs! . . . Do you understand? I will make you rich if I am able to avenge myself, but I will have you killed if you deceive me . . . if you think you can play games with me."

Matteo Lo Vecchio let him vent, standing humbly in the act of listening but with an expression that betrayed a slightly mocking undertone.

When Emanuele finished, he said, "Will Your Excellency allow me to speak?"

"What do you have to say?"

"That the papers will be found. Be patient. We must not expose ourselves to be taken for thieves; it would mean endangering everything, and especially Your Excellency. Leave it to me. I too have a certain account to settle with the Beati Paoli, and by avenging Your Excellency, I will also avenge myself."

He was thinking to himself, "The duchess is protected by the Beati Paoli—a member, not quite, but certainly this protection comes to her from the bastard. She must know many things about that devil of a sect. Therefore, she has to know about the papers, and it may even be that she has them in safekeeping as a precious memory of her illustrious husband, may the devil rest his soul! We must work on the duchess and tear this secret out of her. How? To make a woman in love do what one wants, there's nothing better than jealousy. We'll make the duchess jealous to the point of driving her mad. Let's see . . ."

The birro, with his fertile imagination, elaborated a vast plan of revenge, in which he intended to draw out Don Girolamo, Andrea, Blasco, and Coriolano. Donna Gabriella and Violante, through no fault of their own, would also fall into the trap, but it wasn't something that affected or worried Matteo Lo Vecchio. As for Emanuele, if he should go so far as to humiliate, to shame the two ladies, he couldn't care less; whether or not he managed to take revenge didn't matter to him. For him, Emanuele was only a banner that had to protect him, and then at the right moment, he would throw him into the fire if necessary.

It was a diabolical plan that needed to be studied, but of whose success he hadn't the slightest doubt.

While reassuring the Duke of Motta, he suggested to him some good ways to attack. Andrea, for example, was a man to be trusted with some delicate assignments. In broad daylight, from the corner of Vicolo Sant'Antonio, he had fired a pistol at Don Raimondo, then he had joined the Beati Paoli and had been one of the architects of the plot against Don Raimondo. Oh, he knew him well, that one! To handle the knife? There were few who could match him. He couldn't stomach Blasco; once he had wanted to kill him, and he was a man capable of doing so.

Emanuele listened and thought.

"For heaven's sake! Then why did I push him aside? And if now . . ."

That "now" was left hanging in a reticence heavy with a thousand thoughts.

"Very well! Very well!" he said, dismissing Matteo Lo Vecchio.

Matteo Lo Vecchio ran into Andrea in the antechamber and, dragging him amicably down the hallway, he whispered in his ear, "I have talked to His Excellency about you. You'll see that from now on he will recognize your worth."

Andrea thanked him. An observing eye would have caught an ironic distrust on the face of the former servant of the House of Albamonte, but out of the corner of his eye, the birro was watching Girolamo Ammirata, who stood on the threshold of a balcony facing him, looking at him with the gaze of someone trying to understand what is being said far away from them; therefore he didn't notice anything at all, and he left.

Don Girolamo went out almost at the same time and followed him, while Emanuele was calling Andrea over to him.

CHAPTER 16

As if by chance, Donna Gabriella ran into Violante in the parlor of Santa Caterina; the young girl, accompanied by the Prince of Butera, had gone to visit her aunts. With Easter approaching, Donna Gabriella had also gone to visit her two old sisters-in-law.

It was the first time that stepmother and stepdaughter had been together in a long time. They greeted each other formally, politely, but coldly. They exchanged some meaningless words, and then the duchess came to the point, pretending to inquire about the state of the annulment.

"We hope to conclude it within four or five months," the prince said.

Donna Gabriella seemed saddened.

"But is it really irreconcilable?"

The prince and Violante both had a look on their face that seemed to say, "Can there be a more stupid question than this?"

But Donna Gabriella wasn't daunted; she began with an edifying lecture, rendered more eloquent by the hidden motive that spurred her on. She praised Emanuele, who was rich, handsome, valiant, and had everything to envy as a husband. . . . They didn't love each other? Love would surely come later. Meanwhile, they would avoid more gossip; there had been too much of it, and not all of it benevolent. And although Emanuele didn't show it, he was very much in love with Violante, and he would do something crazy . . .

Violante listened to her with ever-growing amazement and, thinking about Donna Gabriella's walks on the Mura delle Cattive, she wondered if the duchess hadn't been given some assignment by Emanuele. She was reserved. She became suspicious. But the Prince of Butera intervened. Things were already in motion and there was no need to reverse course. Too bad for Don Emanuele. Instead of going to spend the night in the house of a lady of that sort, he should have gone to his house. Come on! These were no longer things to be discussed without failing in the consideration deserving of a lady of "quality." He begged Donna Gabriella not to press on with talk that was so painful for everyone.

The duchess pretended to be sorry. But she felt her anger roaring inside. In those days she had received some anonymous letters that urged her to keep her eyes open, because days of great suffering would be in store for her; a few letters made allusions to unfaithfulness, betrayals of the people who were closest and most dear to her.

Violante's refusal and the prince's words resounded in her ears like the effect of other suggestions, behind which her suspicious mind could see the image of Blasco.

She attempted a retort, by way of a joke, almost whispering in Violante's ear.

"You wouldn't perhaps be . . . in love with someone? . . . Tell me the truth."

Violante looked at her with her face in flames; Donna Gabriella's expression seemed insincere.

"No," she replied brusquely, and from that moment she became somber and silent.

They had understood each other, but Violante stared back at Donna Gabriella's yearning, irascible, tempestuous gaze with a look of haughty disdain.

"Signora," she said, enunciating the syllables, "when my marriage is annulled, I will come to ask these walls for the peace that I have never had since my mother died!"

Donna Gabriella stayed there for another minute, then she took her leave and left with her heart in great turmoil. When she shut herself in her carriage, lowering the curtains so that no one could see her, she abandoned herself to tears of spite, anger, jealousy, hatred. No one could convince her otherwise than that there must be some understanding between Blasco and Violante.

"But I will thwart her!" she thought, sobbing. "I will thwart her!"

Nothing made her more irrational, headstrong, and ruthless than these fits of jealousy.

That evening she planted herself in front of Blasco with eyes that seemed to be blazing, and she threatened him: "Beware! I have proof that you don't love me, that you can't love me. . . . It's useless to deny it. I couldn't believe you . . . but beware, I repeat. I trampled over everything in order to give myself to you completely, all of me! . . . I have lived and still live for you. Well, I will kill you with my own hands!"

She burst into tears after those words, and it took all of Blasco's pity and tenderness to calm her down. But a life of suspicions, anxieties, fears, and fits of madness began for her, from which she would wear herself down and lose that gaiety and that passionate nature that were her most effective charms.

Another anonymous letter arrived in those days:

> *A devoted person, who doesn't want to be seen, could give you some important news about what mainly concerns your beloved. Do not say a word to anyone about this letter, and if you at least want to have the key to what grieves you most, please go by carriage to Strada Colonna; a man near the fountain will approach and ask for alms for the blessed souls in Purgatory. Silence and prudence.*

This letter didn't give her any peace. She was restless until the following afternoon, when she went to the Marina. As soon as she had passed through Porta Felice, a man dressed in the sackcloth of a brotherhood, with his cowl covering his eyes and a box in his hands, came toward the carriage, shaking the box and moaning, "Blessed souls!" Donna Gabriella gestured, indicating that she wanted to give alms.

The man from the brotherhood held out the box and murmured, "Does Your Illustrious Ladyship want Signor Don Blasco to be faithful to you? First of all, you should find out where he has put a little bundle that contains some old documents that belonged to an abbot and that consist of very precious things. . . . It's a little packet, folded in four, wrapped in a paper folio and tied with a thin cord."

"What papers are they?"

"I couldn't say . . . they are writings . . . magical. They are terrifying spells and prayers, and whoever has them is master of the lives of others."

Donna Gabriella gave a start, and a shudder of fear coursed through her blood, but she didn't want to show her belief right away, fearing that some trickery was involved.

She pretended not to have any interest in this business and replied haughtily, "Signore, I don't know why I should care about any of Blasco's papers."

And then she directed the carriage to move on, but the friar implored, "One moment, Your Excellency. Don't chase me away like this. I come for your benefit, and I don't want any remuneration. Thank heavens, I can take care of myself. It pains me to see you waste away like this! . . . Those papers have 'bound' other people."

"Violante!" Donna Gabriella thought, with a shudder of hatred.

"If Your Illustrious Ladyship," the hooded friar went on, "wants to avenge herself and regain Signor Don Blasco, she should try to find out where he has them."

Donna Gabriella wondered, "What interest could this man have in meddling in my affairs?'"

Her doubt was perhaps evident in her eyes, because the friar resumed, "There is another person who is also suffering, and whose recovery depends on rendering null the 'bond.' So Your Most Illustrious Ladyship can see that her peace and that of others lies in her hands. At this time the day after tomorrow I will pass by with my box, in front of the bastion. Come. I beg Your Ladyship to be there."

He paid his respects and moved away, shaking the box and shouting in a mournful voice, "Blessed souls!"

Donna Gabriella remained pensive; those papers, that "spell," that intervention of supernatural things encumbered her state of mind. She believed and then she didn't; her jealousy magnified everything and rendered the most implausible things credible. But what to do? Asking Blasco directly was tantamount to making him suspicious and would be worse. A name suddenly occurred to her: Coriolano. Wasn't he Blasco's great and only friend? Wouldn't he perhaps know all his secrets?

Back home, she hastened to send for him, in order to ask him to come see her. Such a request was more than a little surprising to the Cavaliere della Floresta, who was quick to accept the beautiful lady's invitation.

At the first words with which, after a difficult and elaborate round of entreaties and protests, Donna Gabriella told him about a mysterious packet that Blasco had taken from an abbot, Coriolano became serious. But when she claimed that those papers contained spells and prayers for "bewitching," he couldn't keep himself from laughing.

"Who told you that? My apologies . . ."

Donna Gabriella hesitated, but at Coriolano's insistence she gave in and told him everything.

"Where is that letter?"

She looked for it and handed it to him. The Cavaliere della Floresta glanced at it, rubbed his fingers on the paper, smelled it, and put it in his pocket.

"What are you doing?" the duchess asked.

"Permit me; I need it in order to find out who wrote it."

"Can you find out?"

"Yes, it's my business, do not be concerned. Now I will tell you that Blasco doesn't have any packet."

"How can you be so sure?"

"I'm quite sure. He had only one packet, and it's no longer in his hands."

"Ah! Do you see?"

"Yes, but that packet consisted of anything but spells; they were very serious and terrible revelations about a person, now dead, and they are no longer useful."

"You speak with so much certainty that it perplexes me."

"It is just that that packet belonged to some people of my acquaintance, and it had been stolen from them by a despicable individual—"

"Wasn't it in the hands of an abbot?"

"—of a despicable individual who had disguised himself precisely as an abbot in order to carry out his villainy. Blasco took it away from that scoundrel and handed it back to the people to whom it belonged. That is all."

Donna Gabriella, astonished, looked at him with an open mouth; what Coriolano was saying was so precise and detailed and he spoke with so much confidence that there was no need to doubt what he was saying.

"But why," she remarked, more on account of the astonishment she felt than of any doubt she might still have, "why did that friar of the Blessed Souls want to entangle me?"

"This I will find out, have no doubt. Leave it to me."

That evening, shadows could be seen brushing along the walls of Piazza Santi Quaranta Martiri, behind Casa Professa,[1] and disappearing in the shadow of a little door that mysteriously opened next to the door of the church.

That evening Donna Gabriella had begged, in vain, for Blasco to stay; he had resisted all her seductions, citing some pressing business, which made the duchess suspicious. She fidgeted the entire night, imagining who knows what, pursuing her fantasies, tormenting herself and returning to the little story about spells and incantations, despite Coriolano's assurances. She tossed and turned.

The clock of San Domenico struck eleven o'clock. Donna Gabriella had heard those hours being rung one after the other, and her spirit had grown increasingly dark under the clouds of her imaginings, and her heart had gradually given way to the wave of her irrational misery. She was convincing herself of a truth—such was her belief—that didn't spring from any new fact but was no less terrible and real: that Blasco had left because he had promised some other woman he would spend the evening with her. It couldn't be otherwise. This fantasy had such a grip on her and penetrated her being to such a point that she began to cry. And then, making a sudden decision, she called her maidservant and gave the order to get her everyday portantina ready—the one used for half-mourning—and two volanti without livery.

Her maidservant was surprised by this. So, what was her mistress up to? Had she perhaps gone mad? Donna Gabriella had to repeat the order to persuade her to comply.

A moment later she was leaving the palazzo. She had ordered that they take her to the Palazzo della Floresta. She wanted to convince herself that Blasco was home; she wanted material proof that he was innocent of the betrayal that she was accusing him of.

The door of the palazzo was closed, but the portantina had not yet arrived when it opened, and two men came out. They passed next to the flames of the volanti and from inside the portantina Donna Gabriella recognized Coriolano and Blasco. So as not to reveal herself, she didn't say anything, but as soon as they went past she gave orders to go back.

She said to one of the two volanti, "Did you recognize those gentlemen who just passed?"

"Yes, Your Excellency."

"Good. We must follow them, but without arousing suspicion."

"As Your Excellency commands."

That modest portantina wouldn't arouse any suspicion. At night it wasn't uncommon to encounter one because doctors, midwives, and father confessors

---

1 One of the most important baroque churches in Palermo and in all of Sicily. Also called Church of the Gesù.

had no other means of travel and there were always people being born and people dying. Therefore, Coriolano and Blasco had no reason to think they were being followed.

In fact, having just passed the Church of Sant'Orsola, they disappeared into the shadows of the vicolo that followed, and the volanti were not able to show her where they had entered, because they didn't know. They recognized the vicolo, but the piazzetta was deserted and silent, immersed in the nocturnal shadows, and the little houses, around which stood the ancient tower of the Palazzo Marchese with its beautiful arabesque window, were shuttered and didn't reveal any sign of life. The volanti had a good look around; they didn't see anyone and couldn't make out anything.

Donna Gabriella was distressed. Where could Blasco have gone? Were the volanti certain that he had gone into the piazzetta? And could they be sure that he hadn't come out the other side, from the alley that led to Casa Professa?

"Let's go home," she said in a voice broken by her annoyance and distress.

The procession resumed its way toward the Quattro Canti; it was already late at night and a sense of fear ran through Donna Gabriella's veins. Her fear brought her to her senses, revealing to her the absurdity of this nighttime expedition, which had come to nothing.

They crossed through the Quattro Canti and went down Via Toledo. A carriage preceded by four volanti came toward her at a quick pace and gave her a new fear. She instinctively drew back, as if to conceal herself. By the light of the torches, she had recognized the livery of the House of Albamonte, a sign that Emanuele was in the carriage.

"God! If he could see me!" she exclaimed to herself. "I would be doomed!"

But the carriage continued on its way, as if it hadn't even noticed the portantina; soon after, the noise of the wheels almost abruptly died down. Perhaps the carriage had turned into some side street, which reassured Donna Gabriella somewhat. As soon as she arrived home, she called one of the volanti.

"Go," she said, "to the Palazzo della Floresta and watch what time the cavaliere Albamonte comes back and with whom. Don't move without first having seen him return. . . . And above all, don't let yourself be seen. Be careful. Whatever time you return, have them wake me."

The volante left.

He lurked in a doorway and waited. Midnight sounded, then two hours later, the volante saw two shadows emerge from the darkness, approaching the Palazzo della Floresta; he looked hard and tried to recognize them. One of them in fact looked to him like Blasco; on the other hand, who else could open and go into the Palazzo della Floresta at that hour except the master of the house or his guest? He waited another minute to see if the door would open again, and whether the two who had gone in would come out. When he was convinced that it was useless to wait anymore, he started to leave.

A voice suddenly stopped him.

He turned sharply and saw Matteo Lo Vecchio right on top of him, grinning with a diabolical smile.

"What do you want?"

"Nothing, my son. I was here, I saw you, and since I'm curious, I wanted to see what you were doing."

"And you think nothing of meddling in other people's business?"

"That's right, my young man. Sometimes it's good to meddle. . . . For example, what were you doing here?"

"Whatever I like."

"That's a good answer, but a risky one, because . . ."

Matteo Lo Vecchio quickly drew a pistol from his pocket and, pointing it at the volante's chest and grabbing him by the arm, he continued, "Because if you take a step, if you scream, if you move, I will kill you like a dog."

The volante wasn't a coward, but neither was he a man of great courage; in the face of the pistol, his impertinence faded. Pale, stammering, he asked, "Who are you? What do you want?"

"Who I am doesn't concern you; what I want is easier said than done. What are you doing here? And you better tell me the truth, because I always have a way to make you talk under the lash in the Carbonera or the Vicaria. Your choice."

"What was I doing? . . . But you saw me. . . . I was looking—"

"You are a petty thief, most likely, and you were trying to rob the Cavaliere della Floresta."

"Me? Me, a thief? . . . Oh, who do you think you are dealing with?"

"Don't shout so much. What's your name? What's your trade?"

"Oh, for heaven's sake—"

"You don't want to answer? Be careful, I will hand you over to the patrol, and to the lash."

The volante tried to break free and run away, but Matteo Lo Vecchio held on to him tightly, and with every movement he would raise his pistol. As if under a spell, that gesture calmed the poor wretch.

"Then you don't recognize me? You don't know who I am? Have a good look."

The volante stared hard at his face and said, not without fear, "Matteo Lo Vecchio!"

"Now you will talk, I hope."

"I am the volante . . . a volante of the Duchess of Motta."

"Ah!"

The birro became worried. In truth, he had been too careless in letting himself be recognized, but he could no longer back off; he had to put things right. He quickly guessed why the duchess had sent her servant to spy on Blasco and realized the advantage he could draw from it.

He said to the volante, "Come with me. . . . Come on!"

"Where?"

"Come with me and be quiet."

He pushed him forward, without letting go of him; at the entrance to Via del Bosco they encountered a patrol. Matteo Lo Vecchio let out a distinctive whistle, which made them come rushing.

"Tie up this degenerate," he said. "He's spreading news against His Majesty and says that the Imperials[2] have landed in Milazzo and are coming to take back Palermo."

The volante, dumbfounded, shouted, "But it's not true! It's not true!"

"Be quiet, scoundrel. . . . He's an enemy of the king! Take him to the Vicaria and don't let him escape."

* * *

In those days the fortunes of war were getting worse for the Spanish armies. The Alemanni reinforcements, having entered Milazzo, were making the siege useless. The news had spread throughout the city that since the month of January, Emperor Charles VI had appointed the Count of Mercy as General in Chief, commander of the German troops in Sicily, and that an expedition was being prepared, of some said thirty and others said forty thousand men, and this news was making the people fearful, but it was making the government, who had given strict orders against those who spread the news, even more fearful. This explained Matteo Lo Vecchio's accusation and the terror felt by the poor volante, who was dragged away tied up like a salami.

Matteo Lo Vecchio walked away, rubbing his hands together and saying to himself, "Dear madam duchess, I am sorry for Your Ladyship, but that's a really nice trick that you played!"

---

2 The forces of Charles VI, Holy Roman Emperor and ruler of the Austrian Habsburg monarchy.

CHAPTER 17

Donna Gabriella waited in vain for the volante, not only all night but also the following day, and she didn't know what to attribute his disappearance to. Instead, she received another anonymous note that unsettled her.

It is useless for you to wait for your volante. People interested in putting an end to your spying have made him disappear. Remember how much you know and trust whoever is your friend, and who prays for you to the . . . Blessed Souls.

It was the same handwriting as before. After lunch the duchess was getting ready to go out in her carriage to meet the hooded man, and just as she was about to walk down the stairs, Coriolano showed up.

"Are you going out?" he asked. "I'm sorry. . . . I was coming to ask permission to kiss your hand."

Donna Gabriella felt uncomfortable; Coriolano's gaze was scrutinizing her and seemed to read her completely. She didn't dare dismiss him or allow him to enter.

The Cavaliere della Floresta then smiled kindly and said to her, "I realize that I arrived at a bad time, but I have something to tell you. . . . If you permit me, I will accompany you in the carriage . . . unless it's an inconvenience."

"No, no . . . not at all," she stammered, a bit confused, not wanting to be rude but certainly not pleased.

"Let's go, then."

When they were in the carriage, Coriolano asked her, "Duchess, pardon my indiscretion, but it's in your interest. . . . Where are you going?"

Donna Gabriella blushed without answering.

"Then I will tell you: you are going to meet the friar of the Blessed Souls."

"What can lead you to think that?"

"Your own discomfort . . . and the deserving friar who is waiting for you."

"Oh! How do you know that?"

"I know. It's not important how I know. I know many other things. For example this: that you have brought about the arrest of your poor volante, for a . . . I don't know what to call it."

"Pietro arrested?" Donna Gabriella exclaimed.

"I don't know if his name is Pietro, but he is in the Vicaria, accused of shouting and seditious speech!"

"Him! Pietro!"

"And this for sending him around to spy, in order to find out what time Signor Don Blasco would return home—not having been able to follow him yourself quickly enough—because you wanted to know where he had gone with the Cavaliere della Floresta."

Donna Gabriella blushed, turned pale, and looked with a terrified expression at Coriolano, who was smiling his gentle and subtle smile, upright and measured in the expression on his face, in the way he moved, in his manner.

"Who told you all this?" she murmured, trembling.

"I know, madam duchess; I had promised you that I would find out about something that concerns you, and, as you see, I have gathered a great deal of information, whose truth you can vouch for yourself."

The duchess trembled from dismay, looking with a superstitious astonishment at this man who was speaking so calmly.

Coriolano continued, "Well, I can tell you who that friar of the Blessed Souls is."

"Who is he?" she asked eagerly.

"Matteo Lo Vecchio!"

"Him!" she exclaimed, panic-stricken.

"Precisely. And I will also tell you who had the patrol arrest your volante last night, with that trumped-up accusation."

"Who, then?"

"Matteo Lo Vecchio."

Donna Gabriella was almost overcome by a fainting spell. She stammered with a bewilderment that made Coriolano smile. "Matteo Lo Vecchio. . . . Matteo Lo Vecchio!"

Then she was in the hands of that birro! What did he want from her? Why had he told her all those stories about Blasco? Why had he had her volante arrested? Why? She was bewildered.

She clasped her hands in a desperate yet pleading gesture, murmuring, "I'm out of my mind! I'm out of my mind!"

Then, as if seized by a doubt, she asked, "But are you sure of what you're telling me?"

"Are you still doubting? Then I'll tell you everything that you did last night . . ."

"No, I believe you. . . . Oh God! God! I can't make head or tail of it."

"Don't be afraid, I am here for this reason."

"And Blasco knows everything?"

"Everything."

"Oh God! What will he say? . . . Did he get angry? Was he upset? Tell me the truth."

"Angry, no. Upset, very."

Donna Gabriella was silent for a while. Meanwhile the carriage was emerging from Porta Felice, and the sight of the sea reminded the duchess about her meeting with the friar.

"What should I do and what should I say?" she asked, as if talking to herself.

"Pretend not to know who the friar is, and come to an agreement with him."

"And if he asks me for the papers?"

"Here they are."

He pulled out of his pocket a small packet tied with a ribbon and handed it to Donna Gabriella, adding, "Give him these: they are precisely writings of spells and incantations. You will tell him that you took them from Blasco while he was sleeping. After you've given them to him, ask him what you should do. I will then come to find out what he said, if you allow me."

Donna Gabriella took the packet. She was truly overcome with emotion thinking about the meeting with Matteo Lo Vecchio and about the part that she had to play.

* * *

The birro was there under the bastion, covered by his cowl, with the box in his hand, shaking it and shouting, "Blessed Souls!"

As soon as he saw Donna Gabriella's carriage, he approached as if to ask for alms, repeating his cry: "Blessed Souls!"

Then, while holding out the box, he added with a tone of compassion, "Your Ladyship has suffered! . . . Poor young man! I saw him this morning."

"Who are you talking about?"

"Your volante . . . poor soul, what a pity!"

"Where did you see him?"

"In the Vicaria. I went there for prayers and I recognized him. The poor soul was coming from being tortured. . . . Ten lashes. They don't mess around."

"What on earth are you saying?"

"The truth! . . . He was defending himself, the wretch. . . . But it was clear that it had to turn out like that. . . . Can't you guess who set him up?"

"Who?"

"Who did Your Ladyship have followed?"

In spite of herself, Donna Gabriella was taken aback. Blasco? Could it have been Blasco? Wasn't the birro lying? Even knowing how things had gone, she had a moment of doubt.

Matteo Lo Vecchio added, "But now we'll fix everything. Did Your Ladyship find out anything out about those papers?"

"Yes," Donna Gabriella replied, remembering the part that she had to play, "in fact, I have them here."

"Really?" the birro exclaimed, overcome with joy.

"Yes, I was able to take them, by chance. He had them on his person."

"Ah, so there! I was right!"

One could interpret those words in one way, but they had another meaning to Matteo Lo Vecchio. He was responding to an inner thought and wanted to say, "That's why no one could find out where they were, he had them on his person."

And he added, in a louder voice, "Well, if Your Ladyship wants to give them to me, we can reverse the spell."

"Here they are."

Matteo Lo Vecchio recognized the ribbon, recognized the outer paper, also noting that it was a bit burnt at the corners. A lively pleasure spread over his face; he took those papers, thrust them against his chest, and said, "When Your Ladyship permits me, I will come to bring you the other prayers, and I will be able to tell you who Blasco's beloved is, and what must be done."

An ingenious idea suddenly occurred to Donna Gabriella.

"Come tomorrow evening, to my house."

If the hood hadn't concealed Matteo Lo Vecchio's face, the duchess would have seen the comical grimace he made at that suggestion.

"Your Excellency," he said, "such things are not talked about in one's home; walls may not have ears, but they can hear. Rather, if Your Ladyship deigns to meet me either here or in Mezzo Monreale or wherever you shall direct me, I will come and bring you what is needed."

"In my house, it's like being in church, but I will do as you wish; tomorrow at this time I will go to the Terre Rosse."[1]

"Do go to the Terre Rosse. Very well. I kiss Your Ladyship's hands."

* * *

While Donna Gabriella's carriage moved away in one direction, Matteo Lo Vecchio was hurrying along in another. He walked along the wide road to Porta Termini. When he arrived under the arch of the gate, he took out the packet, impatient to see once again the much sought-after papers, obtained by him so cheaply. He untied the cord, unfolded the paper that served as a wrapper, and took out one sheet; but as soon as he unfolded it, he let out a cry of astonishment.

It was a sheet full of cabalistic signs, triangles, circles, wide-open eyes, monstrous animals, a cross, and strange formulas written in an illegible style, and some in an absurd Latin.

After having looked at it, and looked at it again, he slowly folded the sheet, took another, unfolded it, and gestured in contempt. There were drawings more comical than those on the first sheet.

1 At the time of the novel, a rural area of Palermo.

He didn't want to look any further; angrily, he retied the packet, muttering under his breath, "She got me! She got me! . . . But there's somebody else's hand in this. Who? Don Blasco? The Cavaliere della Floresta? Who? But for Christ's sake! They will have to deal with me! My name isn't Matteo Lo Vecchio if I don't give the duchess a bitter mouthful!"

He went at once to the Palazzo della Motta.

* * *

That evening Blasco said to Donna Gabriella, "Why, then, do you distrust me and torment yourself? How is it possible that you expose yourself to the deceptions of a scoundrel who must have his own objectives in mind? And meanwhile, that poor devil of a volante . . ."

Donna Gabriella sank down onto a footstool, murmuring, "Forgive me, I'm out of my mind . . . but I love you so much!"

"I want you to understand how wrong you have been to be mistrustful. Those papers that the birro asked you to get do not belong to me, nor to you, nor to anyone else. Matteo Lo Vecchio had them taken away from a man who had dedicated his life to restoring to Emanuele, whom he had picked up as an infant, his rank and patrimony."

"Don Girolamo Ammirata!"

"Don Girolamo. They contain a history of crimes."

Donna Gabriella lowered her head sullenly. "I know about them," she said.

Blasco was silent for a moment and it seemed that the terrible past, whose secret they both knew, weighed on them.

He took out from his breast pocket a small, slightly singed packet and went on: "Matteo Lo Vecchio, I don't know for what ends, but certainly despicable ones, had stolen these papers. I took them from him by chance and I kept them; I was about to destroy them but was prevented from doing so. Now that the man they condemned is dead, there is no longer any reason to preserve them. . . . They could do nothing except harm the purest affections of an innocent person, for the benefit of no one. That birro who tried to get them back with your help would surely have made you an accomplice to an infamous act. Do you want this complicity?"

Donna Gabriella raised her head in scornful pride.

Blasco continued, "I knew it well. . . . Here are the papers; you destroy them!"

"Oh no!" she said with an expression of disgust.

So Blasco went over to a candle and lit an edge of the paper, holding the packet so that it would be enveloped and consumed by the flames.

Donna Gabriella felt an urge to snatch those papers and save them from the fire; an inner voice whispered to her, "Those papers are a weapon against Violante." But something vague, obscure, and stronger prevented her from moving, and the same voice murmured with a tone of sadness and regret, "You are saving Violante and ruining yourself!"

The flames consumed the papers to the last shred. Blasco threw to the ground some very light crumpled blackened sheets that disintegrated in a puff, then, passing his hands over his face as if to drive away a shadow, he took on a joyful air and, moving next to Donna Gabriella, he sat beside her and, clasping her hands in his, said to her in his beautiful, youthful voice, vibrant with joy, "Well? Why don't you smile at me? And why are you so silent?"

Donna Gabriella heard her sad inner voice murmur again, "He is happy because he saved Violante!" And she felt her heart tighten and her eyes tear up, but suddenly, in a wild fit of passion, she put her arms around Blasco's neck and pulled him to her, crying out, "No! . . . You're mine! Only mine!"

CHAPTER 18

Matteo Lo Vecchio found his heart enraged by the trick played on him—as he believed—by Donna Gabriella, but as an expert dissembler, he had endured with apparent submission the outbursts of Emanuele, who, thinking he had in turn been tricked by the birro, had nearly tumbled him down the stairs.

Repeating "Your Excellency is right, but I was caught by that demon of a woman," Matteo Lo Vecchio went downstairs in a hurry, evading Emanuele's kicks, but in his heart he swore to take bitter revenge on him and on Donna Gabriella.

The duchess hadn't shown up at the rendezvous on the agreed-upon day or on the following day; it seemed that she wouldn't dare leave the house, so Matteo didn't see her in her carriage or in her portantina, no matter how long he remained at his post.

This disappearance reconfirmed to the birro that Donna Gabriella must have acted that way at Blasco's and Coriolano's behest, and that one of them had assembled that little bundle of cabalistic nonsense. He wouldn't even consider the possibility that the duchess, in her turn, could have acted in good faith.

In his heart he concluded, "Here we have to carry out a widespread attack. Let's see. Three days ago the Prince of Belsito's fiscale was killed; two shots from a rifle at night, and that is the mark of the Beati Paoli. Yesterday evening, the Cavaliere di Sant'Alessio was beaten because he tried to force himself into the home of the fool Carusello—who has a beautiful seventeen-year-old daughter—and no one knew who the thrashers were, and that too is the mark of those devils. This time the cavaliere was the fool, but it wouldn't have bothered them. . . . So the sect is active again. And that was to be expected, now that the Spanish have returned. . . . The Cavaliere della Floresta and that bastard buddy of his suddenly disappeared into the piazzetta of the Santi Quaranta. Where did they go? Into the tower? Into the church? Ah! When I was a boy I used to hear stories that there is an underground, where Sant'Offizio once had its prisons. . . . Listen! Listen! . . . If it's true, then there is no doubt that those devils would go there to hide out."

Roused by his curiosity and personal gain, the birro went to Sant'Offizio in order to look for some of the servants he was friendly with, and in fact, his childhood memory was not unfounded.

About two centuries earlier, even before the Tribunal of the Inquisition had its permanent premises in the Castello a Mare and then in the Palazzo Steri, it had been located for a few years in the Palazzo Marchese, and it was rumored that its prisons were located in the caves or catacombs that extended underneath the Church of Casa Professa and under the piazzetta.

Therefore, it was obvious to him that the Beati Paoli had moved their hideout to that underground, and that with a single blow, more shrewd and better orchestrated than the first time, without much preparation, and without involving too many people, all of them could be caught. What filled him with joy was that he had discovered that Blasco had returned to the fold of that sect; this would allow him to get his revenge in the eyes of the viceroy.

Matteo Lo Vecchio was going on: "So much for those best buddies; but for the duchess, we need to come up with a revenge a hundred times worse. Let's see. She isn't coming, and if I were to draw her into. . . . But that devil Andrea looks so suspicious to me. . . . I bet that he too is back with those other jolly members. Emanuele must be warned."

* * *

Two days later Andrea was dismissed.

He dared to ask the reason for this dismissal, which would drive him away from the house where he had grown up, but the house steward said curtly, "It is by order of His Excellency; he no longer needs your services."

Andrea bowed his head in an expression of sorrow that turned into indignation and hatred.

"Very well," he said, "but he will come looking for me one day . . . and then!"

He left those words hanging, making them sound like a threat, then he immediately went to see Don Girolamo, who had resumed his position as razionale at the hospital, and told him of his misfortune.

"It was to be expected, my friend; that brat isn't the son of the late Don Emanuele but of ingratitude itself."

"It's all the work of the birro, I tell you; but for the Madonna—"

"Shush! . . . *Baccaglio!*"[1]

They set about to spy on everything that the birro was doing, unleashing on his heels a whole pack of bloodhounds, quick of scent, unrecognizable, and above suspicion under the garments of the friars of the Souls of Purgatory or of Ecce Homo, or disguised as street peddlers.

They were able to determine that Matteo Lo Vecchio had frequent dealings with Emanuele, no longer in the Palazzo della Motta but in the suburban regions, and always in different locations. One of these meetings, the longest, had taken place near the Zisa, in an isolated cottage that they looked into. This information made them redouble their surveillance. Coriolano sensed some machinations were afoot,

---

1 "Silence!"

and through Don Girolamo he gave the appropriate orders. A few days passed thus. Matteo Lo Vecchio had become more wary and Emanuele was carrying on a lifestyle that didn't arouse suspicion. The birro had probably figured out that he was being followed and kept under watch.

One morning, in the Church of San Domenico, a stooping old woman who was dragging herself along, leaning on a cane while reciting the rosary, approached Donna Gabriella, who sat in an armchair in front of the Chapel of the Crucifix, in order to ask for alms. The two footmen standing behind the duchess at a respectful distance moved to chase away the nuisance, but the indignant old woman said, "Oh, be off! We are in the house of God, and we are all his children . . . and then"—and she lowered her voice so that only Donna Gabriella could hear her—"Your Excellency may want to know something from me that concerns her. I come from the Monastery of Santa Caterina."

"Ah!"

Donna Gabriella said to one of her footmen, "Give her a few tarì and leave her alone."

The old woman signed herself with the coins, knelt down, and kissed the ground, murmuring, "May the Blessed Patriarch San Domenico and the Madonna of the Rosary give her health of body and soul, and may God reward her, now and at the hour of our death and so be it. Holy Mary, mother of God—"

But the duchess grew impatient.

"What can you tell me?"

"Well, Your Excellency, I always go to the Monastery of Santa Caterina, where they give me alms . . . and she has come to grow fond of me, in her goodness, the granddaughter of the Prince of Butera, who is your relative. Yesterday, when the church was closing, she called me from one of the *comunicatori* of the chapel. She says, 'Anna'—that is the name I use to serve Her Excellency—'will you do me a favor?' 'As Your Excellency wishes,' I say. She says, 'You must go see the Duchess of Motta, who will give you alms, and you will tell her that I send her greetings.' And here I am, Your Excellency."

Donna Gabriella was irritated; this greeting wasn't worth the effort of having listened to the old woman. She dismissed her with a gesture, and the old woman went away, dragging herself along, kissing the rosary.

The following morning the old woman went to the Monastery of Santa Caterina, and after requesting to see Signora Violante Albamonte, she told her the same little story—this time, however, bringing greetings from Donna Gabriella; and this went on for quite a few days, from San Domenico to Santa Caterina and from Santa Caterina to San Domenico. But after four days she didn't find Violante. The young girl, having relapsed into her grief, had left the monastery, and, since the weather was not yet too hot, the Prince of Butera had taken her to his villa in Bagheria in order to recover.

The old woman seemed desolate at hearing this, but upon leaving the monastery she rubbed her hands together, saying with visible joy, "This is better! It couldn't have turned out better than this! If I knew the doctor, I would go and give him a pinch kiss!"

That evening Matteo Lo Vecchio, after having waited for Emanuele to leave the arena at the *firriato*[2] of Villafranca, told him quickly, "We must change everything. Your Excellency will be the judge."

And in a few words he explained to him what he had planned.

Emanuele's face lit up with great joy.

"Splendid! By God! You are a genius!"

* * *

That day Donna Gabriella's suspicious eye noticed an indefinable and feverish look on Blasco's face and in his whole manner, but she kept her painful curiosity repressed, fearful of provoking her lover's resentment; she forced herself to be calm and cheerful, also hoping that this way she could catch some telltale sign that would put her on the right track.

She now lived in a continuous state of anxiety, tormenting herself over every little thing, giving shape to every shadow, magnifying the dangers, even seeing, in the most innocent words or in the simplest acts, revelations of infidelity and betrayals, and constantly interpreting a hidden meaning behind every word.

Blasco was cheerful? She would ask herself, "Why is he cheerful? Has he perhaps obtained some privilege?" Blasco was sad? Then she would ask herself, "Why is he sad? Perhaps he hasn't seen her." If he left earlier, or if he chose one street over another, then she would torture herself with more questions. Her festive nature, her joyful spirit, and the charms that preserved something childlike about her were fading away and dying out; she would spend hours in a misanthropic gloom, looking at the sky with an intense and unconquerable sorrow, searching in vain for a ray of consolation.

* * *

Meanwhile, June was flowing by, sweet and fragrant, like an extension of spring. The entire countryside was turning green and the tall blond wheat was swaying in the plains, waiting for the scythe. The Feast of Corpus Domini, being celebrated with larger crowds due to the return of the priests and friars from exile and due to the renewed benevolence between the Court and the Curia, had also spread a bright gaiety into the little village that had risen around the noble villas.

Violante felt a great relief in that countryside, amid the wild hills, the fertile plain, and the calm blue sea. In the morning and evening, from the thickets surrounding the villa (which still had the semblance of a castle), the high-spirited and

2 A dialect word meaning "large plot of land that is surrounded by walls." RLD, 793.

impertinent greetings of the sparrows would reach her room, and then those of the gentle and melancholy nightingales. At times, however, the deep silence was interrupted by the distant cawing of crows, and in the sweet calm of her spirit, that cawing seemed to Violante like a sad voice of the saddest omens.

The Prince of Butera, after having spent a week in his villa with his grand-daughter, had returned to Palermo, leaving Violante in the company of two old ladies, cousins of the prince, who, as they were spinsters and were being taken care of by the family, would usually go live for a few months in the countryside. All three of them had then been entrusted to the custody of the steward or governor of those estates and of the vassals of the prince.

Other villas stood here and there in the surrounding area: on the hill already loomed that of Valguarnera, standing since 1709; further down the Prince of Palagonia was building his; the villa of Santa Flavia and that of the Prince of Furnari, more ancient, still retained some towers and crenellated walls. The entire region was dotted with farmhouses and villas, populated by fearless people devoted to their masters. Thus the Prince of Butera could be very confident that his women were quite safe in that villa, more so than in his urban palazzo.

One fine day Violante, sitting in her room, heard a succession of gunshots, somewhat distant in the dense woods. She asked what it could be and found out that there were some lords who had come from Palermo to hunt. The hill, in fact, abounded with wild rabbits, and there were wild ducks in the nearby river, the ancient Eleuterio, not yet dried up by the onset of the season.

The hunt had to be plentiful and full of attractions; in fact, after a break (perhaps to have lunch), the hunters resumed, and the gunshots could then be heard much closer.

Violante went to the window; she saw the two ladies who, each one leaning on a gentleman escort, were heading out on a path toward the woods. They were probably going to watch the hunt. At first she felt an impulse of youthful curiosity and was about to say, "Wait, I'm coming too!" But she said nothing, as if something unknown had unconsciously silenced her. Besides, she felt so comfortable in her solitude . . . and at that hour it seemed that the noise of the hunt, attracting curiosity to itself, had created a silence around the villa. Violante didn't see anyone. When the ladies vanished into the thicket of trees, the place seemed deserted.

She sat down, abandoning herself, as she always did, to that inert and vague state of mind that seems to be thinking yet in truth cannot and does not know how to say what it is thinking; it is like wandering about in a succession of fleeting thoughts, none of which can be attained and secured.

The shots seemed farther away but more frequent, and Violante was no longer listening to them.

It seemed that her thoughts were gradually coming together, taking form and shape, melding into one. It was her dominant thought that she was pushing back, in vain; it was in vain that she tried to overrule it under the multitude of other thoughts and images. It would constantly resurface, stronger, more tormenting, triumphantly superimposing itself over everything, taking possession of her mind, permeating her blood, occupying her heart, dominating her entire being, demoralizing her. And then, powerless to react, Violante would surrender herself to it, and her mind had only one, single, dreadful thought: that of Blasco.

So she was thinking about Blasco, not tormenting herself with useless questions, not bitten by the fangs of jealousy, but with that same spirit with which one returns to a gift that has been hopelessly lost, and lost forever! A reserved sorrow, without outbursts, without moans, without pauses—deep, desperate!

She was recalling the memory of a life spent as if in a dream, fading away at the appearance of a dawn made somber by the fog, without sun and without warmth.

The room where she lived was, like the others, slightly elevated from the ground; a man climbing on a chair or on top of a boulder could easily put his hands on the windowsill. The window was open. Violante had gone over to a table and had picked up a prayer book, her only comfort in her solitude.

Suddenly, it seemed to her that the light was intercepted by something; she turned quickly and let out a cry of fear, but before she had time to recover, a man had leapt into the room and had raced to close and bolt the door.

It was Emanuele.

Violante realized she was imprisoned. There was only one way out: the window. She ran to throw herself from it, but below the window was an armed man with the sad face of a convict. She thought she was done for.

"What do you want?" she asked, trembling, barely able to curb the fear that was making her legs weaken. "What do you want?"

Emanuele too was upset, but the turmoil had given him a wild, ferocious, bestial appearance. He answered, "What do I want? Oh, almost nothing, signora, except to settle an account with you, if you don't mind."

"I have no accounts. . . . What passes between me and you is now in the hands of the monsignor judge of the Monarchy. . . . Go away. . . . I will call for help."

"Oh! Oh. . . . I understand, my dear Donna Violante, that the way I chose to enter is not the most proper, but it is surely the quickest and saves me much inconvenience. . . . On the other hand, I warn you that it's perfectly useless to trouble yourself by calling someone, because no one would hear you. The villa is deserted; your peasants are attending the magnificent hunt that I have been organizing from this morning . . . in your honor. . . . Therefore, you are completely in my power and I have, for myself, the inescapable obligation to avenge the ridicule that you had have brought on me."

Violante wasn't hearing clearly; in her emotional state these words sounded indistinct to her ear and she didn't sense in them a significant threat.

She looked at Emanuele, hoping to discover his intentions before they turned into action, almost to anticipate him, and she looked at that window that could have been her salvation but that instead represented another danger.

She thought she saw another dark and menacing figure among the trees; she assumed that there were others around the villa and that she was trapped. This thought discouraged her. If she had had any hope of immediate help or the chance that her cry could reach the peasants in the distance, she would have taken heart; but in the abandonment, in the seclusion in which she found herself, she felt faint, and the awareness of her own weakness increased her distress.

A cold sweat dampened her forehead; she was losing heart. She attempted a defense.

"I haven't done anything to you. . . . I am a poor orphan! . . . What you are saying is wicked, monstrous! Leave me alone, I beg you!"

Emanuele took a chair and straddled it, resting his arms on the back with an air of defiance and mockery.

"Ha! Ha! Ha! . . . You are begging me? That's truly funny. . . . But I am good, I am generous. . . . Come on, come here, come closer. Sit next to me, actually, look here, I'll make myself more comfortable and offer you my knees as the most beautiful seat there can be . . . But come! . . . I am not a monster, I am not; and you are sensible. . . . No? You're not moving? You don't want to come? Then I'll come to you, as Muhammad said to the mountain. Time is passing and I. . . . I am expecting another charming visit . . . here!"

He stood up and moved close to Violante. She felt her legs buckle and leaned against the window jamb, letting herself fall to the floor with her hands folded, and with an expression of terror and prayer, she said, "For pity's sake! Do it for the memory of your mother!"

A shadow passed over Emanuele's face; his appearance changed, and his voice became dark and vindictive.

"Why are you evoking my mother at this moment? . . . You are unwittingly reminding me that I also owe my mother an act of revenge. . . . Do you know, Donna Violante, who killed my mother and who also wanted to do away with me? You don't know? Well, I will tell you: it was the man who usurped my name and my patrimony; it was Don Raimondo . . . it was your father!"

Violante turned red with disdain; her eyes lit up with a fierce blaze that seemed to infuse her blood with sudden vigor.

She jumped to her feet, shouting, "It's not true! You are lying!"

But Emanuele shrugged in disdain.

"It takes more than your misplaced indignation, Donna Violante, to destroy the truth. Through you I will avenge both myself and my mother. . . . Oh! Have no fear, I won't kill you, it would be a sin. . . . Rather . . ."

He approached her, and with the agility of a lion he grabbed her by the wrists, pulling her to him and murmuring, "You are so beautiful and so desirable that the only weapon that can be turned against you is kisses."

The young girl tried to put up a defense, tried to free her wrists, but in vain; she was too weak and her will wasn't strong enough to infuse her with strength. She could feel Emanuele's breath on her face, and the lustful fire in his gaze bored through her eyes and clouded her sight.

And so she screamed in desperation: "Help!"

The sound of a carriage that was racing there resounded on the path; a whip cracked three times. Emanuele counted those blows and said fiercely, "Here's the other one! . . . But too soon!"

Violante didn't grasp the meaning of those words because her heart, revived by a sudden hope, pounded so furiously in her chest that it was taking away her precise perception. Who had come? Was it a rescue? She looked: Emanuele's face blazed with a cruel joy; he wasn't vexed, and he wasn't afraid. Therefore, the person arriving was surely a friend, perhaps a partner in his villainy.

"Come on!" Emanuele shouted. "Let's not waste time unnecessarily!"

And with a violent tug he pulled the young girl to him, pushed her and threw her on the bed. In the imminent danger Violante gathered all her strength; propping up her legs, she tried to set herself against him and free herself, but Emanuele was too strong and was holding her firmly.

"Don't fuss," he said to her. "Anyway, it would be of no use."

There was a violent bang on the door.

Violante thought for a moment that if it was truly help, arriving to aid Emanuele, she was irreparably doomed, and that if she could still put up a resistance, perhaps it would give enough time for the people of the villa to return, and that would be her liberation. Flailing about and preventing Emanuele from subjugating her, she said to him in a broken voice, "Leave me alone! You're despicable! Despicable!"

Two more blows resounded at the door, then it seemed as if an attempt was being made to knock it down. Meanwhile, Emanuele managed to grab a towel and pass it around Violante's arms and waist; he bound and tied her so tightly that she was unable to use her hands. Then it was easier for him to lift her off the ground and throw her on the bed in order to prevent her, though she had already put her feet on the ground, from escaping him.

The door swung open violently and a woman rushed into the room like a fury; but she suddenly stopped in front of Violante and Emanuele, shouting, "Where is he?"

Violante recognized her; a faint hope lit up her face and she cried out, pleading, "Your Excellency! . . . Save me!"

CHAPTER 19

It was Donna Gabriella.

With her face distorted by rage, jealousy, and shock, she looked around and repeated her question: "Where is he? What is the meaning of this?"

But Emanuele, who had already shut the door, replied with a sneer, "I really wasn't expecting you so soon. You certainly must have whipped the horses to death!"

"I don't understand you . . ."

"Your Excellency, Signora Madre, save me!" pleaded Violante.

Donna Gabriella truly wasn't understanding anything. A letter some hours earlier had made her almost lose her mind. It was worded as follows:

> *Signora, a friend who desires your happiness and who is indignant at the insults you receive informs you that you have been cowardly betrayed; if you want proof, have your carriage harnessed, rush to Bagheria, and you will find Signor Blasco in the arms of Donna Violante.*

Like a madwoman, she called for her carriage.

"Crack the whip," she had said to the coachman.

The road had seemed endless to her, and the horses slow. Her mind was pounding with a dark and savage thought: "I will kill them! I will kill them both at once!"

As soon as she arrived, after leaping down from the carriage, not noticing that no servant had come out to welcome her, she went in, opening the rooms one by one, casting a scrutinizing glance into each until an indistinct cry led her to Violante's room. But Blasco wasn't there; and Emanuele's words, unclear but full of a meaning that her muddled mind was unable to grasp, plunged her into a state of suspicious uncertainty.

She looked at Violante, who was on her knees with her arms tied, looking lost, in a state of anxiety; she looked at Emanuele, who was sneering, defiant, ferocious; she sensed something. It seemed to be a trap. But why had they drawn her in too if the victim, as it appeared, was Violante?

She asked again, "So what is going on here?"

Don Emanuele then approached her and, without altering his sneer, said, "Perhaps the madam duchess was expecting to find someone else here. I regret her disappointment, but for now that person has ceded his place to me. Donna Gabriella, it is time for revenge. And I wanted you too to share in the joy of my revenge by witnessing my nuptials!"

Donna Gabriella took a step back, turning red; she sensed that she had been the victim of a deception, but she didn't suspect that Emanuele would plot anything against her. She was aware of only one victim: Violante, who, pale and terrified, was looking at her with eyes in which all her prayers, all her hopes, and all her fears had come together; Violante, who was anxiously trying to read every gesture, every glance, and every tremor in the one who had been her father's wife, who was the lover of the man that she loved, and who was her fiercest enemy.

There are moments when perception, the connection of ideas, and the succession of memories occur with a prodigious abundance and encapsulate an entire life. Violante and Gabriella experienced this moment.

Something deceitful, the intense pleasure not of an unexpected revenge but of one that is desired and then is carried out by others, passed for an instant through Donna Gabriella's heart and flashed on her face. Violante moaned. This thought surfaced in her mind: "They are in this together, and I am done for!"

Emanuele, satisfied with his words, stooped down toward Violante, lifted her off the ground, and placed her on the bed again.

"Signora! Signora!" the young girl cried out in desperation.

Donna Gabriella was suffering and, yielding to a new impulse in her heart, said, "What you are doing is not worthy of a gentleman. . . . There is nothing for me to do here. . . . At least let me go."

But Emanuele, stopping her and laughing boorishly, exclaimed, "Are you leaving? Now, then! . . . But you too are my slave now! Ah, by God! Signora, I have suffered too many affronts for me to renounce this hour of revenge. You are both in my power and I will have you . . ."

And then what was still confused and unclear to Donna Gabriella's mind suddenly appeared clear in all its luridness. She saw Emanuele look around the room as if searching for something. She feared for herself, rushed to the window, and caught sight of a man below; thinking he was there to help, she screamed, "Come! Hurry!"

But instead the man raised his arms, holding a musket, and threatened her: "Quiet, or I will shoot you!"

Her instinct for survival flung her back. Emanuele caught her and wrapped his arms around her, rendering her powerless. Donna Gabriella understood the extent of the danger she was exposed to and sensed that if Emanuele managed to imprison her, to tie her up as he had done to Violante, both of them would be subjected to a despicable abuse; her imagination magnified the danger, and the rage that was still burning in her veins flared up. In her agitation she became energized.

Emanuele, victorious, dragged her toward the bed, saying, "There. . . . You are reasonable, my dear duchess! . . . Set an example for your stepdaughter!"

But as he was bending down to embrace her, he let out a scream, and, pressing his hand against his chest, he staggered back. Quick as lightning, Donna Gabriella, pulling a dagger from her bosom, had plunged it fully into his chest.

"Murderer!" stammered Emanuele with a gurgling sound, and then he fell heavily, moaning, "I'm dying."

Donna Gabriella seemed astonished and unnerved by her own audacity. Violante, terrified and weeping, cried out, "God! God! Signora Madre, what have you done?"

These words shook the duchess. Pale, with disheveled hair, her forehead damp, her lips trembling, and still clutching the bloody dagger, she looked at Violante for a minute; then she suddenly flung the weapon, loosened the towel, violently took the young girl by the hand, and pulled her, shouting, "Come, let's get away!"

An indistinct sound came from under the window, filling the two women with fear. They went out through the corridors and reached the entrance, where two horses harnessed to the carriage were pawing the ground.

Donna Gabriella pushed Violante inside, thrust herself in, and shouted to the coachman, "Whip the horses . . . make haste!"

She said to her footman who had accompanied her, "Kill anyone who tries to stop us!"

The carriage took off nosily, while an extraordinary clamor rose around the villa and gunshots resounded. As they were leaving the villa, a man rushed toward the carriage, shouting, "Your Excellency! . . . Your Excellency!"

But at the threat of the footman, who, faithful to his orders, had leveled a carbine, the man stepped aside and hid behind a tree.

"Who was it?" Donna Gabriella asked from inside the carriage.

"Your Excellency, it was Matteo Lo Vecchio."

"Ah!"

* * *

In fact, it was the birro who was watching him from the lookout points, waiting for Emanuele, sure of their coup; but, surprised at seeing the duchess's carriage racing back, not knowing the reason for this apparent escape, and not having seen clearly who was inside, he was trying to find out. But the carriage vanished down the road. Matteo Lo Vecchio headed toward the villa, but he hadn't gone ten steps when he saw three or four men coming—fleeing, followed by screams, throwing down their weapons in their haste, coming out of the villa and scattering for the farms.

"Ah! Something bad must have happened," thought the birro, and as soon as one of the men passed in front of him, recognizing him, he called out, "Hey there. . . . Wait . . . what happened?"

"They killed the master!"

"What?"

Almost at the same time, two more gunshots resounded. Matteo Lo Vecchio saw some men appear at the end of the path.

"Here," he thought, "we have to rely on our own blessed feet."

And as soon as he turned around, he too ran away, hiding amid the orange groves to escape from view.

Inside the villa there was confusion, shouting, a bustling of people who were coming, going, pushing, distraught by the incident, and uncertain about what could be done.

Emanuele's moaning had attracted the attention of the man below the window, who, after gesturing to a companion lying in wait amid the trees, climbed up to the windowsill so he could look into the room. At the sight of his master gasping for breath, he had let out a cry of terror, but almost at the same time, two gunshots had been fired from the thick of the trees. Other bravacci who were lurking there had leapt out, full of fear, onto the esplanade of the villa, fleeing.

Their fear had infected the other two, and without knowing why or where the danger was coming from, they had fled. Behind them, the steward and a few peasants, having arrived, had fired more shots, and then they had returned to the villa, where in the meantime the two old ladies were arriving, shaken by the gunshots.

Since the hunt was becoming drawn out and the hunters had brazenly spread out in a chain, preventing the ladies from returning to the villa, the steward, suspicious, gestured to his men and respectfully told the ladies that it was late and that the young lady was alone in the house. So they started off—the steward and a peasant in front, the ladies behind, other peasants at the rear. When they were almost at the edge of the woods, the steward saw a man climbing up to the window of Violante's room, and he fired, shouting; the effect of that shot was striking. Caught off guard, the rascals who were lying in wait, believing themselves under attack, fled, and the ladies and the peasants, fearing something sinister, rushed into the house. But a wretched sight presented itself to their eyes: the young man was on the ground, a clot of blood in his mouth, his eyes wide open, overcome by his suffering.

That dead or dying man, the disorder of the room, and Violante's absence filled the two old ladies with fear, and they began to scream. Everyone scattered this way and that trying to find the young girl, while the steward and a few peasants pursued the runaways with gunshots.

"Violante! Violante!"

"Your Excellency!"

No one answered. Their hearts were seized by an unspeakable anguish; their eyes, which had searched in vain, looked at one another with an astonishment filled with anxiety and panic. The old ladies wept, and that young man on the ground, unknown to everyone, immobile in his tragic and horrifying prostration, no one knowing how he had gotten in or who had killed him or why, amplified their terror with the mystery that enveloped him. Everyone crowded around to see him, staying a moment to look at him, to watch him with a silent curiosity, full of conjectures and questions.

The steward bent down next to him and said, "He's still alive."

A voice added, "Run to summon the parish priest."

They cautiously lifted Emanuele off the ground and laid him on that same bed where he had thought he would celebrate his double revenge.

He gave no sign of life; he barely had a pulse. Suddenly, his limbs quivered, his body relaxed, and his head tilted gently on his shoulder.

"*Requia materna!*" murmured the steward in a sad and solemn voice, taking off his hat and kneeling. And all those peasants with sunburnt and wrinkled faces also knelt around the bed, repeating with greater fervor, in their mangled Latin, the invocation of eternal peace for the soul of that unknown young man: "*Requia materna!*"

CHAPTER 20

Donna Gabriella arrived at her palazzo in the grip of a nervous fit and needed help from her footman and Violante to step down from the carriage. She immediately ordered the gates to be closed. She was afraid. Although what she had done was lawful due to her right to defend herself, just the thought of having killed a man filled her with terror. She thought that justice was already on her trail; the birro Matteo Lo Vecchio had seen her, and by now he must have reconstructed the crime and reported her as well.

"Lock all the doors!" she ordered, suddenly trembling at the slightest noise.

Violante had followed her in silence, not even daring to offer her a word of comfort. Her eyes too were filled with the horrific vision: Emanuele, lying on the ground, his eyes terrified in death. That youth's life that was struck down in an instant and that frightened expression were still before her eyes. She was trembling.

Nevertheless, she felt and would admit that Donna Gabriella had saved her; she had saved her by arriving at the villa at the moment when she was about to succumb to Emanuele's loathsome embrace, had saved her by violently killing that overbearing man who seemed already sure of his victory and who was getting ready to carry out a vile ritual before her eyes.

She owed her safety to that woman who had been her fiercest enemy, and toward whom her heart had been seized by hatred and jealousy. Fate, destiny, providence, divine will? She didn't know. Besides, what did it matter? If she wasn't crying now over something irreparable and lost forever, didn't she owe it to Donna Gabriella's intervention and courage? If she was now safe, far from the danger that had threatened her, didn't she owe it to Donna Gabriella? Hadn't her stepmother stamped out, extinguished in an impulse of human charity, the voices of hatred in order to hold out her liberating hands even at the cost of covering them with blood?

When, after hurriedly crossing the drawing rooms, Donna Gabriella, pulling Violante behind her, went into her room and shut herself in, pale, trembling, and suspicious, the young girl threw herself into her arms, and then both of them began to cry.

* * *

At that very moment, Coriolano della Floresta was going into Blasco's room; Blasco was stretched out in a large chair, wandering after his dreams and thoughts with his gaze. Coriolano's demeanor, seemingly troubled by something weighty, surprised him.

"What is it?"

"Emanuele was killed two and a half hours ago."

Blasco leapt to his feet, turned pale, and stammered, "What are you saying? . . . Killed?"

"It's the truth; I just received the news and rushed to tell you."

"But how?"

"He was killed in Bagheria."

Blasco grew even paler and frowned.

"In Bagheria, you said? . . . But then he . . ."

"Yes—pretending to go to a hunting party, he had instead stormed into Butera's summer villa at a time when no one was there except Donna Violante."

"Oh God!"

"It was something that had been plotted beforehand, and so secretly that I had no inkling. However, I ordered a punishment for the informants who didn't let me know about Emanuele's departure so that I could have him followed."

"Leave aside these details, which don't matter to me. . . . Rather tell me—"

"Donna Violante is safe. Emanuele was killed before he could commit a rape."

"Ah! . . . Thank you! But don't keep me in suspense, tell me everything, in the name of God."

"I still can't tell you anything definite, because what I told you is the first news I received. I can only say that Emanuele was killed by a woman."

"By a woman?"

"Precisely. By Donna Gabriella."

Blasco let out a cry of amazement and his face expressed utter disbelief.

"Donna Gabriella? How? Where? . . . But aren't you mistaken?"

"Donna Gabriella had been lured to the summer villa, I don't know why or how; it is certain, however, that she thrust a dagger into Emanuele's chest and that she took Violante with her, removing her from any danger. Go see the duchess, who must have already returned."

Coriolano hadn't yet finished when Blasco had already taken his hat, sword, and long cane and launched himself out the door, saying, "We'll see each other later."

He raced to Donna Gabriella's house with his heart in turmoil on account of what he had heard, and what he didn't know but was afraid of finding out and assumed was very serious. Donna Gabriella didn't want to see him.

Hearing through the door the valet's announcement of Blasco's arrival, she looked grimly at Violante, who had grown paler, and, opening the door a crack, showed her face and said to Blasco, who was standing anxiously in the middle of the drawing room, "Go! Go! You cannot come in. . . . I don't want you here now. . . . Go see the Prince of Butera; tell him to come here at once. Go. . . . You will come tomorrow. Not now, I don't want you here. Do you understand that I don't want you here?"

In the tone of her voice, in her eyes, in the sorrowful torment on her face, there was so much painful pleading that Blasco couldn't insist, and he left. Donna Gabriella closed the door again and approached Violante, who had remained motionless, with her forehead obscured by a shadow.

She looked at her a moment and asked her, "What are you thinking?"

Her voice had taken on a tone that was trying to be harsh, but she couldn't manage to conceal the profound pain that surged in her chest.

Violante raised her large, limpid, sad eyes and replied softly, "Nothing, Signora Madre."

"Did you hear who I was talking with?"

Violante blushed slightly.

"Yes, signora."

A flash of anger blazed in Donna Gabriella's eyes, but it died away immediately; she took Violante's hand and asked in a voice trembling with dread, "Do you still love him?"

Again the flames rose on Violante's face, and she didn't answer. But it was easy to catch sight of the intense emotion in her heart by the frequent throbbing of her arteries, which looked like they were about to burst.

The duchess waited a moment for an answer, then resumed: "Listen to me. . . . I killed a man. . . . I killed him for you. . . . For an instant I cherished the thought that he was going to violate you, because it seemed to me like a way to exact revenge, and I almost would have helped him . . . in order to humiliate you, to vilify you, to destroy you. . . . But then I thought about many other things. . . . And then I wanted to save you. . . . and I killed."

She covered her eyes with her hands, as if to avoid seeing the horrific sight.

Violante, clasping her hands, emotional and pleading, murmured to her, "Signora . . . Signora Madre!"

The duchess raised her head, with her eyes full of tears. She went on: "I killed. . . . Now listen to me . . . for what I did, for the blood spilled . . . for what I am suffering, I beg you to tell me the truth. Will you tell me? Will you tell me?"

"What do you want me to tell you?" Violante asked in a whisper.

"Tell me if you still love him. This thought is stuck here in my brain, like a nail. . . . You know this, he belongs to me now, he belongs to me, he has taken hold of my entire life. . . . Now, perhaps, now that I've killed, he will look at me in horror . . . and yet, you see . . . I saved you, I freed you from that scoundrel, for Blasco, because I felt that this would please him, and that *he* should be grateful to me. . . . So tell me, then. . . . Doubt is more tormenting than reality; tell me if you still love him."

Her words were labored, and her face had the indescribable anguish of great, intense suffering. Violante's heart ached; her sense of mercy prompted her to lie, but her loyalty compelled her not to conceal anything from someone who had begged her so fervently. Loyalty won.

"Oh! Signora Madre, why are you tormenting yourself like this? Well, I will tell you everything—yes, it's better for me and for you. . . . I loved him. . . . I loved him as if in a dream, like something noble, great, sublime, almost divine!"

"Yes, yes," Donna Gabriella stammered fervently. "He is like that."

"But now . . ."

"Now?"

"Now I have solemnly sworn to consecrate myself to God. I will return to the monastery and take the veil. . . . And the world will be closed eternally for me. . . . He never heard a word from me; he never knew whether I had any feelings for him . . . and he will never know! That is what I can tell you."

Donna Gabriella took her hands; in her eyes shone a feeling of gratitude and a truly maternal tenderness, but the sobs that swelled her chest prevented her from speaking.

They were in that state of emotion when the valet came to announce the Prince of Butera.

* * *

Violante departed the same night in a carriage with her grandfather the prince, who was furious not only about the attack on his granddaughter but also, and even more so, because Emanuele had dared attempt such a thing in his house.

He was threatening to have the steward and the peasants who had left the house to the mercy of the first comer hanged, and he regretted that Emanuele was dead, because he would have liked to teach him a lesson himself about the respect that was owed to him. Thank God that the duchess had taken care of it! What a woman! But, all right, goodness! Now he would have to see about freeing her from all her troubles with justice, naturally expecting that the Prince of Geraci would not sit idly by to avenge the death of his grandson.

For the entire journey from Donna Gabriella's house to the Palazzo Butera, the noble gentleman could talk of nothing else, passing through all the shades of anger, indignation, admiration, and pity toward that granddaughter, so young and already tested by a thousand misfortunes.

Violante was keeping quiet and thinking, or at least it seemed like she was thinking; instead, she was crying inside. She had renounced everything that evening, committing herself to something higher, whose solemn and admonishing voice she had heard in the depths of her heart, but now, before the loquacity of her ancestor, she felt the enormity of her sacrifice. And yet, she had never dared hope to conquer Blasco's heart, to be loved by him, to live with him always, always, as she had dreamed in the first blossoming of her youth; on the contrary, knowing him to be her stepmother's lover had nearly stifled the flame of her love under the scorn and the offended pride of her character. So it seemed to her. Instead, now that she had solemnly given it up, she realized that her love was still alive and passionate within her heart and that a dream, a distant hope, had concealed itself deep within her soul. And she was sobbing inside, in the silence of her reserved and impenetrable suffering.

* * *

After Violante's departure, Donna Gabriella, finding herself alone in her room, felt afraid. Why on earth had she driven Blasco away? Wouldn't it have been better to ask him to come back? The solitude of her room, full of sad and frightful visions, was putting a cold fear in her veins!

What if she sent for Blasco? . . . Yes, that would be better. She felt the need to have a friend beside her, to hear a word of comfort, a sweet and tender word, to receive a caress, a squeeze of the hand full of mysteries and confidences.

She pulled the bell cord; to the maidservant who rushed in, she ordered, "Send a volante at once to Don Blasco Albamonte; tell him that I am expecting him, that I need him. Go, hurry!"

Blasco was having supper with Coriolano; he was gloomy and quiet, as if oppressed by the accumulation of events of that day, and the Cavaliere della Floresta hadn't been able to lift him out of that depression. But when a servant conveyed to him the volante's message, he jumped to his feet and said, "I'm coming right away. . . . Permit me, Coriolano."

He arrived at Donna Gabriella's palazzo in a few minutes. The duchess was in a corner of her room, huddled in a large chair, with her eyes staring at the door, waiting in an anguished state of mind, shuddering in her solitude at the slightest noise.

When she saw the door being opened and Blasco coming in, she stood up with outstretched arms, crying out as if to a savior, "Blasco! My Blasco!"

And she fell against his chest, sobbing in a nervous fit. He put her down on a sofa, sat on a lower stool in front of her, and took her hands, comforting her with a tender and caressing voice.

"Don't be afraid! . . . You did the right thing. . . . No one will touch a hair on your head. . . . I am here."

She stammered, "And you will never leave! Isn't that true? Stay here forever. . . . I don't want you to leave anymore!"

"Yes, yes . . . but calm down! After all, you did what you had to do."

"Do you know everything? Do you know how it happened? . . . I went there for you. . . . I thought I would surprise you. . . . I was out of my mind. They told me that you were there."

"Me? . . . What? I know nothing. So tell me."

And so Donna Gabriella, at times interrupting herself, at times becoming excited, then suddenly overcome with fear, told him about the letter she had received, her ride to Bagheria, and of her storming into Violante's room.

"I had decided to kill both of you at once. . . . But instead I found him. . . . Violante was lying on the bed with her hands tied, so helpless, in shock. . . . He had drawn me in . . . had arranged for a horrible revenge. . . . One more minute and Violante would have been ruined . . . ruined. . . . I realized it. . . . Oh, how many sad things suddenly flashed through my mind. Ruined! Ruined forever and to everyone. . . . He hadn't touched her yet. He moved closer to me; I saw nothing more. I stabbed him. I wanted to run away immediately, but I saw Violante there, terrified. . . . I took pity on her, I dragged her with me. . . . When you came today, and I didn't let you in . . . she was here . . . that is why I didn't want you to come in. You must not see her ever again! I saved her. . . . I don't know why. . . . I can't explain it . . . but if I did something for which you are grateful, swear to me that you won't see her anymore . . ."

That story, the tone of her voice, and Donna Gabriella's appearance had gradually aroused a storm of feelings and affections in Blasco's heart. He understood or thought he could see, through her restraint, the entire power of the double sacrifice carried out by Donna Gabriella, but above all he felt toward her a profound gratitude for what she had done on Violante's behalf. There was for him, in the young girl, something more sacred than life itself: the virgin purity that rendered her to his eyes a creature of dreams and surrounded her with all the charms of immaculate things. And of all this, Donna Gabriella had become an armed and avenging guardian, precisely the woman whose mad impulses he had thwarted and had feared, the woman he had seen blazing with hatred at the slightest shadow of suspicion. How and from where had this change come about? What profound kindness was concealed in the intimate mystery of such a tempestuous soul? What frightening breadth did that love have, to have reached the point of saving her hated and feared rival, only because it could please her beloved man?

Blasco was vanquished. He clasped Donna Gabriella's hands, kissed them with tender devotion, and looked at her with a profound and touching joy.

"Oh! Gabriella!" he said, sighing. "Who can reward you for what you have done? If I gave my life for you now, I wouldn't be able to equal your gesture!"

Donna Gabriella looked hard into his eyes as if trying to read into the depths of his soul. She sensed something unusual and new in the tone of his words, and in his kisses a tenderness she had never felt until then. A shadow of sadness fell over her face. That night Blasco was more demonstrative and tender; he genuinely surrendered himself to the joy in his heart, for which no happiness was greater than knowing that Violante was safe, thinking that with his demonstrativeness, with the most tender caresses, he would make Donna Gabriella happy. But instead, the duchess became increasingly melancholy, darker, tormented by a thought: "These caresses are not for me, only for me. He doesn't love me for who I am but for what I have done; thus his heart is not entirely mine. I will never possess him completely. Caring, passion, caresses, they all need something that makes them quiver. . . . I am not loved! I am not loved!"

This thought gradually took possession of her spirit, made her blood run cold, extinguished the flames, and dried up the fountains of her joy. The voice of that thought cruelly and relentlessly said to her, "It's over! It's over for you! His heart is elsewhere; his heart is escaping you, it will always escape you! Over! It's over!"

In an unguarded moment, Blasco said to her, "My dear, I must tell you something that will upset you. I didn't have the courage to tell you before."

Donna Gabriella gave a start. Her inner voice whispered to her with a sneer of bitter triumph, "Do you see? Now he will tell you that he is forced to abandon you."

She looked at Blasco without speaking, questioning him sorrowfully with her eyes.

Blasco went on: "I have orders to leave for camp in Francavilla, at once."

Donna Gabriella's first impulse was to say to him, "I'm going with you too!"

But the words died before they reached her lips; she lowered her head in silence and only then did her eyes fill with tears, for which she could give an apparent explanation.

After a moment of silence Blasco said, "This might be the last night that we spend together."

His voice had the profound emotion of a last goodbye, and Donna Gabriella heard it and burst into tears.

"Yes, yes," she repeated mentally in a fit of anguish. "This is the last night. . . . The last!"

But Blasco was alluding to his possible death in a battle that was expected to be bloody, between the Spanish troops fortified in Francavilla and the German troops that were besieging them from all sides; Donna Gabriella was thinking about the death of his love.

"I am departing tomorrow at noon."

Then she was seized with a horrible thought, her still tearful eyes blazing with all the gloomy light of a uniquely ferocious passion.

"If I killed him," she thought, "he would never belong to anyone else!"

Kill him? . . . And there before her eyes appeared the image of Emanuele lying on the ground, with that bleeding hole in his chest, his lifeless pupils, arrested by the spasm of death in a frightening stillness. Horror coursed through her blood; in the thrill of her fantasy, the image of Emanuele turned into Blasco. She saw Blasco dead, in his room, and then, jumping on impulse to her feet, stretching out her hands, she screamed with an indescribable accent, "No!"

And she fell back into Blasco's arms.

CHAPTER 21

On the evening of June 21, two men were talking to each other like two good friends at the corner of a vicolo opposite the Piazza del Duomo. A patrol passed by; they shook hands, said goodbye to each other, and parted, one to one side, one to the other, as they also waved to the patrol head. It was almost ten o'clock; the streets were becoming deserted. The dark, long Cassaro faded into the shadows, barely broken by the faint light of the sky, which was luminous with stars. A few lanterns bobbing just above the ground briefly penetrated the darkness.

The patrol went by, going down the Cassaro in order to monitor whether the taverns and shops were closed in accordance with the Senate bans. And then, cautious, creeping along the walls without making a sound, those two men returned to the corner of the vicolo where they had been before. This time, despite the heat, they wore sleeveless black capes.

One of them whispered, "Come. He stopped to talk with the patrol."

In fact, looking down the Cassaro, they saw the lantern of the man leading the patrol, not moving, shining on the guards and on a man dressed all in black. Then the man broke away and the lantern moved.

The two men then retreated into the dark vicolo and threw their cloaks over their shoulders, leaving their arms and their carbines exposed. They posted themselves on either side of the vicolo, in two doorways, with their weapons ready.

They heard the tapping of a cane on the pavement gradually coming closer. A man passed by and didn't notice anything; the darkness in that vicolo was so deep that nothing could be seen, not even by the most well-trained eye.

The man went two or three steps beyond the end of the vicolo; the two men lying in wait came out of their hiding places, reached the corner, aimed, and fired.

Two flames pierced the night; the two shots made a tremendous booming sound. The man collapsed to the ground without letting out a moan. The two men went over to him, then bent down and looked at him. "He's dead. Let's go."

They immediately plunged back into the vicolo, but without making a sound—it was as if they didn't have shoes on their feet. When they were shielded by the darkness, they started to run up to Via dei Biscottari, where they resumed their normal stride, as though they were two people peacefully on their way home.

They no longer had their cloaks or their carbines. Some mysterious hands, in the darkness of the vicolo, had made them vanish; any patrol could have stopped them and wouldn't have suspected a thing.

They walked along Via dei Biscottari, went down along Ballarò toward Casa Professa, and hurled themselves into a vicolo. One of them imitated the call of a quail.

Another, similar call answered.

Then they went into Piazza Santi Quaranta Martiri and disappeared inside a small door that closed mysteriously behind them. Meanwhile, the two carbine gunshots, which in the night had sounded like shots from a cannon, had immediately animated and lit up the street. It was suppertime, and naturally those two tremendous booms had made the windows of the nearby houses shake and had interrupted peaceful family gatherings. Men were opening up the balconies and windows; the doors of a few workshops were opening; some suspicious heads were appearing and looking out; they all said the same thing: "There's been a murder!" . . . But no one dared go out, certainly not for fear of some gunshots, but so as not to have any trouble with justice. Meanwhile the patrol came rushing from the end of the Cassaro; three or four half-undressed soldiers were running from the piazza of the Palazzo Reale, fastening their swords or their doublets as they went.

The patrol was the first to arrive, then from the workshops and houses the most curious came out, some bearing oil lamps or lanterns. They all crowded around the fallen man, who lay face down with arms stretched out to the sides, legs wide apart, in a pool of blood.

The patrol head shouted, "Back! Back! . . . Make way!"

The birri started using their halberds to clear the way, and immediately the patrol head bent down and turned over the fallen man, on whose dusty face fell the light of the lamps and of the lantern carried by the man leading the patrol.

A cry emerged from everyone's mouth: "Matteo Lo Vecchio!"

"The birro!"

It was an astonishment to everyone, an astonishment at which it wasn't difficult to feel a certain satisfaction. From the street to those who were on the balconies, to the newly arrived, the news was being given with a gratification that seemed like the outpouring of a long-awaited revenge.

"They killed Matteo Lo Vecchio!"

"They killed that scoundrel the birro!"

A voice sang his eulogy with one word: "Finally!"

And another added as a commentary, "They even took too long!"

"He's dead. Good heavens! Two gunshots, and may God keep us free of him! . . . It's pointless to take him to the hospital. Get a ladder."

Two birri ran to the nearby Duomo, where they were sure to find as many as they wanted, and returned soon after with a short one; they laid the corpse on it and lifted it like a bier onto their shoulders and started off for the Albergheria, followed by a crowd of people who were laughing, cackling cheerfully, going around saying to anyone who would show their faces, and to those they would run into, "They killed Matteo Lo Vecchio!"

"Really?"

There was widespread astonishment and satisfaction; the procession swelled. In no time the dead man had a train of people who accompanied him all the way home, filling that narrow and winding vicolo that leads to the Albergheria from Via Salita del Banditore and that now bears the name of the birro. The guards and the patrol head had to use their pikes to prevent the crowd from invading the little house.

"Throw him away! . . . He's a swine!"

"He doesn't deserve a funeral!"

"He is an excommunicant."

"If the *repitatrici*[1] come, we'll do them in!"

But a woman appeared at the window, looking disheveled and weeping, shouting, "It's not true! It's not true! He was no longer excommunicated. He had been blessed again by the vicario generale!"

But the crowd was cackling. "He was a birro! A birro and wicked!"

The commotion lasted until late, when sleepiness began to thin out the crowd. Then two or three women, dressed in black, with their hair loose, went into the house. Matteo Lo Vecchio was stripped, washed, and dressed in newer clothes, but without shoes, since it wasn't proper for him to meet the Lord with shoes on his feet.

They placed him on the bed, stretched out; they lit candles at his feet, and after they sat down on the floor, those women began to weep, to mourn, to remember the deeds and kind acts of the dead man.

"Do you remember when he came with new shoes?"

"Ah, poor me."

"How handsome he was on horseback!"

"Ah, poor me."

All night, sitting on the floor with their hair unpinned, beating their chests, clapping their hands, the repitatrici, a remnant of the ancient female mourners, lamented themselves before the dead man, who lay with his hands crossed on his stomach and tied with a rosary, his face contorted in a grimace of terror, rendered more frightening by a tragically comical cotton cap.

In the morning more guards came to protect the house from potential aggressions. Judge Don Antonino Negri, alerted by the patrol leader, had given explicit orders, so that the birro, the shrewdest, most hardworking, most frightening of his

---

1 Women mourners who participated in the preparations for funeral vigils or accompanied the funeral service.

birri, had a Christian funeral, like every other good citizen. The vicolo was watched over by guards, who kept in check the rabble and the young delinquents of the nearby market, who were gathering in a manner that was anything but benevolent.

At dawn, the news that Matteo Lo Vecchio had been killed had already spread throughout the neighborhood, and it had aroused a sense of satisfaction in everyone's spirits. The terror that the birro had spread throughout the city, the hatred that he accumulated throughout his career, the tears shed by hundreds of his victims, the cruelty of his ways, all this created a feeling of relief and joy, like a liberation that had been wished for and awaited every day until it finally arrived.

"Blessed are those hands!"

"Blessed are those gunshots!"

Then a rumor began to spread: "It was the Beati Paoli!"

"He had been sentenced to death!"

"May they be blessed, now and forever!"

Via Albergheria was in a state of commotion; there was talk of nothing else besides the death of Matteo Lo Vecchio. Now they were waiting for the funeral rites; they wanted to see if there was any group that had the courage to go with and, as it was said, "escort" the corpse of that excommunicant.

So the vicario generale had absolved him and blessed him again? And what did it matter? He hadn't gotten rid of all the villainies he had committed that were crying out for revenge.

"They should go and throw him in Via dei Cavallacci."[2]

"That one, even dead, will commit his last 'infamy.'"

"Not even San Michele Arcangelo could avoid the birro!"

After lunch, there were the poor of the Seraglio,[3] with the cross and the congregation of the Sciabica,[4] to accompany the dead man. There was widespread astonishment.

"What? What? Is he going to be buried like a respectable Christian?"

They were expressing their outrage, and everyone was murmuring with such threatening and grim faces that it was making the poor and the friars uneasy. Some were apologizing. It had been ordered by Judge Negri. After all, it was a baptized body and he had been absolved; this was the main argument, but it satisfied no one.

A squad of birri and algozini armed with pikes, swords, and long knobbed clubs kept the population in check, but not enough to prevent that turmoil that is a sign of uncontrollable outbursts to come.

Then came the parish. The poor priest cast suspicious glances all around, with an expression on his face that meant "May God help me!"

---

2 The place where carcasses were thrown. SE, 1222

3 Poorhouse. SE, 1222.

4 Congregation of artisans and lower middle classes. SE, 1222.

The procession began. With its hands crossed, the corpse was placed on the bier and lifted onto the shoulders of the porters, preceded by the poor of the Seraglio and by the parish, followed by the friars, surrounded by birri and algozini. But as soon as it emerged from the vicolo and was on its way down to the Albergheria, a murmur arose, like the roar of a distant large wave, that, gradually growing, turned into a storm of whistles, shouts, and insults.

A rabble of half-naked delinquents placed themselves at the head of the mournful procession, chanting in parody, "*Catameo, catameo*, dead is the birro Matteo!"

The birri and algozini, at first with pikes and with clubs, cleared their way roughly, in a bullying manner, but since the crowd and the racket were growing, their bravado was weakening, and from the bottom of their souls a worry rose to the surface about possible dangers to come. Some were cursing Judge Negri, because instead of having the corpse transported at night, without pomp, he had wanted to honor the man with a funeral.

"But do you know what nerve!" was being said in the crowd. "They are going to bury him at Sant'Antonino!"

"That flesh from hell at Sant'Antonino!"

And then threatening cries erupted: "Leave him! Leave him!"

"Put out the torches! It's a disgrace!"

There were the most ardent, who, adding a gesture to their words, blew forcefully and put out the torches.

The leader of the algozini appealed to them: "My friends, be patient . . . after all, he was a Christian; he is dead, absolved by His Lordship the vicario. . . . Have a little compassion!"

"Compassion? Did the birro ever have any for so many poor people?"

The threatening cries grew more violent than ever; a few apple cores flew through the air. The crowd started to bear down on the procession, and the shoving began. At the corner of Via del Bosco, the congregation of the Sciabica, given the bad situation, slipped away.

"Well done! Well done!" the crowd shouted. "That's the spirit! . . . Well done!"

They were cheering, but the cheers were a new threat for those who were still there; the birri and the algozini found themselves exposed to the rage of the growing mob. They held out for a while, ashamed to give in, but when they realized that the turmoil was about to violently erupt, one by one, without drawing attention, some to one side, some to the other, they began to scatter.

When the coffin reached Via Maqueda, there was not a guard to be seen; it was left to the mercy of the emboldened mob, who intoned a *de profundis* of abuses and insults, upsetting the porters who were carrying it. Above the moving heads that poor coffin swayed like an upside-down boat abandoned to the waves.

After arriving at the Monastery of the Assunta and seeing that the church was open, the priest, pale as death, turned, mumbled two incomprehensible Latin words, hastily sprinkled the cross with the aspergillum, and ran into the church, happy to have come through it well and quicker than he would have thought and to leave the problem to others.

Then the eight porters quickened their pace; the Convent of Sant'Antonino wasn't far off and in a few minutes they arrived there, continually followed by the mob, who was singing, "*Catameo catameo*, dead is the birro!"

"That infamous scoundrel is dead, throw him away like a dog!"

The door of the convent was closed. The porters placed the coffin on the ground and knocked; a friar appeared who said, "This is no place here to bury birri."

And he closed the door again.

It was a plain and simple dirty trick. Judge Negri had paid ten onze to have Matteo Lo Vecchio buried in that church. The friars had unscrupulously pocketed the money; now they had the obligation to take the dead man. Of course! Instead, the friars shouted from inside, "Take him away! Take him away!"

Then suddenly, the door opened wide and they came out armed with clubs and threw themselves on the porters, beating the living daylights out of them and repeating, "Take him away! Take him away!"

At that fury the porters fled, and the friars went after them, but they caught up to only one, and they dragged him, threatening to break his ribs if he didn't take the coffin away.

"But I can't do it alone!"

Among the laughing and cackling crowd, there were a few who had compassion for the poor porter and offered to help him; so the sad coffin was lifted again and resumed its way, tottering over the heads. Near there, almost on the bank of the Oreto River, there was a cemetery for the poor people, with a chapel, looked after by a hermit. They started off toward that bend, but the hermit shut the gate and locked it.

"Here? You want to bury the birro here? In the midst of so many of God's poor children? . . . That excommunicant? That scoundrel? You are crazy! There is no room for him here. . . . Go and throw him in the river."

The porters looked at each other; it was starting to annoy them. Oh, were they expected to walk around all day with that dead body on their shoulders, then? They talked it over among themselves and, after opening the coffin, they removed the hard and stiff corpse, a horrible sight owing to the expression of terror on its face under the cotton cap. They stripped him of his clothes, leaving him naked, and having climbed onto the wall of the cemetery behind the church, they hauled him up, lowered him down the other side, and after finding a dry well, they took that wretched corpse with its kidneys ripped open and blackened by its wounds, and they threw it down the well, sending it off with an obscene gesture.

Then they heard the dull thud of the body smashing against the stones at the bottom.

CHAPTER 22

Blasco had returned from the camp in Francavilla on June 23 with two of the Marchese of Lede's messengers in order to take the announcement of the victory of the Spanish forces to the Marchese of Montemar in Palermo.

The letter, written in Spanish, was published soon after in the press by Francesco Cichè, a printer from Palermo, and, as was to be expected, brought about a great sea of lights and pageantry in the Cassaro, *Te Deum* in the churches, and salvos from the bastions and castles.

Blasco had asked for the honor of taking the announcement of what appeared to be a great victory so that he could return to Palermo; he had left Donna Gabriella in such a depressed state of mind that despite the events in the camp and the dangers of a fierce and bloody battle, he had not been able to keep his heart at peace. He was in the grip of an intense anxiety.

On leaving, he had unconditionally entrusted Donna Gabriella to Coriolano.

The Cavaliere della Floresta had replied, "Your urgings are unnecessary. She will have nothing to fear; no one will accuse the duchess . . ."

"But those bravacci—"

"They have already been warned and will not dare breathe a word. . . . Don Girolamo has taken care of it."

"Oh! . . . All right, but there is the birro."

"Don't worry about him. Last night justice was done. . . . Besides, I have informed the Prince of Carini about everything, and it goes without saying that he is not a man to allow a rape to be committed against a woman of his house, and no judge will dare to order her arrest. You can leave without worry."

Without worry? Oh, no; Blasco had lost any sense of calm. Too many sad and painful events had taken place and were weighing on his soul for him to be able to have peace of mind! Another request had come to his lips, and he hadn't dared to express it. Coriolano, who was observing him, smiled subtly, as he would often do: "I understand you, dear friend, without you telling me anything. Don't torment yourself about this at all; I will watch over Donna Violante and will keep you informed about everything that may be of interest to you."

Blasco was not wrong to be worried. Emanuele's death had stirred up a great commotion, all the more so due to the extraordinary circumstances that had accompanied it. Finding the dead body in Violante's bedroom, in the Prince of Butera's villa, seemed inexplicable; but he didn't defend the slain man when the young girl told her grandfather, in all its details, about the attack of which she had nearly fallen victim. The Prince of Butera saw in that act an affront so grievous that the scoundrel's death didn't seem sufficient to expiate him, and he expressed his deep-felt grievances to the Prince of Geraci.

But he, who was fed up with his grandson's recklessness, shrugged his shoulders and said, "What can I do about it? You cannot have any greater satisfaction than this: that I am not taking a step to avenge the death of my grandson."

Justice began its investigations, pretending to assume that the murderous hand had been quite another than that of a woman, not daring to investigate the truth because it would have compromised three of the most important and most powerful families of the kingdom.

But if all that averted a danger that hung over Donna Gabriella's head, it wasn't helping to dispel her fears, which her solitude and her distance from Blasco had only increased.

The distance above all had made her restless and embittered. The dominant thought that constantly gnawed at her brain like a woodworm and filled her with a profound sadness was this: Did he love her? And Violante?

Why, then, wasn't her eye able to penetrate and read into the depths of the hearts of Blasco and Violante? She had gone on occasion to visit Violante in the palazzo of her grandfather, the prince, and had been welcomed with fondness. The prince would run to meet her, would kiss her hands in the proper and formal manner, but with a strong feeling of gratitude, and then would declare, "Here is our heroine!"

But this allusion, evoking a bloody scene that horrified her, would clench her heart in an icy grip.

Even Violante no longer had toward Donna Gabriella that same stiff manner, that proud and reserved demeanor as before; she would kiss her hand respectfully and call her "Signora Madre." Now she was in a unique situation: she was a widow without ever having been a wife; Emanuele's death had rendered the annulment proceedings pointless, and while liberating her from that ill-omened marriage, it still didn't bring her any joy. She aspired to nothing more than to shut herself in a cloister, and without the determined opposition of her grandfather, she would have long since gone back there. One day, when Donna Gabriella had gone to visit her stepdaughter, the subject of the monastery had come up.

"But what cloister! What nuns!" the Prince of Butera exclaimed, laughing. "There's no need for the veil. You got married as a diversion. Now we must get you married in earnest, to a fine cavaliere."

"Oh, no! Your Excellency, forgive me, but I will not marry any man; my resolution is irrevocable. Why do you want to oppose me? Why do you want to make me unhappy?"

"But listen to these ideas. . . . At that age! . . . When you will find a handsome young nobleman, rich . . ."

Violante had become quite pale, as if faced with an imminent danger. Clasping her hands, begging, she had murmured, "Your Excellency is making me suffer. I will never be able to look at a man."

The prince had laughed, but Donna Gabriella had in turn become pale and distressed; she alone had understood the tragedy of that soul, who at the same time had partly opened, then shut herself to love; she alone had heard beneath that "I could never look at a man" what had been left unsaid—that is, that her heart was entirely occupied, taken, overwhelmed by the vision of Blasco. Violante had loved him, she still loved him, she always loved him, she loved him completely, profoundly, intensely! . . . And she was locking away her love with a willpower and resignation that amazed Donna Gabriella, amazed and saddened her, she who wasn't able to renounce her own passion and who trembled and tormented herself at the mere suspicion that they could be rivals for the object of her passion.

Was it out of pride? Out of necessity? Out of gratitude toward her liberator that Violante was forever renouncing all hope of a supreme joy? Was that young girl so heroic, then? She seemed more altruistic to her. And she thought with dismay that perhaps this altruism would make her even more beautiful, more desirable, more beloved in Blasco's eyes, beloved as something loftier, like something heavenly. She felt envy for that creature, struck by a tragic fate, from whose hands she had snatched the cup of happiness. Donna Gabriella had snatched it away from her, had drunk from it in long sips, greedily, had kept it for herself, had left her thirsting and without hope, and yet she envied her for that heroic, noble, silent sacrifice that was her strength.

Envy, yes; but to her astonishment, Donna Gabriella realized that in her heart there was nothing sinister or hateful about that feeling. If anything it was something that could even seem to be admiration and gratitude. She would say to herself, "For me, it is surely only for me that Violante is sacrificing herself."

She had gone home troubled, emotional, humiliated, with her heart full of fears and suspicions, thinking about Blasco's return and what she would have to do to chain him passionately and eternally to herself. How? With what new virtues? At times sad and sinister thoughts would come and torment her. If she hadn't killed Emanuele, Violante would have succumbed; instead of acting unselfishly, she should have resigned herself to becoming the wretched young man's accomplice. What chasm wouldn't she have dug between Blasco and Violante? Yes, but then how and to what extent would Blasco have hated her? Hated? And wouldn't that have been better than living in uncertainty, in doubt, in suspicion? Hated? But that would have given her an opportunity, a reason to avenge herself ruthlessly and to end it once and for all. . . . And then?

* * *

Donna Gabriella had lived in that state of mind during Blasco's absence. Coriolano, who had gone to visit her a few times, had failed to instill her with courage and to lift her from the depression that she had fallen into while she was yearning for, and fearing, Blasco's return.

After Blasco had been to see the General, Count of Montemar, to deliver the letter, he went to visit Donna Gabriella and found her in a state of tremendous anxiety. News had quickly spread throughout the city that a bloody battle had taken place in Francavilla, in which, between the dead and the wounded, about seven thousand men, including generals and senior officers, had fallen on both sides. People were saying that Lieutenant General Caracciolo and Brigadier Taucher of the Spanish Army—who were with the guards and the dragoons at the Convent of the Capuchins, around which they had withstood the greatest attack from the Germans—had perished. A great slaughter of dragoons and guards had occurred. As she had not heard any news about Blasco, that had been enough to make Donna Gabriella tremble for his fate.

Upon seeing him come in, she leapt to her feet and ran to meet him with open arms and with a cry, in which all the voices of her burning and tormented heart trembled: "My Blasco!"

He was warm and tender, but to Donna Gabriella it seemed that his kisses lacked that ardent fervor of passion that she had dreamed about while expecting his return. Whether it was conjecture on her part or reality, it was enough to reawaken her anxieties, fears, suspicions, envies, and dormant agonies, and to make her blood run cold and to dampen her enthusiasm. And then she noticed that Blasco didn't seem to be aware of her sudden lack of warmth. Was he preoccupied by some other thought, then? By that same dominant thought of hers? But Blasco didn't say a word about Violante. On the contrary, he seemed to be avoiding any allusion to her, or even any mention of her. As soon as the possibility of talking about her would arise, he would change the topic and always have another subject ready. Was it out of regard for Donna Gabriella? Was it a pretense?

With a tremor in her voice she asked him, "Will you stay here always?"

"Only for a few days, then I will return to the camp."

She bent her head on her chest in an anguished silence; then she asked him again, "Why don't you take me with you?"

"But it's not possible, my love; we live in tents, sleep on straw thrown on the ground, exposed to surprises. . . . And what sort of people those soldiers are! . . . I would surely have to fight twenty times a day over you; not that this scares me, but you would be in constant distress. No, no; these are not things to even think about, not at all. . . . Besides, the war will not last long. We won't be able to hold out; the Imperials are stronger. Milazzo is in their control, they have half of Messina, they are masters of the sea because they are aided by the English. . . .

You will see that the island will pass to the Emperor and we will have waged war against the Savoy only to create an opening for the Germans to take our beautiful island. From one master to the other, it is always like this!"

He immersed himself in that speech about war and politics that she cared nothing about. Neither the Spanish nor the Austrians nor the Savoy, none of them would give her back Blasco's heart, his love, his peace. If they had gone away by themselves, even far away from the island, to a foreign city, perhaps then she would have regained dominance over that heart that was escaping her. Regained? She wondered if she really had ever had that dominance. She said in a low voice, "What do I care about discomforts? What do I care about sleeping on the ground? I will always be near you, always. . . . I'll disguise myself as a man, as if I were your page."

Blasco laughed. He ran his hand over her hair with a caress and said, "And what about these beautiful tresses, where I take pleasure in sinking my fingers?"

A shudder crept along Donna Gabriella's skin and veins, made of sensations and memories. She lowered her head on Blasco's chest and murmured with profound desperation, "Ah, you don't love me with passion anymore!"

Blasco gave a start. That didn't seem to be the voice of Donna Gabriella, but an inner voice that was reawakening his conscience and was forcing him to confess what he was trying, in vain, to conceal from himself. And yet he stifled that inner voice, made his conscience lie, aroused in his heart all the sweetest memories, all the visions of the intoxications caught on that mouth that was now distorted by pain, all the gratitude, the tender friendship that he was feeling intensely for that woman, aroused all these sensations, all these feelings, so that she would not see the collapse of what had seemed to be passion but had been for him only the impulse of a youth bewitched by beauty and intoxicated by a mouth throbbing with kisses.

He tried to delude himself, to deceive her, to divert her, but in his heart, in Gabriella's heart, a voice sadly repeated, "It's over! It's over!"

Yet he would add: "But I will never again abandon her! I will be her affectionate friend, until death."

* * *

The day continued gloomily. At the time of the afternoon promenade on Strada Colonna at the Marina, Donna Gabriella went to visit Violante, wanting to investigate whether any of her suspicions were well founded.

"Do you want to go for a ride with me in my carriage?" she asked her. "We'll ask for the prince's permission."

But Violante thanked her, saying, "I never leave the house, Signora Madre," and she added, smiling, "My cloistered life has begun here."

The duchess then sat down next to her; she praised some of her embroidery work and then asked her if she had seen anyone.

"Who do you mean?"

"I wouldn't know. . . . I was thinking that a duty call to the prince . . . in his capacity as first peer of the kingdom, having to do with the announcement of victory of the king's forces . . ."

"No, signora, I haven't seen anyone."

"Come on, he surely must have come."

"He? Who?"

"Don Blasco," the duchess said, feigning a nonchalance and an indifference that was, however, betrayed by the flash of her scrutinizing eyes and in the pallor of her lips.

Violante felt something like a jolt. She turned pale but held her stepmother's gaze and answered in a clear and calm voice, "No, he hasn't come; we haven't seen him."

Then Donna Gabriella let out something like a sigh of relief, was kind and affectionate, and took her leave, promising that she would return, and for the first time in a long time, she indeed had herself taken to the promenade at the Marina in order to hear the Senate's musicians, who that afternoon were performing the music of Scarlatti. If she could have turned back or looked on the other side of the walls, she would have seen Violante sink on top of a large chair, hide her head in her hands, and choke back her sobs, but at that moment Donna Gabriella was happy and not thinking about Violante.

* * *

Blasco was not happy, however; neither was he pleased. A burden was weighing on his shoulders and it was oppressing him.

Coriolano needled him a bit, then said, "I want to give you some news that may interest you."

"Interest me?"

"Yes, you. Haven't you considered that due to Emanuele's death, you are the last of the Albamonte, of the firstborn branch."

"Oh! A bastard!"

"It's not the first time in Sicilian inheritance law that an acknowledged illegitimate son is invested with the same rights as a legitimate one and may take the titles and privileges of the house. Manfredi III Chiaramonte was an illegitimate son and was the most powerful of the Chiaramonte, powerful enough to become related to kings. So your birth is not an obstacle. If Don Raimondo had lived, he may have been entitled over you, and Donna Violante could lay claim herself, as her father's heir, to the estates of Motta. But Donna Violante is renouncing all her potential and prospective rights because she is entering a monastery."

"Violante?"

"Yes. What do you expect her to do? The poor girl might have found joy and happiness if she had met the hand that she was waiting for; now all she has left to do is bury herself and her sorrow in the silent tranquility of the cloister."

"We should have left her her father—"

"No. Justice cannot be merciful; justice punishes. It's up to love to spread honey on the wounds. Justice killed the guilty father; love was supposed to bring new life to the innocent daughter. You, Blasco, didn't want to. But let's not talk of the past, let's talk about the future. . . . Don Girolamo Ammirata left eight days ago for Madrid, as your proxy, with the petition to the king for your recognition."

"Oh!" Blasco exclaimed, blushing.

"The petition is joined by a juridical allegation that develops and expounds on our feudal right and by a letter from the Count of Montemar for Cardinal Alberoni."

"But all this—"

"It's an entirely legal matter. In one or two months we will receive the actual letters; the process of investiture will take place, and you will become the most illustrious Don Blasco Albamonte, Duke of Motta."

"Thanks to the blood of two victims and the tears of a third. . . . Oh no, really . . ."

"You are still a boy! Do you really have qualms about taking what is yours just because a thief and an undeserving man succumbed under the weight of their crimes? Come on! These are not things you should think about! . . . I was right to act without your consent; I wouldn't put it past you to have prevented me . . ."

"But who is going to provide evidence of my birth?"

"Ah! Do you think that I haven't gathered the evidence? You have told me more than what was necessary in order for me to procure it; in fact, it was in my possession all along."

"You?"

"Yes."

Blasco looked at him with great astonishment.

"Why?"

"Why do you care to know? It shouldn't be difficult for you to imagine that I don't lack the means to obtain whatever I need."

"That is true."

Their conversation continued for quite a while in this vein.

Blasco felt his heart fill with sudden hopes and an immediate despondency. Something was dismaying him. The Duke of Motta? To do what? What would those riches do for him? Would he become a different man? Would his soul gain or lose something more? And would happiness only then open its doors? Would Blasco da Castiglione die and become a memory? And with an anxious glance he saw, as though in a scenario, his entire past of adventure, of poverty, of slashes of his sword, imprisonments, escapes, dalliances in love, and everything animated by a wonderful gaiety; and he loved that past of his, he loved that life that was now so far away, he loved his status as an abandoned child, lost in the world, that would confront life with a sword at his side, with half a stale loaf of bread in his sack, a beautiful song on his lips, and the splendor of daring youth in his eyes!

That evening, after returning to Donna Gabriella, he was still deeply disturbed by that news, and a cloud darkened his forehead; the duchess felt a pang in her heart and didn't dare to question him. They both spent those hours as if overwhelmed by a greater destiny, as if oppressed by an imminent and looming calamity, and they greeted each other with a pale smile, with a kiss without passion, full of tears, like two people parting in order to travel different and distant roads, along which they will never meet again.

CHAPTER 23

Several days passed by like a slow agony. Blasco was proving himself to be always diligent, prescient, attentive, full of tenderness, but Donna Gabriella seemed to see in that behavior an effort to conceal a truth that she could clearly see.

One morning, knowing that Blasco had been detained by the Count of Montemar, she sent for Coriolano to come and see her. The cavaliere hastened to get there quickly.

"I received a gracious request, and I have rushed here; but permit me to ask what distresses you, because your beautiful face has a painful expression that fills me with dismay."

Donna Gabriella smiled sadly, and her eyes teared up. "I need you, your help, your advice."

"Tell me—I am at your command, happy if I can be of help to you."

They were sitting in the half-light of a large and silent drawing room, she on a sofa, Coriolano in a large chair, with his back to the light, so as to leave his own face in shadow but see clearly that of the duchess.

Donna Gabriella seemed to be collecting her thoughts in order to find a word, an approach, then she said, "You are close to Blasco and you know his most secret thoughts."

"In fact, he gives me the honor of granting me his trust and his confidences, however much I do not solicit them, and I maintain the reserve and discretion that friendship dictates."

"So you. . . . Excuse me, cavaliere, if I peer into your soul and if, perhaps, I oblige you to reveal a secret."

Coriolano smiled. "Some transgressions?"

"Don't smile; the transgression, if you want to call the confidence that I'm asking of you, could mean someone's happiness."

"And if it did not?"

"It will. The sorrow of one may be, or rather is almost always, the joy of another."

"Tell me. If I can prevent a sorrow without failing in my duties of friendship, I will not entrench myself in silence."

"Della Floresta, Blasco doesn't love me."

"Oh!"

"Blasco loves another woman."

"You amaze me! What could make you think that?"

"Think? I am certain."

"Very well. What can give you this certainty?"

"Have you ever loved deeply and completely?"

"Me? Thank heavens neither deeply nor superficially! I am immune . . ."

"Then you cannot understand me, you cannot understand what small, slight, imperceptible signs reveal to a woman that she is no longer loved. She feels it, she senses it in the tone of his voice, in his smile, in the flash of his eyes, in the clasp of his hand, in his soft caress . . . in everything! . . . Blasco doesn't love me anymore, I tell you, and you know it!"

"Me?"

"Yes, you. You are the custodian of his secrets."

"I am, but I assure you, duchess, that Blasco has never said anything to me that could lead me to believe that he has some other love."

"But you have guessed it."

"Oh, forgive me . . ."

"Don't say no. I can read it in your eyes. He is no longer as cheerful as before. He is oppressed by a thought that I recognize, that I have caught . . . and you know it, yes, you know it! . . . Oh, other times, sure of my strength, I would not have cried, would not have abased myself, would not have pleaded as I am doing now. . . . I would have avenged myself. . . . But now . . . now I cannot. I don't know how! I don't want to."

Coriolano looked at her in amazement. Donna Gabriella was wringing her hands; her eyes were blazing, but there were no tears, and her lips were wan and dry.

"Cavaliere della Floresta, I do not want any help from you, I do not want you to use your influence on Blasco's heart. When love comes to an end it cannot ever be resumed. Wood that has been consumed by fire does not burn; ash does not produce flame. . . . No, do not tell him anything, but at least tell me that I am not mistaken, give me the assurance that mine is not a supposition, that everything is over for me, everything!"

"Why do you need to grieve?" Coriolano said to her, moved, but controlling his emotions, and without losing that good-natured calm that was habitual to him. "Why do you torment yourself? Let's suppose that it is as you say; well? Is anything everlasting in this world? We must prepare ourselves for what seems to be the end. You have said that wood that has been consumed by fire doesn't burn. Well, love is a wood that burns; you set it on fire too soon. . . . Mind you, I am following what you are saying, I am not asserting anything because I don't have the facts to do so, just as I don't have any to deny. . . . Have the patience to reconstruct the history of this love and you will see in it the reasons for its end. . . . I will say it better: for its evolving into a tender conjugal friendship. . . . You have been intoxicated, and like all intoxications, even that of love fades away. . . . Be strong; from the blaze of love rises the spirit of sincere, devoted friendship that can fill your life and give you feelings and joys, perhaps not more intense but more serene and more enduring than those of love."

Was Donna Gabriella listening to him? So it seemed, but instead she told herself, "Then it's true, it's true: he doesn't love me anymore, he loves Violante; now it is over, over forever!"

Coriolano carried on, calm and ingratiating: "You are a woman with spirit, duchess, an outstanding woman. Do you think that Blasco does not love you with passion anymore? Do not try to revive the flame; the flickers that it would produce would not even kindle the illusion of love, and it would create greater disappointments, greater pains. Do not try to resurrect the lover but be content with the friend; it will be better for you and for him. They say that true love, profound love is devotion, abnegation, sacrifice; well, if you love him so deeply, as I am seeing in your pain, have the strength to sacrifice some illusions, some desires, some dreams, and in your sacrifice you will find joy."

Those words evoked the image of Violante in Donna Gabriella's mind. She asked herself, "Does Violante love him more than I do, then? She has the strength of self-denial and sacrifice that I don't have, because she loves him more. . . . More?"

The young girl appeared to her as a voluntary martyr on the altar of what she believed was Blasco's happiness, and yet she would need only to say a single word, to hold out her hand, in order to be happy. Unwittingly comparing herself to Violante, Donna Gabriella felt inferior; that querulous pain of hers, that abandoning herself to despair, seemed to her a sign of cowardice. Even worse, it debased her great love.

"Then is it possible," she would wonder, "that this love of mine that consumes me, that is killing me, is not as strong as Violante's?"

She shut herself into her own thoughts, gloomily fixated on that idea of sacrifice.

"Will I appear more altruistic and more worthy of love if I have the strength to give up his caresses?"

After a brief silence she held out her hand to the Cavaliere della Floresta.

"Thank you!" she said to him. "Don't say anything to Blasco about what I have confided to you. . . . Your words have not been in vain. . . . Thank you, my friend!"

Coriolano held her hand gently in his, looking into her eyes as if to read inside that mysterious and many-sided soul.

"Then can I have faith that you will stay strong?" he asked gently.

"I promise you," she answered in a somber voice, as if replying to a hidden thought.

"May I come see you?"

"Yes . . . tonight . . . come for a sorbet. . . . You will see that I'll be fine."

* * *

When Coriolano left, Donna Gabriella buried her head in her hands and remained absorbed in her thoughts, until suddenly, with a resolution that oddly lit up her eyes, she stood up and called for her carriage.

Evening arrived.

Donna Gabriella had been nervous, impatient, and gloomy the entire day, but when she heard the Ave Maria sound, a quiver coursed through her body; she shook her beautiful head and seemed to dismiss the grim thoughts that had troubled her.

That evening she had all the candles lit in the small baroque drawing room where she would always receive her friends. Her face had taken on a charming expression, full of vitality and gaiety, in which a perceptive eye would have detected something restless.

The arrival of a carriage startled her. She rushed to the door to receive the Prince of Butera and Violante.

She took the girl's hands and drew her to her, saying in a vivacious manner, "Oh, how grateful I am that you came!"

But Violante had been struck by a great painful admiration and couldn't help exclaiming, "How beautiful you are this evening, Signora Madre!"

And indeed, Donna Gabriella seemed to have mustered all the seductions of her attire and all the graceful charms of her body in order to be astonishingly beautiful and enchanting that evening.

She replied cheerfully, "Oh, my child, who can be so beautiful as to win you over?"

The prince gave her another compliment, then added, "I leave her to you; I will come later to collect her. I would have gladly accepted a sorbet or a cup of your coffee. . . . I know that it is also your custom, but I must go to the Palazzo Reale. . . . With your permission."

He kissed her hand gallantly and left.

"Come," Donna Gabriella said to Violante, leading her to a small sofa, "we'll spend a few hours together . . . I have so many things to tell you . . . before leaving!"

"Are you leaving?"

"Yes."

"For a long time?"

"Very long . . . I may never come back. This is like a farewell party."

Violante had turned pale; she thought to herself, "She is surely leaving with Blasco."

An intense suffering plagued her heart, but the stern and rigid expression on her face didn't betray her inner emotion.

Donna Gabriella continued: "I'm not sorry, you know. Here everything has become dreadful, gloomy, full of tears, groans, torments. . . . Isn't it true? Tell me, isn't it true?"

Violante looked up and, sighing, she said with a slight tremor in her voice, "We must learn how to endure."

"Yes," agreed Donna Gabriella in a somber tone of voice. Then all of a sudden, having resumed her cheerful manner, she sat down in front of the little harpsichord, painted pale blue with a flower pattern and with embellishments, and she ran her nervous fingers over it. The instrument vibrated with joyful notes that then faded away in a plaintive tremolo.

"Don't you know any piece by Porpora? For example, from *Berenice*?"

"No, signora."

"Ah, right. You are a nun . . . I had forgotten."

She saw the young girl turn pale and unsteady, and she turned; on the threshold of the door were Blasco and Coriolano. Blasco had stopped, in the grip of an intense emotion, astonished, as if he wasn't believing his own eyes, at the sight of Violante in that house, alone with Donna Gabriella. He didn't understand; it was such an unexpected thing that he wasn't sure if he should think it was a miracle or an illusion.

Violante! The young girl that he had no longer seen, had no longer sought, indeed had almost run away from; Violante, whom he always carried in the innermost recesses of his heart, jealously guarded, and whose name he would not even dare to say to himself. Violante, whom he had always refrained from talking about so as not to arouse Donna Gabriella's jealousies, fearing her impulses and her violent acts. Violante was there, before his eyes, alive, palpitating, emotional—there, next to Donna Gabriella, offered to him by Donna Gabriella herself! . . . All this managed to be so beyond his comprehension that he felt confused and couldn't make up his mind whether to enter or not.

Coriolano too had been surprised. He had taken note of Donna Gabriella's enchanting and striking attire, the unusual lighting, and Violante's presence, and he had said to himself, "What does this mean? She is clearly overdoing it."

Donna Gabriella, after enjoying the sight of their astonishment, approached them cheerfully, inviting them to enter.

"Well, gentlemen, would you like to stay at the door?"

Blasco then roused himself and kissed Donna Gabriella's hand, not without astonishment at seeing her more beautiful and more charming than usual, and with a peculiar and strange light in her eyes. He entered like a drunk, with his mind clouded, greeting Violante with a reserve that barely concealed his discomfort.

Coriolano, who had immediately regained control of himself, gave some compliments that broke the ice of that moment and started the conversation. As was his custom, however, he was observing, scrutinizing, analyzing, and nothing could offer him as much material for study as those three tormented souls, forced to conceal their suffering.

Violante was suffering. She hadn't been expecting to run into Blasco, whom she had always avoided; and it wasn't just seeing him again but meeting him there, in the house of her stepmother, the one who had snatched the young man's heart, the one who had broken her dream, the only, the first, and the last dream of a young girl, gave her inexpressible anguish. Oh, why wasn't her grandfather coming, so that she could get away, take refuge in her room, and give vent there, without being seen, to the anguish that was tearing at her soul? . . . And she could no longer impose that rigid and statuesque immobility behind which she had always concealed her deepest emotions; the suffering was transforming her face.

Blasco was silent; a silence full of inexpressible sorrows. All his visions of the past, all his dreams mislaid along life's journey, all his illusions, the full weight of the destiny that hung over his head, everything was playing havoc with his soul; it was an inner martyrdom, but no less terrible than that which was tearing the young girl apart.

But the blustering hurricane with all its carnage, all its upheavals, with all its terrible, horrible, frightful weapons of destruction was in the heart of Donna Gabriella; Coriolano caught sight of it in her nervous manner, in the convulsive motion of her hands, in the feverish animation of her speech, in the sudden and intense glow in her eyes, which looked like those of a haunted woman. While she was playing, Coriolano noticed sudden twitches running through her body. Certainly Donna Gabriella seemed to display a great degree of self-control, but there was something insane about her, which aroused a dismay, a suspicious anxiety, full of terrors of the unknown.

She was playing, and speaking gaily, more often with Coriolano than with Blasco or Violante.

"Aren't you saying anything, my child?"

No, she couldn't say anything; for her it was too overwhelming!

"And you, Don Blasco, have you lost the ability to speak? At least say something nice to Violante!"

How much bitterness, how much poison there was in the smile with which Donna Gabriella said those words!

Then she rang the bell, and to the footman who appeared on the threshold she ordered, "Serve."

A minute later the footman entered with a silver tray on which were placed four little bowls of very fine porcelain with some sorbets shaped like fruits and some engraved silver spoons, and he placed them on top of a little table; then he returned with two more smaller trays, one full of biscotti, the other with two bottles and some small glasses, and after placing them on the little table, he stationed himself on the threshold.

"Go," Donna Gabriella ordered him, passing a handkerchief over her face to wipe away the perspiration.

She served the sorbets herself; Coriolano, who was following her every move, saw that her face had taken on a frightening expression and that her voice was breaking, while she was speaking with greater vivacity and joy.

Then Donna Gabriella chose a bottle. "This," she said, "is for the ladies."

She filled two glasses and moved closer to Violante. Coriolano took a step, staring at Donna Gabriella. He had become pale—a dreadful suspicion had enlightened him. He saw Donna Gabriella's hands, holding out one of the glasses to Violante, shaking with a slight tremor; he saw her face transform and he heard her harsh and gloomy voice say, "Drink, Violante, to our joy."

Violante took the glass.

At that moment Donna Gabriella looked up; Coriolano was in front of her with his eyes blazing like a harsh, unbending, frightening judge. Those eyes penetrated to the bottom of her soul like two blades, like two rays; they pierced her and lit up her frightful dark recesses. Violante raised the glass to her lips. Coriolano's eyes became more frightful.

Donna Gabriella gave a start; with an abrupt gesture she knocked the glass out of Violante's hand, crying out, "No!"

And she drank hers all in one gulp.

"Wretched woman!" shouted Coriolano.

Blasco, who had stayed in a corner, as if immersed in a thought, roused himself. "What is it?"

He looked at Violante and saw her motionless, pale, as if thunderstruck by something unbelievable. He looked at Donna Gabriella; he saw her pass her hands over her face, stagger, and collapse onto a chair!

"Gabriella! Gabriella!" he cried out, frightened.

"My God. . . . What is happening?"

Coriolano grabbed the bottle, quickly hid it, and, going into the antechamber, shouted, "A doctor! . . . Run for a doctor!"

Donna Gabriella had fallen with her head back onto a chair and Blasco had barely enough time to keep her from falling to the floor. Supporting her head with his arm, taking one of her hands, he shook it, questioning her frantically: "What's wrong? . . . What have you done? Speak! . . . My God! Speak!"

Violante, with her hands clasped, her eyes dilated from fright, couldn't utter a word; she looked at Donna Gabriella, Blasco, and Coriolano with a mad terror while Coriolano offered some words of comfort. A cry roused her and awoke her to the precise realization of the tragedy that had taken place.

"Coriolano! . . . Coriolano! . . . She's dying!"

Then Violante burst into tears and, falling to her knees, cried out, "God. . . . God! Have mercy on her!"

Donna Gabriella raised her head; her eyes wandered, searching. They rested on Blasco, on Violante, then they filled with tears; her lips whispered, "Forgive me! . . . Farewell!"

"Gabriella! . . . Gabriella! . . . No! No!" Blasco shouted like a madman.

"Signora! Signora!" Violante was sobbing.

Donna Gabriella, making an effort, raised her arms, searched for Violante's head, and laid a hand on it; she searched for Blasco's, and for a minute her cold hands, with a shiver of death coursing through them, lingered on those stooping and feverish heads.

She said in a whisper, "At least . . . remember me."

A twitch shook her body; a cry tore through her chest.

She raised Blasco's head, her lips searched for him. She whispered, "Farewell! . . . Kiss me!"

Blasco kissed her, crying, repeating, "What have you done? . . . What have you done . . . why?"

"It was necessary," she said.

Those were her last words. Her limbs writhed in a spasm, her lips turned blue, her eyes grew dim; a last twitch of her body and then nothing more.

Blasco fell to his knees, looked at her face, and cried out one more time.

Violante's sobs drowned out his voice. They remained on their knees, bent over that body that only a half hour before had been vibrating with life and beauty.

With a cloth, Coriolano wiped the lips that were no longer smiling, closed the eyes that were no longer seeing, and laid a kiss on the forehead from which all dreams, thoughts, and sorrows had fled forever.

Epilogue

Violante fell ill; visions and terrifying nightmares unsettled her feverish nights; when she recovered, she wanted to return to her monastery and was more resolute than ever about taking the veil.

The image of Donna Gabriella was embedded in her memory, and to think about Blasco seemed to her like a profanation, like a sacrilege, like an infamous rite performed over a tomb that sorrow, sacrifice, and pity rendered sacred.

In the meantime, the royal commissions had arrived that acknowledged Blasco and invested him with his fiefdoms; he became Duke of Motta, which made his life all the more sad and lonely.

His good fortune aroused envy and bitterness. It prompted the Count of Geraci and the Prince of Iraci to spread horribly malicious words about him, suggesting that he had played a part in the assassinations of Don Raimondo and Emanuele in order to become rich and a duke.

Those rumors reached Blasco's ear, and one nice afternoon, after running into the two lords at the Marina, he slapped them in public.

"I hope," he said to them, "that among the many lies you are spreading, you will at least tell this one truth."

The duels followed. Since many young gentlemen couldn't stomach Blasco's good fortune, they complicated the matter, so that Blasco found himself confronted with five duels. The adventure served to restore his good mood. He sent the Prince of Iraci to bed for two months with a stab in his side; he disfigured the Count of Gisia by slashing his nose and lips down to his chin; he cut a few tendons in the arm of a third, rendering it inert for the rest of his life; he disarmed a fourth; with the fifth thought it best not to expose himself to any risk and declared himself satisfied with the wounds . . . of the others.

These duels caused a fury; they made some trouble for Blasco, but a proclamation by Emperor Charles VI, as King of Sicily, granted him a pardon. He became the idol of society and many ladies did everything they could to have him, but Blasco didn't allow himself to be seduced.

Two women, or rather, two images of women, held a place of worship in the depths of his heart: Donna Gabriella and Violante, both of them united in the vision of that fatal and tragic evening.

He tried many times to see Violante; the young girl always refused. But finally the Prince of Butera, who loved Blasco and would have been happy to see him as a bridegroom for Violante (and he already knew everything), arranged things so that the two youngsters could be alone together, for a moment, in a room of the palazzo.

Before Blasco, the young girl trembled.

He said to her, "Would you still want to refuse to obey the vow of a dead woman who, only for us, for our joy, took her own life?"

Violante felt her eyes fill with tears. Blasco took one of her hands, and she did not withdraw it.

And then he said, "Violante, for the sacred memory of that poor woman, I swear to you that I have never loved a woman other than you, you alone, ever since I saw you, as an educanda, pass by in a litter at the Ponte dell'Ammiraglio . . . and I have loved you without hope, in silence, like something sacred. . . . Do you want to be my wife?"

She bowed her head, blushing, but her eyes were lit up by a profound joy.

A few months later they were married.

After a year they had a little daughter.

Violante said to Blasco, "I want her name to be Gabriella."

* * *

Coriolano went abroad.

Don Girolamo assumed the leadership of the Beati Paoli; one of the first things he did was to pass judgment on Nino Bucolaro, who was sentenced to death.

He killed him himself, at night, at the corner of the Church of the Carmine. But he was found out, and in March 1723 he was hanged.

Andrea returned to the house of the Dukes of Motta.

And Michele Barabino?

The good tailor reopened his workshop with capital given to him by Blasco, and every day he would tell his apprentices the story of the great lord, about when, there in the piazzetta of the inn, he had given the birri a thrashing.

"You had to see!" he would conclude. "But even then, and no one knew him, I said to myself, 'This one can only be a prince.' I have a good nose, I do."

THE BEATI PAOLI AND THE IDEOLOGY OF THE "POPULAR" NOVEL

By Umberto Eco
Translated from the Italian by Marina Cappelletto

I t cannot be said that Italian literature lacks a tradition of the historical novel; all novelistic discussions are dominated by this theme, and after all, even *The Betrothed* falls within this literary genre. It would then be easy to define *The Beati Paoli* as a quite late descendant of this trend, and since we cannot attribute to it innovations of the "genre," either at the level of linguistics or at the level of its narrative structures, it should be sufficient to read it for its local value and for the not inconsiderable light it sheds on historical events that are ignored by most (and seemingly by those who are not entirely unfamiliar with the contemporary reality of the island).

In any case, this book presents various points of interest for a sociology of narration. In fact, above all, the correct key to its reading seems to be this: *The Beati Paoli* should not be seen as an example of a "historical novel" but rather of a "popular" novel. In this sense, its ancestors are not Guerrazzi, Cantù or D'Azeglio, but Dumas, Süe, or, to stay within Italy, Luigi Gramegna (author of a vast, unjustly forgotten, Savoy cloak-and-dagger epic oeuvre). Natoli's book has some structural and ideological characteristics of the popular novel that for various reasons render it (other than narratively pleasing) sociologically contemporary.

THE HISTORICAL NOVEL AND THE "POPULAR NOVEL"

Certainly the distinction between historical and popular risks becoming unclear, when one thinks of the popularity enjoyed by novels of a "historical" bent, like those by Scott or by D'Azeglio or by Tommaso Grossi. Undoubtedly, many popular novels, moreover, are also historical novels, and one just has to refer to *The Three Musketeers,* even if it may be possible to demonstrate the opposite, and to recall *The Count of Monte Cristo* or *The Mysteries of Paris* in order to identify popular novels with a contemporary rather than a historical theme. Finally, both the historical and popular novel have their roots in the "gothic" novel; a "historical" novelist such as Guerrazzi, and also the chroniclers of contemporary fiction such as Ponson du Terrail or the authors of *Fantômas*, draw equally freely from it.

Straddling the two genres, Natoli's novel owes much to the "gothic" tradition. To start, see the beginning, where he introduces his main "evil" character, Don Raimondo Albamonte:

> *Not yet thirty years old, he was tall, thin, and high-strung. His pale face might have looked sad, as if invaded by a dark cloud, except when a certain sudden flashing of his eyes made one think of the flicker of distant lightning in an overcast sky. His thin lips were barely outlined, and his mouth looked rather like a long wound that hadn't fully healed. A slim dark mustache spread a little shadow over it, but his hands and feet were like those of a young girl. His hands were pale, small, fine, and thin, with pink oblong nails that nearly disappeared under the fine lace of his cuffs. He seemed to care about his fingernails. He had, in fact, a relaxed and gracious gesture for showing off his hand, raising it to brush away the curls of his wig (in the French style, in fashion at the time) from his forehead.*
>
> *Despite those features, there was nothing effeminate about him. Perhaps, closely examining the corner of his jaw and the curve of his mouth, a soul-searching eye might have detected a selfishness and a lack of human warmth; perhaps, even something feline, namely, patience and ferocity . . .*[1]

This portrait is canonical: it begins with Byron's Giaour and continues until Raphael Sabatini's Captain Blood and Fleming's James Bond.[2] Mario Praz even dedicates an entire chapter of his *Flesh, Death and the Devil in Romantic Literature* to this archetype, and no further comparisons should be necessary beyond this portrait of Schedoni from Ann Radcliffe's *The Italian, or the Confessional of the Black Penitents*, from 1797:

> *His figure was striking . . . it was tall, and, though extremely thin, his limbs were large and uncouth, and as he stalked along, wrapped in the black garments of his order, there was something terrible in its air; something almost superhuman. His cowl, too, as it threw a shade over the livid paleness of his face, increased its severe character, and gave an effect to his large melancholy eyes, which approached horror. His was not the melancholy of a sensible and wounded heart, but apparently that of a gloomy and ferocious disposition. There was something in his physiognomy extremely singular, and that cannot easily be defined. It bore the traces of*

---

1 Translated from the Italian by Stephen Riggio (MC)
2 Umberto Eco, "Narrative Structures in Fleming," in Roland Barthes et al., *L'analisi del racconto* (Milano: Bompiani, 1969).

many passions, which seemed to have fixed the features they no longer animated. A habitual gloom and severity prevailed over the deep lines of his countenance; and his eyes were so piercing that they seemed to penetrate, at a single glance into the hearts of men, and to read their most secret thoughts; few persons could support their scrutiny, or even endure to meet them twice.

In any case, if a quote from the beginning of the book is not sufficient, there is another in the second half: the attempted execution of Don Raimondo in the dungeons, in that mysterious tangle of crypts that crosses Palermo and that, in this case, connects to the underground spaces of the Palazzo Albamonte. From Lewis's *The Monk* forward, the gothic genre makes abundant use of underground spaces and artificial caves, where the bloodiest crimes take place, obviously by torchlight. And this is a "topos" that both the historical novel and the popular novel will never again give up, and the evidence is that, duly modernized by provident Napoleonic city planning, the dungeons return in the form of the sewers of Paris in *Les Misérables* (in which tens of pages are densely populated by dark evocations) as well as in *Fantômas*, the vast epic oeuvre written by Souvestre and Allain in the very same years that Natoli was drafting *The Beati Paoli*. The last avatar of the topos are the sewers of Vienna, this time on the screen, in Carol Reed's *The Third Man*.

Having said this, it is still not clear why Natoli's novel seems to ascribe not to the historical, but to the popular tradition. But certainly the historical novel is born out of aesthetic as well as civilian objectives. About the *Battle of Benevento*, Guerrazzi says, "I did not want to create novels, but prose poems," and about *Fieramosca* D'Azeglio states, "my intention . . . was to begin a kind of work that would revive the national character."

Therefore the historical novel, in addition to its obvious appeal to the "true historian," is a novel with an exhortative setting in which various virtues predominate, offered up as positive models. And it is at such a point that the historical novel is conscious of having functions beyond the mere proposition of a narrative device that generates its own metanarrative reflection at every point, that questions itself about its ends, converses with its readers, as Manzoni does, for example, better than anyone. The historical novel is the offspring of a poeticism that is quite conscious of itself, and it questions itself continually about its own structure and its own function.

The popular novel, on the other hand, in addition to having characteristics that we will look at at a later point and that make up its fundamental ideological nature, is born as an instrument of mass entertainment, and it is not as concerned with proposing heroic models of virtue as with describing with some cynicism characters that are realistic, not necessarily "virtuous," in whom the public can without qualms identify itself in order to extract from them the gratifications to be discussed.

Ettore Fieramosca is an unattainable human model; D'Artagnan, on the other hand, is like everyman. As we will see, Blasco da Castiglione takes more from D'Artagnan than from Fieramosca. (That Manzoni is able to play on "utopian" characters as well as on "lowly" and realistic characters, creating with Don Abbondio-Renzo-Federigo-Fra Cristoforo a sequence of decreasing realism and increasing exemplary idealism, only means that he was able to depart from set patterns; but, on the other hand, even common and lowly characters that do not constitute a moral model in the positive, constitute one in the negative, and they are also necessary in order to inspire the reader to reflect and to take instruction from it—which does not happen with either D'Artagnan or Blasco).

Not questioning itself more than a certain amount on the moral motivations of its characters, the popular novel also does not question its own style. At the conference that took place in Cerisy in 1967 on "paraliterature," a term that was used for the most part to describe the popular novel and its derivatives, paraliterature was given a definition that was designed to distinguish it from Literature with a capital "L": "All that is paraliterary contains nearly all the elements that would constitute literature, other than a concern about its own significance, other than a questioning about its own language."[3]

In fact, the popular novel does not invent original narrative situations, but it combines a repertory of "topical" situations that have already been recognized, accepted and loved by its own public, and it is characterized by the attention paid to the underlying demand of its readers, as is true today of crime fiction. The readers, on their account, do not ask the popular novel (which is a means of entertainment and of escape) to offer them new formal experiences or dramatic and problematic reversals of current value systems, but exactly the opposite: to confirm the systems of expectations that are already present and that have been integrated into current culture. The pleasure of narration, as we have already seen elsewhere,[4] derives from the return of what is already known, a cyclic return that exists within the narrative work itself as well as within a series of narrative works, in a play of interconnected recurrences from novel to novel.

An obedience to this rule grounds the popular novel in its most typical nature, it is not one of its faults. Just like the rules of the game include the multiplication, with each episode, of opportunities for topical returns, and the acceptance of a summary psychology which is applicable to all the avatars of the same novelistic archetype.

---

3   Noel Arnaud, Francis Lacassin, and Jean Portel, eds., *Entretiens sur la paralittérature* (Paris: Plon, 1970), 18. (UE)

4   See our *Apocalittici e integrati* (Milano: Bompiani, 1964), in particular the observations on "Defense of the iterative scheme" and "The iterative scheme as a redundant message" in the essay on Superman. (UE)

Natoli's book shares with the popular novel precisely an extreme unscrupulousness in closely following prior models, the freedom to lengthen events by reopening closed chapters, and the confidence to present as though prefabricated the psychology of its main characters.

First and foremost, almost as though to establish a tie and to give credence to our hypothesis, Blasco can be traced directly from D'Artagnan: daring, penniless, unconventional and a social climber like the Gascon, like him he enters the story on a down-at-heel nag, and when he sets foot in a pub he risks getting thrashed; he has his own Milady (because at least toward the middle of the novel Gabriella touches on the role of a perverse, vengeful woman) who becomes his Constance (Gabriella, like Constance Bonacieux, dies of poisoning while D'Artagnan/Blasco brushes against her already cold lips with one last kiss); he has his Richelieu in Don Raimondo, who at the beginning tries to make him his protégé; he has his Rochefort in Matteo Lo Vecchio, the damned soul of Richelieu/Raimondo; he has his Athos in Coriolano della Floresta. In the middle of the book he has a duel with three Piedmontese gentlemen that traces step by step the duel behind the Convent of the Discalced Carmelites, including the friendship that binds the adversaries from that moment on. He has his siege of La Rochelle and his captain's commission, except that on top of that he becomes a duke at the end, while D'Artagnan must wait for three volumes before receiving his Marshal of France baton, and as soon as he receives it he dies.

The novel, even while condensing the episodes and reopening those that seemed closed, does not disdain at times to cross over to a picaresque structure, with a hero that carries out various wanderings, encounters and reencounters old and new characters, travels through unprecedented misfortunes, and always emerges from them happy as a lark.

As for psychology, it is only Raimondo that maintains a certain faithfulness to his role of evil character. Blasco passes through his various adventures with a certain openness that is halfway between light-heartedness and cynicism. Gabriella appears at the beginning like an angel, then she becomes a kind of Milady de Winter, all coquettishness and homicidal proposals; at a certain point she is transformed into a passionate and devoted lover, and then at the end into a Mary Magdalene who is redeemed by death. It would not be wrong to recognize a model for this emotional complexity in certain Stendhalian heroines, but the analogy ends here. As an artistic creation, Gabriella doesn't really hold water, and neither does the stepbrother Emanuele, whose conversion from a proud young boy to a disgusting little social climber is a little too quick. But these observations are not made in order to find fault with Natoli, because his behavior is perfectly coherent with the narrative poetics of the popular novel; what matters is the intrigue, the staging, the unscrupulous expansion of a narrative that is given free rein and—above all, but we will come back to this—the delineation of a drama between the oppressed and the oppressors with the decisive presence of a charismatic hero, that is, a Superman.

Once Natoli has been ascribed the genre of the popular novel, it will then only be necessary to resolve some historical details. Because the history of the popular novel is today defined by three vast periods, and Natoli's case could seem atypical:

—*first period, or romantic-heroic period*: begins in the 1830s, is parallel to the development of the *feuilleton*, to the birth of a new readership, made up of petit bourgeois and craft workers (see the fate of Süe and Dumas) and it even inspires some narrators that are considered "superior" who take themes, narrative structures, characters, and stylistic decisions from the popular novel, like Balzac;

—*second period, or bourgeois period*: is situated at the end of the nineteenth century, includes the Montepins, the Richepins, the Richebourgs, and our Carolina Invernizio. While the novel of the preceding period was *populistic* in addition to popular, and in some measure "democratic," this period belongs to the age of Imperialism, is reactionary, petit bourgeois, and not infrequently racist and anti-Semitic. The main character is no longer the hero of the oppressed, but a common man, an innocent that triumphs over his enemies after lengthy misadventures;

—*third period, or non-heroic*: begins at the start of the twentieth century and presents antisocial heroes, exceptional beings that no longer avenge the oppressed but pursue their own egocentric plan for power: they are Arsenio Lupin and Fantômas.

Now *The Beati Paoli* appears in the third period, but with characteristics that are typical of the first period. It's a sort of *Leopard* of the popular novel, that is able to revisit a much earlier style in a very spontaneous manner and with happy results. On the other hand, one cannot ignore that through the Sonzogno and Nerbini translations, the novels of the first period were being spread in Italy precisely or still during those years, and so Natoli's journalistic sensibility probably allowed him to sense the relevance, for a mass public, of that novelistic style that he draws from with unquestionable skill.

From the popular novel of the first period Natoli likewise reconstructs the central theme: the Manichean fight of good against evil, lived by a community of the oppressed that is avenged by a Superman hero. And he draws from it also because the very topic that he wants to deal with lends itself admirably to this structure. Whether or not *The Beati Paoli* is the tale of the historical antecedents of the Mafia, the ideological structure of the early serial novel, as defined by Marx, Engels, and Gramsci, seems made to order for giving voice to this evocation.[5]

THE TOPIC OF THE POPULAR NOVEL

In an essay on the popular novel, Jean Tortel,[6] summarizing the characteristics of the three periods cited earlier, but referring in particular to those of the first and third periods, puts forth a sort of compilation that, when applied to a reading of *The Beati Paoli*, seems to have been written for precisely this purpose. It seems appropriate to refer to these pages because they serve particularly well to reveal the constant structures that Natoli also referred to, and they confirm beyond the shadow of a doubt this book's place within the sociological and aesthetic tradition of the popular novel. In it, there is still a Manichean universe that is subject to the two opposite actions of good and evil. Society, while always troubled, is nevertheless always stable.

On one hand, there are those who suffer, passively subjected to both the criminal action of the prevaricators and the corrective action of the benefactors; they are the innocent, at the same time protected and victims. They have no possibility of active participation; they are hardworking people, girls that have been seduced, and the masses that can only wait and hope. In the end the fight, even if it can either lose or save them, doesn't pertain to them, and it passes over their heads. It is a matter that pertains to the heroes and protagonists. When someone emerges from this mass to try to become a protagonist, placing himself at the service of the real protagonists, in the end he gets destroyed, whether he attempts a criminal venture or he attempts to become allied with the hero (a typical example is Chourineur in *The Mysteries of Paris*) but one can see in *The Beati Paoli* the minor followers of the sect that end up on the gallows, while Coriolano possesses a sort of immunity that is a right of his class, but also a mythical necessity, since he belongs to the cohort of Supermen.

---

5   Gramsci's brief but illuminating notes on the popular novel are in *Letteratura e vita nazionale*, part III, "Popular literature"; see in particular pp. 108–111, 116–125 of the Einaudi edition. The observations by Marx and Engels are scattered, *passim*, in the course of *The Holy Family*, which, as is well known, constitutes a polemical-ideological reading of *The Mysteries of Paris* by Eugène Süe. On these interpretations, see our "Eugenio Süe, il socialismo e la consolazione," which appeared as a preface to *I misteri di Parigi*, Sugar, Milano, 1965. A reworking of this study, under the title "Rhétorique et idéologie dans 'Les Mystères de Paris' d'E.S." was published in *Revue Internationale des Sciences Sociales*, XIX, 4, 1967. The text of the Italian preface with an anthology by Marx, Engels, Poe, and Bielinski (the latter of them having said things that have a great affinity to what was said by the fathers of scientific socialism, in reviewing the novel as soon as it was published) appeared under the title of *Socialismo y Consolacion*, Barcelona, Tusquets, 1970. (UE)

6   "Le roman populaire," in *Entretiens sur la paralittérature*, op. cit. (UE)

Against the oppressed and the innocent is a group of dominators, whether they are good or evil. Sometimes the dominator can come from the most miserable classes (like the Rocambole of the early novels) but, having been kissed on the forehead by novelistic destiny, he in fact comes to belong to the dominant class, even under disguise, and from that moment on he never leaves it. This is no different from what happens to Blasco. In any case, a dominator of humble origins does not establish himself as a humble person who asserts the virtues of his own class; he is enlisted by the upper class, and he takes on its manners and ideology.

The dominators, whether they fight for good or evil, use the same methods of fighting: they are antisocial methods, blow by blow, the end justifies the means, justice must triumph even through the sword because, as we shall see applies to the Superman, it is the dominator that becomes a source of justice, and not justice, as the law of society, that determines the actions of the dominator. As the bearer of a law and a morality that society does not yet know or that society is opposed to, the Hero does not impose it by choosing the customary means of revolutionary heroes, that is, the interpreters of popular demands; he does not turn to the people to ask them to ratify with their approval and their active participation the new law and the new morality. He decides to impose it by unknown means, since the official power that he opposes does not accept his justice, and the people, for whom he is fighting, are not called upon to share in its responsibility. His instrument can only be *the secret society*.

From the Society of Jesus as presented in *The Wandering Jew* by Süe, to the Black Coats of Ponson du Terrail, from the children of Kali, also of Ponson du Terrail, to the blood pact of the Three Musketeers, from Balzac's Thirteen to our Beati Paoli, the secret society is the disguise of the hero, and at the same time a secular arm. Being a society grants it at times the legalistic appearance of a social pact, but the fact that it is dependent on the hero's plans marks it precisely as the artifice through which he extends the range of his own power instead of establishing its legitimization. Whether it is at the service of evil or of the avenger, the secret society in the popular novel doesn't differ much in its formal characteristics or in its methods. Rocambole, after his conversion (the turning point is after *The Savage's Death*), kills the evil with the same cold determination with which he previously killed the good. The Beati Paoli don't employ means that differ much from Don Raimondo's, and precisely for this reason Blasco is unable to accept unconditionally their ethics and plans. But Blasco is not the charismatic protagonist of the book, he is not Monte Cristo or Rodolphe of Gerolstein, because this role is taken by Coriolano della Floresta. And even in this Blasco is like D'Artagnan, the action hero, guided in the shadows by the charismatic hero, who is Athos—as Gramsci had sharply perceived. So it is D'Artagnan and Blasco who love, not Athos (destroyed by a tragic love that was almost repressed) and not Coriolano. The charismatic hero (a characteristic that is still present in the superheroes of the comics) is chaste and immune from desire, not consumed by any passion nor possessed by any woman (even Rodolphe of *The Mysteries of Paris*, like Athos, consumes his memories of a distant love and of a disappointment that has Parsifalized him for all the years to come).

Armed one against the other, the dominators form pairs of mortal enemies, whose fight takes place precisely over the head of the commoners that they either persecute or protect. At times the pair is immediately evident (Juve against Fantômas), and at times it is described only by a more accurate observation, as in Natoli's book, where the conflict is not between Blasco and Don Raimondo, but in a parallel way, between Blasco and Emanuele on one side, and Coriolano and Don Raimondo on the other.

The oppositional interplay between the two enemies requires the enemy, as the incarnation of an impediment, to be renewed from time to time, unpredictably, even when the match appeared to be over. Juve's fight against Fantômas, which stretches out for volumes upon volumes without ever coming to an end (in the same way that its present comic form, the story of Inspector Ginko against Diabolik, stretches out) is a textbook case for this mechanism. But *The Beati Paoli* also responds to the prescriptions of its own genre, and episodes are packed away and then renewed; they are retired and then reopened without ever coming to an end, like in the finale of a Beethoven symphony (or better yet, like in a conscious bombastic parody of one) the booming of the bass drum that announces the end of the act reveals, behind the curtain that is about to close, a new conclusion that is beginning again, and so on for hundreds of pages. *The Beati Paoli* begins to come to an end after three-quarters of its journey, and then explodes into a chain of epilogues that never come to a close.

But if the opposition must continually be renewed, it also must base its metaphysical nature (good versus evil) on a humanly dramatic and astonishing fact; and here is another of the constants of the *feuilleton*, the artifice of the *enemy brothers*, that we see habitually revisited by Natoli. The topos of the enemy brothers is often combined (as in this novel) with that of the *antithetical offspring*: the evil father begets the good son who will reestablish justice where he has committed an injustice, or vice versa.

In *The Beati Paoli* the antithetical offspring is doubled and becomes involved in a series of chiasmi, because a profligate father begets a profligate offspring as well as a virtuous one; the offspring are good due to their own innocence regarding the responsibilities of the father (who is good, as an enemy brother, compared to Raimondo), but the two offspring are then one good and the other evil in a reciprocal opposition. As for the enemy brother of the father, he begets a virtuous angel, Violante, who at the end enters into a relationship of kinship with the good offspring/brother, Blasco.

In this interplay of "elemental connotations of a kinship," as we can see, the values become complicated, because no one is either good or evil in the absolute, but each assumes a status when compared to the other. If one wants to find a pattern, this is how this series of relationships could be represented:

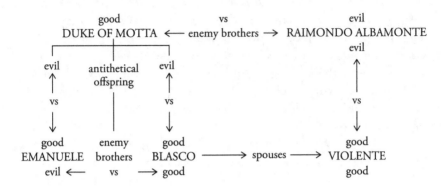

Where one can see that only Raimondo is always evil and only Blasco is always good, and he cannot in the end avoid marrying Violante, who always has the same value, good. With the sacrifice by Gabriella, who takes on within herself the opposing values of the various characters in play, good when compared to Don Raimondo (and evil because in any case she betrays him), good-evil compared to Blasco, good-evil compared to Violante. Her psychological implausibility becomes a certain symbolic necessity at the level of the actantial structures of the drama, and her death is the least that the narrator can devise in order to free the tale from a permanent contradiction that prevents things from resolving themselves (and here the reference is also, perhaps, to certain of Salgari's sweet female slaves, that readers would always like to see marry the hero, because they are more human and appealing than the heroines with their icy and virginal beauty; while the author at the end always has them die miserably because otherwise mythological values would be blown apart, and readers would not be able to put them together again, according to the laws of the popular novel). By the same right, Marx and Engels observe that at the end of *The Mysteries of Paris*, Fleur-de-Marie, virgin prostitute that she was, must die after becoming Princess Amelia because even if the reader may be able to accept her redemption, it is difficult for bourgeois morality to accept the thought that an ex-prostitute, even though innocent, could be awarded the throne. We could say that these odd character figures (often female, but at times also male: see Le Chourineur) of the "betrayed and beaten" serve precisely to introduce into the novel a trace of humanity; because they are devoid of the symbolic rigidity of the other characters, but precisely for this reason they are destined to be eliminated. Oddly, their tragic fate is exactly what in the "cultured" or "committed" novel instead strikes the hero, who is in fact a problematic hero, and the novel (that reflects on its own structure and its own role) cannot avoid leading him to a loss; while the popular novel, presenting us with mythological characters, leads them to success and to one-dimensionality and therefore must give them back to us at the end having been crowned by happiness (or at least, for some, by a serene death, expected due to old age, crowned in any case by something that has to do with a supernatural prize).

To finish up this survey of the constants of the popular novel, we will recall that Tortel (whom we have abundantly cited and as abundantly inserted into this quick compilation) attempts in the end to limit the imaginative "space" of the popular novel, to discuss a typology of this universe where one staging follows the next, and the fight between good and evil seems to regenerate, without fading entirely, not even at the end, leaving open the possibility of a continuation of this dialectic, in a sort of consoling pessimism, or tragic optimism, as if to tell the reader that the contradiction between good and evil is a constant of history, that he will always be a victim to it and that nothing, not even the novel that at this moment is consoling him, will be able to protect him from his fate.

"It's that an obsessive image cannot look out over a space that isn't itself. Here [he is talking about the final discovery in the thirty-second volume of the Fantômas series, where one learns that Juve and Fantômas are brothers], due to a marvelous novelistic invention, the entire symbolic space of the identity of opposites has been filled. An irrational, impossible universe has suddenly petrified into this unlikely and necessary assertion that the two adversaries, the two dominant opposites and equals, are restored to a single unit. Good and evil that have a common origin become a pair of equal forces going in opposite directions. It's a mechanism that the first incredible image put in motion, and that will never stop. Each of the two opposite and inseparable sides pursues its own double, its negative side that it will not reach until the final catastrophe and that alone allows Juve to see his brother's face: 'surely the voice of my dreams had told the truth! . . . .' The structure of the popular novel is pure repetition, obsessive-obsession of a single theme: that of access to domination, taking form in the deeds of the one we have called the hero."

Now, will we not be allowed to use these observations as an apologue, not so much for Natoli's undertaking (dependent on the laws of the literary genre it is a part of) as for the subject that inspires him and that leads him to choose the *feuilleton* form of the first period, almost one hundred years after its first appearance and almost fifty years after its disappearance?

By undertaking to tell the story of a secret society, dominated by a hero who is a promoter of autonomous laws that he overlays on those of society in order to create his own justice and his own rationality, will Natoli not have been forced to assume the laws of *that* genre that alone could give an ideological justification (and at the same time an unmasking, beyond his intentions) to the history that he was reconstructing? Does not the profound nature of the *feuilleton* relate to the fight of a presumed good against a presumed evil that in the end are found to be quite similar? This breed of avengers that are born to defend the people and fatally take on, with their methods, the face of the persecutors that they are fighting, this virtue that lives like a crime (or this crime that presents itself as a virtue) are not they a mark that is shared by the imaginary secret societies of the *feuilleton* as well as by those real secret societies of which the Beati Paoli were one, and it would seem not the last, of their incarnations?

And where is, for imaginary creatures as well as for real ones, the mechanism that gives them this fundamental and decisive ambiguity? And that obsessively pushes them to repeat their own adventure, without ever bringing the game to a close, inventing new faces for the enemy, in a bloody dream, in a tragic game, where good and evil are novelistic abstractions, and dark violence is the reality, from time to time ideologized as an act of solidarity or persecution of transgressors? Will not this original sin perhaps lie in a separation between the Hero and the people for whom he says he is fighting?

And so, we must return to the root of the fundamental myth of the popular novel, the figure of the hero as Superman. That superman who, as Gramsci had well observed, before he appeared in the pages of Nietzsche (or those of his Nazist ideological falsifiers) appears in the pages of the populist and democratic popular novel, as a bearer of an authoritarian solution (paternalistic, self-guaranteed, and self-founded) of the contradictions of society, over the heads of its passive members.

THE IDEOLOGY OF THE SUPERMAN
AND OF THE SECRET SOCIETY

The tradition that we have decided to call "popular novel" is born and is established in France after Émile de Girardin founds *Musée des familles* in 1833. Of course, one could speak of the popular novel in reference to the oldest Anglo-Saxon narrative tradition, that from Richardson's *Clarissa* and from the novels by Fielding or Defoe, passing through the masterpieces of the *gothic novel*, arrives at Dickens. It is really about the emergence of a narrative for the bourgeoisie, influenced by the fact that women also start to become consumers of novelistic goods. But there are various contributing factors that characterize the French popular novel of the period being discussed: the popular press promoted by Girardin reaches even the humblest classes of the population, and we know that during the release of *The Mysteries of Paris* in installments, even the illiterate would meet in building lobbies to have the adventures read aloud to them. It is the birth of a new public that the popular narrative is talking to, but also talking *about*. The plebes, the subordinate classes, are beginning to become the subject of the tale. In addition to *The Mysteries of Paris*, one may also think about *The Wandering Jew, Les Misérables*, even to arrive at the characters and the proletarian universe of Turin that appear in the pages by Carolina Invernizio. The French popular novel does not only talk about the masses to be able to sell to the masses; in fact it is responding to the impact of a general political and social environment, it is happening at the same time as the birth of socialist movements, (*The Mysteries of Paris* predates by a few years the barricades of 1848), it is written by narrators who in one way or another feel they are involved in a "democratic" fight. Süe, as we know, makes use of his dandyistic experience to become first a socialist reformer, and in the end a revolutionary socialist; Dumas fights against the Riancey amendment that threatens freedom of the press; Hugo is pervaded by populistic turmoil and socialism that is at once moderate and mystical. . . . The popular novel of the first phase presents itself as being democratic, unlike that of the second phase, which it is already beginning with Ponson du Terrail, who instead uses crime and the plebes as a background for the undertakings of his troubled characters, without any interest in social investigation.

But even when it is *truthfully* democratic, the nineteenth century novel does not escape a fate of mystification, and for reasons that are fairly clear. As we demonstrated in our examination of Süe, the ideology of these authors is social democratic-reformist. The format of the novel itself compels them to make this choice, or this choice leads them to use that format; the constant narrative arc of the popular novel requires crises and contradictions to arise within the adventure, and then, due to the appearance of a deus ex machina, that the contradictions resolve themselves and that there be a return to order. It is the extreme depauperization of the structure of Aristotelian tragedy, except that there the arc would end in a "tragic" catharsis (and the discussion of the poet revolved around the clash between man and fate) and here instead the catharsis, for reasons of salability, must be optimistic. The narrative structure that needs a crisis to be resolved by an optimistic catharsis requires the universe to produce some fissures, but ones that can be corrected by an action of reform. The popular novel cannot be revolutionary, because otherwise even the narrative model, in which the public recognizes itself and that gives it pleasing consolations, would be blown to bits. In a narrative, revolution happens at the level of "other" narrative forms that prefigure a different definition of the world, or that, in any case, assert the impossibility of accepting the world as is. For this reason, Balzac is not Dumas, because Lucien de Rubempré kills himself, Père Goriot dies, and Rastignac wins, but at a high and dismal price. Stendhal is revolutionary because Julien Sorel cannot pursue his dream of success in the society of the Restoration. Dostoyevsky is revolutionary because the failure of his heroes is a criticism of the official order of the universe.

Unable to be revolutionary because it must be consoling, the popular novel is forced to teach that, if there are social contradictions, there are forces that can resolve them. Now these forces cannot be the popular ones, because the masses have no power, and if they take power, we have revolution and therefore a crisis. The ones doing the resolving must belong to the dominant class. Since, as the dominant class, they would not be interested in resolving contradictions, they must belong to a breed of avengers that can foresee a broader and more harmonious justice. Since society does not recognize their need for justice and would not understand their plan, they need to pursue it against society and against its laws. In order to be able to do this, they must be endowed with exceptional qualities and a charismatic power that can legitimize their apparently subversive decision. This is the birth of the Superman.

The three musketeers act as supermen, superimposing their skills at distinguishing good and evil on the nearsighted legalistic consideration of official authorities, and they decide on the execution of Milady or, in *Twenty Years After*, on the salvation of Charles I and the death of Mordaunt. But in fact, out of all of them, the bearer of charisma and the one who makes the ultimate decisions, taking on himself their tragic responsibility, is Athos. In the series on the French Revolution by Dumas, the charismatic hero is Joseph Balsamo, who practically decides, with the swindle of the queen's necklace, to cause the Revolution to break out. In order to do so, he, who already has supernatural powers, because he is the immortal Cagliostro, also makes use of a secret society, the sect of the Illuminati of Bavaria (which, interestingly enough, attracted the legitimist sympathies of Joseph de Maistre; the secret society that decides on good and evil is intimately reactionary and is acting according to its own mystical principle without seeking a relationship with the masses who were looking for Marat or "Père Duchesne"). Monte Cristo is a superman who decides on punishment for all the wicked without having any doubts at all as to the legitimacy of his action (guaranteed by his enormous economic power) and he also confirms his charisma with external apparitions inspired by Oriental displays. Rodolphe of Gerolstein of *The Mysteries of Paris* is a superman who, from the heights of his legal charisma, makes judgments according to what he can put his claws into, and—as decided by him—that are seen as sacrosanct even in the inhumane torture forced upon the notary Jacques Ferrand, the blinding of the Maître d'Ecole, the final destruction of all the transgressors, just as the prize to the good, which he in fact gathers within a model farm where he paternalistically dispenses happiness and safety (as long as they do not rebel against his decisions).

In the imperialistic phase of the *feuilleton* the wicked supermen may be Rocambole and Fantômas, but when the former mends his ways, he still functions as a charitable superman.

And in the end, Coriolano della Floresta is a superman. A characteristic that they all share is to decide for themselves what is best for the oppressed commoners and how they should be avenged. A superman never entertains the thought that the commoners can and should make their own decisions, and so he is never inclined to enlighten or consult them. In the heat of his virtue, he constantly banishes them to their own subordinate role, and he acts with a repressed violence all the more mystifying since it is disguised as Salvation.

So inevitably his revolt becomes a settling of accounts between rival Powers, which are two facets of the same reality. The moral reasons, or the historical necessity that gave rise to the secret society, do not count; what counts is its refusal to reveal itself and solicit the popular consciousness. In this way, the secret society, a collective incarnation of the superman, fails in its illusory plan of resistance and liberation and becomes a different form of dominion. Born against Power or against the State, it acts like a State within the State and becomes a Secret State, without hope.

Whoever submits to its fascination lives his dreamlike adventure like a reader of the popular novel, who asks the fantastical page to console him with images of justice, managed by others, to make him forget that in reality justice is taken away from him.

And so, the circle of our reading of *The Beati Paoli* closes, and not so much the subject as the narrative form that the author has been led to make use of in having to relate it becomes for us an ethnological document, an anthropological spy on recurring behaviors, the reflection of an ideology. It is also, as it always is for those who are able to read the vicissitudes of a society in the mirror of literature, the beginning of a civil critical discussion.

ACKNOWLEDGMENTS

M y wife, Laura, and I began taking lessons at Scuola Italiana of Greenwich Village following a tragic event in 2008. We lost our daughter Melissa after her brave and mighty year-long struggle with leukemia. I felt a longing to do something with Laura that would help us find a way forward. Why not study Italian together?

Beatrice Muzi, the school's founder, was and still is our guide and teacher. One day she set down a massive novel before us, *I Beati Paoli* by Luigi Natoli. Captivated by the story, I decided to translate it. Thus, a principal debt is owed to Beatrice for years of nourishing lessons. Her late husband, my guitar teacher, Allan Evans, was an early supporter. His lessons on Reverend Gary Davis were nourishing of the musical kind. But *I Beati Paoli* would not have made its way into English without the wise and deft editing of Marina Cappelletto, who teaches at Scuola Italian.

Thanks to Amy Berkower at Writers House for her efforts to find a home for my translation. A shout-out to Dan Weiss, my former colleague at Barnes & Noble, for introducing me to Scott Waxman at Waxman Literary Agency. Radius Book Group's editorial director Mark Fretz provided invaluable guidance and made sure my vision for the book was executed to my satisfaction. Evan Phail and Julia Sloan managed the publishing process. Kudos to editor Eliza Dee, whose skills helped wrestle to the ground quite a few passages in need of grammatical surgery, and to proofreaders Marilyn Burkley and Amy Martin for scouring the text with such diligence. The maps were expertly rendered by Julie Witmer.

A high five to designer Alan Dingman for his powerful covers. M.J. Rose, founder of AuthorBuzz, steered the marketing plan. Ann-Marie Nieves of Get Red PR ably handled the outreach.

Through our trips to Sicily, the people we have come to know did not directly contribute to this work, but they must be acknowledged. Peppe Mendola, dear friend and cofounder of Essence of Sicily, opened the island to our eyes and hearts. Cofounder of Essence of Sicily, Viviana Buscemi, welcomed us into her family home in my ancestral town of Burgio during Easter celebration. Vito Ferrantelli, ex-mayor of Burgio and expert on Sicilian ceramics, and his wife, Lilla, have become special friends. One will not find a better guide in Sicily than Marcella

Amato. We thank her for the surprise of showing us the secret entrances to the Beati Paoli's caves. In Burgio, guide Letizia Bilella escorted us up a steep path to discover Via Riggio, where my great, great grandfather Leonardo Riggio lived. Our family and the distant family we discovered in Burgio share a common ancestor, Giovanni Riggio, born about 1500. But ever more meaningful is having established a true kinship with the late Giuseppe "Peppino" Riggio, his children Gioacchino, Silvestre, and Nicoletta, and their families.

Sergio Intorre, researcher at the University of Palermo, read my introduction and advised on how to best translate the many institutions and titles of eighteenth-century Sicily. Thanks to Dr. Anita Bestler and historian Louis Mendola. His Eminence Lorenzo Casati, Orthodox Archbishop of Palermo, gave advice on several passages written in Sicilian.

Un grande abbraccio to the wonderful Adriana Trigiani for her encouragement and support! And to the writers Lisa Scottoline, Lorenzo Carcaterra, Jo Piazza, and Jill Santopolo. *Grazie mille!* Mark Moskowitz, my literary companion, was my first reader. He immediately grasped the epic nature of what I was attempting and provided steadfast encouragement. To Jim Mustich, longtime bookselling compatriot and an early reader.

Thanks to all my colleagues and to all the booksellers at Barnes & Noble, especially to Mary Ellen Keating for her professional and personal support. We were fond of saying that B&N was a purpose-driven company and that working in a bookstore is "an education in itself."

My brother Len, a man of boundless creativity and generosity of spirit, opened the world of books to me on an audacious, mind-expanding journey. In memory of my late brother, Jimi, a much-needed source of courage in our most difficult time. His spirit and good heart embodied the perfect marriage of Neapolitan sunniness and Sicilian pride.

My profound wish is that this translation did not have to come into being, but now that it has come to pass, Melissa's presence in it is undeniable. Our daughters Laura and Christina have been a constant source of the kind of emotional fuel that a father needs. The pride I have in publishing Sicilian Avengers pales in comparison to the pride of having two loving, caring daughters who face every opportunity and challenge with courage, determination, and intelligence.

My wife, Laura, has been my stalwart supporter and traveling companion through an adventure-filled life. We call ourselves *i due vagabondi* because we find no greater joy than in being together in some unfamiliar place turning a corner and serendipitously discovering something new and wonderful. I dedicate this translation to her, the woman I love: my wife, my life partner, my best friend.

GLOSSARY

Algozino: Sheriff

Banditore: Town crier

Birro: Policeman

Bravaccio: Bully, thug

Campiere: Private rural guard and overseer

Catapani: Provisions officer who collects fees for the display of goods

Cavaliere: An untitled noble, usually any son of a count or baron, regardless of whether he had been invested in a knightly order, as in the Cavaliere della Floresta in *Sicilian Avengers*; also, a lady's escort or a gentleman

Duomo: Cathedral

Educanda: Young girl receiving her education in a monastery

Fondaco: A trading post, with rooms and stables

Fondacaio or **Fondacaro**: Keeper of the fondaco or trading post

Gabellieri: Tax collector

Grano: Sicilian silver coin

Osteria: Simple restaurant

Palazzo: Palace, more typically a large urban residence

Piazza: Town square, or large open space in front of a church or public building

Ponte: Bridge

Porta: City gate

Portantina: Sedan chair

Portantini: Carriers of portantina

Razionale: An accountant

Signore(a): Lord, lady; also, a form of address to a man or woman

Tarì: Sicilian gold coin

Via: Urban street

Vicolo: Narrow street

Vicoletto: Very narrow street or alley

Volante(i): Young servant assisting the master by running ahead of the carriage, performing errands

Zia: Literally "aunt" but also used as an informal title of respect

NOTES

Unless credited, notes are by the translator.

Interested readers will find more extensive notes at www.sicilianavengers.com.

PART ONE

CHAPTER 1

1. *a public ceremony took place in Sant'Offizio*: The public execution of the condemned by the Tribunal of the Inquisition, called the "act of faith" or auto-da-fé, was considered by the populace as entertainment. This is one of the few times that Natoli—evidently due to the necessity of carrying out the plot of the novel—indulges in historical inaccuracy. No public execution of the auto-da-fé actually took place in 1714. However, there is scrupulous adherence to reality in the description of the ceremony. AC, 349.

CHAPTER 4

1. *demesnial cities*: Under Frederick, feudal towns were controlled by their resident lords, but *demesnial* cities also existed that answered directly to the Crown and were administered by local councils of minor nobles called *jurats*. Louis Mendola and Jacqueline Alio, *The Peoples of Sicily: A Multicultural Legacy* (New York: Trinacria, 2014), 77.

CHAPTER 5

1. *From Villagrazia*: Natoli: *Grazia*, a town today called Villagrazia, in the southern countryside of Palermo.
2. *That Our Lady of Light*: The cult for the Madonna del Lume; a confraternity with this name existed in the Capo. AC, 373.

CHAPTER 8

1. *Ustica*: A small island in the Tyrrhenian Sea.

CHAPTER 10

1. *Institutes of Justinian*: A unit of the Corpus Juris Civilis (Body of Civil Law), the sixth-century codification of Roman law issued by order of the Byzantine Emperor Justinian I.

2. *Palazzo Pretorio*: The Praetorian or Magistrate's Court, made up of three judges, dealt with civil cases. The judges came out of the eastern door of the palazzo, where the writing *Pax Huic Domui* ("Peace be to this house") had been put back in the nineteenth-century restoration; from there begins the Discesa dei Giudici, called before the seventeenth century "Salita della Corte del Pretore."

3. *frequented by all these advocates*: Natoli: *causidici*. Those who acted or appeared in court on behalf of a party, even though they were not actual lawyers.

4. *Partinico*: Town about twenty miles from Palermo, an excellent wine-producing area.

5. *zecchinetta . . . primero*: Zecchinetta is an Italian version of lansquenet; primero is a sixteenth-century Italian card game.

6. *Abbazia del Parco*: Abbey of Santa Maria di Altofonte, built by Frederick II of Aragon, completed March 25, 1306.

CHAPTER 14

1. *Bianchi*: La Compagnia del SS. Crocifisso, called "Bianchi" for their hooded white tunics, was made up solely of aristocrats. The procession led the condemned to the gallows in Piazza Marina. AC, 441.

CHAPTER 15

1. *He had reached Ballarò*: Natoli is probably referring to the area of the Ballarò market, the oldest and biggest market in Palermo.

CHAPTER 17

1. *Meanwhile, the militia had surrounded:* in this scene Natoli refers to *le compagnie rurale, i compagni d'arme,* and *campagno d'arme,* which translates to "rural companies" "comrades in arms", and "fellow soldier". As he describes, these "forces", under the direction of feudal barons, were composed of thieves, bullies, murderers... the cream of the crop of the banditry that roamed the rural areas. They have been described as both "rural police" and "rural militia". We have chosen to use "militia" and "solider" as more apt English words to describe forces that imposed law and order in a way that does not equate with a contemporary definition of police.

CHAPTER 18

1. *Have you informed our notary?* Italian notaries are legal professionals, responsible for recording property transactions, debts, and loans; creating wills; and authenticating documents, agreements, and contracts.

CHAPTER 19

1. *by the beard of Michelangelo*: Bongiovanni is suffering from dementia. He appears to be invoking the Renaissance master in the same way as one would invoke the Madonna, as in "By the Madonna!"

2. *Tressette*: One of Italy's national card games.

3. *Your mouth still stinks of milk*: an idiomatic expression meaning "you're still wet behind the ears."

CHAPTER 21

1. *the revolving wheel*: a system known as *ruota dei* proietti, used in churches and foundling homes. The *proietti* (literally "projectiles") were children who were thrown away, that is abandoned by fathers who did not want to recognize a child born out of wedlock or by families that were unable to care for a child due to extreme poverty. The wheel was installed in a door that was half inside and half outside. Alerted by a knock on the door or the sound of a crying baby, a woman on the inside would turn the wheel while the ones depositing the baby could slip away without being seen.

CHAPTER 23

1. *the cave in Denisinni*: the Denisinni district is west of the city.

CHAPTER 25

1. *Padre Mongitore*: Antonino Mongitore (1663–1743) was a Sicilian presbyter, historian, and writer, known for many and important works on the history of Sicily and Palermo.

CHAPTER 27

1. *Ecce Homo dei Biscottari*: There were numerous wood-burning ovens in Via Biscottari in the Albergheria. Near the arch at the western end that connects Palazzo Sclafani to the buildings facing it is a shrine of the Ecce Homo, with an image of the humble and merciful Christ that has elicited the popular saying *pari l'Ecce Homu di viscuttara*, meaning a "gaunt and battered person." AC, 526.
2. *the bells of the Castellana*: Castellana is a commune of Palermo. The tolling of the bells of the parishes of San Nicolò all'Albergheria, Sant'Antonio Abate, and Santa Lucia al Borgo were the closing signal for activities in the city and for the emergence of night patrols, after which people were prohibited from wandering the streets without a special permit. AC, 531.

PART TWO

CHAPTER 1

1. *Marchese de Lede*: Felipe-Emmanuele de Bette (1672–1725), Belgian military commander in Spanish service.
2. *Count of Modica*: The County of Modica was a feudal territory within the Kingdom of Sicily from 1296 to 1812.

CHAPTER 2

1. *Ruggero Settimo*: (1778–1863), Italian politician, diplomat, and patriotic activist.

CHAPTER 3

1. *Santa Rosalia*: The Feast of Santa Rosalia lasts for three or four days and ends on July 15 with the solemn procession of the remains of the saint. AC, 556.

2. *Numancia Dragoons*: The regiment was created during the War of the Spanish Succession; in June 1718 it took part in the siege and capture of Palermo.
3. *calabresella*: An Italian card game for three players.
4. *Holy Virgin of the Pillar!*: Our Lady of the Pillar. According to traditional belief, Mary, standing on a pillar and holding the child Jesus, appeared to the Apostle James while he was preaching in what is now Spain. She asked him to build a church on the site, promising that "it will stand from that moment until the end of time in order that God may work miracles and wonders through my intercession for all those who place themselves under my patronage."

CHAPTER 4

1. *the beautiful stage that was erected in 1681*: This was called the Teatro Marmoreo. In the summer, musicians were paid by Palermo nobles to entertain the citizens during the *passeggiata* on the Marina. AC, 571.

CHAPTER 5

1. *his former home*: Refers to Palazzo Branciforte, behind the Oratorio di Santa Cita.
2. *the Conservatorio dei Dispersi, or the Buon Pastore*: The conservatory was founded as an orphanage in 1618 at the behest of the viceroy, Count de Castro, with the name Orfanatrofio del Buon Pastore (Good Shepherd). Music was taught beginning in 1721, and by 1747 music was taught exclusively.

CHAPTER 11

1. *He got laid*: An admittedly modern translation of Natoli: *Ne aveva fatta qualcuna,* which could translate as "he had done one (a woman)."

CHAPTER 12

1. *Alemanni cavalry*: The Alemanni (all men) were a confederation of Germanic-speaking peoples that settled on the Upper Rhine River.
2. *Count of Modica*: Bernard of Cabrera and Foix, Count of Modica (1350–1423), a Catalan nobleman.
3. the Mastro di Campo: the pantomime of the struggle of the *Mastro di Campo* to conquer the hand of the queen that was usurped by the king. It was represented in the popular districts of the Kalsa and the Albergheria during the celebrations for Carnevale. It has become a popular festival in the commune of Mezzojuso that has been held for over two centuries. AC, 627.
4. *confetti*: sugarcoated almonds.
5. *Barcellona Pozzo di Gotto*: town about twenty-five miles west of Messina. AC, 624.

CHAPTER 13

1. *Mura delle Cattive*: A stretch of the city walls overlooking the sea, above which was an elevated promenade; widows would take walks there due to its discreet position with respect to the much-frequented waterfront. AC, 632.

CHAPTER 15

1. *The duchess is courting someone*: Natoli: *La signora duchessa fa all'amore*. Not meant to imply something sexual; the duchess is pursuing Violante for her own underhanded reasons. Over time *fare all'amore* has evolved into *fare l'amore*, "to make love" or "to have sex."

CHAPTER 16

1. *Piazza SS. Quaranta Martiri al Casalotto*: Built in 1294; the Holy Forty Martyrs were a group of soldiers belonging to a Roman legion, who in AD 320 were arrested for being Christians. Given the choice of apostatizing or suffering death, they remained firm in their faith. They were condemned to be exposed naked to the winter cold and died from frostbite in the city of Sebaste in Armenia.

CHAPTER 18

1. *Feast of Corpus Domini*: Also known as the Feast of Corpus Christi (Latin for "Body of Christ"), it celebrates the real presence of Jesus Christ in the Holy Eucharist.

CHAPTER 21

1. *the corpse of that excommunicant*: In Palermo several confraternities took on the task of accompanying the dead to cemeteries outside the city, which were mainly allocated for the poor and the derelict. AC, 684.

CHAPTER 22

1. *Manfredi III Chiaramonte*: Sicilian nobleman (died 1391). Of French origins, he was given the County of Modica, then one of the most powerful fiefs in the Kingdom of Sicily.

CHAPTER 23

1. *Porpora*: Nicola Porpora (1686–1768), Italian composer and singing teacher.

FURTHER READING

Luigi Natoli wrote over twenty-five novels, including *Coriolano della Floresta*, the sequel to *I Beati Paoli*. Many of his books are in print and available from these Italian publishers: Sellerio Editore, Palermo; I Buoni Cugini Editori, Palermo; and Dario Flaccovio Editore, Milan.

Almost every building, church, and monument in this novel still exists, so interested readers can use it to compile a tour guide for a planned visit to Palermo. I found that books written by travelers many years before Natoli's time were especially enjoyable because they offer a glimpse into what must have been a picturesque, enchanting place. But then, again, it still is.

Bestler, Anita. *The Sicilian Mafia: The Armed Wing of Politics*. Wiesbaden: Springer, 2023.

Blaquiere, Edward. *Letters from the Mediterranean; Containing a Civil and Political Account of Sicily, Tripoly, Tunis, and Malta*. London: Henry Colburn, 1813.

Caico, Louise. *Sicilian Ways and Days*. New York: D. Appleton and Company, 1910.

Campbell, Angus. *Sicily and the Enlightenment: The World of Domenico Caracciolo, Thinker and Reformer*. London, New York: I.B. Tauris, 2016.

Chirco, Adriana, *Antiche strade e piazze di Palermo*. Palermo: Dario Flaccovio Editore, 2019.

—, *Palermo City Guide*. Palermo: Dario Flaccovio Editore, 1998.

—, *Palermo al tempo dei Beati Paoli*. Palermo: Dario Flaccovio Editore, 2016.

Chirco, Adriana, and Mario di Liberto. *Quattro canti di Palermo: L'ottogono del sole*. Palermo: Dario Flaccovio, 2013.

Dennis, George. *A Handbook for Travellers in Sicily*. London: John Murray, 1864.

Dummett, Jeremy. *Palermo, City of Kings: The Heart of Sicily*. London: I.B. Tauris, 2015.

—, *Sicily, Island of Beauty and Conflict*. London, New York: Bloomsbury Publishing, 2020.

448

Finley, M. I. *A History of Sicily: Ancient Sicily to the Arab Conquest*. London: Chatto & Windus, 1968.

Holcroft, Thomas. *Travels through Germany, Switzerland, Italy, and Sicily*. Translated from the German of Frederic Leopold Count Stolberg. London: G.G. and J. Robinson, 1797.

Maraini, Dacia. *The Silent Duchess*. New York: The Feminist Press, 1992.

Mendola, Louis. *The Kingdom of Sicily, 1130–1860*. New York: Trinacria Editions, 2015.

Mendola, Louis, and Jacqueline Alio. *The Peoples of Sicily: A Multicultural Legacy*. New York: Trinacria Editions, 2014.

Montemagno, Gabriello. *L'uomo che inventò i Beati Paoli*. Palermo: Sellerio Editore, 2017.

Muccioli, Antonio. *Le strade di Palermo*. Rome: Newton and Compton, 1998.

Norwich, John Julius. *Sicily, An Island at the Crossroads of History*. New York: Random House, 2015.

—, *The Normans in the South, 1016–1130*. London: Faber & Faber, 1967.

—, *The Kingdom in the Sun, 1130–1194*. London: Faber & Faber, 1970.

Paton, W. A. *Picturesque Sicily*. New York and London: Harper Brothers, 1898.

Quennell, Peter. *Spring in Sicily*. London: George Weidenfeld and Nicolson, 1952.

Scottoline, Lisa. *Loyalty*. New York: G.P. Putnam's Sons, 2023.

Sladen, Douglas. *Sicily, the New Winter Resort*. New York: E.P. Dutton, 1907.

Smith, Denis Mack. *A History of Sicily: Medieval Sicily, 800-1713*. New York: Viking, 1968.

Trevelyan, Raleigh. *The Companion Guide to Sicily*. Woodbridge: Boydell & Brewer, 1996.

von Goethe, Johann Wolfgang: *Italian Journey: 1786-1788* (Penguin Classics Reissue). London: Penguin Books, 1992.

Luigi Natoli

Luigi Natoli (1857–1941), patriotic and fervent republican, teacher, journalist, scholar of history, and called "the last of the archetypal popular writers," was the author, in addition to a great number of histories, critical essays, poems, theatrical texts, schoolbooks, and over twenty-five serial novels, published under the pseudonym William Galt. Through them he set out to compose an epic of the freedom of the Sicilian people. Among those that stand out, in addition to the legendary *I Beati Paoli*, are the sequel, *Coriolano della Floresta*, and *Calvello il Bastardo*.

At the age of three, he was imprisoned, together with his entire family, in the Vicaria prison in Palermo, because his mother had dressed her children in red shirts in order to greet Garibaldi's arrival in Sicily. Everything the family owned was confiscated or burned. "The family risked dying of hunger, if not for the mercy of a prison guard, who every so often secretly brought them a bowl of pasta and beans. 'I was saved by a plate of beans,' Natoli recalled."[7] Their strained financial circumstances haunted him until his last days but contributed to the development in him of a most deeply rooted and fervent freedom of thought and expression. As a child, he frequented libraries, became an autodidact, and, as his talent for writing blossomed, he began writing for the *Giornale di Sicilia*. At twenty-three, he taught Italians in gymnasiums (junior high schools). Forced by circumstances to travel all over Italy, from Rome—where he stayed three years—to Pisa, Sardinia, and Naples, everywhere he went he socialized in literary circles. He became friends with other Italian writers, including Federico De Roberto, Luigi Capuana, Salvatore Di Giacomo, and Giuseppe Pitrè. Fervently secular and anticlerical, he worked indefatigably and cultivated his passion for history and culture, in particular for that of Sicily, dividing his time between work commitments—which could not be postponed because of the need to support a very large family—and frequent visits to historical archives and libraries. His assiduous and intense study of the Sicilian history and the vicissitudes that forever troubled the island instilled in him a profound feeling toward his homeland that permeated his writing, and he maintained a prodigious literary output throughout his lifetime.

---

7   Gabriello Montemagno, *L'uomo che inventò i Beati Paoli* (Palermo: Sellerio Editore, 2017, 19–20).

From his two marriages (his first wife died very young; the second, Teresa Gutenberg, was the daughter of the man who became his publisher), he had several children. He educated them on the basis of the same approach to culture and study that he had put into practice with his own students, one inspired by moral rectitude, which could be implemented by being faithful to the principles of respect for everything and everyone (including different political beliefs) and of loyalty and honesty. It so happened that his children, raised by the same principles of education, ended up with different political convictions, and all of them led lives of great fervor.

His rejection of Mussolini and the fascist regime resulted in the banning of some of his books. But until his last breath, Luigi Natoli opposed the abuses of those in power. And to the priest who, in his last days of life, promised to remove his books from the ban as long as he agreed to withdraw the book on Fra Diego La Matina—in which he tells how embezzlement between the Spanish rulers and the clergy brought about the condemnation of the friar to the stake by the Inquisition—he gave his most firm refusal, encouraging him to tell his superiors that "history cannot be recalibrated or covered with a veil. And neither he nor the pope have such power." His rich literary production gave him great fame but little financial benefit.

In his will, he wrote, "I didn't pursue my work for commercial gain, but only for the joy that it gave me."